BREAKING THE PUCKING RULES

LA VIPERS

TRACY LORRAINE

Kodie Rivers.
Hockey god.
Single dad.
And thanks to my father—his coach—he's completely off-limits.
But that only makes him more irresistible.
I know better than to think there's a future with a man like him.
His priorities are clear: his daughter and his career. No room for
complications. No space for me.
But after years of watching him from the sidelines, I'm done just
looking. I want one night. One little taste to quiet the wild
fantasies about the man I can't have.
When my dad's ticket to the LA Vipers' annual charity
masquerade falls at my feet, I know I should put it back. But the
mask gives me the courage to be someone else for one night.
Someone bold enough to go after what she wants.
And I want him.
One night. No names. No consequences.
But will it be enough, or will it only add more gasoline to my
already out-of-control obsession?

"Learn the rules like a pro, so you can break them like an artist."
- Pablo Picasso

ALSO BY TRACY LORRAINE

Falling Series

Falling for Ryan: Part One #1

Falling for Ryan: Part Two #2

Falling for Jax #3

Falling for Daniel (A Falling Series Novella)

Falling for Ruben #4

Falling for Fin #5

Falling for Lucas #6

Falling for Caleb #7

Falling for Declan #8

Falling For Liam #9

Forbidden Series

Falling for the Forbidden #1

Losing the Forbidden #2

Fighting for the Forbidden #3

Craving Redemption #4

Demanding Redemption #5

Avoiding Temptation #6

Chasing Temptation #7

Rebel Ink Series

Hate You #1

Trick You #2

Defy You #3

Play You #4

One Reckless Knight (Jodie & Toby)

Reckless Knight #7 (Jodie & Toby)

Reckless Princess #8 (Jodie & Toby)

Reckless Dynasty #9 (Jodie & Toby)

Dark Halloween Knight (Calli & Batman)

Dark Knight #10 (Calli & Batman)

Dark Princess #11 (Calli & Batman)

Dark Legacy #12 (Calli & Batman)

Corrupt Valentine Knight (Nico & Siren)

Corrupt Knight #13 (Nico & Siren)

Corrupt Princess #14 (Nico & Siren)

Corrupt Union #15 (Nico & Siren)

Sinful Wild Knight (Alex & Vixen)

Sinful Stolen Knight: Prequel (Alex & Vixen)

Sinful Knight #16 (Alex & Vixen)

Sinful Princess #17 (Alex & Vixen)

Sinful Kingdom #18 (Alex & Vixen)

Knight's Ridge Destiny: Epilogue

Harrow Creek Hawks Series

Merciless #1

Relentless #2

Lawless #3

Fearless #4

Callahan Billionaires

By His Vow #1

By His Rule #2

By His Play #3

<u>Seattle Saints</u>

Broken Saint #1

<u>LA Vipers</u>

Breaking the Pucking Rules

<u>Never Forget Series</u>

<u>Never Forget Him</u> #1

<u>Never Forget Us</u> #2

<u>Everywhere & Nowhere</u> #3

<u>Chasing Series</u>

<u>Chasing Logan</u>

<u>Standalones</u>

Naughty & Nice

WOULD YOU LIKE A FREE BOOK?

Get your free copy of The Mistakes You Make, the prequel to my dark college romance series, Maddison Kings University. Subscribe to my newsletter for your free copy!

1

———

CASEY

The second Dad's name pops up on my screen, I can predict what's coming.

"Hey, kiddo. I'm really sorry, but I need a raincheck on breakfast."

A sad smile pulls at my lips. I got too used to our Wednesday morning breakfast dates during the off season.

That's all over now.

He hesitates then adds sheepishly, "Any chance you could do me a favor, though?"

"You got it," I say.

"I left my bible on the kitchen counter..." he trails off.

A laugh spills free.

"Would you like a coffee as well?"

"You're too good to me."

"Someone's got to be," I tease.

"Love you, Care Bear."

The call cuts and I take the final turn toward the house I grew up in.

Killing the engine in the driveway, I waste no time in climbing out and finding my key.

The second I open the door, familiarity rushes over me. The scent of happiness and safety fills my nose.

I love this place. Always have, always will. I have so many fantastic memories here—my father being the main one.

As I step into the kitchen, I find the room in its usual state of chaos, and I can't help but smile. Dad isn't the cleanest or most organized of people, unless it comes to work.

Collecting a stray glass and mug, I dump them in the sink, doing my bit to help.

I'm twenty-three. I shouldn't care that he's busy and blown off our date. But the sad truth of it is that it's the only date of any kind I've had in...longer than I want to admit.

A loud sigh passes my lips.

Glancing around the room, I quickly locate what I came here for.

It's not a real bible. My father doesn't have a single religious bone in his body, unless you count his lifetime commitment to hockey. I'm pretty sure he's prayed to that puck a few times over the years.

His bible is his life. His calendar, his playbook...his everything.

He starts a new one immediately after the end of each season and begins filling it with notes for the next one.

By the time the season is upon us, it always looks like it does now: bursting at the seams, full of scraps of paper with plays scribbled on them, notes about players, and phone numbers. Women's phone numbers.

I shake my head.

Dad is a good-looking man. After years of playing hockey, his body is still something to be proud of. And as the single head coach for the LA Vipers, he is hot property with all the desperate women in a fifty-mile radius.

He's not interested, though.

He's too focused on his job, on his team, and on me.

Don't get me wrong, when I was a teenager, I loved that I didn't have to share him with anything but hockey. But now that I'm older, I do wish he could find someone to enjoy life with.

I lift the bible from the counter and tuck it under my arm

before heading back to my car, placing it safely on the passenger's seat.

Walking through the arena is almost as familiar as walking into Dad's house.

It's my second home.

Some of my earliest memories are from here, watching Dad utterly destroying his opponents on the ice.

I loved it just as much then as I do now. Hockey isn't just a game. It's a lifestyle. One I can't imagine not living.

Sucking in a deep breath, I walk toward the rink where I have no doubt I'll find the man I'm looking for.

The scraping of skates on ice and men shouting get steadily louder, and my speed increases.

If I could, I'd spend all my days sitting in the stands watching them train. Watching Dad boss them around.

The second I turn the corner, my eyes fall on the rink, and without meaning to, they search out number fifty-five. It's been the same since he was traded here last season.

Kodie Rivers is a hockey god.

Always has been and always will be.

I'm honored to get the chance to watch him in action.

The truth is, I've been watching him for years. Since he first took to the ice in college.

Even in high school, he was the best, and that allowed him to have his pick of colleges. And things have only gotten better since.

Especially for me.

When it was announced that he was coming to LA, I thought all my Christmases had come at once.

There's just one tiny issue...

I'm the coach's daughter.

It doesn't matter how much I might obsess over a player; it's never going to happen.

They wouldn't risk losing the respect of my father. A night with me isn't worth it.

I get it. I do. And before Kodie joined the Vipers, it never really bothered me.

I saw them all as adopted uncles, big brothers, and friends.

But now...

I used to have photos of him stuck inside my high school textbooks. I'd have had them on my bedroom wall if I didn't think my dad would lose his shit over it.

I've followed Kodie's career, his life, ever since he first stole my attention all those years ago.

And now that he's here, I'm no less intrigued by him. If anything, I'd say my slight obsession is worse.

Managing to rip my eyes away from his form speeding across the ice, I spot Dad.

Determined to look like a woman in control of her life, I hold my head high, clutch his bible tighter to my chest and keep walking.

He's just a hockey player. Just a man.

No big deal.

But it is a big deal. He's Kodie fucking Rivers.

Gritting my teeth, I do my best to stuff down the excitable hormonal teenage girl who seems to pop up every time I'm anywhere near him and focus on the task at hand.

Noticing movement in his direction, Dad looks up. The second he discovers it's me, his entire face lights up.

"Care Bear," he mouths, making my cheeks burn red.

I'm not sure I'll ever truly feel like an adult when I'm in my father's company. Somehow, no matter how old I am or what I've managed to achieve, I still feel like a little girl.

I continue around the rink, and I've almost reached him when two players slam into the plexiglass beside me. A startled shriek rips from my lips as I twist around to see who it is.

My breath catches, my heart racing even faster when I lock onto a pair of mesmerizing dark brown eyes that I'd know anywhere.

I try to swallow, but my mouth has gone completely dry.

Never before have I been this girl. I've been surrounded by hot hockey boys all my life. Sure, I've crushed on a few, but none of them have caused the kind of reaction that Kodie Rivers does.

It should be illegal.

As much as I'd love for him to look excited to see me, the only expression on his face is one of irritation. I guess that's understandable when you've just been body checked by a teammate.

I have no idea if he recognizes me—I pray that he does, but I can understand that I'm probably not as big a part of his life as he is mine. He gives me a curt nod of acknowledgement, and that alone is enough to cause a riot of butterflies in my stomach.

Get a fucking grip, Casey.

I force myself to look away and at the much more amused-looking man behind him.

Lincoln Storm.

Now, if there was a player who would probably throw caution to the wind and be willing to hook up with the coach's daughter, it would be Linc.

He's been a Viper since his rookie year. He's a great player... in both senses of the word. He works hard and he plays harder.

The opposite of Kodie, who lives a much quieter life.

Linc smirks at me in accomplishment, and a beat before he releases Kodie, he winks. That should be the move to give me butterflies, but nope. There are none for him.

A deep growl fills the air as a shadow falls over me.

"Eyes off my daughter, Storm." The warning in Dad's voice makes my stomach knot. I risk glancing over and find Dad glaring daggers at one of his best players. "Drop and give me fifty," he commands.

Knowing he's fucked up, Linc instantly pushes back and drops to his hands on the ice.

Dad watches him for a few seconds, but once he's happy he's driven off any potential suitors, he turns to me with a soft smile playing on his lips.

"You're an angel," he says, his voice suddenly softer and calmer.

"It's not like it's out of my way," I tease, looking up at him and smiling.

Sure, he has a few more wrinkles and a couple of gray hairs at his temples these days, but James Watson is still a very good-looking man. I can't blame women for acting the way they do around him.

"Even still. Appreciate it, kiddo."

Linc finishes his punishment and he and Kodie take off across the ice again to join the rest of the team, who are watching with amused expressions.

After taking his bible and coffee, Dad promises to make up for missing breakfast by taking me out to dinner instead.

Not wanting to take up any more of his time, I stretch up on my toes to give him a kiss on the cheek and wish him a good day, and then I walk away from the rink without looking back.

The second I pull my car door open, something flutters into the footwell. It must have fallen out of Dad's bible.

With a frown, I reach over and retrieve an envelope. I'm about to turn back and take it to Dad when the messy, unfamiliar writing across the front steals my attention.

Coach Watson, I know you don't want to go, but here is your ticket. Please don't waste it.

It's signed by the team owner.

My heart rate begins to increase as I predict what's hiding inside.

Climbing into my car, I look around the lot nervously. It's deserted, but it doesn't stop me from slumping lower in my seat as I tuck my finger under the unsealed flap. My hand shakes as I pull out the single ticket inside.

My stomach twists with anticipation.

For years, the LA Vipers' fundraising department has organized a masquerade ball in the weeks leading up to the preseason.

Getting your hands on a ticket is like finding unicorn shit.

Every single year, my dad is given one. And every single year, he donates to the cause but refuses to attend, saying that it's not his thing.

I've begged for his ticket every year since I was seventeen, to no avail.

It's not that he's trying to keep me away from hockey. That would be really hard, considering I also work for the franchise. But it would be safe to say that he likes to keep me at arm's length from the team.

That wouldn't have been the case if I were a boy. Hanging out with all the hot hockey players would have been a requirement. I'm not sure it's fair that just because I was born with a vagina, I'm barely allowed to hang out with them.

It was fine when I was little. I was welcomed in as if I were one of their own kids. But as I hit my teen years, as I grew boobs, Dad started limiting my visits.

The team has changed a lot since then. There are only a handful of veterans now who remember me as a kid. I guess that's the issue.

I clutch the slip of paper tighter, feeling like the kid holding the golden ticket.

I shouldn't.

Dad will kill me if he finds out I've taken it.

He'll know, a little voice screams, but one look at the arena and I swallow it down.

Dad won't know. Every year that ticket goes in the trash.

It's a masquerade ball...what if no one finds out?

If I can secure a good enough mask and dye my hair, then no one has to know. Not Dad, not Gary, our GM, or any of the players.

For one night, I'll just be a woman at a party.

A party that a certain number fifty-five will be attending...

2

KODIE

"Aw, you look handsome, Daddy," Sutton says as I enter the living room.

Hearing her sweet voice might make me feel better about myself, but it does little to enthuse me about the night ahead.

I didn't go last year. Sutton was sick and I had little choice but to cancel. I'm not going to be so lucky tonight.

If there were any way to get out of it, I would have. But it's expected that every player on the Vipers' roster attends the event.

I don't mind a charity event on the whole. I'm more than happy to support any good cause and to give back. But a masquerade ball is the thing of my nightmares.

A shiver runs through me.

I fucking hate masks.

I know they're not real masks. Not like the kind that kids run around wearing at Halloween. But I still can't see people's faces, read their expressions, understand what they're thinking, and that unnerves me.

"Thanks, Peanut," I say, trying to summon up a little excitement.

"I wish I could come. I could have a pretty, glittery dress."

"One day," I promise.

Sutton, my daughter, is seven going on seventeen. I love her something fierce, but man, she is a challenge I never thought I'd have to deal with. Especially alone.

"Doesn't my boy scrub up well," Mom sings, stepping into the living room with smoothies for both her and Sutton.

I shake my head, wanting their focus off me and my dinner suit.

I don't do smart. I spend my life in sweats or my practice uniform. This is...this is too much.

"Do you have a date?" Sutton asks, making this situation even worse.

"Ohh," Mom coos. "I want to know this too."

Excitement sparkles in her eyes.

For years, she's been trying to encourage me to get back on the market.

I get it. She wants me to meet a nice woman who'll become a stepmom for Sutton and allow her to enjoy some of her free time instead of being my permanent nanny.

But it's not that easy.

Nice women aren't the ones I'm usually surrounded by.

I've learned my lesson. I've got the scars to prove it.

My eyes shift to Sutton.

Her mom was one of those who left their mark and forever made me skeptical about the female population. The women some of my teammates hook up with also don't help the situation.

"No, I don't have a date. I've already got enough beautiful ladies in my life."

Mom shakes her head while Sutton blushes.

"Come and wave me off?" I ask before spinning around and stalking toward the front door, where I have a car waiting.

"Can you bring me back any chocolates?" Sutton asks as she rushes after me.

"You got it."

"And don't eat them like you did after that other event you went to."

I gasp, spinning around and glaring at her.

"I didn't eat them. They didn't have any."

She raises one eyebrow as if she doesn't believe me.

Chuckling, I pull her in for a hug.

"Be good for Gran," I whisper.

"When aren't I?" she asks, looking up at me with wide eyes and an innocent grin on her lips.

"Hmm...I'll be here when you wake up. Pancakes before training, yeah?"

Her smile only grows.

"Love you, Peanut."

"Love you too, Daddy."

She gives me a big squeeze that makes my heart skip a beat.

I may not have expected my life to turn out like this, but I also couldn't imagine anything else.

"Go and wave from the living room," Mom says, ushering Sutton away.

I cringe, aware that she's about to say something I don't want to hear.

She stares at me with a warm, loving expression as Sutton's footsteps fade.

"Spit it out then," I say, needing to get this over with.

"It's okay to enjoy yourself tonight."

"I'm aware of that, Mom," I mutter, feeling like a child who doesn't know what's good for me.

"Do you?" she asks, her eyes widening to emphasize that she doesn't think so. "We've been here eighteen months and you haven't once done something for yourself."

"I don't need anything," I argue. My life is Sutton and hockey. That's it. Everything else is... inconsequential.

There will come a time when my focus will have to shift, but it's not now.

"Kodie," she whispers. "I just want you to be happy."

"I am. I play for a fantastic team, and I have my family around me. I promise, I have everything I need."

She sighs, thankfully letting it go. For now, at least. I know she won't drop it forever.

"Try to look like you're enjoying yourself," she urges as I pull the front door open and wave to my driver.

"I don't need to bother; I'll be hiding behind this thing," I say, holding up my mask.

Mom laughs, shaking her head in both amusement and disappointment.

"Make sure she goes to bed at a decent time," I call, attempting to regain control and remind her that I'm a thirty-year-old man with a successful career and a mostly well-behaved daughter.

Mom waves me off. "We'd better not see you until sunrise."

She closes the door before I have a chance to comment.

The second I stepped out of the car, the cameras began flashing, but I didn't miss the paparazzi's audible sigh of disappointment when it became clear I wouldn't have a woman on my arm tonight.

I did what I had to do and smiled for the cameras with my stupid mask in place.

The event itself is just like I expected. Elegant, exclusive, expensive.

It's not my idea of a good night out, and certainly not any of the reasons why I wanted to become a professional hockey player.

But apparently, it's a part of the job.

The second I'm inside, I make a beeline for the bar.

The season is starting soon, so I need to be sensible. But that doesn't mean I don't start the night with a little Dutch courage.

The scotch is burning down my throat when I sense someone step up beside me.

I glance over at a woman in a black fitted dress.

Of course.

"Hey," she purrs, looking up at me through her intricate mask.

"Hi," I reply politely before pushing my empty glass across the bar and taking a step back.

"Are you here by yourself?" she asks shamelessly while her

eyes drop down the length of my body, probably trying to weigh up whether I'm a player or not.

Just as my lips part, Linc, Fletcher, our captain, and his wife, Reese, walk across the room.

"I'm meeting someone. Enjoy your night," I say before darting away.

"Evening, Big D." Linc uses the nickname the team has given me with a wide grin as I approach.

"Evening," I mutter.

"Did we just watch you turn down a drink with a hot woman?" he asks as if he's just witnessed the crime of the century.

I glance back at her, now latched onto another victim.

"Wasn't my type."

"Funny, we hear you say that a lot," Linc teases while Fletch and Reese watch on curiously.

"Well, it's true. If you had a bit more taste, maybe you wouldn't end up at the clinic every other week."

"Oh, burn," Fletch mocks.

"Once," Linc argues. "I had to go once. Will you let it go?"

"Sure thing." I wink before turning to Reese.

"This is incredible," I praise.

She's the Vipers Foundation senior coordinator and responsible for all of this.

"Thank you, Kodie. And thank you for your support."

I'm about to respond when a harassed-looking kid with a clipboard and an earpiece comes rushing over to her.

"I'm sorry, please excuse me."

"Shall we check out the auction?" Fletch asks.

"Sure. I could really do with a vacation on a yacht right now," Linc says, earning himself a slap on the head from our captain.

"You should be so lucky."

We walk around everything that's up for auction, balking at the figures that have already been written down.

I'm not sure this will ever become normal.

Growing up, things were hard. Dad was a mechanic and Mom worked at our local grocery store. They always ensured that

I had everything I needed, but there was never any spare money. Especially once I started playing hockey.

My hobby was a huge drain on my parents' finances, and it was something that, even as a young teenager, I never took for granted.

If it weren't for them working their asses off and putting me and my dream first, I would not have gotten here.

I just wish Dad got to see where I ended up.

We get stopped by a handful of people to talk about the upcoming season, but everyone is polite and they don't take up too much of our time. It's one of the things about events like these. Only a certain type of person is invited, and they understand the desire for a degree of privacy, so they mostly leave us to our evening.

"They're going to be serving dinner shortly," Fletch says after checking his watch.

"I'll meet you there," I say, excusing myself to use the bathroom.

I do what I need to do before standing at the sink to wash my hands and staring at myself in the mirror. I look ridiculous, but then, so does everyone else here.

I take a little longer than necessary, preparing for the small talk that's sure to fill the next few hours of my life before I leave the safety of the bathroom.

Pulling my cell from my pocket, I find a photo message from Mom of her and Sutton snuggled on the couch, ready to watch a movie.

I'm too busy wishing that I was at home with them to bother looking up, and two seconds later, I collide with someone.

"Oh shit, I'm so sor—" My words are cut off when I find a petite woman in a stunning emerald green dress wobbling on her heels before me.

Without thinking, I reach out and wrap my arm around her waist, steadying her before she hits the floor.

It's not until she's back on her feet that my eyes collide with hers.

My breath catches. They're so green.

"I'm sorry. I wasn't paying attention. Please," I say, gesturing for her to continue toward the ladies' room.

Holding her head high, a sexy smile pulls at her lips before she muses, "It was nice bumping into you," and walks away.

I blink, watching her go.

"Enjoy your night," I call before she gets too far away.

She shoots a coy glance back over her shoulder before she disappears.

3

CASEY

I walk on unsteady legs toward the main room where the food is about to be served.

My breather in the bathroom did absolutely nothing for my nerves. I almost talked myself out of coming a million times as I was getting ready. I picked up my cell more times than I can count to call my best friend, Parker, so she could either encourage me or talk me out of it.

But I didn't.

No one knows I'm here tonight. No one knows my intentions, and that is how I intend for it to stay.

I was already a wreck just being here, but the second I collided with Kodie...I'm pretty sure my entire nervous system shattered all over the expensive carpet beneath my feet.

Sure, I've spoken to him before. But I'm just his coach's daughter. There's a line that's been drawn between us.

Tonight is different.

I'm no longer off-limits.

Instead, I'm the brunette in the green dress who made him do a double take.

That was an accident, of course.

Of course, I totally didn't see him coming, distracted by his own thoughts, and just...kept going in the hope we'd crash. Nope. Not at all.

Sucking in a deep breath, I step into the main room where all the tables are arranged for tonight's meal.

Almost everyone has found their seats already. There are just a handful of vacant chairs. One of which is mine.

And guess who it's next to…

Also not entirely a coincidence. Not that I'd ever confess to it.

My stomach flutters wildly and I force myself to put one foot in front of the other.

Everyone around the table is locked in conversation. All but one person.

I can't say I'm surprised. He's not known for his friendly, chatty nature.

He seemed to be a lot more lighthearted when he was in college. But over the last few years, he's become more closed-off, more pensive. I can understand why, after everything he's been through.

I might not have all the details, or even all of the correct ones, but they're enough to know that the events of the past have changed him.

Mustering as much courage and confidence as I can, I reach for the back of the empty chair and pull it out. "Is this seat taken?" I ask lightly, knowing full well that it isn't, and slowly lower myself down.

It takes him a moment to look over, but the second he does, recognition sparks in his eyes.

"Hello," he rasps, a small, endearing grin pulling at the corners of his lips.

He's pleased to see you.

I fight my smile, not wanting to scare him off only seconds after I've taken my seat.

"We meet again," I say coyly.

"So it seems," he muses, glancing toward where my name tag should be.

Yeah, I'm smarter than sitting at a place setting with my father's name on it. I removed that baby long ago.

"So, are you enjoying your evening?" I ask in an attempt to avoid any awkward conversation about our names.

His eyes bounce between mine for a few seconds, forcing me to wait for whatever it is he wants to say.

"Honestly?" he finally asks.

"Stranger to stranger? Sure. Be as honest as you like."

His brows lift. I'm not sure if it's in surprise or shock, but he leans forward a little, allowing his masculine scent to flood my nose and make my attraction hit all-new heights.

He smells really fucking good.

"This isn't really my kind of thing," he confesses.

"So why are you here?" I ask innocently.

He shrugs one shoulder, forcing my eyes down to admire just how well his shirt fits his muscular body.

He's lost his jacket since we collided by the bathrooms, and he only looks hotter because of it.

The soft fabric of his shirt wraps around his solid upper arms, shoulders, and chest like it's a second skin.

Without thinking, my teeth sink into my bottom lip as I continue to let my eyes wander, imagining just what it might be like to unwrap that shirt from his body. Quickly followed by his slacks...

"It's a good cause," he finally says, dragging my eyes up to his.

Despite the mask that covers half of his face, I see something in his expression that has never been there before.

Intrigue.

Heat blooms between my thighs at the thought of him wanting me.

Is this actually going to work?

Am I going to manage to flirt my way to ticking off the very top item on my bucket list?

"That it is," I agree. "So, what do you do when you're not enjoying one of these wonderful events?"

He shakes his head, a grin still on his lips.

"How about we keep the serious stuff out of the conversation tonight?"

"That sounds like my ideal kind of night. So, stranger, tell me something... *unimportant* about yourself."

"Uh..." He pauses for a beat as servers begin to place entrees on our table. "I have a scar here," he finally says, tapping on the side of his mask, letting me know it's hidden beneath.

"Yeah?" I'm beyond curious as I reach for my knife and fork.

"From an ex. Threw her shoe at me when I told her we were done."

"What?" I blurt, almost choking on the Parma ham and goat cheese tartlet I'd taken a bite of.

Kodie shrugs like it's no big deal.

"And don't tell me...you picked her up at an event like this. That would explain why you hate them. You think all the women here are crazy."

He laughs.

"No, she wasn't the kind of woman who'd be here tonight. Too..."

"Hot-headed?" I offer.

"Something like that," he agrees as he cuts the corner of his tartlet off and pushes it past his full, kissable lips.

My tongue sneaks out to lick a crumb from my mouth—or at least, that's what I hope he thinks I'm doing as I watch him chew.

"So, what about you?"

"What about me?" I echo. "A woman has never thrown a shoe at my head."

"What crazy shit has a man done when you've broken his heart?"

I shake my head. "I haven't broken anyone's heart."

"I'm sure that's not true," he assures me as he demolishes his entree in record time. Proving he was subjected to Dad's intense preseason training schedule today.

"Trust me, it is. No one has ever cared enough about me to throw anything. We can't all be special like you," I mock.

He freezes for a beat, and I mentally kick myself. *Strangers, remember?*

Thankfully, they spread the team throughout the tables. Whether it's to allow everyone to mingle or to prevent any questionable behavior from them, I don't know. I've heard many, many stories about the players' nights out. I've longed to join them for years, but it's just another thing that the coach's daughter isn't allowed to do.

Kodie is the only Viper at this table. I recognize a couple of others, but I can't place who they are. Hopefully, that can be said for them, too.

If anyone knows who I am and screws this up for me...

My stomach knots. Not only would Kodie run as fast as possible, but my father would find out, and that can't happen.

My biggest fear is disappointing the man who has given me everything.

Being here? It's the biggest risk I've ever taken in my life.

But sometimes...sometimes you just have to follow your gut. And right now, mine seems to be leading me right into Kodie Rivers, a place I've wanted to be forever.

"Come on, you must have a story," he urges.

I do have a couple of stories. Mostly of being caught doing things I shouldn't be by my father. Probably the reason he threatens bodily harm on his team should he discover they've come anywhere near me. But I can't risk confessing to those.

"Since we're being honest, I'm the one who's usually left with a battered heart." He frowns. "I don't have very good taste in men. Or I didn't before I made my oath."

"Your oath?" he asks, falling for my trap.

"Yep. I no longer do anything that lasts more than a night."

"One night?"

I nod. "Exactly. That way, everyone has fun—or at least they should—and no one gets hurt."

"That's very—"

"Unladylike?" I offer, giving him an out if he wants to be sexist about this.

He shakes his head, smiling. "Not at all. I was thinking more... safe."

"That's what I'm going for. Hit it and quit it."

Kodie snorts, barely stopping himself from spraying the entire table with the sip of water he'd just taken.

"I'm not sure I've ever met a woman like you before," he finally confesses once he's managed to swallow his water and take a breath.

"Well," I start, shamelessly shifting a little closer so that our thighs press together beneath the table. "Maybe tonight is your lucky night."

As if I timed it, the server returns to take my plate, giving me an excuse to lean even closer.

"What do you say, stranger? Wanna make tonight an experience you'll never forget?"

My heart slams against my ribs as the question rolls off my tongue.

Never before have I been so forward. But this might be my one and only chance, so I figure I have nothing to lose.

If he says no, then I can take my lonely ass up to my hotel room and sulk with room service and a cheesy rom-com.

If he says yes, then...well, who the hell knows where this night could go?

A laugh of disbelief erupts from him, his eyes flitting around my face—or more so my mask—as if he's searching for something.

My heart jumps into my throat in fear that he's going to figure it out.

He's seen me in person more times than I can count. But has he ever really *seen* me?

Is he one of those people who pays attention to anyone who is in the room, or does he only focus on what's important, happily letting everything else go? It stings a little that I might be so insignificant that he forgets me the second I turn my back, but it would be naive of me to believe it's any other way. "You're making a lot of assumptions there."

Shit.

He's right.

If I truly have no idea who he is, then I have no reason to know he's single.

I make a show of glancing down at his ring finger. "You're at an event like this by yourself, talking with a stranger instead of having a beautiful woman on your arm."

"What if I'm craving a beautiful man?"

"U-uh—" I stutter, unsure what I should say to that.

"I'm joking." And just to prove his point, as he twists slightly in my direction, he shifts his arm behind me and rests it on the back of my chair, making our position look even more intimate.

My temperature spikes as I gaze up at him. His simple black mask might cover half of his face, but he's still devastatingly beautiful with a thick layer of scruff covering his jaw. I'm incredibly glad he didn't shave that off.

I could hardly blame that woman at the bar earlier when she pounced on him mere seconds after he arrived.

There was a moment when I thought he was going to go for it. She was stunning; he had every right to. But if the media is anything to be believed, then he would do exactly what he did.

That leaves me with a huge question, though...why hasn't he already shot me down?

4

___

KODIE

"Who's the woman? She's smoking," Linc asks the second he comes to stand beside me at the bar. Although, his attention is focused on the woman I've left sitting alone so I can get us drinks.

A grin curls up one side of my mouth as the bartender passes over a glass of scotch for me and champagne for her.

He's not wrong.

She is the best-looking woman I've seen in quite some time, and that's saying something, considering she's hiding her face. But it's more than just her pretty eyes and smile, or her banging body. She's...different.

Sure, I'm used to forward women, but she isn't like the desperate puck bunnies.

She's...mesmerizing, and I'm nowhere close to ending our night.

Not that I think that's an option after what she said earlier.

"What do you say, stranger? Wanna make tonight an experience you'll never forget?"

Fuck. Do I?

If I'd followed my own plan for the night, I'd already be at home and in bed. But as it is, I'm still here getting her another drink, hoping that there are many more to come.

"Jealous?" I ask, not willing to go into any details with him. Not that I really have any

I have no idea who she is. And that's fine.

No, it's more than fine.

It's perfect.

Excitement and nerves collide within me.

It's been so long since I've done this. In all honestly, I don't have a clue what I'm doing.

That last time I dated...

This isn't a date. It's a hook-up, I tell myself. *Just one night, and where it leads is up to us.*

"Fuck, yeah. Did you see who I was seated next to?"

I shake my head.

"Of course you didn't; you were too busy being lured in by the beauty in green. I can't blame you though, man. It's about time you succumbed to your baser instincts and proved to us all that you're not actually a robot without any needs."

My brow wrinkles, my expression hardening. "That's not—"

"I'm joking. Enjoy her." He winks before leaning a little closer to the bartender to place his order.

With our drinks in hand, I return to the seats we secured after the meal in the secluded back corner of the room.

She was the one to choose them, and I was more than happy to oblige.

The fewer people who come over and talk to me, the higher chance I've got of ending this night anonymously.

"Hey," she says with a wide smile as I place her glass of champagne in front of her and lower myself to the seat.

As I do, my thigh brushes against hers, sending a potent shot of adrenaline and lust straight through me.

We weren't sitting this close before...

"So, what do you think about those two?" she asks, picking up her drink and tilting it toward an older couple on the dance floor set up in the middle of the room.

"They're an old married couple," I guess.

"Really?" she asks, sounding skeptical. "See, I've been

watching them while you've been gone, and the little touches and naughty whispers...I think they're lovers."

In our quest to withhold any information about ourselves, we've turned our attention to those around us, trying to predict what their lives are like.

Of course, I know many of them, and it's given me great pleasure to make up bullshit stories about their lives. My favorite has been that Linc is secretly gay and using all the women he's hitting on as a cover.

"What's funny?" she asks, noticing my smirk.

"You," I say, my smile growing. I'm pretty sure it's the most genuine one I've given anyone aside from Sutton and my mom in a very, very long time.

"Well, I'm glad I amuse you."

"You more than amuse me, stranger."

She sucks her red-stained bottom lip into her mouth, and a powerful urge to steal it for myself hits me out of nowhere.

"Is that right?" she breathes, her voice taking on this sexy rasp that hits me right in the balls.

"Yeah."

"So where do you see our story going, *stranger*?" she asks, tilting her head to the side and looking entirely too tempting.

"Well," I muse before swallowing down my scotch in one mouthful. "I'm hoping it continues outside this room."

"Maybe...in my hotel room?" she offers as she takes a sip of her champagne and looks up at me coyly through her lashes.

"You really are serious about tonight, huh?"

"Once I've made a decision about something, I always see it through. Nothing worse than living with regrets."

Reaching up to rub the back of my neck, I mutter, "You got that right."

In a flash, the champagne in her glass vanishes, and she hops to her feet.

"Dance with me," she says, holding her hand out.

"Uh..." I hesitate. "I'm not really a dancer."

"Bullshit. I bet you've got all the moves," she assures me, moving her hand closer.

Shit.

"Does anyone ever say no to you?" I ask as I reluctantly slide my palm against hers.

Heat rushes up my arm the second we connect.

She waits until I'm on my feet and staring down at her much smaller frame before responding.

"More than you'd think."

I narrow my eyes at her, not believing it for a second.

"Come on, stranger. Show me what you've got."

The dance floor is pretty busy, but that doesn't mean I don't gain the attention of several of my teammates. I have no idea what Linc has said to them, but they look intrigued.

Refusing to hold eye contact with any of them, I focus on the woman leading me right into the center of the crowd.

Her sparkling green dress hugs every single one of her curves, showcasing her slim waist, full hips, and killer ass.

The thought of running my hands over her, opening the zipper that runs the length of her back, and discovering what's beneath makes my dick jerk in excitement.

As if dancing in front of all these fuckers isn't going to be bad enough already. I really don't need to do it while rocking a semi.

Finally, she comes to a stop and spins around.

I swear to God, the second her eyes collide with mine and her hands land on my chest, everything around me ceases to exist.

Was it like this with women before? Or has it just been so long that I've forgotten the thrill of it? No wonder all the guys think I'm a freak of nature for not indulging at every opportunity.

Her tiny hands slide higher before she attempts to wrap her arms around my neck. I'm too tall for her to get anywhere close, but points for effort.

Unable to keep my hands off her, I press them against the small of her back and gently drag her closer, ensuring that our bodies are fully pressed together as we begin to move to the music.

It's the most intimate I've been with a woman in years, and I'm in public, yet...I don't care.

"See," she says, smiling up at me. "You're a great dancer."

"And you're not a very good liar."

She freezes at my words, and I kick myself for such a stupid comment.

"I'm sorry, I didn't mean—"

"It's okay. I'm not lying, though. Best dance partner I've had in quite a while."

"I'll take that," I say as the song changes to something a little more upbeat. Although, neither of us speeds up. Instead, we remain moving to the song that only we can hear for a few more minutes.

But as the next song begins, my little troublemaker decides to up the ante. She spins around in my arms, sticks her ass out, and finally begins moving in time with the music.

Well, okay then.

Pushing aside my usual fears and insecurities, I allow myself to let go and dance with her. It's something I haven't done since college, but two songs in, I can't deny that it feels good.

All my stress, the pressure that is constantly pressing down on my shoulders, all the expectations of me just vanish.

And as each song melds into the next one, I become more addicted to both the feeling and the woman in my arms.

I'm too lost in her to notice that another guy approaches through the crowd.

My brows pinch and my lips purse as he approaches my stranger, his eyes studying her with interest.

The second she notices him, her movements slow. She stares at him as he silently makes it known that he wants his turn next. Without realizing it, my grip on her hips tightens as a wave of something I'm not sure I've ever felt before floods through my veins.

Mine.

He steps closer, and I fear my possessive grip gets so tight that she'll have bruises in the morning.

She shifts in my hold, and for a horrifying second, I think she's going to slip away from me and join him. But just before I have to decide whether I'll back away and run off to lick my wounds or fight for the night I thought we'd planned, she makes the decision for me.

Spinning in my arms, she gives him her back, making it more than obvious where her interests lie tonight.

I want to say I take the victory privately, but that would be a lie. When I look up and meet the guy's gaze, I've got a smug-as-fuck grin on my lips.

Irritated by the blatant rejection, he slips back into the crowd, probably on the hunt for his second pick for the night.

Rising on her toes, she whispers in my ear, "You don't need to look so pleased with yourself, you know."

"Why not? I just won gold."

Half of her face might be hidden, but that doesn't stop me from seeing the way it transforms with her wide smile.

"And to think, I was expecting tonight to be boring."

"Same," I agree.

"I only booked a room so I could leave when it got dull and go and watch movies in bed with room service."

"So you didn't plan on seducing a stranger tonight?" I ask, raising a brow.

"Well, I mean...if the opportunity presented itself, it would have been rude to waste it."

She drags her fingertip along the line of my jaw, making my stomach knot, and my semi becomes...well, not so much a semi.

Her smirk tells me that she can feel it pressing against her.

And the second her delicate touch gets to my bottom lip, the situation becomes even more urgent.

"You really are a troublemaker."

I didn't think it was possible, but her smile turns even more wicked as she continues to drag her fingertip across my bottom lip, observing me closely.

Her tongue licks across her own as if she's imagining tasting me just like I am her.

"I think I'm done here," she finally says once her eyes jump back up to mine.

Removing one hand from my waist, she dips her fingers into the top of her dress and pulls out a small, black card.

Without saying anything, she slips it into my shirt pocket.

"Give me ten minutes," she says before taking a step back.

I let her go, my excitement and nerves stopping me from reacting. But just before she slips away, I reach for her.

My fingers wrap around her wrist, and I gently pull her back so I can whisper in her ear.

"I'll follow your rules for now. But once I get up there, I'll be the one in charge."

5

KODIE

She walks through the room with her hips swaying and determination in each step, and reality slams into me.

She's going up to her hotel room to wait...for me.

Holy fuck.

With my eyes still on her, I make my way off the dance floor.

"Bro, where's your girl going?" Fletch asks as I pass him unknowingly.

"U-uh—"

"Is everything okay?" he asks, his hand curling around my shoulder and forcing my attention to him.

"Y-yeah. Everything is great."

He looks in her direction just in time to see her flee through the double doors.

"Your dancing wasn't that bad," he mocks as if it'll make this situation better.

Sucking in a deep breath, I attempt to get my shit together.

I've got a decision to make.

Follow through and potentially have the best night of my life.

Or bail and go home and...always regret it.

Her words from earlier come back to me. *"Nothing worse than living with regrets."*

Would I ever forgive myself if I called a car and disappeared instead of seeing where this could lead me?

She's already told me that she isn't interested in anything more than a night. And she clearly has no idea who I am.

It's safe to let go and enjoy myself, right?

"Kodie?" Fletcher asks, his brows pinched with concern.

"She hasn't left. She's—"

"O-o-ohhhh," he sings, predicting what I'm about to say. "You should go. You should *definitely* go," he encourages, his eyes wide and excited.

"Fletch, I don't—"

"Your secret is safe. Just...make the most of it. See you at practice," he says before clapping me on the back and none-too-gently shoving me forward.

It hasn't been long enough yet, so instead of making my way upstairs I head toward the hotel bar.

One for the road...or should it be, one for the elevator?

Once I've ordered and taken a seat, I pull the card from my pocket and open it.

Inside is her keycard, and her room number scrawled on the opposite side.

My stomach flips as I wonder what she's doing right now.

Cleaning up?

Getting changed?

No sooner is my third scotch of the night placed in front of me than I have the glass against my lips.

"Fuck," I hiss as it burns all the way down.

This certainly isn't the evening I thought I was going to have.

But...when in Rome, and all that.

Placing some bills on the bar, I take off in search of the elevators that will take me to the tenth floor—and hopefully the brunette in the green dress.

My foot taps and my fingers fidget nervously as the car climbs higher through the building. But it's not until I step out that a thought hits me.

Will she have taken her mask off?

If she has, will she expect me to do the same?

I glance over my shoulder, contemplating turning back, but the thought only lasts for a millisecond.

I may not want her to know who I am, but I can't back out now.

With my eyes tracking the numbers on the doors, I finally find the one I want.

One-zero-five-five.

Fifty-five...that's my number.

Any doubt I had vanishes as I stare at it.

My gut instinct screams that this is the right thing to do, so without allowing my head to get involved, I knock on the door twice.

Silence.

Once again refusing to listen to my fears about her not being on the other side, or this being a setup, I tap the key to the small black box beside the door and crack it open.

"H-hello?" I call, realizing for the first time that I don't have anything to call her.

"Come in." The second her seductive voice hits my ears, every muscle in my body relaxes. But it only lasts for a second, because the next thing I know, her sweet perfume is luring me in.

I don't see the room. It could be any color. Hell, it could be empty, for all I know.

The only thing I see is her.

She's standing in the center, still in her green dress and, thankfully, still wearing her mask.

Fuck. We're really doing this.

Swallowing down my apprehension, I remember who I am.

Or at least, who I used to be.

I come to a stop when there's only a foot between us and just stare at her.

Neither of us says a word. We don't need to. Our eyes and our bodies do all the talking for us.

One second, nothing is happening, and the next, I'm surging toward her, sinking one hand into her hair and clamping the other on her ass, pinning her tiny body against mine.

Her shriek of shock is swallowed the moment my lips connect with hers, and I kiss her just like I wanted to downstairs.

There is no soft and gentle. No easing in. We dive straight into exactly what we want.

It's wild and it's filthy. It's everything she promised me.

Our masks collide, but neither of us makes a move to remove them, letting me know that she's just as happy to stay anonymous as I am.

My heart races to the point I'm sure it's trying to beat out of my chest, and my skin prickles with the need to feel her touch on every inch of me. But nothing compares to the state of my dick.

Fuck. I've heard the term "so hard it's painful" many, many times in my life, but I've never felt it as wholly as I do now.

The pain is fucking real.

And something tells me that the second she touches me, I'm going to embarrass myself beyond belief.

I need to take the edge off.

The only person who's touched my cock in...longer than I can remember is me.

Fuck, that is mortifying.

Tightening my fingers in her hair, I drag her back, severing our connection.

I blink twice in disbelief when there are a few inches between us.

How is she even more beautiful than she was downstairs?

Not willing to lose myself in my thoughts, I dive into action.

"Turn around," I demand, and she follows orders without missing a beat.

I knew there was something right about this woman.

She stands confidently, her slender shoulders bare and the zipper of her dress taunting me.

Moving forward, my fingers clasp the tiny bit of metal resting between her shoulder blades as my lips press against her neck.

"Oh god," she whimpers as I kiss a trail along her shoulder, slowly pulling the zipper down.

The moment I pass her hips, the dress plummets to the floor, leaving her beautifully naked beneath.

"Have you been walking around like this all night?" I ask,

palming myself as I take in the delicate curve of her spine before it hits the fullness of her ass.

"Maybe," she taunts.

With a smirk, I shake my head and walk around her to the other side of the bed.

I give myself a moment in the hope of controlling my raging arousal before I turn around and get a proper look at her.

She almost knocks me on my ass.

Fuck. She's perfect.

There are so many things I could say in this moment, but we're not here for conversation or compliments. We're here for one thing and one thing only.

Pleasure.

"Come here," I demand.

Being dominant in the bedroom isn't new to me. I learned early on that I loved being the one in charge; I loved watching a woman bend to my wishes.

But this is the first time it hasn't come naturally to me.

It's because it's been so long and I'm out of practice.

Or at least, that's what I tell myself.

After stepping from the mass of fabric around her feet, she moves closer, her hips swaying and her breasts bouncing gently as she moves.

I take in every inch of her skin. Her breasts are the perfect handful, one slightly bigger than the other. Her rosy pink nipples begging to be pinched and sucked, and her hairless pussy is already glistening with desire.

My mouth waters as I wonder if she'll taste as sweet as I imagine.

"Good girl," I praise when she stops in front of me.

Her eyes widen, but the slight smile on her lips and the way she wiggles her hips lets me know that she likes it.

"Now what?" she asks, happily playing the game.

"Get on your knees and take my dick out."

All the air rushes from her lungs, but although she might be surprised, she doesn't back down from the challenge.

Instead, her knees hit the thick carpet beneath us, and she eagerly reaches for my waistband.

She moves with such fervor and haste that I can't help but wonder if it's been as long for her as it has been for me.

No, it can't be. Not a woman this sexy and tempting.

My body flinches violently when she tucks her fingers beneath the fabric of my boxers.

Squeezing my eyes closed, I pray to whatever sex deity there might be up there to stop me from embarrassing myself.

I'm not sure it'll be enough.

My eyes pop back open the second she begins to tug the fabric over my hips.

I stare down at her in disbelief as she does exactly as she's told.

But instead of focusing on the task at hand, her eyes are staring up into mine.

My breath catches as my dick springs free and I send up another prayer.

Every single muscle in my body is pulled tight, waiting for what comes next. But...nothing happens.

Instead, she rests her hands on her thighs and waits, her eyes not wavering from mine.

Shit.

"Do you want my dick, Troublemaker?" The second I say the word "dick," her eyes drop, and fuck if the way they widen and her lips pop open in surprise doesn't give me the confidence boost that I need.

She licks her lips before nodding. "Yes."

"Then you're going to need to prove you deserve it."

I don't need to give her any more instructions. That's all she needs.

Her slim fingers wrap around my shaft, and she strokes me twice before leaning forward and licking around the head.

Ho-ly fuck.

How I don't blow then and there as I watch her get started is anyone's fucking guess.

"More." The plea falls from my lips without instruction from my brain. But when she takes me fully in her mouth, I don't regret it. "Fuck. Fuck," I grunt as my fingers sink into her hair so I can hold her in place.

The guys are right. I am missing out.

"Jesus," I groan as I hit the back of her throat.

Still, she stares up at me with her large, emerald eyes.

Even if I wanted to, I couldn't look away.

She's...addictive.

She works me like she's been doing it all her life, hitting all those magical spots that threaten to make me come long before I'm ready. But as much as I might want to hold off and make this last forever, I also really want to fuck her.

I can't do that yet. Not until she's taken the edge off.

If we're doing this—and it very much looks like we are— then we're doing it properly. I don't want a quick wham, bam, thank you, ma'am. I want the full one-night stand experience. One that will leave me exhausted yet satisfied tomorrow. One that will get me through the next God knows how many depressing years of celibacy.

"Yesss," I moan as she does...something that makes my head almost implode.

Fuck.

There is not a single chance of me forgetting this night for a very, very long time.

Whether that's going to be a blessing or a curse, I'm yet to figure out.

6

———

CASEY

His dick swells, stretching my lips wider a beat before the first drop of salty cum lands on my tongue.

My eyes are still locked on his face, or the parts of it I can see. I'm addicted to his reactions. The way his jaw tenses beneath the scruff and his neck ripples when he swallows. The way he bites down on his bottom lip and the way he gazes down at me with fire burning bright in his eyes. What were nicely styled curls a few hours ago are now a tousled mess on his head, the front falling forward and into his eyes as he watches me.

Even with the mask in place, he looks hot as hell and everything I expected. He is everything I ever wanted and dared to hope for. And we've barely even started.

Aside from a kiss, he hasn't even touched me yet.

But I know it's going to be worth the wait.

I suck him through his orgasm, swallowing down every drop. This is going to be the one and only time I get to experience this. I want to savor every moment...

You're being weird, Casey.

Sitting back on my haunches, I let his dick slip from between my lips before wiping my mouth with the back of my hand.

He stands there, a huge, looming presence before me with his pants around his hips, beneath his softening dick. He looks just as much of a god as he does on the ice. The only thing that will make it better is to strip him bare and get to see firsthand just how much ink covers his skin.

"Get on the bed."

Faster than I thought I could move, I scramble to my feet. My head spins, thanks to the glasses of champagne I've had tonight. I'm far from drunk, but the bubbles have certainly helped loosen me up and alleviate my nerves.

As I crawl onto the bed, I try to ignore the thought that pops into my head.

You're in a hotel room with your teenage crush. The man who's featured in all your dirty fantasies since you were thirteen.

Being rational about this isn't going to get me anywhere. I'll end up an anxious mess who doesn't look like she knows what she's doing.

I might not have a wealth of knowledge where sex is concerned, but I know enough to be confident that I can rock his world. And anyway, if the stories about him are true, he hasn't seen any action in a very long time, so it's not like I'm going to be compared to anything.

He moves to the end of the bed as I settle in the middle with my head on the pillow and everything on display.

How is it fair that I'm naked and he's fully dressed? My eyes drop to his dick. *Almost* fully dressed.

I could have predicted it, but I'm pretty sure he has the most perfect cock I've ever seen.

Movement a little higher catches my attention, and when I look up, I find him pulling his bowtie free before he begins undoing his buttons.

My stomach does a little flip and I have the sudden urge to grab my cell and film his strip tease.

I refrain in favor of enjoying every single inch he reveals, instead of giving away the fact that I know who he is and swiftly putting an end to the night.

I've seen him shirtless at the facility, and also in the many, many photos of him I've stared at over the years, but none of them compare to this moment.

He's not just getting naked because he's about to change to hit the ice, or to jump in the shower after practice. Nor because he's being paid to model something.

He's doing it because he wants to fuck me.

Oh my god, Kodie Rivers is going to fuck me.

The over-excitable teenage girl who lives inside me is having a party right now. But on the outside, I'm a demure, sexy woman waiting to be fucked within an inch of her life. Hopefully.

My fingers twist in the sheets beneath me as he loses the shirt, toes off his shoes, and then finally pushes his slacks and boxers down his legs.

He makes me wait a couple of seconds, but it's so worth it, because when he stands to full height again...holy fucking cow.

I was wrong. This man isn't just a god. He's a...he's a...

My brain cells misfire as he presses one knee into the mattress and reaches for my ankles.

My breath catches as fire burns up my legs, colliding with the inferno already growing inside me.

"Argh," I cry out as he drags me exactly where he wants me before sliding two tattooed hands up my calves. He pauses at my knees for a beat, and then he spreads them wide open.

His eyes immediately drop to my pussy, and his Adam's apple bobs as he swallows.

"Oh god," I whimper, desperate to twist my fingers in his messy hair and hold his face against me for the next hour.

He takes his time lifting his eyes up my body, almost like he's memorizing me, before our gazes lock.

He leans closer, and then closer still. At some point, I stop breathing, but everything kickstarts in a heartbeat when his lips gently brush the inside of my knee before he begins kissing a trail to where I crave him the most.

"Fuck," I groan when his hot breath races over my sensitive skin.

His eyes hold mine as he swipes his tongue across my clit.

I gasp before biting my lips closed for fear that I'm going to cry out his name.

Do. Not. Ruin. This. Now.

Pride glitters in his eyes as he does it again and then begins to suck on my clit.

He's good. So fucking good.

All of my dirtiest fantasies are coming to life, and I am fucking here for it.

He eats me like a man who hasn't indulged in a decade.

With my fingers twisted in his curly hair, I hold him in place, desperate for him to keep going—not that I think he's about to bail. He is fully invested.

"So fucking sweet," he mumbles against me, the vibrations of his deep voice rolling through me and dragging my release that little bit closer.

My legs tremble around his head, and my back arches as he sucks on me.

But the second his fingers join the party, I almost lose it.

Not yet.

Please, not yet.

I force my eyes to remain open, fighting against their desperation to close so I can fully focus on the man who's doing this to me.

I want to watch every moment so I can relive it over and over again once it's nothing more than a memory.

"Oh fuck," I cry as he pushes one digit inside me.

My muscles clamp down on his finger as I fight against my body's need to crash.

Sucking in a deep breath, I try my hardest to hold off, to make this last as long as I possibly can.

It's a little awkward with his mask still firmly in place, but its coolness feels so good against my heated skin. Although, not as good as the scruff that covers his jaw. The scratch of that on the soft skin of my thighs is next level.

"FUUUCK," I gasp when he adds a second finger and curls them deep inside me.

He easily finds my G-spot and goes to town.

"Shit. Fuck. Fuck. I'm gonna..."

I gulp down lungfuls of air as he builds me higher and higher.

All I can see is him as I teeter right on the edge of what I already know is going to be the most intense release of my life.

"Oh fuuuuuuuck," I moan, unable to keep it inside as he finally pushes me over the edge.

Pleasure like I've never known races through my body, making every single one of my muscles tremble with the strength of it.

I swear, fireworks actually explode within me. I see the flashes behind my eyes. My eyes that I still refuse to close.

And if his constant eye contact with me tells me anything, it's that he doesn't want to miss anything either.

The thought that tonight could be as huge for him as it is for me flickers through my mind. But there's no way. Sure, we might be ending a dry spell for him, but he isn't living out his wildest dreams right now.

The truth is, if I were to remove my mask and he were to recognize me, he probably wouldn't even remember my name.

Shoving that depressing thought deep, deep down, I focus on the here and now.

This is what I wanted.

One night with the man I've lusted after as long as I can remember.

Just one night to live out my wildest fantasies.

Once he's confident that I've finished, he swipes his tongue up the length of me again before sitting up and pulling his fingers from inside me.

My body weeps at the loss, and I have to clamp my lips closed to stop me begging for more.

"Anyone one ever told you how hot you look when you come?" he asks, his lips still glistening with my release. Lifting his fingers to his mouth, he sucks them clean.

My cheeks burn red hot, but I can't fight the smile that pulls at my lips.

"I don't remember," I breathe.

It's true. Everything I've ever experienced before with a man now pales in comparison.

Tonight is going to be my benchmark for every encounter going forward.

The only problem is, I'm not sure anyone is going to match up.

After sitting up, Kodie shuffles toward the end of the bed, and my stomach sinks at the thought of him leaving.

"Where are you—"

He holds his slacks up and pulls his wallet from the pocket. The sight of the condom packet makes a rush of air spill from my lips.

It's not over.

He returns to his position between my legs, and the second he lifts the packet up to open, I reach out and swipe it from his fingers.

There is no way I'm missing an opportunity like this.

"Hey," he complains, although he doesn't sound like he really means it.

I'm about to open the foil when something catches my eye. "Uh...this expired, like, eighteen months ago."

He stills, and a second later, the most incredible thing happens.

He blushes.

Kodie freaking Rivers is naked on a bed with me, and he's fucking blushing.

This is just too awesome for words.

"Oh, umm..."

Lifting his hand, he combs his fingers through his messy hair, looking a little confused.

Poor man has too much blood in his dick to be able to think straight.

"It's okay. I've got us covered," I say, swinging my legs off the bed and jumping to my feet. "Lie back. Let me take care of this," I shoot over my shoulder as I shove my hand into my overnight bag and pull out a new box.

"And you told me you wanted a quiet night with a movie," Kodie mutters, eyeing the full box.

"Always be prepared. You never know what kind of stranger you're going to meet. Now," I say, gesturing for him to lie back.

I know he told me that he was in charge in this room, but he's going to have to concede for a moment.

If he lets me indulge, I'll repay the favor after.

"I promise to make it worth your while," I sing when he hesitates.

"Fine," he says, flopping onto his back and offering himself up.

I study him for a moment. The bed suddenly looks a hell of a lot smaller with his giant frame on it. But it's not just his physical size that takes up so much space. It's also his confidence.

He hasn't shown a single sign that he's second-guessing this, and fuck, I can't even describe how fucking epic that makes me feel.

Ripping open the condom packet, I crawl between his legs and get ready to move this night to the next level.

7

KODIE

I'm mesmerized as she rolls the rubber down my shaft.

Handing over control isn't something I do lightly, but the way she looked at me through her mask when she asked me to switch positions...I couldn't say no.

I was too intrigued to see what she was going to do.

Eating her out...Fuck.

I can still taste her on my tongue.

She's addictive.

My dick jerks in her hold as she rolls all the way to the base.

She stares at me for a moment before her eyes jump to mine and she starts moving.

The second she's in reaching distance, I wrap my hands around her waist to support her as she straddles me.

Precum leaks from my tip at the thought of her sinking down on me.

She's tight, I know that from just finger-fucking her. I can only imagine how this is going to feel, or how I'm meant to hold off from coming the second I'm inside her.

I had hoped the blow job would have taken the edge off. It did...for about five minutes.

Now, I'm riding a knife's edge again.

Her palms land on my shoulders, her touch burning all the way down to my dick.

Releasing her with one hand, I hold my cock up ready for her.

My heart pounds, and my fears about blowing this—pun intended—are very real. But like fuck am I ending this now. It's only just started.

Slowly, she lowers herself.

The heat of her pussy scorches me even through the condom long before we connect.

My teeth grind as I wait for the inevitable, but when it comes...Christ...I am not ready.

"Fuck," I grunt as her pussy stretches around me. Her heat, the softness, the tightness.

Holy fuck.

How am I going to go back to not having this in my life?

"Oh god," she whimpers, her arms already trembling as she continues to sink lower.

She's so small, it's hard to imagine how she takes all of me. But she does.

She takes me so well.

Almost too well.

"Jesus, you're—fuck," I mumble, unable to come up with anything more intellectual.

"Yeah. It's...Christ," she groans as she pushes herself up, changing the angle and forcing me even deeper.

With both my hands on her hips, I help her move.

I'm enthralled watching her as she rides me. Her tits bounce, loose locks of hair sway around her shoulders, and her eyes sear into mine.

It's almost like she's trying to imprint herself on my soul.

She doesn't need to try very hard. I'm pretty sure she's already there.

"Oh my god, yes," she cries, taking it at a speed she loves, grinding her hips every time she has all of me inside her.

It's fucking mind-blowing.

"Fucking love your dick," she announces as her orgasm begins to build.

Mine is too, but I'll do anything I can to hold it off and make sure she gets at least two first.

I can't say that I've always been such a gentleman. But she deserves it.

If all we're having is tonight, then it needs to be memorable.

Hell knows it already has been for me. But I might just be another notch on the bedpost for her.

She hasn't been shy about how she lives her life, which I appreciate, but I also haven't missed the irony in the role reversal. It's usually the hockey players who want the one-night stands, not the girls. They all secretly want commitment, weddings, and babies.

"I'm gonna come all over your dick, stranger."

"Fuck, yeah, you are,' I agree, both desperate and terrified to feel it.

Please don't force me over the edge with you. Not yet.

Unable to stop myself, I shift one of my hands so I can press my thumb against her clit.

She cries out at the added sensation, and not ten seconds later do I get the pleasure of watching her fall apart on me.

Best fucking thing I've seen in a while.

I let her ride it out, but the second she comes back to herself, I flip us over.

I may have handed her control, but it had an expiration time. A bit like the condom I was going to use. Not my finest moment.

Momentarily, a little fear trickles through my veins as I consider just how differently this could have ended...

Don't go there.

Do not go there.

Wrapping my hand around the back of her thigh, I push her knee to her shoulder, fully opening her up for me before I drag my dick through her folds and push back inside her.

"Yes," she cries as her walls ripple around me.

Forgetting how slowly she fucked me, I pull out and instantly thrust back in.

The headboard bangs against the wall, but I don't give a fuck.

She's had her soft and gentle. Now...she's getting fucked, Kodie Rivers style.

She shouts, screams, moans, and mewls as I take her hard and fast.

Her tits bounce, her skin glistening with exertion as sweat begins to bead my brow and run down my back.

"Fuck. This is...This...you..." I have no idea what I'm saying, but words just spill free of their own accord. My brain isn't in control now; my body and my pleasure have completely taken over. "Come for me, stranger. Let me feel you strangling my dick again."

"Oh god," she cries as the bed continues to bang.

Her nails scratch down my back, marking me up nicely as she climbs higher and higher, taking me right along with her.

"Yes, yes. Harder. Please. Give it to me."

So I do. I give her everything I've got until we both find our releases.

Pleasure like I've never known rocks through my body. The rest of the world may as well cease to exist. The only thing I can feel is her. Is pleasure.

It was never like this before.

I'm sure of it.

This...this is...

Her.

With that terrifying realization slamming into me, I collapse on top of her trembling body with my dick still inside her.

"Oh my god," she gasps as her hands slide up my back and tuck my face into the crook of her neck as I fight to catch my breath.

I know I should probably be making a move now that we're done, but I can't. Well, that's a lie; I can, because I'm more than capable of pulling my head from her shoulder and finding her lips. I kiss the corner of her mouth, but it's not enough. I need more.

Lifting my weight from her, I reluctantly slip from her body and remove the condom. A coldness I'm not sure I've ever felt before rushes over me.

Placing my hands on either side of her head, I deepen the kiss, not willing to end our night yet.

It seems that the feeling is mutual, because she wraps her legs around my waist and pins me to her.

Our kiss is just as wild as our first. Our tongues twist, our teeth clash, and our masks collide. For the first time tonight, I get the urge to say fuck it and rip the thing from my face.

But I don't.

I know I can't.

Instead, I lose myself in her.

In only seconds, I'm hard again and ready for the next round.

Blindly, I reach for another condom and roll it on without breaking our kiss.

"More?" I mumble into her mouth.

"More," she agrees.

I shift a little awkwardly and slide my arm beneath her back, lifting her from the bed and depositing her in my lap.

With her arms wrapped around my neck, she lifts up to allow me to angle myself properly, and then she sinks down once more.

We sigh in both relief and pleasure as we connect again.

Why does this feel so...natural? Like I belong?

There's no slow movement this time, but equally, there's no hard fucking. It's just...frantic. The kind of "I must have you now" sex. Like our bodies already know it's the last time.

Our hands are everywhere; our lips just as manic as we kiss, suck, and nip any bit of each other's skin we can get to.

With her grinding down, and me thrusting up, her orgasm quickly builds, and before long, she's throwing her head back and crying out as she comes again.

Twisting my fingers in her hair, I drag her back to me before she's finished so I can come inside her.

Her hands go to my hair and we make out like a pair of teenagers. I'm so consumed by her kiss that I don't notice the strap around the back of my head slip away. But the second my mask drops from my face, we both freeze.

She pulls back before I have a chance to get it back into place, and dread rushes through my veins.

My heart jumps into my throat, and it only gets worse when I look back at her and find her staring at me in awe.

"Fuck," I hiss as I lift her from my body and climb from the bed.

I fucking hate that I do it, and from the way her brows knit together, she does too.

But I have to.

Without thinking, I pull the condom off and drop it into the trash before I reach for my clothes.

"Wait," she cries, scrambling across the bed, closer to me. "It's okay."

Something in her voice gives me pause.

"You already knew, didn't you?"

She swallows thickly, her lips pressed into a thin line.

"It doesn't matter. Everything I said to you was true. This was just about tonight."

A bitter laugh spills from my lips.

"Like I haven't heard that before," I scoff.

"I mean it," she assures me. "Tonight...it..." It's her turn to laugh, but there isn't any amusement in it. Instead, it's full of self-loathing. "Tonight has been the best night of my life. But I swear to you, it's between us. Our little secret."

I stand there with my slacks in hand and my dick still hanging out, staring at her in disbelief.

Leave, Kodie. You need to get the fuck out of this room and away from this woman.

"Our little secret?" I repeat. "Why?"

She shrugs. "Because it was fun? Because not everything needs to be plastered over the internet? Because we're two consenting adults who can let go without consequences?"

"Hit it and quit it, right?" I ask, hating the way it sounds now that we're in this situation.

But despite the desperate urge to drop my clothes and crawl back into bed with her, I refrain.

"Right," she agrees. "But as per my rules, we've got until sunrise," she offers with a smile.

I consider it. I really fucking do. Temptation is sitting right before me, looking devastatingly beautiful and perfectly messed up.

"Take off your mask." The demand is out of my mouth before I've really thought about it.

Her mouth opens and closes, but her hands never lift from her lap.

I don't know what difference it makes, really. This was always going to be a one-night stand, whether we knew each other or not.

But now, it only seems fair.

"I-I can't," she whispers, ripping her eyes from mine and staring down at the carpet.

"Why?"

"Because...because I just can't, okay?" she says with a little more strength in her words.

The moment her gaze returns to mine, I know that she won't be talked around.

"Okay, then," I say flatly as I pull my boxers up my legs. "I guess we're done here."

"No, plea—" She cuts herself off and bites down on her lips to stop from begging. After taking a deep breath, she changes tack. "Thank you for tonight. I'm not sure you'll ever know what it meant to me."

I narrow my eyes, still suspicious as fuck about what all of this was about and how fast she's going to sell the story to the press. But there's fuck all I can do about it now. Offering anything for her silence will only make the situation worse. I'll just have to grin and bear it.

I don't say anything. I can't. I don't have any words.

Instead, I dress in silence with her watching my every move.

With one final look in her direction, I walk toward the door.

I've got my fingers around the handle when her voice floats through the air, making me pause.

"I meant what I said, Kodie."

The second she says my name, all the hairs on my body stand on end.

"Our little secret."

My nostrils flare with irritation.

I want to believe her. I really do. But life has taught me to trust no one.

"We'll see," I say flatly before pulling the door open and walking away.

If only forgetting what happened inside that room would be so easy...

8

KODIE

"Daddy," Sutton sings, scaring the ever-loving shit out of me.

I sit upright on the couch, my eyes sore and tired, my vision blurry.

She races toward me with a wide smile and jumps into my arms.

All the air rushes out of my lungs as her small body collides with my larger one. But the second she wraps her arms around my body and squeezes me tight, everything feels that little bit better.

No sooner had I walked out of my stranger's hotel room last night than I climbed into the back of an Uber.

I requested he drive me the long way home in the hope that the journey would help me clear my head.

It did fuck all.

By the time I silently slipped into my house, I was still a mess.

I stopped in the kitchen for a bottle of water, and instead of going up to bed, my ass hit the couch. And that's where I stayed.

After turning my cell off, I finished the bottle of water and laid back.

Despite my exhaustion, I didn't fall asleep for hours.

Instead, I tortured myself with memories of everything that happened last night.

From the moment the troublemaker in the pretty green dress ran into me, until she called my name just before I ripped the door open and marched away.

How could I have been so fucking stupid?

So fucking naive?

It's not like I haven't been there before, or witnessed it with my teammates time and time again.

I know exactly what happens next.

It was okay to have my private life splashed all over the internet when I was young and unattached—hell, it was even relatively safe while Sutton was a baby.

But now?

My little girl is seven.

She has access to the internet—albeit limited. She loves watching ESPN for hockey news; she finds all the things she can and soaks it all up like most little girls do about their favorite pop stars.

The thought of her seeing some woman run her mouth about the night she spent with me fucking terrifies me.

Sutton is already grown up for her age, seeing as she's been forced to live this life with me. I want to at least try to keep her a kid for as long as possible.

The last thing she needs is to be reading about what I get up to behind closed doors.

"Why are you still in your suit, Daddy?" Sutton asks when she sits back and looks at me.

"I was tired when I got in. Fell asleep on the couch."

"That won't be very good for your performance," she points out helpfully.

"I know," I mumble, feeling like a child who's been caught raiding the snack cupboard.

"Preseason is upon us. We need you in top form. We're going to the playoffs this year. I can feel it."

The smile she gives me makes my chest tighten.

"Yeah?" I force out, my voice rough with emotion.

"Yep," she confirms confidently. "You have the best team not only in the conference but in the league this year."

Pride for my girl swells within me.

"I know Henderson's trade was controversial, but I think Coach knows what he's doing."

A laugh bursts out of me.

"I told him so as well. I think he was pleased with the feedback."

"Oh, I'm sure he was."

Her expression is hard and focused. "I also mentioned that he should consider Rodrigo from the Jets. I think he would bring something to the team."

Reaching out, I tuck a lock of hair behind her ear. "I'm sure he's given it some serious thought, Peanut. Are you hungry?"

A smile brightens her previously serious face and she hops off my lap. "Starving," she cries, running for the kitchen.

I shake my head, a grin playing on my lips.

"Still want pancakes?"

She rolls her eyes. "Obviously. With Nutella, and strawberries, and cream."

"I'll see what I can do," I say as I grab a mug from the cupboard and place it under the machine, grabbing another for my mom knowing she won't be far away.

"Did I smell coffee?" the woman in question asks the second she walks into the kitchen.

"Yep, Daddy's having coffee."

I don't turn around to see Mom's expression, but her stare burns down my back.

"Is that right? Did Daddy have a good time last night?"

"He slept on the couch."

"I am in the room, you know," I bark.

"Oh, we know. We just also know that we don't get any details out of you."

"Oh, was there any chocolate?" Sutton suddenly remembers.

"Uh..." I think back to the night before, but I can barely even picture the table or the decorations, let alone if there were any chocolates. All I can see is *her*.

"Daddy," Sutton complains at my lack of attention.

"It seems like Daddy might have been too distracted to search for chocolate, sweetie," Mom says with a conspiratorial glint in her eyes before they drop to my neck.

Panic shoots through my veins.

Tell me she didn't leave a mark.

"Would you also like pancakes, Mom?" I ask, trying to change the subject.

She studies me closely as she takes the stool at the island beside Sutton.

"That would be lovely, thank you."

Sutton and Mom spend the next forty-five minutes grilling me about the night before. Mom's eyes light up when Sutton asks if there were any pretty girls with beautiful dresses.

I mumble some kind of non-committal response that nowhere near satisfies Mom's need for information.

"I'm going to look online when you're at training," Sutton announces.

My stomach tightens as fear shoots through me.

"That's okay, isn't it, Daddy?" she asks, letting me know that I failed at keeping my reaction from my face.

"Just make sure you do it with Gran," I say, reminding her of the rules regarding internet use.

"Of course."

"Granny is interested too," Mom quips.

"Okay, great. I'm going to shower. I need to be at the arena in thirty."

I rush out of the room, leaving them talking about what color dress Sutton would wear if she were allowed to go last night.

"Fucking hell," I groan, scrubbing my hand down my face as I take the stairs two at a time.

The second I kick my bedroom door closed, I undo my shirt buttons and shrug it from my shoulders. My slacks and boxers go next, and I walk into the bathroom wearing nothing but the ink that covers my skin.

Without overthinking it, I stand in front of the mirror, my eyes going to my throat.

"Thank fuck," I hiss when I don't find any evidence of the night before.

I lean a little closer to double-check that she didn't leave her mark on me, but there's nothing.

Shaking my head, I step into the shower and turn it on, letting myself get hit with ice-cold water in the hope it might wash away the memories of last night.

Who was she?

And why did she refuse to remove her mask?

"**R**ivers." I wince as his deep voice booms down the hallway. "Wait up."

Our captain's footsteps ring out around me, getting closer with each one he takes.

"Hey," I say when he finally catches up to me a few feet from the dressing room door.

"Whoa, you look like a man who had a good night," he announces the second he gets a look at my face.

"Can we not?" I groan as he pushes the door open and steps inside.

The dressing room is quiet, but then I guess that's to be expected seeing as I'm early.

Our training session doesn't officially start for almost an hour.

"Oh, shit," he gasps. "Didn't it happen?"

"Fletch," I groan.

"She looked so fucking into you. I can't believe—"

"Good morning, lights of my life," Lincoln sings as he bursts into the dressing room like it's his personal stage. "How the fuck are we all after a fan-fucking-tastic night?"

"Jesus," Fletch mutters, scrubbing his hand down his face.

"Aw, Cap, was the ball and chain too exhausted after her big night to celebrate?"

"Fuck you," he scoffs.

It's a well-known fact that Fletcher Ferguson doesn't talk about sex with Reese. I admire the hell out of him for it. I've played with plenty of guys who did the opposite; it's disrespectful as fuck, if you ask me. Your relationship with your wife—hell, even your serious girlfriend—should be sacred, not locker-room gossip.

"One day, man. One day we're going to discover what Reese does to keep you in a perpetual good mood."

Fletch chuckles but doesn't agree to anything.

"But while we wait for that day to come, I think we need to discuss last night with Rivers."

Turning my back on both of them, I pretend to look busy. It's never going to work, but I try nonetheless.

"Yeah, she was banging," Linc says, trying to bait me.

I clench my jaw as an image of her dancing with him flickers through my mind.

I have no doubt he'd have tried his luck with her if I hadn't gotten there first.

Linc is a player in every sense of the word. A woman as beautiful as my troublemaker wouldn't stand a chance.

She's not yours, a little voice pipes up.

It was a one-night thing. She said so herself...

My cell burns a hole in my pocket.

I still haven't turned it on for fear of what might be written about me this morning.

"Not often I miss my chance with the hottest girl at a party because of Rivers."

Irritation burns through my veins, but I refuse to take the bait.

"Of course, it's not too late. I'm sure she'd appreciate experiencing a real man after spending the night with him. Something tells me he's better at scoring on the ice than he is in bed. And she looked like a woman who knew exactly what she wanted."

My shoulders tighten with my need to say something, but I swallow my words.

Doing so will give me away.

"Storm," Fletch warns.

"What was her name, Rivers?"

"Shut the fuck up," I seethe before pulling my hoodie over my head and throwing it onto the bench.

"Unless, of course, I'm wrong. Unless you *are* seeing her again," he taunts.

Pulling my water bottle from my bag, I squirt some into my mouth before spinning around to glare at Storm.

"None of your fucking business," I state, my eyes locked on Linc's.

His fucking smirk is so cocky, my fist curls with the need to wipe it from his face.

"Come on, bro," he teases. "Who is she? And was she as banging in bed as she was in that dress? That was where you slipped off to, right?"

"She is none of your fucking business," I repeat.

"Oh, you totally banged her," Linc states smugly. "Dude, I'm seriously delighted for you. Although, I would have hoped it would have chilled you out a bit. You're tense as fuck."

"I'm tired," I mutter.

"Fucking knew she'd be a wild one. It was in her eyes."

"How the fuck would you know anything about her eyes when she was staring into mine all night?"

I regret the words when accomplishment glitters in his eyes.

"And if you want to know the details, I'm sure she's already blasted it over the internet for everyone and their wife to read."

Slamming my palms against his chest to force him out of the way, I storm out of the dressing room and head toward the gym to get my session started early.

9

———

CASEY

Safe to say, I didn't get much sleep Friday night.

All night, I chastised myself.

Firstly, for being so lost in the moment that I managed to dislodge his mask. If I didn't do that, how long would it have continued for?

Or was it always going to end there?

I might have since left my hotel room, but the memories of my night with Kodie Rivers will stay with me forever. But the moment he walked away without looking back...that one is going to haunt me.

One question has cycled round and round my head ever since the moment the lock clicked into place...

Should I have removed my mask?

I know the real answer.

I'd have put Kodie in an awful position, forcing him to either own up or keep a secret from one of the most important men in his life. From his teammates.

I couldn't do that to him.

Just like I would never, ever sell our story from that night.

The details are going to my deathbed.

A smile plays on my lips as I think about it.

It was everything I hoped it would be.

Do I wish I could do it all over again? Of course I do. I'd never say no to another round with Kodie Rivers.

Do I think it will ever happen? Nope. Not a chance.

And do you know what? I'm surprisingly okay with that.

I set out that night with one quest in mind, and I succeeded.

I'm one happy and satisfied girl.

Or at least, that's what I tell myself as I stand in front of the bathroom mirror, staring at myself.

My hair is finally back to the color it should be, after four washes.

Now, I'm just me again and no one is any the wiser.

Casey Watson, daughter of the infamous LA Vipers ice hockey coach, James Watson.

A pained sigh falls from my lips.

It was fun being someone else for the night.

Being wild.

I may never have done anything as risky as that before, but it was a little reminder that Fun Casey still exists somewhere.

Somewhere between work and life, I've lost her. It was nice reconnecting with her, even if it was only for a few hours.

Scraping my hair back into a ponytail, I apply a light coat of makeup before returning to my bedroom, stuffing my feet into my sneakers, and swiping my bag from the floor.

It's Sunday morning, and there's only one place I need to be right now.

Nerves flutter in my stomach as I drive toward the arena, despite the chance of seeing him being slim.

Unless the guys have a Sunday home game, they'll be enjoying a well-deserved day of rest. Dad should be, too. But that doesn't mean I haven't bumped into him here before now.

Unlike usual, when I pull up outside, I pause for a moment.

At some point, I'm going to have to face him. But as much as that terrifies me, I think him glancing my way and dismissing me is worse than him learning the truth.

Will I be able to live with being such an inconsequential part of his life when he has always been such a huge part of mine?

Swallowing down the inevitable disappointment, I kill the engine and shove the door open.

With my bag and my skates over my shoulder, I head inside.

"Casey," the young girl behind reception says with a smile as I walk inside. "You're late this morning."

"Busy weekend," I lie.

I may have had a wild Friday night, but since returning home the next morning, I haven't left the apartment.

"Well, hopefully an hour on the ice will sort you out."

Here's hoping.

"Thank you," I say softly before walking farther into the building that's basically been my second home all my life.

Before Dad started coaching here, he was a proud LA Vipers winger. To this day, he still leads the team in the most goals scored in a career.

A few have come close, but no one has matched him quite yet.

He's a hockey legend.

Players want to be on this team purely because of him.

They dream of being as good as he once was.

It's incredible, and I'm so fucking proud of him.

Every single day, he inspires people. No, not just people; he inspires players that are already at the top of their game.

I shake my head as I push the door to the rink open and take a deep breath.

Home.

I lower myself to a bench, take my sneakers off, and begin lacing up my skates.

Once I'm ready, I sit up straight and look at the ice.

It's full of families and skaters of all different ages and abilities.

I watch a couple of kids who can't be more than four racing around the middle like little rockets and smile.

That was me once upon a time.

I vividly remember Dad's proud smile as he watched me.

I've been addicted to the freedom the ice provides ever since.

When I was a kid, all I wanted to do was follow in my father's footsteps.

I joined my first girls' team at age six, and I played until I was fifteen.

But everything eventually got too much, and I quit.

It's something I'll probably always regret.

Mom wouldn't have wanted me to quit.

I may not have been as good as Dad, and I may never have made the PWHL, but I loved it. And when I stopped playing, I lost a massive piece of myself for quite some time.

I blow out a heavy breath as everything I've fought to overcome presses down on my shoulders.

Get on the ice, Casey.

Everything is better when you're on the ice.

Pushing to my feet, I walk to the gate and straighten my spine.

I step out and then glide away.

The second I do, every muscle in my body relaxes.

I find my place amongst the skating crowd and let go of everything that's weighing me down.

I don't count how many laps I do—not that it matters. I'd keep going all day if I could.

But eventually, the ice begins to empty, and over in the corner, the first of the kids' teams congregates to begin their practice.

The sight of the girls in their team uniforms hits me right in the chest.

Slowing to a stop at the exit, I step off the ice and wobble on shaky, tired legs toward the bench where I left my bag.

I might skate most weeks still, but I don't have the stamina I used to.

Lowering my ass, I take a moment to catch my breath.

Before I lean forward to remove my skates, the girls take to the ice.

I sit there, unable to look away as they start their warm-up laps before embarking on some drills.

Longing to be out there suited up and doing the thing I always loved pulls at my muscles.

I'm too old now; I'd probably break every bone in my body if I even attempted to play. But it's nice to live vicariously through them.

They look so tiny out there, but they certainly don't look vulnerable. They're little savages, and I love it.

I always enjoyed being faster and stronger than most of the boys at school. Looking back, I'm pretty sure many of them were scared of me. Explains why I didn't have a boyfriend until much later in life.

I tug off my skates as the girls all crowd around their two coaches, eagerly listening to instructions.

They split them into two teams and select two girls as goalies. They take half the rink each and line up to take shots.

Silently, I do a little cheer for each girl who sinks the puck in the net.

I completely lose track of time watching them as they start a game.

Before I know it, parents are beginning to appear at the other side of the rink, ready to collect their daughters, and I finally place my skates in my bag and head off.

When I return to my car, I feel lighter, almost like I'm ready to tackle returning to work and looking Dad in the eyes without feeling guilty as fuck.

He's always been pretty perceptive when it comes to me. Even when I was a hormonal teenager, he could take one look at me and know what I needed.

If he even suspects anything, then he'll be like a dog with a bone until he gets the truth.

Thankfully, with preseason upon us, he should be a little distracted.

The Vipers' first exhibition game is just over a week away. The guys are already hard at work getting ready, and I know that despite his experience, Dad feels the pressure of the upcoming season more and more every year.

He shouldn't. He's a fantastic coach, and the entire organization loves him. But I guess it's easier said than done.

Lowering my ass to the couch, I wake my cell up as I drink my coffee and look through all the photos that have been posted of Friday night.

I did the same more than once yesterday, but that doesn't stop me from doing it again for fear that there will be one of me that will allow someone to recognize me.

Confident that I'm safe, I take myself to the shower. I've got some work I want to do for tomorrow, but my only other plans for the day include watching some kind of documentary on Netflix.

I really am living the dream right here.

"I've just pulled up outside," Parker says the second I answer her call. "Let me in."

"Hey, it's nice to speak you too," I tease.

"Oh, shush. I have tacos."

"You totally should have led with that," I mock as I pull my cell from my ear and find the app that will grant her entry to the building.

She laughs down the line before saying, "See you in two," and cutting the call.

A few minutes later, my front door slams, and my best friend's footsteps move toward me. But before I see her, the scent of the food she's brought with her hits my nose.

My stomach growls, and I sit forward, ready to accept her gift.

"Good to know which one of us you want more," Parker teases when I make grabby hands for the bag. She clutches it to her chest and sticks her tongue out as she stalks past me.

She places the bag on the coffee table before going to the

kitchen and grabbing everything we need as if she's in her own place.

"Have I told you you're the best?"

She glances over at me before throwing her long red hair over her shoulder and dropping onto the other end of the couch. "Nowhere near enough."

Parker and I first met in kindergarten, and we've been best friends ever since.

It helps that her dad was also a hockey player, so we had a lot in common that other kids couldn't understand. Mostly, our obsession for the sport we grew up surrounded by.

Silence falls as we dive into our tacos. But the guilt I'm carrying over keeping such a huge secret from her never leaves me.

"So..." she eventually mumbles around a mouthful of food. "I saw something interesting earlier when I was scrolling through images of the masquerade ball on Friday night."

"Oh?" I ask, my heart rate increasing as fear shoots through me.

If anyone was going to recognize me hiding behind my mask, it would be Parker.

"Yeah. See...at first, I thought I was seeing things, but the more I looked, the more I convinced myself I was right." My face begins to burn, and my stomach knots.

Risking a glance at her, I find her narrowed, suspicious eyes drilling into me.

She knows.

Fuck.

"Parker," I hedge.

"Casey," she shoots back.

My hands tremble as I stare down at my food, which I suddenly can't stomach.

Parker and I don't keep secrets from each other. Especially not ones as big as the one I'm keeping from Friday night.

"Don't make me ask."

"Fuck," I breathe, closing my eyes for a beat.

"I fucking knew it," Parker shouts as if she's just won the Stanley Cup.

"Parker."

She turns toward me, bouncing with excitement on the couch.

"I need to know everything."

The breath I didn't know I was holding comes rushing out of me.

Of course I want to tell her. Parker knows everything there is to know about me.

I trust her with my life, but sharing this...it feels like I'm betraying the promise I made to Kodie.

"Casey, you're scaring me."

"Parker, you have to promise to never tell anyone about this. No one aside from me and you know I was there."

10

KODIE

"Yes, Sutton. You've got this," I bellow as she gets the puck and flies down the left-hand side of the rink, dodging two members of the other team to line up a perfect shot.

As she pulls back her stick, I hold my breath and pray.

I get nervous for my own games; I'd be lying if I said I didn't. Especially big ones. But I am never, ever as anxious as I am for one of Sutton's.

I try not to be that dad who barks orders and pisses her coaches off from the stands, but every now and then, the words just slip out.

My eyes are glued to her as she takes the shot, hitting the puck with enough force to send it flying past the pint-sized goalie and straight to the back of the net.

"Yes," I hiss, attempting to be a little quieter than before since I can't help myself.

I've been brought up to be competitive and cutthroat on the ice. Even the humblest players struggle to rein it in after years of it being encouraged.

The other parents around me cheer as Sutton finds me behind the plexiglass and comes racing over.

Lifting her hand, she presses it against the board, waiting for me to high-five her.

"Great work, Peanut," I say as her team gets ready for the face-off.

"She's got your talent," the dad standing beside me says.

A wide, proud smile curls my lips.

I wasn't surprised when at four years old Sutton announced that she wanted to play ice hockey. It was pretty much all she knew. But that didn't mean I loved the idea of letting her on the ice. I know firsthand just how hard it is. How fucking painful it can be.

Allowing her to go out there knowing that she's going to get injured at some point breaks every single fatherly promise I've ever made. But I also remember exactly what it was like watching it on TV, going to the rink and seeing these larger-than-life men shoot the puck, looking like it was the easiest thing in the world.

I was in awe of them from as early as I can remember. Hell, most days I still am.

I might be one of the NHL's top goal scorers, but even now, I look at my teammates, at other players in the league, and I feel a trickle of what I used to as a kid.

The only difference now is that I'm lucky enough to be standing on the ice with them.

No, I'm not fucking lucky. I fucking hate that saying.

I've worked my ass off to get where I am today.

Life hasn't been easy, and nothing has fallen in my lap.

I put every single hour I could into hockey, into trying to succeed at college with Dad's diagnosis of early onset dementia and then his declining health. My dream of being drafted was seemingly impossible. But I did it. Then only a couple of seasons in, I had had the added pressure of becoming a single dad.

It's been hard.

Really fucking hard.

But it has been so fucking worth it at the same time.

As long as Sutton enjoys playing and it puts that incredible smile on her face, then I'll be her number-one supporter. Always.

I just wish that I didn't have to miss so much of her season because of mine.

I'd love to be standing front and center for every single one of her games.

I stand there with a permanent grin on my face as the girls finish their game. Sutton's team wins. But while I'm proud of her win, and her goal and assists, what really causes emotion to crawl up my throat is the way she makes a point of interacting with the losing team and the rest of her teammates.

Win or lose, she's always the same.

I like to think that she's learned it from me, but I can be a miserable fucker even after a win, so I'm not sure.

It shows me just a hint of the kind of woman she's going to be, and...

Fuck.

I get choked up just thinking about it.

It's bad enough that she's turning eight soon.

Thinking of her as a teenager right now is hard enough, let alone a grown-up.

I shake my head trying to banish those thoughts of the future as their coach dismisses them, and Sutton immediately turns toward me with her helmet under her arm and races my way at full speed.

I open the bench door with ease as she approaches me, and launches herself into my arms the second her blades hit the edge.

"We won, Daddy," she cries happily.

"You did," I say, carrying her over to the bench so she can take her skates and pads off.

As I undo her laces, she chatters on about the plays they chose and how well they worked.

"Aurora lost the puck right at the last minute. I couldn't believe it; she was so close, but then I remembered what you did in that game against the Wildcats. I did it. Just like you did. They didn't have a clue what I was doing until it was too late."

She's practically vibrating with excitement on the seat, and I can't wipe the smile off my face.

"Hungry?" I ask her.

"Starving," she confesses.

With her bag over my shoulder and her tiny hand in mine, we

say goodbye to her teammates and the other parents and head out.

We drive to our favorite after-practice diner and slip into our regular booth at the back.

Neither of us reaches for the menu. We don't need to. We have the exact same thing every time we come here.

It's our Sunday treat when I'm in town.

The rest of the week, we eat like the athletes we are. I'm not over the top with it. I allow her treats every now and then, but I also think it's important to teach her that if she wants to be a professional one day, she needs to understand how much of a part nutrition can play.

I remember watching kids struggling because of the shit they ate. They weren't as alert or as fast when it really mattered. I also remember them dropping out. Of course, there were a million other reasons as well—food isn't the be-all and end-all—but fuck, it's crucial.

"Two cheeseburgers, loaded fries, a side of onion rings, a strawberry milkshake, and a soda, right?" Clarissa, our usual server, asks with her pad poised and a smile on her face.

"One day we're going to surprise you by ordering a hot dog and mac and cheese," Sutton tells her with a smirk that is scarily similar to mine.

"I'll look forward to it," Clarissa says before ripping her eyes from my daughter and focusing on me. "I do love it when people take me by surprise."

I force a grin in her direction in the hope that this time she'll get the picture.

I like her. She's sweet and good at her job. But she's at least ten years too young for me.

"Okay, well...I'll go and grab your drinks, then."

"Clarissa has a crush on you, Daddy," Sutton informs me.

"She's just a hockey fan," I explain, but if the way Sutton's brows lift tells me anything, it's that she doesn't believe a word of it.

"Then why has she never asked for your autograph?"

"Uh..." Because the place she'd like me to sign isn't

appropriate in a full diner with an almost-eight-year-old watching? "No idea, Peanut. Are you looking forward to school tomorrow?" I ask, quickly changing the subject.

She lets out a heavy sigh, her previous happy expression faltering a bit.

"I guess," she muses, reaching for the salt dispenser.

"Sutton," I prompt.

It takes her a few seconds before she lifts her eyes from the table and focuses on mine. "Miss White put Adrian at my table."

"Ah, I see."

Adrian also plays hockey. He's good. But...he's not as good as Sutton, which pisses him the hell off.

I get it. All hockey players want to be the best. I understand his ego, but also...Sutton is better. And I'm not just saying that because I'm her father.

And unfortunately, this kind of jealousy is something that Sutton is going to have to learn how to navigate.

Being a hockey player is hard. But being a kick-ass female player...I can't even begin to understand what that'll be like.

When I was at school, we were seen as gods. Did it go to our heads? Abso-fucking-lutely. But I suspect is doesn't work for the girls in the same way.

And the rivalry between the boys' and girls' teams... something tells me that it's going to be savage.

"Has he said anything to you?"

She shakes her head. "Not yet. But he will."

I scrub my hand down my face, wondering what makes me qualified to dole out advice on calm conflict resolution when I'm surrounded by physical fights on a weekly basis.

"I know it's hard, but you're going to have to ignore him. But tell me if he does or says anything, okay?"

"Daddy," she begs. "You can't get involved."

"I can and I will," I state.

"But his dad..." Had a career in the AHL and ended up retiring with an injury before he managed to play a single NHL game.

"No one hurts my little girl, Sutton. No one."

She smiles at me, her eyes glassy with emotion.

"I love you."

"I love you too, Peanut," I say as Clarissa returns with our drinks.

The next morning, I stand on the playground and watch as Sutton saunters into school. She doesn't run like many of the other kids, but she's also not clinging to my leg and screaming like a handful of others, either.

She's calm, composed, and maybe even a little stoic.

She wasn't herself this morning, and I know it's because of Adrian.

I scan the playground, looking for him, but come up empty.

I fucking hate that she's scared. But what can I do?

It's a part of growing up we all have to handle.

Just because I want to wrap her up in cotton and never let her get hurt, it doesn't mean I can.

Just like that first time I watched her get on the ice and train.

I've got to trust that she can handle it and be here when it gets hard.

She turns back when she gets to the door, and finally, her beautiful smile appears.

She waves frantically before slipping into the building.

With a heavy sigh, I spin around and head back to the car.

I love the start of a new season. It comes with so much promise, so much possibility.

But it also comes with a cost.

Summers with Sutton are incredible—just the two of us against the world. But now...I'm going to be away as much as I am here, and I'm going to miss out on so much.

Mom is an incredible grandmother. I know she does a fantastic job caring for Sutton in my absence, but it still pains me not to be the first one she sees on those days. I'm not the first to hear about her successes and failures. I don't get to go to her school performances or all her games.

I'm pretty sure the guilt over being a half-time parent will always weigh heavily on me.

I pull into my parking space at the arena, still lost in my morose thoughts.

This place is my home now. I may only be starting my second season here as a Viper, but everything about the place feels right.

It reminds me every day that coming here was the right decision.

We all needed the fresh start, and—Adrian aside—we're happy here.

Forcing down my unease, I head inside and join the rest of my team on the ice for drills.

"Rivers," Coach says with a nod as I pass him, ready to get started.

"Coach."

Our eyes meet, a silent understanding passing between us.

There aren't many guys in my daily life who appreciate the pressure of both hockey and being a single dad, but Coach is one of them. It's one of the biggest reasons I knew we'd be okay when I was traded here.

Coach gets it. He understands my life and where my head is.

And for that, I'll forever be fucking grateful.

———

11

CASEY

I've been on edge at work all week.

Sure, there might be quite a bit of distance between my office and where the team usually is, but that doesn't mean I don't flinch every time someone walks in the office or cringe anytime anyone asks me to do them a favor. I can count on one hand the number of times I've been asked to go down there. I usually make my own excuses so I can see Dad and get a little hockey fix. But that doesn't mean it's impossible.

I've spent the last five days trying to force my night with Kodie Rivers out of my head and focus on work.

It's not just the guys with a new season to prepare for. The anticipation is here in the offices, too.

We have social media campaigns to finalize, and graphics for the next few months to check over. All of our new season merchandise has already dropped in the store. Seeing it—and seeing fans buying it—is so rewarding. There is so much behind-the-scenes stuff that people overlook, and I fucking love being a part of it.

I love seeing what next season's jerseys are going to look like before anyone else; I love getting involved with everything fans see on socials, on our website, and everywhere. Anytime I see a poster, or a t-shirt that I've had a hand in designing, a little thrill goes through me.

I might not be on the ice and wearing the pads, but I am still very much a part of this incredible hockey family.

No matter what, I always knew my future was going to be under this roof; it just took a few years for me to figure out my place.

The day I learned that I had secured an internship in the design department was one of the best days of my life.

Coming here every day, being surrounded by something I love so much...it's everything.

Our first exhibition game is Monday, and I'm already buzzing for it.

It's been a long few months without the excitement of a game after we failed to make the playoffs last year.

"Have a great weekend, Casey," Bianca, my boss, says as she leaves the office for the weekend.

Aside from me, she's the last to leave.

"You too," I call before she disappears, leaving me alone in our office.

Silence falls around me as I save the design I'm working on and close my computer.

With a nervous sigh, I tidy up my desk and pull my purse from my bottom drawer.

I check my cell, but when I don't see anything from Dad cancelling our plans for tonight, I stuff it back into my purse before making a pit stop in the bathroom.

Standing in front of the mirror, I stare at my reflection.

I look like me again, and while it might be necessary, I can't help but miss the woman I was last Friday night.

I'm a fairly confident person, but the dark hair and the mask allowed me to shed my insecurities and be the woman I know I can be.

I was fearless. I knew what I wanted, and I went for it.

Hell, did I go for it.

Running my fingers through my light locks, I let out a sigh as the butterflies in my belly get wilder.

I wouldn't say that I've avoided going to the rink since, but...

Okay, I've avoided it.

I have no idea how I'm going to feel when I see him, and honestly, I'm quite happy to put off finding out.

But the time has come. Dad had to cancel our Wednesday breakfast again, but he promised to make it up to me tonight by taking me to my favorite restaurant.

I told him it's not necessary, but he's insistent, and if there is one thing I've learned over the years...you never say no to James Watson.

I touch up my lipstick, wipe some stray makeup from under my eyes, give myself a little pep talk, and take off.

He won't even look twice at me. I have no idea why I'm so nervous.

I'll just pick Dad up and we'll be on our way. No stress; no drama.

The familiar scent of the rink helps to settle some of my nerves, but my knees are a little weak as I walk closer.

Dad is in his favorite spot, and there are only a couple of players doing drills.

I force myself to focus on Dad and not even attempt to identify who is on the ice.

As far as I know, we currently have a full roster, so it could be any of the twenty-three players getting ready for the season out there.

The chance of it being him is slim.

But despite telling myself this, my heart rate only increases as I get closer.

Dad spots me, and his face lights up. I relax as I walk up to him and accept his embrace.

"Here she is," he muses. "Missed you this week, Care Bear."

Guilt threatens to swallow me whole, but I force it down.

It won't be the first week we've barely seen each other, and I'm sure it won't be the last. But still, neither of us likes it.

"You too. Are you ready to go?"

"Yeah, the guys are putting in some extra hours. They don't need me."

"Aw, they always need you, old man."

"Hey now, enough of that." He laughs. "Let me just grab my stuff and we'll head out. You good here?"

"Sure thing," I say, taking a step back and allowing him to go and get what he needs.

With nothing else to distract me, I lift my gaze to the ice and watch as three players speed around before each taking a shot at the goal.

Tingles rush across my body.

He's there. Number Fifty-Five. He's one of them.

All three score, but one is significantly more impressive than the others.

The line of his body in the seconds before he shoots. The speed and strength of his shot. The way he follows through as the puck sails into the net.

Every muscle in my body pulls tight at the thought of that impressive body. He was so in control.

He knew exactly what he wanted, and he took it.

They continue for another couple of minutes before he turns and skates away from the goal.

My heart jumps into my throat as he lifts his head...

And his eyes lock on mine. I cringe.

His celebratory smirk lasts for another second before it falls, realization slamming into him.

My stomach twists.

He reaches up and rips his helmet from his head, but his eyes don't leave mine.

"You," he mouths, making acid rush up my throat.

"You fucking with us or not?" someone barks from behind him.

He blinks before shaking his head in disbelief.

"Ready, kid?" Dad calls, successfully stealing my attention.

That guilt I felt earlier returns full force, mixing with the nausea.

He wasn't meant to recognize me.

No one was supposed to recognize me.

"Yes," I say, mustering up as much confidence as I can before turning my back on Kodie and walking away at my dad's side.

I want to think it has the same devastating effect that his walking away had on me, but something tells me we're worlds apart in our opinions over that night right now.

Oh well. I got what I wanted.

#1 bucket list item checked off.

I'm ready for my next challenge.

"**A**re you okay?" Dad asks after we've taken our seats and placed our order almost an hour later. "You barely said anything on the way here."

"Of course," I say with a forced smile. "It's just been a long week."

"Tell me about it," he says, dragging his fingers through his too-long hair.

He needs a cut, but like always, it falls to the bottom of his to-do list. It's not like he has anyone to impress.

"How have the guys been this week? Are they ready?"

He scoffs, pretending to be offended that I had the audacity to even ask.

"Of course they're ready. We're going all the way this year."

I smile at him, hope seeping through my veins.

I want it for him—for all of them—so badly. It's been too long since the Vipers lifted the Stanley Cup. They deserve it.

He loses himself talking about the guys' performances this week and the upcoming exhibition games. I try really fucking hard to focus and say the right things. But it's a challenge.

All I can think about is that moment back at the rink.

Kodie knows.

He knows he committed the ultimate sin and fucked the coach's daughter.

Nausea hits me, and I press my hand to my stomach as I consider how he must be feeling.

I lied to him.

I played him.

I broke every fucking rule in Dad's playbook to get what I wanted.

I might have won, but right now, it doesn't feel like that.

"Are you sure you're okay? You're really pale."

"Maybe I'm getting sick," I say quietly.

"Should we go?" he offers, looking concerned.

"No," I say firmly. His brows dip, and I force a smile on my face. "Life is about to get crazy; we don't know when we'll get this chance again."

His eyes bounce between mine, searching for the truth. "Okay," he finally concedes. "But once we've eaten, I'm taking you straight home."

I nod. As much as I want to be with him right now, my guilt's getting the better of me. I really need to lock myself in my apartment and attempt to figure out what the fuck I'm going to do now.

I force myself to eat as much as I can, but despite loving the food here, it's like chewing on cardboard. Dad devours his steak like usual, so I know the issue is with me and not my meal. Before long, he's paid the bill and is ushering me out of the restaurant to deliver me home.

"I'll get your car dropped off," he tells me as he pulls up outside my building a while later.

"No, it's okay, I'll—"

"Casey," he warns in his deep, don't-mess-with-me tone.

"Okay, thank you."

"Anytime. Go and get some rest. I'll call you tomorrow."

Leaning over, I press a kiss on his cheek before climbing out of the car. Once I'm inside the building, I turn and give him a wave, letting him know that I'm safe.

The second he turns the car around and drives away, I press my hand to my stomach and breathe, "Oh my god."

12

———

KODIE

Casey Watson.

I spent the night with Casey fucking Watson.

No wonder she wanted to keep her identity a secret.

Over the past week, I've come up with every conceivable reason as to why my mystery woman refused to reveal her identity to me.

But it never even crossed my mind that it was because she was Coach's daughter.

"Fuck," I breathe, lifting both of my hands to my head as the water rains down on me.

Everyone else has left. I'm finally alone and able to freak the fuck out.

Coach is...Coach is like a father to me.

To all of us.

It fucking kills me that I've unknowingly disrespected him.

And not just once, either.

Sure, I may have only spent one night with her, but I've thought about my mysterious masked woman constantly over the past week.

Hell, I've jerked off daily to my memories of that night.

And now I discover she's the most forbidden woman in my life.

79

Pressing my palms to the cold tiles before me, I hang my head as shame, regret, and disbelief rush through my veins.

I should have known.

How the fuck didn't I know?

A frustrated groan rumbles deep in my throat as I tip my face to the ceiling, letting the water rush over my skin. Unable to contain it, my lips part and a loud roar erupts as my fist slams against the tiles.

But it doesn't help. I'm not sure anything will.

Turning off the water, I grab a towel, wrap it around my waist, and head back to my stall to get dressed.

My heart jumps into my throat when I find one of our third-line defensemen with his pants halfway up his legs and a guilty expression on his face.

He's a rookie fresh out of college. Green as fuck but cocky as hell.

I remember it well.

"I'm sorry," he blurts. "I-I wasn't listening or anything."

I glare at him, and he dresses even faster than before.

"I wanted to put in an extra hour at the gym and—"

"Shut the fuck up," I bark.

He slams his lips together and swallows nervously.

Ripping my eyes from him, I continue toward my stall.

He doesn't say another word.

I'm not surprised.

I've got quite a reputation around here. One that I'm more than happy about.

The second he's dressed, he shoves his stuff into his bag and disappears, muttering a quiet goodbye and see you tomorrow as he flees.

"Fuck's sake," I groan once I'm alone again.

Pulling my cell from my bag, I open up a browser and search my name for recent news.

Just like she promised, there is nothing about a wild night of debauchery after the masquerade ball.

I didn't think it was possible. Why else would a woman want to spend the night with me?

I'm a miserable motherfucker with a job that has me away from home half the time and a daughter that takes up the rest.

I'm more than aware that I'm nothing more than a paycheck and a boost up the social ladder for women.

It's why I don't do what I did that night.

But now I understand why our tryst hasn't hit the headlines.

Selling her story would put her at risk.

Sure, she could do it anonymously, but these things have a way of being uncovered.

Clearly, that's too much of a risk for her.

So why do it in the first place?

Why risk turning up to an event where numerous people could recognize her?

She could have any man she wants. A man not on our roster.

I take the long way home in the hope that the drive will give me some clarity.

It doesn't.

As I pull up my driveway, my head is still a mess, but the sight of the front door opening and Sutton running out with a smile on her face just about drags me from my thoughts.

Killing the engine, I push the door open and climb out just as she launches herself at me.

"Hey, Peanut," I say, lifting her into my body.

Her little arms wrap around my neck, and I blow out a long breath as I hold her.

When my world is in chaos, she is the only one who can bring me back to Earth.

"Have you had a good day?"

"We baked cookies," she says excitedly. "Come and try one. They're still warm."

"Try and stop me," I say as I lower her to her feet. "How was school?"

"Meh," she says, waving off the question as if it isn't important.

I smirk. She reminds me so much of me when I was a kid.

If it wasn't hockey, I didn't want to know.

"How did you get on with your spelling test?" I press.

She spent an hour going over and over her list of words last night.

Just like me, she struggles academically. I wish I could make it all easier for her. But unfortunately, there is no easy fix.

I just hope that she keeps trying to overcome it. I'd hate to see her give up because it's too hard.

"Yeah, it was okay," she says before running back to the house.

"Sutton," I warn as I follow her.

Swinging the front door closed behind me, my nose leads me toward the scent of freshly baked cookies in the kitchen.

"Eight out of ten," Sutton says as she studies the cookies to select the one she wants me to have.

I beam, so fucking proud of her. "Peanut, that's amazing."

She shrugs. "Still got two wrong," she mutters under her breath.

"And I missed two attempts at scoring during practice today. I still sunk eight into the net, though," I say, hoping she sees it differently if I bring a puck into it.

Her eyes lift, a smile lighting up her face.

"You should do that in a game. Everyone would lose their minds if you scored eight."

"Exactly. Just like I'm losing my mind over the fact you worked really hard for that spelling test and got eight right. It's amazing."

Color rises on her cheeks.

"Going to get ten next week," she states.

"Me too," I tell her, lifting my hand for a high five. "Thank you," I say, taking the oatmeal and raisin cookie she offers me. "Oh my god," I mumble around a mouthful. "These are amazing."

Her smile grows, proud of herself.

"So, what are we doing for dinner tonight?" I ask, turning to look at our weekly planner.

"Tacos," Sutton cries excitedly.

"Ah, yes. It's Friday."

Sutton does a little celly dance before dragging her stool to the refrigerator so she can get the ingredients out.

Cooking with Sutton is one of my favorite things to do. Hell, anything with her is my favorite. But after a long day of training, it's the perfect time to catch up.

She tells me about her day at school, giving me all the gossip before she turns it on me and asks all about my practice and training session.

She eats up all the details like she always does as she chops peppers like a pro.

Obviously, I don't say anything about my big revelation of the day, but thoughts of that moment on the ice when I looked into her eyes and my entire world crashed around my feet are right at the forefront of my mind.

I fucked Casey Watson.

Coach is going to kill me.

I shake my head, lost in my own thoughts.

No. He won't, because he's never going to find out.

"Go and get cleaned up," I say as I put the cooked ground beef into a bowl and slide it across the island.

Movement across the yard catches my eye, and I watch as Mom lets herself out of the pool house.

Noticing me, she lifts her hand in a little wave, but she doesn't come over.

She's a fucking angel.

Honestly, I don't know what Sutton and I would do without her.

From the moment Sutton's mom left without a backward glance, my mom stepped up.

She already had Dad to look after, but that didn't stop her.

She allowed me to continue playing the game I love, all the while knowing that my daughter was being cared for.

The thought of employing a nanny and trusting them with my baby girl is terrifying.

And there was very little chance I would meet anyone and leave the job to them.

Mom is our guardian angel.

Tonight, she's going out with the group of friends she's made here.

She was reluctant at first, but I refused to let her follow us here and then just hide away in the pool house.

She deserves to get out and enjoy herself. She deserves friends. Hell, if it happens, I'd love for her to find someone again. Of course, it'll be weird as fuck to see her with someone who isn't Dad, but she deserves to have that kind of love in her life again.

"I'm ready," Sutton squeals, sliding across the kitchen tiles in her socks.

Hopping up onto the stool beside me, she immediately dives into dinner.

She makes up two tacos before diving in as if she's the one who's been training for our first exhibition game all day.

We spend the evening hanging out watching ESPN. I can imagine it's not what most dads and daughters do together on a Friday night. But to us, it's perfect.

"You're coming to my game Sunday, right?" she asks, hope in her eyes.

"Of course." She asks me that before every game she knows I'm home for. As if I'd miss a single one.

I live for Sutton's games even more than I do my own.

Her smile grows.

"Good. I'm better when you're watching."

"The feeling is mutual."

With Sutton tucked in bed, I take another shower in the hope of washing the day off me before dropping my ass to the couch again.

Unease continues to drip through my veins. Questions over what I should do next race through my head.

The sensible side of my brain tells me to just ignore it all.

She told me very confidently that it was one night and one night only.

So what, I now know who she is?

That doesn't really change anything.

Does it?

She was happy to have one night with me and then continue with her life like nothing happened.

If she hadn't turned up at the rink earlier—if I hadn't turned around and looked her in the eyes—I never would have figured it out.

I'd be sitting here now, blissfully unaware that the woman I can't get out of my head is the daughter of my coach.

The daughter we've all been very firmly told to stay away from.

If I'd known...

A bitter laugh spills from my lips as I consider what would have happened if I had found out.

At what point would I have stopped it?

What would I have done if she'd removed her mask when I'd asked her to?

Freak out. That's what I would have done.

My stomach knots tighter as I think about how I've betrayed Coach.

If he finds out...my life here could be over.

He could trade me in a heartbeat.

I may have only had one season here in LA, but it feels...right.

Sutton is happy here. She loves her team, and school—mostly. And Mom has friends who are helping to bring her back to life. I can't rip that away from her.

And anyway, if I don't ignore it—ignore her—like it never happened, what's the other option?

Talk to her?

I shake my head. I can't do that.

I can't be anywhere fucking near her.

My memories are enough.

The thought of having her scent in my nose again is just too much.

The only thing I can do is remember what she so confidently said.

She wanted a one-night thing.

It was enough for her, so it has to be enough for me.

I'm putting Casey Watson and our night together firmly behind me.

I have a season to focus on.

I wake Saturday morning to my cell ringing on my nightstand.

With a groan, I reach over and crack an eye open to see who it is.

Swiping the screen, I bring it to my ear.

"Yeah?" I croak.

Laughter hits my ears, and I cringe.

"Jesus, someone had a good night," Parker teases. "Why wasn't I invited?"

"I—I—" I clear my throat in the hope of making my voice work. "I didn't go out," I tell her honestly.

I didn't do anything last night other than toss and turn in bed, reliving the moment yesterday when he looked into my eyes and discovered the truth.

I can't decide if I'm mortified or thrilled that he recognized me.

That excitable teenage girl inside me is doing backflips over the fact he clearly didn't forget about me the second he walked out of the room. But the sensible side of me knows that I fucked up.

I underestimated him. And now...now I don't know how he's reacting to the whole thing.

I want to say he doesn't care, that he can put that night into a neat little box and focus on the upcoming season.

But I'm fucking terrified that he can't, and that it'll be my fault if he's not fully focused.

A laugh erupts. Who the hell do I think I am?

That night might have blown my mind and set the bar for any future man I may sleep with, but it doesn't mean I had the same impact on him.

He might be going through a dry spell—if the gossip is to be believed—but that doesn't mean I was anything memorable.

He's previously been linked to numerous actresses and models.

I will have been nothing compared to those.

He didn't even know who I was at the time, so there was no thrill of doing something he shouldn't be for him.

Not that I think he's the kind of man to break the rules for the fun of it.

Lincoln would, but not Kodie.

"What's so funny?" Parker asks, wanting in on my private joke.

I can't help but laugh again.

"Are you sure you're okay?" she asks, sounding a little more concerned.

"Yeah," I say, trying to believe my own words. "Yeah, I'm fine."

"You sound it," she deadpans. "I was calling to see if you fancied breakfast and a trip to the mall, but I'm making it compulsory now."

"What if I have plans?" I tease, rolling onto my back and staring up at the ceiling.

I don't. I have no plans this weekend. But that's not the point.

"Then cancel them. Unless, of course, it's with your mystery man from last weekend..."

"Parker."

I may have confessed that I was at the masquerade ball—I couldn't exactly do anything else, after her detective stint—and I may have admitted that I hooked up with someone, but despite her pleading, I didn't give a name.

I hate lying to her. Parker and I tell each other everything.

But this...telling her about Kodie...I don't want to break his trust. But at the same time, I'm not sure I'm going to be able to keep it in.

Especially now that he knows.

I need advice. I need to talk it out. And I can't do that with anyone else. I certainly can't go to Dad with this little issue.

"Okay, I'll pick you up in thirty. If he's there, kick his ass to the curb. I'm coming for you, girl."

"No kicking needed. I'm alone," I tell her as I throw the covers off and swing my legs over the edge of the bed.

"Boring," Parker complains.

"I'm getting ready. See you in thirty."

We hang up and I throw myself in the shower to get ready for a day of retail therapy with my best friend.

<hr>

I step out the front door of my apartment exactly thirty minutes later, just as Parker pulls into the parking lot. The top of her car is down, and her red hair is pulled back into a sleek ponytail. As usual, she wears a tank and leggings. You can take the girl out of the gym, but you can't take the gym out of the girl.

"Hey," I say, dropping into her passenger seat.

"Hey," she says, glancing over at me before taking off again. "You look tired."

"Thanks," I mutter as I put my sunglasses on and enjoy the warm fresh air rushing over my face.

"Long week at work?"

"Something like that," I mutter cryptically.

"You know what you need, a nice massage." I groan when she shoots me an evil grin.

I know the kind of massages she gives and that's the last thing I need in my life right now.

"You've seen him, haven't you?"

I groan. "You're not going to let this go, are you?"

"Casey, you had a night with a masked stranger. I swear, that's the hottest thing I've heard in...a very long time. I need more information. Hell, I need a mystery man of my own."

I can't help but laugh, but something in it makes her look my way with her brow pinched.

"What?" I ask, not liking the way she's looking at me.

"You're stressed. Your shoulders are tight as hell. Something is going on."

The sigh I let out only confirms what she already knows.

"Fill me with caffeine and I might just spill," I mutter.

A smirk covers Parker's face as she presses her foot harder to the gas. "Consider it done."

Twenty minutes later, I'm sitting in the back corner of Starbucks, waiting for Parker to collect our orders.

As I wait, I pick at my croissant, but I don't enjoy it. I may as well be eating sand.

My stomach rolls with nerves and guilt. I haven't spoken a word yet, but it's already hitting me.

"Here you go, a venti caramel latte with a double shot," Parker says, placing the large mug in front of me.

Abandoning my croissant, I wrap my hands around it in the hope that the warmth will settle everything inside me.

It doesn't.

"Go on then," she encourages before lifting her own croissant and taking a massive bite.

"The guy I hooked up with. He—"

"He's a Viper, and you're panicking that your dad will find out?" Parker blurts, as if she's been holding herself back all week.

I glare at her.

"What?" she asks innocently. "It was obvious. You wouldn't be so tight-lipped about any other guy."

I shake my head. Parker knows me better than anyone, I shouldn't be surprised that she can read me like a book. "He found out who I am," I confess.

Silence follows my admission.

"What?" Parker asks when I widen my eyes and gesture for her to react in some way.

"Parker, this is bad. Like, really fucking bad."

"Why? You had a hot night with a player, and now he knows who you are. So what? It's not like you want to marry him and have his babies."

I school my features.

I have never in my entire life written "Mrs. Casey Rivers" on any single piece of paper just to test it out and see how it would look...how it would feel.

Nope, not once.

"Or...maybe you do?" Parker teases, a smirk playing on her lips.

I lift my hands to my cheeks. "Is it hot in here or is it—"

"You and your wild fantasies?"

"Look," I state, holding her eyes. "I'm not under any illusion that this is the beginning of anything. It was a one-night thing," I say, slumping in my chair. "I just...I just wanted to see what it was like, and I knew I'd never get another chance."

The second Parker's eyes widen, I know she's figured it out.

I mean, I was going to tell her anyway but...I guess I don't need to now.

"Oh. My. God," she breathes, unable to keep the delighted smile off her face. "You didn't."

I shrug one shoulder, trying to look nonchalant.

"You slept with Kodie Rivers."

I squeeze my eyes closed; as she whispers the words, I'm back in that hotel room with his dark brown eyes staring down into mine.

"Keep it down," I hiss. "I promised him that—"

Parker looks at me flatly. "Who the hell am I going to tell?"

"I know you're not going to tell anyone. I just...I promised him that it would never get out, and in turn, he wasn't meant to know who I was."

"But he figured it out. How?"

"Well, it wasn't from the mole on the side of my neck like you," I say, rolling my eyes.

"If you had as good a night as you've made out, I bet he'd recognize it too."

I groan in frustration.

"No, seriously. How did he figure it out?"

"I met Dad at the rink last night after work and he was on the ice. He turned around, looked at me, and...he just knew."

A wide smile spreads across my best friend's face, and I inhale in preparation for what's to come.

"You rocked his fucking world."

I laugh, all the air puffs from my lips.

"I'm not sure that's true."

"Oh, come on. Don't even pretend you haven't read every single word that's been written about him in the press. He hasn't been connected with a woman since he moved here."

"I know," I muse.

"Many have tried, it seems."

"Parker," I breathe. I really, really don't need to hear what she's going to say next.

"And yet you, Casey Watson, managed to seduce him in one night—even with half of your beautiful face covered."

I groan and drop my head into my hands.

"That isn't helping," I mutter.

"I'm so fucking proud of you, Case."

I shake my head, refusing to look up at her.

"Don't be weird."

"I'm not. You set a goal and you fucking smashed it. Did you ever think you'd be able to sit in front of me and say, I, Casey Jessica Watson, have screwed my childhood crush, the man I've been obsessing over for at least a decade, and that it was the best night of my life?"

"I never said it was the best night of my life," I muse, peeking at her through my fingers.

"Babe, you didn't need to. I can read it in your eyes."

"Fuck," I breathe.

"Say it," she taunts, her eyes glittering with excitement.

"Fine. It was the best night of my life, and he's...he's just as much of a god in the bedroom as he is on the ice."

She bursts out laughing, causing a few people to look over.

"Well, there you go then. I guess it is true what they say about hockey players."

I shake my head, but I can't deny that she's right. Hockey players have a reputation for a reason.

"You already knew it was true. That's why you refuse to sleep with one. You know no other man will satisfy you after."

She scoffs, refuting my statement.

We both know it's not the reason why she stays as far away from hockey players as possible, but I still like to tease her about it.

"So, now what?" she asks, dragging the conversation back to my issue.

"Exactly. Now what?"

She studies me for a moment, considering my options.

"I guess it all depends on how much you want to tease him."

"I can't. If Dad finds out—"

"But what if he doesn't? You want a do-over, right?"

"It was one night. One night that I'll never forget. I don't need another."

"Bullshit," she coughs.

"I can't. It's not fair to him."

"Okay, fine," she concedes. Or at least I think she does. "So, you don't want to hear my ideas then?"

14

KODIE

I stand in the tunnel, listening to the starting line up being announced with hope in my veins.

First exhibition game of the season.

Of course, a lot of things can change.

But I can't help but feel like this very first game sets the tone for everything to follow.

My name is announced as I lower my skate to the ice, and the fans go crazy.

Keeping my gaze down, I skate to the middle of the rink, trying to focus on what's to come.

More players are announced, and with each one, the crowd gets wilder.

They've been waiting months for this.

Hell, we all have.

I love the off-season. I get to spend my time focusing on Sutton and being a father. But something is always missing. Hockey runs through my veins. It always has and always will.

It's a part of my DNA. It's a part of Sutton's, too.

I smile to myself as I do a lap, thinking about her game the other night.

They won six to nothing. And my girl scored four of those goals.

Fuck. I was—I am—so fucking proud of her.

She was on top of the world, and the smile on her face only grew with each goal she scored.

I'm sure many of the other parents think that her skill is because of me. Because I push her to be the best, spend hours training with her. But the truth of it is, it's her.

I didn't push her into hockey. Quite the opposite, in fact. I would have been more than happy if she wanted to paint, dance, box, anything. All I want for her is to find something she loves and to enjoy spending time doing it.

Her skill, the hours she put in perfecting it, it's her drive to succeed, not mine.

Of course, my knowledge and years of experience help her, I won't deny that, but she knows what she wants, and she's going for it. I'm pretty sure she would even if she didn't have my full support. She's fucking fierce, and I hope she never loses that fire and determination to win.

As I skate around to the board where the rest of the team is waiting for the game to start, I glance at the spot she'd sit in.

But she's not there.

I hate having evening games when she can't come.

She does, too.

She used to beg me until I almost cracked. The sight of her tear-filled eyes and wobbling bottom lip used to wreck me.

But it's Monday night. She has school tomorrow.

I need to be a responsible father. Her education has to come before hockey. Even if she hates it.

That doesn't mean she won't be watching, though.

She'll be sitting at home with Mom right now, wearing her jersey with her eyes glued to the screen.

I come to a stop and look directly at one of the cameras aimed at us. I have no idea if it's the one that'll stream directly into our living room, but if it is, Sutton will know it's for her.

Coach gives us a few final words before we line up, ready for the face-off.

Squeezing my eyes closed for a second, I picture the trophy that we all crave.

Preseason game one.

The first step toward lifting it.

The first of eighty-two season games.

Each of those games will help determine our fate.

Sucking in a deep breath, I open my eyes—and it's not the official or even the puck that steals my attention.

It's her.

Sitting right behind our opponent's net is Casey Watson.

Her attention is already on me.

My teeth grind so hard, I'm sure I'm about to crack one.

It might have been three days since I discovered the identity of the woman who rocked my world last weekend, but I haven't figured out what to do about it.

I was hoping that maybe I could just ignore it. Ignore her.

I mean, really, how often do I see her?

But standing here right now, I realize that locking her in a neat little box and stuffing her to the back of my mind is going to be easier said than done.

I haven't been able to forget a second of our time together. It's only worse now that I can put a face to the body, to the desperate moans and sexy pleas for more.

"Fuck," I hiss through gritted teeth as I force my eyes from hers.

But they don't move very far, and the second they lock on what she's wearing, I really fucking regret it.

She's wearing...she's wearing my fucking jersey.

Shock renders me useless, and without me knowing, the puck drops, and the game starts around me.

"Fucking focus," I bark at myself, taking off after our opponent's forward, who won the drop. "FUUUUCK," I roar when he sinks it into the net not twenty seconds later.

With my heart in my throat, I line back up to go again after watching the other team celebrate their first goal of the new season.

First game...it sets the tone for what's to come.

I refuse to be so up in my head over a woman I can't have that we lose this fucking game.

There are only thirty seconds on the clock, and we're tied.

It looks better than it did at the end of the second period when we were down by two.

We've fought hard. Harder than I'd like for our first game.

But it is what it is, and all we can do is push harder.

I fly down the left side of the ice and watch as Fletch passes to Linc.

Both of our opponent's defensemen turn on him, leaving me wide open.

Linc's eyes lift and find mine instantly.

He keeps going and fakes a shot at the net, instead sending the puck my way.

I catch it, and without looking up, I shoot.

The arena erupts, the goal horn sounds, the lights flash, and the front row fans pound on the glass.

Pride shoots through my veins, but it's not as powerful as it usually is. Much like everything recently, the happiness is grayed out.

I lift my eyes from the net a beat before Fletch and Linc jump on me, and the only person in the crowd I see is her.

She's on her feet, her arms above her head and her lips parted as she screams in delight.

Our eyes collide again, and suddenly, everything comes back to me in full, sparkling color.

I don't get a chance to enjoy it because my teammates surround me, congratulating me on winning our game.

The celebrations continue as we shake hands with the other team and do a victory lap.

It takes every ounce of willpower not to look at her as I pass her, and I almost succeed, but my head takes on a life of its own and turns to her.

Her smile is wide, and her cheeks are flushed.

Fuck. She looks hot. And it's even better because she's wearing my jersey.

It doesn't mean anything, I try to tell myself.

I bet she has everyone's jerseys, and she'd smile at Linc exactly the same if he'd just won the game.

My heart skips a beat at the thought of her being with some of the other guys.

The thought makes my teeth grind, and the image of one of my teammates in my place that night has bile rushing up my throat.

I glance back at her unintentionally as more thoughts and questions race through my mind.

Has she been with the others?

Are they all keeping the same secret that I am?

I shake my head.

Surely not.

She's not like that...is she?

Casey might be a regular at the rink, but I've never seen her flirt with any of the guys. From what I can tell, she's always professional, and in turn, they treat her with the respect that she deserves—and Coach demands.

Sure, Linc flirts his ass off, but that's just who he is. But almost everyone else is too terrified to piss off Coach. Looking at Casey the wrong way is probably the fastest way to get ourselves benched and then traded. Something none of us want.

The LA Vipers are a family.

I've been tight with my team before, but the Vipers are different. Every staff member here is a part of the family, whether you're a cleaner, the Zamboni driver, or work in the ticket office.

It's a family that I would like to remain a part of, which means it's even more critical now than ever to put Casey Watson behind me.

My career, my daughter, and my mom are too important to fuck this up.

"Nice work, Rivers," Coach says, slapping my shoulder as I step off the ice. "You're on post-game press after that."

"Wonderful," I mutter under my breath as I walk away from him.

Freshly showered and in my suit, I make my way out of the arena and straight to my car.

Coach likes us all to head up to the friends and family suite after the game to celebrate together, but when Sutton is at home, I avoid it in favor of seeing her.

I know he gets it. He's been a single dad for years.

Another potent shot of guilt hits me.

Dragging my hand down my face, I continue forward, putting much-needed space between me and the woman who will no doubt be wearing my jersey.

Is she waiting for me up there?

Locking down those kinds of thoughts, I climb into my car and head for home ready to focus on tucking my daughter into bed.

She's usually asleep by the time I get back, but knowing that I won't get to talk to her about the game until the morning never stops me from leaving at the first possible opportunity.

The house is quiet when I walk through the front door.

"Great game tonight." Mom says from her spot on the sofa. The highlights play on the screen in front of her, and I watch the playback of my goal.

I can't deny that it was a good play. I might have scored the goal, but it was very much a team effort.

"You didn't even look up," Mom laughs.

"You say that like I don't know what I'm doing," I tease. "Sutton okay?"

"Of course. I'm surprised you didn't hear her screaming for you when you scored."

A wide smile spreads across my face.

"I recorded some of it."

Mom passes me her cell, and I hit play on the video.

"YES, YES, YES," Sutton screams. "THAT'S MY DADDY RIGHT THERE." And then she dives right into her celly dance as if she just scored the winning goal.

My chest tightens as I play it again.

Fuck, I love that kid.

"I'm going to go see her and then go to bed," I say, my voice rough with emotion.

"You got it. Sleep well."

"You too."

As silently as I can, I climb the stairs and slip into Sutton's room.

Her star nightlight illuminates the ceiling, allowing me to get to her without tripping over the million stuffies that have already been kicked from the bed.

Coming to a stop beside her, I spend a moment taking her in. Her lips are parted, her eyelashes resting on her rosy cheeks, and her hair is a mess across the pillow. She's still wearing her jersey—standard for a game night—and she's hugging her matching LA Vipers bear.

The store manager had it specially made for her when I was traded. It hasn't left her side since.

"Sweet dreams, Peanut," I whisper before kissing her forehead.

"Daddy," she rasps, her arm reaching for me. "You won."

"We did."

"Proud of you," she whispers, her voice getting quieter with each word as she slips back to sleep.

I stand there for a few more moments, focusing on what's really important in my life.

As she begins snoring softly, I back out of her room and walk into mine.

I strip down to my boxers and climb under the covers.

But despite needing to, I'm not ready to sleep. My body is still too amped up from the game.

Back in the day, I'd have gone out with the team to decompress. Win or lose, we'd always go out to let off some steam.

But those days are behind me now. Even when we're away, I don't join them.

I'm not that guy anymore.

I'm a father, and I have to put that before anything else.

Hockey might be my calling in life, my career, but Sutton is my entire world.

15

CASEY

"Stop looking at the door like he's about to walk through it. You know he's not," Parker says after the game.

"I'm not," I mutter, although we both know I'm lying.

Dad sent Kodie to do post-game press, so he'd be late even if he was planning on attending. Which he never does.

"Come on, let's get a drink," Parker says, threading her arm through mine and dragging me to the bar.

She orders for both of us, and I force myself to keep my back to the door as we discuss tonight's game.

Parker might have no interest in bedding a hockey player, but that doesn't mean she's not as obsessed as I am.

Her ultimate dream is to become an athletic trainer for the team. Other than playing when she was a kid, it's the only thing she's ever wanted to do.

Over the years, I've teased her relentlessly about how badly she wants to get her hands on their muscles. She laughs it off, but I've always wondered what it would be like. To get up close and personal with a pro hockey player. Sure, I may have dabbled while at college with a few members of the team, but after what I experienced last weekend, I now know just what a different league they're in. What a pro athlete can do in bed compared to a college player... well...

My blood heats, and I can't stop the blush from rising on my cheeks.

"Oh my god," Parker gasps. "You're thinking about him."

"Parker," I hiss.

"Sorry, sorry," she says, looking around with a guilty expression on her face.

Suddenly, the door opens and a buzz of excitement rolls through the room as everyone turns to see if it's their loved one about to walk through the door.

I try not to look as excited, but I'm pretty sure I fail if Parker's giggle tells me anything.

It's all for nothing because our captain, Fletcher Fergurson, and Lincoln Storm come bouncing into the room.

Fletch marches straight toward his wife, Reese, and wraps her in his arms.

Linc, on the other hand, lifts his arms in the air and shouts, "Who's gonna win the Stanley Cup this year?"

I laugh as a chorus of "LA Vipers" ripples around the room.

"If anyone was going to break the rules, I'd have put money on it being him," Parker whispers as Linc makes his way through the room, greeting his teammates, friends, and family.

"I'm not interested in Linc," I say, seconds before he approaches us.

"Pretty sure that makes me and you the only ones in the country who would turn him down."

"Ladies," the man in question says as he wraps an arm around both of our shoulders. "How did you enjoy watching me play tonight?"

"Oh, were you on the ice?" Parker quips. "I thought you'd been benched."

"Funny, Donnelly. Really fucking funny. In case you missed it, I was the one who set up Big D for his epic winning goal."

"Oh, yeah. We saw him do that. Kodie Rivers is the best winger in the league."

Linc lifts his hand to his chest. "You wound me, Donnelly."

"I'm under no illusion that your ego can handle it."

Linc chuckles before someone else catches his attention, and he leaves us alone.

The rest of the team joins us, and not long after, Dad also appears.

He makes a beeline for me.

"Great game tonight," I say, my wide smile matching his.

During practice and games, he's so serious and stoic, completely focused on the job at hand. But after a win, he turns into the fun-loving man I remember from childhood.

"It was. The guys did a fantastic job."

"And as humble as ever," Parker teases.

The next hour passes with excited chatter about tonight's game, along with discussions about our first road game.

The team is heading to Vancouver for Wednesday's game. I hate being left behind and having to watch them on TV. But seeing as I have a job here, I can't just hop on a flight and follow them.

Eventually, the team and their wives and girlfriends begin to disappear. I know exactly where most of them are going.

The Fractured Compass.

It's a dive bar a few streets over from the arena that the team has claimed as theirs.

I'm desperate to go and hang out with the team after hours.

If things were different, if my father wasn't their coach, then maybe I would.

Who am I kidding? I wouldn't stand a chance of talking to these guys if I weren't thrust into this world by Dad.

I'd like to think that no matter what, I'd be a fan. But who knows?

"We should go," Parker suggests, reading my expression.

I shake my head. There have been a few occasions where I've hung out with them after games, but that's usually because it's someone's birthday or we have something big to celebrate.

I might be a part of the LA Vipers franchise, but I'm not a part of the team. Not really.

We're not friends. We're acquaintances. They're nice to me

because they're too terrified not to be. But equally, they keep me at arm's length because they have to.

"I'm tired. I'm just going to head home."

Parker lets out a long, disappointed breath.

"Yeah, same."

Guilt twists me up inside. She wants to go. She wants to hang out with the team, soak it all up.

"One day," I promise her.

After saying goodbye to Dad, we head out.

"Sure I can't tempt you?" Parker says as I hit the blinker that will take us toward her apartment and away from the bar. "He's not going to be there."

"No, I need to go home. I've got a busy day tomorrow."

She smiles sadly at me but doesn't say anything else about it.

After dropping her off, I head home with tonight playing out in my head.

Kodie has never spotted me in the crowd before. Or, if he has, then I haven't noticed.

But the second his eyes landed on me earlier, something happened. And the moment he looked up at me after he scored and won the game...

It felt like...

I squeeze my eyes closed as I stop at a red light.

It felt like it was for me.

Lock it down, Casey.

You probably didn't feature in a single one of his thoughts tonight.

There is no way he'll crawl into bed tonight and think about that eye contact, remember how it was when you were together.

My thoughts run away with me as I pull into the parking lot outside my building and picture him lying in bed with his hand wrapped around his dick, groaning my name.

Fuck's sake, Watson. Get a grip.

He doesn't care about you.

The only thing important to him is his future here.

"Fucking hell, come on," I scream at my TV as Vancouver steals the puck and shoots off down the ice, scoring again.

We're losing three to one, and the clock is counting down too fast.

I'm on the edge of my seat as the puck drops and Fletch wins the face-off.

He passes to Kodie, who takes off with Vancouver's defense right on his tail.

My heart is in my throat as he gets closer to the goal. But just before he gets there, the other Vancouver defenseman—Cooper Nash—bodychecks Kodie.

"Motherfucker," I cry, now on my feet, unlike Kodie and the asshole who took him down.

The whistle blows and play stops as they right themselves.

Kodie barks something, and the Vancouver player turns on him and steps right into his space.

"Shit," I whisper as I wait, not breathing..

Fights on the ice are common, but it's very rare that Kodie gets involved.

Unsurprisingly, it's usually Linc. Or Killer, one of our starting D men.

My heart slams against my ribs as I wait to see what's going to happen.

Members of both teams move closer, ready to get involved if necessary.

The Vancouver captain reaches out to pull his man away, but he's not having any of it. He's gunning for a fight.

Kodie lifts his chin, and I gasp, waiting for fists to start flying.

I can't decide if I want it to happen or not.

Watching him fight will be hot as hell, I have no doubt. But also...his daughter.

It's the last thing she needs.

I've only seen her a handful of times. We did a family day last year that she came to. Honestly, she was the cutest thing I've ever seen, walking around wearing her dad's jersey with pride.

But mostly, Kodie keeps his family life private.

I can't blame him. I think I'd do the same thing.

I'm just about convinced he's agreeing to fight before he skates away.

I breathe a sigh of relief and lower myself back to my couch.

Fuck. That was intense.

Both teams line up for the final face-off, and I'm forced to watch as Vancouver steals the puck and scores the final goal of the game.

"Fuck," I sigh. Disappointment sits heavily in my stomach.

I feel it for Dad. For the team. For everyone.

Throwing myself back on the couch, I keep my eyes on the screen, or more specifically, our number fifty-five.

The camera doesn't pan that close as he skates toward the exit and steps off the ice, but it's close enough to see the hard set of his jaw. Anger and frustration roll off him in waves.

Linc rushes up behind him, clamps his hand on Kodie's shoulder, and says something.

Kodie isn't having any of it, though, and shrugs him off.

My heart sinks.

I don't move from my spot as I watch Fletch and Dad do post-game press before highlights from the other games tonight are shown.

"Onwards and upwards," I mutter, walking to my kitchen to get a glass of water.

Adrenaline still races through my veins, and that's from just watching the game. I can only imagine what it must be like to be a part of it.

My phone pings on my coffee table, and it lights up, showing a picture of Parker and me last season in our jerseys. We traveled to Las Vegas for a game. It was incredible. Not only did the Vipers win, but we had an epic weekend.

We've already booked our tickets for when we play Vegas later in the season, and I can't wait.

Parker: That was rough.

Parker: Thought your man was gonna start throwing punches there.

Parker: Do you think he's sexually frustrated? Maybe he needs a hand with that…

Casey: Knew I shouldn't have told you.

Parker: 🤐🤐🤐

Casey: You're a nightmare.

When she doesn't reply immediately, I find my conversation with Dad.

Casey: Onwards and upwards x

It's the words he used to say to me after a loss.

I remember vividly walking out of the dressing room after a hard game, choked up and fighting back tears and falling straight into his arms.

"Losing is a part of the game," he used to whisper to me. *"You can't be a winner if you can't handle the losses."*

Dad: You can't be a winner if you can't handle the losses. Love you, Care Bear.

I smile.

Casey: Love you too. See you soon x

As I stare at our thread, I can't help but wonder if Kodie has anyone messaging him, letting him know that they were watching, that they care and that a loss is okay.

Sadness seeps through my veins. Everyone deserves to have someone on their side.

16

KODIE

"Ugh," I grunt, throwing my bag onto my bed in the hotel room I'm sharing with Linc before watching it bounce off and land on the floor with a thud.

Pretty much sums up everything about tonight.

A total fuck-up.

I knew it was going to happen.

Cooper Nash.

I shake my head as I swipe my bag up and place it on the chair beside my bed.

He's been a pain in my ass for years now.

The fact that we were friends once is laughable.

We went to fucking school together.

Played side by side for years.

But we went to different colleges and then got drafted to different teams, and our once-innocent friendship has turned into this toxic competitive bullshit that I can't stand.

It wasn't me. It was all him.

The first time we played against each other in college, I was excited to see him. Thought we could go out after the game and catch up.

But the second I stood before him on the ice, I realized that the man in front of me wasn't the person I once knew.

All hockey players are competitive. It runs through our veins. But Cooper...he's taken it to the extreme.

Our friendship is long gone now. Every time I see him, I can't help but feel sorry for him.

Sure, he's focused and has an incredible record—not quite as good as mine, but still good. He plays for a great team, but somewhere along the way he seems to have forgotten that it's possible to be a good player and a decent person.

I can't put all the blame at his feet, though. His dad and uncle were both ex-NHL players. The pressure they put on him was ridiculous. Even at a young age, they wanted him to be the best. Back then, though, he could also enjoy the fun of the game and the dream.

It seems that all of that has gone by the wayside.

"It's not the bag's fault," Linc mutters from behind me.

More often than not, we're put together. Usually, I don't complain.

We might be wildly different, but we get on well.

He's the version of me I barely remember from my college and early NHL days.

He's the life and soul of the party. He never takes anything—aside from hockey—too seriously. He's generally a happy-go-lucky guy who's happy to entertain as many of his adoring female fans as possible.

Shrugging off my suit jacket, I pull my tie from around my neck, loosen a few buttons, and fall onto my bed.

"That guy is a fucking asshole," I mutter.

"What's new there?" Linc asks, leaning against the wall with his arms crossed over his chest.

"Fucking hate losing to him."

"I hate losing," Linc shoots back.

I glare at him.

"You know, you're even grumpier than usual," he points out helpfully.

My teeth clench, making my jaw tick with irritation. I can't exactly argue with him.

The pressure of preseason, our first loss, and the fact that I can't seem to get Casey out of my head...yeah, I'm a miserable motherfucker.

I grunt some kind of response as I stare up at the ceiling.

If it weren't so late, I'd video call Sutton. But she will have been in bed long ago. With any luck, she fell asleep before the end of the game, but it's wishful thinking. I fucking hate being lured into something on the ice that she shouldn't be witness to.

"It's because you got laid," Linc surmises as he pushes from the wall. He stalks around his bed before sitting on the edge and leaning forward to rest his elbows on his knees, studying me.

"We're not talking about this," I mutter.

"You might not be, but I am."

Squeezing my eyes closed, I fight to keep my breathing even.

"Probably a stupid question, but...have you seen her again?"

"Who?" I ask, keeping my eyes closed.

His laugh booms around me, but there isn't a lot of humor in it.

"You're funny."

No, I'm not.

I'm pissed, and I want to be at home.

"Are you going to see her again?"

Cracking one eye open, I glare at him as hard as I can praying he gets the message and fucks off.

He should be at the bar already, hitting on women. If I'm lucky, he'll find one to spend the night with and leave me the hell alone.

"Dude, come on. Give me something here," he begs. "I just want to see you happy. And that night...you were happy. Hell, I'm pretty sure I actually saw you smile."

"Fuck off; I smile."

"You grimace at best."

Forcing my cheeks up, I smile at him.

"Grimace. You look about as happy as someone who's just been told their grandmother's died."

"Can you just...leave?"

"Nope. Not unless you're coming with me."

"I'm not—"

"You need to blow off some steam. Let go of...whatever is weighing you down."

"I'm fine."

"You're a liar," he counters. "Come for a drink."

I don't know why he's asking; I hardly ever go out with them, even when we are on the road.

"Linc," I warn.

"One drink, just one, and then you can come back here and cry into your pillow."

"I don't cry—"

He raises a brow, a smirk pulling at his lips.

"Come, or I'll stay too and keep asking you questions about your lady in green. She looked good in Vipers colors. I wonder how hot she'd look in your jersey? Probably not as good as she'd look in mine."

Something red hot shoots through me as my stomach knots up and my fists clench at my sides.

"You want her," he teases.

"I don't," I counter. "I don't even know who she is."

It's a bare-faced lie. But it should be the truth.

I was never meant to know who she was.

Fuck.

It would be so much easier if that were still the case.

She may have lingered in my head, in my fantasies for a while, but eventually, the memories of her would have faded.

But now...

Now I'm going to see her at home games, at any time she finds an excuse to come to the rink during practice. It might well be innocent, to see her dad. She might stand by what she said and never do or say anything about it again. But even the promise of her presence is enough to drive me out of my mind.

My confession has the opposite intended effect, piquing Linc's interest.

"You don't know who she is?" he repeats.

Pushing myself up so I sit against the headboard, I look at him, begging him to get this over with.

"No. I don't know who she is."

"But you fucked her, right?"

"I went back to her hotel room," I say, refusing to go into details.

"Aaaand...watched Disney Plus?" He quirks a brow. "I saw you kiss her on the dance floor. There's no fucking way you went and watched a movie."

"Whatever we did or didn't do, she never removed her mask."

"Kinky, Rivers. I like it," he says, waggling his eyebrows like the tyrant he is.

I drag my hand down my face.

"Does she know who you are?"

I swallow thickly, my Adam's apple bobbing in my throat.

Apparently, that's enough of an answer for him.

"So she knows who you are, and yet, she hasn't come to find you?" he muses, like this is an algebra equation he needs to figure out.

"It was a one-night thing."

"The women who want to sleep with us never want it to be a one-night thing," he states, probably referring to the hordes of women he's had to turn away over the years.

"Well, then I lucked out, because this one was happy with one night."

"And she hasn't sold the story to the press? I can see it now: 'first woman to bed LA Vipers' top scorer in years tells all about mystery winger.'"

"You're not funny," I grunt.

"Wait...how many years had it been, exactly?"

I shake my head. Mostly because I want him to stop, but also because it was so long that I'm not even sure anymore.

Making a decision that I hope will result in him shutting the hell up, I swing my legs off the bed and mutter, "Are we going for a fucking drink or not?"

His eyes burn into my back as I march toward the door and pull it open.

"You coming, Storm?"

"Hell yeah!" He jumps to his feet and races after me, fist-pumping the air.

I already felt out of place as I followed Linc into a bar a few blocks over, but it only gets worse as we approach the booth the guys are sitting in.

One by one, they look up, and the second their gazes land on me, eyes widen and chins drop.

I fucking hate it. Mainly because it makes me feel like an asshole.

All these guys welcomed me from my very first training session a year ago, and I've thanked them by...mostly being absent.

And it's not just me. They've welcomed Sutton and Mom, as well.

Whenever there have been family events, or even just at the games Sutton attends, they always make the effort to say hello to her. They've made her feel as much a part of the team as I am. It's something I'll forever be grateful for.

I guess I should probably start showing them.

"Shift over, Marilyn," Linc says, none too gently shoving our rookie, Hayden Monroe, in the shoulder, forcing him to make space for us.

It's a big booth, but put a handful of hockey players in it, and it looks tiny. Much like when Sutton tries to put her stuffies into her Barbie house.

Fletch gets the attention of the server before my ass hits the bench, and he orders another round of beers.

"I don't usually—"

"Just one. With your team," Fletch says, turning to me with an understanding expression on his face.

The conversation drifts to tonight's game and what an asshole Cooper is. I don't argue the point.

I may have fond childhood memories with him, but every time I come up against him as an adult, another one of them withers and dies.

The second my beer is placed in front of me, I act on instinct and reach for it.

A groan rumbles deep in my throat at the familiar taste.

"Good?" Linc asks with a smirk.

"Yeah," I agree.

"See, it's not so bad hanging out with us, is it?"

Guilt knots up my insides that my teammates might think I don't want to spend time with them.

That's not it at all. It has nothing to do with them and everything to do with me.

Putting tonight's loss behind us, we focus on what's to come. We still have six more exhibition games; hopefully, it'll be enough time for us to find our footing as a team and embark on our most successful season yet.

"So, how was your first road game as a Viper, Marylin?" Flech asks our rookie.

"Yeah, good," he says, shrinking a little under our attention.

"Wow," Fletch laughs. "I'm glad it left an impression on you."

I think back to my first week of preseason. It was the most overwhelming week of my life.

Just like our rookie, I had all the confidence, and I knew I had the skill. After being at the top of my game at college, it was unnerving to suddenly become the bottom of the pile again.

There's something about our rookie, though.

He'll be fine. Give it a month or two, and he'll have found his place.

I'm looking forward to seeing what he can bring to the team.

I've watched his college games; I know what he's capable of. I'm sure everyone around the table does as well.

"Right," Fletch says after finishing his beer. "I'm heading back to speak to Reese."

We stand to allow him out. He says goodbye to everyone before turning to me.

His hand wraps around my shoulder, and his eyes find mine. "It was good to see you tonight, Big D."

My lips purse at the nickname.

Unlike what people assume, it actually stands for Big Daddy.

Which...honestly, I'm not sure is better or worse.

"You should hang out with us more; I know it would make Coach happy." I swallow thickly as that guilt returns. "We're going to the playoffs this year. But to do that, we've got to do it together," he states with a look that makes me want to return to my hotel room with my tail between my legs.

Instead, I force a nod. "Yeah."

"Great. See you in the morning. Enjoy the rest of your night," he calls to everyone before he disappears.

"So whipped," Linc says as I lower myself beside him.

"Yeah," I agree. Although really, is that a bad thing?

For the very briefest of moments, I wonder what it might be like to have a woman waiting for me at home after a game.

No, not a woman.

Casey.

"You're thinking about her again, aren't you?" Linc teases.

Shaking my head, I reach for what's left of my beer and try to focus on doing what Fletch just said: enjoying my night.

Thankfully, Linc doesn't mention my mystery girl again until we're back in our hotel room a little over an hour later.

"You need to find her," he says as the door closes behind us.

A laugh spills from my lips.

"I don't need a woman in my life. And I certainly don't need to run around town looking for one."

"Did she leave a glass slipper behind?" Linc asks unhelpfully. I shake my head as I toe my shoes off.

The only things she left were the memories of the best night of my life.

And the desire to do it all over again.

17

CASEY

The arena erupts as Lincoln Storm nets what is going to be the final goal of the game.

Six to one.

The Vipers were on fire tonight.

Lights flash and the goal horn sounds as the floor beneath my feet vibrates, everyone stomping and shouting for their beloved team.

This is what hockey is all about.

The sense of belonging, of family. Of being able to turn to the person sitting beside you and know they've got your back.

Parker hollers as Linc laps up the praise in the middle of the rink like the cocky asshole he is.

"Be careful; if he hears, he might think you like him," I shout in her ear.

She immediately stops, her top lip peeling back.

"I'm not screaming for Linc. I'm cheering for my team. They fucking killed it. All of them."

"They did," I say, unable to wipe the smile from my face as the team congratulates each other. "Hayden Monroe smashed it, too."

"He was a good draft pick," Parker agrees, watching the rookie get attacked by the others after his kickass performance tonight.

The losing team disappears off the ice, leaving just our Vipers behind. The majority of their fans that came to watch have already left. I get it—it's disappointing to see your team lose—but I'm always here to the end, no matter the score. Hell, the guys need it more if they've lost.

Dad catches my eye from behind the boards, and I give him a little curtsey. He's buzzing from that win. I can sense it from here. Unable to accept the praise, he gestures to his team, still joking around on the ice.

Glancing back at the team, my breath catches as I find Kodie looking this way.

For a moment, I think it's an accident, but when he doesn't immediately drag his eyes away from me, I realize it probably isn't.

"Casey?" Parker shouts in my ear, but I'm powerless to rip my gaze away.

"Holy shit, Case," Parker laughs.

But then his eyes drop to my jersey, and he's gone. Like it never happened.

Only it did.

My body knows it did. And so does Parker.

"Okay, even I need a cold shower after that," Parker says as the guys finally make their way off the ice.

"I don't know what you mean." I try for nonchalance, but I fail massively.

"He wants you," she states as we begin to file from our row.

"It doesn't matter if he does. He can't have me." I don't mean for there to be so much bitterness in my tone, but it's there, and there is no chance of Parker missing it.

"But what if you can?" she asks, playing devil's advocate.

"There are a million reasons why I can't."

She steps beside me as we make our way to the friends and family suite. "But are they really good enough? The way he looked at you, Case. That was..." She fans herself with her hand. "So fucking hot."

"All of them are good enough," I force out, hating that my words might be true.

Would I like the chance of a repeat and then to maybe see if things could go anywhere? Sure. I'd be an idiot not to.

But we can't.

That night has to be enough.

He has other things that need his attention, and I...I have a life that I love that doesn't involve getting hot and heavy with one of the men who've been warned off me.

But doesn't that only make it more tempting to break the rules?

We step inside, excited chatter about the win filling the room.

"We need drinks," Parker says immediately, dragging me to the bar.

"Okay," I laugh, happy to follow her lead.

She orders while I'm looking around the room.

I recognize almost everyone, and more than a few wave and smile at me in greeting.

I'm about to spin around when a slightly older woman catches my eye. But it's not her who really captures my attention; it's the little girl she's leaning down to talk to.

Sutton Rivers.

I swear to God, she is the cutest kid I've ever seen.

She isn't just wearing her father's jersey but the whole uniform, and she's clutching a bear stuffy to her chest that's in a matching outfit.

Her eyes sparkle with excitement. Looking at her, you'd have no idea that it's more than likely past her bedtime.

"She's cute, huh?" Parker muses, having seen who has captured my attention. "Looks like us as kids."

She does. "Nah, she's cuter than you ever were."

Parker gasps, and when I turn toward her, I find she's got her hand over her heart.

"Brutal, Case. Brutal."

Laughing, I turn to get our drinks.

"Uh...shots?" I ask, staring at the four small glasses in horror.

"Yep," she agrees, lifting her first one. "Tonight, we're letting go and having fun."

"Sounds dangerous," I tease, hesitantly eyeing the two shots before me.

"We haven't had a good night out in forever. Come on."

She gives me her best puppy eyes, not that I really need convincing. She's right. We are long overdue a night out.

Without saying a word, I reach for the first shot.

"One for fun," I say, holding it up.

"And one for luck," Parker says, lifting her glass to tap mine.

"Ugh," I complain after swallowing. It burns all the way down to my stomach. "I think we might be too old for shots.'

"Bullshit. No one is ever too old for shots."

"I'll remind you of that in the morning," I tease.

"It'll be worth it," she says, reaching for the second.

"Really?"

"Really."

I can't lie; the second one goes down a little easier. The buzz it gives me only adds to that from tonight's win, and I'm on my way to being ready to dance the night away.

It's a little over thirty minutes later when the team begins to join us.

I know he's coming—his mom and daughter are here. But this time, I don't stare at the door, waiting for him to appear like a lost puppy.

That eye contact earlier was enough for me to handle.

Anymore and I might end up really embarrassing myself.

The image of me humping his leg appears in my head, and I can't help but laugh.

"Is this a private joke, or can anyone join?" Parker quips.

"It's nothing. I just..." My words trail off as tingles run down my spine.

"Just what?" she pushes.

He just walked in.

Inhaling through my nose, I try to focus on Parker, but I can barely even remember my own name.

"Daddy," ripples through the room, and I lose my fight to keep my eyes off him.

My head twists just in time to see her jump into his arms.

He engulfs her small body in a hug and presses a kiss on the top of her head. It's adorable.

"You were amazing tonight."

He whispers a response, but his voice is lower and less excited, stopping me from hearing his words.

"That final assist was incredible. But not as good as your first goal. That play was perfect. Monroe is good, too; he was a good choice. I've already told Coach."

Parker snorts a laugh. Apparently, she's listening too.

"She's you fifteen years ago," Parker whispers.

"Uh...I don't ever remember giving Dad's coach advice."

"Something tells me he might say otherwise," she counters.

Turning away from father and daughter, I start to argue. "I did—" But the second I look into Parker's glinting eyes, my words vanish. "Fine, maybe I did once or twice. I was right, though."

"James always said you should have become a coach," she says as our fresh drinks are placed before us.

I smile, although I can't deny the desire to coach isn't there. "Maybe in a different life. I'm happy with what I'm doing."

"Yeah," she agrees. "Same." It's bullshit. Parker might have the career she always wanted, but she isn't happy with her current job. She really wants to be here on the Vipers' medical team. But positions are like gold dust.

It'll happen. She needs to be patient.

It's another thirty minutes before Dad and Fletch appear. Fletch is fresh from the shower and as per usual, the second he spots Reese in the crowd, he walks straight into her arms.

"Care Bear," Dad calls—a little too loudly, considering we're surrounded by people.

"Great game, Coach," Parker says. "Casey and I were just talking about when she was little and used to tell your old coach what plays to run."

Dad's face lights up with a wide smile before a chuckle erupts. "You always had a good eye," he tells me.

"Exactly."

"You still do. I've made use of your ideas in the past."

Pride swells in my chest. I know he has; I've seen him call plays that the two of us have discussed over the kitchen island.

"Breakfast tomorrow morning?" he asks, as if I hadn't already agreed to it.

"You got it, old man," I tease.

"Coach," someone calls, making him look over his shoulder.

"Gotta go. Be good tonight. Don't do anything I wouldn't do," he warns before stalking off.

"Oh, Casey is definitely imagining doing things you wouldn't do with your number fifty-five."

"Shut up," I hiss before grabbing my vodka and Coke and swallowing a large mouthful.

"I bet you that by the time this season is over—hell, by the end of the year—you'll have gotten up close and personal with him again."

My cheeks blaze red hot.

Fuck. I really hope she's right.

"**P**arker," I groan as she pulls me toward The Fractured Compass.

The drinks we've already consumed have left me with a nice buzz, but I'm not drunk enough to happily go along with her wicked plan.

"Casey," she states authoritatively. "I'm not about to line up the entire team and ask you to blow them."

"I should hope not."

She pauses for a moment as if she's considering the thought herself.

"You don't want a hockey player. They're all egotistical jerks, remember?"

"Still a hot image, though."

"Jesus," I mutter.

"Anyway, what I was trying to say is that you're allowed to go to a bar where they might be, Case."

"Where they are," I correct. There is no might about it.

"So what? You're a grown-ass woman. It's not like you're going to work your way around the team and make it hella awkward for everyone. You're as much a part of the Viper family as they are. You're allowed to celebrate a win with them."

I think back to all the warnings Dad has given me over the years. He's trying to protect me and stop me from getting my heart broken. I respect that.

But also...

Parker's right. Those warnings are old. I'm a fully grown adult who can make my own decisions.

I internally cringe.

My heart isn't getting involved in this.

I was just ticking off a bucket list item before I find "the one," settle down, and never get the chance.

It was a one-off.

Something that won't be repeated, and certainly not with another member of the team.

"Okay, fine. But if Dad has something to say, I'm sending him your way."

She waggles her brows. "Oh, you can send Daddy Watson my way any day."

My top lip peels back.

"Gross," I mutter, shoving her out of the way so I can get to the door. I need a drink to help me forget that comment.

"What? He's got that hot older thing going on. And he's no longer a player, so..."

"Just for that comment, you're buying the drinks."

"Atta girl," she says excitedly as she follows me into the bar.

Music and loud chatter hit my ears the second I step inside, and as I round the corner, my eyes immediately land on the booths filled with hockey players.

It's not like they're hard to find. They're all stacked with muscles and unbelievably hot.

I don't know what it is about hockey players' DNA. They're

not only gifted on the ice, but they're always ridiculously good-looking.

It's really not fair.

I scan the faces, mentally ticking off who's here and who's not, when my eyes snag on a face I was not expecting to see.

Kodie Rivers doesn't go out drinking with the guys after a game.

He goes home and tucks his little girl into bed.

But not tonight.

He's...here.

And he's looking right at me.

18

KODIE

Every muscle in my body tenses, and my lungs depress as if I've just been hit in the chest with a stick.

I knew it was a risk when I agreed to join the guys for a drink tonight. But from what I've heard over the past year, Casey doesn't follow the team out after a game.

I can only assume that's because her father has told her not to.

Exactly why she refused to take her mask off two weeks ago.

She isn't allowed to fraternize with the team just as much as we're meant to keep our distance from her.

After Fletch told me how good it was for me to show my face after our Vancouver game, Coach pulled me into his office and none too discreetly demanded that I put in a little more effort with the team.

He fully understands my other priorities but also knows how vital team bonding is.

He's been in my position, so I have to trust that he knows what I need to do to be both the best hockey player and father I can be.

I thought it was going to be safe. I could have a beer with the guys and then head home so I could be up early to spend time with Sutton before I was needed back at the arena.

I was confident that I could handle both going into the season. Until she walked in.

Hell, what am I saying? The second I saw her sitting behind the net as I stepped out onto the ice earlier, I knew that life was never going to be easy again.

Not when she refuses to get out of my head.

Linc spent the rest of our trip trying to pull information out of me.

I refused to give him anything, instead sticking with my story about not knowing who she was.

It's how it was meant to be.

I played better tonight. Instead of being distracted by her eyes on me, I was able to harness it and turn the heat of her stare into determination.

I hate to give her the credit, but I'm pretty sure she's the reason I was tonight's top goal scorer.

The moment she sees me sitting amongst the team, her steps falter, and the blood drains from her face.

Something stirs inside me.

Satisfaction and a little relief.

I'm not the only one who's just had the world tugged from beneath them.

The only problem is I don't know the reason for her shock.

It's been two weeks since the ball. A week since I discovered her identity. She's had every opportunity to seek me out. It's what a puck bunny would have done.

They're relentless in their quest to bag a player.

But she hasn't. Other than turning up to my games, wearing my jersey, and holding eye contact a couple of times, she hasn't made a move.

I can't help but wonder if I'm thinking about all of this way more than I should.

Am I building it up to be something bigger than it is?

She told me that she only wanted one night. Was that really the truth?

I feel like a jerk assuming that one night wouldn't be enough. Apparently, I'm now the cocky asshole I used to be.

She brings it back up in me, though.

The need to be noticed. To be wanted.

Although, if I'm being honest, I've never been genuinely needed by a woman before. They might have wanted me for a fun night or two to let off some steam and earn some bragging rights or a story to sell. But not a single one ever cared enough to actually need me.

It doesn't matter, though. I've got Sutton for that.

She makes me feel needed and worthy every day.

I don't need any more than that.

Conversation continues around me, but it's like time stops as we stare at each other.

Memories of that night flicker through my mind like a movie. No, not a movie. A porno...but better.

It was real.

So painfully fucking real.

"What do you think, Big D?" Fletcher's voice floats around in my head, but it's not strong enough to pull my attention to him. "Big D?"

Finally, I turn to look at Fletch and the rest of the guys at our table.

"Uh...yeah."

"Excuse me," Linc says, sliding from the booth and making a beeline for Casey and Parker.

"Fucking dog," Fletch mutters as he tracks Linc's movement toward the bar. Or, more specifically, Casey, after he clocks what's on her jersey.

He waves to the bartender and orders drinks for both of them.

"You know who that is, right?" Cole Hansley, our goalie, or Handsy, as he's fondly known, says, throwing his arm around our rookie's shoulder.

"Uh..." Marilyn studies both of them.

There's no way Coach hasn't said anything to him. The rest of us have been warned more times than I've had hot dinners about staying away from his daughter.

Unless, of course, he isn't concerned she'll go for the baby of the team.

Something hot and uncomfortable rushes through me at the thought of her looking at him—or any of them—the way she did me that night.

"C-Coach's daughter, right?" he asks, proving that he's not as unaware as he often appears.

"The one on the left, yeah. She's off-limits, unless you want to say goodbye to your career before it's started."

"What about her friend?"

"Parker Donnelly? I'd stay well clear of that one, too."

"Why?"

"You've heard of Everett Donnelly, right?"

Monroe frowns for a second before realization hits. Everette Donnelly is not only the Seattle Bandits star defensemen, but he's also Linc's best friend and Parker's big brother.

"Oh, shit. No way."

"Rett's little sister."

Hayden huffs and slumps back with his hands folded over his chest. It's a move I'm more used to seeing on Sutton than one of my teammates.

"Well, this fucking sucks. Who can I hit on in this bar?"

The guys look around. "Anyone but those two."

"But they're by far the hottest."

"Probably best not to lead with that line," Fletch suggests.

"What the fuck do you know about picking up women these days?" Handsy asks with a smirk.

"From watching you lot, I know exactly what you shouldn't do," Fletch laughs. "Right, I'm out. Got a hot woman waiting on me."

After a quick round of goodbyes, he disappears, the first to leave just like last time. But seeing him walk away, dividing his time between his two great loves—his career and his wife—solidifies my belief that I can also do the same.

I should follow his lead and go home.

When I told Mom I'd been instructed to join the team after the games, she unsurprisingly agreed. Even Sutton was happy about it. She told me that I should go and celebrate all my goals with my friends. That it's what she'd want to do if she were in my skates.

I shake my head as I remember the firm way she glared at me, ensuring that I did as my coach and captain said.

Linc glances over from the bar, having seen Fletch depart. He studies me closely, probably expecting me to be next. But as much as I might want to get home, I can't force my legs to move.

Especially not while he's standing a few inches too close to the woman who seems to be a constant presence in my life these days.

"Another round?" Handsy asks, but while everyone else agrees, I decline the offer.

Over the next hour, I try my best to keep my eyes off Casey, but it gets harder and harder, especially when it becomes obvious that she's drunk.

Linc has thankfully moved on to more hopeful targets. He might flirt his ass off with Casey and Parker, but he likes his job and his balls too much to take it anywhere further.

Unfortunately, there are other guys in the bar who don't have a death wish hanging over their heads, and not ten minutes after Linc leaves them does some other asshole try his luck.

Casey stares up at him from her seat on the stool and throws her head back, laughing at what I'm sure was a shit joke.

My fists curl under the table.

The guys talk around me, but thankfully, they're too lost in their conversation about our next game to pay any attention to me.

My heart jumps into my throat as Casey slides off the stool and, on unsteady legs, starts toward the bathroom, focusing intently on where she's going.

As she passes, her addictive scent hits my nose, and my cock jerks as I remember that she tasted even sweeter than she smelled.

The guy she left behind takes her stool and turns his full attention on Parker, but that doesn't concern me.

I'm still trying to convince myself to leave when she returns.

The sight of her jersey stirs those unwanted feelings that hit me earlier, and my breathing increases.

She should not affect me like this.

As she passes, she pulls her cell from her purse, swipes the screen, and puts it to her ear as she turns to leave. But before she gets to the door, she stumbles and crashes into the wall.

Parker looks over with concern, but Casey waves her cell at her to explain where she's going before reaching for the door.

It's too heavy, and she fumbles with it for a few seconds before finally getting it open and disappearing outside.

I should ignore it. Ignore her. I should wait for her to come back and then leave.

But I can't. The temptation is too much.

"I'll see you guys tomorrow," I say as I push to my feet. I don't know if they hear me or even respond. My sole focus is the door and the woman on the other side of it.

Warm air rushes over me as I step outside and leave the air conditioning behind.

"I-I can't hear you. The reception is crap," she slurs down the line. The sound of her raspy voice hits me right in the chest. An ache forms behind my sternum. "Are you there? Can you hear me?" she asks, almost shouting at whoever is on the other end. "Ugh. I'll call you tomorrow," she finally says before giving up. "Useless piece of shit," she mutters to herself as she drops her cell into her purse and spins around.

I swear her gasp is big enough to suck all the air from around us.

Being close to her again...it's dangerous.

My fists curl, attempting to stop me from reaching for her.

Everything that night was so easy.

I even danced with her, for fuck's sake.

I don't dance.

Hell, I don't do any of the things I did that night.

"Kodie?" she whispers, suddenly sounding a hell of a lot more sober than a few moments ago.

The sound of my name rolling off her lips does bad things to me. But worse than that, it makes me want to do filthy, wicked things to her all over again.

"H-how are you?"

She takes a step forward, probably intending to return to the bar, but in my head, she's moving closer to me.

Whatever she's attempting to do, she fails the moment her foot catches on the pavement, and she stumbles straight into me.

19

CASEY

His large hands wrap around my upper arms as he catches me with ease before I crash into his big, hard, muscular body.

Memories of the first night this happened flicker through my mind.

Oh for a repeat of that...

Damn him.

How is it fair that he's so hot?

Heat burns down my arms from his touch, shooting straight to my core.

I shift my thighs together as the ache intensifies.

Coming here tonight was a bad idea. But it's too late to do anything about it now.

He pushes me backward, righting me on my feet again.

But the second I look up, I discover that this isn't a happy reunion.

There is no joy on his face. None of the lightness from that night. Just anger.

His lips press into a thin line before he rasps, "What the fuck are you playing at, Casey?"

I blink up at him as the sound of my name rolling off his lips hits me full force.

God, I wish I could have heard him moaning that in my ear.

Desire pools between my thighs.

I was wrong.

One night with Kodie Rivers wasn't enough.

I need more.

So much more.

"I-I'm not playing at anything," I shoot back. "I came out with Parker for a drink."

His jaw ticks with irritation, and the urge to lean forward and lick the pulsating spot is almost too much to ignore.

"I wasn't expecting you to be here."

Irritation flashes across his face.

His eyes hold mine captive. I don't know what he's looking for, or if he finds it.

The team is right inside. One of them could come out at any moment and catch us like this.

My heart rate continues to increase as his familiar manly scent flows through my nose.

"I'm leaving. This...This..." He gestures between us as he fights for something to say.

Behind me, the door opens and the loud music from inside the bar spills out.

My heart jumps into my throat, but I don't react as fast as Kodie.

His giant hand grips mine tightly for a beat before he drags me around the corner.

All my breath rushes from my lungs as my back crashes against the rough wall.

"What are you—" His burning palm covers my mouth, and my eyes widen.

"Shush," he hisses, his expression tight and panicked as we wait.

I'm not sure what he's expecting. Surely, one of his teammates isn't going to come out to find him?

He's a grown-ass man who can do whatever the hell he wants.

They were probably expecting him to leave ages ago. I know I was.

My heart flutters as I consider that he might have hung around because I was here.

It's silly and naive, but I can't help it.

Our eye contact holds as silence falls around us.

No one calls out for either of us. No one does anything.

My heart pounds so hard, blood whooshes past my ears, and my head spins, but it has nothing to do with the alcohol I've consumed tonight.

A car races past before blaring its horn. My entire body flinches, and I swear Kodie moves closer.

The thought of him trying to protect me is almost too much.

Long seconds pass with nothing but eye contact before he finally lets his hand slip from my mouth.

His warm, beer-scented breath rushes over my face. He's so close that all I'd have to do is stretch up on my toes and our lips would collide.

"What are you doing?" I whisper, needing to know where this is going.

Please let it be where I want it to be.

His eyes bounce between mine as if he's battling some kind of internal war.

My breath catches when his arm lifts and his hand wraps around the side of my neck, his thumb resting on my jaw.

"Kodie," I whimper, unable to keep it in.

I wanted to moan his name so badly that night, but I couldn't. I couldn't let him know the truth.

His chest heaves, the heat of his body searing the front of mine.

I swear time ceases to exist as I silently beg him to kiss me.

Me.

Not the woman in the mask, but *me*.

Casey Watson.

The forbidden daughter of his—

He leans forward, and my eyelids lower as my tongue drags along my bottom lip in preparation.

Kiss me. Please.

Kiss me.

His lips are a hair's breadth from mine. He's going to do it.

He's going to—

"Casey?" My best friend's voice pierces through the air, and he jumps back as if I burned him.

No.

"Kodie?" I whisper as ice quickly replaces the lava that was filling my veins only moments ago.

"Go," he instructs, his voice hard and commanding.

He sounds just like he did that night when he was making dirty demands, but this is a very different situation. It takes everything I have not to sob in disappointment.

"Case?" Parker calls again.

"This isn't over," I state quietly before I step out of the alleyway he'd pulled me into.

"Hey, what's up?" I ask, attempting to sound innocent and failing miserably.

Her eyes hold mine for a beat before they jump to the darkness behind me.

"What were you—Oh my god. Were you with him?"

"Shush," I hiss, glancing back over my shoulder as if he's going to walk out and make his presence known.

He's not. He will hide as if he's ashamed of being anywhere near me.

I know that's not true—hell, I hope it's not. His hiding and not wanting anyone to know what happened between us is a hell of a lot more serious than a little bit of shame.

His entire career, his life as he knows it, is at stake.

And yet, he was about to kiss you...

My eyes fill with tears, and I look away, embarrassed that I'm getting emotional over this.

It must be the alcohol.

"Casey?" Parker whispers in concern.

"I'm just going to call an Uber and head home."

"I'll do it," she says, pulling her cell from her purse.

"No," I say a little firmer than before. "You stay, enjoy the rest of your night. That guy was into you. You should—"

"I'm not interested in him, Case. I'm worried about you, though."

She taps the screen, ordering a car. "Two minutes," she says before putting it away again.

"I'm fine. I'm just being silly. Coming here tonight was a mistake," I confess.

"Was it?" she asks, linking her arm with mine as we wait. "Case, that man has barely taken his eyes off you from the moment you walked in." Her words are spoken quietly so that no one else would hear, but they hit me with the force of a defenseman slamming someone into the boards.

I shake my head, refusing to believe her words.

"He was probably wishing I'd leave," I mutter dejectedly. "He thinks I'm playing games."

"Pfft," Parker huffs. "Then he needs to get to know you better."

"He can't. We can't. I just need to forget it ever happened."

Her hopeful expression dies. She knows that isn't going to be possible. She knows just how much that night meant, how much he means to me. Even if I don't really know him. Even if he's only a figure in my fantasies. He's still a part of my life. One I never expected to be within touching distance of. But he's here now.

I set all this in motion, and I'm going to have to deal with the consequences.

"Casey," she sighs.

"It's fine. I just need to pull my big girl panties on and move on with my life."

She smiles sadly at me as our car pulls up to the curb.

She climbs in first, and just before I follow, I look behind me at the alleyway he's loitering in.

He's watching me. Electricity shoots through me the second our eyes connect, and I wish it was enough for him to step out of the shadows and stop me from leaving. But no matter how much I pray for that to happen, I know it won't.

A heavy sigh rips from my lips a second before I turn away and climb into the car.

Parker doesn't say a word. She doesn't need to. A lifetime of friendship means she knows. So instead of saying anything, she reaches over and takes my hand in hers, squeezing in support.

The journey is mostly in silence, and when we pull up outside of my apartment building first, I tell her that I'll call her in the morning before climbing out and heading inside.

If it were a different night, I might have invited her up. But right now, I just want to be alone.

Maybe we can have a do-over of our night out tomorrow.

My limbs are heavy as I plod through my apartment to my bedroom. The second I'm there, I drag my jersey from my body and throw it down on the bed.

My eyes snag on the name and number printed across it.

I wore this one tonight as a test. It was stupid.

I have a full roster of the Vipers jerseys, and I rotate them.

Of course, since Kodie signed, I've secretly favored his.

I've never really thought much of whose I'm wearing. Or at least, I didn't until the first exhibition game on Monday when I made a point of selecting Kodie's. I wanted to see his reaction to me wearing his jersey after discovering that I was his mystery woman.

Just like I wanted to see if he would react to me wearing Linc's tonight.

Maybe he was right earlier when he accused me of game-playing. Maybe that is exactly what I'm doing.

I strip the rest of my clothes off and pull out a t-shirt to sleep in before making my way to the bathroom to take my makeup off.

The second I look at myself in the mirror, I let out an exhausted sigh.

We shouldn't have gone to The Fractured Compass tonight. We should have gone to one of our usual places away from the team.

It was a risk. One that didn't pay off.

Or maybe it did, if you consider getting close to Kodie again winning.

He was going to kiss you.

Damn Parker for coming to find me when she did.

I brush my teeth and climb into bed, running those few minutes with Kodie over and over in my mind.

If Parker hadn't come out, if we hadn't been interrupted, where could tonight have gone?

Probably nowhere, a little voice pipes up.

But that voice doesn't stop my imagination running on overdrive and I picture us stumbling into my apartment, his lips locked on mine, his hands on my body.

My hand slips down my stomach as I picture exactly what I'd want him to do to me. How he'd command me to do his bidding and I'd love every second of it.

It doesn't take me long to find my release, and I fall asleep with filthy thoughts of Kodie still buzzing around my head.

20

CASEY

Buzzing drags me from a deep sleep.

"Stop it," I mumble, not ready to wake up yet.

I don't know what time it is. I refuse to open my eyes to check, but it's definitely too early to be awake on a Saturday.

I just begin to drift back off to sleep when it starts up again.

"Ugh."

I reach for it on my nightstand, but instead of grabbing it, I knock it off and it hits the floor with an obnoxious thud.

"For fuck's sake," I complain before forcing my eyes open to search for it.

It continues buzzing across the floor, Dad's name lighting up the screen.

A memory from last night hits me.

That's why I went outside.

He called me, and it was noisy as fuck in that bar.

Panic hits me, and my eyes jump to the clock. But I sigh in relief when I realize I still have an hour before he's meant to be picking me up for breakfast.

Definitely too early for a Saturday morning.

"H-hey," I croak when I finally lift my cell to my ear.

"Ah, good morning to you to, Care Bear."

"It's too early."

"Did you go out drinking with Parker last night?" he asks, a teasing lilt to his voice.

Guilt knots my stomach as I think about being in the same bar as the team. Sure, I only really spoke to Linc and Kodie; the others kept their distance. But still, it goes against everything he used to tell me.

That was years ago, though.

"Maybe," I answer coyly.

"Sorry I interrupted your night. I just heard something you might be interested in."

"Oh?" I ask, my curiosity piqued.

"Are you still good for breakfast?" he asks.

"Yeah, of course."

"Perfect. I'll pick you up in an hour."

"Wait," I cry before he has a chance to hang up. "What's the thing I might be interested in?"

"You'll have to wait and find out. See you in an hour."

"That's not fair," I complain.

He chuckles down the line before hanging up.

I humph as I drop my cell to the bed.

Such a tease.

With no other choice, I throw the covers back and pad to the bathroom to attempt to make myself presentable enough to step out of the building.

After two coffees and a shower, I feel a little more alive.

I didn't drink that much last night, just enough to have a nice buzz going, but that doesn't stop me from feeling like I pulled an all-nighter.

I know why I feel hungover.

It's him.

The effect his touch has on me. His almost kiss.

I tossed and turned all night, my head full of filthy dreams of what I want to do to him.

Getting myself off only scratched the surface.

I need his hands, his tongue, his cock.

"Fuck," I hiss as I stand at the kitchen window, waiting to see Dad's car turn into the lot.

It was hard enough to put Kodie out of my head when he didn't know who I was, when I thought I'd had my one shot. But that all changed when he learned the truth. And after he almost kissed me last night...shit. I don't stand a chance of putting that night behind me. My crush on him is burning hotter than ever.

The thought of not seeing him again until the Vipers' next home game doesn't sit well with me.

They're out of town for road games at the end of the week. They're not playing here again until next Sunday.

That's too long.

Watching him through a screen isn't going to cut it.

But what am I meant to do? Stalk him wherever he goes in case I get a chance to continue what we started last night?

That's crazy.

Let it go, Casey.

But as solid as that advice is, I'm not sure I can take it.

The second I spot Dad's car, I grab my purse from the side and make my way down to meet him.

"You look better than I was expecting," he says, chuckling to himself as I drop into his passenger seat.

"Thanks," I mutter as I strap myself in, although a small smile plays on my lips.

I love my dad so much. He's always been my number one. I have just as much fun hanging out with him as I do with Parker.

"Did you have a good night?" he asks as he pulls back out of the space.

Guilts twists up my insides.

"Yeah, it was okay. We had a lot to celebrate."

"It was a good game," he muses before we dive into a deep dissection of everything that happened.

It's always been this way. Even when he was playing. I used to live for the morning after a game where I'd get my father's undivided attention as we critiqued the game the night before. It didn't matter if it was a win or a loss; we'd do exactly the same.

He'd ask my opinion on things, and it would mean the world to me that he cared about what I had to say.

Those mornings we spent together and the analyses we did

made me a better player. He used to tell me that it helped him, too. I really hope it did and that he wasn't just saying that to make me feel good.

We're still in the thick of it as Dad pulls up outside our favorite diner, and we head inside.

Sylvie's face lights up as we walk in, and after grabbing two menus and the coffee pot, she races over.

She's been serving us here since I was a little girl, and she's just as excited to see us—okay, Dad—as she was back then.

"Good morning, how are you?" She beams at us as if our presence has made her entire week.

"Good morning, Sylvie," Dad says as we slide into our usual booth. "I'm good. This one partied a little too hard last night, so she's going to need extra special treatment."

I roll my eyes and groan.

"He's just jealous he's too old to have the same kind of fun," I say, glaring at him across the table.

Sylvie chuckles, her cheeks blazing red as her eyes flick between me and Dad.

"Great win last night," she says, focusing on him.

"Thanks. Hopefully, we're set for a good season."

"Oh, I do hope so," she says while filling our mugs. "Did you need the menus, or are you ready to order?"

She asks this every time we come despite the fact we haven't looked at the menu in years.

"I think we're good to go," Dad says before we both give her our usual orders.

She knows exactly what we want, but she still writes it down and double checks if we'd like anything else.

Dad watches her leave, and I study him with a smirk.

"You could just ask her out, you know," I point out.

His body tenses and his eyes snap to mine.

Sylvie is hot. She was barely an adult when we first started coming here, but now, she's a woman. A woman who clearly has a crush on my father.

Dad waves it off. "She's not interested in an old man like me."

"Sure," I say with a smile.

"So, what did you want to talk to me about?" I ask when there's a break in our conversation. It's been bugging me since he mentioned it.

He smirks. He knows what his comment has done to me.

"You can be mean when you want to be," I tease.

He chuckles before resting his elbows on the table, his eyes on mine.

"There's going to be a position opening up for an assistant coach for the girls' under eight team."

Excitement jumps in my stomach a beat before the anxiety hits.

For a long time, I dreamed of coaching and guiding young girls to become the women of the future. But years have passed, and while I might still think about it at times, I've mostly let the dream go.

I chose a different path.

"You should apply," Dad states with all the confidence in the world.

I shake my head. "I don't have any experience or training. I can't—"

"Casey, you have a lifetime of experience and training. You've talked about this for years. This is your chance."

Butterflies flutter wildly in my stomach as possibility begins to overtake my initial fears.

Dad's right. Hockey runs through my veins. It always has.

I do think I could be a good coach, and the idea of watching the girls grow and improve lights me up inside.

But am I good enough? Or will they take one look at me and laugh, knowing that I'm riding on the back of my father's career and success?

"Just apply, Care Bear. What's the worst that can happen?"

They can tell me that I'm not good enough.

Able to read my thoughts, he reaches over the table and takes my hands in his. "Fear is good, Casey. It's what pushes us out of our comfort zones and allows us to achieve things we never thought possible.

"Maybe this isn't your time, and that's okay. But what if it is?"

What if it is?

"I'll send you all the details, then leave it up to you," he says, trying not to push me too hard. "For the record, though, I think you'd be an asset to the league."

Sylvie returns to fill up our barely touched coffee, and our conversation changes to our upcoming week and the Vipers' next exhibition games.

As always, the food is amazing, and we leave with full bellies and smiles on our faces.

As we step into the late morning sun, my cell starts ringing.

Dad goes ahead and climbs into the car. I pull it free, finding Parker's face smiling at me.

"Hey," I say, lowering my ass to a bench.

I don't dare get in the car for fear of what will fall from my best friend's lips.

"How are you feeling?" Parker asks.

"Good. Just been for breakfast with Dad."

"I was referring to last night. I've been worried about you," she confesses.

"It's fine. I...I just need to put it behind me and move forward."

"But what if—"

"Dad just told me about a coaching position for a girls' team," I blurt.

"Oh shit, for real?"

"Yeah."

"You've got to apply," she encourages, just like Dad did.

"They'll want experience and—"

"You've got experience, Case. You did that summer camp, remember?"

"I just helped out. I wasn't a coach."

"You have to do it," she says again, ignoring the roadblocks I put in place. "You'll regret it if you don't."

I squeeze my eyes closed.

She's right.

Not knowing will be far worse than being turned down. Wondering what if would haunt me.

"Promise me that you'll apply," she begs.

I nod despite the fact she can't see me.

"Casey," she warns. "Apply, or I'll do it for you."

"Okay, okay."

"Good. Perfect. I've booked us mani-pedis and an ice bath for this afternoon."

"U-ugh," I stutter, not expecting her to say that. "I am not getting in an ice bath, you Satan."

"I want to cheer you up, and I noticed last night that your nails need a refresh, so..."

A smile curls at my lips.

"Sounds great, thank you."

"I'll pick you up at two."

"Okay, but can you...can you pick me up from the arena?" I ask, making a spur-of-the-moment decision.

"Of course. Any reason, or are you just going to watch Kodie skate?"

My mouth opens and closes as I try to find an answer. "No, I'm going to write my application. I figure the surroundings might inspire me."

I'm also hoping to sit in the shadows and watch practice, yes.

Parker chuckles, seeing right through me.

My phone pings with an incoming message.

"Okay, well, I hope inspiration strikes. I'll see you soon."

She cuts the call before I get a chance, and I find a message from Dad on my screen.

I open it, and the coaching position details appear before me.

My stomach knots and my hands tremble.

What if this is the right time?

21

———

CASEY

Over the years, I've experimented around the arena to find the perfect hidden spot.

When I was younger, I used to come here after school and do homework while Dad was working, and not much has changed. I've just switched up homework for actual work.

Being here always inspires me. There's something about the energy of watching the guys on the ice, listening to the whistles, the shouts, and the laughter.

It's addictive.

Dragging my eyes from my cell, I watch Dad waving his arms around as he explains something to his forwards alongside his assistant coach.

The players listen to every single word, soaking it all up.

The image before me morphs into one of me standing before a handful of girls, all of them gazing at me like I'm the most important person in their world at that moment. That I can help bring all their dreams to fruition.

Can I, though?

Dad and Parker might have the confidence in me, but will others?

Just because I've grown up around hockey, just because I've played, just because my father is head coach of the LA Vipers, it doesn't mean I'll be any good at coaching.

Dad and his assistant step back and the guys skate off, ready to put whatever they were just told into practice.

As always, my eyes follow number fifty-five.

It's an obsession I'm not sure I'll ever overcome.

I never feel more at home than I do when I'm here like this. It's where I belong.

Hockey is my life, and I desperately want to share that passion with those who will become the future of the sport I love so much.

Looking back down at my cell, I try to put everything I feel about ice hockey into words.

If nothing else comes of this, those who read it will know just how dedicated I am.

I know that I should probably let Dad read my application, maybe even Parker, but I can't wait.

If I don't hit send right now, there's a chance I'll talk myself out of it.

There is no time like right now.

My heart is in my throat as my thumb hovers over the button that could very well change the course of my future.

I already have a full-time job, but that doesn't matter. I will always find time for hockey.

Hell, I'd do this coaching job for free, given the chance.

I figure that if I get it, the only thing that will change is being able to attend road games.

I don't go to all of them, but I like to go to a handful throughout the season.

But it'll be worth it. Seeing those girls doing what they love, helping them improve, watching them win their games...It'll be *more* than worth it.

My hand trembles as I wait for my email to show as sent, and the second it does, my stomach turns over as if I'm going to be sick.

This was not the way I expected my day to go when Dad woke me up this morning.

I remain hidden in the shadows, watching the guys practice until Parker messages to let me know that she's outside. Kodie is still on the ice, and it takes every bit of strength to walk away from him.

It's ridiculous. He doesn't even know I'm here.

"I thought I was going to have to drag you out," Parker laughs as I drop into her car.

I chuckle, but I don't really feel it.

"Shit, what happened?" she asks, reading my reaction.

"Nothing," I mutter as she pulls away.

"Did you see him?"

"From a distance, yeah. He didn't see me."

"Casey, you need to—"

"I applied for the job," I confess, needing to change the subject.

"You did?"

"Yep. Now we wait." Just saying those words puts me on edge. Waiting to hear back is going to be hell.

"You'll get it. They'll be stupid not to."

"We'll see," I muse, hoping like hell she's right.

I want it.

I want it so fucking bad.

***

The next morning, I find myself back in my favorite seat, waiting for the under eights team to take the ice.

It's their first game of the season, and I can feel the apprehension in the air.

The coaches have everything set up for them, and I've got a notebook in hand.

I figure that if I'm lucky enough to get an interview, I need to have first-hand experience with the teams, the coaches, and the players.

Parents from both teams fill the seats below me, each nervous for their daughters as the coaches give their pre-game speeches.

I imagine what I would say to them in this moment.

It isn't hard to come up with something. I've had a lifetime of pep talks from Dad—mostly before games, but also about life in general. When school was hard going, or I had a test I didn't feel prepared for, he was always there with uplifting words that gave me a confidence boost.

Once they're ready, both teams burst onto the ice with applause and cheers from the parents watching.

Goosebumps rise across my skin as they take their positions and wait for the puck to drop.

I swear, I have a smile on my face the whole time they're playing.

It's not the first youth game I've watched, but this time, it means so much more. Just having the chance to possibly work with these young players is a privilege.

It's a tight game, and teams are tied two-to-two. But two minutes before the end of the third period, our number fifty-five shoots off around the side, successfully evading the other team's defense before taking a shot that has everyone in the arena holding their breath.

A proud laugh erupts from my throat as the puck hits the back of the net, and the girl who scored it immediately begins a celly dance that has the whole place smiling.

Maybe it's got something to do with the number, but I find myself completely enthralled by her.

When the final whistle blows, all players on our team form a huddle, and they being chanting something I can't make out. The coaches descend on them, congratulating their girls on an incredible win.

Pride swells in my chest, and I fight to drag in my next breath.

I want to be down there with them.

Because they're all incredible sportsmen, they shake hands with the opposing team before they disappear off the ice, searching for condolences from their parents.

Our team, on the other hand, bounds off the ice, excited to celebrate their first win of the season with their loved ones.

As they skate off, my eyes linger on one player as she awkwardly runs on her skates toward her—

"Fuck," I breathe as she launches herself into a very strong and familiar pair of arms.

The Polar Bears' number fifty-five is Sutton Rivers.

Of course it is.

I shake my head. It should have been obvious from the second I saw her jersey.

My heart is in my throat as he spins her around. She's lost her helmet, allowing me to see her wide smile.

I lean closer, desperate to hear the laughter that no doubt spills from her, but I'm too far away.

Ripping my eyes from her happy face, I look at her dad.

My breath catches, and the rest of the stadium disappears when I find the most incredible smile lighting up his face.

On any normal day, he's grumpy as fuck. Even after a win, his smiles are generally more of a grimace or a smirk. He smiled that night, but as amazing as it felt to be at the reason for it, I now realize it was nothing like the one he gives his daughter.

Because that smile? It's...life-altering.

I want him to smile at me like that.

It's stupid, fickle, and impossible, but the desire is there all the same.

He puts her down a few seconds later before dropping to his knees and helping her out of her skates.

I'm completely enthralled by them.

And when I quickly glance around, I discover that I'm not the only one.

More than a few moms are blatantly staring at him.

Something hot and uncomfortable rises in me, and I quickly realize it's jealousy.

He's mine.

He's not. He's so far from mine it's laughable.

But I want him to be.

Once Sutton has removed her pads and has her sneakers on, the pair of them say goodbye to the others who are lingering around—mostly moms who are hoping for a shot with the pro hockey player. They walk toward the exit hand in hand, talking animatedly, I assume about the game.

Lifting my hand, I rub the spot above my heart as the image of them morphs into one of me and Dad all those years ago.

I don't remember it at the time, but I bet all the moms were making moon eyes at him then as well.

Shaking my head, I look down at the notes I've written as the ten and under team gets ready to take over the ice.

The thought of this being a regular thing on Sunday mornings makes excitement flutter in my stomach.

Looking at their season schedules online, it seems that both teams train and have games on Sunday mornings or Wednesday evenings depending on when the Vipers' games are.

Pulling my cell from my pocket, I check my emails.

I shouldn't be disappointed; it's the weekend, and I only sent my application yesterday.

But I am.

I want this.

And not just because it'll be another way to see Kodie more often. That is just a very welcome bonus.

The next team doesn't fare so well and ends up losing their first game. It sucks, but it also means I have plenty of notes about places they can improve by the time the final whistle blows.

Confident that I can walk into an interview—assuming I get one—and talk honestly about both teams and their performances, I head out of the arena and into the LA sun.

Lowering my sunglasses from my head, I locate my car and make my way home.

The second my ass hits the couch, I turn the TV on to ESPN and open a new browser on my cell before typing one my favorite search terms.

Kodie Rivers.

I already know he keeps his private life, and more importantly, his daughter, out of the media. But after seeing them together today, I need more.

I need so much more.

22

KODIE

I almost kissed her.

I almost fucking kissed her.

It's been five days since I nearly gave in to my baser desires.

Thank fuck Parker called her away, because I honestly don't know what would have happened next.

One taste of her wouldn't have been enough; I know that for a fact.

Five fucking days.

I fall back on my bed and stare up at the ceiling.

I swear, I've never lived five longer days in my life.

The irrational, horny part of my body begs me to do something about it.

When I was called into a meeting with our head of PR, Hailee, earlier in the week, the temptation to "get lost" and end up in Casey's office was almost too much to ignore.

I just managed to restrain myself, although I kicked myself for it later that night when I laid in bed thinking about her with an aching erection. Again.

That almost kiss lives rent-free in my head. I've even struggled to shift it during practice, which is unlike me. Normally, nothing else exists while I'm on the ice.

And now that we're heading out of town for our next two

exhibition games, I'm going to lose any chance of seeing her until our next home game on Sunday.

It'll have been over a week.

It's probably a good thing.

Soft footsteps move closer before Sutton joins me in my bedroom.

"Are you packed, Daddy?" she asks, hopping up on the bed and lying next to me.

"Yeah."

"What are you looking at?" she asks innocently.

What I wouldn't give to be seven again and not understand having to stare at a blank wall—or ceiling—when life gets too much.

"Nothing, just relaxing."

"You've got a big few days," she tells me.

First Chicago and then Utah.

Both teams beat us more than once last year. We've got everything to prove.

No pressure.

"But I'm confident that you've got this."

I can't help but laugh as I roll onto my side to look at her.

"Thanks. I'm sorry I'm going to miss your practice tonight," I say quietly.

I fucking love my job, but I hate that doing it well means missing out on so much with Sutton.

"It's okay. You'll be at our next game."

"I will," I agree.

"Come on, you need to make me breakfast before school," she says before sitting up and grabbing my hand, attempting to pull me from the bed.

Sutton might be strong and powerful in her own right, but she doesn't stand a chance.

"I thought you were making me breakfast this morning," I tease.

"If you would let me fry the eggs, I would."

She would too.

My independent daughter would happily be the one running the house, given the chance.

"Go and grab everything we need and I'll be right there," I say, sitting up and watching as she skips out of the room.

I sigh, dragging my hand down my face.

I fucking hate leaving her.

Mom does an incredible job looking after her in my absence, but it's not the same as having her actual parent taking care of her.

Guilt twists my insides. It's becoming an all-too usual feeling these days.

It was bad enough when it was just dad guilt over not being present enough for Sutton. But add what I've done with Casey into the mix and I'm drowning in it.

If only it was enough to stop me from wanting to do it again.

I throw a couple more things into my suitcase before joining my daughter in the kitchen.

She gives me one of her widest smiles as I step up beside her. She's trying to silently reassure me. I fucking love her for it, but I hate it at the same time.

I'm meant to be the one reassuring her, not the other way around.

Together, we make breakfast and enjoy our last few minutes before leaving for school.

She chatters away about our game tomorrow night, seamlessly relaying traded players' stats. I swear, if her teachers taught her math in relation to hockey, she'd get top marks across the board. The girl is a freaking genius when she has a reason to apply her knowledge.

My heart is in my throat when we pull up at school. She finally falls quiet as we sit there for a moment, watching her classmates head inside.

A low groan comes from my daughter, and I glance over to see her eyes narrowed as she glares at someone across the playground.

I don't need to turn around to see who it is, but I do nonetheless.

"Is he still bothering you?" I ask as Sutton tries to burn holes in the back of Adrian's head.

"He's a jerk," she mutters angrily.

I want to chastise her for calling him that, but honestly, he is. So is his father.

We played against each other during college, and I don't have any good memories of the experiences.

"Unfortunately, dealing with people like Adrian is a part of life."

"I know. I just wish his dad still played so he could get traded to the outback of nowhere."

"Not sure they have hockey teams there, Peanut," I joke.

"NHL ones, no. But AHL…"

I just about manage to contain my snigger at the expression on her face.

Man, I lucked out with this kid.

I was smugly informed the other day that Adrian's team lost their first game this season, and he came into school on Monday like a bear with a sore head.

I feel for the kid; losing sucks. But if he's going to make it further than his dad did, then he's going to need to learn how to deal with it.

Losing is a part of the game. It's how you deal with it that determines if you can be a professional athlete or not—something his father never learned.

I fear that the apple may not have fallen too far from the tree.

"Be the bigger person," I remind her.

"I am. I only rubbed our win in his face a little bit."

"Good girl. I know it sucks, but you've just got to grin and bear it."

"Karma will get him eventually."

Hopefully, karma will be a hockey stick to the face…

"Yep. You'd better go," I say when the stream of kids begins to lessen.

"I know. I'll be watching tonight after practice," she promises. "And Friday."

"Come here," I say, reaching for a hug from my girl. I squeeze her almost as tightly as she squeezes me. "I'll be back Saturday. Think about what you want to do in the afternoon."

"Can we skate?" she asks, making me laugh.

"If that's what you want. But we can do something else," I offer.

"I'll think about it," she confirms before pulling back and swallowing thickly.

My own eyes burn as I watch her battle with her emotions.

"See you Saturday. Good luck," she says before pushing the door open and climbing out.

"Love you, Peanut."

"Love you too, Daddy."

My chest compresses as her sweet words float around me.

She gets halfway across the playground before she spins around and waves at me.

Once she sees me wave back, she takes off running and slips into the building.

I drive to the airport feeling like the world's shittiest father.

We might have more money than we know what to do with thanks to my career, but that's not what's important.

I'd still do my job if I got minimum wage; I love it. It's what I was born to do.

***

"Whoa, who pissed on your Fruit Loops this morning?" Linc says, dropping into the seat beside me as we get ready to take off.

We've got Chicago tonight and Utah on Friday.

This is what our lives are going to be like for the next seven months—and that's if we don't make the playoffs.

"I'm fine," I say unconvincingly once he's settled.

"Did you want to tell your face?" he teases.

"I'm going to ask if I can room with someone else," I warn.

"You wouldn't," he taunts.

"Try me." He holds my glare for a few seconds before his smile cracks and he begins laughing.

"You'd have nowhere near as much fun with any of the other guys."

"I heard that," Fletch says as he twists around in front of us. "Not my fault I'm taken and don't bring bunnies back every night of the week."

"He's got a point," I say, side-eying Linc.

Honestly, he isn't that bad.

There have only been a handful of times I've had to make myself scarce because he's brought a bunny back to our room. If it were a regular thing, I would have demanded to room with someone else.

Most of the time, he's a great roommate. He reminds me of me a few years ago. Before life got hard and complicated.

Secretly, I quite like living vicariously through him. I'm not going to fucking tell him that, though.

"Our couch is always open for you, Big D," Handsy offers, but knowing he's just as bad as Linc, I don't take the offer seriously.

"Thanks, appreciate it. Storm is gonna be a good boy this trip, though, aren't you?" I say, ruffing up his hair like he's a child.

"Fuck off. I'm always a good boy."

"Not from what I've read," Fletch mutters. "Remind us why Hailee ripped you a new one recently...something to do with stumbling out of a club with two...wait, no, three bunnies in tow."

"It was a one-off," Linc scoffs.

"What, a one-off for that month?" Handsy teases with a laugh.

"What's Linc done?" Marilyn asks, taking the seat on the other side of the aisle.

"What hasn't he done?" Fletch chuckles.

"Probably best not to tell the rookie all of Linc's dirty tales. Might give him ideas," Handsy points out.

"Oh, now I definitely want to know," Marilyn says, rubbing his hands together in interest.

Thankfully, Coach commands our attention, and all conversation about my state of mind or Linc's sexcapades die.

That is, until Linc and I get to our hotel room later that day.

We managed a win, which, after the first period against

Chicago, I didn't think was going to be possible. But thanks to two epic goals from my roommate in the third period, we took the win and hopefully proved that the tide is changing this year.

We've learned from last year's losses, and we are back with a vengeance.

Everything about the game felt wrong, though. I kept looking to the crowd behind the goal, expecting to see her there.

But she wasn't.

I shouldn't care, but disappointment hit me every time I glanced up, out of habit.

How I can go from not noticing her to being so hyperaware of her absence is beyond me.

"So, I've been thinking about your mystery woman," he says almost as soon as the door has closed behind us.

"Please don't," I beg.

"Not in that way," he says. "I've got enough of my own to contend with."

"Christ," I mutter as I drop my suitcase onto the bed and kick off my shoes. "Don't you have a date or something?"

"Nope. Thought I'd hang out with my buddy tonight and celebrate our win."

"Wonderful," I deadpan.

"We're meeting the guys downstairs in twenty."

My lips part to decline the invitation, but then I remember that I'm meant to be embracing spending time with the team.

It's not a hardship. They're a great bunch of guys. I just...I'd rather be here alone and maybe, just maybe, scroll through Casey's Instagram account.

It's wrong. So fucking wrong. But I made the mistake of typing her name in on Sunday morning when I woke up hard and desperate.

I'm fucking ashamed to admit it, but I found an image of her wearing my jersey last season and I...fuck...I came all over myself while staring at it.

"Anyway," he says, distracting me from my sinful thoughts. "I've been thinking about the guest list that night."

"Shit. I wouldn't do that. You'll pop a blood vessel or something," I tease.

"Fuck off. I've got the smarts."

"Sure you have," I laugh as I grab my toiletry bag and lock myself in the bathroom for a few minutes.

I'm not worried about him digging into the guest list. It's not like he'll find her name on it.

23

———

CASEY

"You can work remotely tomorrow afternoon, right?" Parker asks the second I answer her call as I get out of my car on Thursday morning and head for the arena.

In the front office, it's not always that obvious that the team is away, but I still feel their absence.

The atmosphere is different. It's stupid, but I'm acutely aware of it.

No one else has ever mentioned it, so I figure I'm just being weird, or that I love the game more than them.

"Uhh...I guess so. Why?" I ask, curious.

"I booked us flights."

My chest gets all light and hopeful.

Please, please say what I think you're about to.

"Flights for..."

"Utah, duh."

Oh my god.

"You want to go to the game, right?"

"Of course I do."

"Perfect."

"Have you booked a hotel?" I ask as I tap my security pass to allow me access to the building and walk inside.

"No, I thought you might want to sweet talk your dad to see if he can get us a room at the team's hotel."

"I can try, but I'm happy to stay anywhere."

"But you'd prefer to be close to *him*, right?"

"Parker." I force a smile on my face as one of the women from the PR office passes me.

"What? Just imagine it. He has no idea that you're coming, and he scores the winning goal, looks up, and there you are in his jersey, screaming his name from the top of your lungs. After, he could slip you his hotel room key and the two of you could spend the night celebrating. Swoon."

There isn't a single inch of my body that isn't interested in the fantasy she paints.

I want it. I want it so bad, but I'm also a realist and I know it's not going to happen.

"Unlikely, but I like your thought process."

"There is always a chance."

"And what about you? What would you be doing while I was living out my wildest fantasy?" I inquire before I step into my office.

"I'm sure I could find a way to entertain myself."

"Careful, Park. I might start thinking you do actually want to spend the night with a hockey player."

"Ugh, as if. No offense."

I chuckle as I lower my ass to my chair and turn on my computer.

"The lady doth protest too much, methinks."

"Dude, do not quote Shakespeare at me. I know what hockey players are like. I lived with my brother long enough to know the dirty truth."

"They're not all as bad as him," I counter.

"Still not risking it. I will not spend the night or even an hour with a professional athlete. I want a man whose dick is bigger than his ego."

"Well, I think you might find—"

"Do not finish that sentence. I've read enough online about the size of my brother's...ego. Ugh."

I can't help but laugh as I picture her shuddering.

She's not wrong. Everett Donnelly has a reputation that rivals

Linc's.

When they were together, they were notorious. It's a good thing that they play for different teams now.

"One day, someone will come along and change everything."

"Not a chance," she states firmly. "Shit, I need to go. My client just walked in."

"Okay. Send me the flight details. I'll speak to Dad."

"You got it. Eee, I'm so excited."

She hangs up, leaving me buzzing.

Watching the game on the TV is great and all, but it's nothing like being there in the flesh.

Parker and I have been to a Utah game before. Their fans are wild. It's going to be a good night. And if Dad can get us into the team hotel, then…

I refuse to think too much about what comes at the end of that sentence.

All I know is that I need to see Kodie again.

Confident that Dad will already be up working on his plan of attack before their flight this afternoon, I hit call on his contact and see if I can make magic happen.

"This is the best idea you've ever had," I tell Parker as we step off the plane the next afternoon.

It doesn't matter that it's raining. Nothing could dampen my spirits right now.

The second I told Dad that we were coming, he promised to secure us a room and tickets to the game.

He also said that he'd send a car to collect us from the airport.

Of course, we're more than capable of doing that ourselves, but I appreciate the shit out of him trying to take care of me.

"Well, I don't like to brag, but…"

We're already three cocktails in, and I feel amazing about this little impromptu trip.

I'd been feeling a little off as this week went on. I haven't heard anything about the assistant coaching job, and I'm getting antsy. Even a rejection at this point would be better than nothing.

I may still not believe I've got the skills they'll be looking for, but the more I think about those two girls' teams I watched on Sunday, the more I want it.

Hell, I more than want it.

We climb into the back of the car and chat away as we're escorted to the hotel.

Dad and the team are already at the arena, getting ready, but I message him to let him know we've landed safely and that we'll see him later.

After checking in, we drag our luggage to the elevator and head toward our room.

I don't know what floor the team is staying on, but secretly, I pray that we're on the same one.

Images of sneaking out of our room and into another in the middle of the night flicker through my head.

Parker whistles appreciatively as we step inside our room.

"Daddy Watson did us good," she praises as she looks around.

I groan. "Please don't call him that," I mutter as I follow her inside.

She isn't wrong; the room is sweet, and it has an even better view of the city.

Parker chuckles wickedly.

"Let's get ready, get food and more drinks, and then head to the arena," she says before pulling her cell from her purse and reading a message.

A frown pulls at her brow.

"Everything okay?" I ask.

"Yep," she states before pushing it into her back pocket and unzipping her suitcase.

The arena is buzzing with excitement when we enter, and it only adds to my anticipation.

We find our seats and watch as the Utah fans sing and chant for their team.

It's weird going to a road game and not being in the majority in the stands.

The Vipers have a nice number of supporters here, though, so we're in good company as we get swept up in the pregame excitement and sing along with beers in hand, waiting for the game to start.

Not much later, both teams hit the ice to furious rounds of applause. The entire stadium vibrates as everyone cheers and stomps their feet.

My heart races as we watch our boys warm up and get ready to hopefully annihilate Utah just like they did Chicago two days ago.

They struggled against both teams last year. I know how important it is to Dad that they turn things around with them, even in exhibition games.

"Start as we mean to go on," he told me as if I was one of his players in the dressing room.

"Fuck, I love it when goalies do those warm-ups," Parker sighs as Handsy drops to the ice and begins grinding his hips.

"You don't want a hockey player, remember?"

"Never said I did. I'll happily watch one, though."

"Can't beat a bit of hockey porn," I laugh.

"How much do you think he'd charge to do that naked?"

"Parker," I gasp.

"What? Handsy is hot."

"Yeah, he's also had his hands on almost every bunny in LA." Hence the nickname.

She waves me off, finishing her beer as Linc skates around our side of the rink, his eyes on the crowd, riling us up.

He's forever the showman. I'm pretty sure he'd be on stage if he weren't a hockey player.

"Jesus, who does he think he is?" Parker mutters as Linc gestures for the Vipers fans to get on their feet.

Obviously, everyone does. We're all powerless but to follow orders.

He begins clapping as we all chant excitedly, his eyes scanning the faces staring down at him.

He continues showing off and lapping up the fans' attention until Fletch barks at him to get off the ice.

The players might momentarily leave the ice, but the excitement in the arena doesn't wane as we wait for the game to start.

Not too long after, the starters are being announced, and they play the national anthem before the teams get into position.

Calm settles over the arena for a beat as we wait for the puck to drop, but the second Utah wins possession, a loud roar rips through the crowd.

It only lasts so long, though. Our rookie intercepts it and makes a killer pass to Kodie, who flies down the wing and sails it straight past their goalie.

I'm on my feet before the puck hits the net, my drink flying out of my hands and soaking the guy in front. Whoops.

The guy turns to look at me, a scowl set on his face, but thankfully, he's a Vipers fan, and lets it go.

"FUCK YES," I scream, jumping up and down as the lights around the stadium flash and the fans in Vipers' green and white go wild.

Kodie and Linc collide in a celebration before Kodie turns to us and does his standard celly dance.

It doesn't matter that I've seen it more times than I can count over the years; I still love every second of it.

The game resumes and Utah quickly levels the score.

And that is how the game continues.

We hit the back of the net, and then only minutes later, they do the same, bringing us even again.

It's a fantastic game, but equally as frustrating, because just when we think we're going to steam ahead, they catch up.

We head toward the end of the third period tied. The puck drops and Utah claims it and races toward their goal.

Their fans are on their feet, shouting and screaming for them to get the win.

But then, out of nowhere, Monroe appears and steals the puck.

A roar of frustration erupts as I watch him fly down the left side of the ice and head toward Kodie.

He's battling to get free, and at the very last minute, he breaks away—just in time for Monroe to pass him the puck. He spins and takes the shot with a second left on the clock.

My heart is in my throat. I swear every single Vipers fan around me sucks in a breath as the puck sails through the air.

And then it happens. It hits the back of the net and chaos erupts as the final whistle blows.

Kodie flies in front of us before he's engulfed by every single Vipers player as they celebrate his last-minute goal.

They jostle him so much, his helmet falls off and he ends up on his back on the ice.

He's laughing with a wide smile lighting up his face when he finally gets to his feet again—until he looks up and his eyes lock with mine.

His smile falters and his expression—hell, his entire demeanor—completely changes.

My heart sinks, hating that my presence is ruining what should be an epic moment for him.

"Shit," Parker hisses next to me. Clearly, every single person around me is witnessing his unfiltered reaction to seeing me here.

"I need to leave," I mutter, bending down to pick up my trash.

No sooner have I ripped my eyes away from Kodie does Parker reach for me. "Wait," she shouts. "Look."

With my heart in the pit of my stomach, I follow her command and look back at the ice.

Kodie's eyes are still on me, but the shock has lessened.

"He's...he's smiling, Case. At you."

My knees buckle.

Thankfully, I catch myself on the seat in front of me.

But by the time I've steadied myself, he's gone.

"He wants you," Parker states.

"It was shock," I mutter, trying desperately not to obsess over how close he was to kissing me last weekend.

My stomach clenches with anticipation; my eyes still locked on him as he continues to celebrate the win with his teammates.

"We need to find what room he's in tonight. You need to go to him."

"I-I can't do that," I stutter.

But while I might argue. I can't deny that I don't clench my thighs in anticipation of doing just that.

If I were to knock on his hotel room door, would he open up? And if he did, would he let me in?

The thought of him sending me away hurts. I can only imagine how bad it would be if it were to happen.

I can't risk that. Can I?

As the team begins to leave the ice, I lose myself in thoughts of what the night could hold.

Kodie is about to step off the ice just behind Linc when he turns around and looks up. But it isn't any of the other fans he searches out.

It's me.

His eyes drop to my jersey, and one side of his mouth kicks up.

"Oh my god, Casey," Parker squeals.

His gaze lifts again, and something powerful crackles between us.

Right there and then I decide that I'll risk being turned away from his hotel room.

Anything to do with Kodie Rivers is a risk worth taking.

24

KODIE

She's here.

Casey fucking Watson is here.

In Utah.

Possibly in this very hotel right now.

Probably with her father.

Fuck.

FUCK.

"Does winning give you the shits or something?" Linc barks through the bathroom door.

We arrived back about fifteen minutes ago, and after agreeing to meet the team at the bar, we came up to our room. I swiftly locked myself in the bathroom for a moment alone to process what the fuck happened at the arena.

She's here.

"I'll be out in a bit."

"We're gonna be late," he points out

"Then go. I'll meet you down there."

"Or you'll pussy out of it."

"I won't. I'll be there."

How could I possibly pussy out of it when she's likely to be down there?

With her father...

No. He never drinks with the team after a game.

But he might with his daughter…

"Promise?" Linc asks, sounding much like Sutton when she wants to make sure I'm going to follow through on something.

"Yes. I promise."

Shaking my head, I pull my cell from my pocket and press play on the video Mom sent me of Sutton watching the end of the game when I scored.

She launches from the couch so fast that she's a blur before jumping on the coffee table, shouting and screaming at the TV.

Linc mumbles something on the other side of the door as I read the message Sutton sent after the video.

> Mom: You are amazing. I'm so proud of you, Daddy. I love you, Sutton xxx

She's in bed now, so she won't see my reply until Mom shows her first thing in the morning.

Knowing that my daughter is proud of me makes my chest ache in the best kind of way. Sadly, though, it doesn't lessen the panic raging inside me from seeing Casey standing among our fans wearing my number again.

If only she knew just what seeing her like that does to me.

Finally, I take a piss, wash my hands, and step out of the bathroom, assuming it's safe.

But no sooner have I stepped around the corner does my heart jump into my throat and a grunt rips from me.

"I thought you'd left," I bark, my pulse racing.

"Decided I didn't trust your promise," he states.

"And I've decided you're an asshole."

"Original," he mutters.

"Whatever," I say before quickly changing out of my suit in favor of a pair of jeans and a T-shirt.

"Ready?" he asks, his eyes alight with anticipation for the night ahead of us.

My stomach turns over with a mixture of nerves and excitement.

If she is down there…what am I going to do?

I haven't propositioned a woman in years.

Do I even want to?

Yes, yes you do.

Another night with her, now you know who she is, and it'll get her out of your system...

Here's hoping.

Wiping my hands on my thighs, I turn to look at Linc. "Yep, let's go."

I march toward the door before he has a chance to respond and pull it open.

If I don't leave this room right now, I might talk myself out of it. And I already know that I'll regret not taking this chance.

"Whoa, someone is keen," Linc laughs as he catches up with me to the sound of the hotel room door closing behind us.

I don't respond. I can't.

All I can think about is her being at the bar and still wearing my jersey.

The guys are already sitting around a large table with drinks when we get there, and the second they spot me, a round of cheers goes up, ensuring that every pair of eyes in the bar turns to me.

I shake my head and give each of them a warning glare as I fight with my potent need to scan the entire bar, looking for her.

Who am I kidding? She might not even come.

That moment I thought we shared at the arena may have all been in my head.

Forcing myself to continue forward, I take a seat next to Calvin, aka Killer, and Milo McKenna, aka Brit, our first-line defensemen, as Linc drops next to Monroe—but not before he ruffles his hair, messing up the style he probably spent ages perfecting.

"Fucking epic work tonight, Marilyn," he praises as two beers and two shots magically appear before us.

I eye the shot suspiciously. It's been years since I did one, and I'm not entirely sure I liked them all that much back then.

"Don't be a pussy," Handsy mutters, watching me closely.

Movement to my left catches my eye, and when I glance over, the entire world stops.

Casey walks into the bar as if she's walking down a catwalk in slow motion. Or that could just be the way I see it.

Her long blonde hair is now down, hanging around her shoulders like silk.

Instantly, an image pops into my head of her on top of me, her hair surrounding both of us, making it seem like only the two of us exist.

My heart slams against my ribs and my cock jerks in excitement.

She's got her sight set on the bar as Parker says something beside her that causes her to throw her head back laughing.

The sound floats over to me, and my temperature spikes.

I can't end tonight without at least talking to her.

Who am I kidding?

I want to do a hell of a lot more than that.

"Kodie," Killer barks. "Are you going to do that shot or what?"

A huge part of me wants to shove it away, stand, and march straight over to her.

I could throw her over my shoulder and walk out of here, allowing everyone to understand my intentions.

She's your coach's daughter. You shouldn't be looking, let alone touching...

I reach for the shot and lift it to my lips.

Without thinking too much about it, I swallow the vodka, letting it burn down my throat.

"That's what we're talking about," Linc says before waving to the server for more.

Absolutely not.

As the guys fall back into their previous conversation, discussing tonight's game and our performance, I let my eyes drift around the bar.

There are more than a few tables who are none too discreetly watching us. Quite a few are also wearing Vipers colors. But for now, they're happy to just be in the same place as us. Something tells me that won't last forever, though. As the drinks flow, they get braver.

Hoping that I'm being inconspicuous, I turn my attention to a tall table over by the windows.

My breath catches the second my eyes lock on hers.

She was waiting for me.

Swallowing thickly, I look away and back to the guys, but I don't hear a word they're saying; my head is too full of her.

Needing something to do, I reach for my beer and drink over half of it without coming up for air.

My skin tingles with awareness, and fire burns through my veins.

She's still looking at me.

I focus on the guys ribbing Monroe for a comment that I totally missed, but I soon find my eyes drifting back over to Casey. And just like I was expecting, she's watching me.

Parker has her back to me, but there's no chance she's missed the fact that Casey is paying her zero attention.

Look away, I silently beg.

If any of the guys notice, I'm fucked.

Our next round of shots arrive, but I don't reach for mine. I need a clear head tonight.

Sliding mine across the table, I gesture for Monroe to take it.

"You sure?" he asks, his own already empty.

"Yep."

"Pussy," Linc scoffs.

Ignoring him, I drain the rest of my beer, already planning my escape.

I figure an hour is enough to humor them before I make my excuses.

I swear, time stands still as I sit there waiting for the right moment to slip away.

Linc, Killer, and Monroe have excused themselves and headed toward the bar to chat up a bunch of bunnies who've entered—although none of them seem to have stolen Linc's attention, because he's wandered over to the table Casey and Parker are sitting at.

My blood begins to boil and my heart races as he turns his panty-melting smile on Casey.

Mine.

Gritting my teeth, I attempt to watch them without making it obvious.

It helps when a round of cheers goes up from where Killer and Marilyn are. As I watch them dance, I pray that it'll be enough to steal away Linc from Casey.

But the motherfucker stays put.

Leave, Kodie. Just leave and go back to your room and go to bed...

If only it were that easy.

With a glance around the table, I thankfully discover that everyone is lost in their own conversations. I finish my second and final beer of the night before excusing myself to the bathroom.

I force myself not to rush, but I regret that the second a fan steps up to the sinks beside me and tells me how awesome I was tonight.

Now, don't get me wrong, praise from a fan is great. I always love a good ego boost, especially on a night like this where we have everything to celebrate. But right now, the only place I want to be is out there, making sure Casey isn't going to spend the rest of the night celebrating with a player who isn't me.

She's not like that, a little voice says. But as much as I want to believe that, I don't actually know Casey.

Finally, he allows me to escape the bathroom after signing the back of a receipt for his kid. The second I emerge, my eyes scan the bar for them.

I breathe a huge sigh when I find Linc still standing at their table. Although, I'm not thrilled by the wide smile playing on his lips as he gazes down at Casey.

Red-hot jealousy shoots through my veins.

It shouldn't be there.

She isn't mine.

But I can't help it.

I'm not done with her.

I'm almost at the table when the three of them notice my approach. The fact that Casey isn't as aware of my presence as I am of hers pisses me off.

But what else can I expect?

She probably hasn't given a second thought to our night together.

She got what she wanted.

"Oh, hey," Linc says when he finally turns to me. "You know Casey and Parker, right?"

I glare at him. Even if I hadn't spent the night with Casey, I'd still know who she fucking is.

And Parker Donnelly—everyone on the team knows her too, thanks to her big brother.

"Yeah," I mutter.

I look at Parker first. She smiles up at me with interest sparking in her golden eyes.

Steeling myself, I turn my attention to Casey. The second my eyes connect with hers, desire shoots through me, ending right in my balls.

"Ladies," I greet, my voice unusually deep and raspy. "I hope Storm has offered to buy you both a drink."

Linc scoffs, but Parker is the first to respond. "Pfft. Storm wouldn't know how to be a gentleman if it bit him in the ass."

Linc rears back, offended. "I know exactly how to treat a woman, thank you very much."

"Pulling hair and slapping ass might be fun, but we're more than just sex dolls, you know."

I snort in amusement as Linc's chin drops.

Clapping him on the shoulder, I say, "She's got a point there, man."

"The fuck do you know?" he mutters as I gesture for the server to get the girls two more drinks.

My eyes collide with Casey's again, the air between us crackling. I pray that it's only us that can feel it. If they notice, we're fucked, and I'm not ready for Coach to kill me just yet.

I need another taste of her first.

"Shouldn't you be over there choosing your bunny for the night?" Parker asks Linc as she jerks her head toward the other side of the bar.

"The night is still young. Thought I'd come over here and make them all jealous by chatting you up first."

Parker's face screws up in disgust.

"I don't think that's going to work for you, hot shot."

He leans closer to her, getting in her space.

She attempts to get away, but she just bumps into the wall.

"I appreciate your concern, Donnelly, but I'm more than aware of what works for me."

"Asshole," she hisses, making Casey chuckle.

The sound is like music to my ears. The only thing that would be better is her moaning.

25

———

CASEY

My heart is racing and my hands are trembling as the server approaches with two fresh drinks for me and Parker, courtesy of Kodie.

I don't want to read into that action, but I can't help it.

He's come over to chat after that intense moment between us at the arena. It has to mean something, right?

As the server steps up to the table, Kodie moves a little closer, until his body is right beside mine.

His warmth burns down my arm, but that has nothing on the way his fingers brush across my back as he rests his hand on the back of my chair.

My thighs clench as heat pools between them, and without thought, my head twists until I'm craning my neck looking up at him.

His eyes drop to mine, and the subtlest of smirks curls his lip.

Oh. He meant to do that.

A million butterflies take flight in my stomach.

Dragging my gaze away, I reach for my drink and hold it up.

"Thank you for this. And congrats on an epic game."

"You're welcome. Thanks for coming to support us," Kodie counters.

Parker's eyes burn into me, but I don't look up at her. I can't.

"What about me?" Linc asks like the asshole he is. "I had a great goal and a handful of outstanding assists tonight."

I smother a laugh at the expectant puppy dog look on his face as he glances between me and Parker, waiting for some praise.

He really is barking up the wrong tree if he's expecting any nice words to come his way from that direction.

She had a point earlier; why is he standing over here when he could be with a bunny?

Suspicion gnaws at me. I glance up, my eyes jumping between the two of them.

Does Linc know?

Has Kodie sent him over here as some kind of wingman?

But despite my concerns, I don't see anything untoward in either of their expressions—not that I really know them well enough to read properly.

"You were great," I offer, aware that Parker won't humor him.

"Aw, thanks, Casey. So glad you noticed."

I roll my eyes and laugh at him, but it's cut off abruptly when Kodie's thumb brushes my back again.

"I'm calling it a night," Kodie suddenly blurts, turning all attention on him.

"Dude, it's still early," Linc complains with a pout.

"And we've got an early flight. I've got plans tomorrow."

"Just one more?"

"No," Kodie states, leaving no room for argument. "Don't wake me up when you stumble in later."

"I can't make those kinds of promises," Linc says with a smirk before Kodie grazes his knuckles across my back one final time, sending sparks shooting in all directions.

My skin continues to tingle as I watch him walk away.

I should avert my gaze, but I can't. They're glued to him, to his large, powerful body as he marches across the bar as if he owns it.

Linc says something, but I don't hear anything other than his deep, rumbling voice and then Parker as she cusses him out.

I'm about to force myself to look away when he pauses and glances over his shoulder.

His eyes find mine instantly, and it takes my breath away.

No words are said, but they're not needed.

My stomach knots and my mouth goes dry

He wants me to follow him.

He's inviting me up to their room.

It's over in a heartbeat, and he's disappearing around the corner.

Turning back to the table, my trembling hand reaches for my drink and I quickly swallow it all.

"Excuse me, ladies. I need to visit the little boys' room."

Linc steps back and disappears, leaving me alone with Parker.

"What are you waiting for? Follow him," she whisper-hisses across the table.

"I can't," I say, thinking with my head, not my vagina.

"Casey," she sighs. "You might never get this chance again. He wants you."

I shake my head.

"It's a bad idea."

"Aren't all the best ideas concealed as bad ones?" Parker raises a brow and waits impatiently for what I'm going to do. "Go now or you'll miss him."

I glance back at the exit and picture him waiting in the elevator for me.

"I need another drink," I mutter.

"You're going to regret this," Parker warns as I slip from my chair and move toward the bar.

"Nothing good can come of it," I say as she steps up beside me.

"Ladies, are you trying to run away from me?" Linc says from behind us when he returns.

"If only we could," Parker mutters.

As Linc gestures for the server, Parker leans closer and whispers in my ear. "You'll forever regret not taking this chance, and I refuse to allow you to live with that."

"It's too late now," I argue, my chest constricting. She's right.

"It's never too late."

Before I have a chance to say anything, Parker turns to Linc and smiles up at him like he's the best thing to ever grace the planet.

My brows furrow, because that is far from what she thinks of her brother's best friend.

She's up to something.

A drunken laugh erupts as I walk down the hallway almost twenty minutes later, counting the numbers on the doors until I find the one I want.

Eight-three-two.

I should have known the second Parker smiled at Linc instead of sneering at him. But it worked because he told her their room number without little thought.

"Fuck," I hiss, shaking my arms at my sides as I begin to second-guess this decision.

I thought I made the right one earlier when I didn't follow him.

But Parker is right.

If I don't make the most of this opportunity, it may never happen again.

This might be my one and only shot for a repeat.

He knows who I am, and it seems that he still wants me regardless of the consequences.

Blowing out a shaky breath, I smooth my hands down my jeans, fluff up my hair, and give the girls a jiggle. I'm wearing his jersey, there isn't exactly anything on show, but still. I feel better about myself once I'm sorted.

"Just do it, Casey. Worry about the consequences tomorrow."

Rolling my shoulders, I hold my head high and lift my knuckles to the door.

My knock sounds like a gunshot in the silent hallway.

When nothing happens and there's no movement inside the room, I begin to panic.

What if I read that entire situation wrong?

What if he didn't want me to follow, after all?

"Fuck."

I take a step back, ready to run away and pretend that this didn't happen, when there is a shuffling noise from the other side of the door.

My heart jumps into my throat, and I'm pretty sure I stop breathing.

"I swear to God, Storm, if you've lost your fucking key agai—" Kodie's words are cut off the second the door opens a few inches and he finds me, not his roommate, standing on the other side. "Casey?" His brows pinch in confusion and his hand lifts to rub the back of his neck.

He's shirtless, and his pants are open.

He looks hot.

Unbelievably hot.

"I-I'm sorry," I blurt, clearly having got the wrong end of the stick.

Shame and embarrassment burn up my up my neck and to my face, no doubt turning it a mortifying shade of red.

"I'll just..." I take a step back. "I'll just go and—"

"No," he barks before reaching out and twisting his fingers in the front of my jersey.

I shriek as I'm dragged forward.

One second I'm getting ready to run and hide, and then next, Kodie has me pinned against the closed hotel room door.

I stare up at him in disbelief as my chest heaves and my body burns with need.

His eyes search mine. It's almost as if he's trying to convince himself that it's really me. That I'm really in front of him.

"I didn't think you were going to come," he says, his voice low and raspy. It hits me right between my legs, making me even more desperate for him.

"I-I wasn't sure if I was imagining the invite," I whisper as he nudges his knee between my thighs.

"Can't stop fucking thinking about you," he confesses, leaning closer.

His lips are so close to mine, the heat of them burns.

Tilting my chin up, I search them out, desperate for him to touch me. But he doesn't allow it.

"Tell me not to do this, Casey," he begs.

His eyes bounce between mine, his expression tight and tortured.

He's riding the fine edge of wanting to do the right thing but needing to do the other, just like I am.

"I-I—" I stutter before swallowing and licking my lips. "I can't. I want you."

Not a second after the confession falls from my lips does he claim them.

A loud moan erupts before he sucks the bottom one into his mouth, gently sucking.

Heat blooms in my core as he pushes his thigh farther between mine.

His fingers wrap around the back of my neck, his thumb pressing against the underside of my jaw, tilting my head exactly where he wants it before his tongue pushes past my lips.

I sag against the wall, against his thigh, as we collide, his taste filling my mouth.

I didn't think I'd get to experience this again.

My hands slide up his thick arms before I loop them around his shoulders.

His other hand drops to my waist, and he drags me from the wall and into his hot and hard body.

The groan that rumbles up my throat is nothing but pure filth as his hand slips under my jersey in search of bare skin.

I shamelessly dry hump his leg, desperate to get as much of this man as I can.

"You taste even better than I remember."

Oh my god.

I cry out in disappointment when I'm suddenly lifted off his thigh.

"Oh god," I moan when he wraps my legs around his waist and walks me through the room, his lips still on mine.

"Kodie," I cry as he drops me, letting me crash to the bed.

I stare up at him in disbelief.

Already this is so much better than our first time.

I can see him. All of him. Well, almost.

He watches me closely, his heated eyes flitting around my body as if he doesn't know where to look first.

I'm still fully dressed; I'm not sure what he really wants to look at—maybe aside from the fact I'm wearing his number. That's a big deal to many players. It's a mark of ownership.

I did consider that it could be a step too far. But I couldn't stop myself.

"I always knew you were trouble," he muses as he reaches up and combs his fingers through his curls.

My chest heaves and my thighs clench.

Having him standing there looming over me might be things dreams are made of, but I need more. So much more.

"Please," I whimper, forcing him into action.

He tugs both of my sneakers off, letting them crash to the floor before peeling my socks from my feet and then curling his fingers under the waistband of my jeans and dragging them over my hips and off my legs.

"The fuck are you doing to me?" he mutters as he stands to his full height again.

My eyes run down his exposed chest, taking in all his ink until I get to his open waistband. I swallow thickly as I take in the way his slacks are straining against the thickness of his erection.

"I shouldn't be doing this. I shouldn't be fantasizing about the things I have been. It's wrong. So fucking wrong."

I hate the torn expression on his face.

Hell, I more than hate it. I feel it. Right down in the depths of my gut. But there is no other option.

Anything else would be...it would be unfair on us.

This chemistry...we need this.

We deserve this.

26

KODIE

Unwilling to wait for me to sort my shit out, Casey sits up and reaches for my waistband.

In a heartbeat, she has the fabric around my thighs, her fingers circling my length.

"Fuck, Casey. Fuck," I bark, my hips jerking forward with my need for her to move. Although, the second she does, I'm pretty sure I'm going to blow.

"Get out of your head. This is happening."

I nod, unable to form words as she leans forward and licks my tip.

"Fuck," I groan, sinking my fingers into her hair, holding her in place.

She's right. This is fucking happening.

One way or another, I need to figure out how to get her out of my system tonight.

I have a fleeting concern about Linc and the fact he'll appear at some point to crash, but then she wraps her lips around the head of my dick and all thoughts clear from my mind.

The only thing that matters right now is her.

"That's it," I groan, pushing myself deeper into her mouth—not that she needs the encouragement. "Fuck, Casey. Your mouth is sinful."

My grip on her hair tightens, but she doesn't complain. If anything, it only spurs her on to take me deeper.

My balls ache as pleasure builds at the base of my spine.

It really was as good as I remember.

No, that isn't true.

It's better.

"Fuuuck," I groan as my release surges froward.

With one hand wrapped around the base of my dick, she lifts the other one to play with my balls, and I fucking lose it.

Staring down at her wearing my fucking jersey, I shoot my load down her throat. My loud groan bounces off the walls around us as she takes it all.

My head spins as pleasure shoots through every inch of my body.

Fuck. I needed that.

Once she's confident I'm done, she pulls back and licks the tip clean.

"Fuck, you're something else," I muse as she rests back on her palms and gazes up at me.

I swear to God, she's the most tempting fucking thing on the planet.

You shouldn't be touching her, a little voice whispers, but it's so quiet, it's easy to shove it aside as I grab her thighs and force her to lie back on the bed.

"Gonna eat your pussy while you're wearing my number," I tell her as I drag her panties down her legs. I ball them up and lift them to my nose, inhaling the scent I've been craving since walking away from her that night.

Her eyes widen and her lips part as she watches me get my fill of her.

Stuffing them under the mattress for later, I kick my slacks and boxers off and drop to my knees. I spread her wide, my attention zeroing in on her pretty pussy.

"So fucking perfect."

Leaning forward, I trail kisses down her thigh, stopping before I get to the spot she really wants me.

"Kodie," she complains, her fingers twisting in the sheets, her hips lifting from the bed in an offering.

Hearing my name rolling off her lips in nothing but a desperate plea isn't like anything I've ever experienced before.

My cock jerks, already hard again for the next round.

But that won't be happening until I've heard her screaming my name.

I didn't realize how much I missed that our first time, but now I crave hearing it over and over again.

Shifting to her other thigh, I give that the same treatment, loving the way her entire body is trembling with anticipation.

"I thought you said you were going to eat my pussy," she complains.

"Be a good girl and I might," I taunt, kissing the patch of hairless skin right above her clit.

It's the ultimate tease, and she groans in frustration.

"Please, Kodie. Please."

"Fuck," I breathe, my eyes locked on hers.

Silently, she dares me to take exactly what both of us need as her sweet scent fills my nose.

My mouth waters and my cock is painfully hard all over again.

Will it ever be enough with her?

I'm fucking terrified it won't.

If tonight isn't enough to get her out of my system, what happens next?

I shake my head, refusing to worry about what comes next when she's lying right here like an offering.

"I don't ever want you in Storm's jersey again," I demand like a possessive asshole before giving her what she wants.

"KODIE," she cries, her hips jumping from the bed, but with one arm pressed across her hips, I hold her in place as I begin sucking on her clit. "Yes, yes, yes."

"So fucking sweet," I mutter against her.

Her fingers thread in my hair, and she attempts to drag me closer.

"More. Please," she begs.

Lifting my hand, I find her slick entrance and push two fingers inside her.

She's tight, and knowing just how fucking insane it's going to feel pushing balls deep inside her makes my cock twitch impatiently.

"Oh my god," she cries when I curl my fingers, gently grazing her G-spot as my teeth pinch her clit.

Continuing to pin her to the bed, I don't let up until she's moaning and coming all over my face.

Best fucking feeling ever.

I lick and suck until she's limp and exhausted.

Her eyes are barely open as I pull my fingers from inside her and climb to my feet. But the second I push those digits into my mouth and suck them clean, they open again, desire sparkling.

Twisting around, I grab my wallet from the side and pull out some new condoms.

Did I purchase them with memories of Casey filling my head? Maybe.

Did I also slip them into my wallet on the very slim chance that I might run into her again? Also maybe.

Casey's eyes light up when I drop four onto the bed beside her.

It's wishful thinking. We're on the clock here. At any point, Linc could return and put an end to this.

Briefly, I glance at the door. I've deadlocked it from the inside, but that isn't going to stop him from interrupting.

If he returns while she's still here and it's locked, he's going to demand to know why.

We should have gone to her room instead.

"Kodie?" Casey questions, her voice quiet and unsure.

I turn, my eyes finding hers, and something potent and addictive shoots between us.

No, I'm nowhere near ready to let her go.

Pressing my knee into the mattress, I settle between her legs and reach for her.

"As much as I fucking love seeing you in my jersey, I want to see your body," I explain, removing her jersey and bra in a rush, my hands immediately cupping her breasts.

Casey's head falls back on a moan as I pinch her nipples.

"Yes," she whimpers as I duck my head and suck.

Her hands wrap around my shoulders as she arches back, offering herself up to me.

My body burns in the best possible way.

Little shots of pain head straight for my dick as her nails rake my skin.

"Need you inside me," she moans as I kiss up her chest in search of her lips.

"Patience," I muse before claiming her lips in a life-altering kiss.

I didn't realize anything was wrong in my life, but the second she's in my arms, everything feels right in a way I've never experienced before.

She shifts in my hold and when I pull back, I find that she's got a condom pinched between her fingers, the wrapper already discarded on the bed.

"Sit back," she instructs, and I'm powerless but to do as I'm told, remembering how incredible it was to watch her roll the rubber on last time.

The second she's done, she lies back, offering herself up for me.

Her eyes are dark, her lips swollen and her chest heaving. Her nipples are hard and needy. And as I drag my gaze down her stomach, I find her pussy glistening and desperate.

"Kodie," she whimpers, her voice rocking through me, feeding my desire.

My eyes jump to hers again, and suddenly, our connection becomes overwhelming.

As much as this should just be sex, fucking to get it out of our systems, the tightness in my chest leads me to believe that it could be more.

And I can't afford that.

Needing to squash whatever it is that's crackling between us, I reach for her waist and flip her over.

It'll be easier if she's not looking at me with those big green eyes.

"Hands and knees," I bark before pulling my arm back and spanking her ass.

She squeals in surprise, but she doesn't shy away. Instead, she pushes her ass toward me, silently asking for more.

"Dirty girl," I muse before wrapping my hand around my dick and guiding it toward her.

Precum leaks from just the thought of pushing inside her again.

"Kodie," she moans, glancing back at me over her shoulder.

My heart slams against my ribs the second I look into her eyes.

It's too much.

Everything is too fucking much.

Reaching out, I wrap her long, wavy hair around my fist and shove her face into the pillow, stopping her from looking at me as I push just the head inside her.

My eyes slam closed as pleasure surges through me.

I'm barely even inside her, and yet, I swear it's better than anything I've ever experienced before.

"Kodie," she begs.

Fuck. I can't take hearing that.

Thrusting my hips forward, I fill her in one quick move, making her cry out, her body jumping up the bed with my power.

I tighten my grip on her hair, my other hand wrapping around her hip as I pull out.

"Oh my god," she whimpers, her pussy rippling around me.

The sensation is insane, and I grit my teeth, attempting to control my body. I've already blown too fast once.

This is going to be the last time we're together, and I don't want her to look back and laugh.

Squeezing my eyes closed, I thrust back inside her before setting a punishing pace.

I don't know which one of us I'm torturing. Her because she's so goddamn perfect that I can't help wanting to keep her, or me for being so weak, for breaking the rules, for being selfish and taking what I want without worrying about the consequences.

Whatever it is, I take it out on her body—and she loves every single moment of it.

As the bed slams against the wall, she cries out, begs, and whimpers, taking everything I give her.

When she comes, it takes every ounce of my self-control not to fall over the edge with her.

I tell myself that I need to give her two. Or three, if you count the previous one.

I want her to walk out of this hotel room satisfied, and hopefully with some good memories.

My chest aches at just the thought of what I'm going to have to do once this is over.

It can't happen again.

I can't risk my career, my life.

As much as it might hurt. I'm going to have to turn my back on her and find a way to put her behind me.

Easier said than done when it seems that the Vipers literally flow through her veins. Just like her father.

My coach.

Never in my life have I disrespected someone I admire and look up to like I am right now.

Shame burns through me, but it's not as hot as the desire.

That'll come later.

I'm going to fucking drown in it.

But right now, I need her, and I'll allow myself to indulge one final time.

Tightening my grip on her hair, I pull her body up so her back is pressed to my front.

My other hand slides down her stomach until my fingers hit her clit.

"Oh god. Kodie. Yes." Her head falls back against my shoulder as I keep fucking her.

"Come for me, Casey," I groan in her ear, barely holding back.

"Yes, yes, yes," she chants as I pinch her clit and send her crashing over the edge.

Her pussy grips me in a tight hold as her orgasm takes her, and I can't hold mine back any longer.

"Fuuuuck," I groan as my movement falters and I allow myself to be swallowed whole.

Fire shoots through my veins as I unload.

It's fucking insane. But long before I finish, I already regret it.

Because I know I'm never going to experience it again.

No other woman is ever going to stand up to Casey.

No one.

Releasing her, I let her crash to the bed as I suck in greedy lungfuls of air and climb to my feet.

I'm pulling the rubber from my softening cock as I stalk to the bathroom.

I don't look back to see her. I can't. She's going to look beautifully fucked; her chest will be heaving as she tries to catch her breath, and her skin will be glistening.

If I see it, I'll want another round.

But this isn't about what I want.

It's about doing the right thing. Finally.

I pause when I'm in the bathroom doorway and close my eyes, summoning the courage to do what I need to do.

Blowing out a long breath, I find the words that need to be said.

"You have five minutes to grab your shit and get out." My voice is rough and cold, and I fucking hate it. But I don't know what else to do.

Not a second later, I slam the bathroom door, flinching at the loudness.

For the longest time, I stand there in the middle of the bathroom, talking myself down from going back out there, apologizing, and telling her what I really want.

But I don't.

Instead, I wait, listening to her movement before eventually, the hotel room door is opened. The second it falls closed behind her, I stumble forward, catching myself on the counter.

I keep my head down for fear of what I'll see reflected in the mirror before me.

But eventually, I can't put it off any longer.

Guilt and shame threaten to swallow me whole as I look myself dead in the eyes.

"Goodbye, Casey," I whisper as if it'll help.

It won't.

27

———

CASEY

I practically run down the hallway on unsteady legs with tears in my eyes and my heart in my throat.

That was...

That was everything...until it wasn't.

Everything I thought I'd made up in my head about last time...the connection...the chemistry...it was all there. Hell, it was even better than the last time, because we weren't hiding.

We both knew who the other was, and it made it so much more intense.

I knew last time that I shouldn't have been with him. But this time, he knew it too, and I swear it made our desire burn even hotter.

As I round the corner, spotting our hotel room and my escape, I reach into my pocket for the keycard. But it's not there.

My heart plummets as I frantically check my other pockets.

I have my cell, but there is no sign of the keycard.

"Fuck," I hiss, spinning around to look down the hallway as if I just dropped it.

Unsurprisingly, there is nothing there.

Lifting my hand, I comb my fingers through my knotty sex hair and groan.

I have two options.

Go back and ask for it.

Or call Parker.

A bitter laugh erupts. There really is only one option.

There is no way I can face him again so soon.

"Hellooo," Parker sings after picking up on the third ring.

I squeeze my eyes closed, embarrassed by this entire situation.

"Please can you let me into our room? I've lost my key." My voice is quiet and cracked with emotion.

Voices float down to me, and I cringe at the thought of any Vipers staff seeing me. I don't doubt I look thoroughly fucked, and I'm not wearing any panties.

The asshole stole them.

Or worse. It could be my father.

My stomach turns over. He'll take one look at me and know I've been up to no good.

"Can you hurry, please?" I whisper as I move closer to the wall in an attempt to make myself disappear.

"I'm coming. I'm coming right now. Don't move."

A laugh spills free.

Where the hell am I going to go?

Thankfully, whoever the voices belonged to disappear in the opposite direction, leaving me anxiously hopping from foot to foot as I wait for Parker to rescue me.

The handprint on my ass burns, and my pussy is deliciously tender. At least she's happy she got another round.

I attempt to detangle my hair with my fingers, reliving one moment over and over.

Something in his eyes...changed.

He flipped me and shoved my face into the pillow.

And it wasn't just dominance this time.

It was like he suddenly couldn't bear to look at me.

I'm chewing my nail when Parker finally rounds the corner.

"Oh shit," she gasps the moment our eyes connect, and her pace picks up.

The second she's in front of me, she opens her arms to hug me.

"Please, just let me in," I beg.

The longer I'm out here, the more chance I have of being seen, and I refuse for them to see me falling apart.

Parker nods and quickly taps her key to the pad before pushing the door open and allowing me to rush inside.

She doesn't say anything until the door slams closed, but as soon as it does, she demands to know what's happened.

My tears burn hotter, but I fight to keep them from falling.

He doesn't deserve my tears.

It was a hookup.

No. It wasn't. It was closure.

I laugh, and Parker frowns in concern. "Casey?"

I shake my head and look up at the ceiling, willing my tears to disappear.

"It was nothing," I lie.

"Yeah, I'm not buying that. Try again."

When I look at her, she's staring at me with one brow lifted and her hands on her hips.

I sigh. "We hooked up. I left. But I must have left my key behind."

She studies me closely, silently urging the words from my lips.

"Fine, he sent me away when he was finished with me like I was nothing more than a bunny he'd never think of again."

Anger radiates from Parker in waves, her lips pursing and her fists clenching.

The thought of her stepping up to him and throwing a punch is almost enough to make me laugh.

She's so small, and he's so...not.

"That's bullshit, Casey," she spits. "You're not a bunny. You're so much more than a bunny. You're his coach's daughter, for fuck's sake."

And that right there is exactly the problem.

Reaching up, I swipe the few tears that escaped from my cheeks.

"Yeah, exactly. I'm his coach's d-daughter." I try to keep the emotion out of my voice but fall at the last hurdle.

"Oh, sweetie."

Parker steps closer and pulls me in for a hug.

I don't respond. I don't need to. Kodie Rivers has always been my dream man. Since the very first time I saw him online, I was borderline obsessed. And nothing has changed.

No. That's a lie. Everything has changed.

I've shared the same air as him, I've tasted him. And now...I want him more than ever.

Even if he is a massive asshole.

I allow myself a few seconds to absorb my best friend's support before dragging in a few shaky breaths and pulling back.

"I'm going to shower. All I can smell is him."

Emotion burns up my throat as I walk to the bathroom.

"You need to talk to him," Parker says before I disappear from her sight.

I shake my head and close my eyes.

"Kodie and I have never talked," I confess. "It's probably for the best if I just slip back into the shadows and watch him from afar."

The words cause a physical ache in my chest, making it hard to breathe. But it's the right thing to do.

Kodie and I aren't and never have been friends. Hell, until the night of the masquerade ball, I'm not sure he even knew I existed. We've had two nights together. One where he had no idea it was me, and another...

A sob bubbles up, and I clamp my hand over my mouth to stop it from erupting.

"Casey, I think—"

"It's fine, Parker. I got what I wanted, and now it's over." I just need to figure out a way to be okay with that.

I sleep like shit. While Parker lightly snores beside me, I toss and turn, getting more and more pissed off and agitated.

His dismissal repeats over and over in my head until I want to scream.

The sad thing is, I get it. I really fucking do.

We shouldn't have been together again.

We shouldn't have been together in the first place.

I did all of this. I instigated it all. I put him in this awful position. I deserve his anger, his frustration.

But despite knowing that, it doesn't stop it from stinging.

Being with Kodie...it was so much more than anyone else I've ever been with.

It's probably just because I've fantasized about him for so long. Maybe because he's forbidden.

But whatever it is, I already know that no one is going to compare to him.

Kodie Rivers has ruined me for anyone else.

Was it worth it?

Yes. One million times, yes.

"Good morning, Care Bear," Dad says as Parker and I approach the table he booked us for breakfast. "Oh," he adds when I get closer, his eyes darting over my face before settling on the dark shadows under my eyes. "Late night?"

"Something like that," I mutter as I lower my ass to the chair and search for the server with the coffee pot. I am in need like never before.

"We're not all old and sensible like you, Coach," Parker teases as she sits beside me.

"Less of the old, thank you," he mutters.

Thankfully, Parker is happy to keep the conversation flowing, and the second she congratulates Dad on an epic game last night, the two of them get into it in the same way that Dad and I usually do. Any other morning, I'd feel left out, but right now, I don't feel anything but broken and exhausted.

What Kodie did last night shouldn't matter.

It was a bit of fun. Something we both needed to get out of our systems.

It's not like I expected him to make some big declaration of love and that we'd run off into the sunset together.

I just wasn't expecting him to be so...cold. So harsh.

I drink three cups of coffee before our breakfast is delivered, and despite my stomach growling in hunger, I struggle to swallow any of it.

Instead, I poke the eggs and bacon around my plate while keeping one eye on the entrance.

There is a massive table on the other side of the restaurant with a number of team staff sitting at it. It's where Dad would usually be, but he excused himself to spend time with me. Guilt twists my insides. He's abandoned his team, and I can barely string two words together.

The rest of the team will appear at some point, and I have no idea how I'm going to react to seeing him again.

I have no doubt that he won't even look over, let alone spare me a second of his time.

He said everything he needed to last night.

We're done. Over.

Not that we were ever a thing.

I let out a pained sigh as my fork clatters to my plate.

"Are you sure you're okay?" Dad asks with a deep frown marring his brow.

"It was the shots," I mumble, hoping it's enough to pacify him.

"It's easy to forget that we're not eighteen anymore."

Dad's eyes open wide at Parker's comment. "You were both underage at eighteen," he points out.

Parker coughs. "I meant twenty-one, obviously."

Dad rolls his eyes and shakes his head at her.

"Sure, you did."

"Ah, come on, old man. I know it was a long time ago, but you must remember what it was like."

Dad's lips part to say something, but he doesn't get a chance, because there is a loud ruckus at the entrance.

Without instruction from my brain, my head snaps around just in time to see the majority of the team spill into the restaurant.

My stomach twists, and my chest compresses as I scan the faces.

For a few seconds, I don't think he's with them. But then Linc and Cole, our goalie, part.

All the air rushes from my lungs as I study him.

The asshole looks as perfect as ever.

I don't know why I'm surprised. I wasn't expecting him to lose any sleep over what happened last night.

Under the table, Parker grips my hand and squeezes in support.

I tell myself to look away, not to look bothered by his presence. I almost manage it, but then he looks up.

I swear, it's like being slammed into the boards by a giant D man.

Needing to look like the bigger, uninterested person, I rip my eyes away and focus back on Dad, who's also watching his team, probably looking for signs of hangovers from the night before.

A few of them make a detour our way to say good morning, but most head straight to their table and begin ordering endless amounts of food.

"We should probably get going," Parker says. "We need to be at the airport soon."

I nod in agreement.

"You're coming to the game tomorrow?" Dad asks.

"Of course." Just because one member of his team is an asshole, it's not going to stop me from watching a sport I love.

"And let me know if you hear anything," he reminds me.

"I will, but it's the weekend. I'm not expecting—"

"You could get the call anytime," Dad says. He wants me to get this coaching job so bad. I appreciate his support, I really do, but as excited as I am, the reality of coaching Kodie's daughter is beginning to hit me a little too hard.

Maybe it isn't my time, after all.

28

———

KODIE

I hated myself the second those words fell from my lips.

But what else could I do?

We both knew what that was.

Closure.

Getting it out of our system.

And the easiest and best way for her to know it can't happen again was to end it firmly.

Even if I hate myself for doing it.

I couldn't go out there, clean her up, and then embark on round two.

It would have only made both of us want more.

Linc could have come back at any moment.

And then what would have happened?

Would he have told Coach, or would he have kept our dirty little secret?

I refuse to drag anyone else into my mess.

It's already bad enough that we've both found ourselves entwined in this.

It's her fault. She did this, a little voice pipes up.

If she hadn't tricked me, seduced me that night, I wouldn't be here right now with guilt eating me from the inside out.

The worst of it is, I'm not sure I'm going to be able to leave it where we did last night.

Everything feels wrong.

I lied to her.

I lied to her and made her feel like what we had was nothing more than a quick fuck.

I treated her like the bunnies of my past. But that's not who she is or what she deserves.

The guys chat happily around me about their plans for the afternoon and evening once we land back in LA, but despite having a date with Sutton when I get home, all I can think about is the woman sitting across the restaurant.

She looks utterly defeated, and it's my fault.

Everything inside me screams to go over and talk to her, to apologize.

But I can't.

She's sitting with Coach.

Even if she wasn't, I couldn't go over. Not with all the guys watching.

Linc could do it and no one would question him.

But me?

Not a chance.

So instead, I drag my eyes away and stare at the menu as if it's the most interesting thing I've ever read.

Eventually, both Casey and Parker push their chairs back to leave.

We might be on the other side of the restaurant, but I can see from here that Casey has barely eaten anything.

Another thing to add to my guilt levels.

Without looking in our direction, she says goodbye to her dad and then she and Parker head for the exit.

My heart is in my throat as I wait to see if she's going to look back.

She shouldn't. I don't deserve even a second of her attention. But I still want it.

I want her to look into my eyes and see how much I regret how things ended last night.

I thought I was doing the right thing.

Being with her last night terrified me.

It was so much more than our first time.

Knowing who she was and how many rules we were breaking became too much.

The guilt. The desire. The connection...

Add those to the beer, the high of the win and the exhaustion, and I was fucked.

Royally fucking fucked.

By the time they get to the exit, I'm attempting to come to terms with the fact she's not going to look back at me. Maybe I'm not the reason she looks exhausted and didn't eat any of her breakfast. Maybe she met back up with Parker in the bar and...

My body tenses at the thought of her having a second round with someone else.

She had every right to. Especially after the way I treated her.

What if she found another member of the team to cheer her up?

What if it was Linc?

He didn't appear for a few more hours, and when he did, he stumbled into the room, crashing around and cursing in his awful attempt not to wake me up. He was about as quiet as a fucking hippo on ice skates.

Luckily, I'd been lying there awake, questioning my life choices.

It couldn't have been Linc. He might be a flirt, but he's not stupid.

Not like me, apparently.

I'm fucked.

Just when I think they're both going to disappear around the corner as if we're not sitting here, Parker looks back.

But she isn't looking at just anyone. Her eyes immediately find mine and then narrow in warning.

I sit back as if she physically struck me, my heart slamming against my ribs.

She knows.

Not only that; she wants to hurt me for what I've done.

"Fuck," I whisper-hiss the second they're out of sight.

"You okay, man?" Handsy asks, and when I glance over, he's studying me closely.

"Y-Yeah, of course. Just looking forward to getting back to my girl." It's not a lie. I'm desperate to see Sutton. I just wish she was my only focus.

"I don't know how you do it," he says, clearly happy with my excuse. "Dealing with bunnies is hard enough, but a kid? Fuck, bro."

"It's just life," I say with a shrug.

"Yeah, I guess. I'm not ready for that shit yet, though."

"You say that like I was," I mutter.

He rubs the back of his neck in thought. "No, I guess you weren't."

"Best thing that ever happened to me, though. My girl's—"

"She's fucking awesome," he says with a smile.

I love how much my teammates care for my daughter. They haven't spent all that much time with her, but it doesn't matter. She's just as much a part of the Vipers family as I am.

"Yeah," I say with a laugh. "She really is."

"You've done a solid job," he states.

"Doing my best, man."

I am. I'm trying really fucking hard to give Sutton the best start in life. It's not easy when I'm away for half of the year, but... I'm doing my best.

***

"What's that?" Linc says as he walks into our hotel room ahead of me just over thirty minutes later.

He bends down and swipes something from the floor beneath my bed.

Panic shoots through my veins.

Casey's panties.

I stuffed them under the mattress for later...

If he's found them—

"A...keycard?" I don't mean for it to come out as a question, and he frowns in response.

"No, it's a fucking chicken. What does it look like?" He rolls his eyes, looking at me like I'm an idiot.

"Alright," I mutter, moving closer to my bed when he backs toward his.

"Is it yours?" he inquires.

"Uh...n-no, I don't think so."

"Well, is yours in your pocket?"

I pat my slacks. The temptation to lie is strong.

"Yeah, mine is here," I say, pulling it free and holding it up.

"Huh. Weird."

My heart is like a runaway train in my chest.

He doesn't know.

How could he?

My fingers twitch with the need to pull that pair of panties from the bed.

It would be wrong to stuff them into my suitcase and take them home.

Nothing will stop me from doing exactly that, though.

I might have fucked everything up last night, but I'm not leaving those behind.

"Maybe the cleaners dropped it or something," I reason, needing to get out of this fucking conversation.

"Yeah," he says, tapping the card to his chin as he thinks. "Yeah, you're probably right."

He places it on the desk.

My heart lurches as he studies me.

His lips part, and I swear an accusation is about to fall from them.

Thankfully, I'm wrong.

Although, I barely relax when he does speak.

"Guess we'd better get packed. Wouldn't want to be on Coach's naughty list."

"No," I muse. That is definitely not a place I want to be. But I fear that I'm far beyond the naughty list at this point. I've got a one-way ticket to hell for what I've done.

The moment Linc disappears into the bathroom to gather his shit, I flip the sheet back.

"Oh fuck," I whisper when I find her Vipers-green G-string poking out.

I have it balled in my hand in a heartbeat.

"What was that?" Linc calls.

"Nothing."

Unable to stop myself, I lift her panties to my nose and inhale for three blissful seconds. Memories from our time together slam into me, making my temperature spike and my dick stir to life. Not allowing myself to indulge, I shove the panties deep into my small suitcase. I'll have to find a special place to hide those.

In only a few minutes, we're both ready to head back to LA for a few hours of rest before our home game against Seattle tomorrow.

"What time is Rett getting in?" I ask as we make our way down to reception so we can get the team bus to the airport.

"About four, I think."

"Any plans?"

He glances over at me, probably wondering why I'm so interested in his plans with his childhood best friend, but I figure it's better to keep him talking so he doesn't go back to the mystery keycard.

The second he held it up, I knew who it belonged to.

And it leaves me with the question...what did she do when she left me?

She couldn't get into her room, and she wasn't wearing any panties.

None of the ideas that pop into my head are good ones.

Not long after we join the guys, we're hustled onto the bus, and then before I know it, we're on the plane heading for home.

"Daddy," Sutton squeals, her little feet pounding against the tiles that cover our ground floor.

No sooner have I bent down to greet her, she launches herself at me, her small arms around my neck, and squeezes me as tightly as she can.

"I missed you so much," she whispers, her voice cracked with emotion.

My chest constricts. I'm the one who's caused her anguish by being away.

The beginning of the season is always the hardest.

In only a few weeks, it'll feel normal again. But after having the summer together, being apart hurts.

"I missed you too, Peanut. Have you had fun with Gran?"

"Yes. We made cookies," she says excitedly. "Do you want one? You should have one," she says before I have a chance to respond. "You deserve it. Your goal last night was insane. I was on my feet shouting and screaming."

I chuckle as I let her take my hand and drag me to the kitchen.

"Oh wow, look at these," I say, taking in the tray of green and white iced cookies.

"They're Viper cookies. I was going to talk to Coach about getting them made. Fans at the game would love them."

"I'm sure they would. Is this one mine?" I ask, pointing at one with the number fifty-five on it.

"Yep, that's all yours. There's a container over there with one for everyone. Will you take them tomorrow?"

Walking over, I study the container she pointed at, and just like she said, there is a numbered cookie for every member of the team.

"Of course I will. The guys will love them. Good luck cookies. You think we need extra luck tomorrow?" I ask.

She thinks for a moment. "Seattle has been killing it with their exhibition games. Rett has been on fire. I think it's going to be a tight game."

I smile at her, appreciating her honesty, but mostly astounded by her.

I always thought I knew my shit as a kid, but I had nothing on this girl.

I'm so fucking proud of her.

"I just need to grab a drink and something to eat and then we can head out."

"Gran said we couldn't go skating and that I had to choose something better."

"Okay, so what did you decide on?"

"The zoo," she says with a wide smile.

"You got it, Peanut. Get ready to go and we'll leave in thirty."

"Okay, Daddy. I'm so glad you're back, I love you."

"I love you too," I call after her just as Mom rounds the corner.

"Hey, sweetie. Welcome home." She smiles at me, but she looks a little concerned.

"Hey. These are incredible," I say, pointing at the cookies, hoping it'll be enough to distract her from the questions in her eyes.

"Yeah, she did a great job. You don't look like you've been sleeping. Is everything okay?"

I love my mother dearly. There is no way I could do what I do without her. But sometimes, I wish she wasn't so entwined in my life.

"Yeah, everything's great. Sutton and I are going to the zoo. Are you com—"

"Nope. You two enjoy the time together. I'll be here when you get back...in case you want to talk about anything."

Inhaling deeply, I release it through my nose as I silently tell her to quit it.

But all she does is smile back at me with nothing but love and support in her eyes.

It might ease some of my anxiety, but nothing will ever squash the guilt.

29

CASEY

"Fighting fire with fire, huh?" Parker muses as I join her in my living room, having gotten changed for tonight's game.

She met her brother this morning for breakfast before coming here to laze on my couch all afternoon.

"I don't know what you're talking about," I say coyly as I walk past her.

It took me a while to decide what to wear tonight. There was only one thing I knew for certain that I *wasn't* wearing...his jersey. There was no way I was giving him the satisfaction of seeing me in that again.

I had the rest of the team to choose from, but I needed one that would prove my point should Kodie care enough to look in my direction tonight.

"The hotpants and boots are a good touch," Parker laughs. "You're giving great bunny vibes."

I swallow nervously, suddenly questioning my decision.

"Is it too much?" I ask, looking down at myself.

I've never been a puck bunny, nor do I want to be one. And not just because Dad would have a coronary if he saw me flirting with the players.

But the chance to make a point tonight was too much to deny.

"After what he did? Not a chance," she states confidently. "You look hot, and he's going to lose his mind when he looks at you."

My stomach knots and my hands tremble.

I'm not sure if I'm ready to see him again. But I refuse to miss a game I love because of one idiot player.

I'm starting to understand why Dad has insisted I never date his players. It makes things complicated. Especially when it goes wrong.

"You look like you're about to throw up," Parker points out.

"I feel like I might."

"You need a shot," she states before jumping to her feet and rushing into my kitchen.

"Pretty sure that's the last thing I need," I call after her.

I've barely eaten all day, so a sip of alcohol will go straight to my head.

"We're going for food. It'll soak it all up," Parker reasons as she pours us a shot each and turns to me with a wicked smile.

"Tequila," she says, in case I didn't know what I had in my cupboard. "Perfect start to the night."

"You do know we both have work tomorrow, right?"

"We're not getting drunk, just...liquid courage. One for fun," she says, lifting her glass to her lips.

"And one for luck," I finish before swallowing the whole thing in one go. "Ugh," I complain as it burns down my throat.

It only takes a few seconds though for it to begin working its magic.

"Right, let's go before this really hits me," I say, grabbing my purse and looping it across my body.

"You don't need to tell me twice."

In contrast to my choice, Parker is wearing a generic Vipers hoodie tonight. I can only assume that's to avoid antagonizing her brother, who is about as happy with her dating players as my dad is me. Not that he really needs to worry; the only interest she has in getting up close and personal with them is to cause them physical pain.

By the time we get outside the building, Parker has an Uber

waiting for us, and in only a few short minutes, we're being dropped off at our favorite Mexican restaurant a couple of blocks from the arena.

As per usual, the place is a sea of green and white jerseys and there is anticipation in the air.

A rush of excitement goes through me.

Screw Kodie and his bullshit. He's not going to ruin tonight for me.

We're shown to our table, and Parker immediately orders us the biggest margaritas on the menu.

A collective gasp sucks all the air out of the arena as Everett Donnelly crosschecks Kodie into the boards.

The whistle blows, but the penalty isn't called, sending the Vipers fans into chaos.

"Your brother is on fire tonight," I quietly muse to Parker.

"He isn't called the best grinder in the league for nothing."

"Pfft."

Usually, I celebrate Rett's achievements just as much as I will the Vipers'. But not when he's playing against my team and slamming my players into the boards.

Tonight, he's the enemy.

Play restarts and the Vipers fans continue to riot over the ref's decisions.

"Is Rett paying this guy off or something?" I mutter, anger obvious in my tone as he stops another of our advances with questionable techniques.

"He's going to start a war if he keeps going," Parker says. "Although knowing Rett, that's probably what he's trying to do."

I can't help but chuckle. Rett is nothing if not a showman. He loves nothing more than having his face on the front page and splashed all over social media. He doesn't seem to care if it's because he's done something good or something stupid—and the latter is more common. I feel for the Seattle PR team having to deal with his antics.

The game continues in a similar fashion, with us getting our asses handed to us.

The fans around us get angrier and angrier as they watch in horror as Seattle scores again.

With their expressions set with determination, the Vipers get into position for one last chance to gain some ground before the final whistle blows.

"Yes," I scream when the puck drops and Fletch quickly passes it to Kodie.

My heart is in my throat as he flies toward the goal.

Almost the entire arena is on their feet, waiting to see if he can end the game with a goal like in Utah.

But just as he's about to take the shot, Rett appears.

The two of them collide, and Kodie's shot goes wide. A collective groan of frustration ripples through the stands.

The whistle blows, and the fans who hadn't already abandoned the game start to file out.

Disappointment is heavy. I get it. No one likes to see their team lose. Hell, no one wants to lose. But it's all part of the game.

And nowhere is that disappointment felt more than on the ice.

Kodie climbs angrily to his feet, stumbling a little as he recovers from the hit. "Oh my god," I gasp as he shoves a celebrating Rett, forcing him to crash into the boards.

Kodie hasn't had a good game. Every one of his attempts was thwarted by Rett or one of the other Seattle defensemen.

Kodie shouts something at the defenseman, but we're too far away to hear.

Whatever it is has Rett's entire body tensing before he spins around and gets in Kodie's face, shouting right back.

"What the fuck is he doing?" Parker mutters.

Rage ripples from them, the air is thick with it as the rest of the players watch everything unfold before them.

I watch in horror as they rip their helmets off, sending them clattering to the ice.

"Kodie doesn't fight," I whisper, my voice barely audible over the sounds of the arena.

"That doesn't look like a man who doesn't fight," Parker muses as Kodie rips his gloves off, standing skate to skate with Rett.

"You need to stop him," I beg as I reach over and grip her forearm.

"I can't. Even if I went down there and tried, that idiot doesn't listen to me. And what exactly would I say? Please, big brother, don't hit the player that Casey's been secretly banging?"

"Christ," I hiss, combing my hair back with my free hand.

Thankfully, Fletch, Linc, Handsy, and a few of Rett's teammates pull them away from each other.

Nothing but potent irritation rolls off Kodie as Linc turns him away from Rett.

Just before he shoves him toward the gate, Kodie looks up.

My breath catches as our eyes collide.

Refusing to get lost in him—or give him any kind of indication that I care about how things ended the other night—I turn my back on him.

The second I do, I realize my mistake.

Or not...

My skin tingles. I don't need to look back over my shoulder to know he's glaring pure hate at my back. Or more specifically, my jersey.

"Oh shit," Parker whispers. "He really doesn't like that."

Good.

"I don't care what he does and doesn't like," I lie as I snatch my empty cups from the floor and stalk toward the stairs to leave.

"Casey, wait," Parker calls, catching up with me as I storm down the stairs.

Out of the corner of my eye, I can see Linc skating beside Kodie before they step off the ice and disappear.

Finally, I'm able to breathe.

Banging on the plexiglass rips my eyes back to the rink, and I find Rett pounding his fist on it, grinning up at his sister.

"Fucking moron," Parker mutters. I glance back in time to see her flip him the bird, which he gives her one right back.

It's easy to forget what a nightmare the two of them were growing up.

"I need another drink," I mutter to myself as I round the corner.

"I didn't think you wanted to stay," Parker says, stepping up to me.

"I don't. I'm not." I've already explained to Dad that I've got an early start in the morning and that I'll skip the after-game drinks so he's not expecting to see me.

"Oh, come on. Just have one. I know Rett wants to catch up."

"I can't," I argue. I don't know if Kodie is going to be there. Dad mentioned that he'd asked Kodie to spend more time with the team off the ice, which explains his presence after the last few games. I can't risk seeing him. My heart can't take it.

"Okay," she says, her hand squeezing mine in support.

"You should still go, though."

"Without you? Not a chance. Come on." She hooks her arm through mine, and together we walk toward the exit.

It feels wrong not to go up and commiserate with the team and their friends and family. But it's not a place I can be tonight. The more space I put between me and Kodie right now, the better.

"One of my clients told me about this dessert restaurant with the most incredible cheesecake. We should go check it out."

"As long as there aren't any hockey players there, I'm in."

30

KODIE

Everything about tonight has been a disaster. Long before I even arrived at the arena, things were spinning out of my control.

Sutton accidentally dropped a carton of OJ on the kitchen floor. It went fucking everywhere, and I'm ashamed to say I lost my shit.

I was already running late and the last thing I needed was to get on my hands and knees and clean that shit up.

I felt like a piece of shit the second I snapped at her, but I couldn't hold it in.

I've been trying to put a brave face on it, but the truth is, I've been drowning since the moment I sent Casey away.

The guilt of doing that on top of what I was already dealing with has been too much.

She deserves to be treated so much better than that.

She deserves so much better than me.

That's exactly why Coach warns every player off her. He knows what assholes we can be, and he wants us as far away from her as possible. It's understandable. I'd want the same for Sutton. Although, something tells me that I'm not going to stand a chance. Hockey is just as much her life as it is mine. I just have to hope that the only playing she'll do with them will be on the ice while proving to them that she's better than they are.

Anger from tonight's game burns through my veins. My muscles are tense, and my fists clench and unclench as I think about how good it would have felt to throw one into that asshole's face.

I don't know what I did to piss him off, but he was gunning for me from the moment he hit the ice.

I'm not a fighter. I never have been. But every now and then, even I can admit that it's the only way to shatter the tension.

I slam my palms into the dressing room door, and it swings back and crashes into the wall.

The atmosphere in here is tense, the weight of the loss hanging over every single member of the team.

There is only one person who seems to be in high spirits, and the second he speaks, my eyes shoot to him.

"Tell me she didn't look hot as fuck, wearing my number," Marilyn announces, a cocky fucking grin on his lips.

My teeth grind, instantly knowing who he's talking about.

There is only one reason why Casey was wearing the rookie's fucking number tonight.

Because I'm a weak-ass prick who couldn't do the right thing.

"Oh come on, you can't honestly tell me that none of you have tapped that? She's fucking banging."

I'm moving before I've considered the consequences.

Monroe's back collides with the wall. He's already shed his pads, and the force of the hit knocks the air from his lungs. My forearm presses against his throat as I pin him with a dark look.

"The fuck did you just say?"

He attempts to swallow before his lips part, his eyes wide and shocked.

"Well?" I prompt.

"I-I'm s-sorry," he forces out. "I-I didn't—"

"Leave it, Big D," Linc says, attempting to drag me back.

I give Monroe another warning glare before taking a step back. As I do, the dressing room door swings open and Coach stands there, his eyes scanning the room as he assesses the mood.

"Well," he starts as he walks deeper into the room. He eyes Monroe standing flat against the wall with his chest heaving before giving each of us an accusatory look. "That wasn't great."

I shake my head as I rip my pads off before dropping my ass to my stall, while Coach points out our failures on the ice tonight.

By the time he's done, all I want to do is go home, kiss my girl good night, and crawl into bed. But it's not going to happen yet.

I made Coach a promise, and I fully intend to follow through. Turning up for a few drinks for team bonding is easy. Even if it does very little to soothe the guilt over breaking another more serious promise I once made him.

The mood in the friends and family suite isn't all that much better than in the dressing room, but at least most of them have had a few drinks to take the edge off the loss.

I scan the room, looking for the one person who can brighten my mood no matter what, but then I remember that it's Sunday night and Mom has already taken her home.

With Sutton not here, I quickly find myself searching for someone else.

I shouldn't. I should forget about her. But I can't.

There is so much I want to say to her, but most importantly, I need to apologize.

Honestly, I don't even know where to start when it comes to trying to explain the other night. I'm just hoping that a simple, "I'm sorry," will be enough.

It fucking won't. Nowhere close. But what else am I meant to say?

I can hardly tell her the truth.

Shaking my head, I make my way through the crowd, still searching for her.

But she's not here.

My heart slams against my ribs as disappointment rocks through me.

I just needed to see her.

With my chest tight and my muscles heavy, I make my way to an empty table at the back of the room. I nod at a few people who attempt to interact, hoping that my expression will be enough to scare them away.

They all watched me play tonight. They know that I'm in a bad place.

Fuck. I knew it long before I stepped onto the ice.

I couldn't get out of my own head, and I knew it was going to affect my game.

And I only have myself to blame.

What I did Friday night...

How I hurt her.

It's driving me fucking crazy.

I'm alone with nothing but my thoughts for a blissful four minutes until a familiar voice asks, "The fuck was that about in the dressing room?"

I look up as Linc slides a beer in my direction.

"He was being disrespectful," I grunt.

Seeing Casey wearing Linc's jersey was one thing. I could deal with that; she was taunting me, and I got it. But seeing her wearing the rookie's? It fucking got to me.

Hell, she could have been wearing anyone's but mine tonight and it would have fucking got to me.

Linc studies me, and I'm fucking terrified of what he can see.

I'm fucking this all up. Coach is gonna find out, and I'm gonna find myself traded.

My heart races and my hands tremble. Reaching for my beer, I wrap my fingers around it and hold tight, hoping to quash it.

It doesn't fucking work.

"You've been off all night," he notes. "Did you want to talk about it?"

A laugh threatens to bubble up, although there is no joy in it. Just pain and bitter disappointment in myself.

"Just feeling the pressure of the season, I guess," I mutter, finally feeling brave enough to lift my beer from the table. Thankfully, my hand is a little steadier and I don't slosh it all over myself.

Instead, I swallow a couple of large mouthfuls in the hope the cool liquid will settle me.

From the way Linc sits back and studies me, I'd say that he doesn't believe a word of it.

His lips part to say something that I'm sure to hate, but the words never break free. I never thought I'd be thankful to see Rett, especially after he's been riding my ass all night, but he storms across the room at the perfect time, stealing Linc's attention.

It's not unusual to see members of the opposing team after a game in here. Hockey families are tight, and I'm not surprised that he's here on the search for Linc and his sister.

"Dude," he hollers, earning everyone's attention. "Great game."

His demeanor is the complete opposite of mine.

"Not exactly true," Linc says as Rett joins us.

"The best team won, I think you'll agree. Your offense was off tonight." Rett slides his eyes to me, but I don't back down.

Sure, I might not have had my best game tonight, but I refuse to sit here and get shit for it.

"Whatever," Linc scoffs. "It'll be different next time we meet. When it really matters."

"Sure, bro. You keep telling yourself that." Rett claps him on the shoulder before looking around your room. "You seen my sister?"

"Nah, not since she crawled out of my bed this morning," Linc deadpans.

Internally, I do a little celebration as anger and pure disbelief flicker across Rett's face. He quickly covers it before slugging Linc in the arm.

They do this little skit every time they're together. Linc riles him up about sleeping with Parker, and Rett attempts to pretend he doesn't care.

I smother the sigh that wants to pass my lips.

"I thought she was gonna be up here. We fly out first thing in the morning," Rett explains.

"Don't know what to tell you, man," Linc says before offering to get him a beer.

I sit there silently, fearing that I might be the reason for Parker's absence. She'll be with Casey, staying as far away from me as possible.

As Linc stands, I drain my beer and get to my feet.

"I'm heading out."

"What?" Linc gasps, we've barely just got here.

"I know, but I'm wiped. And I want to be up to take Sutton to school tomorrow."

"Yeah, it's been a long week," Linc agrees, as if he has any fucking idea what I'm dealing with right now.

"See you at practice?"

"You got it, man."

I look at Rett and my nostrils flare. What I want to do is flip him the fuck off. But what I settle on is a curt nod before I make my way from the room.

Thankfully, Coach has registered my attendance, but he doesn't attempt to talk to me. He's also searching the room for someone he isn't going to find.

Just over an hour later, I finally strip down to my boxers and crawl into bed.

Mom was still waiting for me and, much to my delight, wanted to know why I was so off my game tonight. I pacified her by saying I was exhausted after traveling and quickly got the hell out of there.

I gently kissed Sutton good night before closing myself in my bedroom.

But the second I'm alone, my head starts spinning, and all the images flickering around like a movie are of her.

Casey Watson.

She left straight after the game because of me.

Guilt twists around me like barbed wire, making my skin prick and my chest tight.

Before I know what I'm doing, I reach for my abandoned slacks and pull my cell free. Her Instagram page is the last one I searched, and I pull it up in only seconds.

My teeth grind when I find a picture of her and Parker from tonight. Casey proudly wears her Monroe jersey.

That should be your number, a little voice screams in my head.

I scroll through the other images she posted of tonight. She and Parker drinking margaritas bigger than their heads. A platter full of tacos, the game, and then ones from later this evening eating dessert together.

While Parker might be in many of the images, I barely register her existence. My attention is locked on my troublemaker.

The longer I stare at her, the more my temperature picks up.

I'd hoped letting myself have her once I knew her identity would have given me some closure and got her out of my system. But I fear it's done the opposite.

Now, all I can think about is apologizing for my bullshit and proving to her over and over again why she should forgive me.

It would break every goddamn rule...

But isn't that what they're made for?

I battle with my conscience, my thumb hovering over the message button.

The need to reach out burns through me, and eventually, it becomes too much to ignore.

CASEY

I'm in the bathroom taking my makeup off when my cell pings with a notification.

Assuming it's Parker, I ignore it and continue with what I'm doing.

The events of the night spin through my mind, and as usual, thoughts of Kodie aren't far away.

I hated seeing him struggling on the ice. It was jarring. He's usually so strong and together; watching him fumbling plays and shots really didn't sit right with me.

He's better than that.

I tugged my boots and Monroe's jersey off as soon as I stepped into my apartment.

The second Kodie looked at it, I regretted the childish decision.

I don't want to be the girl who plays games to get attention, although I fear it's what I'm turning into. That's how all this started after all.

I also don't want to be the girl who breaks all the rules, but here we are.

Shedding the rest of my clothes, I pull on a tank and pair of sleep shorts and crawl into bed.

After getting comfortable and switching the TV on to watch highlights from tonight's games, I grab my cell.

I tap on the Instagram notification without thought, but when the messages open, my heart jumps into my throat.

Kodie Rivers has sent me a message.

And it's not from his public account, the one I've shamelessly scrolled through a million times over the years. It's from the private account that is locked up so tight I've often doubted if he lets anyone in.

"Oh my god," I whisper as I tap to open the message.

I don't know what I'm expecting to find staring back at me.

Sure, I know what I want. But I have very little hope that this is an apology and a Kodie Rivers booty call.

A girl can dream, right?

Hesitantly, I open the message, and the second the words appear before me, all the air rushes from my lungs.

> Kodie Rivers: I'm sorry.

I sit there with my mouth open, blinking in disbelief.

All thoughts leave my head, all possible replies vanish, and I lower my cell into my lap as I stare blindly at the TV.

The Vipers – Bandits highlights are playing, and I get the displeasure of watching Rett grind Kodie into the boards over and over again. It was bad enough seeing it firsthand, but watching it again makes it look even more brutal.

Rett really is going for it. And it only takes a few more highlights of the game to really appreciate just how much he had it out for Kodie. Rett plays rough, as he always has. But he was gunning for Kodie tonight.

Before I know what I'm doing, I've found his contact and I've hit call.

I'm not expecting him to answer—he'll be out celebrating their win. But after only a couple of rings, the call connects.

"Good evening, Watson. Calling to congratulate me on an epic performance tonight?"

I grunt in response, which makes him laugh.

"Parker told you, didn't she?"

"No idea what you're talking about." There's something in his voice, though. Parker and Rett are close. It doesn't matter that they're now in different states; they still talk almost every day. And Parker is pissed at Kodie. It makes total sense that she's mentioned something and set her brother on payback for what Kodie did to me the other night.

"Rett," I breathe.

"Your boys got their asses handed to them tonight, Watson. They need to have a very hard look at themselves before the season starts."

I let out a sigh, hearing the unspoken words.

"They're ready," I state confidently, making him scoff. "Just you wait. The tables will turn."

"I'd like to see them try. I gotta go, Watson. I can see two bunnies with my name on them."

"Still a pig, I see," I tease.

"Living my best life while I can. Who knows when these knees will give out."

I laugh. "Enjoy your celebrations while you can."

"Cheers. See you soon."

"Rett?" I call before he hands up.

"Yeah."

"Thank you, but despite what Parker says, I don't need anyone else fighting my battles for me."

"No idea what you're talking about, Watson," he says before cutting the call.

Silence fills the line, and I slump lower in my bed, feeling stupid for not figuring it out earlier.

Opening Instagram again, I stare at his message.

My heart flutters. He'll have seen I've read it.

Mentally, I come up with numerous replies. I even tap a few of them out.

But I never hit send.

None of them feel right, and I don't want to send anything that I'm going to regret later.

Instead, I put my cell on silent and turn it face down on my nightstand.

The TV continues to play, but I don't see any of it, and

eventually, I turn it off and lie in the dark, reliving the events of the past few weeks over and over until I pass out.

***

"Hello, this is a message for Casey Watson. My name is Lisa Kirk. I'm calling regarding the assistant coach position you've applied for. We'd love to invite you in for an interview to discuss the position further. If you could get back to me at your earliest convenience so we could discuss availability, that would be fantastic. Speak soon."

It doesn't matter that I've listened to the message no fewer than five times this morning and called them back to schedule my interview—butterflies still erupt in my belly when I hear it again.

"See, I told you that they'd want you, Care Bear," Dad says with a proud smile.

A mixture of nerves and excitement shoots through me.

"I'm scared," I confess.

Dad looks at me with a soft expression. It's not one that many other people see while at the arena. He's usually riding players' asses, pushing them harder and harder to get the results they need, both on and off the ice. I'm grateful that he can put the coach in him aside for a few moments to be a dad.

"You're going to kill it, Casey. You're going to be an incredible coach, and those girls are going to love you."

I blow out a shaky breath.

"I hope so."

"I know so. Do you need help preparing for the interview?" Dad offers.

I want to say yes, but then I watch him smother a yawn and I swallow down my request.

They arrived back this morning from the penultimate exhibition game before the season starts.

It was another painful loss for the Vipers. It was a hard watch last night, and I know Dad is reeling from it, trying to figure out how to learn from it and move forward. He doesn't need to be babysitting me when he has more important things to be doing.

"Nope. I've got this," I say, putting as much confidence into my voice as possible.

"You have," he says with a smile.

"So have you. The Vipers are going to make the playoffs this season. I can feel it."

"Maybe we'll both have teams that go all the way," Dad counters.

I blow out a slow breath as I allow myself to picture it.

"Is everything else good with you?" Dad asks. "I hate the transition from spending the summer with you to basically living here."

"I'm good," I say with a smile.

I'm not lying. Not really.

Everything is great, especially with this new opportunity right here for the taking.

But as excited as I am about the possibilities, there is still something else—someone else—taking up way too much of my headspace.

I still haven't replied to Kodie's message.

It sits there in my inbox, taunting me every time I open Instagram.

He also hasn't sent a follow-up, so I can only assume that he was trying to shed some guilt over the whole thing. That or he got one too many hits in the head courtesy of Rett that night. I could reply, but realistically, where is that going to get me?

He doesn't want me.

And honestly, that's for the best.

We can't date. There is no kind of future for us.

He needs to focus on the season, on his daughter. And I need to focus on my job and hopefully, my new coaching gig.

Dad's eyes narrow, and my stomach clenches.

His lips part and I hold my breath, dreading what he's about to say.

Dad prides himself on knowing everything about his team. If he were to find out about me and Kodie...

"You're coming to the barbeque on Sunday, right?"

I force a smile onto my face. Dad invites everyone to his

annual preseason barbeque—all the Vipers' staff, the players, and their families.

It's always been a big thing, and as a kid, it was up there as one of my favorite days of the year. As an adult, I still love it, even if I have to act a little cooler about spending time with NHL gods.

"Of course I'll be there," I say.

"It's going to be a good season, Care Bear."

I smile at him. "It is. I'll leave you to it," I say, rising from the chair.

"You're gonna get this job, Case. And you're gonna be the best assistant coach in the girls' league."

I leave his office with a wide smile. I'm too lost in thoughts about tomorrow's interview and what could possibly come after to look up, and the second I round the corner, I collide with what might as well be a freaking bus.

I shriek before stumbling back. I trip over my own foot, and the world falls from beneath me.

My breath catches and I brace myself for the hit, but a beat before I swear I'm about to collide with the floor, a pair of large hands wrap around my waist and right me.

"Thank—" My eyes lift and collide with a chocolate brown pair that haunts my dreams. "K-Kodie," I breathe like an idiot.

The second I breathe in, I'm hit with his scent. It wraps around me like the world's most erotic hug, making my body react in ways it shouldn't.

I want to hate him for what he did last week, for the cold way he dismissed me. But after watching him get slaughtered on the ice the last two games, I can't deny that my anger has ebbed away a little.

His eyes bounce between mine.

My heart slams against my ribs, and damn it if my thighs don't clench.

I swear, every second feels like a minute as he continues to hold me up, his giant palms burning my skin.

"S-shit," he finally hisses before releasing me and taking a huge step back. "Are you okay?"

"Y-yeah," I say, smoothing my blouse down before tucking my hair behind my ears.

"Are you?" I ask as if he doesn't get hit by men who weigh four times my body weight on a daily basis.

"Yeah, Troublemaker. I'm good."

The second his nickname for me rolls off his tongue, every muscle in my body sags.

I didn't realize how badly I needed to hear that.

Silence falls between us, but it's not awkward. Hell, it's anything but. It's charged and full of all the unspoken words between us.

"It's good to see you," he finally says.

"Mmm."

"I-uh…" He rubs at the back of his neck.

Oh, nervous Kodie is so freaking cute.

"I messaged you."

I nod. "You did."

He frowns, clearly not expecting that response.

I guess I shouldn't be surprised; all these guys are used to bunnies who will immediately ask how high when they tell them to jump.

"You didn't reply."

"I wasn't aware that was necessary."

He shrugs one shoulder. "Would have been nice to know if you accepted my apology."

"Do you deserve it?" I don't mean for the words to sound quite so bitter.

"Uh…" He looks away from me for a beat. "No, I guess not."

"Well, there you go then. Excuse me, I should probably…" I step forward, expecting him to move aside considering his huge body takes up the majority of the hallway.

"I meant it, Casey. I'm sorry."

I suck in a breath as the sincerity in his words rocks through me.

"What I said—"

"Don't," I snap, risking another look up.

If he says anything to make me doubt what he said...well, neither of us needs that.

He's one of my dad's best players. And if luck is on my side, then I could be about to become his daughter's coach as well.

We've already broken enough rules; we don't need to be shattering any more.

"I get it. All of it. I understand, and if it makes you feel better, I do accept your apology. I'm sorry as well. I put you in an awful position. It was selfish and—" My words die as he steps closer, stealing every single one of my senses.

He drags his bottom lip along his teeth. Desire sits heavy in my lower stomach, remembering just what those lips are capable of.

He releases it and his chin drops, as if he's about to say something, but another voice fills the hallway, forcing us to jump apart like naughty little kids.

"Yeah, I'm coming right now," Dad barks—I assume into his phone—as his footsteps get louder.

"Shit," I hiss before finally darting around Kodie and disappearing down the hallway.

"Rivers?" Dad says, surprise in his tone. "Everything okay?"

"U-uh, yeah," he replies unconvincingly. "Meeting," he mutters before heavy footsteps move away from me.

Without waiting around to find out what happens next, I rush down the hallway and jam my finger against the elevator call button to take me away.

32

KODIE

The buzzer sounds, the lights flash, and our fans go wild as we break our losing streak with an epic win at home for our final pre-season exhibition game.

This is the fucking thing I live for.

Spinning around, I search the crowd for my girl.

A wide smile spreads across my lips, and a laugh erupts when I find her on her feet, her arms in the air, jumping up and down, screaming my name.

Fuck. She is the best thing that's ever happened to me.

I glance at Mom, who's much more composed in her celebration. She smiles at me and nods while Sutton continues bouncing beside her.

"Love you, Daddy," she mouths, making my heart ache in my chest.

I didn't think it was possible to love another human being this much. And I swear it only gets stronger every freaking day.

I keep my eyes on her for a few more seconds before I can't help but search for someone else.

She's here, and she's been driving me crazy.

I expected her to turn up wearing someone else's jersey again, but to my shock—and delight—she's back to mine.

I don't want to say it's the reason I've played like I actually know what I'm doing again—unlike the last two games—but having her supporting me, on my side again...fuck, it feels good.

She still hasn't replied to my message, but seeing her wearing my number again makes me think that maybe she will. Or that maybe she's asking me to follow up.

Fuck, it's tempting.

She's so fucking tempting.

She smiles at me, and I swear it rocks the ice beneath me.

The air between us crackles just like it did in the hallway the other day.

I wanted to kiss her so fucking badly. Despite being right outside her dad's office, I've regretted not doing so ever since.

She looked so fucking beautiful and smelled fucking delicious.

She might be off-limits, but I want her again. And it's getting worse with every day that passes.

Touching her on Thursday, no matter how innocently, only stoked the fire burning inside me.

Now, with this win under our belt and the high I'm riding from both my assists and goal tonight, my need for her is an inferno.

"Great game, man," Handsy says as he skates up to me with his helmet under his arm and a wide smile on his face.

"I should be the one congratulating you on your shutout. Epic, man. Fucking epic."

"Ah, it's only the beginning."

"Fuck, yeah," I agree as the rest of the team huddles around us, celebrating as our loyal fans continue to chant.

Best feeling ever.

"D addy." I hear her excited squeal the second I step into the room before there's a flash of light brown hair as she flies toward me.

"Hey, Peanut," I say, lifting her from her feet and wrapping her in my arms.

The attention of others burns into me, and I know without looking up that it'll be the women.

It's the same everywhere I go with Sutton.

The bunnies are bad, obviously. But since becoming a single dad, I've started attracting a whole other group of women.

Ones who want to be Sutton's new step-mommy.

Yeah, no thank you.

I swear, some days, I can't go fucking anywhere without attracting attention.

I understand why the guys think I'm crazy for not embracing it while I have it, but I don't have the energy for women—anyone, actually—who only want me because of my career and daughter.

It's bullshit.

"You were amazing tonight," Sutton praises as I lower her back to her feet.

"So were you," I tell her with a smile. "I could hear you screaming from the ice."

Her smile lights up her entire face, and the sight makes my chest contract.

"Hey, little Riv," Linc says, stepping up behind us and holding his fist out for her to bump.

She beams at him and touches her knuckles against his as if she's one of the team.

"I hope that's a Storm jersey you're wearing," Linc teases.

Sutton scoffs before placing her hands on her hips. "There will only ever be one name and number on my jersey," she states fiercely.

Linc shoots me an amused glance before he reaches out and ruffles her head.

"I look forward to the day another player enters her life," he teases.

"Never going to happen." The glare she gives Linc makes me laugh.

"We'll see."

He ducks off as Mom approaches. "Great game," she says.

"Thanks," I mutter as I attempt to discreetly glance over her shoulder, searching for someone else.

"Are you sure you don't want to go out with the guys tonight?" she asks, dragging my attention back.

"Nope, not tonight. I want to put my girl to bed," I say, squeezing Sutton's hand a little.

I cleared it with Coach earlier that I wasn't hanging around after the game. The only place I want to be tonight is at home.

Next week, we're heading out for our first road games, and I'm going to miss the hell out of her. I'll be able to spend time bonding with the guys then. Sutton is my priority right now.

There's movement behind Mom, and as the crowd parts, I get my first look at Casey.

She's got her back to me, allowing me to see my name and number on her jersey.

The sight of it hits me right in the balls.

Mine.

I grit my teeth at the memory of having her body pinned against mine the other day, even if it was only briefly.

The need to breathe her in, to slide my hands down her body burns through me.

As if she senses my attention, she slowly turns around and her eyes lock on mine.

It's like a shot to the chest.

My breath catches and my temperature spikes.

We're surrounded by people, many of whom could be watching this exchange, but with her eyes on me, it's like we're the only two in the room.

"Daddy?" Sutton says, tugging on my hand and successfully ripping my attention from Casey.

I turn back to her and listen as she tells me about a particular play that she was impressed by tonight.

I allow her to sweep me up into her game analysis as I lead her and Mom from the room before I do something stupid like change my mind.

My skin is still tingling, and my blood is surging with desire as I climb into bed a couple of hours later.

After putting Sutton to bed, I stripped out of my suit and hit the bike in my home gym in the hope of banishing some of the energy buzzing through me.

I knew it was going to be pointless. It's not post-win adrenaline I'm dealing with. It's something I haven't battled with in years.

Desire.

The sheets brush over my skin and I groan as I lie back against my pillows, my cock fully hard and aching.

For her.

Closing my eyes, I will my body to calm down.

Over the last few years, it's become easier and easier to somewhat shut off this part of my brain. Sure, I still had needs, but I became used to taking care of them myself.

My life was hockey and Sutton; anything that fell outside of that just wasn't important enough to be a focus of mine.

But then there was her...

She shattered everything I'd told myself.

Broke through the lies I'd forced myself to believe about what I wanted.

My cock jerks, resting on my stomach, as I think back to how close I came to kissing her right outside her father's office.

All I could think about was her. Her sweet taste, her soft curves, her pretty pink pussy.

"Fuck," I groan, my fingers sinking into my hair and tugging until a shot of pain races down my spine.

It doesn't help.

My head is still full of her and my body...fuck, it craves hers.

Before I can stop myself, I reach toward my nightstand and grab my cell.

The fact she still hasn't replied drives me to the brink of insanity.

She told me she accepted my apology to my face; I should be able to let it go now.

That was what that night was about.

Closure.

But I didn't fucking get it.

I open Instagram and check her profile. As predicted, there is an image of her tonight proudly wearing my number and wishing us good look.

That's basically all her profile is.

Hockey.

I may not know all that much about her, but it's clear that hockey runs through her blood.

It makes me wonder what she was like as a kid. Was she like Sutton, giving her dad a detailed analysis of her performance after every game?

Did she play?

Hell, I don't even know if she can skate.

There's a selfish part of me that hopes she can't so that I can be the one to teach her.

Who am I kidding? Her father is James Watson. Of course she can skate.

After staring at the images of her tonight for a minute or two too long, I tap the message icon.

Instantly, my unanswered message appears.

I stare at it, irritated that she couldn't even send me a thumbs-up.

No, scratch that. That would have been worse than nothing.

Nothing good comes from a thumbs-up.

A middle finger would be preferable to a thumb...

My mind drifts to the gutter, wondering which Casey would prefer.

Both...

Fuck.

I run through several message options, some dirtier and more questionable than others.

I was in college the last time I sent filthy messages to a girl; it feels fucking weird.

I'm a grown-ass man. I'm a father.

I should be past getting nervous about messaging a girl.

> Kodie Rivers: Good to see you chose the right jersey tonight.

The second I hit send, I regret it.

I was going for teasing, but reading it back, it sounds patronizing.

Jesus. I'm screwing this up before it's even started.

In a rush, I close the app. If I can't see it, I can pretend it didn't happen.

I attempt to distract myself with sports news and scores from today's games, but I don't register anything I read.

Throwing my cell to the bed, I swing my legs off and pad through to the bathroom to take a piss.

Easier said than done when I'm rocking a semi.

Fucking Casey.

She's not even here, and she's causing fucking trouble.

It takes longer than it should to do my business, and I'm busy convincing myself that I won't have a reply as I stalk naked back to my bed.

But as I approach, I notice my screen is alight with a notification.

My heart jumps into my throat, and I surge forward, snatching it up.

Instagram message.

My hand trembles as I tap to open it, and the second I see who it's from, all the air rushes from my lungs and I collapse on the bed.

> Casey Watson: Don't flatter yourself. You play better when I'm wearing it…

A laugh bursts out of me.

> Kodie Rivers: We've only lost one home exhibition game. How would I know what you were wearing for our road losses?

My heart is a runaway train in my chest as I wait for her

response.

I already know it's going to floor me. That's what Casey Watson does to me.

She takes everything I thought I knew about myself and my life and throws it into a fucking blender.

Casey Watson: I watch road games in nothing but a pair of panties with your number on.

33

CASEY

My laughter rings through my silent apartment as I picture his response to my message.

It's not true, obviously.

But I kinda want it to be.

I can see myself lying on my couch in only a pair of green and white panties with the number fifty-five stamped on my ass, sending him pictures to open when he gets off the ice.

Only if they win, of course.

I giggle again.

Clearly, the vodka Parker and I consumed tonight is having an effect.

I want to say the alcohol is the reason I replied tonight. But it's not.

The truth is that I've been typing and deleting replies to his apology for days. And it only got worse after our interaction outside Dad's office.

My obsession with this man is growing to the point I can no longer control it.

At least toward the end of last week I could somewhat distract myself with prepping for my interview. But now, while I'm dealing with the anxiety of waiting for the outcome, thoughts of him are slipping back in again.

I laugh at myself. As if they ever really left.

He's been a constant in my thoughts and fantasies for years now. I don't expect him to go anywhere anytime soon.

My cell pings, and I lift it from the counter, my blood already at a boiling point from just the couple of messages we've exchanged.

Was I disappointed when he walked out of the suite earlier with his little girl's hand in his? Hell yes. But I also understood it.

As a kid, I loved it when Dad came home with me after a game. He gave so much of himself to his team, to hockey as a whole, that getting him to myself was huge. I used to embrace every second I could have him just being my dad, and I have no doubt Kodie's daughter feels the same.

She's so freaking cute. I saw her with her grandmother, wearing her small Kodie Rivers jersey. And the way her entire face lit up when Kodie stepped into the room...I swear, my heart and ovaries exploded right there.

> Kodie Rivers: I'm going to need to see photographic evidence of that, Troublemaker.

"Of course you are."

Placing my cell back down, I stare at myself in the mirror as I braid my hair, ready for bed. My eyes are glittering with excitement, and my cheeks are flushed. I don't need to look down to know my nipples are hard and pressing against the soft fabric of my tank.

Happy with the outcome, I tie it off with a scrunchie, snatch my cell from the side, and turn the light off as I slightly sway toward my bed.

I've got a nice buzz on, and I'm nowhere near ready to crash yet.

We could be in for a fun night...

> Casey Watson: I don't know what you've heard about me, Rivers. But I'm not the kind of girl who sends booty shots to players.

> Kodie Watson: Thank fuck for that. I'd have to kill any of them who've seen beneath your jersey.

My heart thumps at his possessiveness. And of course, I can't help but make it worse.

> Casey Watson: Of course, they've all seen me in a bikini. You are coming to the BBQ tomorrow, right?

> Kodie Rivers: I'll be there.

> Casey Watson: Better bring your boxing gloves. My bikini is all ready to go. I'm going to need someone to rub sunscreen on my body. Do you think Monroe is up for the job?

I can practically hear his warning growl in my ear. It sends a chill down my spine, causing goosebumps to erupt across my skin.

> Kodie Rivers: Monroe? You want Monroe touching you? The kid will probably jizz in his pants the second he gets close. He's already gunning for you after you wore his jersey the other day.

> Kodie Rivers: That was a mistake, by the way.

> Casey Watson: Some might say mistake, others might say excellent plan. It sure got the attention of the player I want.

> Kodie Rivers: And one you don't...

> Casey Watson: Says who? How do you know I'm not building my perfect hockey harem?

> Kodie Rivers: Casey...

The shudder that rips through my body is ridiculous, considering he's nowhere near me.

"Get a grip," I hiss at myself.

I'm such a fucking whore for this guy.

Not that I can really blame myself. He's a certified hockey god.

And his moves off the ice...just as good as I always hoped they be.

Biting my bottom lip, I tap out my reply.

Casey Watson: Yes, Daddy?

Heat surges through me as I picture his eyes darkening before tracking down my body, giving away exactly what he wants.

Me to submit.

He may not have had the chance to fully unleash his kinks yet, but I've seen hints of what he likes. And hell if I don't want the chance to experience it all.

I squeeze my thighs together, attempting to quell the pulsating that is only getting stronger and stronger.

Kodie Rivers: Will you be a good girl for me?

"Holy fuck," I gasp, my hips rolling as if he's in the room with me and I'm desperately trying to tempt him over. Not that I think he'd need it.

I could see everything he wanted in his eyes earlier.

It crackles like a livewire between us.

Casey Watson: Will you punish me if I'm not...

Kodie Rivers: You have no idea, Troublemaker.

Kodie Rivers: Where are you?

Casey Watson: At home. In bed.

My stomach tumbles and everything south of my waist clenches.

Kodie Rivers: Wearing?

I suck in a deep breath as I debate whether to lie or not.

Casey Watson: Tank and panties.

Kodie Rivers: With my number on?

I giggle as happiness washes through me.

I always suspected Kodie was my perfect man. I just never could have imagined he'd be this perfect.

Casey Watson: Maybe…

Casey Watson: What about you? Where are you and what are you wearing?

He doesn't reply as quickly this time, leaving me on edge.

He'd better not be about to tell me that he put his daughter to bed and then went out with the guys.

Kodie Rivers: In bed.

Kodie Rivers: Naked.

"Yesss."

Kodie Rivers: And hard as a fucking rock.

All the air comes rushing out of my lungs.

This man.

This fucking man.

Kodie Rivers: What about you?

Casey Watson: What about me?

A coy smile pulls at my lips as I wait for his response.

Kodie Rivers: Spread your thighs, baby.

Unable to do anything but what I'm told, my knees fall to the mattress.

Kodie Rivers: Good girl. Now push your hand inside your panties and tell me how wet you are for me.

Jesus.

I've dabbled with a little phone sex in the past, but it has never been anything like this.

I swear to God, I'm about to combust from just reading his words.

"Oh my god," I gasp as I do what I'm told and brush my fingers against my swollen clit. "Why aren't you here?" I complain as I circle it a couple of times before pushing lower.

A filthy groan spills from my lips as my fingers slip easily inside my body.

I'm embarrassingly wet, considering I'm alone.

Kodie Rivers: Casey?

"Oh god," I moan.

Casey Watson: So wet for you...

Kodie Rivers: Fuck, I wish I could see you.

My eyes lift to the video call option...
No, Casey. Don't do it.
If you see him...
I shake my head.
If I see him, I'll want more.
I'm already taking more than I should.

Casey Watson: Have you got your hand wrapped around your cock?

Kodie Rivers: Yes. Fuck, yes. Trying to imagine it's you.

Casey Watson: Same. But I don't touch myself like you do. I can't make myself come like you can.

Kodie Rivers: Fuck, you're killing me here.

Casey Watson: What would you be doing if you were here?

Kodie Rivers: I'd have my face buried in your pussy. I'd have your juices all over my mouth.

His words have my release surging forward faster than I can control.

My fingers move quickly as warmth begins to bloom from my core.

"Oh god."

Kodie Rivers: And I'd have two fingers inside you. I'd curl them, finding that spot that makes you cry out my name.

I picture him fisting his cock as he types these words, his muscles taut and his skin glistening with exertion.

Fuck, he's unbelievably hot.

Kodie Rivers: You're going to come all over my face and fingers before I stretch your pussy open with my dick.

"Oh god. Oh god."

Kodie Rivers: Then I'm going to take you bare, fill you up before sitting back and watching as I leak out of you.

"Fuck. Fuck. Kodie motherfucking Rivers," I cry out, my body convulsing as pleasure consumes every inch of me. "Oh my god. Fuck."

My chest heaves as aftershocks keep firing off, extending my pleasure.

I don't know how long it takes me to come back down from my high, but when I do, I discover that I've dropped my cell.

"Shit," I hiss, sliding my hand around the sheets to find it.

The second it hits my finger, I pull it free and wake it up.

Kodie Rivers: Fucking addicted to your pussy, Troublemaker.

Kodie Rivers: So hot. So tight. So fucking perfect.

Kodie Rivers: Are you being a good girl for me?

Kodie Rivers: The thought of you lying there, playing with yourself as you think of me is so fucking hot.

Casey Watson: I've been doing it for years.

My confession ensures my heart continues racing.

I should probably keep my obsession with him to myself. It'll do nothing but make me look like a creepy stalker.

He doesn't need to know about my collection of posters I have of him, how I used to hide them everywhere I could so Dad wouldn't find them.

Kodie doesn't reply, and I can only imagine why.

Nerves take hold. Maybe I shouldn't have said that.

It's weird, right? Bringing up a teenage crush during sexy talk with the man who you've been crushing on for years?

But then I think about another reason why he might not be replying.

Did he drop his cell too...

The thought of him coming all over himself while talking dirty to me is almost enough for me to go for round two. If it weren't for my need to keep messaging him, I might.

There's always later...

The memory of this exchange is going to come in useful for a very, very long time.

Kodie Rivers: I'm gonna need to change my sheets.

The smile that curls at my lips is ridiculous.

Casey Watson: Just imagine if I were there too...

Kodie Rivers: In my dreams...

Casey Watson: Don't worry, I can guarantee you'll be in mine tonight.

When no more messages follow, I begin to think that's it. That he's used me to get off and then dropped me.

With a dejected sigh, I head toward the bathroom to clean up.

The high from my orgasm has sadly faded. But it's my fault.

I keep allowing myself to get involved with him, knowing it can't be anything.

But it's so good in the moment.

If only I were someone different.

I'm all up in my head when I straighten my messy sheets and crawl back into bed. Tonight has been full of all kinds of highs, but it's ended on that low.

But then...

My cell pings, and I scramble to get it.

The second I see his name, a huge rush of relief spills from me.

> Kodie Rivers: Are you going to be able to look at me with a straight face tomorrow?

I smirk.

God, I can't wait.

> Casey Watson: I have a good game face. What about you?

> Kodie Rivers: I don't plan on being traded any time soon. My warning about the bikini still stands, though...

> Casey Watson: You're a big boy. I'm sure you can control yourself.

> Kodie Rivers: Glad you noticed...

> Casey Watson: Impossible not to.

> Kodie Rivers: Tomorrow is going to be the best kind of torture.

> Casey Watson: I can't wait. See you tomorrow, Big D 😊

34

CASEY

"Oh my god," I squeal the second I pull up at Dad's the next morning and see a very familiar face walking out of the driveway next door.

Jumping out of my car, I race toward Freya and throw my arms around her.

Freya and her parents have lived next door for as long as I can remember. She's a few years older and used to babysit me when I was younger.

"I didn't know you were back," I cry as she returns my embrace.

"Surprise," she says, although there isn't as much pep as I would expect to be in that word.

Pulling back, I study her.

"Frey?" I question, concerned.

"I'm sorry. I'm okay, really." She blows out a long breath as she fights to get it together. She's far from okay.

"Come on," I say, taking her hand and leading her to the swing seat on Dad's porch.

The second we sit down, words begin tumbling free.

"It's over, Case. He sent me home.'

"Oh shit," I gasp, retaking her hand and squeezing for support.

Freya had been working in Las Vegas, something her parents

hated with a passion, but she was adamant that she wanted to experience more.

Well, she got more in the form of a famous rock star who swept her off her feet and whisked her off on a world tour.

I should have known something was up. The photos stopped coming.

At the beginning, she'd send me one from every place she went. Then it dropped to once a week, then every now and then. And then nothing.

I assumed she was just busy.

She had the world at her feet, literally—one of the planet's hottest men in her bed at night.

How wrong was I?

"I've been in London for a couple of months trying to figure out what I'm going to do next."

I nod, aware that she's got family there now.

"I've just...I've got nothing without him."

I have no idea what to say to that.

"You'll figure it out. There are so many opportunities here, Frey," I say, hoping to sound supportive and not condescending.

"I know," she breathes, looking down at her feet. "I'm heading toward thirty, and I've just gone from flying around the world, spending nights in some of the most luxurious hotels and bars, to living back at my parents'. It's...a lot to process."

"And you had no idea?" I regret the question as soon as it falls from my lips. She clearly doesn't want to talk about it.

She shakes her head, her watery eyes meeting mine again.

"I'm such an idiot, Casey."

"No. No, you're not. He's an asshole for not seeing how incredible you are."

She sucks in a shaky breath before wiping her eyes.

"I'm sorry. I'm okay. I've made some dishes for your dad's party, and said I'd help today in the hope of a distraction."

I can't help but smile at her. "Freya, an entire roster of hockey players is about to descend. There is no better distraction in the world."

A laugh bubbles out of her before she confesses, "There may have been an ulterior motive. My ego could do with a boost."

"Girl, you don't have to worry. My boys will fix you right up with one look at you in a bikini."

"Here's hoping," she says with a weak smile.

"I think it's time for a mimosa, don't you?"

Together, we walk into Dad's kitchen. "Oh wow," I gasp when I find the island covered in dishes full of food."

"I may have gotten a little carried away," Freya confesses. "I didn't get to cook much when we were travelling, or at all really. It felt so good."

When I glance over, she has a little twinkle back in her eyes.

She's going to be okay. It's just going to take a little time.

We don't really need to do anything else. Everyone who's coming today will bring food with them. By the time all the players and their families are here, we'll have more meat for the grill than we know what to do with, so instead of food, we embark on organising drinks. After having our mimosas, of course.

I love hosting. I have since I was a little girl. Looking back, I can't help but wonder if I was overcompensating for the fact Mom was no longer here to do it. But I genuinely loved it. And it only got better when Dad would tell his teammates and other staff that I did it all. They'd look at me with awe and pride in their eyes and it would light me up.

I desperately wanted to be accepted by the team—hell, the entire organization. I wanted to be a part of it. I wanted to be them.

I smile to myself as I remember how floored I always was when player after player used to walk into our house as relaxed as if it was their own home.

Those men were my idols. I was in awe of all of them. Their strength, power, determination, their resilience—it still blows me away all these years later. It doesn't matter that the men turning up today are the next generation of players from those I grew up with; they're still just as incredible.

Most of them bloody well know it, too.

"I needed this," Freya says as she takes her first sip of mimosa as heavy footsteps rumble down the stairs.

"Ah, you found her," Dad says, looking between the two of us with a smile.

"Ugh, put it away, old man," I tease.

"Enough of that," he chastises as he grabs a t-shirt from the back of a dining chair and pulls it on. "Sorry about that." He shoots a look at Freya, letting me know that he's apologizing—and dressing—for her benefit.

I glance over at Freya and unsurprisingly find her ogling him. Not in a blatant puck bunny kind of way—more a "wow, he's cut for an old man" one. I'm weirdly proud that my dad can cause that kind of reaction still.

"I can't believe you didn't tell me she was back," I chastise lightly.

"Thought it would be a nice surprise. This all looks incredible. I've missed your cooking, Freya."

Freya's cheeks brighten at the praise.

"Is it too much?" Freya asks nervously.

"Nothing a team of professional hockey players can't demolish," I say with a laugh.

"True that. Right, I'm going to double-check the grill. They should be here soon."

A bolt of nervous energy races through me, and my gaze darts to the window that showcases the driveway.

No one yet. But there will be. And as much as I teased Kodie last night about keeping a straight face this morning, the closer it gets to seeing him, the more I'm worried about how I'll react.

Will everyone look at me and know I had a Kodie Rivers–induced orgasm last night?

Oh my god.

I spin away from Freya as my cheeks burn red.

They're all going to know, and Dad is going to find out and—

"Casey?" Freya's concerned voice cuts through my panic.

"I'm okay. Just feeling a little lightheaded. I think I celebrated too hard last night."

"It was a good game. Dad was going wild for it." Her father is a massive Vipers fan. He couldn't believe his luck when we moved next door. He fanboyed for quite a while over Dad.

I chuckle before moving toward the door. "I'm just going to get some air." But instead of moving toward the backyard, I dart toward the stairs.

I take them two at a time and in less than a minute, I'm in my childhood bedroom.

Walking over to the Juliette balcony, I throw the doors open and suck in a deep breath, staring out at the perfect blue sky.

Instantly, I feel a little better.

Curling my fingers around the railing, I tip my head back and close my eyes. I force myself to breathe and relax.

I can't influence the people making the decisions about the coaching job. I can't control Kodie's reaction to me when he turns up. All I can do is focus on the here and now.

What I can do is catch up with an old friend and hopefully make her see that she can still have some fun while we get Dad's place ready for his guests. Then I can kick back and enjoy spending time with some of the world's most incredible people.

With the warm fall breeze flowing around me, I let myself get lost in my thoughts. I don't hear movement downstairs, and it's not until there's a knock behind me that I come crashing back to Earth.

"Oh my god," I gasp, spinning around to see my best friend striding into the room. "Jesus, you scared the crap out of me."

Parker studies me closely before muttering an apology. "What's going on?" she asks, her eyes bouncing between mine. "Why are you up here hiding? Freya said...yay for her being back by the way."

"I-I'm not hiding," I stutter, sounding like that's exactly what I'm doing.

"Did something happen?"

"Damn it, Parker. Can you stop reading me so well?"

She smirks. "It's not hard, Case. You're not a hider, and yet here you are shut away in your childhood bedroom as if you're scared to face something...someone?" she guesses, her brow lifting.

"I'm not—I was just—"

Her eyes open wider, silently willing me to tell the truth.

"Okay, fine. Something may have happened with Kodie last night," I confess.

A wicked smile twitches at her lips.

"I hope it was him getting on his knees and groveling after what happened in Utah," she says firmly.

"Uh…"

"Casey," she whines. "Do not let him get away with that."

I wave her off. I get it. What he said was awful, but I refuse to forget what I've done to him and be the kind of woman who gets hung up on a man's mistakes while ignoring her own.

I played him, and quite frankly, he played me right back. Touché.

"It's not that simple," I argue.

"It really is." Silence falls between us as her glare gets more intense. But eventually, I win, and her need to know the details gets the better of her. "So, what happened? Did he turn up at your door like a stalker in need of a celebratory blowy?"

"I wish," I mutter, conjuring up the image of him standing at my front door looking all hot and desperate.

"So?"

"He messaged me last week to apologize," I say, filling her in on the details I've held back recently. "I didn't reply. But last night he messaged again and…well…one thing led to another and—"

"Explains why your eyes are so glazed," she points out with a smirk. "Even at a distance, he can make you cum that hard, huh?"

"Jealous?" I tease.

"Yes and no," she hedges. "So you're hiding up here, abandoning Freya, because he's coming with his daughter and you're freaking out."

"Yes and no," I echo.

"I think you mean yes, Casey."

I throw my hands up and groan.

"What if everyone can see it?" I ask, voicing my concerns. "What if I can't keep my eyes off him and others start to notice?"

"Casey," she says softly, moving a little closer. "Are you really worried about your reaction to him, or is this about how he's going to react to you?"

I hold her eyes, waiting for her to explain, but my heart is already racing, telling me that she's nailed it.

"You've been living with his mega crush on him for years. No one has noticed yet, so I don't think you have a problem, even if things have escalated. I think you're worried about him—"

"He can control himself. You've met hockey players, right?"

"Yeah, babe. I know them," she states. "But that's the thing. Deep down, you don't want him to control himself. You want him to walk in here and be obsessed with you. You don't want him to be able to take his eyes off you. You want him to be jealous if another player—hell, another person—talks to you. You want to be his everything, and you want every fucker to know it."

Do I?

Is that what I'm really afraid of?

"It's okay to feel that way, Casey. It's okay to want to be the center of his world."

"But I can't be," I counter. Even with all the reasons why we can't be together. "He's got a daughter. She is, and always should be, the center of his world."

"I wasn't putting you up against her. Completely different categories, babe." She drops her voice to a whisper, but despite the volume, the words smack me upside the head. "He can have you both."

All the air comes rushing out of my lungs and noise erupts from downstairs. My heart jumps into my throat, fear surging through my veins.

"They're here."

"You're going to need to come to terms with the fact that today, Kodie is likely to ignore you." Her statement hurts, but I understand it. "He stands to lose a hell of a lot more than you do if this comes out. Your dad could trade him in a heartbeat and uproot his entire life. His daughter's entire life. That won't happen to you."

"You also need to figure out what you want and where this is going, because the longer it goes on, the worse it's going to get."

"I know," I whisper weakly.

A door slams and deep, booming voices filter up to us.

"Are you ready to put on your game face?" she asks.

Blowing out a calming breath, I move toward the mirror and check myself over.

I might be wearing a tank and shorts now, but beneath it is the bikini I teased Kodie with last night. Let's see if I'm going to be brave enough to show him.

"Come on," Parker says, taking my hand and tugging me away. "You look gorgeous. He's going to be walking around with a semi all day."

I snort a laugh as we descend the stairs.

"So when did Freya get back?" she asks.

"I have no idea. She surprised me earlier."

"Yeah, well. Fuck her ex. It's his loss. Today, the three of us are going to have some fun."

Despite her words, and my agreement, my nerves are at an all-time high as we turn into the kitchen where the voices stem from.

Parker squeezes my hand in support, and it's needed—because no sooner have we stepped into the room do a dark and hungry set of eyes turn on me.

35

KODIE

Sutton was up with the sun this morning running as usual, chattering at a million miles a minute. But for the first time in quite a long time, she wasn't the only one who woke up with a spring in her step and excitement shooting through her veins.

The second I opened my eyes, I reached for my cell and re-read last night's conversation like a pussy.

I didn't care. I needed it. And fuck, if it wasn't almost as hot as it was last night.

I woke up hard with thoughts of her in my head, but reading her words, picturing her getting herself off as she messaged me...fuck.

I'm so fucking fucked.

Thankfully, I was able to get ten minutes alone in the shower to fix the situation before I dived head-first into being a father.

"Is it time to go yet?" Sutton asks as she chases a ball around the kitchen island with a hockey stick.

I chuckle and glance at the clock.

If she got her way, we'd be first at Coach's house. I, however, would rather be fashionably late.

Today is going to be all kinds of torture. I might want to spend as much time with Casey as possible, but doing so while her father, the team, and my daughter are with us isn't quite what I have in mind.

Plus, there's every chance she wasn't lying about that bikini...

I drag my hand down my face and glance at the bags sitting at my feet and the platters of food on the counter.

Sutton had the best day of her life when we attended Coach's barbeque last year. The team was new to both of us, and they invited us in and made us feel like we belonged, just as I'd hoped.

My only regret is not paying enough attention to my new coach's daughter. She was there—I remember seeing her. But I was so concerned about ensuring Sutton was happy that I didn't have much time for anything else.

Something tells me that this year will be different.

"Yes, we can go now," I concede, making Sutton squeal in delight.

She immediately reaches for her Vipers rucksack and throws it on her back before grabbing the grocery bag full of chips and crackers.

The rules are that we bring meat and beer, but when Mom and Sutton went shopping yesterday, they went a little over the top.

I throw my own duffle bag over my shoulder before grabbing the platters of marinated meat ready for the grill that Mom prepared and follow Sutton as she bounces out of the house.

The twenty-minute drive to Coach's house passes in the blink of an eye, and Sutton's face is practically pressed against the window as I pull into the drive behind a handful of cars. I breathe a sigh of relief that we're not first. I'm not sure I'd cope being in a house with only Casey and Coach.

My heart slams against my ribs.

What are you doing, Kodie?

I shake my head. I have no fucking idea.

I know what I should do. I should walk away and force the memories of Casey to the dark depths of my mind.

But I'm not going to.

I can't.

She's too addictive. Too tempting.

Holding back from messaging her this morning was one of the hardest things I've ever done.

I'm trying really hard not to look like a crazy stalker.

A laugh bubbles out of me without instruction from my brain.

"Are you okay, Daddy?" Sutton asks from the back seat.

Chastising myself for letting her see that I'm barely holding it together, I suck in a calming breath and turn to look at her.

"Of course. Excited for today."

"Me too," she says with a wide smile, which I can't help but return.

"What are we waiting for, then?" Without overthinking, I push the door open and climb out.

Our arms loaded with goodies, we make our way to the front door.

Thankfully, someone sees us coming, and the door opens before I have to figure out how to ring the bell with no hands.

"Little Rivers," Killer announces, ignoring me and turning his attention straight to Sutton. "Ah, and you brought Big D with you, too."

Sutton sighs. "Someone had to drive me. I can't reach the pedals yet."

Killer barks out a laugh as he gestures for Sutton to enter.

"Can I help you with your bags?" he asks her, like the gentleman he most certainly is not.

She happily lets him take the weight before instructing both of us where to put everything. It doesn't matter that she's only been here once before; she owns the place. Everyone else who's already here watches the scene play out with amused smirks on their faces.

"Little Rivers, bossing it as ever," Linc says, coming over to bump knuckles with her.

I watch happily as everyone else greets her.

"Good to see you," Coach says, dropping to his haunches. "There are some kids already playing field hockey in the backyard if you want to—" Laughter rips through the air as she races toward the open doors and disappears from our sight before he can finish his sentence.

"I think we know who's going to captain that team," Reese, Fletch's wife, correctly guesses, earning another round of laughter. "Your daughter is a firecracker, Kodie. I love her."

"She's sure something."

"All the drinks are outside; the grill is already fired up and..." Coach's words trail off as someone else walks into the kitchen, and my eyes lock on hers.

Holy shit, she's beautiful.

The voices and laughter surrounding me vanish.

Her green eyes darken as she moves closer, and my blood begins to heat, my cock forgetting about whatever hand action it had this morning.

There's movement behind her, but I don't pay whoever it is any mind as my eyes drop down Casey's body, finding her wearing a wide armed Vipers tank and a tiny pair of denim shorts.

She's totally wearing a bikini under that...

"Daddy. Daddy."

Someone tugging on my hand brings me back to myself, and when I look down, I find Sutton looking between me and Casey with a small frown on her brow.

"H-hey, Peanut, what's up?"

"We're going in the pool. Is that okay?" She stares up at me with her large, brown eyes, and I have a very firm word to myself to keep my reactions to Casey in check.

It's not just Sutton watching. It's the entire fucking team.

It's Coach.

"Of course. I'll be right out, okay?"

She nods happily before racing away, pulling her t-shirt off as she goes, revealing her swimsuit beneath.

"You made a really fucking cute kid, Rivers," Parker announces as she steps up to the island beside a woman I don't think I've ever seen before.

"Thanks," I mutter, rubbing the back of my neck as I watch Sutton disappear around the corner. "I should probably—" I thumb over my shoulder and turn around.

Thankfully, everyone else is also moving outside, and I pray that no one noticed my lapse in judgment.

"Casey, do you need any help with anything?" a familiar voice says.

I look back over my shoulder just in time to see fucking Monroe step up to her, already wearing nothing but a pair of swim shorts and a shit load of muscle.

Fucking asshole.

"Uh...no. I think I'm okay," Casey says, sounding confused. "Go and enjoy yourself."

"I don't mind," he mutters before turning to the other woman. "Hi, I'm Hayden but everyone calls me either Monroe or Marilyn."

Parker and Casey smother a laugh while the other woman looks at our rookie with sympathy in her eyes.

"Hi, I'm Freya."

"And she's not interested," Parker adds for her.

"Here, take this bowl out." Casey concedes, giving Monroe a smile that makes me want to claw his eyes out.

"Shall I come back?" he offers like an eager little puppy.

"No, go and enjoy yourself."

"Rivers, you want to put those hands to use as well?" Parker asks, turning all attention onto me.

"Sure," I agree, shooting a Casey a look.

"Take these. Just make sure they stay in the shade. No one wants a hard baguette in their hand." Parker's eyes hold mine, mirth dancing in them as both women on either side of her snort.

"Parker," Casey cries as I take the breadbasket.

"I'll do my best to keep it soft," I inform her flatly before turning around.

Their sniggers fill the air as I move away from them, and I can't help but smile.

I was right. Today is going to be a whole new kind of hell.

"BOMB," Handsy shouts before racing to the pool, curling his gigantic goalie body into a ball, and landing right in the middle of the water, splashing everyone around us.

"Uh, you got us wet," Parker calls.

Parker has proved to me today that she's as much of a handful as her best friend. The third one of their little trio is much quieter, though. She's spent most of the day hiding behind her sunglasses with her head buried in a book.

"It's what we're good at," Linc barks back, making her face twist with frustration.

Linc, Killer, and Monroe all run toward the pool and jump at the same time, causing a tidal wave to cover Coach's backyard. Kids squeal in delight, the women sitting around sunbathing cry out in irritation, and the rest of the guys laugh.

Coach turns from his spot at the grill and shoots us an amused smirk. Man, I'd have loved to have known him when he was a player. Something tells me that he was a fun teammate to have.

It's a pretty fucking perfect afternoon, apart from the fact Casey is on the other side of the yard, lying on a lounger with those fucking shorts undone and a tiny green bikini top doing very little to hide her tits.

All the guys have looked; I've fucking seen them. Thankfully, all but Monroe have kept their distance. He's the only stupid motherfucker who's been shamelessly trying to entertain all three of them. He's not getting anywhere, which is giving us all more entertainment than I think he's aware of. Even if I want to rip him a new one every time he so much as glances at Casey.

"Daddy, come and get in the pool," Sutton calls from her giant pink inflatable donut that's bobbing on the water.

"Sure," I say before pushing from my lounger and standing to full height.

Fire burns down my side, and I glance over at Casey. She's wearing big, dark sunglasses, but I know she's watching me.

Reaching behind my head, I drag my t-shirt off with one hand, exposing my torso to her.

Parker wolf whistles, apparently watching the show too, but I don't bother looking at her.

Combing my fingers through my hair, I stalk toward the pool's edge, letting Casey get her fill before diving in.

The water is a little too warm after the summer heat to do anything about the fire that's raging inside me.

I surge up beneath Sutton, and without her seeing me, I flip her out of her donut.

She screams before going under.

"Daddy," she squeals the second I lift her up. "That wasn't what I meant."

Furiously, she wipes water from her face.

"Oh, what did you mean then? This?" I say before throwing her, letting her splash back under the water.

This begins a very loud and boisterous game as all the kids demand to be thrown around by their fathers or anyone who's willing to get involved.

Every time I glance in Casey's direction, she's watching.

"Oh no, don't you dare," a familiar voice screams.

Spinning around, I find Linc closing in on Parker, who's relaxing on her lounger wearing nothing but a fire-engine red bikini and a pair of sunglasses.

"Lincoln Storm, walk away from me right now," she demands loudly.

He might have his back to me, but I can picture the cocky smirk playing on his lips.

She hops up and begins backing away from him, but she's forced to turn to the left, leading her closer to the pool.

"Shit," she shrieks before she takes off running.

If she thinks she can outrun him, then she really needs to reconsider, because not three wide strides later does he catch her, wrapping his arms around her waist. He launches both of them into the pool, her scream piercing the air for a few seconds before they go under.

Laughter erupts around us, and when I glance back at Casey, I see that she's got a wide smile playing on her lips, joy radiating from her.

"You gonna join her?" I shout over.

"Nah, I'm okay here," she replies with a smirk.

"Ah, come on, Watson," Monroe predictably calls. Of course he wants her to strip down and get wet.

She's too busy focusing on him to notice that Killer and Handsy have slipped behind her lounger, both dripping with pool water.

"Yeah, Watson. I didn't have you down as a scaredy-cat," I taunt.

I can't see through her glasses, but I'd put money on her shooting daggers at me right now.

Her lips part to say something, but it's too late; they're on her.

36

CASEY

"Get off me," I scream as their grip on my upper arms tightens and my ass leaves the lounger. "Freya, help!"

I kick out and attempt to twist out of their hold, but it's pointless. And all Freya does is laugh. Traitor. I'm battling not one but two professional hockey players. I don't stand a chance.

I'm still wearing my shorts and my glasses are on my face, but that doesn't stop either of them. Thank fuck my cell is on the lounger, because I would be pissed if they stopped me from messaging a certain player that I've been discreetly eye-fucking behind my tinted lenses all afternoon.

Fuck, he's hot.

All rippling muscle and inked-up skin.

Delicious. And I want a taste.

"No, please," I cry as they carry me kicking and screaming toward the pool's edge.

"Sorry, Watson," they say in unison before throwing me toward the water.

Sucking in a breath, I squeeze my eyes closed and prepare to go under.

I hit the water with a hard slap and sink beneath the surface.

"You're both jerks," I cry when I come back up and wipe my hair from my face.

The pair of them are still standing on the edge, looking far too pleased with themselves.

Lucky for me, Dad has my back—and he and Freya's dad both silently step up behind them and give them a hard shove.

Shock covers both of their faces before they tumble forward, right toward me.

I attempt to swim away, but I already know I'm not going to be fast enough.

This is going to hurt.

Everything happens so fast. One minute my arms and legs are thrashing as fast as I can manage to get away, and the next, I'm being hauled against a very large, very hot, and very hard body.

Oh god.

Kodie's arm bands around my waist, keeping me out of the firing line as Killer and Handsy tumble into the pool, covering both of us in water.

"Holy shit," I cry.

"Pretty sure I just saw your life flash before my eyes," Kodie whispers in my ear. "And I didn't like it because I barely featured."

Oh, holy fuck.

All the air rushes from my lungs as the guys pop back up and begin goofing around with the others in the pool.

Shamelessly, I grind my ass back against him. It's too tempting not to when I can feel the length of him pressing against me.

"There are kids in this pool, Rivers," I shoot over my shoulder.

"Yeah," he grunts. "You're causing me a real big problem, Trouble."

I can't help but snigger.

"Do you want to play with us?" Sutton asks, having swam closer to us.

Her beautifully familiar dark eyes stare up at me, silently begging me to say yes.

Could I say no to this little girl even if I wanted to?

I'm powerless with her, just like I am with her father.

"Of course, I'd love to."

Still trapped by Kodie's strong arm, I reluctantly twist to get free. It takes a second for him to release me, but he does.

"We're playing volleyball," Sutton tells us as Fletch and Monroe set up my old net across the pool, dividing us into two teams.

"Ready?" Fletch shouts, holding the ball above the net.

Everyone agrees, and he launches the ball into the pool.

Both sides of the net are a mixture of players and kids, though with the heights of our players, I'm not sure the kids, or me and Parker, are going to stand a chance here.

Thankfully, I soon discover that the guys can be a little less competitive when off the ice, and they allow the kids to get involved.

"I got it," I call when the ball comes flying in my direction.

I jump as high as I can with my arms in the air, but a beat before I make contact, I'm hit from behind.

"Fuck," I grunt, my mouth filling with water as I go under.

But my annoyance of missing the shot is soon forgotten when a large hand slides up my stomach and grips my boob.

Desire shoots straight to my core.

It's a bold move from Kodie. But he isn't the only player here.

Let the games begin.

By the time we surface, his hands are firmly off my body, but that doesn't mean that I'm not aching for him.

My blood is simmering, and my need for him is growing by the second.

It's a dangerous game, but it makes it so much more fun.

I'm fully aware of his every move beside me, and I can only assume the same can be said for him.

Sutton makes a hit and we both celebrate as it goes flying over the net and gets missed by one of the kids at the front.

"Well done, Peanut," Kodie says, giving her a high five. The move makes my chest constrict. They're too freaking cute together.

"That's five to three," Fletch calls from the sidelines where he's playing ref.

"Come on, we've got this," Kodie says competitively before getting into position.

Linc hits the ball and it flies toward us. Both Kodie and I move, ready, but this time, I'm not going for the ball. I've got something else I want to get my hands on.

Our shoulders collide, and I pray that I've done a good enough job to make it look like I wanted the ball before my hands sink under the water, over the waistband of Kodie's swim shorts, and down the length of his cock.

We're both submerged, but I feel the deep groan he lets out as I squeeze him, turning his semi into a full-blown erection.

It's naughty. We're surrounded by his teammates, my father, his daughter. But I can't help it.

He makes me wild and rebellious.

I come up with a wide smile playing on my lips, my clit swollen and desperate for more.

He shoots me a look, and it's nothing but pure fire.

I'm in trouble now, and I can't fucking wait to take my punishment.

The game continues for another ten minutes, giving me more than a few opportunities to cop a feel and ensure Kodie remains deliciously hard and ready for more.

We're announced the winners, and after a round of high fives to celebrate, I swim toward the edge and pull myself out so I'm sitting on the tiles.

"I'm going to get a drink. Join me?" I shamelessly ask Kodie, knowing full well he can't leave the water yet.

His smile is pure malice, and it hits me right between the legs.

"No, don't go yet," Sutton cries.

I quirk a brow.

Saved by his daughter.

Parker climbs out on the other side of the pool, looking like a glamor model in her red bikini with water running over her curvy body. More than a few of the guys drool after her as she moves around the pool toward me.

"Cocktail?" she asks, holding a hand out.

She makes it look like she's oblivious to the guys' attention. But she's not. She's eating it up and showing them exactly what they can't have.

She gets off on the power. It's about the only time hockey players aren't the ones with all the control.

"Absolutely," I agree, climbing to my feet and walking away with an extra sway in my hips. My soaked shorts cling to me, but I make it work.

"He's so fucking gone for you, Case," she whispers as we approach Dad's makeshift bar and grab a couple of solo cups.

"Parker," I hiss.

"What? No one is listening. They're all too busy playing, and your dad is bossing the grill."

She begins grabbing bottles of alcohol and sloshing a random concoction into the cups.

"What the hell are you making?" I ask.

"It's inspired by sex on the beach. It's called, grope in a pool."

"Parker," I whisper-hiss.

"What?" she asks innocently. "You cannot tell me there wasn't a little fondling going on back there."

I drop my head to my hands. "Fucking hell."

"It's okay. It was totally discreet. No one would have known."

"You know," I cry.

"Yes, but I also know you're already bumping uglies. No one else does."

I groan. "What am I going to do, Parker?"

"Talk to him instead of fucking him? Talk to your dad?"

Both are incredibly sensible suggestions that I really don't have the bandwidth for right now.

Of course, I could talk to Kodie. But I'm pretty sure I already know how that'll end. And as for Dad, what exactly would I say? "Hey, Dad, you know how you've always told me to stay away from your hockey players? Well, I'm currently fucking one who probably doesn't want any kind of future and is going to break my heart, but I'm doing it anyway." I'm sure that would go down like a lead fucking balloon.

"I need—"

There are several screams and a loud splash behind us.

"I get it if you don't talk to your dad, but you at least need to talk to Kodie, find out where his head is at."

"Parker," I sigh. "He's a professional athlete and a single dad. There isn't any space in his life for me. This is just a bit of fun while it lasts."

"But what if it's not?" she urges.

I raise a brow. "When did you become such a romantic?"

"I'm not. I just know that if there is one man on this planet that you want a happily ever after with, it's Kodie freaking Rivers."

"It's a dream, Parker. A dream that I know will never come true."

The strength of Parker's cocktail helped me process those painfully truthful words a little better. But the reality is that they're a bitter pill to swallow.

No matter how much I want Kodie, no matter how much fun we have, I'll never be important enough. And I shouldn't be.

I wasn't that much older than Sutton is now when we lost Mom. It was awful, heartbreaking, confusing, and all I wanted was to have Dad around me twenty-four-seven.

As far as I know, Sutton hasn't lost her mom. She's just... absent. It's not the same. But despite the differences, we're both kids of single fathers and professional athletes. That's hard. Really fucking hard.

I can't even begin to imagine what it would have been like if Dad had met someone. If he'd allowed someone else into our little family unit.

As much as I want Kodie, there is no way I want to be the woman who comes between him and Sutton. Their bond is so special, unbreakable. I would hate for either of them to feel like I was threatening that.

"You've got man problems, haven't you?" Freya asks after we've been sitting silently for a little over ten minutes.

Parker is on the other side of the yard with Reese and a couple of the other women. Every now and then, their laughter floats over to us, but I'm nowhere near intrigued enough to go and find out what they're laughing about.

Kodie is now out of the pool and drinking beer with Linc and Fletch while Sutton plays with Monroe, Killer, and Handsy, along with some of the other kids.

Dragging my eyes to the quiet girl beside me, I contemplate lying. But what's the point? She knows.

"Isn't it always," I mutter, lifting my drink to my lips.

It's just soda. After the cocktails Parker made earlier, I need it.

"Yeah," she muses, sadly.

"You want to talk about it?" I offer.

She shakes her head.

It's been quite a few years since Freya and I spent any real time together. I don't know all that much about the man who's recently broken her heart other than what I've read online, but I see just how much he's hurt her.

"Men are jerks," I offer up, making her laugh.

"Amen to that," she agrees, holding her cup up for me to tap mine against. "Who needs one, anyway?"

My eyes automatically drift back to Kodie.

Me.

But I don't need just any man.

I need him.

37

KODIE

Draining my bottle of beer, I sit back and watch Sutton playing with some of my teammate's kids with a wide smile on her face.

Like always, my stomach knots with self-doubt.

I do everything I can for Sutton. But I'll forever be worried it's not enough.

She hangs out with the other guys' kids a couple of times a year at events like these. She's been invited by their moms to playdates and things, but it's almost always when we're on the road for games. I already put way too much on Mom. She doesn't need to be dealing with playdates on top of school, homework, hockey practice and games, and everything else that comes with a child.

But if her mother were here...

No. Not her mother.

We're both better off without her in our lives.

The day she abandoned her duties as a parent and left me to raise my daughter was the best decision she ever made.

But someone.

Someone who could be a mother figure. Someone who would allow Mom to be the kind of grandmother she deserves to be.

I let out a heavy sigh as Sutton dives through the giant donut floatie before popping up on the other side.

I just wish I could give her everything. But as hard as I might try, it's impossible.

"Peanut," I call while her head is up.

Instantly, she twists around and smiles at me.

"Thirty minutes," I say, making her happiness falter.

She wants to complain, but she doesn't. It's a school night, and she knows the rules.

"Okay, Daddy," she says, her lips drawing into another smile. This one doesn't reach her eyes, and I hate myself for it.

I look around Coach's backyard, at my teammates and their families all enjoying themselves. They make it look so easy.

Life. Hockey. Families.

I know I'm not failing, but I can't help but wonder if I'm running at eighty percent on everything.

With a sigh, I climb from the lounger and ask the moms who are sitting closest to me if they're okay to keep an eye on Sutton while I'm gone before swiping my bag from the floor and heading inside to change.

As much as I might want to spend the night here watching Casey in her sexy bikini, I need to leave.

I need to put some space between us. We've already crossed enough boundaries today.

Anyone could have seen us fooling around in the pool.

It was dangerous and risky.

I should have been more self-aware. But in the moment, all I could think about was her.

Touching her. Tasting her. Burying myself inside her and never letting her go.

"Fucking hell," I mutter to myself as I slip into Coach's house.

Noise floats down from the kitchen, and as I turn the corner, I spot a flash of blonde hair before the red head walks around the island with a smile on her face.

Despite my body begging me to join them, I force myself to move in the opposite direction.

"Whoa," I cry, grabbing onto Parker's upper arms to stop her from stumbling backward. "Are you okay?"

She gazes up at me with glassy eyes. Whatever she's been drinking, it was strong.

"Yeah, Rivers. I'm good. Are you?" Her eyes twinkle. It's all I need to know that she's aware of what was happening with Casey earlier.

"Yeah, I'm good."

She continues to look up at me for a few seconds before her eyes drop to my bag, and then she glances back over her shoulder in the direction I was heading.

"Oh, um...The bathroom is busy. Lincoln is—" She sucks in a breath before blurting, "There is another one. Upstairs. Bathroom, that is."

"I don't mind waiting. I just want to change," I say.

"You should go upstairs. First door on the right. You can't miss it."

"It's o—"

"Just go. Coach won't mind. Promise."

She stands before me, clearly unwilling to let me past. Not that a five-foot-nothing woman will stop me from going anywhere I really want to go. But I concede. My swim shorts are damp and I'm more than ready to get out of them.

"Okay." I spin away from her and take the stairs two at a time.

The voices from the kitchen fade as I turn the corner, my eyes locked on the first door on the right.

Everything is silent up here. Confident that I'm about to find the bathroom empty, I reach for the handle and swing the door open.

I already have a foot inside the room before reality hits me.

This isn't a bathroom.

And it isn't empty.

"Shit," I mutter, my eyes locked on Casey holding a towel to cover the best bits of her naked body.

"Kodie?" she asks, her eyes wide and much more alert than her best friend's.

That's when it hits me.

"P-Parker said," I stutter like a moron.

"Close the door," she whispers, her eyes holding mine as she continues to clutch the towel to her chest.

My heart thumps against my ribs as my grip on my bag tightens.

"Casey," I breathe, my head and my body at war.

My head screams at me to walk out and find an actual bathroom. But my body...fuck, my body. It's hers. Every goddamn inch of it.

I move without instruction from my brain and the door clicks closed behind me a beat before my bag hits the floor.

Her towel is next to go, fluttering to the carpet and revealing her beautiful body beneath.

"Fuck," I grunt, taking in her full breasts, peaked nipples, slim waist, and rounded hips.

Her chest heaves, her lips slightly parted as she fights to catch her breath.

"Kodie, please."

"Jesus, Casey. What the fuck are you doing to me?"

In a heartbeat, I'm across the room. I have her tempting body in my arms and her lips on mine.

She groans into our kiss, and my already hard dick swells until it hurts.

Nothing we've done so far has come anywhere close to getting this woman out from under my skin.

My fingers twist in her wet hair and I drag her head back, positioning her exactly where I want her as my tongue sweeps into her mouth, tasting her, claiming her.

Her hands slide down my back, making me shudder with need before they slip beneath the fabric of my shorts.

"Casey," I groan as her palms slide around to the front of my body. "Fucking hell."

I pull back as she wraps a hand around my cock and squeezes with just the right amount of pressure.

My head rests against hers as I take a moment to appreciate just how fucking incredible she is.

There was something about her from the very first moment I crashed into her outside the restrooms that night. Nothing that has happened since has dampened it. If anything, since knowing the truth, my need for her has only grown.

"We shouldn't be doing this," I state, a little rational thought slipping in.

"Is it going to stop you?" she asks, her green eyes begging me to keep going.

It should. It should be enough to stop me.

Her father, my entire team, my daughter, are downstairs.

But despite knowing that, there is nothing that could drag me away from getting what I need right now.

Dropping my hands to her waist, I effortlessly lift her feet from the floor before placing her on the edge of her desk.

A groan rumbles in my throat as her hand slips away from me, but I swallow it down. It'll be worth it.

"Spread your legs. Show me."

She swallows thickly before doing exactly as she's told.

"Good girl," I praise, my eyes holding hers for a few more seconds before they drop to her pussy. "So fucking pretty."

Reaching out, I drag two fingers through her wetness.

"Oh my god, Kodie," she moans, her head falling back as her hips jump from the desk.

"So fucking wet for me. Have you been walking around like this all day?"

"Yes," she confesses, spreading her legs wider in the hope of getting more.

"What do you need?"

"You, Kodie. I need you," she demands impatiently.

"Gonna need more than that," I tell her, slowly circling her clit.

"Shit," she gasps. "I need...I need you inside me. Last night... all I wanted was you stretching me open."

"Just last night?" I tease.

"Every night. Right now. Always. Kodie, please."

"Jesus, Trouble," I grunt before pushing two fingers inside her.

My teeth clench as she clamps down on me.

"Fuck, you're so fucking tight," I groan, my cock weeping to push inside her and feel her strangling me.

"Yes, Kodie. Yes. Fuck."

Leaning over her, I claim her lips again in a filthy kiss. There is no finesse. We're all tongues and teeth, but we don't care.

"Kodie. Oh my god," she pants as I kiss down her throat and across her chest.

As I continue to finger-fuck her, she arches her back, thrusting her tits closer.

Fucking perfect.

Wrapping my lips around one of her perfectly pink nipples, I suck her into my mouth.

She cries out, louder than before, and I quickly reach up to cover her mouth.

I don't know how soundproof this house is, and I really don't want to find out.

Alternating between sucking, nipping, and licking at her nipples, I curl my fingers, finding the spot that's going to make her shatter.

She moans behind my hand, her cheeks and chest getting redder and redder as she edges closer to her release.

Her body trembles. "Are you going to come for me, Casey?"

She nods, mumbling *yes* into my palm.

"Good girl. I want you to come all over my fingers. Then, I'm going to fill you up. I'm going to stretch this pretty pussy with my cock, and I'm going to take you right here in your bedroom with everyone else downstairs."

Her pussy tightens around me.

"Who owns this pussy, Trouble?"

"You," she mumbles, making me regret covering her mouth. I need to hear that it's mine like I need my next breath.

But I can't risk it.

If someone were to hear us...

"Me?" I ask, and she nods frantically.

"You're not going to leave this room until your pussy is dripping with my cum." She trembles violently as her orgasm hits. "No one else will know. But we will. We'll know you're mine.

That's it, baby," I praise as she rides out her release. "Fuck, I can't wait to push inside this pussy. It's all I can fucking think about."

Once I'm confident she's not going to scream, I let my hand slip from her mouth and tug at the ties around my waist.

"Oh my god," she whimpers as I slowly pull my fingers from her body.

They glisten beautifully with the light of the sunset that's streaming through the windows.

Her eyes are wide as I move them to my mouth and taste her as I shove my shorts down, letting them drop to my ankles.

As I pull my fingers from my mouth, her eyes roll down my body until they lock on my dick.

She licks her lips, and it jerks as I picture her on her knees for me.

Such a fucking beautiful sight.

But it's not happening right now.

We have limited time, and I need to be inside her.

Stepping closer, I spread her thighs wider before dragging my dick through her juices, coating myself in her.

"Kodie," she gasps, watching where we're about to be joined.

"You're going to need to be quiet," I remind her.

She nods. "Please. I can be whatever you want me to be."

A smile pulls at my lips, and somehow, I manage to swallow the words that want to spill free.

You're everything.

Holding myself at the base, I push just inside her.

My teeth grind as the sensation overwhelms me.

I can barely control myself.

Thankfully, it seems that I'm not the only one.

"Fuck me, Kodie. Please. Fuck me."

38

———

CASEY

"**F**uck. Fuck. Fuck," I chant as Kodie's hips thrust forward, his dick stretching me in the most mind-blowing way.

His teeth grind, making his jaw pop as he gazes at me with dark, hungry eyes.

One hand is locked around my hip, the other wrapped around my throat, his fingers tightening in warning.

"Quiet," he growls. The depth of his voice sends tingles racing through my body.

I nod, clamping my lips shut.

There isn't a chance of me doing anything that will put a stop to this.

I don't know why he's here. I don't know how he found me. But I don't care.

He's here, and that's the only thing that matters.

I groan when he circles his hips, his cock buried deep inside me.

"Fuck, this pussy," he mutters as he slowly pulls out and slides back in. "Fucking heaven."

"Yours," I say again, wanting to see his eyes flash with possession like last time.

His grip on me tightens, sending fire shooting toward my pussy.

275

"Oh god. Kodie."

The second his name rolls off my tongue, his control snaps.

His hips thrust forward with such force, the desk beneath us shifts, colliding with the wall.

"Shit. Kodie," I gasp as I grip his shoulders harder to hold on.

He's like a man possessed.

My heels dig into the top of his ass, attempting to pull him even deeper. I don't think it's possible, but I'm happy to try.

I need every single part of this man I can get.

"Yes. Oh god. Fuck," I gasp as he continues his relentless thrusts.

I'm louder than I should be, but with the desk banging back against the wall, I'm not sure it matters.

Heat rises between my legs as my release builds.

"Casey," he groans before leaning over me and stealing my lips.

His kiss is wild and messy. It's everything.

"Come for me," he demands before shifting his hold on my hip and pressing his thumb against my clit.

I cry out as his fingers squeeze my throat tighter, cutting off my air.

I'm flying.

Fucking soaring.

"Come all over my dick, Casey. Show me how much of a whore you are for me."

His words are fucking kryptonite, and I shatter.

I lose all sense of my surroundings—of any words or noises coming from my mouth. The only thing I'm aware of is him as he swells even bigger inside me before his own orgasm claims him, and he drops his head to my shoulder.

Wave after wave rolls through me, and he works me through every single one until I'm a trembling, sweaty mess.

His lips move against my damp skin, and I swear his tongue sneaks out, licking me.

I shudder as he softens.

My muscles clamp, desperate to keep him inside me, to make our connection last a little longer.

It's pointless. He might still be touching me, be inside me, but I can already feel him pulling away.

He releases a long breath, and the warm air rushes over my chest, making my nipples harden again.

But as much as I might crave round two, I already know it isn't going to happen.

Hell, round one probably shouldn't have happened.

We're in my dad's house.

Everyone is downstairs.

His teammates. His coach.

Fuck. His daughter.

Regret slams into me.

What the fuck were we thinking?

"Kodie, I'm s—" My words shrivel and die on my lips as he stands to full height, his eyes focused on my pussy.

His jaw clenches so tight, I'm sure he's about to crack a tooth. His chest heaves, his muscles pulled tight.

He's freaking out.

He—

Fuck. We didn't use a condom.

"K-Kodie," I stutter, closing my legs to hide the evidence of what we just did.

"No," he growls, his giant hands gripping over my knees to keep me spread for him.

My breath catches at the dark, possessive look in his eyes.

He's freaking out, but it's about more than what we just did.

"It's okay. I've got an IUD, and I'm clean. I swear to you."

He swallows thickly, not saying a word as he reaches forward, drags two fingers through our combined release, and pushes them inside.

"Kodie, fuck," I gasp.

It takes him a few seconds to react, but eventually, he looks up, his eyes locking on mine.

"You look fucking incredible with my cum running out of you, Trouble."

All the air rushes from my lungs.

"I've never..." He lifts his free hand to comb his wild curls back, conflicting thoughts warring behind his eyes. "Fuck. We shouldn't have done that."

"It'll be okay. Even if it weren't safe, I'd never—"

He silences me with a kiss. It's just as heated and as reckless as before and I cling to him, desperate to keep him to myself for a little bit longer.

"I've got to go," he finally says, our lips still connected.

"I know," I say softly, fighting the emotion that crawls up my throat.

"This was...you are...fuck, Casey." His soft, confused chuckle fills the air. "You're driving me fucking crazy."

"I'm sorry."

"No. Don't be sorry. I don't think it's a bad kind of crazy."

"Oh."

He pulls back and looks me dead in the eyes.

"I don't know what's going on here, but..." My breath catches. "But I'm not sure I can stop."

"Kodie, I—"

His fingers press against my lips.

"Don't," he warns. "There's every chance I'll never leave this room if you say anything like I think you're going to." I nod in understanding. "I'm gonna go. I'm gonna take Sutton home and..." He shakes his head, a small smile playing on his lips. "Hell, I'm probably going to go home and freak out," he confesses. "But this. Fuck, Casey. This," he says, cupping my cheek tenderly.

"This what?" I whisper, desperate to hear the end of that sentence.

"This...you...it's not enough. I don't think it'll ever be enough."

My heart soars at his words, but they're not enough to stop the chills when he steps back and finally allows me to close my legs.

I sit on my desk in a puddle of our cum, watching as he dresses.

The room is silent, aside from our heavy breathing.

There is so much I want to say, but I can't.

He's right. He needs to get his daughter and go home.

It's Sunday night. She has school tomorrow.

He's a father. He can't be wild and reckless like this.

He has responsibilities.

Once he's dressed, he stands to full height and studies me.

"Casey, this was—"

"Don't," I whisper. I don't know if he's about to say something good or bad, but I can't deal with either right now.

He nods and moves across the room.

The second the door closes, all the air rushes from my lungs, and I slip off the desk, collapsing on the floor in a sated, exhausted mess.

"Oh my god," I breathe, staring into the room as the last few minutes of my life float around in my head.

I was dreaming, right?

That was a fantasy.

But it felt so real.

"This...you...it's not enough. I don't think it'll ever be enough."

God. Kodie Rivers didn't really say that to me, did he?

It's too good to be true. There is no way this is real.

Time passes as I sit there on the floor, reliving everything that happened. I can't bring myself to move. If I do, I'm admitting that it's over. And if I step back into the shower and wash his scent from my body, I'm effectively erasing the evidence. And I want it. I want him.

"Oh shit," I gasp when footsteps approach my door a beat before the handle rattles and it opens. "Wait," I cry, desperate to stop whoever it is.

I shift on the floor, attempting to cover up as much of myself as I can, but it's pointless. Anyone would know exactly what just happened in here with one look.

I breathe a sigh of relief when a head pokes around the corner and I find my best friend smiling at me with wicked intent sparkling in her eyes.

"You're welcome," she sings before collecting my abandoned towel from the floor and handing it over.

"Thank you," I whisper.

"Damn right. Tell me I didn't just win the best friend of the year award."

"Parker," I sigh.

"Oh, come off it. You can't tell me that Kodie Rivers didn't just come up here and fuck your brains out. It's written all over your face."

"Christ," I mutter as I wrap my towel around myself.

Parker squeals. "You've got that glow."

"What glow?"

"You know, that after amazing sex glow. Man, I'm so jealous right now."

"I just got fucked by one of Dad's players in his own house. In my childhood bedroom."

"In the childhood bedroom where you used to hide posters of said player and fantasize about him. How fucking hot is that?"

"How disrespectful," I counter, cringing at my own actions.

I am the worst daughter in the world.

Dad has asked only one thing of me. Don't get involved with his players.

And look at me.

I'm a disgrace.

"Okay, sure. If you look at it that way, then—"

"Parker," I snap.

"Casey, you're a grown-up now, and there is something between the two of you. It's electric."

"It's wrong."

Parker lowers her ass to my bed and rests back on her palms.

"Look, I know it's cliché and whatever, but...what if he's the one, Case? What if all of this is one big love story that'll have a happy ending?"

"And what if it has disaster written all over it?" I counter.

She raises a brow, a smirk twitching at her lips. "Life is unpredictable, Case. You've got to take every opportunity when it arises in case you never get the chance again."

—

By the time I showered and found the courage to go back downstairs, most people had left. Not that I cared about most people. There were only two I was interested in.

The house was tidy, but funnily enough the backyard looked like a hockey team had barrelled through it, so Parker, Freya, and I, along with Dad and Freya's parents, embarked on the job of putting it back together again.

By the time we were done, the sun had long set and the temperature had dropped.

Dad offered to make more food and drinks, but all I wanted to do was lock myself in my apartment and obsess over everything that happened today.

Pathetic? Maybe. But I don't care.

I'm living out my ultimate teenage girl fantasy, and I'm more than happy to drown in memories of experiencing what it's like to be touched, kissed, and fucked by Kodie Rivers.

I don't bother putting any lights on in my apartment. Instead, I make my way through to my bedroom and change into my pajamas.

With my cell in my hand, I crawl into bed and get comfortable.

Hope swells within me that I'll wake it up and find notifications to say he's messaged.

But the second it lights up, I find emails and messages from everyone but him.

I quickly reply to Dad to let him know I'm home safe and send a gif in reply to Parker before going through everything else.

But he's not there. He hasn't reached out.

A lump climbs into my throat as I think about his words being nothing but post-sex bullshit.

He won't be the first man to say things he doesn't really mean while riding out an orgasm, and I'm sure he won't be the last. But staring at the evidence that he clearly hasn't thought about me since stings.

Maybe it was a one-off.

He's had his fill today, and that's all he needed.

Forcing myself to put my cell down, I slip lower in my bed and curl up on my side.

He's just doing the right thing, Casey.

No matter how much you might want him, he's not yours to take.

39

KODIE

We have two days before we get on a flight for our first road games of the season.

We won't be back for two weeks.

My heart aches just thinking about the time away from my girl.

I hate leaving her, but there's no other option.

She spins back around on the playground and waves, a beaming smile on her face.

I wave back, but my smile is nowhere near as genuine as hers.

It's the same at the beginning of every season. It's like I'm being ripped in two.

Sutton is my life. So is hockey.

This is how it needs to be.

I sit there long after she's disappeared into her classroom, my thoughts running at a mile a minute. Just like they were last night.

I've barely slept, and I have no doubt it's going to affect my performance today.

The guilt I've been battling to keep down threatens to explode.

Not only did I disrespect Coach last night, but I'm going to disappoint him today as well.

I'm a fucking embarrassment.

I fucked his daughter under his own roof.

The need to confess my sins burns through me.

But what good will it do?

I'll find myself traded before I've even left his office.

He won't want me around if he knows the kinds of thoughts I'm having about his little girl.

My stomach turns over. The thought of Sutton having to deal with men—players—in her future makes me want to give it all up and move to the middle of nowhere so it can be just the two of us.

I never really thought about how players treat the bunnies at the beginning of my career, when I was living the high life and fucking as many as I could. It was a part of the job. Work hard, play harder, and have the fucking stories plastered all over the internet. But then Sutton came along, and I took a good hard look at reality.

And I really didn't like what I saw.

Closing my eyes, I rest my head back and take a breath.

I need to get to the arena. Cromwell, one of our PTs, is waiting on me.

You took her bare, you fucking idiot, a little voice pops up as I continue to sit there.

It's been a constant in my head since the moment I realized.

It was so fucking stupid. A risk I should not be taking.

My life is already hard enough. I don't need to be adding anything else to it.

Sure, Casey assured me that if she wasn't already on birth control, she would have dealt with it. But...would she?

I might have fucked her a handful of times now, but I don't know her. Not really. And saying things like that in the moment are very different from the reality of having to actually do it.

"Fuck's sake," I mutter before starting the engine again and finally pulling out of the space.

A laugh erupts from me as I think back to only a few weeks ago, when I told myself I was going into this season with a clear head and focus.

Wishful thinking at its finest.

How was I to know a woman in a green dress would crash into me and turn my life upside down?

"Whoa, you look like shit," Linc says when I join him in the gym after PT.

"Thanks," I mutter.

"Thought you'd have slept like a baby after all the fun and games yesterday."

Refusing to let his words affect me, I climb onto the bike beside him and start moving to expel some of the pent-up energy surging through my veins.

"What's wrong? Cromwell poke all your sore spots?" he asks, glancing back at the door to the PT office.

"Something like that," I mutter, putting my ear buds in and drowning him out.

I want to say it helps, but it doesn't. Without his constant voice, my mind wanders back to her. To last night. To watching my cum run out of her pussy.

Mine.

My jaw tightens, and my grip on the handlebars becomes painful.

Fuck.

Squeezing my eyes closed, I refuse to let the vivid images of her distract me. Instead, I make them fuel me.

My legs pump harder and harder, my heart pounding as I fight to drag in the air I need. Sweat pours from me, soaking my shirt, but I don't stop. I can't. If Linc notices, he doesn't say anything. Or at least, not loud enough for me to hear over my music.

Eventually, though, I run out of steam. My legs slow and I lean forward, resting my head on my arms as I suck in breath after breath.

I have no idea how long I stay there—although it's not fucking long enough—before a hand clamps down on my shoulder, scaring the ever-loving shit out of me.

I glance up and find Linc standing beside me with a deep frown.

"Let's go shower and eat," he says simply before stalking off.

Unable to argue, I follow on shaky legs.

The rest of the guys are in here working out, but most of them are too lost in their own heads themselves to notice us.

Fletch and Handsy do, though, and not two minutes after I've hit the shower do I hear them join us in the dressing room.

"Fuck's sake," I mutter under my breath. I know where this is going.

They keep the conversation light and focused on hockey as we clean up and dress. But the second we're sitting down with food in front of us, they change tack.

"What's going on, Rivers?" Linc asks, his eyes boring into mine.

I shrug one shoulder and drop my gaze to my plate.

I've played hockey all my life, been surrounded by teammates, some of which I've been closer to than others, but never have any of them actively sat me down to discuss feelings and shit.

Even when I discovered I was going to be a father and all the fucking bullshit that followed, everyone mostly just left me to do my thing. Hockey was my solace then. Being at the arena, on the ice, was the only time I was able to push reality aside.

Despite what's going on right now being less life-changing than becoming a parent, I'm struggling to find any relief from it. Casey...she's in my head twenty-four-fucking-seven. It doesn't matter how hard I push, how fast I skate; she's always there. Taunting me. Tempting me. Reminding me what a fucking awful human being I am.

I've disrespected the one man I admire more than any other.

James Watson is a hockey god. A fucking legend.

And I've done the one thing he asks us not to.

I've touched his daughter.

No, it's worse than that. I haven't just touched her, I've—

"Come on, man. We're worried about you." Fletch's words rattle around in my head, banishing my previous thoughts.

I've never had teammates who care like this. I've never had them fighting this hard to be my friends, despite having my walls built so high they're impossible to scale.

"It's a girl, isn't it?" Handsy says with a knowing smirk.

"Yeah," I confess. "It is. I've spent all fucking summer with Sutton, and we're about to leave for a two-week stretch. I fucking hate it."

"That's tough, man," Handsy says, although considering he's chronically single, I'm not sure he really stands a chance of empathizing.

"I get it," Fletch says. He's the closest here to understanding, seeing as he leaves his wife behind almost every time we go. Sure, she flies out to join us for some games, but she's got a job and a life here. I can't help but wonder if it's why they don't have kids yet. Leaving is really fucking hard. "It fucking sucks, man."

"Yeah," I muse, spearing a carrot with my fork and pushing it into my mouth.

Linc remains quiet, his eyes still on me, I fear looking for a lie.

He won't find one. Leaving Sutton is a huge part of my issue right now. It's just not all of it.

"Is she coming to any of our road games?" Handsy asks, forcing me to look over at him.

I shake my head. "She's desperate to come to Boston, but it's too far. She's got school and her own team to think about."

"We need to go to one of her games," Fletch announces.

I can't help but laugh at the image of them all in the stands, watching Sutton and her team chase the puck around. It's not the kind of game they're used to.

"Yeah, we should," Linc agrees.

"You can't go just to hit on the moms, moron," Handsy mutters as he reaches out and slaps Linc upside the head.

"That's not what I meant. The girls' and women's leagues are growing. We should show our support."

We stare at him, seeing right through his bullshit.

"And if there just so happens to be a hot hockey mom, then..."

"Fucking hell," Fletch mutters.

Fletch is right, though; we should go. Sutton would love that.

"We should surprise her," Linc adds before pulling his cell out. "When's her next game?"

My heart swells to the point it hurts. They're right. She would love it if they turned up to support her.

Sliding my own cell from my pocket, I pull up her game schedule and make a plan with the guys. It's not fucking easy. With our own games and training, we don't have a lot of time to play with.

"That's perfect," Fletch says as we finally agree on a Sunday game later in the season. "I'll see if any of the others want to come. We can take her out to celebrate her win after."

"I like your confidence," Linc teases.

"Hell yeah, she's a Rivers," I agree.

"Are we inviting any of her friends to join us? Maybe those with single moms."

Laughter erupts at our table, earning a few curious glances from the others around us.

Vipers staff litter the arena restaurant, but Casey isn't here. I can't decide if I'm disappointed or relieved that I don't have to try to act normal while she sits only a few feet away.

We might work for the same franchise, but thankfully, our paths hardly ever cross. I'm more likely to see her when she comes down to visit her dad. If I'm up in the offices, it means I'm doing PR, and I try to avoid that as much as possible. The less I'm in the spotlight, the more chance Sutton has at a normal life. It's wishful thinking, but I try my best.

Thankfully the conversation soon turns to our upcoming games. I want to say it's enough to distract me, but it's not.

My cell burns a hole in my pocket, just like it has done from the moment I left her.

I wanted to message her. I was fucking desperate to. But I stopped myself.

What the hell would I even say?

I can't apologize again.

I already said more than I should have. I told her way too many truths that I can't take back.

"Oh shit," Handsy teases as Coach walks in with a stern expression on his face. "Someone is in for a kicking."

My heart jumps into my throat as I watch James Watson march through the restaurant like a man on a mission.

I swear, I don't breathe, convinced he's about to come over here and announce to the entire restaurant that my time as a Viper is over.

But he doesn't, and I have to fight not to let the relief show on my face. Instead, he turns toward a table of medical staff and begins talking animatedly with our team doctor.

"Ohhh, someone is getting benched," Linc sings like an asshole.

Fletch immediately begins chastising him, but my attention is dragged away from them when a familiar body appears at the entrance, her eyes scanning the room for someone.

I wait frozen, my heart racing, to see if her eyes will find mine.

But they don't. Instead, they lock on someone else, and she races excitedly through the room to get to him.

I sink in my chair, disappointment pulling at my muscles.

I want her to run to me like that.

Coach notices her a beat before Casey bounces up to the table. She says something, and his face instantly lights up. His arms open, and she falls into the embrace.

"Oh shit. Looks like someone got some good news," Handsy says, watching the same scene play out.

My teeth grind as jealousy drips through my veins.

"I'll see you guys back downstairs," I mutter before shoving my chair back and marching toward the exit.

40

CASEY

"I did it. I got the job," I whisper excitedly to Dad, aware that I've just totally interrupted his conversation with Eddie Phillips, the team doctor.

Dropping whatever they were discussing, Dad turns to me with a wide smile on his face.

"Of course you did, Care Bear. I didn't doubt it for a second."

Internally, I squeal in excitement.

I thought I was going to throw up when the number came up on my cell. I was already enough of a mess after a fitful night's sleep full of dirty thoughts about a certain player.

Emotionally, I'm beyond fragile right now. If they turned me down, I'm pretty sure I'd have spent the day sobbing in the bathroom.

I should have just messaged him. An answer about where his head is would have been easier than all the what-ifs.

Doesn't mean I did, though.

Where's the woman from the masquerade ball? The woman who took the bull by the horns and went after what she wanted?

She's hiding scared, that's where she is.

She had a taste of what she wanted, and now she's afraid to put her head above the parapet in case it gets shot off.

What am I talking about? Of course it's going to get shot off.

That night, all I wanted was a few hours.

Now?

I want everything.

Damn him.

Kodie Rivers has always had the power to turn me into a crazy woman.

Well, here she is.

"I'm so proud of you," Dad says, releasing me from his embrace, but I'm only half paying attention. Movement on the other side of the restaurant catches my eye, and I glance over to find Kodie storming toward the exit. His shoulders are slumped, his head down. He looks defeated.

My heart slams against my ribs, my previous excitement draining out of me.

Every single one of my instincts screams for me to chase after him.

But I can't.

And now, it's not just because he's one of my father's players, but I'm one of his daughter's coaches. Everything has just got even more complicated.

"Thanks, Dad," I muse, turning my attention back to him. "I'm so sorry, I totally interrupted."

"It's okay," he assures me. "Dinner tonight to celebrate?"

"Sounds great. Let me know when you'll be finished," I say, stretching up on my toes to kiss his cheek before spinning around and marching in the direction Kodie disappeared in.

The second I'm around the corner, I pick up speed, hoping to catch up to him.

Heavy footsteps echo down the hallway, letting me know I'm close. "Kodie, wait," I whisper-hiss, desperate to stop him but also terrified someone will hear.

Thankfully, as I turn the next corner, I find that he's stopped. But I quickly discover it isn't for me; instead, he's staring down at his cell.

I slow my pace as he swipes the screen and lifts it to his ear.

"Yes, this is him. Is everything okay?" He asks in a rush, fear lacing his voice. My heart jumps into my throat.

I may not know Kodie all that well, but there's only one person on the planet who could make him react like that.

Sutton.

"Okay, good. No, no. I'm glad you called me." He pauses, listening before huffing out a laugh. "Of course she did. Okay, if anything changes, call me. If I don't answer, call the arena. Someone will get me." He nods despite the person not being able to see him. "Okay, thank you. Bye."

He takes a step back, colliding with the wall.

"Shit," he hisses, combing his fingers through his hair.

"I-is everything okay?" I ask quietly as I continue my approach.

He startles despite my soft voice, and I cringe.

"Sorry, I didn't mean to...I wasn't eavesdropping, I promise. I was just—"

"It's okay," he says, cutting off my rambling.

"Are you sure? Is Sutton okay?"

He lets out a laugh as he rubs the back of his neck.

"Yeah. She got into a fight with a kid at school."

"A fight?" I balk.

"Adrian Scott," he mutters through clenched teeth. "Ever heard of Theodore Scott?"

I think for a moment. "AHL?" I ask making Kodie's brows shoot up. "Injured before he was called up to the NHL. Wait... wasn't he on your rival team at college?"

Kodie stares at me with an open mouth.

"H-how do you know that?"

I shrug, my cheeks burning. "Stalker, remember?"

"*I* barely remember some of the guys I played with at college."

My blush quickly spreads down my neck. Why the hell did I say that?

He drags his hand down his face, getting over his shock.

"But yeah, Adrian is his kid. He and Sutton...they don't get on."

I can't help but chuckle as memories from my own childhood

come back to me. "Adrian probably feels like he has something to prove."

"Yeah, like how to not be an asshole like his father. He isn't doing a very good job."

"I may have only met Sutton a couple of times, but something tells me that she can hold her own."

"And that would be why school just called me to say she has a bump on the head but is refusing point-blank to allow them to pull me out of practice to collect her."

"Shit, is she okay? I can go and—'

"She's fine," he interrupts before I can offer my services. I don't know what I'm doing. I have a job I should be doing; I don't have time to play babysitter to Kodie's possibly concussed daughter. But also, if he needed me to, I'd look after her in a heartbeat. "I'm sure her teammates hit her harder than Adrian ever could."

I snort a laugh.

"Sutton is awesome. She's a real credit to you."

Kodie's breath catches. "Thank you. We're both just...trying our best."

"Is everything okay? Back there, you looked a little—"

"Everything's fine. Just the season starting, a stretch of road games. You know how it is."

"Yeah," I muse, searching for the lie.

"I should get back. Tomlinson will be on my ass if I'm late for training," he says, referring to his offensive coach.

"Yeah, me too."

His eyes bounce between mine before dropping to my mouth.

Without instruction from my brain, my tongue sneaks out and wets my bottom lip.

Desire pools between my thighs as I think of all the things he can do with his mouth.

"Kodie?" I blurt as he takes a step back.

"Yeah?" he rasps, his voice deeper than it was a few moments ago.

"Are we...is everything okay after..." I kick myself the second the words pass my lips. I sound like a needy girlfriend, and I hate it. I'm just...low-key freaking out, and I need to know there's still hope here. Maybe not for a relationship or anything serious, but for something. Anything.

I'm not ready to say goodbye to Kodie Rivers yet. Nowhere fucking close.

"I really need to go," he says, turning around and walking away.

"Fuck," I breathe the second he's out of earshot.

Could I have fucked that up any more?

"You're starting tomorrow night?" Parker asks from the other end of my couch. There's a giant meat feast pizza between us and bottles of beer on the coffee table.

"Yep," I confirm as I reach for another slice.

Last night, Dad took me to my favorite Italian restaurant to celebrate my new position, and tonight Parker wanted her turn. Only, I point-blank refused to go out again. I wanted a night in with fast food and beer. Parker pouted for all of two minutes before she agreed. She turned up less than thirty minutes later, already wearing her pajamas for a night in.

"They want me to find my footing before their current assistant coach leaves."

"Fair enough. Case, I'm so buzzed for you. Those little girls are going to freaking love you." I don't realize I react to her comment, but she must read something on my face. "What's wrong?"

I let out a breath. "You do realize Kodie's daughter plays on the team I'm going to be coaching, right?" Her mouth opens and closes as she processes.

"I think I knew that. I just...fucking hell, Case. Could you possibly make this any more complicated?" I shrug. "Does he know?"

I shake my head. "I should have told him. He deserves to know. But—"

"Casey," Parker warns.

"I know. I know. I spoke to him yesterday, but he was so...off. He'd just had a call from the school about Sutton being in a fight, and he said he was stressed with the season starting. But it seemed like more."

"Because you're a Kodie Rivers expert?" Parker asks, quirking a brow.

"More than you are," I mutter under my breath.

"They leave tomorrow morning?" she asks, changing the subject.

"Yep."

"For two weeks?"

"Uh-huh."

"Are you going to message him? Remind him of everything he's missing back home?"

"Parker," I groan.

"What? You know you want to."

"Yeah but—" I slam my lips shut.

"But?"

"But he hasn't messaged since Saturday night. He got his fill. What if he's done?"

"Casey, that man is nowhere near done with you. He's just freaking out. He doesn't want to want you, but he does."

"That's not helpful."

"Why isn't it? Right now, you're doing exactly what he wants you to do. You're being distant and allowing him to think you're not interested. He's probably thinking the exact same thing you are of him. He's probably at home right now, assuming that you've had your fill."

"I haven't," I cry.

"You know that. I know that. But does Kodie?"

I mean, I'd like to hope so, considering how hot we are together. But then again, I did tell him that I only do one-nightstands. I promised him that I'm not a bunny who wants to trap him into something.

"Message him," she encourages. "Let him know you're going to miss him. Tell him you'll be at the other end of the phone should he need to celebrate or commiserate while he's away."

"He'll share a room with one of the guys. I doubt that'll be—'

"If he wants to sext you, he'll find a way, Casey. He just needs to know it's an option."

"I don't know."

"I do," she says, reaching out and snatching my cell before I have a chance to stop her.

"Parker, what the hell are you doing?" I shriek as she begins typing.

The second I lunge for her; she hops off the couch and skips to the other side of the room.

"There. Done. You can thank me later."

41

KODIE

"Who is that?" Sutton asks, peeking over my shoulder.

"No one," I snap before putting my cell to sleep and placing it screen down on the counter. "How's your head?"

"Daddy, it's fine," she sighs. "I barely even hit it. Miss White was totally overreacting. I'm so annoyed they called you."

Folding her little arms over her chest, she rolls her eyes, looking the epitome of a drama queen.

"Peanut, you hit your head. They have to call; it's their job."

She shakes her head, her eyes going again. "It's just ridiculous. I take harder hits on the ice right in front of you. No one goes crying to you then."

"You have a helmet on," I counter.

"Oh yeah, because that stops it from hurting," she deadpans.

I mean, she's got a point.

"Sutton," I sigh.

"Sorry, Daddy," she says with the sweetest smile. "But I promise, I'm okay. Hopefully, Adrian has a nice bruise forming though."

"Oh my god," I mutter, dragging my hand down my face.

"He deserved it. He was being mean."

"That doesn't mean you should be fighting, Sutton."

"If I were a boy, I'd have waited until we were on the ice," she informs me. "Every time I look at him, I picture slamming him into the boards."

I just about manage to smother my laugh.

I'm raising a savage.

If they ever have the opportunity to play a game against each other, it's going to be a bloodbath.

"Remember, Sutton, a good sportsperson—"

"I know, I know," she says, interrupting me. "I promise I'll do my best not to let it happen again."

I stare at her, unable to do anything but accept that.

"Just focus on being better than him. Don't stoop to his level."

"You got it, Daddy," she says, smiling up at me, her eyes glinting wickedly.

There is no way this is the end of this rivalry. Something tells me that it's going to haunt us for years.

Getting Sutton away from Adrian and his family would probably be the only benefit to me getting traded if Coach finds out about everything. The only problem is that no matter where we are, there will always be Adrians. Sutton will always be a girl in what is predominantly a male sport. It's getting better, but there is still a long way to go for female hockey players to get the recognition they deserve.

"Go and get ready for bed, Peanut," I say, watching as she skips out of the room.

Once she's out of sight, I drop my head into my heads and suck in a few calming breaths.

Parenting is really fucking hard.

Picking up my cell, I look at Casey's message again. My heart swells at her concern about Sutton.

I'm about to respond when, "Daddy," echoes down to me. "I can't find Vincent."

With a huff, I put my cell in my pocket and go in search of her bear.

I find him abandoned on the couch where we were watching

ESPN earlier, and after tucking him under my shirt, I head up to see her.

"Did you find him?" I ask.

"No," she mumbles around her toothbrush.

"Damn," I muse, my eyes taking in her green and white bedroom.

She may have supported me at my old team, but she wasn't all in like this. One of her conditions for moving to LA was that she wanted a Vipers bedroom. Obviously, I agreed, and no sooner had I secured the house than I instructed a designer and decorators to make her dream come true.

One wall is covered in lockers, which she uses for her clothes, instead of drawers. There's a huge Vipers logo on the opposite wall and two jerseys in frames above her bed. One is mine, and one is hers. Every time I look at them, I swear my heart will explode.

She runs the faucet, finishing up before her light footsteps move in my direction.

"We need to find him, Daddy. I can't sleep without—" Her words cut off and a smile pulls at her lips when she rounds the corner and finds me standing there with a bear-shaped lump under my T-shirt. "Daddy," she laughs.

"What?" I ask innocently as she reaches for her beloved bear and wraps him in her arms, hugging him tightly. "Into bed, Peanut."

She does as she's told, and I perch myself on the edge and read her story. Mom and I spend hours searching for books for her. Most girls want princesses and unicorn books, but my daughter is all about sports. We've found some good ones, but we read through them faster than the authors can write them. Sutton keeps talking about writing her own. I have no doubt that'll happen at some point.

I can't help but smile at my daughter's tenacity. Fuck, I love her.

"Sweet dreams, Peanut," I say once we've finished a chapter.

"Night-night, Daddy. Sweet dreams."

Dropping a kiss on her head, I put her book away, turn on her nightlight and quietly walk toward her door.

"I love you. See you in the morning."

"I love you too."

Her words ring in my ears as I make my way down to my own bedroom.

After changing into athletic clothes, I grab my EarPods and make my way to my home gym to burn off some energy.

The whole time I'm working out, my cell taunts me from my pocket.

I should reply to let Casey know that Sutton is okay. But if I do, I'm not going to be able to stop. She's too fucking addictive.

I push myself until my muscles are trembling before staggering back up the stairs to my bedroom so I can shower.

It's been hours since that message came through when I finally fall into bed and open the thread again.

> Kodie Rivers: Sutton is fine; thank you for asking. The hit didn't knock the sass out of her.

My message shows as read immediately, and my heart lurches.

Was she waiting for me?

> Casey Watson: Glad to hear it. Scott Jr is hurting, though, right?

I can't help but laugh. Of course, Casey has the same thoughts as Sutton.

> Kodie Rivers: According to Sutton, his bruise should be glowing by now.

> Casey Watson: Good girl. Can't let these boys win.

> Kodie Rivers: Is that right?

My eyes are glued to my screen, and my pulse increases as I wait for a reply like a teenage boy with a crush.

I'm a grown-ass man; I shouldn't be this excited about receiving a reply from a girl.

No. A woman.

Casey might be younger than me, but that doesn't mean she's not all woman.

God. A groan rumbles deep in my throat as I think about just how much of a woman she really is. Those sinful curves, full tits, perfect pussy.

And now, I'm hard again.

> Casey Watson: Yep. It's important that boys know not to mess with us. It's not their fault that they won't understand our superpower until they're a little older.

> Kodie Rivers: Superpower?

> Casey Watson: Yep. What are you doing right now?

A smirk pulls at my lips.

You want to play, baby?

> Kodie Rivers: Just finished working out. Fresh from the shower and naked in bed. You?

Her response doesn't come as fast this time, and I start to wonder if I've pushed her too hard.

She only messaged to check on Sutton. Maybe she doesn't want to dive headfirst into flirting.

Christ. Could it be any more obvious that I've been out of the game for a long time?

> Casey Watson: Same. Although not the working out part. I was eating pizza and drinking beer with Parker. She wanted me to tell you you're welcome, by the way.

I frown for a moment before realization slams into me.

> Kodie Rivers: Are you naked, too?

Delete.

> Kodie Rivers: What are you wearing?

Delete.

> Kodie Rivers: She played a dangerous game.

> Casey Watson: Worth it, though. No?

My dick jerks just thinking back to last night.

> Casey Watson: I'm still a little sore.

"Fucking hell," I moan. "Don't tell me things like that, baby girl."

> Kodie Rivers: I'm sorry. I lost control a little.

> Casey Watson: NEVER apologize for that. EVER.

> Kodie Rivers: I guess it's a good job I'm away for the next two weeks, then. Give you a rest.

> Casey Watson: I'd rather you weren't...

> Kodie Rivers: Fucking hell, Trouble. What are you doing to me?

> Casey Watson: Hopefully making you hard and desperate...

My groan ripples through the air.

> Kodie Rivers: You have no idea.

Unable to ignore it any longer, I wrap my hand around myself, stroking slowly.

> Casey Watson: It gets me so hot, knowing I'm turning you on.

> Kodie Rivers: Touch yourself. Imagine it's me.

> Kodie Rivers: Tell me exactly what you're doing.

Every time I come with Casey's name on my lips, I crave the next time more than the last.

It's turning into an addiction I'm not sure I'm going to be able to kick.

It doesn't matter that she's not physically with me; I'm fucking dying for her.

The last thing I want to do right now is leave town for two weeks.

Leaving Sutton is always hard. But now, it's not just her I'm leaving.

Fucking hell. Me and Casey. We're not even a thing.

It shouldn't be bothering me that I'm putting hundreds of miles between us, but it is. I'm really un-fucking-happy about it.

Maybe it's for the best.

Time apart might give us both the space to do the right thing.

Instead of seeing her, I'll be spending every day with her dad —the perfect reminder to stay away.

But those thoughts are shattered to smithereens every time I see her name flash up on my phone.

Before I went to sleep last night, I made what might have been the monumental mistake of sending her my phone number. I don't know why it feels like such a big deal. Maybe I'm a bit old-school, but having it feels huge—like we've taken another big step into a place we really shouldn't be.

My cell dings as I say my final goodbye to Sutton at the school gates. I ignore it, focusing on my daughter and fighting my emotions. She's struggling, too, but being the stubborn little girl she is, she fights it and tries to hide it from me.

I both love and hate that she does.

Seeing her fall apart is really fucking hard. But I really wish she didn't feel like she had to be strong all the time. I hate that she'll spend the next two weeks missing me, worrying about me.

She knows to take the media with a pinch of salt, but if

anything comes out about me, whether it be an injury or that I'm not starting for whatever reason, she'll freak out.

I love that hockey is such a huge part of her life, but at times, it's also a curse, because she knows it all. She also knows the risk I put myself in every time I step on the ice.

I don't pull my cell free until she's slipped into her classroom. Then, I welcome the distraction from the pain in my chest.

Trouble: Safe travels today. I hope Sutton is okay x

I blow out a long, slow breath as my eyes linger on that little kiss.

"Fuck."

This woman has got me all tangled up in knots, and something tells me that this road stretch is going to be one of the hardest I've ever experienced.

Kodie: Have a good day. Speak later?

Trouble: Try and stop me

42

CASEY

My hands tremble as I lace up my skates, ready to hit the ice for my first coaching session.

I mean, I'm not expecting to actually do much coaching tonight. I'm just here to see how it all works before I take over.

"Casey, it's good to see you again," Megan, the head coach, says, a soft smile playing on her lips. "Have you met Nancy before?" she asks, gesturing to the woman beside her.

"No, we haven't," I say, offering her a smile.

"Okay, before we start, I thought we could have a quick run-through of the team," Megan explains. "From what you said in your interview, it seems you already have some experience watching them."

My cheeks burn just like when I confessed to my Sunday morning guilty pleasure of hiding in the shadows, watching them.

"Knowing their numbers and chosen positions is only half the job, though. I don't know who the girls are really, and that is just as important."

She smiles at me, and I instantly relax.

This is where I'm meant to be.

I'm inside the arena that I love, helping girls play the sport that has shaped my entire life.

I breathe a sigh of relief and listen as Megan talks through each girl on her roster.

Only ten minutes later, the sound of little girls' chatter hits my ears, and I look up just in time to see the first members of the team walk toward us with their parents trailing behind, mostly with heavy bags.

"Good afternoon," Megan calls. "Get yourselves ready—I've got someone to introduce you to."

Every set of eyes turns to me. I'm not surprised; I'm the obvious new addition.

More girls arrive and get their skates on with the help of their parents. But as I scan the group, I can't help but notice Sutton's absence.

She should be here. She was on Megan's list. And from the way Megan spoke about her, I'd say it's highly likely that she's this team's MVP.

"Okay," Megan says, glancing around, mentally doing a head count.

Her eyes collide with Nancy's, and an unspoken question floats between them.

Kodie only left this morning. He'll be beside himself if something has happened.

Discreetly, I check my cell. Not that I really think he'd call me if there was an issue.

I'm no one. Just the off-limits woman he's fucking behind everyone's backs.

"Before we hit the ice this afternoon, I want to introduce you to—"

"I'm so sorry," Kodie's mom calls as she and Sutton come running toward us.

"No problem. Come and join us," Megan says softly as a frantic Kathleen pulls skates from the bag over her shoulder and drops to her knees.

"It's okay, Gran. Go and sort the car out. I've got this," Sutton says, taking control of the situation.

"Goodness," Kathleen sighs as she drops onto the bench beside her granddaughter.

It takes everything in me not to walk over and give her a hug. I remember all too well how hard it was when Dad used to go for away games. Especially a stretch as long as this one. And for it to be at the beginning of the season as well? It's tough, even for the veterans.

Sutton pauses what she's doing, drops her laces, and turns to her gran. "It's okay, Gran. We made it safely. That's all that matters. You can go."

Oh, my heart.

Kathleen studies her granddaughter for a moment before hopping back up, kissing her cheek, and rushing away again.

My legs move without instruction from my brain, and in less than three seconds, I'm on my knees before Sutton, reaching for her laces.

"Let me help you with that, sweetie," I say softly.

She turns to look at me. I'm sure she's about to tell me that she can do it herself—which I don't doubt—but her stubbornness falters when her eyes land on my face.

"Hey," I say with a smile that's at odds with the guilt twisting me up inside.

I still haven't told Kodie about this.

I should have. I know I should have. But I'm terrified that it'll just give him yet another reason to end this thing between us.

"Hi," she says, her eyes bouncing between mine as she figures this out. "You're our new coach, aren't you?"

My smile grows.

Fuck. I love having that title.

Coach.

"I am. Is that okay?"

Her eyes light up, and I relax a little. "Okay? That's more than okay. Your dad is amazing."

I chuckle.

So is yours, sweetie. So is yours.

"Well, let's hope I'm good too, huh?"

"You'll do great," she assures me as I finish up her skates and stand.

"Everyone, I'd like to introduce you to your new assistant

coach, Casey Watson," Megan says, turning all attention to me again. "Just like you guys, Casey started playing hockey from a very young age, and she won numerous leagues and competitions over the years. You might also recognize her as the daughter of the Vipers head coach, James Watson."

All the girls stare at me with wide, excited eyes.

God, I really hope I'm good at this and can give them the guidance they deserve.

"Hey, everyone," I say, waving awkwardly. "I'm so excited to be working with you. I can't wait to get on the ice and see what you've got."

They all smile and say hello as Megan takes the register and the parents either get settled in to watch the hour session or excuse themselves to run errands.

"Come on then, my little bears," Megan says as she opens the gate and lets them flood onto the ice.

I'm frozen for a moment, struck by a million childhood memories.

I lived for this time on the ice. It was my favorite time of the week. The only thing that topped it was when Dad and I hit the ice together. I fucking loved that. He'd show me everything he knew, helping me work on skills I was struggling with.

Finally, I force my legs to move, and I follow them out. But the second my skate hits the ice, regret slams into me.

I shouldn't have quit when I did.

Playing hockey was my life, and for a while after Mom died, it was my lifeline. But as I got older and the rebellious teenager that lived inside me stood up, my focus turned to other places.

I wanted to hang out with friends, party, and drink.

I wanted to drown the memories of the past. Of Mom taking me to practice and sitting on the sidelines at every single one of my games.

I didn't want to feel the heart-wrenching loss when I stepped off the ice after a defeat and she wasn't there to hug me and tell me I did great.

Everywhere I looked, there was this huge black gaping hole in my life.

It wasn't so bad when I was with friends, doing things I never did with her.

"Right, ladies. Warm-up drills," Megan announces, and off they go. They're like little rockets, so confident and strong. All I can do is stand there in the middle of them, grinning like a fool.

—

"How'd it go?" Parker asks as I drop into the chair opposite her and accept the Cosmopolitan she slides toward me.

"Amazing," I say, barely able to contain my grin.

"I knew you'd smash it."

I take a sip of my drink and reflect on the evening's events.

"The girls are incredible. Coach Megan is awesome as well. It was weird, though, being a part of a girls' team after everything."

For a while after giving up, I didn't even skate. I couldn't; it was too painful.

But eventually, my need to be on the ice came back. I never played again, though. The closest I've got to the game is supporting Dad and the Vipers.

"She'd be so proud of you," Parker says quietly.

Emotion burns the back of my throat, making my nose itch.

I know she would. Even if she'd be disappointed I quit.

"I felt her with me," I confess.

Parker reaches across the table and takes my hand in hers, squeezing in support.

I know it sounds weird, and I'm not sure anyone who hasn't lost someone close to them would understand.

"I kept looking around as if she was watching. It was... comforting. Like she was approving."

"Of course she approves," she says like it's the most obvious thing in the world.

I blow out a breath and drain my cocktail.

I shouldn't. I haven't eaten yet. But I need something to take the edge off.

Tonight was...unexpected in a lot of ways. But at the same time, it felt so right.

And now, we sit here surrounded by Vipers fans waiting for the game to start.

I wanted to go home and watch it in peace, but Parker refused to allow that.

She knew I'd most likely be sulking over the fact I can't be there in person—and she'd be correct—so she insisted we come to our favorite sports bar and watch with everyone else.

"How was Sutton?" Parker asks.

"Her usual Sutton-self," I say with a laugh. "She's so—"

"Much like Kodie?" Parker finishes for me.

"Well, yeah. The confidence of that girl. I pray she never loses it."

"She might just stand a chance, with the right coach."

"She knew who I was straight off the bat," I confess, anxiety twisting my stomach.

"Of course she did. You're a fucking legend, Coach Watson."

Ripping my eyes from her, I stare down at the empty glass before me.

"Do you think she's told him already?"

Parker shifts to look at the TV on the wall opposite. I do the same just in time for the Vipers to be announced.

Fletch bursts onto the ice, quickly followed by Linc and... Kodie.

My eyes lock on him, watching as he skates a lap while the Vipers fans in the crowd shout and scream.

"Nah, she's a good kid. She'll know not to give Kodie mind-blowing news before a game."

"She wouldn't know it's mind-blowing, though, would she?"

I watch as our defense gets into position and Handsy drags his stick along the crease, marking his territory.

"I guess not," I muse as a server comes over with a tray loaded with food.

Chicken wings, fries, and onion rings are lowered to our table before Parker orders more cocktails.

The puck drops, and a loud roar erupts around us as Fletch

takes possession and skates off with a defenseman hot on his heels.

Focusing, I allow myself to get lost in the game as I devour way too many carbs and far too much alcohol for a work night. Thank God for Uber.

I stumble through my front door a few hours and far too many cocktails later, my throat raw from shouting and screaming. The guys played a fucking fantastic game, and Handsy provided us with our first shutout of the season. Fucking epic for game one. Long may it continue.

I grab a bottle of water as I continue toward my bedroom. I need to down this and curl up in bed if I stand any chance of getting to work on time and not being hungover in the morning.

But there's something I need to do before I pass out.

I toe off my sneakers and strip out of my leggings before stepping in front of my full-length mirror. Turning my back to it, I drag my hair over my shoulder so the name across the back is on full show. Then, I pull up the hem of my jersey, twisting the excess fabric in my hand until it's pulled tightly around my waist, showing off my Vipers-green panties.

Opening the camera on my cell, I arch my back and look over my shoulder, directly into the camera, before snapping the picture.

Without overthinking it, I send it to the newest addiction to my contacts, a little thrill shooting through me the second I see it's delivered.

Time to celebrate, baby.

43

———

KODIE

I'm resting back on my bed while Linc fucks about with his hair after what was an incredible first game of the season.

All I want to do is crawl into bed, turn the lights out, and message Casey.

It's only been three days since I touched her. Two days since I saw her and we exchanged filthy messages that left me coming all over my stomach like a horny fucking teenager.

I need more.

I'm like a fucking junkie who needs his next fix.

But I fear that another taste of her won't be enough.

I'm not sure any amount of her will ever be enough.

And that's a fucking problem.

"Are you nearly ready?" I groan.

I get it. He wants to go out tonight and pull a bunny. But he's Lincoln Storm, starting winger for the LA Vipers. No puck bunny on the planet is going to turn him down because he has a hair out of place.

His eyes meet mine in the mirror and narrow in warning.

"Just because you don't care about looking your best, doesn't mean the rest of us don't."

"Everyone else is already in the bar," I point out, waving my cell at him with the group chat open.

He turns back to the mirror, poking his hair again before stepping away. "Fine. This will have to do."

"Oh yeah, it looks awful. No one is going to want to fuck you with hair like that," I deadpan.

"You're funny," he seethes.

"I'm really not. I'm impatient."

"Yeah, to get back here to go to bed like a miserable fuck."

"Nothing wrong with sleeping. We've got a long two weeks ahead of us."

"We will if you don't lighten up. Unless there's another reason you want an early night..." He taunts.

"We have seven back-to-back road games. I'm not ending this stretch on my knees."

"Nah, man. I'm not getting on my knees for anyone."

"Wonderful," I mutter. "The women you hook up with are so lucky."

"Damn right, they are. Why do you think they're always begging for another ride?"

I side-eye him as we make our way toward the elevator. "Because of the size of your bank account?"

"Oh, it's to do with size alright. But nothing to do with money."

I scoff. "You keep telling yourself that, man," I say, patting him patronizingly on the shoulder.

"Fuck off," he scoffs, twisting away. "How're things with your puck bunny, anyway."

My irritation levels rise, and it takes every ounce of my self-control not to slam him back against the wall for disrespecting Casey. Instead, I grit my teeth and seethe, "She's not a bunny."

"Ooooh, so it's serious then?" he asks, hearing the possessiveness in my tone.

"No, it's not. I don't have time for serious. It was just a bit of fun." The words are like ash on my tongue.

It's the truth. It has been fun. But it feels entirely too serious right now.

My cell burns a hole in my pocket. I should have messaged her. Asked her if she'd had a good day. If she was watching the game. I mean, I assumed she would be. She seems like a pretty hardcore fan. I played as if she was watching...whatever the fuck that means.

Jesus. I'm a fucking mess.

I haven't played with the intention of impressing a girl since I was in high school. "Ah but you want it to be, don't you, Big D?"

"Can you leave it?"

"Who is she?" he pushes. "Someone I know?"

"She's..." I hate myself before the next words even leave my lips. "No one."

"Uh-huh," he mutters, seeing right through me. "I'm gonna figure this out." Panic shoots through me.

We've been careful—if you forget about the pool groping and fucking her in her childhood bedroom—but that doesn't mean that someone won't work it out if they look hard enough.

"Good luck with that."

Thankfully, the second we walk into the bar, Linc is distracted from asking me questions about my mystery woman and happily accepts one of the shots that's waiting for us.

"About fucking time," Handsy mutters.

"Storm was having a bad hair day," I explain as I lower my ass to a free chair, avoiding the shots and ordering a beer instead.

I meant what I said to Linc earlier: I don't want to finish this stretch on my knees. I'll celebrate with the guys, but I draw the line at two beers.

Everyone is excited and boisterous as we celebrate the best possible start to the season we could get. As the night goes on, the married and taken guys disappear—I'm assuming to get some alone time with their other halves—leaving the single guys to work their way through the bunnies who have discovered where we're drinking until they make their choice for the night.

Linc seems to have chosen a redhead. She's hot, but she's got nothing on Casey.

Standing, I make my way over to tell him that he's going to need to find somewhere else to bang her because I'm going to bed. At least if he's distracted for a while longer, I might just get a little quiet time with Casey.

Pulling my cell from my pocket, I glance at the time.

"Shit," I hiss as I make my way over. It's late in LA. I might have already missed her.

"Alright?" Linc says as I approach.

"I'm calling it a night," I tell him. "Please be quiet when you decide to join me." I'm hoping the hard glare I give him is enough of a warning to keep the bunny as far away from me as possible.

To be fair to him, he's only brought a girl back twice, and that was at the beginning of last season when he was hoping that despite my attitude I might have been interested in joining.

Hard no.

Back in the day before I was a father, I'd been known to party just as hard as the rest of the team. But everything changed the day I learned my life as I knew it had ended. I made myself a promise right there and then to be the kind of man that my future child would look up to and be proud of. No way in hell would they be reading articles online that I was out fucking any bunny who looked my way just for the fun of it. Sure, if Sutton looks back far enough, she'll find some. But nothing past the day I learned of her existence. There are enough people in the world setting bad examples for the next generation; I wasn't going to be one of them.

"I'll do my best," he says, turning to look at his bunny. "You got a room here, baby?"

She slides her hand up his chest before biting her bottom lip and shaking her head.

Of course she hasn't gone to the expense of a hotel room when she knows the men she's trying to bag have more than enough to splash around.

"Well, we'd better see what we can do, seeing as my roommate isn't up for a party."

His comment has her attention turning my way.

Her eyes bounce between mine before dropping to my lips.

Oh, hell no.

"Shame. We could have had some fun."

"I'm sure," I mutter as my cell buzzes in my hand.

I lift it without thinking, and when I find a message from Casey, excitement shoots through me.

She's still awake.

Desperate to see what she's sent, I tap the notification. The second the photo appears, I swear, my eyes almost pop out of my eye sockets.

"What was that?" Linc asks.

I lower my cell and drop it into my pocket to ensure it's hidden.

No one is seeing my girl like that.

"Nothing."

Linc's brows lift. He's clearly aware that whatever was just on my cell was far from innocent.

"I'm gonna go. Try not to get into trouble."

Trouble...yeah, Casey really is trouble.

My fingers curl into a fist as I imagine bending her over and spanking that perky ass until it's rosy red and she's begging for more.

Fuck.

Linc barks a laugh. "You know me better than that, Big D."

I shake my head as I walk away.

"Enjoy your *alone time*," he taunts, his voice carrying too well across the bar. I don't look back at the guys, but I know they heard, and I'm sure they're all wearing knowing smirks.

Assholes.

I swear I don't breathe until the elevator doors close behind me, cutting me off from everyone in the bar.

The temptation to pull my cell out and study the image I got a brief look at is tempting. But I refrain.

Instead, I wait until I'm alone in our hotel room and lying on my bed in only my boxers.

I'm already hard, my underwear doing very little to contain it.

Once I'm comfortable, I unlock my cell, open our message thread, and make the image full-size.

"Fuck me," I groan, taking her in.

She's wearing my jersey, but she's hiked it up around her

waist and is posing with most of her ass on show in a pair of Vipers-green lace panties. And the sexiest thing about it? She's looking me dead in the eyes. I feel that connection to her through the phone despite the miles between us.

My cock jerks, my balls aching for her touch.

If only that were possible. I don't know when I'll see her next. But fuck, I can't fucking wait.

> Kodie: Is that what I get for scoring the winning goal tonight, Trouble?

> Trouble: Thought you might want to know that I was wearing your jersey.

> Kodie: Fuck yeah, I do. Did you watch the game wearing only that and those pretty panties?

God, the image of her home alone, watching my game with her hand inside those panties, is almost too much to bear.

> Trouble: As much as I want to lie to you and say yes, I was actually in a bar with Parker and a load of Vipers fans.

> Kodie: You were wearing pants, right?

A wave of possessiveness rocks through me. I swear, I'd kill any other motherfucker who got to see her like this.

> Trouble: Yep, and a bra.

> Kodie: Christ. You're killing me here.

> Trouble: Are you alone in your room?

> Kodie: Yeah, left the bar the second I got your message. Been waiting for an excuse to leave so I could speak to you.

Fuck, was that too honest?

> Trouble: Really?

My heart races. I sincerely hope that's a good really.

> Kodie: Of course. Celebrating with the guys is fun and all, but I'd rather be celebrating with you.

> Trouble: Wish I could be there to celebrate with you in person.

> Kodie: What would you do if you were here right now?

I bite down on my bottom lip, allowing my dirty imagination to run away with itself as I wait for her to type her response.

Those little dots bounce for the longest time, and by the time it comes through, I've got my boxers around my hips and my dick in my hand.

> Trouble: I'd be crawling between your legs, tugging your boxers down, and dragging my tongue up the length of your cock.

"Christ," I groan, stroking myself a little faster.

> Trouble: Then I'd suck you to the back of my throat, and I wouldn't stop until you've come in my mouth.

> Kodie: Definitely a better way to celebrate than with the guys.

> Kodie: What next?

> Trouble: Well, you might be the one celebrating, but I'm getting mine too, so I'd continue crawling up your body until I'm sitting on your face.

> Kodie: Fuck yes, baby.

Safe to say, that by the time Linc lets himself in, and somewhat noisily gets himself ready for bed, I'm almost satisfied. Doesn't mean I'm not lying in bed with another raging hard-on as I think about everything she sent me tonight, though.

My Troublemaker is a dirty, dirty girl, and I fucking love it.

44

———

KODIE

With my cell in my hand, I stalk toward the door that leads to the small balcony attached to our room.

Linc is still passed out, flat on his back and snoring like a fucking freight train.

I'm not sure what time he appeared last night, but I was still awake, thinking of my girl back in LA, curling up in bed still wearing my jersey. Or at least, that's what she told me she was going to do.

She'd come all over herself and then went to sleep wearing my name and number.

Fuck. Does life get any better than that?

Yes, you asshole. She could be naked and falling asleep in your arms.

I shake my head as I pull the door open and step outside.

If I were a real asshole, I'd make this call in the room and wake him up, but while he might deserve it, I don't want to deal with his tired, moody ass as we get on a plane and head toward our next location later.

"Daddy," Sutton squeals the second the call connects.

"Hey, Peanut," I say, resting my forearms on the railing and staring out across the city before me. "How was school yesterday?"

"Meh, that's not important," she says. "Let's talk about your

319

game. Daddy, it was incredible. You couldn't have had a better start to the season."

"It was a really great game."

"I wish I was there," she complains.

"I know. I wish you were there too. So, how was school? Everything okay with Adrian?"

"Ugh," she complains, and I smirk as I picture her rolling her eyes. "He was...you know, his usual self."

"But no fighting?"

"Nope. I held myself back from knocking some sense into him."

"Well done," I say, trying desperately not to laugh.

"Oh my gosh, you'll never guess what," she suddenly says.

"What?" I ask, having learned a long time ago that she doesn't actually want me to guess. Not that I'd be able to even if I tried. Sutton is nothing but random with her exciting news.

"I got a new coach."

"Oh yeah? Any good?"

"Yes. She's amazing. I can't wait to see what she can teach us."

"That's awesome, Peanut. Are you guys ready for your game on Sunday?"

"I hope so. But we lost against them last year, so the pressure is on."

"You've got this. Gran is going to video call me so I can watch."

"Yesss," she squeals. "I hope I play as well as you did last night."

"Nah, you'll play better."

We chat for a few more minutes before Mom calls out that she needs to leave for school.

"Call me tonight?" Sutton asks.

"Of course. Have a good day—try to stay out of trouble."

It doesn't escape my attention that that is a phrase I seem to be saying a lot recently.

"You too," she giggles. "Send me pictures."

"You got it." It doesn't matter where I am, or how similar the hotel rooms we stay in are, Sutton always wants photographs of everything so she can experience it with me. "Have a good day. I love you."

"Love you too, Daddy."

She cuts the call, and I let my hand drop, along with my head.

I used to live for all the traveling. I loved spending just one or two nights in each place before moving on. There was a time when I didn't believe it was possible to become bored and homesick. I was wrong. And speaking to Sutton only makes the longing for home worse.

Sucking it up, I lift my cell again and open my messages. It's not just Sutton I need to speak to before the day really starts.

> Kodie: Good morning, Trouble. I hope you slept well wrapped n my jersey.

My cock jerks in my sweats just thinking about it. The image of her lying on her front with my name on full view pops into my head, only she's been wriggling around and the fabric has risen, showing off her pert ass in those green panties.

I groan, slipping my hand beneath my waistband to squeeze my swelling dick.

Closing my eyes, I allow myself to get lost in the moment as I picture myself crawling onto the bed at her feet, tucking my finger under the lace covering her, and dragging it aside so I can see her sweet pussy.

I swallow roughly as I imagine myself leaning forward and licking her gently, letting her taste flood my mouth as I wake her up with my tongue.

> Trouble: Good morning, handsome. I slept like a baby surrounded by you. I hope you slept well too x

"Good morning, handsome." A deep, booming voice comes from behind me, and I jump a fucking mile.

My hand holding my cell descends for my pocket in a poor attempt to hide the evidence.

The truth is, as I push my hand into my pocket, the fabric of my sweats stretches over my more-than-obvious semi, which Linc gets an eyeful of.

"What has been going on out here, Big D?" he teases.

"Can you just fuck off?" I grunt.

"So you can jerk off in public and risk it ending up online? Absolutely not. I'm a better teammate and friend than that. Get yourself in there and finish the job in private."

Oh, for the love of God. "I wasn't jerking off."

He raises a brow, his eyes dropping to my waist again. Thankfully, this conversation has killed any desire, and my erection has sunk like a fucking rock.

"Damn, did I ruin your flow?"

"Fuck. Off. Storm."

He smirks at me. "You sure are cranky when you get cock-blocked."

Relenting, he holds his hands up in defeat and backs toward the door. "I need to shower anyway. I smell like pussy."

"Wonderful."

"Breakfast in twenty?"

"Sure," I mutter as he disappears, closing the door behind him.

Really, the only thing I want to be eating right now is Casey.

Kodie: I slept like shit. Kept dreaming of this hot woman sleeping with my jersey on. The things I want to do to her...

I should stop. I know I should stop.

But I can't.

The hit of adrenaline I get every time I send a message and am forced to wait for a reply is too fucking good.

Trouble: Mmm...tell me more, Big D.

"Fucking hell."

Kodie: I'd prefer to show you...

Trouble: What day and time are you back?

Bending over, I rest my head on my forearm on the railing. "Not fucking soon enough."

Another win, and I'm flying high from a goal and two assists tonight.

We're on fucking fire, starting the season as we mean to go on.

We have a long way to go, but I'd be lying if I didn't say I was feeling confident about the playoffs already.

Something is clicking. Our synergy is on point, and I really fucking hope we can keep it that way.

Two games of this seven-road-game stretch, and we're bossing it.

Once again, I'm sitting in the bar with the guys celebrating, but while they're all laughing and joking, I'm anxiously awaiting a message.

There's been nothing since her pre-game message where she wished me good luck, told me that she was wearing my jersey, and promised to celebrate our win with me later.

It's been hours. The high of the win is buzzing through my veins, and so is my need for her. My patience is running out fast.

It's another thirty minutes of attempting to look like I want to be here when my cell eventually buzzes.

The second I feel it, I'm out of my seat and saying goodbye to the guys.

I don't even bother checking to see that it's her.

I know it is.

Excitement shoots through my veins as ideas of what she could have sent to celebrate tonight's win run through my head.

My foot taps impatiently as the elevator moves to our floor at a snail's pace.

I burst through the door, shed my clothes, and dive into bed in record time with my cell in my hand.

I wake my cell up with more enthusiasm than I've ever had in my life, and the second my eyes land on the notification waiting for me, my heart sinks.

It's an Uber Eats offer.

"You have got to be fucking kidding me," I groan.

I thought I'd turned off all my notifications. I didn't want to be teased with the prospect of it being her every time my cell buzzed.

I glance down at my tented boxers and sigh.

Needing my fix, I open Instagram. Unsurprisingly, her name is at the top of my search bar. The second I tap it, her account appears, and my eyes eat her up.

There's a new image from this morning before she started work. She's smiling into the camera, looking as beautiful as ever. Her eyes are twinkling, and I like to think I know why...

Just like I have done a million times since I figured out who my mystery girl was, I scroll through her photos, my eyes lingering on my favorite ones.

She told me she'd message me if we won. I trust that she will.

I also trust that she's going to torture me by making me wait for it.

My girl knows exactly what she's doing.

It's another long ten minutes before I finally get what I've been craving.

"Holy fuck," I groan, my eyes wide, my grip on my cell tight enough to crack the screen.

Heat sears through my veins as I stare at her.

The small green panties are back, and so is my jersey—but this time, she's lying back on her bed with the fabric pulled up to show off the curve of her waist and more than a generous amount of underboob.

My mouth waters, and every muscle in my body tightens as this morning's fantasy of crawling up the bed between her legs and eating her until she screams comes back to me.

Goddamn, she's so sexy.

Beautiful. Caring. Smart.

Fuck. She's everything I didn't know I wanted or needed in my life.

> Kodie: I am so fucking hard for you right now.

> Trouble: You killed it tonight. Congrats, Big D 😊

> Kodie: Fuck, I wish you were here.

> Trouble: Five more games, and maybe we'll get to celebrate in person.

A groan rumbles up my throat at the thought of being able to touch her, taste her, push balls deep inside her, and make her mine.

> Kodie: I can't wait. You might need to book the day off work…

> Casey: Oh, big promises.

> Kod e: You know I'm good for it, baby.

45

CASEY

The hours after a Vipers' road game have become my favorite part of the day.

I've always loved watching the guys play, but since this thing with Kodie started, it's hit a whole new level.

My infatuation with him was always borderline obsessive. But now...fuck. He's completely ruined me.

He's not even in the same state and yet he consumes every single one of my thoughts.

If I'm not planning my next celebratory dirty picture, then I'm obsessing over the previous one.

I still think the first one is my favorite. My ass looked particularly good in that shot.

So far, they've won all four of their games. They're having a killer start to the season, and I'm buzzing for them. But realistically, their winning streak has to come to an end eventually, and I'm not sure how I feel about that.

I'm loving sending him filthy images more than I should be.

Although, I can't lie...I have a very good idea about what's going to happen when they lose.

I fight to hold back my smirk.

So far, this little thing hasn't been tit for tat.

There has only been tit. And I am so ready for the tat.

I'm not even going to be greedy and hope for a full-frontal.

Just his arms, pecs, V lines. Fuck, give me a shot of the man's thighs and I'll be a happy lady.

I haven't revealed anything in my photos yet. So far, they've been very tasteful and the ultimate tease. But there are only so many ways I can drive him wild wearing his jersey and a green pair of panties. At some point, I'm going to have to up the ante.

A mixture of nerves and excitement shoots through me at the thought of sending him a more revealing picture.

It's not like I haven't dabbled with naughty pictures in the past, but I've never sent one to an NHL god. I've never sent one to the man I've spent all my teen and adult years lusting after.

My stomach knots anxiously. Sending any kind of photo is always a risk, especially when it's to someone as high-profile as Kodie. If someone were to snatch his cell...

I make a mental note to talk to him about locking those photos down. I mean, I'm sure he does. The last thing he needs when he's back is to find Sutton looking at me.

Sutton.

I squeeze my eyes closed as my heart clenches.

Sutton and the Polar Bears won their game on Sunday. It was incredible, watching them dominate the ice. I was one proud mama bear. I loved every second of it, and all I wanted to do was pick up the phone, call Kodie, and tell him just how amazing his daughter is. But I couldn't.

He hasn't said anything about my new job, so I can only assume Sutton hasn't told him. Guilt eats at me. I need to tell him before someone else does.

I just...I keep finding much more exciting things to talk about instead. And also, I don't want to do it through text. That needs to be a real conversation, and as of yet, we haven't had one of those.

I'm desperate to hear his voice instead of just reading his words, but I also understand the position he's in. He's sharing a hotel room with Linc, so we have to be discreet.

I guess there's a part of me deep down that knows he could be lying when he tells me he gets off during our down-and-dirty messaging. That he could have Linc on the bed next to him as they watch the game highlights. I smother the sigh that wants to spill from my lips, trying to look like I'm paying attention to the design meeting I'm sitting in.

When I said Kodie has stolen all my thoughts and focus, I wasn't lying.

***

"No, come on, you motherfucker," I scream at the TV as one of the Hurricane's D-men slams Linc into the boards.

Linc spins on him and gets right in his face.

We're down two to one, and there are only a few minutes left in the third period. We don't have time for Linc to lose his shit and end up in the box.

"Get it together, Storm," I mutter.

I'm standing on my coffee table like a fucking lunatic, wearing Kodie's jersey, my lucky panties, and a pair of Vipers athletic socks like they're leg warmers.

"Oh, for fuck's sake," I cry when Linc launches an attack and the whistle blows. "Moron," I grunt, jumping down and lowering my ass to the couch as Linc skates toward the box with blood dripping down his chin.

Irritation and desperation ripple through the team as they get into position to start again.

With Linc out, everyone has to work harder to avoid giving away another goal.

It must be a bitter pill to swallow after four incredible wins.

"Come on, Handsy. You've got this," I cry, surging to my feet again as Killer and Brit fight to stop the Hurricanes offense getting close to the goal. "Yes, yes, yes. NO," I scream when they suddenly take a shot, and it flies straight to the back of the net. The goal horn sounds, and the Hurricanes fans go wild.

Linc is released from the box, but it's too little, too late. Only a few minutes later, the game ends with our first loss of the season.

We all knew it had to come, but it doesn't stop it from hurting.

The guys look totally defeated as they congratulate the winners before skulking off the ice to lick their wounds.

"Fuck," I hiss before turning the TV off, unable to bear watching the Hurricanes soak up the praise from their home crowd.

I miss the guys. I miss home games. I miss Dad. But more than anything, I miss Kodie.

I've watched him from afar for so long that I should be used to it. But he allowed me to get closer; he allowed me a taste, and now he's been ripped away again. It's fucking hard.

Reaching for my cell, I pad through to the kitchen to get a fresh drink as I think of what to send him.

Usually, I wait until I know he's back at the hotel after celebrating with the team. I don't want to get in the way of the festivities. Tonight, though...

> Casey: Number 55 was the hottest player on the ice.

I let out a sigh and second-guess my message as soon as it shows as sent.

> Casey: PS the Hurricanes suck

Laughing to myself, I turn to my fridge and grab a can of soda.

The second I get back to the couch, I check to see if he's read my messages.

He has.

My heart jumps into my throat as I stare at the screen, waiting to see if he's going to reply.

But the dots never start bouncing.

"Damn it."

Tapping out of our conversation, I find the one with Dad instead and send him our standard commiseration message after a loss before I turn the TV back on to catch the highlights of the other games tonight.

Every few minutes, I check my cell.

I know it's ridiculous. He'll be in the locker room getting reamed by Dad. Either that or showering with the guys.

I quickly shake my head to remove that image.

"Come on, just give me something," I whine like a needy girlfriend.

I hate myself for it, but I also can't stop it.

I sit there impatiently as ESPN plays and I scroll through social media. Usually, I'd be taking a million sexy shots in the hope of getting the perfect pose. But not tonight. I'm sticking by my decision.

Annoyed that I've still had no response, I tidy up and head for my bedroom to get ready for bed.

The second I'm there, I check my cell again.

Nothing.

I won't sleep yet, but I want to be ready for him.

When my cell does finally buzz, excitement twists my stomach, but it doesn't last long.

I feel like the worst daughter in the world for feeling disappointed that Dad is the one who replies first.

It's over an hour later when my cell finally pings, and the contact I've been waiting for illuminates my screen.

In my rush to open it, I catapult it across the bed.

"Motherfucker," I mutter as I pick it up and swipe the screen.

55: Agreed, they suck.

55: PS Thanks, beautiful.

Casey: How are you feeling?

55: Like I've been hit by a truck. Lennon worked his magic, so hopefully, it won't be too bad tomorrow.

Lennon is the team's head athletic trainer; he'll have done a good job fixing Kodie up. I fucking hate the fact that he's hurting because of those assholes tonight though.

Casey: You let someone else get their hands on you...

55: Trust me when I say it was nowhere near as fun as having your hands on me. Pretty sure someone tortured him in a previous life and he's after revenge. He's brutal.

Casey: I've heard plenty of players get 'excited' during sessions...

55: It was Linc, wasn't it?

I can't help but burst out laughing.

Of course, I'm talking about guys Parker has worked on. As of yet, they haven't been hockey players.

Casey: My lips are sealed.

Casey: What are your plans for tonight?

55: The guys are hitting the bar.

Casey: You all deserve a drink after that.

55: I'm not going.

Casey: Oh?

55: I'm not feeling very sociable. There's only one person I want to hang out with right now.

Casey: Is that right?

55: I'm also waiting for my post-game photo...

Casey: Ah...about that...

55: What? Don't tell me that my night is about to get even worse 🫤

Casey: So...

I smile to myself as I imagine him staring at his phone impatiently.

Casey: I was thinking...

Casey: You win, and you get a treat.

Casey: You lose and...

55: Trouble?

Casey: You lose, and I'm the one who gets the thrill...

Casey: I think it's only fair, don't you? You're over there collecting all the spank bank material, and all I've got is memories.

Casey: You have no idea how badly I want to look at you while I get myself off...

55: You're bad 😼

Casey: I know. Be bad with me, Big D. Let me see what you've got.

I bite down on my bottom lip as if he's watching me.

55: You don't know what you're asking for.

Casey: Oh, I think I do.

I sit there cross-legged on my bed, waiting for a response, but it never comes.

Is he doing what I asked? Or is he ignoring my request?

My head spins with possibilities as the minutes tick on.

If he's anything like me and needs to take at least one hundred shots before settling on one, then I could be in for a long wait.

"Oh my god," I shriek when my cell lights up before me.

My hand trembles as I reach out to swipe the screen.

Our chat appears, but the image is gray, still loading.

Until...

"Oh my god. Kodie Rivers, you are a fucking god."

46

KODIE

I throw the towel I used to cover up my junk onto the counter and march out of the bathroom, naked, with my cell in my hand.

My heart is racing, my stomach twisted with anticipation.

I haven't sent a picture like that to anyone since I was in college.

I was just a boy then.

Now, I'm all man. And I just fucking wish I got to see Casey's reaction.

Confident that Linc won't be back for a while yet, I flop down on my bed with everything on show.

I can't say I was surprised by her request, but it does bring a whole new kind of challenge to our next game if I want to see more of her.

A laugh spills out of me. I'm fucking dying to see more of her. And not just through a screen.

With each game, I'm one closer to getting back to LA. Back to my girl.

And back to Casey.

My cell buzzes, cutting off my thoughts.

> Trouble: Wow. What I wouldn't do with that if it were right in front of me.

My dick jerks as my own ideas flood my head.

Trouble: We'd lose the towel, though. That thing is in the damn way.

I smirk. There was no way I was going all in on a nude when she's been teasing me mercilessly.

Kodie: It's all yours…

Trouble: Christ. I'm so hot for you right now.

Kodie: Are you wearing your jersey?

Trouble: You know I am.

Kodie: Prove it.

And not a minute later, she does.

"Fucking hell," I groan, staring at a picture of her on her bed, wearing my jersey, her legs spread. I can't see anything, but it doesn't matter. My memories are good enough to picture it.

I quickly tap out a response, using her words against her.

Kodie: What I wouldn't do with that if it were right in front of me.

Trouble: Are you still alone?

Kodie: Baby, I'm lying here on my bed, hard as fuck for you. Yes, I'm alone.

Her response isn't as fast as previous ones, and I start to wonder if I said the wrong thing.

But the second her message does pop up, I discover the reason for her hesitation.

Trouble: Video call?

My heart jumps into my throat as I stare at those two words. Fuck. I want to. I really fucking want to.

> Kodie: Missing me that much, baby?

Delete.

> Kodie: Do I want to see your sexy body through a screen? Is that even a question?

Delete.

> Kodie: Sure.

Kodie Rivers, you're a fucking loser.

Thankfully, I'm dragged out of my self-deprecating thoughts when her call appears on my screen.

A shot of nerves goes through me.

It's ridiculous. I've been with this woman. I know her intimately. Why is a video call so daunting?

Without overthinking it, I scoot back on the bed so I'm resting against the headboard and accept the call.

My breath catches when she appears before me.

She's so fucking beautiful. And of course, she's wearing my name and number.

"Hey, Big D. How's it going?"

"Really?" I groan. "Do you have to adopt that nickname?"

She smirks into the camera. "I like that I know it's got a double meaning."

"You know I shower with the guys on almost a daily basis," I point out.

"Oh, Christ. Now there's an image."

"Hey, now. Get them out of your head right this second."

Her smile turns wicked. She knows exactly what she's doing.

"I'm not interested in a single other player on our roster, Rivers. You don't need to worry about that. There's only one jersey I'm wearing right now."

"Jesus, Casey," I groan as if in pain.

"How are you feeling? Tonight was—"

"I'm not thinking about that right now," I blurt.

"I know, but you took a few hard hits and—"

"I'm fine, baby."

"I bet that's not what Lennon said when you were crying like a baby on his table."

"Shit, did you talk to him already?" I ask, making her laugh.

The sweet sound hits me right in the chest.

Fuck. I want to hear that every fucking day for the rest of my life.

"Nah, he prefers to have our chats in the mornings. He's wiped after working all of you over."

I glare at her through the screen, waiting to see if I can break her.

"Casey," I growl.

"Yes, Kodie?" she asks sweetly.

"Whose jersey are you wearing right now?"

The little minx has the audacity to pull at the fabric to double-check.

"You're in so much trouble," I tease.

She bites down on her bottom lip and looks up at me through her lashes.

"What are you going to do about it from all the way over there?"

One side of my mouth curls into a smirk.

"Prop your cell up on your pillow, then get on your knees in the middle of the bed," I demand.

She shuffles around for a few moments.

"Like this?" she asks coyly, lifting her hand to tuck her hair behind her ear. "Now what?"

"Spread your thighs."

As she does, I wrap my hand around my aching length. The tip is already glistening with precum. Swiping my thumb through it, I use it for lubrication, biting back a moan.

"What are you doing?" she asks, letting me know that I'm failing to cover my reactions.

"Waiting for you to do as you're told."

"Is that all?" she taunts.

"Anyone would think you want me to take you over my knee

and spank that ass until it's glowing with my handprint."

She trembles at my words, and it does little to calm the raging inferno inside me.

"Oh god. That's hot," she moans as she finally follows orders and spreads her thighs.

"Trouble," I groan when she drags her hands up her legs, taking the fabric of my jersey with them. "Are you missing something?"

My eyes are locked between her legs.

Even in the low light of her bedroom, I can see how wet she is.

Fuck. My mouth waters for a taste.

"Uh...no, I don't think so."

She might be trying to look all innocent with her hands resting on her thighs, but everything else gives her away.

Her chest is heaving, her cheeks are rosy, and her eyes are blown with desire.

"I want to watch you get off, Trouble. Show me how you do it when you're alone and thinking of me."

She groans, her hips grinding in her search for friction.

"God, I miss you," she rasps.

I swear, my heart fucking stops.

"Not long now and you can show me just how much in person."

Her eyes widen. "Is that a promise?"

"Be a good girl for me, and maybe I'll do the same in return."

The honest answer is *fuck yes, that's a promise.*

I'm as desperate to be with her in person as I think she is to be with me.

I'm fucking aching for her.

"I'd better make this good, then," she muses.

Fuck me. She's sitting on her bed, in my jersey, her legs spread and her cunt on display, about to show me how she gets herself off. On what planet wouldn't this be good?

"Damn straight. I need cheering up, remember?"

She shakes her head, her eyes locked on mine as her fingers dance up her thighs, heading toward where we both need them.

I swallow thickly as she gets to the juncture of her thighs.

"Kodie," she gasps as her fingers finally collide with her needy little clit.

Her head falls back as her back arches, the fabric stretching over her chest letting me see the press of her hard nipples.

"Fuck," I grunt, loving every single thing about this.

The only way it could be better was it if were in person.

"So fucking hot. That's it, play with your clit, baby. Pretend it's me touching you."

Her head lowers and her eyes lock on mine.

"Are you stroking yourself?" she asks, her voice rough with desire.

"Y-yes."

"Let me see," she demands.

This whole time, she's only seen my face and the top of my chest.

Shifting a little, I stretch my arm out, letting the camera capture me from head to waist.

"Oh my god," she moans, her eyes feasting on my body.

Fire burns through my veins, colliding in my balls.

"Fuck, Casey."

Knowing she's watching me makes this so much hotter.

It's only been a minute or two, but I'm already riding a knife's edge.

"Kodie," she counters, lifting her free hand to squeeze her boob through my jersey.

Fuck. This is going to be spank bank material for the rest of my goddamn life.

"Keep talking to me. I want to come while listening to your voice."

"Shit," I curse, forcing myself to slow down so I don't blow before her. "I'm so fucking hard for you right now, Trouble. You have no idea how much I wish I could bend you over and bury my dick deep inside you."

"You want to fuck me with your name across my back?"

"Fuck, yeah. I do. I want to own you inside and out."

"Oh god, Kodie. I'm so close."

"Same."

"I'm gonna...fuuuck. Kodie." Her eyes slam closed, her mouth opens, and her body convulses as her release consumes her.

So fucking beautiful.

I'm so lost to her that I don't hear movement outside until it's too late. I sit up, my heart in my throat.

Then, there's a deep voice. A familiar deep voice.

"What is it?" Casey asks breathlessly as she comes down from her high.

"Fuck," I bark, jumping from the bed faster than should be possible after what I've endured tonight.

The lock disengages as I round the corner to the bathroom, and Linc steps inside, his eyes on his cell, but the second he notices movement, he looks up.

His eyes widen, but I don't hang around long enough to see any other reaction. I dive through the bathroom door, my cell clutched tightly in my hand, and slam the door.

"What just happened?" Casey demands as I fall back against the now-locked door.

"Linc," I whisper. "Linc came back."

Her eyes widen to the point they must hurt. "Did he...did he see me?"

"What? No. Fuck no. I'd never let that happen."

"Okay good," she says, her body slumping on her bed, her hand no longer between her thighs.

"I'm sorry. I didn't think he'd—"

"Not your fault," she says softly as she drops back onto the bed, grabbing her cell and holding it above her.

"I'm going to fucking kill him," I groan, glancing down at my still-hard dick.

"Did you come?" she asks, her eyes searching my face.

I shake my head. "Fucking asshole."

She smirks at me. "Nothing we can't fix. Get comfortable, Kodie. I'm about to finish what we started."

Pushing from the door, I place my cell on the counter, allowing Casey a full-frontal shot of my body.

"Fuck, yeah. You're still hard, huh?" she muses, her eyes

locked on my cock. "You're going to do as you're told, okay?"

"Yeah," I groan as the sound of Linc moving around on the other side of the wall floats through.

Focus on Casey. You'll have to deal with him the second you step outside this room.

He'll want answers.

"Wrap your hand around your dick." Instantly, I do as I'm told, and with her voice floating around me, my lost release surges back to the surface almost instantly.

"Fuck. Yeah." I bite back her name for fear of being overheard as she continues talking.

"That's it. Let me watch you come for me," she demands, and I'm fucking powerless but to give her want she wants.

Pleasure shoots from my dick as I come all over myself, my eyes locked on hers through the screen. "Fuck. Fuck. Fuuuuck."

"I want to watch as you do that over my tits," Casey confesses, causing little aftershocks to shoot up my spine.

"You're gonna be the death of me."

"I really hope not. I've got plans for you, Rivers."

I jump a mile when the door knocks.

"Are you done yet, lover boy? I need to take a piss."

"I'm sorry," I whisper to Casey.

"No need. Soon, there won't be any distractions."

"God. I can't wait."

"Message me before you fly tomorrow?"

"You got it. Night, Trouble."

"Goodnight, Big D."

I groan as she cuts the call, leaving me standing in the middle of the bathroom in a puddle of my own cum.

And they say the life of a pro hockey player is glamorous.

"Dude, you've got five seconds before I piss on your pillow."

"Fuck's sake. Hang on."

After quickly mopping up my mess, I pull the door open and face my overly amused roommate.

His smirk grows as I glare at him.

"You've got some explaining to do, Big D," he warns before shooting past me to piss.

47

KODIE

I've pulled on a pair of boxers and have ESPN playing in the background by the time Linc emerges.

He doesn't say anything as he strips out of his clothes, grabs his cell and a bottle of water, and joins me on the bed beside mine.

But that doesn't mean he hasn't got a million and one questions spinning around in his head. And I also know he's not going to let me off easy. He's just biding his time. Torturing me.

I barely breathe as he gets settled, keeping my eyes glued to the TV.

Minutes pass, and my anxiety only grows.

"You're really going to make me ask, aren't you?" he finally says, breaking the tension that's settled over us.

"No, I'm not going to make you do anything," I mutter.

He chuckles. "Of course. So...go on, then."

"Nothing to tell," I say, trying and probably failing to look like I'm invested in the TV.

"I know we've only known each other a little over a year, man. But it's enough to know that what you were doing tonight isn't your usual post-game routine."

"How do you know that's not what I used to do instead of going out for drinks with you?" I cringe at my own words. I shouldn't be encouraging this. I think my brain is still fried from the orgasm.

He laughs. "Because you weren't," he states. "Come on, who is she?"

"Nope, not going there."

"Dude. I need to meet this woman. She's clearly knocked you for six. She's got you smiling, for fuck's sake."

"I smile," I complain.

"Yeah, when Sutton is in the room," he counters.

I don't respond. How can I? It's not like he's wrong.

"She looks good on you," he finally says.

I shake my head.

Casey might be a good influence on me in some ways. But in others, she's distracting. If my head weren't so far in the gutter during tonight's game, maybe we wouldn't have lost so badly. Maybe if I were focused on the job at hand and not the photo I thought I was going to receive this evening, we could have secured a win.

"Is she hot?" he asks, changing tack.

I scoff.

"What? I don't even know what your type is. We were wondering at one point if you were gay."

My brows lift. "I've got a daughter," I counter.

"Crazier things have happened," he mutters.

"I'm not gay."

"From what I heard just now, I can confirm."

"You were listening?" I balk, my previous panic returning.

"I wasn't against the door with a glass to my ear or anything. But you weren't exactly quiet, bro. Although, I get it. She had a sexy fucking voice."

Dread sits heavy in the pit of my stomach.

It didn't even occur to me that he might recognize her voice.

I'm going to fuck this up for us. There's no doubt in my mind that I'll be the one.

Just look at what's already happened. I unknowingly walked into her childhood bedroom and fucked her on her desk with her father and the rest of the team downstairs. And I've let her get me off on a video call with Linc right on the other side of the door.

"Turned me on a little, if I'm honest."

"Seriously," I mutter.

"What? I'm just a mere, red-blooded male."

"You're a pig."

"And someone is getting all jealous and possessive over their mystery girl. If you won't tell me who she is, how am I going to—" I cringe as the cogs fall into place. "I know her, don't I?" he says on a gasp.

"Lincoln," I warn.

"Don't you *Lincoln* me," he shoots straight back.

"I need you to stop."

He turns to look at me with a raised brow.

"You could just tell me."

My hard glare is clearly enough of an answer.

"Rivers, you're my man. Whoever it is, your secret is safe me with. Bros before hoes, right? Shit, unless it's Reese," he says in a panic, referring to Fletch's wife. "Or Cour—"

"I'm not with anyone's wife, Linc. She's single."

"Well, she's not, is she? She's yours."

Our penultimate game of this road stretch ends with a win in overtime.

My mind is spinning as I follow the guys back to the visitors' dressing room, ready to change and head back to the hotel.

One game to go.

Three more days and there won't be a phone between us.

She could be in my arms.

Fuck. I want it.

Her.

I want her.

Coach tries to keep spirits high as he gives us his post-game speech, but I'm barely listening. Mentally, I'm already in that hotel room, waiting for Casey.

"So, what's the verdict on drinks tonight?" Linc asks me.

"Ugh."

"It won't just be me who gets suspicious if you keep blowing us off to...well..." He wiggles his brows, making me roll my eyes.

"I'll be there for a drink."

"And you'll put a sock on the door handle so I'll know if you're in the middle of something when I return?"

"Or you could go and find your own fun."

His thoughts wander. "Here's hoping."

I never actually asked him why he was back so early the other night. To be honest, I don't want the details. But it's unlike him not to lose himself for hours with bunny action.

Thankfully, Monroe steals Linc's attention, and I can go back to focusing on what the rest of my night has to offer.

Fuck, I hope I get to watch her come properly this time. Once I'm showered, dressed, and ready to leave, I discreetly pull my cell from my gear bag.

> **Trouble:** Tough game. I'm confident that you're still going to score tonight, though.

"Ohhh," Linc sings behind me, forcing me to shove my cell back into my bag. "Is that her?"

"Fuck off," I grunt.

He holds his hands up in surrender. "Fine, fine. You keep your secrets."

I shake my head, not wanting to get into this with him while in a dressing room full of ears, throw my bag over my shoulder, and head out.

I'm the first on the bus, but that suits me.

Sinking low in my seat, I pull up my chat with Casey.

> **Kodie:** Promised Linc I'll go for a drink when we get back.

> **Trouble:** Making me wait for it, huh?

> Kodie: You know how much I love it when you beg.

Heat stirs within me.

It's only been two days.

Before Casey, I went years without any action. How have I become so needy in such a short space of time?

> Trouble: You want me on my knees for you, baby?

> Kodie: You have no idea.

Our filthy messages continue until there's movement at the front of the bus.

"There you are," Linc mutters. "Should have known you'd be getting frisky somewhere."

"Jesus. One video call and I've got a rep."

"Nah, I'm just yanking your chain. You know I'm fucking stoked for you."

He drops into the seat beside me and taps my knee like a patronizing jerk.

Everyone else joins, and only a few minutes later, we head off.

The last thing I want to do is go for a drink, but Linc is right. If I want to keep everything under the radar, I can't give them a reason to look harder.

***

Despite wanting to be alone with Casey, hanging out with the guys isn't actually a chore. I may not have spent much time getting to know everyone last year—I was too focused on keeping my head down and doing a good job— but the Vipers are a great group. Eclectic as fuck, but then, from my experience, that makes the best team. It may have only been a few weeks since I was instructed by Coach to make more of an effort, but already, these guys feel like family.

Beside me, Fletch's cell lights up on the table.

"Right, I'm calling it a night," he says, standing and slipping it into his pocket. "I've got a hot woman waiting on me to wish her good night."

A couple of the guys groan, ribbing him about his ball and chain, but he takes it all with a smile.

"Same," I say, draining what's left of my beer and following him out.

Linc notices from where he's chatting up two bunnies and gives me a little wave, his brows wiggling.

"Jesus," I mutter.

"Everything okay?" Fletch asks, turning back to see what's going on.

"Just Linc being Linc."

Fletch chuckles. "Ah, the good old days."

"How do you do it?" I blurt without really thinking it through.

"Do what?"

Reaching up, I rub the back of my neck nervously. "Juggle hockey and a serious relationship."

"Dude, you have better experience with that shit than I do."

"I've never had a serious relationship," I confess.

"I was talking about Sutton," he explains. "You know more than anyone how hard juggling two lives can be. At least with Reese, she understands. This was my life before she came along. She was never under any illusion that she'd be able to change me. She knew she had to fit in. It's different with a kid."

"And she's okay with it? All the traveling?"

"She has to be. There isn't really any other option. We were all born to play hockey. It's in our blood. Until we're told we physically can't play anymore, everything else in life comes second to the game. You know this as well as I do."

"Yeah," I muse.

He studies me as we step into the elevator. "Have you found someone, Rivers?"

"I-I— I've found something," I confess. "I wasn't looking. I don't need anyone. My life is already busy enough, but—"

"She just stormed in and found herself a place to slot in as if she's always been there?" he asks, making it sound like he knows exactly what I'm talking about.

Hell. He does. He has Reese.

"Yeah, something like that," I mutter as we head to our floor.

"I'm not going to lie to you. Relationships for pro athletes are fucking hard. But when you find the right one, it's more than worth trying to figure it all out." When I don't respond, he continues. "Is she a hockey girl? Does she get it?"

I think about Casey and the life she's lived with James Watson as her father.

"Yeah, she gets it." She probably gets it more than I do.

"Good. That's a good start. Just...be open and honest with her. And...figure out ways to be creative in your time apart. Makes it more exciting when you return," he says, clapping me on the shoulder.

"Yeah...we're, uh...trying."

"Good man. See you in the morning, yeah? One more game, then we can go home."

Home.

Whenever I've thought of home before, it's been my house, wherever that might be. So why when he says the word does my mind immediately take me to wherever Casey is? I fear I've got a real problem here. And the fact that her father is my coach isn't the biggest one.

I'm pretty sure I'm falling for Casey Watson, and there's fuck all I can do to stop it.

48

___

CASEY

"Yes, Rivers," I scream, watching our little number fifty-five flying toward the goal with the kind of skill some professionals would be jealous of.

I'm sure having an NHL-playing father helps, but even a professional can't teach that kind of talent. She might have hockey in her blood, but this is more than that. She was born to play.

I'm so proud of her and her team. Watching them kicking ass on the rink is one of the best things about my week.

Sutton manages to fake left, losing the defenseman who's trailing her, as she races around the back of the net. She does this little spin thing and shoots before her head has caught up with her body.

The puck flies into the top left of the goal, and the Polar Bears parents scream with excitement.

The Angels goalkeeper stands there looking utterly stunned—as does Megan, and most of our team, to be fair.

Sutton, on the other hand, looks totally unaffected by that epic display of talent.

She didn't even look at the freaking goal.

This girl is something else.

It takes the team a second before they dive on Sutton,

celebrating her incredible goal, which puts them even further in the lead.

They've got this game in the bag, even with half of the third period to go.

Our players change shifts, and the second Sutton steps off the ice, she approaches me, her expression set in her usual game face.

She's so freaking serious, and I know exactly where she gets it from.

"Sutton, that was incredible," I say, a wide smile on my face as I drop to my haunches to speak to her on her level.

But my smile falters when I see tears in her eyes. "Sweetie, what's wrong?" I ask, reaching out and squeezing her shoulder—not that she can feel it with her pads.

Her bottom lip trembles.

"I've been working on that trick with Daddy, and he wasn't here to see it."

"Oh, sweetie."

What she's feeling right now...I remember it all too well.

"He'll be so excited to hear all about it later. And he'll be so proud of you."

She nods. "I know. I just...I miss him."

Me too.

Before I know what's happening, she's surging forward and wrapping her little arms around me. It's awkward with her equipment on, but she doesn't let that stop her.

Unable to do anything but hug her back, I squeeze her tight, hoping that I'm helping. Over her shoulder, my eyes find her gran, sitting with the other parents watching our game. Sympathy oozes from her. She's well aware that Sutton is struggling, and she doesn't know how to help.

Honestly, until Kodie is standing before her, nothing will.

"Just a couple more days, sweetie," I say, desperate to take her pain away.

She sniffles, pulling her game face back on.

"I know. And I'll do that again."

"You absolutely will," I say with confidence. "Go and get a drink. You'll be back on again soon."

She nods at me before waddling off on her blades. I keep my eyes on her as I stand to my full height and try to breathe.

"Is she okay?" Megan asks without taking her eyes off the ice.

"She's fine."

Megan nods before shouting, "Rivers, Smith, Andreev—get back out there."

Instantly, they're on their feet and moving toward the gate for another shift. The only difference to watching the pros is that they can't jump the boards.

Pulling my cell from my pocket, I prop it up the best I can to capture footage of the game. I may not send it to him today, or even this week. But I'm sure he'll appreciate anything he misses when it comes to Sutton.

As predicted, we hold our lead until the end, winning the game five to nothing.

The Polar Bears are ecstatic as they celebrate another win, but just like always, they make sure to take their time to shake hands with the other team.

After a brief post-game speech from Megan, the parents come and join us while the girls tug off their skates and lose their pads.

"Coach C," a little voice calls as I'm tidying up.

Looking over my shoulder, I find Sutton running toward me.

Her arms open, and when she wraps her arms around my legs this time, she's not hindered by pads.

"Thank you," she says quietly.

"Ah, sweetie, I didn't do anything."

My stomach twists when she gazes up at me with her large, chocolate-brown eyes. They're the exact same color as her dad's.

"I know you understand," she says.

I nod, attempting to swallow the lump in my throat.

"I understand how hard it is to have your daddy away so much. But do you know what else I know?" I ask her.

Her face lights up as if I'm about to tell her the world's biggest secret.

"When he's back, he'll make up for every moment he was gone."

She blinks, attempting to banish her threatening tears.

"He always does. He's the best."

"Don't get me wrong, I appreciate the shit out of this impromptu spa trip, but I'm assuming you have an ulterior motive than just having a girls' day," Parker says with a smirk as she glances over at me from her lounger.

The idea struck me during my video call with Kodie last night. They're flying back Wednesday morning, and I want to be ready should he take our dirty video calls to the next level.

Fuck. I hope he will. I think I'll die if I don't get his dick inside me soon.

Sure, having his voice in my ear as I come is great, but I need more. So much more.

I made more than a few calls this morning in the hope of finding somewhere that could fit us in last minute. Really, I just need a good wax. But I want the full works. I want to be fresh and smooth for our reunion.

Oh god. Butterflies go wild in my stomach just thinking about being with him again.

"Maybe," I confess from behind my mimosa.

"I'm assuming it also has something to do with you not wanting to come out last night."

"Mmm."

Parker laughs. Between her clients and my busy schedule this week, we haven't managed to catch up. Parker knows Kodie and I have been messaging, but I haven't dived into confessing to our video calls yet.

"When are the guys back?" she asks, turning her attention to the calm water of the pool before us.

"Wednesday afternoon, I think."

"You think," she teases. "You can try to be flippant all you like, but I know for a fact you have their flight number and you're ready to track the shit out of it."

I shrug. "I miss Dad."

Parker snorts. "Oh yeah, that's who's got you pulling favors for a last-minute waxing session...your father."

I laugh, sipping on my drink.

"So, what's the plan then?"

"There isn't a plan." She gives me the side-eye, clearly not believing a word. "I mean it. We haven't talked about what happens when he gets back."

She raises a brow.

"We've talked about seeing each other and being together in person instead of through a screen. But it's all in the heat of the moment. I'm trying really hard not to fixate on anything he says when he's about to come. Or when he's riding the high of an orgasm. We all know that men say everything and anything in those moments."

Parker shifts on her lounger so she's facing me.

"Tell me more about all these orgasms."

I shake my head, laughing before embarking on the CliffsNotes of our video calls.

"Man, that's hot," she sighs, fanning herself dramatically.

"Yeah," I muse, thinking of some of the kinkier moments. "It is."

"Mostly, I'm just shocked that grumpy Kodie Rivers is willing to dirty talk and jerk off on camera."

"You make it sound so..."

"Dirty?" she asks.

"Well, yeah."

"It is. It's dirty, filthy, hot, kinky—"

"Okay, okay," I laugh. "I get it. You know, you sure sound a little jealous."

"Of hot-as-hell phone sex? Of course I am. I can't even find anyone decent to do it with in person, let alone via video."

"There are plenty of interested guys out there, P."

"Mmm. Have you seen them, though? They're not exactly the quality I'm after."

"Maybe if you were less picky."

"Oh, that's rich. How many guys have you turned down because they're not your beloved Kodie?"

"Okay, could you make me sound like any more of a stalker? And, I'll have you know, I've never turned down a guy because they're not him. I've never been under any illusions that I had a chance with him. All of this...it's a dream. I keep thinking that I'm going to wake up and discover that none of it was real."

"I can assure you, it's real," she says, finishing her mimosa.

"Yeah, but for how long? This past week and a half have been great. We've...enjoyed ourselves. But it can't last, surely? He's going to come back, life will get busy with Sutton, and—"

"What did he say when you told him about coaching her team?"

"Uh..."

"Casey," she chastises.

"I know," I sigh. "I know, okay? I just...what if he calls it off because I'm her coach now?"

"And what if he doesn't?"

"I..." I pause, attempting to imagine my life without Kodie in it. Without trying, he's become such a massive part of my every day. He's always in my thoughts. If I'm not reflecting on one of our many exchanges, then I'm scheming up what I'm going to do or say next. It's become an obsession.

The nights he's traveling or too busy to call or message, I feel like someone has removed a limb. It's ridiculous, because it's only been a few weeks since the masquerade ball. We've only been together twice. But...it's just so right. Everything with him is so easy.

"I know I should have told him. And I will."

"When?"

I shrug.

"When the time is right."

"Casey, you can't have him just turn up to practice and see you there. You'll totally blindside him."

"I know. I'll tell him before Wednesday's practice," I assure her, but even as I say the words, nerves flutter inside me.

The thought of telling him and him calling time on this...fuck, it'll kill me.

I know I'm going to have to let him go at some point. But I'm not ready yet.

Honestly, I'm not sure I'll ever be.

He's not just the only man I've lusted after since I can remember; he's so much more than anything I ever read about him online.

Yes, he's an incredibly talented player, but he's also the kindest man, a supportive father, a thoughtful lover, and I'm quickly discovering a loyal friend too.

He's the whole package, and I want every single inch of him for as long as I can have him.

"Linc walked in on us the other night," I blurt.

"What?" Parker gasps. "Oh my god. What did he say?"

"He doesn't know it's me. Or at least, Kodie hasn't said he does."

"Shit. You do know that the longer this goes on, the more chance you have of being caught?"

"Of course I know that. What's the chance it'll be over before anyone figures it out?" I ask hesitantly.

"Honestly?"

"Of course," I say, although really, I'd probably be happier if she lied to me.

"Almost zero. The second Linc figures it out, he'll chirp to anyone who'll listen."

"Linc isn't that bad," I argue.

"You don't know him like I do."

"If you say so," I mutter before a member of staff appears to call me to my waxing session.

Man, I hope this is going to pay off.

49

———

KODIE

The hotel room door slams back against the wall a beat before my roommate saunters in with a smirk playing on his lips and mischief dancing in his eyes.

We've got less than an hour before we need to leave for the arena for tonight's game. I don't have the time or patience for his shit.

"What?" I grunt as I lie on my bed with my cell in hand.

I just got off a call with Sutton, and I'm tired of being away from her. I'm so ready to go home and be a dad again.

Just one more game. One more night. "I'll give you one last chance," he offers making my brows pinch.

"The fuck are you talking about?"

His smirk grows as he stands right at the end of my bed with his hands on his hips.

My pulse rate picks up as unwanted fears spin around my head.

"Casey Watson."

The second her name rolls off his tongue, I swear my heart plummets so fast it actually leaves my body.

"I don't know what you're talking about," I lie, my voice a little too rushed and an octave higher than usual, giving me away in a heartbeat.

"Oh, is that right?" Linc teases. "So...you're telling me she's not the woman who took her father's place in the masquerade ball? She's not the sexy masked brunette in the green dress you hooked up with that night? She's also not the woman you've been video-calling since the moment we left LA? She isn't the one you jerk off over every fucking—"

"Stop," I beg. "Please, just stop."

One of his brows quirks as he waits for me to either confirm or deny the charges.

Fuck. Linc knows.

My heart rate is out of control as I stare at him, panic spreading through my veins, engulfing me and threatening to drag me under.

You're going to fuck up your entire life because of a woman.

Is she worth it?

I could continue trying to lie.

But what's the point?

He knows.

And if he knows...

"You can't say anything," I blurt.

"Holy fuck, you really are banging Casey Watson," he announces as if he didn't actually believe the accusation he walked in here with.

"Jesus Christ," I groan, dragging my hand down my face.

"Kodie Rivers, the team's good boy, the sensible single dad who never does anything wild, is fucking Coach's off-limits daughter. Fucking hell, I didn't see that coming."

"Yeah, well, you and me both, asshole."

"Careful who you're insulting here," he teases, trying to lighten the tension.

Fuck. It's so thick, I can barely breathe.

Or that could be the band wrapping around my chest and getting tighter every second.

Fuck.

This can't be happening.

I rub the heel of my hand against my chest, right above where I'm sure my heart is about to explode.

"Shit," Linc says, pressing his knee to the mattress. "Are you okay?" His brows pinch as concern covers his face.

Swinging my legs from the bed, I begin pacing back and forth, my head spinning a mile a minute.

"Does anyone else know?" I ask, his eyes following my every move.

"I haven't told anyone, if that's what you're asking," he says sincerely. "To be honest, I don't think anyone else really knows you've got a girl. I've made a few jokes about it, but I don't think they've taken me seriously. No offense, but they're used to you being a boring, celibate fuck, so..."

I shoot him a glare.

"Everyone gets it, man. Sutton is your priority. I know we tease you, but we fucking get it."

"Thanks," I mutter.

"You could have told me at the beginning. I've got your back, man."

"I'm so fucked," I interrupt, finally coming to a stop in front of him.

He blinks a few times as he looks up at me.

"It's not that bad."

"Not that bad?" I echo. "Did Coach not give you the speech about staying away from his daughter?"

"Well, yeah, but—"

"There is no but, Linc. Casey is his little girl. He's her Sutton. He doesn't want any of us near her for a very good reason."

"He doesn't want guys like me near her. You're...you're different."

I shake my head. "W-what?"

"He doesn't want her to be treated like a bunny. He doesn't want her to be used and discarded when someone else comes along. But that's not what you're doing, are you?"

"What?" I ask again as if it's the only word in my vocabulary.

"You're not using her. You're not fucking her because she's available. You're fucking her because you want her."

"Is there a difference?"

He chuckles, sending a wave of irritation rushing through me. "For a smart guy, you're a fucking idiot, Rivers."

My teeth grind as I stare at him sitting there on my bed, resting his elbows on his knees, staring up at me with mirth dancing in his eyes.

"Casey isn't a bunny, is she?"

"Fuck no," I state.

"Exactly," he says, rising to his feet as if he just won something.

"If you wanted an easy fuck, you'd be screwing a bunny right now. But you're not."

"I didn't want an easy fuck. I didn't want a fuck, period."

He laughs again, and my lips purse.

"You swore off women to focus on your game and your daughter. I fucking get it, man. But a guy still has needs, and our hands only get us so far."

I glare at him.

"Casey isn't an easy fuck you can just walk away from."

Just hearing the suggestion sends a fire roaring through me.

"She's endgame."

"E-endgame?" I stutter like an idiot.

"Oh, come on, man. You can't honestly stand there and tell me that you're only in this for shits and giggles. You're different— and in a good way, I might add. She's changed you. I swear to fucking God, I've seen you smile more in the last few weeks than I did all of last year. You're still just as focused, but it's different. It's like you've got more to fight for. And you're more fucking fun."

I'm not sure I believe that last point, but I'm not going to argue.

"What are you saying exactly?"

His smile grows, and I smother a groan.

"You're so fucking gone for her. It's cute, really."

"I-I'm not—"

"Dude, argue with me all you like. I see you. I see those heart eyes you get every time you receive a message from her. I see your excitement after every game because you know you're closer to talking to her. You've got it fucking bad, and you know it."

I comb my fingers through my hair, dragging it back until it stings.

Silence falls between us as he allows me space to gather my thoughts.

"What the fuck am I going to do?"

"**R**eady for this?" Linc says, clapping me on the shoulder before we leave the dressing room, ready to hit the ice.

We're playing Vancouver again tonight, and I need my head in the game more than ever.

Cooper fucking Nash is going to be waiting for me.

If I'm lost in thoughts of Casey and what our future might hold, he's going to see—and he's going to use it to his advantage.

"Yeah," I say as we make our way to the ice.

The air around us vibrates with Vancouver fans' excitement, but, I don't feel it.

All I feel is dread.

I'm distracted. All I can think about is the fact that Linc knows. And all I want to do is go home and see her.

Basically, I'm a fucking mess who shouldn't be allowed to face off against anyone tonight, let alone Cooper Nash.

The buzzer sounds a beat before we're announced, and one by one, we shoot out onto the ice.

Lights flash, music plays, and the Vancouver fans cheer, excited for what's to come.

"Long time, no see," Nash mutters as I pass him.

I shake my head, trying to remember a time when it wasn't like this between us. The memories get hazier each time we meet and he proves to me what an asshole he grew into.

Whatever.

He's not important.

I need to focus on the win and the private celebration that will follow.

Shut her out.

She'll be waiting for you after. Right now, you have to focus.

"Motherfucker," I grunt as I collide with the boards, Nash's weight following a beat later.

"You're playing like a pussy, Rivers," he says in my ear. "Bet your daughter is more of a man than you on the ice."

We're almost halfway through the third period, and this asshole has been getting under my skin all fucking game.

So far, I've managed to keep a lid on it. But the second he brought Sutton into it, my grip slips.

Pushing from the boards, I spin on him.

"The fuck did you just say to me?" I bellow, my fist curling in his jersey, dragging him so close our helmets collide.

"I said you're a bigger pussy that Sutton."

The red haze descends, and before I manage a conscious thought, I throw my stick to the ice and rip my gloves off.

"Get her name out of your fucking mouth," I roar before my fist collides with him, knocking his helmet to the ice and sending him rearing back.

Blood gushes from his nose and the ref blows the whistle, but I'm beyond listening—and so is Nash as he flies at me.

My helmet is next to go as he lands a solid hit on my jaw.

There's a little voice in the back of my head screaming to stop. Sutton is watching. Casey is watching.

But I can't. This asshole has had this coming for a long fucking time.

Our fight continues until I'm finally dragged away by Linc, Killer, and Brit, my breath heaving, my adrenaline pumping.

"Enough, Rivers," Killer barks as Nash is shoved away by his own teammates.

"The fuck were you thinking?" Handsy demands, skating over and stopping in front of me.

They're right— it's been a fucking battle to keep the score even to this point. Having me in the penalty box isn't going to help things.

With little choice but to leave the ice, I lift my hand to wipe the blood trickling down my chin before collecting my stick and helmet and skating toward the box.

Nash shouts something at me, but the blood rushing past my ears thankfully means I don't hear it.

I'm forced to sit there as Vancouver lines up for a power play.

Guilt rages inside me, and it only gets worse when the puck hits the back of our net and the goal horn sounds.

Nash glares at me from his spot on the bench the whole time.

One of their team doctors tries to patch up his split brow, but he keeps knocking her hand away.

Sure, I'm the better player out of the two of us, not because of skill, but because of focus and dedication—and I got drafted first, but it's time to fucking get over it.

The game ends in a loss, and I feel its weight pressing down on my shoulders as we return to the dressing room.

"That guy was a fucking asshole tonight," Fletch says, stepping up to me.

I grunt a response. It doesn't matter how much of an asshole he was; I shouldn't have let him get to me like he did.

Falling into my stall, I tip my head back and close my eyes.

Everything fucking hurts, thanks to Nash's attacks tonight, but nowhere is as tender as my fucking heart.

I'm done being away. Now that we've finished our final road game, I just want to be home.

I need my girl...

Both of them.

50

———

CASEY

Watching Kodie on the ice tonight was horrible. Nash was after him. That was obvious almost from the moment the puck dropped.

He was on a mission, and apparently, violence was the answer.

It was the roughest game I've seen in a long time. How we didn't sustain any serious injuries is beyond me.

It wasn't just Nash. The entire Vancouver team came out as if they had something to prove. It's not like they lost their exhibition game, either.

Whatever it was, I fucking hated it.

And what I hated even more...there was a very high chance that Sutton was watching.

All I hope is that she went to bed before the third period, so she didn't have to see her dad fighting.

I don't know what Nash said to him while he had Kodie pinned to the boards, but I can imagine.

There's only one thing in this world that Kodie cares about more than his career, and that's Sutton.

I know a little of the history between Kodie and Cooper. They grew up together. They played on the same team for years until they went to college.

Curiosity to know more burns within me, but I already know I won't be demanding answers tonight.

I have no idea what kind of headspace Kodie will be in after that game. Hell, for all I know, he won't be interested in a chat tonight.

Pain lashes at my insides at the thought alone.

I want to be his safe place when shit gets hard. But I understand that there's a very good chance I haven't earned the right for that yet. I fucking want to, though.

I lie on my bed, waiting for a response. I messaged him a few times during the game. I knew he wouldn't read them, but I wanted him to know that I was right behind him when things didn't go his way tonight.

The messages now show as read, but he hasn't replied.

What if tonight is going to be the first night after a game that we don't talk?

It'll fucking kill me. But there isn't much I can do about it.

It's not like we're together or anything.

We're...I don't know what we are.

Fuck buddies?

Each other's dirty secret?

My cell buzzes and my heart jumps into my throat. But it quickly sinks again when I find Parker's name staring back at me.

> **Parker:** That game was brutal. Are you ready to brighten Rivers' night?

> **Casey:** I'm waiting to hear from him. Radio silence so far.

> **Parker:** He's probably having a drink with the guys. He deserves it after all the hits he took tonight.

> **Casey:** Yeah, probably.

A heavy sigh passes my lips, and I rub the ache in my chest in the hope of abating it.

Parker: Stop worrying. That guy is crazy about you.

"Get out of my fucking head," I mutter, staring at the screen. It's freaky how well she knows me.

Casey: Even if that's true, it doesn't mean anything. He's a hockey player, remember?

I don't know why I'm baiting her. I guess I need the reality check of her telling me that no players can be trusted with anything beyond pussies and orgasms.

Parker: He isn't just a hockey player, though, is he?

"Damn you, Parker Donnelly. Damn you."

Casey: We may be about to find out...

Parker: Trust him.

I blow out a breath as I sink lower on my bed.

My Vipers jersey rises higher, exposing more of my stomach. I've tied the excess fabric at my side to give me a sexier look, but I'm starting to wonder if I shouldn't have bothered.

Anxiety wars within me, and I'm on the verge of calling it a night when my cell lights up. Only, it's not with a message like I was expecting; it's a video call.

My stomach flips as I reach for it and answer in a rush.

"Kodie?" I whisper when I get nothing but wall on the screen.

"Shit," he curses darkly.

Just that one word has butterflies erupting within me.

Seconds later, the camera switches and I get my first look at him.

"Oh god," I groan, taking in his glistening body fresh from the shower. Water droplets cover his taut, inked-up skin and he's wearing nothing but a towel wrapped low on his waist.

Best sight ever.

The teenage girl with a fierce crush on this man does little backflips inside me.

He's silent as I roll my eyes up his body. I'm breathless, but the second he lowers himself to the bed and looks into the screen, I gasp.

"Kodie," I breathe, my fingers twitching with my need to reach for him. "Your face."

His lip is split and swollen, and his cheek is glowing. The bruising is already darkening.

"I'm okay," he says weakly.

He rubs the back of his neck as pain and regret flicker through his eyes.

"What happened tonight?" I urge, desperate to take some of his suffering away.

He shakes his head. "It was...it was just a bad game."

"I know you two used to be friends," I confess.

He snorts. "Yeah, used to be. Nash is an asshole who's trying to prove something. I fucking hate playing against him."

Silence lingers between us. I hate not knowing how to help him, how to reach him.

"I don't want to talk about him, Trouble," he says, focusing back on the screen.

This time, there's something different in his eyes. There's heat but there's also a vulnerability there.

"Oh yeah. Did you have something else in mind?"

"You know I do. But we lost..."

"Ah, so you did. You owe me something, Rivers."

Concern still lingers, but I can't deny the excitement at his willingness to continue with our game.

"Mmm," he rumbles, rubbing at the scruff on his jaw.

Fuck, I want to feel that between my thighs almost as much as I need my next breath.

Soon...

"Pretty sure you've seen everything already," he teases.

"Doesn't stop me from wanting to see it again," I counter. I move the camera away from my face, allowing him to see what

I'm wearing. "Just like this…I've worn the same thing every time we've spoken. I bet you're far from bored of it."

"Fuck no. I'll never be bored of this sight. I can't deny that I want more, though. You've seen all of me through the screen, and yet, you've hidden parts of yourself."

"Delayed gratification," I taunt. "How do I know that you won't lose interest if I show you everything? You might not want to see me when you're back."

"You're kidding, right?"

I shrug, playing innocent.

"I'm fucking dying for you, Trouble. Look," he says as he stands and allows me to see just how tented his towel is.

Biting down on my bottom lip, I stare at the fabric, wishing I could banish it with nothing but willpower alone.

Kodie looks hot as hell like this. But nothing will ever beat him naked.

"Let me see," I whisper. "Show me how hard you are for me."

A thrill goes through me, ending right at my clit.

God, he's not the only one dying for some in-person action. I swear, I'm going to combust the second he touches me.

"What am I going to get in return? I've had a really hard night, remember?"

"Playing the sympathy card, huh?"

"I need distracting from the pain." He ducks down so I can see his face again, and I burst out laughing at his pout.

"Aw, my poor baby," I whisper as I drag my hand from my waist and up my stomach.

His eyes track the movement, darkening with every inch.

"I want my hands on your body," he muses, almost as if he's talking to himself. "I want to feel those curves, the heat of your skin. I want to drown in your sweet scent with your addictive taste on my tongue."

"Jesus, Kodie."

"Keep going," he encourages as my hand skims over my ribs.

He swallows thickly, and I let my groan break free as my fingertips tuck under the fabric of his jersey and graze my boob.

"More. Let me see those perfect tits, Casey."

Oh god. My hips roll and desire blooms within me as he rasps my name.

Sexiest sound ever.

I keep going until my hand is entirely under the jersey.

His jaw tics with desire and irritation.

"Oh my god," I moan, my back arching as I squeeze myself.

"Casey," he snaps.

"So good. My nipples are so hard for you. Begging to be sucked on."

"Casey Watson, if you don't show me your tits right now, I'll—"

I pause, my eyes locking on his.

"You'll what, Daddy?"

He shakes his head, his lips pressed into a thin line.

"Test me and find out."

Oh god. I want it all. Every single thing he can give me. The good, the bad, and everything in between.

"Lose the towel, big boy," I tease. "You're the one who lost tonight, not me."

"Fucking brat," he mumbles as he takes a step back, allowing me to see all of him.

Good boy.

My breath catches as his hand goes to the fabric around his waist.

"Please, Kodie. Show me what you've got," I rasp, hoping like hell I sound sexy and not wanton.

He tugs at the towel, and not a heartbeat later, the fabric flutters to the floor, leaving him standing there deliciously naked.

"Jesus," I mutter, and it gets even worse a second later when he wraps his hand around himself and strokes slowly.

He is my every fantasy come to life.

"You're so much hotter than my imagination ever was," I blurt.

He smirks, more than a little happy with himself.

"Now, your turn, Trouble."

Adjusting myself a little, I squeeze my boob again and pinch my nipple.

"Kodie," I gasp, driving him wild.

"Casey."

I smile at him innocently. "Oh, sorry." Propping my cell against my pillows, I shift around again so I'm on my knees in the middle of my bed. It's my favorite position to tease him in.

Releasing the tie at my ribs, I wrap my hands around the hem of his jersey and pull it up.

I swear, he stops breathing as he watches me inch it up my body.

Fuck, I love the power that shoots through me in moments like these.

This strong, powerful adonis of a man needs me.

It's a heady experience.

"Holy shit, you're beautiful," he says in a rush as I expose myself to him.

His eyes are focused on my tits as he drags his bottom lip between his teeth.

"When can I see you in person?"

"Name a time and date, and I'll be there."

"Tomorrow," he blurts, his movements getting faster as he continues to stroke his dick. "We land about twelve. Can you get the day off? Work from home? Anything."

Oh my god. He's serious.

He wants to see me the second he lands.

"Yes," I agree without even considering if I actually can.

I'm too lost in Kodie to know what day tomorrow is, let alone if I can get time off for a dick date.

"Fuck, yeah. I'm gonna come for you, Casey. I'm gonna come for you, and I'm gonna spend all afternoon fucking worshipping you."

51

KODIE

nock. Knock. Knock.
I shake my head as the hotel room door opens.
"Is it safe to enter?" Linc asks, a teasing lilt to his voice.
"I messaged you, asshole."
"No naked bodies?"
"No," I sigh.
"Damn, that's disappointing," he announces, slamming the door closed and marching inside.
"Hey," he says, finding me in bed watching TV. "Fun night?"
"I don't kiss and tell."
"Well, lucky for me, you're a few miles apart, so there was no kissing..."
"You're insufferable," I complain.
"Maybe so, but you know you lucked out, getting me as a roomie."
"Did I?"
"Hell, yeah. And anyway, who else would put up with your surly ass?"
He walks into the bathroom, leaving that question hanging in the air as he gives me little choice but to listen to him piss and then brush his teeth.

"Tonight fucking sucked, huh?" he finally says after stripping down to his boxers and falling into bed.

"We've had better games," I mutter.

As much as I know we're going to need to analyze what happened tonight, I'd rather just put it behind me and never think about it again.

"What's the deal with you and Nash, anyway? He was an asshole last time we were here, but tonight, he was like a dog with a fucking bone."

I shrug. "Fuck if I know."

"You grew up together, didn't you?"

"Stalker much?"

I find it weirdly endearing when Casey confesses to knowing details about my life that prove she's done more than her fair share of Googling my name. But for Linc to do it? That's just fucking weird.

"Might have looked you up when your trade was announced," he admits.

"Lovely. Find anything worth noting."

"Aside from the stats?"

"They speak for themselves," I say confidently.

"Not as good as mine, but whatever."

I scoff. "Believe what you want."

"I'm serious, though. Did you fuck his future wife or something?"

I think back to our years together. "He's never been serious enough about anyone to care about that shit."

"So, you might have?"

"It was college, and we were horny hot-shot hockey players destined for the draft."

"Say no more," he says with a laugh.

"I dunno, man. After we got drafted, he just turned into a competitive asshole."

"Fair enough. This life, the adoration, it can go to some guys' heads."

"Some guys," I tease.

He shoots me a side-eye, and I can't help but laugh.

"See," he says, pointing right at me. "This is exactly what I was talking about earlier. You're fucking laughing, man. It's beautiful."

"Uh...thanks, I think."

"So, am I right to assume that your night improved once I left you alone?"

"Mmm."

"Oh, come on, you gotta give me more than that."

"It was great, and I'm feeling much more relaxed now. How's that?"

"Barely scratches the surface, but whatever."

"Seeing as you're back this early, I'm assuming it does more scratching than a bunny."

"I wasn't interested."

"Oh? Trouble in paradise?"

"Nah, all's good. It just...gets a bit much sometimes. I'm sure you remember."

"Yeah," I muse.

"So, what's the plan now? We're gonna be home for what? Just over a week?"

"I don't know," I confess.

"You want to see her, right? Continue what you've started?"

I shoot him a sideways glance.

"And you're going to tell Coach."

My body locks up at the suggestion.

"Kodie," he warns.

"We're not telling anyone anything."

"But—"

"There are no buts. I don't know what this is or where it's going. It might be nothing."

"You don't want it to be, though, do you?"

I stay quiet as I roll that question around my head for a few minutes.

The honest answer is no. I don't want this thing with Casey to be nothing. I want it to be something. No—I want it to be everything.

But is that nothing but a pipe dream?

Guys like me don't end up with girls like her. At least, not guys who already have commitments and not enough time to give her the attention she deserves.

Being with me... she'd get short-changed. She can never be my number-one priority. Sutton will always come first. Thankfully, Linc doesn't push for an answer. He doesn't need to. He knows it just as much as I do.

Instead, we turn our attention to the TV and dissect the highlights of the other games tonight.

Tomorrow, we return home. This two-week stretch has been one of the longest I've ever experienced, and I'm more than ready for it to be over.

I wake with a start, my heart racing. Sitting up, I find the hotel room in darkness with Linc snoring beside me.

Reaching for my cell, I discover it's only been thirty minutes since we switched the light out.

I lie back again, listening to the pounding of my heart as it begins to slow.

I stare up at nothing, and my mind runs away with itself.

I quickly find myself counting down the hours until I can see Casey again.

I told her to book the day off and demanded she send me her address, which she did instantly.

Was it a bit presumptuous of me to assume she'd be willing to drop everything to spend the afternoon together? Probably. Do I care? Not one single bit.

My need for her after our exchanges over the past two weeks knows no bounds.

It'll be easier once I've had her. It will lessen, and I'll be able to think straight again. Or at least, a little straighter.

Before I know what I'm doing, I have my cell in my hand, and I've pulled up one of the airline apps in my travel folder.

I tell myself that I'm just seeing if there are options. But I know it's bullshit.

The second I see an earlier flight, I'm leaving.

Coach won't care. I'll bend the truth a little and say I had a family commitment come up. Tomorrow's just a travel day. It's not like anyone will miss me.

Ten minutes later, I'm the proud owner of a ticket for the first flight to LA, taking off in just over an hour.

Fuck.

I'm going home.

No, not home. I'm going to Casey. Right fucking now.

In a rush, I jump out of bed and pull on my suit before gathering up as much of my shit as I can find in the dark. Once I'm fairly confident I have all the important stuff, I throw my bag over my shoulder and tug my suitcase toward the door.

Linc doesn't so much as stir.

With my palm pressed against the door, I close it slowly before pulling my cell out of my pocket and calling a car.

As I'm standing outside the hotel, I begin to second-guess my rash decision. But as the car pulls up, I figure it's too late to back out now.

"Holy shit," the driver gasps once I've climbed in. "You're Kodie Rivers."

"Hey," I say, not really in the mood to talk.

"Shit, man. My kid loves you. Any chance you could sign something for me?"

"Sure thing." He rummages around in his glove compartment before pulling out a battered old notebook. He finds a page and a pen and passes them back.

"Thanks, man. He's not going to believe this. It's going to make his whole year."

I smile at him in the rearview mirror as I pass it back.

"Shit. Airport. Right, let's go."

As he sets off, I pull my cell out and open Instagram.

For my plan to work, I need some help, and there is only one person I can go to for it.

I glance at the time and cringe. If she doesn't answer, I'm fucked, and all of this will be for nothing.

But if she does...

52

CASEY

I stir awake and roll over in bed, more than ready to drift back to sleep.

I don't need to look at the clock to know that it's still too early.

It might be reckless, but I did exactly what Kodie suggested and put in a last-minute request for annual leave tomorrow—or today now, I guess. Bianca messaged me straight back, letting me know that she'd accept it first thing this morning. I never, ever do anything last minute like this. I feel guilty as hell. But I'm not letting anyone down. I've got a to-do list as long as my arm, and it'll still be there on my return.

Snuggling back down, I just begin to drift off when a noise has my eyes popping open.

My heart races as I listen, waiting for confirmation that whatever it was isn't inside my apartment.

But that isn't what happens; instead, there's another noise and movement in my room.

My lips part, and a blood-curdling scream is about to rip from my throat when a large hand covers my face.

A familiar scent washes over me as the warmth of his palm burns my skin. "Don't freak out. It's just me."

His hand slips free, allowing me to speak. "K-Kodie?" I rasp, my voice rough with sleep. "W-what are you—"

"Shush," he breathes as he takes a step back.

I want to argue and demand he returns, but then the sound of clothing being removed hits my ears, and I swallow the words.

Oh god.

He's here.

"I thought you were coming back this afternoon," I whisper as clothing hits the floor.

My room is in darkness, but my eyes are adjusting, and I can make out his shadow as he moves.

"Couldn't wait," he muses, and my heart tumbles in my chest.

He came back early.

Desire races through my veins, and heat floods my core.

He's here. He came back early for me.

"I booked the first flight I could get. Left Linc snoring in his bed."

"Am I dreaming?" I whisper into the darkness as the sheets are lifted from my body.

A shiver runs down the length of me, goosebumps chasing it, but it's not from the cold. It's him.

It's always him.

"No, baby. You're not," he rasps as he climbs in beside me, wraps his hand around my neck, and searches out my lips.

"You're here," I repeat, still unable to believe this.

He's here. In my bed. And...I slide my hand down his toned back to his...And he's naked.

Miracles do happen.

"Oh god," I whimper as his warm breath rushes over my face before his lips brush mine.

"I couldn't wait any longer," he repeats. "I need you."

His grip tightens and fireworks shoot down my body as I hitch my leg up to wrap around his hip, needing him closer.

A needy whimper spills from my lips as his tongue pushes inside, greedily searching for mine.

He's here.

He couldn't wait any longer.

Twisting my fingers in his hair, I kiss him back as if he's the air I need to breathe.

For a few seconds, our kiss is soft and slow, but that soon changes as the electricity crackling between us sparks, flames exploding everywhere.

Our kiss turns wild and messy as our tongues tangle and our teeth clash, our hands roaming over every inch of skin we can touch.

"Wait," Kodie says, sitting up in a rush and ripping his body from mine.

"Come back," I complain, reaching for him with grabby hands like a toddler who's lost her snack.

Suddenly, light fills the room, and I wince, my eyes watering as they fight to adjust.

The second I see him, my breath catches and I reach for his face.

"I'm okay," he whispers as my thumb gently brushes his split bottom lip. It looks worse in person.

I shuffle to my knees as he sits back, my hand dropping to my side.

"Fuck," he grunts, dragging his hand down his face as he stares at me, his eyes molten. "You look—" He swallows thickly.

"It's my new favorite sleep shirt," I say, tugging the bottom of my jersey up enough to show my green panties.

"I know, but...it hits different in person."

My smile grows, and movement at his waist has my gaze dropping.

The second my eyes lock on his dick, my mouth waters.

He's right. It really does hit different in person.

Our chests heave as we stare at each other, chemistry crackling loudly.

Time stands still. It's like we're standing on the edge of a cliff, getting ready to dive off.

"Kodie," I cry—except when he jumps, it's not into the abyss. It's into me.

His arms wrap around my waist as he flips me back and spreads my legs with his knees, settling between them.

"Fuck, I needed this," he mutters before claiming my lips again.

His hands start on my thighs before sliding under my jersey, gliding up my ribs until he cups my breasts.

"Yesss," I hiss.

It felt good when I did it earlier, but my touch was nothing compared to his.

He lights me up inside in a way I can never achieve.

Ripping his lips from mine, he pushes the fabric up my body before cupping my breasts and ducking down to suck one of my nipples into his hot mouth.

"Oh god, Kodie," I moan, my back arching from the bed, my hips grinding in the hope of finding some friction.

I claw at his shoulder, desperate for more—desperate for him to be closer, to be inside me.

"Please," I beg. "Please, I need you."

"Jesus Christ, you drive me fucking crazy," he says after releasing me with a pop and dragging the jersey from my body, discarding it without a second thought.

Sitting up, he stares down at me. His attention burns in the best possible way as his eyes feast on my skin as if I'm the only woman in the world.

Oh, to be that to him.

"Kodie?" I whisper, sensing that I've lost him.

But the second he hears his name on my lips, he turns feral.

And I am fucking here for it.

His fingers tuck under the lace covering my hips before he tugs sharply, the sound of ripping fills the air.

"Oh my god, you didn't," I gasp as he pulls the ruined underwear from my body, leaving me naked before him.

The smirk playing on his lips is everything. My every fantasy come to life.

I wish it were possible to freeze time so I could really appreciate the look of adoration and desire on his face right now. So I could savor the way his attention and touch make me feel.

I already know that no amount of time I'm lucky enough to

spend with Kodie is going to be enough. I want to make the most of every second I have with him.

His hands slide from my knees down my inner thighs until he presses, spreading me open for him.

His heated gaze locks onto my bare pussy, and I mentally give myself a high five for finding that spa.

Totally worth all the phone calls and the high price tag it came with.

Dropping to his stomach, he watches as he drags two fingers through my folds before notching them inside me.

I moan, words of encouragement stuck beneath the lump of emotion that's crawled up my throat as I watch him gaze at me with such reverence and awe.

This can't be real. It just can't.

Things this good don't happen to me.

But then, he leans forward, and everything is forgotten because his tongue...

Kodie Rivers' tongue is something that deserves to be worshiped.

The speed, the pressure, the way he circles it...it was designed to be licking my pussy, I swear.

"Kodie, fuck. Yes," I scream, my fingers sinking in his hair as I try to pull him closer. It's not possible, but fuck, I need it.

Pushing his fingers deeper, he curls them against my front wall as he sucks on my clit.

Shit. I am not going to last.

I may have gotten off every single time we've connected this week, most recently with the sound of his voice, but it's not the same as having him here, having his tongue on my clit and his fingers inside me. The only thing better will be his dick.

"Oh fuck," he groans, the vibration of his deep voice pushing me closer to the edge. "What are you thinking about that made you strangle my fingers like that?"

"Your dick. I want your dick inside me, just like you promised," I gasp as he picks up speed, fucking me with his fingers.

"You can have my dick," he promises. "But not until you've come on my face, baby."

"Oh god, please."

He flattens his tongue against me and moans.

"Holy fuck, Kodie. Kodie. Fuck. Fuck," I cry as my orgasm crests and I fucking fly.

Lights flash behind my eyes as I shatter into a million pieces.

He works me through it, ensuring I ride out every second of pleasure before he sits up and wipes his hand across his glistening mouth.

"So fucking hot," he mutters as he shuffles forward.

My chest heaves, my heart races, and my muscles twitch from the power of that release, but I'm nowhere near done.

The sight of him with his dick in his hand ready to take me is enough to start the beginnings of a second orgasm.

The ink on his arm ripples—as do his abs— as he gets into position.

"Haven't been able to stop thinking about this pussy," he confesses as he presses the tip against my entrance. "About you."

My greedy pussy tries sucking him in, but he holds back, reminding me who's in charge here.

"Kodie, please. Fuck me, please," I whimper, beyond desperate to feel him stretching me open, ruining me for any other man on the planet.

He chuckles, but there's very little humor in his expression.

Reaching up, I wrap my hand around the back of his neck and drag him down to me.

I'm under no illusion that I can physically force him to move anywhere, the man is a beast, but he humors me, his nose brushing mine tenderly.

"Please," I whisper, my body trembling with need.

"Fuck, as if I can say no to you."

His lips slam down on mine at the same time his hips punch forward, filling me in one swift move.

I cry out in surprise as my body fights to adjust to him.

He holds himself inside me, giving me a chance to get used to the invasion before it all becomes too much.

"I'm okay. You can move now, please."

He licks deep into my mouth as he rests on one forearm so he can grasp my hip with his other, keeping us anchored together.

Slowly at first, he moves, small thrusts that make me shudder with need, but after a few moments, he begins to drag his dick all the way out before pushing back in.

"Goddamn, you feel better than I remember," he groans, his forehead resting against mine as he sucks in greedy breaths, our eyes locked on each other.

I've been with a few guys before, but I have never felt anything like this.

This kind of intimacy is on a whole different scale.

My body continues to tremble as he moves inside, but he never picks up pace. He never actually fucks me.

Does that mean he's making...

Nope. Not going there.

He's just tired. He flew home in the middle of the night, and this is all he's got.

It's bullshit.

He's a professional hockey player. We all know they have stamina in spades.

He's doing this on purpose. He's building me up and breaking me down all at the same time because this is what he wants.

Oh god.

Emotion burns up the back the back of my throat, making my nose itch and my eyes burn.

Fuck. Do not cry while he's inside you, Casey.

You'll scare him off.

Sliding my hands back into his thick curls, I search out his lips, needing as much distraction as I can get.

He kisses me back just as eagerly as he lifts my ass from the bed, allowing him to hit me deeper.

"Oh shit," I gasp into his kiss.

"Come for me, baby. Let me feel you strangling my dick."

He circles his hips, working my clit and giving me the extra push I need.

"That's it. Be a good girl and do as you're told, baby. You always look so beautiful, coming all over me."

"Kodie," I cry.

"That's it. Give it to me. Then I'm going to fill you up. Can't fucking wait to watch my cum spilling out of you."

"Yes, yes, yes," I chant as his filthy words and ridiculously talented dick push me over the edge.

"Christ," he grunts. "Fuck, Casey. You're fucking perfect."

His roar echoes off my walls as he follows me into his release, his cock jerking violently.

Best wake-up ever.

53

KODIE

"How did you get in here?" Casey asks now that our breathing has returned to normal.

After coming inside her, I collapsed to her side and dragged her body into mine. Now, we're lying chest to chest with our legs entwined and our arms wrapped around each other.

I've never been a cuddler, unless you count with Sutton. I never saw the appeal. Once I'd gotten what I wanted from a woman, I was out.

But this...this is...nice.

No. That's a shitty description. It's fucking everything.

After the last couple of weeks of only hearing her voice through the phone or seeing her through a screen, being able to hold her...well, it's almost as good as feeling her strangling my dick. Almost.

An unexpected laugh erupts from my chest. The noise shocks her just as much as it does me, if the way she rears back so she can see my face properly says anything.

"What?" she asks, her own smile stretching across her pretty face.

"You owe Parker," I confess.

"Oh, I do, do I?" she asks with a laugh.

"Yeah, she said that being woken up so you could get railed by a hockey god was going to cost you."

"She did not say that."

I shrug. "It's what I heard."

"Of course it was. I'm amazed she complied; she can be a bitch when she hasn't had enough sleep."

"I guess I got lucky," I say, leaning forward for another kiss.

Fuck. I'm addicted.

I have her wrapped around me like a spider monkey, but it's still not enough.

My hands slide over her curves, learning all the lines of her body. Seeing her through a screen and not being able to touch her has been torture. But now that she's here in my arms, I realize it was so worth it.

Pushing up on my elbow, I force her to lie back as I tuck my face into her neck, breathing her in before sucking on the soft skin beneath her ear.

"Oh god."

"Not God, baby. Rivers. Kodie Rivers."

"Christ. You might seem different to all the others, but really, you're just a hockey player, aren't you?" she teases.

"It runs through my blood, Trouble. Just like I think it does yours."

"Mmm," she groans as I kiss down her chest.

"Can't get enough."

"Take it all," she offers, shamelessly spreading her thighs.

My hand automatically drops to her pussy, and I drag my fingers through her. My cock jerks as I push my cum back inside her.

"Yesss," she hisses.

I work her until she's begging and precum is leaking from my tip, then I flip onto my back and lift her onto me.

Handing over control never used to be a part of my playbook, but everything is different with Casey.

I groan as she grinds her hot pussy against my shaft.

This is what I've been dreaming of every single minute of every single day since I left.

"Kodie," she whimpers, lifting her hands to her hair as she teases me.

The move lifts her tits, and my hands move on instinct, cupping them both and pinching her nipples between my fingers.

She arches into me, desperately seeking more.

"Put me inside you, baby. Let me feel your pussy sucking me deep."

She doesn't need to be asked twice. Immediately, she reaches for me and lifts up a little before teasing me at her entrance.

My teeth grind with impatience.

"Casey," I hiss.

She smiles at me, and I swear that, along with the desire in her eyes and her incredible body above mine, causes my soul to leave my body.

That is, until she drops down on me, and then I swear my soul leaves my body.

Ho-ly fuck.

"Ride me. Take what you need. Let me watch you fall apart."

With our eyes locked, she does exactly as she's told, riding my dick like a fucking goddess.

I watch her in awe, teasing her breasts, skimming my hands over her curves.

She's a fucking vision.

"You're close," I tell her as her grip on my cock increases.

"Yes," she gasps. "More. Give me more."

Slipping my hand to her front, I brush my thumb against her clit.

"That's it. Fuck, Kodie. Fuuuuuck," she cries, her release ripping through her.

My free hand wraps around her ribs, helping to hold her up as she loses herself.

Watching her is enough to push me over the edge with her, and it only takes a couple of thrusts for me to fall as well.

She collapses on my chest, our bodies sweaty and our chests heaving with exertion.

"I'm so glad you came back early," she confesses.

I can't help but laugh, and the second I hear the sound, I think back to what Linc said.

He's right. Since Casey snuck her way into my life, I do smile and laugh more.

Long may it continue.

"Me too, Trouble. Best decision I've made in a while."

We fall silent as our bodies come down from their highs, and before I know it, my exhaustion claims me and I drift off with Casey still lying on top of me.

"The fuck is that?" Casey groans as an alarm drags us both from sleep.

"My alarm," I rasp as I roll her off me so I can dig it out of my pants pocket.

"Why?" she complains.

I glance back at her, a laugh spilling from my lips. She looks so sexy wrapped in nothing but her sheets. Her lips are still a little swollen from our kisses, and she's got marks all over her chest.

Something wild and possessive rises in me as I stare at them.

Mine.

"I want to surprise Sutton and take her to school."

Instantly, Casey's expression softens.

"Aw, she'll love that," she breathes. "What are you waiting for? Go, go." She actually tries to shoo me from her bed.

Climbing to my feet, I stand there naked, looking down at her with a frown lining my brow.

"You want me to leave?"

"No, of course not. I want you to stay right here and spend the day in bed with me. But you can't. Turning up and surprising her will make her whole year."

"Fuck," I breathe.

"What?" she asks, sitting up in the middle of her bed and staring at me with wide, curious eyes.

"You get it," I admit.

"What? Of course I get it. Sutton...she's your priority always. You never have to question if I understand that."

I continue staring at her, wondering what I did to be so lucky to find her.

"Once upon a time, I was Sutton," she says softly.

Pressing one knee to the bed, I wrap my hand around the back of her neck and pull her to me for one more kiss.

The second I release her, I march into her bathroom and find a washcloth to clean her up with.

I'm not used to caring for someone else. Sutton might be my top priority, but Casey isn't far behind.

"What are you doing?" she asks when I return with the wet cloth in hand.

"Cleaning you up, what do you think?" Quickly, I rip the covers from her and crawl onto the bed. "What?" I ask when she sits there frozen.

"No one has ever done that before."

Anger shoots through me that no one has taken care of her properly, but at the same time, I puff my chest out, because I intend to show her just how things should be.

"Lie back," I encourage.

She does, and I gently press the warm cloth to her.

"There, all clean and ready for another round."

"Big promises for someone who's leaving," she teases, snuggling back into the sheets as I pull on the suit I abandoned a few hours ago.

"Don't worry. The second Sutton is at school, I'm coming right back. And you'd better be exactly where you are now."

"Oh?"

Stepping up to the bed, I lean over her, now fully dressed. "Don't be a brat, Casey."

"And what if I am?" She flutters her lashes, and my hand darts out, collaring her throat.

Her eyes widen in surprise as she sucks in a breath.

"Test me and find out," I say darkly.

Her green pupils are swallowed by black as desire washes through her.

I smirk, tightening my grip for a beat and cutting off her air.

"I'll be back soon, baby. Be a good girl for me."

Leaning down, I steal one last kiss before I force myself to walk away.

After grabbing my carry-on and suitcase I had discarded in her living room, I make my way out of her apartment, feeling like I've left a piece of myself behind.

As I ride the elevator down to the ground floor, I call a car.

Thankfully, there's one right around the corner, and not five seconds after I've walked out into the morning LA sun does it appear before me.

With one look up at the building where Casey's apartment is, I let the driver take my things and climb into the back.

I close the door as quietly as I can and lower my luggage to the floor as Mom and Sutton's soft voices float around me.

My heart is in my throat as I toe off my shoes and creep toward the kitchen.

Surprising Casey was a rush, but so is this, only in an entirely different way.

Happy they don't seem to suspect anything, I step into the doorway and wait.

It takes two seconds before Mom looks up. Everything happens so fast it's almost a blur. For the briefest of moments, pure, unfiltered fear covers her face. But then, she registers who's standing there and the most incredible smile appears.

Sutton notices her distraction and turns to see what's happening.

She freezes in pure shock as her brain tries to figure out what's happening. But it doesn't matter; her body has already figured it out. Wearing the brightest of all smiles, she launches herself from the stool and flies at me.

"Daddy," she screams.

Her cry fills the kitchen as her body collides with me.

I sweep her off her feet and wrap my arms around her.

"You're here," she breathes as I suck in a deep hit of my girl.

"Surprise," I chuckle as my emotions threaten to get the better of me.

Long minutes pass as we stand there just holding each other, making up for all the cuddles we've missed while I've been away.

"Would you like some breakfast?" Mom asks after I've carried Sutton back and placed her on her stool.

My stomach growls right on cue.

"Yes, please."

But she doesn't immediately move. Instead, she studies me closely.

My heart jumps into my throat. What can she see?

"You need to ice your face," she finally says.

"Does it hurt, Daddy?" Sutton asks, dragging my attention back to her.

"Nah, it's fine."

"I can't believe Nash did that. What was wrong with him last night? His cross-checks were brutal. He should have been in the box long before you were. It was a joke."

"Forget Nash. What have you been up to, Peanut? Tell me everything," I say as Mom begins frying more bacon.

Usually, I'd tell her no and do it myself. She's already done more than enough these past two weeks. But I'm starving and exhausted, and I'm in desperate need of some Sutton time.

And that does it; she sucks in a breath and then unleashes the last two weeks of her life on me.

All the information makes my sleep-deprived head spin, but I wouldn't have it any other way.

54

KODIE

"It's good to have you home," Mom muses as I pull her in for a hug when Sutton runs upstairs to finish getting ready for school.

"It's good to be home," I confess as we part. "How has everything been?" I ask, aware that no matter how bad things get while I'm on the road, she'll lie and tell me it's all good.

I appreciate the fuck out of her for it, even if it drives me crazy, not really knowing what's going on with my own family.

I get it—she's trying to protect me and ensure I'm fully focused on the task at hand, but also, I just want to know.

She stares at me. "I think you and I have bigger things to discuss right now, don't we?" One of her brows lifts, and I instantly feel like a little boy who's been caught stealing food from the kitchen.

"Uh...do we?" I ask, wracking my brain for clues.

"We do."

Our stare holds as she stands there with her hands on her hips, trying to glare a confession from my lips.

"I don't know what you're talking about," I finally say, utterly confused.

This is what happens when I don't get any sleep. Or was it the orgasms that frazzled my head?

Mom smirks, her eyes dropping to my neck. On instinct, my hand lifts to cover whatever she's looking at.

"You smell like women's perfume and *s-e-x*," she sounds out the final word, as if that makes it better.

Fuck.

"Something you need to tell me?"

"Uh..."

"I'm assuming you picked those up after your flight."

Jesus fucking Christ.

I rub my scruffy jaw as I attempt to come up with a response.

"Is she...is she someone?" she asks with so much hope in her eyes that it makes my chest ache.

"Uh..." *Fuck's sake, Kodie. Find some fucking words.* "No?"

"No?" Mom asks skeptically.

"Shit," I hiss, entwining my fingers behind my neck and tugging. "I don't know. Maybe."

Mom doesn't react for a beat, but then the most incredible smile spreads across her mouth.

"Oh gosh, really?"

"Mom," I warn. "Don't get excited."

I swear, she's practically bouncing on the balls of her feet. "I'm not." I give her a look, and she attempts to wipe the smile off her face. "I promise I'm not."

I shake my head, because she's doing a really good fucking job of looking indifferent right now.

"I'm going to have a quick shower," I say, backing away from her.

I should have known that I'd smell of Casey, but I was too up in my head to really think about it.

Showering before I left her place would have been the most sensible thing to do, but it's a bit late now.

"Good idea," Mom agrees, still trying to hide her smile.

Ripping my eyes from her twinkling ones, I grab my luggage before jogging up the stairs.

"Aren't you taking me to school, Daddy?" Sutton asks with a frown as I pass her on the way out of her room.

"Of course. I'm just going to shower quick, and I'll be right there."

Her expression brightens before she sings, "Okay," and runs down the stairs to find Mom.

Dumping my stuff onto my bed, I strip out of my suit for the second time this morning and step naked into my bathroom.

I step up to the mirror and instantly see what Mom clocked.

"Fuck's sake, Casey," I laugh as I stare at the mark she left on my neck.

Of course, it's only fair. Her chest was littered with my own. But she's still in bed, or at least she should be. She isn't gracing others with her presence and pretending everything is fine.

With a contented sigh, I step into the shower and turn it on, letting myself get blasted with cold water. If the thought of returning to Casey and spending the day with her isn't enough to perk me up, then the chill will do it.

In only a few minutes, I sadly no longer smell like Casey and sex, and I'm dressed in jeans and a Vipers t-shirt, ready to take Sutton to school.

Checking my cell before I drop it into my pocket, I find a message that makes my heart flutter in my chest.

Calm down, Rivers. She's just a girl.

I close my eyes for a beat.

All the air comes rushing from my lungs when the photo loads on my phone. It's her twisted up in the sheet, looking all sexy and well-fucked.

Trouble: Being a good girl and waiting for my man to return.

My man.

I am so fucking screwed.

"Have things with Adrian been okay?" I ask as I take the final turn to Sutton's school.

I don't look over, but I know she rolled her eyes the second his name left my tongue.

"He's…his normal self."

"Look on the bright side. While he's being his normal self, he's not being worse," I offer.

"I guess. His team also won on Sunday. He's been telling anyone who will listen that he scored the final goal. It doesn't sound like it was very impressive. I heard one of the boys in the other class saying that the goalie wasn't even paying attention."

"Let him get his praise where he can and remember how freaking awesome your own winning goal was," I tell him.

When she called me on Sunday after the game to tell me what she'd done, she was buzzing. I was devastated not to be there and see her make that winning goal. But it is what it is.

She told me that her new coach was super stoked about it, and that helped. Of course, Mom was there in the crowd as well, cheering her on in my place.

"Don't worry, I won't forget that. You're going to be at my game on Sunday, right?"

"As long as you're at my game on Saturday," I counter.

"Try and stop me," she says with a smile.

"Come here, Peanut," I say, holding my arms out for a hug before we're forced to part again.

While I might hate leaving her, I drive away from school after watching her safely slip inside her classroom in a much better mindset than the last time I was here.

With nowhere else to be today until pick up other than in Casey's bed, I head that way, only pausing to grab coffee and breakfast for Casey.

Only, as I pull up, I realize I have a problem.

Opening my contacts on the screen, I find the person I called in the middle of the night for a little bit more help.

"Ah, good, you came up for air," is Parker's way of saying hello.

"How do you know I'm not ringing for life support?" I counter.

"Lucky for you, I've already spoken to Casey, and she's given me the delicious details of your sordid night, sparing you the job, so I'll just say...you are welcome."

"I appreciate it. But—"

"Ahhh," she laughs. "There it is."

I blow out a frustrated breath.

"Trust me, if I didn't have to call you, I wouldn't."

"Fine. She's a thirty-two D and/or a size six."

"What?" I splutter, my head spinning.

"What? You're calling because you want to buy her slutty lingerie, aren't you?"

"No, Parker."

"Shit, my bad."

"If I wanted to do that, I'd just look at the sizes she wears."

"Okay, so...what did you want?"

"I need her coffee order." I cringe as I say the words. It seems so stupid now, but I didn't want to guess and get it wrong.

"Oh," Parker laughs. "I mean, it's coffee; you can't exactly go wrong."

"Okay, but what's her favorite? Her treat?"

"Aw, Kodie. Don't make me think for even a moment that I could be wrong about hockey players."

I chuckle. "We're not all bad."

"Diamond in the rough, huh?"

"Casey doesn't seem to have any complaints."

"Not from what I've heard, no. Good job, Big D."

I shake my head, scrubbing my hand down my face. "So, coffee order?"

"Are you ready?" she warns, making me frown. How bad could it be?

"Always."

"Venti iced caramel macchiato with an extra shot made with oat milk, extra caramel sauce, half the ice and sprinkled with a little salt."

I narrow my eyes as I attempt to remember that blur of words.

"Got it?"

"Umm..."

"Kodie?"

"Yeah," I ask, my head spinning.

"The fact you called and asked makes you better than any other guy Casey has been with before." My fists clench at the thought of any man being near my troublemaker.

I don't respond. How can I?

"I know this might not be a big deal to you, but I promise you, being with you is a huge fucking deal to Casey. Please, don't hurt her."

"Parker—"

"No, listen for a moment," she says firmly. "If this is just a bit of fun, then that's fine, just make sure she knows that. Don't allow her to think it could be more if you know it can't be."

"Yeah," I agree, although I'm not entirely sure what I'm agreeing to.

Do I want this to be just a bit of fun that I can walk away from in a few days, weeks, or months? No, I really fucking don't. But equally, do I want this to turn into something serious?

I sink lower in my seat as that question sits heavy on my shoulders.

I don't think it's about whether I want it to or not; it's about whether it can be possible.

This isn't as simple as boy and girl finding something with each other. I come with a whole truckload of baggage that no woman deserves to deal with.

"Kodie?"

"Yeah," I breathe.

Silence fills the line as Parker battles with what to say.

"Be honest with her and yourself. The only way this will end badly is if you're not."

My lips part to respond, but Parker cuts the call, obviously wanting to have the final word.

"Fucking hell," I mutter, dragging my hand down my face before I push the door open and head inside to order her...fuck. What was her drink again?

I get into Casey's building with the codes Parker gave me just as easily as I did under the cover of darkness—but everything is different this time.

Casey knows I'm coming. Hell, if she's done as she was told, she should be waiting for me.

Desire stirs low in my gut. I'm already sporting a semi and I'm not even in the same room as her yet.

I've had her twice this morning. Shouldn't this incessant need lessen? Shouldn't my itch be scratched already? But if anything, I'm just as desperate as I was in the middle of the night with only one thing on my mind.

The control panel flashes green, and the lock disengages, allowing me entry into her apartment.

I slip inside and listen for a moment. It's silent.

Assuming she's followed orders, I step deeper into the apartment, but the second I round the corner, I discover I'm wrong.

Casey isn't lying in bed naked and waiting for me like I demanded.

She's standing in the kitchen, sipping on a cup of coffee, wearing my jersey and another pair of those fucking green panties.

My jaw tics as I take her in, my cock going full mast, pressing against the unforgiving fabric of my jeans.

"What are you doing?" I demand, my voice deep with desire.

She smirks, looking up at me through her lashes as I approach with our breakfast.

"I needed a drink."

"You're not in bed."

"I know, but—"

"No buts, Casey. You defied me."

She bites down on her bottom lip, and my cock jerks.

"Sorry, Daddy," she whispers. "Are you going to punish me?"

55

CASEY

Casey

Butterflies erupt the second I hear the front door open.

I have time to run back to the bedroom. He probably would be none the wiser. But honestly, where's the fun in doing what you're told?

So instead of running, I adjust his jersey around my waist, attempt to smooth down my wild sex hair, and rest my ass against the counter in the hope I look even a little bit alluring.

Each of his footsteps rock through me, but I refuse to cower. Instead, I use his approaching presence to strengthen my resolve.

He booked an earlier flight so he could see me sooner. He's come back after dropping Sutton at school. It all leads me to believe he really wants this.

If it were a quick hookup to take the edge off what was building between us this week, he'd have gone after he first had me. But he didn't. Instead, we cuddled.

Fuck.

I cuddled with Kodie freaking Rivers, and it was awesome.

I hold my breath as his shadow appears a beat before he steps around the corner.

His eyes widen the second he sees me, and his lips press into a thin line.

Oh, he's pissed.

I'm fucking giddy. Who knew I could hold the power to shake this incredible man?

I hold my head higher as his eyes run down the length of me.

"What are you doing?" he growls, the rasp of his voice hitting me right between the legs.

My pussy should be done. We had two very intense rounds in the middle of the night. But that doesn't seem to be the case. Instead, she seems to have forgotten she's already had more thrills than usual for this time of the morning.

He approaches, eating up the space between us in a few short strides, sucking all the air from the room as he does.

"I needed a drink," I say coyly, fluttering my lashes at him like I'm all innocent.

"You're not in bed," he states.

"I know, but—"

His jaw tics, his fists clenching at his sides.

He's huge, strong, powerful, and nothing but corded muscle. But I'm not scared of him. Instead, I'm desperate, needy, and craving another taste of him. "No buts, Casey. You defied me."

I bite down on my bottom lip praying it stops a groan from breaking free.

"Sorry, Daddy," I whisper. "Are you going to punish me?"

Oh, please. Give me everything.

He moves again, abandoning the takeout coffee tray and paper bag on the counter before grabbing my hand and dragging me from my spot.

I race behind him, my heart pounding a mile a minute.

He leads me out of my kitchen and into my modest living area before he drops onto my couch.

It's a decent-sized piece of furniture, but suddenly, with his hulking frame on it, it looks tiny.

With his hand still clutching mine, he tugs me closer so I'm standing right before him.

"What are you going to do?" I ask, my voice barely a whisper as my excitement and anticipation get the better of me.

His grin turns dangerous, and I shriek when he suddenly tugs on my arm, giving me little choice but to bend over and lie across his lap.

"Kodie, what—" My words die as he gets me into position and realization hits. "Oh my god," I whimper as his hand slides up the backs of my thighs before kneading my ass.

He's going to spank me.

This is my punishment for being a bad girl.

Heat blooms in my lower stomach as my core floods with desire.

He's barely touched me, but already, my panties are ruined.

"What did I tell you to do?" he demands.

"To...to stay in bed and wait."

"And what did you do?"

"Got up."

"I told you to be a good girl. And what have you been?"

"Bad. I've been bad."

"And what do bad girls get?"

Fucking hell. This is too much. I'm squirming on his lap like a desperate little whore.

"Punished," I gasp. "Please, Kodie."

His hand leaves my ass, and my body locks up in preparation for what's to come.

Another whimper spills free a beat before his palm collides with my ass.

I cry out as my body jolts forward, my feet leaving the floor as pain blooms on my ass cheek, warmth spreading through my body. Instinctively, my hands shoot behind me, in a pathetic attempt to cover myself.

He tsks in disappointment, and they fall away again.

"You're going to take ten. Count for me," Kodie demands, his voice deeper than I've ever heard it.

"One," I gasp, still recovering from the hit.

He does it again. This time, I'm almost prepared for it.

"Oh my god," I cry as the pain shoots straight to my clit.

My ass might be burning already, but it has nothing on the way my pussy is throbbing with need.

"You're counting, remember?"

"Two," I whisper before quickly counting three, four, and five.

By the time he hits six, seven, and eight, I'm riding a knife's edge.

No one has ever spanked me like this before. Sure, I've had the odd slap during doggy style, but this is very, very different.

"Nine," I cry, my voice hoarse, my body limp despite the desire coursing through my veins.

He rubs the sting, his calloused hand gently scratching at my tender skin.

Tears fall freely from my lashes. I'm breathless, and my core is clenching on nothing, desperate to be filled.

When he pulls back, I suck in a deep breath, both ready for this to be over and desperate to keep going all at the same time. It's a heady feeling. One I could become addicted to a little too easily, given the chance.

"Ten," I all but scream as he connects again. "Fuck, that was..."

"You did so well, baby. Such a good girl for me. And look at this ass." His hand rubs over me. "So pretty."

I light up at his praise. I swear to God, he could ask me to do anything right now and I would without question.

"Kodie," I whimper.

Knowing exactly what I need, he hooks his finger under the edge of my panties and pulls them aside.

"Fuck," he grunts. "You're soaked."

I know. I'm fucking dying here.

"Please."

"So fucking beautiful."

I cry out when his fingers connect with my swollen, sensitive skin, coating himself in my juices, before sinking two inside me.

"Oh my god. I'm so close."

"You're a bad girl, Casey Watson. But you're my bad girl."

"Yes, yes."

"You're going to come all over my fingers before you swallow my dick. Are you ready for that?"

"So ready," I gasp as he holds me right on the edge of my release.

"My perfect whore," he muses, and that's it. I shatter.

My release rocks through me, my body convulsing on his lap as wave after wave drags me under.

It goes on and on. I swear it's the longest orgasm I've ever experienced. It's exhausting and exhilarating all at the same time.

Kodie doesn't stop until I've sagged in relief, and then he gives me only thirty seconds before he's gently moving me to my knees between his parted thighs.

"Take my dick out, Trouble."

I scramble to do as he says, my need to have his taste on my tongue at an all-time high.

The second I've released him, I rub the precum on his tip before stroking him, once, twice.

"Enough," he growls. "I want your pouty lips wrapped around me."

He shifts slightly, making it easier for me, before resting his hands on either side of his hips, allowing me to take my fill.

And I do.

With one hand wrapped around the base of his shaft, I lick around his tip, savoring his taste before sinking down on him.

The low growl that rumbles in his chest is all the encouragement I need, and I hollow my cheeks, relax my throat, and take him as deep as I dare.

Unable to keep his hands to himself, he twists his fingers in my hair and helps to control my movements. But at no point does he force me to take him deeper. He allows me to control the pace; he's just there with me.

"Push your hand into your panties and play with your clit," he demands, his deep rasp suddenly filling my apartment.

I don't need telling twice. Sliding my hand down my stomach, I tuck my fingers beneath the edge of my panties and almost instantly discover just how true his words from earlier were.

My fingers slide through my folds with ease, and I circle my clit as I continue to suck him.

"Don't you dare come," he warns.

I shake my head, so he knows I'm not ignoring him.

In only seconds, my next release is growing, my already weak legs trembling. And I'm not the only one, because Kodie's cock is swelling, stretching my lips even wider.

But just before I think he's about to shoot down my throat, his grip on my hair tightens, and I'm pulled from his cock.

I stare up at him in disbelief, only a string of saliva connecting us.

"I'm not coming in your mouth, baby," he explains before pushing to his feet and lifting me from the floor as if I weigh nothing more than a feather.

Spinning around, he places me on my knees on the couch.

"Rest your arms on the back and stick your ass out," he demands, his hands wrapping around my hips to help me out.

The second I'm where he wants me, he drags my wet panties down, leaving them around my knees before he steps forward.

"Oh god, please," I beg, arching my back more in the hope he'll find my entrance faster. "Kodie, I need you."

"Fucking love it when you beg," he groans as he rubs himself through my wetness.

"Fuck me, Kodie, please. I need your dick inside me."

He pauses at my entrance and notches just the tip in.

My body sags in relief.

"Only because you asked me nicely," he says before pushing in so slowly it makes my eyes cross.

"Holy shit."

"Sensitive, baby?" he asks. I swear I can hear the cocky smirk that's no doubt playing on his lips.

"Yes. So good. More. Deeper. Faster."

"Fuck. I'm pretty sure you were made for me," he groans as he bottoms out.

It's so deep like this. So deep and perfect. He hits me in all the right places.

"Need you to come for me again," he demands as one of his hands slips from my hip and down to my clit.

"Yes," I cry, my back arching in my need to take him even

deeper. I don't care if it's not possible; I need it. "Kodie. Kodie. Fuck. YESSSS."

I clamp down on his dick as I fall over the edge again. How many orgasms this powerful can you have before you legit die of pleasure?

"Casey," he booms as his dick pulses inside me, spilling everything he has. "Holy fuck," he groans as his release continues. I know the fucking feeling.

The second he's done, he folds over me, wrapping his arms around my ribs and tucking his face into my neck.

"Tell me you've got a bathroom with a really big tub in it?" he murmurs.

"Uh...I have a bathroom with a normal-sized tub," I counter.

"It'll have to do," he says, twisting me around and laying me on the couch.

I can't help but smile as he walks away. In only seconds, he's returning with my iced coffee—ice long departed.

"What are you smirking about?" he asks, studying me. I probably look like a mess with my hair in every direction and my panties bunched around my knees.

He doesn't seem to notice.

"Wondering why you're not naked."

His smile grows.

"I will be once I've fed you. Breakfast is cold. You good if I warm it up?"

"Knock yourself out," I say. "But could you at least take your top off?"

He laughs but humors me by reaching behind his head and pulling it off in one slick move.

How do guys do that? And why is it always so freaking hot?

56

CASEY

After warming up my cold bagel, Kodie brought it over and sat beside me as I ate. We were silent, but it was perfect, and I had the most incredible post-sex glow.

Once he was happy that I'd been fed, he swept me into his arms and, with my direction—not that it's hard in my small apartment—he carried me to the bathroom and sat me on the counter as he filled the tub with hot water and bubbles.

Then, and only then, did I get my wish, and he stripped down to nothing, giving me a nice little show.

He then peeled my jersey off and carried me to the tub.

I wasn't lying when I told him that I had an average-sized tub, and it was a very, very snug fit. But I wasn't complaining. I was snuggled up with a very naked, very hot Kodie Rivers. I was living my best life.

He made sure to clean every inch of me, and despite me trying to heat things up again, he was the perfect gentleman, telling me that I needed to rest before he took me again. It wasn't an if, it was a when, and I couldn't freaking wait.

So instead, we talked. He told me about his trip, about his game, and the guys, and in return, he asked me about work, and Parker, and Freya. He listened to every single word I said as his fingers trailed up and down my arm, ensuring that my desire for him continued to bubble just under the surface.

My addiction to my hockey god is officially off the scale now, and I don't stand a chance of quitting.

By the time the water got cold, I was curled up on his chest, fighting against sleep.

As soon as Kodie noticed, he lifted me out, wrapped me in one of my huge, fluffy towels, and carried me to my bed.

Naked, he crawled in with me, and with his big body wrapped around mine, I drifted off to sleep, happy, content, and very, very satisfied.

I wake who knows how many hours later to the most incredible sound.

Kodie laughing.

A smile tugs at my lips. I wish I could bottle that sound and keep it forever. Right alongside his scent. Needing another hit, I roll over to the pillow he was lying on and breathe in deeply.

Addicted. Utterly addicted.

I'm unable to make out what he's saying as his deep tone rumbles through my apartment, and while I don't want to eavesdrop, my need for him is too strong to deny. Throwing the covers back, I swing my legs over the edge and stand up. My muscles pull in the best kind of way, and as I move, tenderness between my thighs makes itself known.

Worth it. So freaking worth it.

After swiping my robe from my chair, I make my way to my connected bathroom to freshen up.

"Dude, are you serious right now?" Kodie barks as I slip silently into the kitchen, although the second my eyes land on him, my movements falter.

He's standing in front of the windows in only a fitted pair of boxer briefs. The fall sun lights up his body, making his tattoos almost look like they're glowing and highlighting his incredible muscle definition.

I stand there unnoticed, completely ogling him. The thing is with Kodie, he's not only beautiful on the outside. It's the man I'm getting to know who hides beneath the surface who's really taking my breath away.

The dedicated athlete, the caring father, the thoughtful lover, the supportive friend.

All of it.

Shit. I'm falling harder and faster than I can control.

This wasn't meant to happen.

It was meant to be a bit of fun. Knocking off the top item on my bucket list. I wasn't meant to fall for him.

"No, I know." He sighs. "She's going to fucking owe us."

Whoever's on the other end of the line speaks.

"Oh, great. Yeah, I'll really look forward to that."

He nods.

"Yep, okay. Sure." He laughs again at it hits me right in the chest. "Yeah, I will. Yes, she will too."

I frown; surely he's not talking about me?

"You got it. Bye."

As he hangs up, another huge sigh passes his lips. I want to ask him and help fix whatever's bothering him. But are we there yet? Will we ever be?

Wanting to announce myself before he turns around and finds me listening to him, I surge forward.

"Hey," I sing a little too chirpily. Could I sound any guiltier?

He startles before spinning around, making my breath catch all over again.

How is this real?

I'm still convinced that this is all a dream that I'm going to wake up from at any moment.

The smirk on his face points to the fact there isn't actually anything wrong, and I breathe a sigh of relief.

"Everything okay?"

He continues studying me for a few seconds before stalking toward me.

"Yeah, it was just Linc."

After placing his cell on the kitchen counter, he comes to a stop right in front of me. His hand wraps around the back of my neck before he ducks to brush a sweet kiss on my lips.

"He knows about us," he confesses while we're still connected.

Ice floods my veins as his words register.

I pull back in a panic and stare up at him with my heart pounding.

"H-He—'

"He won't say anything," Kodie assures me with confidence.

I shake my head. Linc is one of the biggest gossips I've ever known. As soon as he learns anything, he spreads it far and wide. Okay, sure, he's usually chirping about rivals, doing his best to rile them up and cause drama, but still.

The fact he knows...

Fuck. It makes me nervous.

"Did you tell him?" I ask. I hate that it comes out sounding so accusatory.

I've told Parker. Hell, I needed to tell Parker. I'm pretty sure I'd have exploded by now if I hadn't confessed. I'd be a hypocrite if I was angry at him for doing the same thing.

Sure, Kodie and Linc might have built a friendship since Kodie's transfer, but how close could they really be. They've only known each other a year.

It's fine. It's going to be fine.

"No," Kodie confesses, nervously rubbing at the back of his neck.

"Then how—"

"He figured it out."

"Shit," I hiss. "How?" I repeat.

A laugh tumbles from his lips. "Turns out your disguise that night wasn't actually all that good."

"Oh my god," I breathe. "He's known all this time?"

Kodie shrugs one shoulder. "Seems that way. He's only just confessed that though."

"I knew he was my biggest risk that night," I mutter under my breath.

Out of all the players on the Vipers roster, Linc is the one I've known the longest, although we've never been close. But if anyone wasn't going to be fooled that night, it would have been him.

"It's going to be okay, baby. He'll keep our secret."

I stare up at him, my heart in my throat.

Is that all I am? Kodie Rivers' dirty little secret?

Once upon a time, I would have said it would have been everything to me. In a way, it is. But is hiding what we've found as if we're doing something wrong really what I want?

No.

I want to shout and scream from the rooftops that I'm with this incredible man. I want to nestle my way deeper into his life and ensure he keeps smiling and laughing like he does when he's with me. It's a heady feeling, a high like no other, and I'm not ready to lose that yet.

I nod as I force the emotion down. I don't want to ruin what we've found here because of my insecurities and fears.

He doesn't want a serious relationship. He isn't looking for anyone to join his family. I get that; I really do.

I just have to find a way to be okay with it.

"Yeah, okay."

Reaching out, he cups my jaw and brushes his thumb across my bottom lip.

"I don't know about you, but I like what we've got going on at the moment," he says, his voice barely above a whisper.

"Me too," I agree softly.

"My life is complicated, and most days I feel like I'm being pulled in a million different directions. I won't lie, adding you into the mix adds a whole new one, but as complicated as it might be, I can't imagine it any other way at this point."

"Kodie," I breathe.

"I can't put a label on this, and I'm nowhere near ready to figure out how we move from the place we're in right now. I'm not sure there even is another place, if I'm really being honest. But that's not to say that I don't want to see if there might be."

My eyes burn with tears, and I fight as hard as I can to stop them.

It might not exactly be what I want to hear, but it's something.

It's a start.

It's him trying to reassure me without freaking himself out by moving too fast.

"I'm sorry, Casey. I wish I could offer you more, but right now—"

Reaching up, I press two fingers to his lips, cutting off his words.

"It's okay. I understand," I promise before stretching up on my toes and replacing my fingers with my lips.

"You look different," Parker says. I shrug as I walk toward my kitchen with her hot on my tail.

After Kodie left earlier to pick Sutton up from school, I messaged Parker with a brief update, and she told me that she was coming over the second she finished with her final client of the day.

"Don't know what you're talking about."

"Of course you don't," she mutters as I reach into the cupboard to grab two glasses for the wine she brought with her. "You're glowing."

"I've barely slept, so it isn't through rest."

"I hate you," she teases.

"I know. Getting banged six ways from Sunday by a hockey god is a hard job, but someone's got to do it."

"Was it that good?" she asks, her eyes locked on me as I turn around and begin pouring.

"It was better than that."

"Gimme," she says, making little grabby hands for her glass.

With a chuckle, I slide it closer and watch as she swallows a large mouthful.

"I need to get laid," she complains. "I'm torn between needing all the details and wanting to shove my face into a pillow and scream with jealousy."

"Just know that every time with Kodie has been a million times better than any other guys I've ever been with. He's..." I take a moment to think. "Gentle yet rough, demanding yet giving."

"Sounds confusing," she muses.

"It's perfect."

"Jesus. You have legit hearts for eyes. You are so gone for him."

I take a sip of my wine, needing a little liquid courage for what I'm about to say.

"Yeah, and it's a problem."

"Case, you're happier than I've ever seen you. How is that a problem?"

"Because I'm going to end up with a broken heart."

She stares at me, and in her eyes, I can see that she knows I'm right. But those aren't the words that spill from her lips.

"But you might not."

"I appreciate the positive thinking, I really do. But let's be honest here."

"There is nothing to say that this will all end badly. If he feels even half of what you do for him, he might surprise you."

"Parker," I sigh. "He's a father. He doesn't have time for me in his life. His job is...as demanding as they get."

"He came home from Vancouver early to see you. He still saw Sutton and took her to school, and then came back to spend the day with you. Those aren't the actions of a man who can't make time for you."

"Today was an exception. It was a travel day. Once training starts up again tomorrow, I'll be pushed aside."

"Or you might not."

I love Parker to death, I really do, but I'm not sure I can cope with much more of her positivity. She's usually the more level-headed one out of the two of us. I'm the dreamer, the one whose glass is always half full, but for the first time in as long as I can remember, we've switched roles.

"Anyway, how did he react to you being Sutton's new coach?"

My teeth sinking into my bottom lip is all the answer she needs.

"Casey," she chastises.

"It's fine. Hailee has sent them to some community outreach thing tomorrow afternoon, so he can't make it to training anyway. It buys me a few more days to figure out how to tell him."

57

———

KODIE

I glance at my watch, hating that Sutton's training session is in five minutes and I'm stuck here.

Usually, I love spending time inspiring young hockey players, but right now, this event for high school players hoping for a future in the league is the last place I want to be.

I want to see my girl cutting up the ice and getting ready for her game on Sunday.

Hell, I wanted to pick her up from school and be a dad to her again while I'm at home, but after a strength and conditioning session and an afternoon on the ice, then having to race across town to get here on time, it just wasn't going to happen.

Hailee, our director of public relations, wanted as many of us here as possible and wasn't accepting any excuses to get out of it.

She might only be five-foot-two with a waist that's probably smaller than my thigh, but she's a force to be reckoned with. None of the guys say no to her. I understand why, too. I've heard the stories of the kinds of things she makes you do if you don't follow along with her plans.

I smirk as I remember a story Linc told me about the time she forced Killer to spend an afternoon at our local bird sanctuary after he refused to attend some other event she'd planned. He's shit scared of birds and had to stand there with a glove on as an eagle of some sort landed on his arm and ate a dead chick from his

412

hand. Not his finest moment, but it's safe to say, he's never refused to follow orders since. Something tells me Hailee knows most of the guys' secrets and is more than willing to use them against us.

She sure as hell knows my weakness—youth hockey. Especially girls' youth hockey. Sutton has opened my eyes to just how lacking the support is. I'll do anything to help raise awareness and open the opportunity for more girls to get involved.

I watch the rest of my teammates chat to the boys who've come. They sign whatever they're handed, laugh, and give advice where necessary. It's great, but I can't help but feel like something is missing.

All the young athletes here are male. Of course, that might be because there aren't many girls interested in hockey at this school, but I find that hard to believe.

"Hey, sorry. Is there any chance I could get your autograph?" a boy, probably no older than fourteen, asks, handing me a Vipers jersey and a marker pen.

"Of course," I say with a smile, reaching for the pen.

"Thank you so much. My sister is going to be so stoked. She loves you."

"She should have come," I say absently as I sign the fabric.

"She's outside with a couple of friends," he admits.

"Why?"

"They wanted to see if any other girls turned up. I've tried telling them that this event is for everyone, but they feel a bit awkward."

"That's bull—" I just about manage to cut myself off.

"I agree. It is bullshit." He lowers his voice. "Bailey is a better hockey player than most of the guys here."

"Is that right?" I muse. "You wanna take me out to meet her?"

"U-uh..." he stutters, looking around at the crowds of boys waiting their turn to speak to their idols. "You'd do that?"

"Yeah, of course. We're meant to be inspiring hockey players of the future, and your sister is a player, right?"

"Yeah. Her dream is to play in the Olympics," he explains.

"Okay then, lead the way."

He spins around and marches across the room like a man on a mission, and I don't waste a second following him.

We're almost at the door when someone shouts my name, forcing me to stop.

"Where are you going?" Hailee asks as she storms over, her eyes narrowed in suspicion.

I might want to leave so I can go and watch Sutton, but she should know that I'd never walk out of an event like this without at least clearing it with her.

"Going to meet someone outside."

Her eyes narrow even more, if that's possible.

"It's my sister," the kid explains. "She and her friends didn't want to come in and—"

"Come on," I say, gesturing for Hailee to follow us. It won't be a bad thing for our PR director to experience firsthand just how little support the girls get compared to the boys.

I squint as we step out into the bright late afternoon sunlight and scan the area.

Over on the left, sitting on a bench, are three girls.

They're too busy chatting to notice as we move toward them, but it only takes a couple of seconds for the middle one to notice our approach, and her eyes widen and her chin drops.

"Oh my god," she gasps. "Oh my god. Oh my god. Oh my god."

The other two look at her with wrinkled brows until they follow her line of sight.

"Oh my god," they both repeat simultaneously.

"Afternoon, ladies. Which one of you is Bailey?" I ask as they continue to freak out.

"Uh...m-me," the middle one stutters before surging to her feet and sticking her hand out. "Oh my god, I can't believe you're standing right in front of me."

All the blood has drained from her face as she lifts her hand to cover her mouth. I'm pretty sure she's seconds away from passing out.

"God, I'm so sorry," she says in a rush.

"It's okay. Here, your brother asked me to sign this for you," I say, holding out the jersey that's still in my hand.

"Wow, that's..." She turns her attention briefly to her brother, her eyes filling with tears. "Did you really ask him to do that?" she asks in disbelief.

Her brother shrugs as if it's nothing.

"Your brother tells me that you play. That you're hoping for a chance at the Olympics."

She nods frantically. "Y-yeah. I mean, that's the dream."

"What about your friends?" I ask, casting them all glances.

"We play, but we're not as good as Bailey," one of them explains.

"Tell me about your team, and your plans for the future," I prompt. Looking at them, I'd say they're older than the boy who approached me. Fair play to that kid; he deserves Brother of the Year for what he just did.

Bailey chats away, barely coming up for air.

"You know, you deserve to be in there just as much as all the boys."

"I know," she says softly. "It's just awkward."

"The problem is," one of her friends pipes up, "Bailey could outscore any of the boys in there. That makes her a target. They all refuse to believe they could be beaten by a girl. But they would be."

I nod, not doubting a word of it.

"I know a little girl a bit like that," I muse, thinking of Sutton.

I hate that there's a chance she could still be experiencing the bullshit with Adrian into her teen years. I hate even more that it could get worse. Right now, it's just one boy, but by the time she's in high school, I do not doubt that it'll be more.

"I'd love to come and catch one of your games sometime," I say, even more convinced that she's going to hit the deck any moment.

"Oh my god, stop. You're kidding, right?"

"Absolutely not. This sport needs more girls like you, Bailey. All girls' and women's teams deserve the attention the male teams get. You're just as talented, and with everything you face, you're much more resilient."

"Wow, that's just...wow."

"You should call your team, get them down here. The Vipers would love to talk to them."

She nods enthusiastically as her friends pull their cell phones out.

After getting her head coach's name, and a million and one thank yous from the girls, Hailee and I head back inside.

"That was a really nice thing to do."

"I don't need to tell you that growing awareness for women's ice hockey is one of my passions." Hailee is more than aware. I've turned up in her office on more than one occasion demanding equal representation with our charity work and affiliations with youth teams.

"It'll happen," she promises me.

"Maybe you can come to one of their games with me. Meet the staff and the girls. See if there's something we can do," I suggest hopefully.

"When you get the dates, send them on."

I nod, accepting her words before glancing at my watch again.

"Am I keeping you from something, Rivers?"

"Sutton is training. I haven't seen her on the ice for a couple of weeks."

A soft smile appears on her lips. "Go," she whispers.

"Really?" I ask, afraid to get my hopes up.

The guys have still got a few hours here yet. The number of boys in the room is only growing.

"Yes. You just made that girl's entire year by making her feel seen. You validated her as an athlete. She'll never forget it. Now, go and see your little ice demon. Go and make her smile as well. She deserves it. She's been a long time without her daddy."

"You're the best, Hails," I say before rushing out of the building as fast as my legs will take me.

I don't bother saying goodbye to anyone; they'll all understand.

I'm in my car and heading across town in only a few minutes.

I make a quick pit stop for a packet of Hershey's Kisses, Sutton's favorite treat, before pulling up to the arena. No sooner have I killed the engine, am I on my feet and racing toward the rink where I know Sutton is going to be.

I hear them long before I see them, their high-pitched voices shouting and cheering each other on, their passion and dedication clear in their voices.

They may all be under eight, but it doesn't matter; hockey is their everything. This time on the ice will hands down be the best part of their day.

I remember it well.

With a fond smile playing on my lips, I round the final corner. The rink appears before me. The girls always look so tiny out there, even in their pads. I'm so used to the guys cutting up the ice that it always takes me by surprise to see their small bodies flying around.

I watch them shooting pucks into an open goal two at a time as I approach.

Sutton doesn't see me; she's too focused on her next turn.

I stand there at the boards on the other side of the rink to the rest of the parents as Megan, her head coach, shoots a puck toward Sutton.

She catches it instantly before skating forward and shooting.

I holler the second it hits the back of the net, and Sutton spins around with a wide smile on her face that makes my heart tumble in my chest.

"Daddy," she mouths.

She skates up and presses her gloved hands to the plexiglass.

I do the same.

"You came," she shouts.

"I managed to get away early."

Her smile widens.

"Gran is over there," she shouts, pointing over her shoulder. "Go and watch."

Lifting my eyes, I look across the rink. But Mom isn't the first person I find.

Instead, my eyes lock onto another familiar set of eyes.

A green set.

A set that I can't stop fucking thinking about.

Confusion wars within me as she stands like a rabbit in headlights.

"What's Casey Watson doing here?" I don't mean to say the words out loud, but they spill from my lips regardless.

"Oh, didn't I tell you?" Sutton shouts. "She's our new coach."

58

CASEY

My heart slams against my ribs. The entire arena slips away from me. The only thing—the only person—I can see is Kodie standing on the opposite side of the ice behind the plexiglass, staring at me as if I'm a ghost.

Oh god.

He wasn't meant to be here.

My blood runs cold.

He's looking at me as if he doesn't know me, not like I'm the woman he did all kinds of ungodly things to barely twenty-four hours ago.

Another girl on the team shouts in celebration of her goal, and I manage to rip my eyes away from Kodie's and focus on my job.

Coaching, Casey. You should be coaching.

Just pretend he's not here.

Fuck. That's easier said than done.

I'm frozen on the ice as the last few girls take their shots.

Out of the corner of my eye, I watch as Sutton rejoins her team and Kodie walks around the rink toward where his mom is sitting.

My stomach twists, the lunch I had hours ago threatening to reappear. Steeling myself, I try to focus on the task at hand. But honestly, running away right now seems like a much better option.

"Right, team," I call getting the girls' attention.

They skate over to where I'm standing, eager to hear what's next.

Something settles inside me as twelve pairs of excited eyes hold mine.

"Fantastic work out there, guys. Some of the Vipers would be jealous of those goals. Now, we're going to spend the next fifteen minutes working on our stick handling and passing before our friendly game to end our session."

I glance up to see Megan already setting out the cones in two lines down the ice. I was buzzing when she told me that today's session was mine to plan and lead. Or at least, I was until Kodie showed up. Now, I'm a mess, and I'm questioning everything I'm getting the girls to do. What if he doesn't think it's enough? What if he thinks I should be pushing harder? What if—

I blink, forcing my worries from my head as I skate around the team and begin explaining their drill.

With three players at each end of the cones, Megan and I drop the puck, and the first girl takes off, weaving her way through, showing off her agility on the ice as well as her puck control.

Once she's completed the course, she passes the puck to the next girl, who takes off back down through the cones.

"That's it, keep the speed up," I encourage as the girls weave in and out, so fluid and relaxed on the ice.

Aurora effortlessly weaves between the last two cones before she gets ready to pass to Sutton.

My eyes follow the puck as it leaves her stick and lands right on target. Sutton takes off with the kind of ease I'm used to seeing from the professionals.

As she embarks on the course, my gaze lifts to her father. I find him watching his daughter with nothing but love and awe in his eyes, and my heart tumbles.

That man is literally everything.

His attention doesn't leave her until she's passed to the next player, then he sits back, his eyes moving straight to me.

I swallow thickly.

His face is expressionless, so different to how he looked yesterday while we were hanging out, and I mentally kick myself for not pulling up my big girl pants and just telling him about this.

How badly could it have gone?

A shit ton better than it's going right now.

Forcing myself to move, I turn my back to him and focus on my girls.

Once they've done two rounds of the drill, Megan hands out colored vests to go over their jerseys, turning them into two teams, and we stand back as they battle it out.

Pride for these girls oozes from my every pore. Watching them put everything they've learned in our session to practice during a game, even if it is just a friendly one between themselves, is amazing. I can only imagine how Kodie feels, watching his baby boss it on the ice. With only a couple of bumps and girls skidding across the ice after a collision, we bring the game to an end and finish off our session.

After wishing them all a good rest of their week, we watch them wobble off on their skates toward their waiting parents.

"Good session, Coach," Megan praises.

"Thanks," I mutter, my stomach knotting tighter and tighter. "I'm going to check in with Mila, make sure she's okay after that fall."

Megan nods as a mom approaches to speak to her.

Swallowing down my nerves, I hold my head high and walk toward the benches where the girls are getting sorted.

Once I reach Mila and her mom, I drop to my haunches.

"How are you feeling?" I ask, my eyes bouncing between hers, searching for a lie.

It's not just the professionals who will put on a brave face and try to cover up any pain.

"I'm okay."

"Are you sure? It's okay to say if it hurts. I can get someone to check you over if you need—"

"I promise, I'm fine."

"Okay," I say, rising to my feet and focusing on her mom.

"She's tough," her mom muses as movement behind her catches my eye.

"She is. They all are. Any problems, though, you let us know." Mila's mom agrees before she turns her attention to her daughter and begins to help her pack up her gear.

"Hey, Coach C," a familiar voice says. "Great session today."

I can't help but smile. "Thanks, Sutton."

"You know my dad, right?" she says, grabbing my hand before I have a chance to do anything and marching me over.

"U-uh...yeah, we've...met." The final word comes out as a whisper as Kodie's angry eyes lock on mine.

"He's taught me everything I know," Sutton announces proudly.

"Maybe you shouldn't say that in front of one of your coaches, sweetie," Kodie's mom offers, cringing.

"Ah, it's okay..."

"Kathleen," she finishes for me.

"We should really get going," Kodie suddenly says.

"Daddy, Coach C used to play as well, didn't you?" She looks up at me with the widest, most innocent of eyes.

"Um...yeah, I did," I confess awkwardly. "My daddy taught me everything I know, too."

Kodie makes a scoffing noise, and my eyes shoot to his. "I very much doubt that's true," he seethes.

My chin drops, shock rendering me useless.

"Kodie," Kathleen snaps in shock while Sutton looks between me and Kodie with wide eyes.

"We need to go," he states before spinning around, swiping her gear bag from the floor, and stalking toward the exit.

"I'm so sorry," Kathleen breathes. "I don't know what's gotten into him."

"Daddy can be grumpy when he's had a long day," Sutton adds, desperately trying to defend him.

"It's fine. I know how hard your daddy and the team work. Go and be nice to him, okay?"

If it's possible, her smile grows wider.

"You've got it, Coach. See you Sunday."

"Not if I see you first," I tease before walking away, my heart threatening to beat out of my chest.

"Everything okay?" Megan asks as I join her in sorting out equipment ready for the under tens.

"Yeah, everything's great," I lie.

"Casey, for fuck's sake," Parker complains. "Didn't I warn you that something like this would happen?"

"Yes," I sigh, flopping back on my couch and holding my cell above my face so I can still see her on the call.

"See, if you'd have just told him..."

"I know," I snap. "I fucking know. I just...I didn't want to lose him earlier than necessary."

Parker sighs, her expression softening.

"I know, babe. But you should have told him when you first got the job."

"What do I do now?"

It's been hours since he walked away from me. I worked with Megan and Jamie with the under tens, and then Megan and I chatted about applying for my coaching certification for just over an hour. But despite the time that has passed, I haven't heard a single thing from Kodie.

I think the radio silence might be worse than anything else.

At least if he were shouting at me, I'd know how he felt.

"Has he said anything?"

"Nope."

"Then you need to make the first move." I know that. I do. I just...don't want to.

I've always had this deep-rooted fear of upsetting my dad. He was always away so much that when he was at home, the last thing I wanted to do was disappoint him. That familiar feeling is taking up room right now.

I've disappointed Kodie, and I hate myself for it.

It's all my own fault. I could have prevented it. But I was scared.

I was terrified that if I told him, it would be just another reason why we couldn't be together. Another reason to end this sooner.

Then, we wouldn't have had yesterday, and that would have been a travesty.

Yesterday was everything to me. Everything.

"What if it's over?" I whisper, voicing my greatest fear.

"What if it's not?" Parker counters. "Only one way to find out."

We end the call, but before I pluck up the courage to reach out to Kodie, I roll off the couch and pad toward the bathroom.

I'm running numerous options through my head as I pee, none of which give me any hope.

I lied to him. He has every right to back away now.

My cell dings as I make my way back through my apartment, and my heart jumps into my throat.

Maybe it's all okay and I'm overreacting. Maybe he was just busy with Sutton and waiting until she's in bed.

Maybe I'm just lying to myself.

When I get to my phone and the message lights up, my heart sinks.

Dad: Ten minutes out with takeout. Get ready.

"Shit," I hiss, guilt twisting me up inside that I forgot.

Casey: I'll be ready.

Despite forgetting that I agreed to have dinner with Dad, we have a lovely night together catching up. However, I never lose the elephant in the room, which is the huge secret I'm keeping from him.

He tells me about their two weeks away, filling me in on the stupid things the guys did to the rookie, and the events and charity opportunities that Hailee dragged him to. He also excitedly tells me about how he returned home to a freezer full of premade meals that Freya made for him, which allows a little more guilt to trickle in. And I explain about my coaching and the girls I'm working with.

It's a nice evening, but at no point do I forget what happened this afternoon, and at no point does my cell ding to announce an incoming message.

The thought of my time with Kodie being over brings a lump to my throat.

"Are you okay, Care Bear?" Dad asks as I stop at my door to see him off.

His eyes bounce between mine, and my stomach sinks.

What can he see?

"Yeah, of course. I'm just so glad you have you back again." It's not a lie; I miss him now when he's away just like when I was a kid.

"Aw, I'm glad to be back too. It'll be good to play on our own ice again."

"I can't wait."

"You'll be there Saturday?"

"Absolutely."

"Breakfast before I go in?"

"You got it."

He gives me one final hug before we part and he disappears down the hallway, leaving me standing there with tears filling my eyes.

The truth is, I'm not okay. Not even close.

Locking my door, I head back into my apartment to tidy up and send the message I've been putting off.

But as I step into the kitchen, my cell vibrates across the counter, and the message I've been both hoping for and dreading is there.

55: One new message.

My heart is in my throat as I stare at the screen, praying this isn't going to be as bad as I fear.

Eventually, I manage to convince myself to swipe and discover the truth.

> 55: This has been fun, but I think this is also where it needs to stop.

59

KODIE

The number of times I typed and deleted different versions of that same message was a joke.

But I couldn't help it.

I'm freaking out.

When Sutton told me about her new coach, I didn't give it a another thought. I certainly didn't consider for one second that it could have been Casey.

I mean, why would it have been?

As far as I know, she's never done anything like that before or even been interested in it.

A bitter laugh spills from my lips.

How the fuck would I even know?

I don't know Casey.

We might have spent hours talking over the past two weeks, but our conversations have been a little one-tracked. We haven't really talked about our hopes and dreams for the future. We haven't talked about our fears or our insecurities. We've talked about—and had—a lot of sex. And we talked about hockey. Lots of hockey.

I mean, I'm not complaining. It's been fucking epic.

But walking into the arena and finding her coaching Sutton and the girls tonight proved to me how little I know the woman slowly taking over my life.

Since Sutton told me about her new coach, she's only had good things to say. It only occurs to me now that she never told me her name.

But why? It's not like Sutton to leave details out.

The message is read almost instantly, but it takes at least a minute for the dots to bounce. My heart lurches into my throat.

I didn't send that message to invite a reply. In fact, I settled on it in the hope she'd decide against replying.

I'm doing the right thing by cutting this off before we get in any deeper.

She's the daughter of my coach.

She's the coach of my daughter.

Fuck me, this is beyond complicated.

It's better to end it now.

It'll be easier this way.

We can focus on what's really important.

Our jobs.

The dots continue bouncing, making the dread that's only been growing since I walked out of the arena and away from her earlier to get heavier and heavier in my gut.

I was an asshole to her.

Mom chastised me over it the second Sutton was out of earshot, demanding to know what my problem was.

Of course, I didn't tell her.

But I have a feeling she might be seeing a hell of a lot more than I want her to.

Those hickies on my neck after I spent the night with her, and then my reaction today.

Fuck.

I need to lock it down.

Mom knowing is one thing.

Linc is another.

But anyone else?

Combing my hair back from my face, I tug until it hurts.

But still, the dots keep bouncing.

I'm either going to receive the world's longest reply, or she's doing exactly what I was before I sent that message.

Write.

Delete.

Write.

Delete.

I hate that I could be causing her pain.

I just...why didn't she tell me?

Anger bubbles under the surface, battling with a million other emotions I'm struggling to get in line.

Getting frustrated with those dots, I abandon my cell on the bed and throw my legs off the side.

I need to move. I need to—

Everything stops when my cell pings, the screen lighting up.

She replied.

There's a part of me that doesn't want to look.

I just want to forget all about this afternoon.

If I'd just stayed talking to those kids...

No, I needed to know the truth. Who the hell knows when she was going to tell me?

"Fuck," I hiss before reaching for my phone and tapping on the notification.

> Trouble: I'm so sorry.

That's it?

All those bouncing dots, and that's all she has to say?

"Fuck. FUCK," I roar, throwing my cell back down, tugging on a pair of sweatpants, and marching to my home gym.

I don't stand a chance of sleeping now.

The next two days pass in a blur of confusion.

I never hear anything else from Casey, and I don't catch a single sight of her at the arena.

I know she's there, working upstairs, but at no point do I go in search of her.

I have no idea what I'd say even if I did see her.

I'm torn between pulling her into my arms and kissing the life out of her or shouting at her for lying to me and leaving me feeling like she's ripped something out of my chest.

I fucking hate it.

I'm off my game. I'm fucking awful company to be around—even worse than usual.

My teammates have seen it. My coaches have seen it.

Hell, even Sutton has asked me what's wrong.

It's fucking embarrassing.

I'm a professional athlete. I'm a father. And yet I've been completely thrown off track by a five-foot-something woman with pretty blonde hair and stunning green eyes.

My gear bag lands on the floor at my feet with a loud thud as I fight to keep my groan inside.

We've got our first home game of the season tomorrow, and I'm going to find my ass benched if I can't sort this shit out.

"Daddy," Sutton squeals, her tiny feet pounding against the floor as she runs to me.

"Hey, Peanut," I say, trying to shove everything else aside.

She's already in her pajamas and ready for bed.

I wanted to get home earlier tonight, but practice ran over, and then I had a PT session.

"Are you ready for tomorrow?" she asks excitedly.

"You know it," I lie.

I feel less prepared for a game than I have in my entire life.

I just can't get my head in it.

I'm always looking over my shoulder, expecting her to come and visit Coach. Every tap of heels, I think it's her. Every sweet female scent, my brain tells me it's her, even if it smells nothing like her.

It's driving me fucking crazy.

We weren't even a thing, and yet not seeing her, not talking to her...it's like I've lost one of the most essential parts of my life.

"Come on, we made cookies," Sutton says, wriggling out of my arms before taking my hand and dragging me toward the kitchen.

"Oh wow, these look amazing," I say, taking in their handiwork.

"Here you go," Sutton says, proudly handing me the jersey-shaped Polar Bears blue and yellow iced cookie with the number fifty-five written on it.

"Thanks, Peanut."

"Before the game tomorrow, we're going to make them for the Bears. I think Casey will love them."

My breath catches at the sound of her name, successfully inhaling a bit of cookie. I fight the cough, but it's no use.

"Daddy, are you okay?" Sutton asks with a concerned frown as I attempt not to cough up a lung.

"Uh huh," I grunt as I take the glass of water Mom is holding out for me. "Your team will love that," I add once I'm able to speak again.

"Why don't you go and brush your teeth, sweetie? Your dad will be up in a few minutes."

"Ow." Sutton might complain, but she doesn't hesitate to follow the rules.

"Get your book ready," I say. "We're going to finish it tonight, aren't we?"

"Yep. And they're going to win the championship," she shouts before disappearing around the corner.

Mom waits until Sutton's footsteps fade away before she speaks. "Are you ready to talk about it yet?"

"Mom," I breathe.

"What? It's eating at you, and I don't need to be at practice to know it's affecting you on the ice."

I stare at her. "There's nothing wrong with my game," I say defensively.

"I know you, Kodie," she says.

"Great," I mutter, backing out of the room. Sutton won't be close to being ready yet, but I need to get away from this.

I'm not ready to talk about her, confess my mistakes, or have Mom look at me with disappointment.

I'm just...

Fucking hell, I'm a mess.

"I'm just gonna…" I thumb over my shoulder before turning my back on her.

I've just stepped into the hallway when the doorbell rings.

I pause, not used to hearing the sound. No one ever comes here, and I'm not expecting a delivery.

"I'll get it. You go and spend time with Sutton," Mom says, stepping up behind me.

"Just get rid of them," I mutter before taking the stairs two at a time and leaving her to it.

Sutton is still in her bathroom when I get there. I lower my ass to her bed and arrange her stuffies in the way I know she likes. Anything to attempt to keep my mind from wandering to Casey.

It's Friday. She's probably getting ready to go out with Parker.

Closing my eyes, I can see her as clear as day, putting on a sexy dress and some fuck-me heels. My fists curl at the thought of other men leering at her. Something explodes within me the second I think about her dancing with someone, his hands all over her. I shoot to my feet, unable to remain sitting as the image plays out like a movie in my head.

Will she invite him back to her apartment? Will she let him fuck her in the same bed I did?

My heart races and my hands tremble as I remember us together, getting tangled up in her sheets. But it's not my face; it's a stranger touching what's mine.

"I'm ready," Sutton sings, bouncing into the room before diving onto her bed and snuggling under the covers.

Focus on your daughter, Kodie.

Focus on your job.

<hr>

I spend just over thirty minutes with Sutton. I read the final two chapters of her book before we spend ten minutes reviewing the characters and the plot. My girl is nothing but critical, but I love that she's able to give constructive feedback. I'm not sure Coach feels the same, but he always humors her.

Seeing Casey coaching Sutton's team the other day made me wonder just how much he really does understand. Was Casey the same when she was little? Sutton said Casey used to play, but did she also tell her dad and his coach how to improve their games like Sutton does?

After turning her night light on, I walk across her room and pull her door closed, wishing her a good night before heading back downstairs.

I'm aware that I'm probably about to walk directly into a one-woman firing squad, but locking myself in my bedroom will only make this all worse.

But when I get to the kitchen, it's empty.

I frown, looking around to see where she's hiding.

Movement in the yard catches my eye, and I groan the second I discover who was at my front door on a Friday night.

I step out to the sound of Mom's voice. "Ah, here he is. You've got a friend," she says as if I'm ten.

"I thought I said to get rid of whoever it was," I mutter.

"Lovely," Linc teases, lifting his bottle of beer to his lips, looking comfortable as fuck on my lounger. "Grab a beer, man. We're chilling."

"Are we?" I question suspiciously.

"Yes, you are," Mom agrees, pulling a bottle from beside Linc's lounger, popping the top, and passing it over. "I'm going out in twenty minutes, so you'll have the place to yourself. It was great seeing you, Lincoln. Good luck tomorrow night."

Mom spins on her heels and marches toward the pool house.

"Dude, I think your mom just winked at me," Linc teases.

"For the love of God," I mutter as I drop to the lounger beside his. "Why are you here?"

"You know, it's so fucking awesome to feel wanted," he deadpans.

"Mmm."

"I thought it was for the best I come and bang your head against a wall so you can focus tomorrow night. We can't lose our first game of the season on our own ice."

"We won't," I assure him.

"We will if you can't pull your head out of your ass. The fuck is going on? You and Casey fallen out already?"

"Don't," I warn.

"Try again. I'm not leaving until we've talked this out."

"What are we? Thirteen-year-old girls having a slumber party?"

"I mean, I'm down for a pillow fight if you are."

"Fucking moron," I mutter, taking a pull on my beer.

"Come on, hit me with it."

I'd rather just fucking hit him.

"Casey is Sutton's new coach."

Linc takes a few seconds to digest my words before he turns to look at me with his brows pinched.

"So?"

60

CASEY

"You really mean business tonight, huh?" Parker asks as we filter into the arena with the other Vipers fans excited for tonight's game. We invited Freya to join us, but she couldn't even be convinced with the promise of margaritas and tacos.

"Don't know what you're talking about," I shoot over my shoulder.

"Sure you don't," she muses. "I thought wearing another player's jersey was brutal, but somehow, I think tonight is worse."

Finding our row, I make my way down to our seats.

"I don't know what you're talking about. I'm wearing the jersey of the man I'm here to support tonight," I explain, glancing down at my vintage Vipers jersey with *Watson* on the back.

"Exactly," Parker agrees. "The second Kodie sees it, he'll understand the message."

"There is no message," I lie.

I stood in my closet for a good five minutes before I decided what to wear to tonight's game.

There was no way I was wearing *Rivers* on my back, especially after what we did while I was wearing it after his road games. And I didn't want to torment him by wearing Linc's or any of the other guys'. That's just asking for trouble, and I don't have the energy for those kinds of games. So, I settled on wearing Dad's. After all, he's the reason I'm here tonight. Okay, that might be a lie as well, but he's the main reason.

"Sure, whatever you say," Parker says before taking a huge gulp of beer.

She had late clients this evening, so we weren't able to grab dinner before the game like we usually would.

"I still think you should call him later, claim your prize."

"Are you suggesting we're going to lose?" I ask in horror.

"I guess that depends if your man out there is as heartbroken as you."

"Firstly, I'm not heartbroken," I state, despite the fact my heart currently feels like it's been put through a meat grinder. "And secondly, I doubt he's given me a second thought."

She gives me a sympathetic look. "Girl, you *know* that's not true."

I shrug. There's a part of me that really wishes she's right. But she can't be. It's been three days since I sent that apology message, and I haven't seen or heard from him.

If he were missing me, or even slightly heartbroken, then surely he'd have reached out?

You haven't.

All of this is my fault, I'm more than aware of that.

If I'd just told him...

The volume of the music around us increases as the seats fill with fans ready to cheer on their beloved Vipers.

"You should message him good luck," Parker suggests.

"I can't."

"Sure you can."

"It might make it worse," I reason.

"Or it might make it better," she counters.

My cell burns red hot in my pocket as I consider it.

Deciding that I should risk it, I pull my cell free, but just before I wake it up, an excited voice hits my ears.

"Coach C! Oh my god, we're your game buddies."

I look down the row of seats to find Sutton beaming at me. She's in full Vipers gear and she's clutching her bear who's also branded up. She looks beyond cute, and her excitement to see me makes my heart ache even more than it already was.

My eyes shoot to the ice despite the fact I know he's not on it. The guys have already done their warmup. Usually, I'd make sure I was here early enough to watch. It doesn't matter how many times I've seen him out there rolling those hips; it'll never be enough. But tonight, I couldn't face it. Seeing him play is going to be hard enough. Watching those moves would be physically painful.

Kodie isn't going to like this. But what the hell can I do about it? Those are their seats, and I refuse to leave mine. Sure, I could watch from the friends and family suite. I could probably even sweet-talk my way into the team box as well, depending on who's working security tonight. But I don't want to. I want to be down here, feet away from the plexiglass so I flinch whenever someone slams into it. I want to be close enough to see the expressions on the players' faces. I want to scream, knowing they can hear me, not just blend into the crowd. And from the look on Sutton's face, she wants that too.

God, I remember being her age and arguing with Dad about being safer in the family suite. Screw that. I didn't want to watch him from a distance. I wanted to be right there, able to see his face the moment he scored.

"I'm so excited," Sutton squeals as her and Kathleen take their seats. "It's been so long since I saw Daddy on the ice."

Yeah. It's been far too long.

"They're going to kill it tonight. I can feel it."

"I hope you're right," I say before looking up and greeting her gran, who's also proudly wearing a number fifty-five jersey.

She studies me closely, and my stomach knots.

She knows.

My heart begins to race as I fight to say something that isn't going to make me sound like a moron. But words no longer exist.

Instead, I smile awkwardly and swallow a massive mouthful of beer.

Fuck. This is bad.

Turning to Parker, I whisper-shout in her ear.

"His mom knows."

"What? What makes you say that?"

"She saw his reaction the other night, and the way she just looked at me. She knows."

"That might be a good thing. She could be on your side."

"Or she might hate me."

"Casey," Parker sighs. "No one could ever hate you."

My lips part to respond, but the lights dip as spotlights flash around the crowd, signaling the start of the game.

My cell buzzes in my pocket and my heart lurches into my throat. But when I pull it free, I don't find the name I want staring back at me.

> Freya: I hope you have a good night. Watching at home with Dad x

"She should have come," Parker says when I show her the message. "It would have done her some good."

I can't argue with that. But also, I understand. She needs time to put everything behind her. I have every confidence she'll find herself again.

"Please welcome your Vipers to the ice," echoes around the arena. The crowd are on their feet, shouting and screaming, waving flags and banners as one by one, our players burst through a cloud of smoke and out onto the ice.

Fletch is first, then Linc, and then...

All the air rushes from my lungs the second I lock eyes on Kodie.

Fuck. I miss him.

It's only been a couple of days, but everything feels wrong without him.

Sensing my reaction, Parker takes my hand, squeezing in support, as Kodie does a lap of the ice, his eyes locked on the first few rows of the crowd, searching for someone.

He's looking for you.

He knows where you sit.

He wants—

His eyes land on their target, and his face lights up as the little girl beside me screams, "Daddy," at the top of her voice.

Kodie skates right up to the board and blows her a kiss.

All the women around us scream, pretending that was directed at them, despite knowing the truth.

Kodie only has eyes for his girl. And rightly so.

He backs away from the plexiglass and is about to turn around when he looks up.

My breath catches as his eyes find mine.

All happiness from seeing his daughter is instantly wiped away, replaced by irritation.

Ouch.

He holds my gaze for a few heart-wrenching seconds before his eyes lower. The second he sees my jersey, the muscle in his throat tightens, and his lips press into a thin line.

Parker's grip on my hand tightens, and the side of my face burns. I don't look around, but I can picture Kathleen glancing between us with a knowing, yet concerned, look.

His eyes might be hiding behind his visor, but it doesn't mask the anger and the frustration.

I'm frozen as he glares at me. I need to look away, but I can't.

Eventually, he has to move to get into position, and if anything, the moment he takes his eyes from me is worse than the glare.

A sob rips up my throat, and before I know what I'm doing, I rush past Parker and those next to her to get out.

Tears burn my eyes as what feels like a giant elastic band wraps around my chest.

I can't breathe.

Thankfully, everyone moves out of my way quickly, and before I know it, I'm racing toward the bathroom as others still enter the arena a second before the game starts.

"Casey," Parker calls from behind me as I rush inside, the door slamming back against the wall.

"Oh my god," I gasp, my fingers wrapping around the edge of the sink as I hang my head, closing my eyes tight. "Fuck."

"Hey, it's okay," Parker soothes.

"Nothing is about this is okay, Parker," I snap a little more forcefully than I was intending. "I've fucked everything up."

Pressing my hand to my chest, I fight to drag in the air I need.

"I've been lying to my dad, sneaking around behind his back. And for what?"

She stares at me.

"Nothing. For absolutely nothing. Going to that ball was the stupidest thing I've ever done," I hiss. "I should have just forgotten about him when he moved here."

"Casey," Parker says, a little firmer, before gripping my upper arms and forcing me to look at her. "Breathe, okay? Deep breath in." She does it with me. "And out."

She repeats it a few more times until she's confident I've calmed down a little.

"It's too late to start second-guessing your decisions now. What's done is done. All you can do is deal with the future.

"I know you're hurting, Case. But it won't always be like this."

I hold her eyes, my own swimming with unshed tears.

"I miss him," I whisper so quietly, I'm not even sure she hears me.

"So tell him. Tell him how you really feel. Tell him what you want." Her eyes bounce between mine. "Will it help? Maybe, maybe not. But at least you'll know that you've said exactly what's in your heart. You'll never regret telling him the truth."

I sniffle, desperately trying to keep the tears in, and nod.

"You make it sound so easy."

"Nothing about love is easy," she says. "But sometimes, it's worth the pain—or at least, so I've heard."

All the air comes rushing out of my lungs as a door opens behind us and someone moves closer.

Glancing over, I find a familiar face with an empathetic smile on her lips.

"Parker's right," Reese, Fletch's wife, says as she steps up to the sink and washes her hands.

"You missed the puck drop," I say, unable to think of anything else to say.

Reese chuckles. "Nervous wee. I'm the same before every

game. It never gets easier. Nerves for Fletch before a game, I mean. The relationship stuff gets easier," she assures.

"Does it?" I whisper.

"If you've found the right one, yeah."

She studies me for a beat, as if she'll be able to read the answers on my face.

"I wasn't eavesdropping, but I was right there. Am I safe to assume that the man who has you twisted up in knots is out there right now wearing a pair of skates?"

Tipping my head back, I stare up at the ceiling.

I can trust Reese. She's been a part of the Vipers family for a long time. But that doesn't mean that confessing to my sins comes easily.

"Yes."

"Look," Reese says when I finally look back at her. "I don't expect you to give me any more than that, but let me just say this...being with a professional hockey player is hard. Really hard. Their training schedule alone is nuts, but then you add the road games and...I swear, during the season, it can feel like I don't really see him for months at a time. I know I don't really need to tell you this—you've lived this life longer than I have. I just...I want you to go into whatever this is with your eyes open."

I nod. "I am, thank you."

Reaching forward, she squeezes my hand.

"I need to get back out there. But if you need anything, you've got my number, right?"

I nod, appreciating the offer, and then she's gone.

"You've gotta talk to him, Case. If you don't, you'll regret all of this more than you already do."

61

KODIE

As I get into position, ready for the puck to drop, the only thing I can think about is her.

I knew she'd be here tonight.

I also knew that seeing her was going to hit me like a fucking freight train. But the reality was way worse than I was expecting.

"Fuck," I breathe, rubbing my gloved hand over the spot on my chest that hurts the most.

I know I'm doing the right thing by putting an end to all of this, so why does it hurt so much?

All I want to do is jump the board, pull her from her seat, and wrap her in my arms.

Fuck, I need her.

And that fucking annoys me. I've gone through life never needing anyone.

Sure, women have been useful over the years to give me the relief I craved. One—who I'd rather not think about—brought me the greatest gift of all, Sutton. But I've never *needed* one.

Until Casey.

I didn't realize just how hard life was, how fucking miserable I was, until she crashed into my life. Hell, it isn't really a life. More of an existence.

Of course, my life has meaning. I have Sutton and hockey.

Both of those are more than enough to focus on and keep me busy. But I can't say that I was really living.

Being with Casey...she sparked something inside me that I'm not sure ever existed before. Like a fuse just waiting to be lit.

Focus on your job.

Focus on the game.

Focus on the puck. On the win.

I almost feel like I've got it together, but then, I make the colossal mistake of looking back in her direction.

Sutton is on her feet, chanting with the rest of the crowd. But Casey...she's...gone.

I stand frozen, staring at her empty seat as everything happens around me.

The puck is dropped, and Fletch wins it and takes off toward the goal.

"Rivers," Killer barks as he shoots past me.

"Fuck," I hiss, taking off to do my fucking job.

I don't look up again until we change shifts, but even then, I keep my eyes down until I'm on the bench.

My body sags in relief when I discover she's back.

Thank fuck.

The next time I hit the ice, I do it knowing she's watching, and I put my all into it.

The ache in my chest never leaves, but as I make an assist, putting us in the lead, the pressure lessens.

At least I'm not fucking everything up.

The arena erupts as the final buzzer sounds, securing our first home win of the season, and the first thing I do is search for them in the crowd.

My girls.

She's not yours anymore.

That reminder is like a bucket of ice water thrown right over me.

I go through the motions of celebrating our win before finally following the guys off the ice and toward the dressing room.

They're all buzzing, already planning the rest of their night. I barely listen to a word of it. I already know my plans, and they don't involve discovering if Casey is going to be partying with the team or not. I'm going to take Sutton home, listen to her analyze our game, and tell me all the things she thinks Coach needs to know.

A small smirk plays on my lips as I think of my girl.

She makes even the worst of days worth the effort. No matter how bad things get, I can always rely on her to make me smile.

"Come on, Big D. Just come for one," Monroe begs, clearly oblivious to my current mood. Everyone else seems to understand, because they've mostly left me to myself.

"No," I grunt as Coach steps inside the room to a round of cheers before he gives us his speech.

"Fletch, Rivers, you're on post-game press. The rest of you, get the fuck out of here."

"Fuck's sake," I mutter under my breath. The last thing I want to do right now is answer questions.

Coach knows Sutton is here and that I'll want to get back. He's also more than aware that I choked out on the ice earlier tonight. He's punishing me for it.

"Coach," I mutter in agreement before reaching down to untie my skates.

Exhaustion seeps through my body, my joints aching.

It's going to be a long time before I get home tonight.

I stand in the shower at home a few hours later with my hands pressed against the tiles, letting the water hit my shoulders and run down my back.

I messaged Mom before going to the press room, telling her to take Sutton home and that I'd meet them there.

It hadn't been an overly brutal game, but I was in need of a session with Lennon before leaving the arena, and I didn't want them waiting for me any longer than necessary.

We won tonight. If this were last week, I'd be waiting for a message from Casey to celebrate.

But this isn't last week. It's this week, and everything has gone to shit.

The only thrill I'm likely to get tonight is if I deliver it with my own hand.

A pained sigh slips past my lips.

Is Linc right?

Does any of the noise surrounding us really matter?

So what, her dad is my coach?

So what, she coaches my daughter?

Does any of that really matter if there's something real between us?

Is it real, though?

All I do know is that what I feel when I'm with Casey, I've never experienced before.

But is that because it's forbidden?

The thrill of the chase. Sneaking around in the shadows.

Is that what I really want, though?

She deserves so much more than to be someone's dirty secret.

The man she's with should be proudly walking around with her, showing her off, publicly claiming her as his—not sneaking around and hiding how they feel from the rest of the world.

As I watch the water swirl down the drain, I realize that I'm not getting any closer to the answers I need.

The only real thing I know is that I'm terrified.

Terrified to admit how I really feel about Casey, but at the same time petrified of doing anything about it.

There is so much at stake. So much at risk. Things that neither of us can afford to mess around with.

Reaching for the dial, I turn the shower off. With a towel wrapped around my waist, I pad to my bedroom, pull on a clean pair of boxers, and practically fall onto my bed.

Two ice bags sit on my nightstand, and I reach for them, placing them over my knees.

I can only assume the adrenaline ran out faster tonight, knowing that I don't have Casey to come home to. But fuck, everything hurts. At least the pain in my chest has taken a back seat.

I've just gotten comfortable when my cell dings.

My heart jumps into my throat, but I quickly talk myself down.

It won't be her.

I left her last message on read. That sent a very clear message.

But what if it is?

With my heart in my throat, I reach for it.

"Motherfucker," I mutter when I see who the message is from.

Storm: Message her.

Kodie: Fuck you.

Storm: Not interested. But Casey is here, and she is looking F.I.N.E.

A growl rips up my throat. The thought of Linc, or anyone, touching her makes me feral.

My hand trembles as I angrily tap out a reply.

Kodie: Stay the fuck away from her.

Storm: Bro, you're so fucked.

Kodie: You will be too, if you go anywhere near her.

Storm: Maybe you should come and make sure I don't. Monroe is looking too…

He's baiting me. I know he is. But fuck if there's not a massive temptation to drag some clothes on and go and see for myself.

When another message comes through, I assume it's Linc attempting to press a few more buttons, so when I pick my cell up and find someone else's name, I almost drop it.

Trouble: Great game tonight. Sutton was so proud of you. She really is a great kid.

"Fuck," I breathe.

Seeing them both up there in the crowd tonight, jumping up and down, screaming for us—for me—is a sight I'm not going to forget for a long time.

It was also a complete headfuck.

I have never, ever allowed any woman I've hooked up with anywhere close to Sutton. Hell, in the early days before I swore off women, most of them didn't even know I had a kid. Easier that way. Less risk. Puck bunnies can be…a lot. Thankfully, I've never experienced it, but I've had teammates who have had issues with stalking in the past. I never, ever want to subject Sutton to anything like that. It was why I stepped away from that way of life. Her safety was so much more important than me getting a bit of action.

Kodie: Thank you. And I agree, she's the best.

Trouble: So's her dad.

"Christ. You're fucking killing me here."

There are so many things I could reply with, but each one is more dangerous than the last.

In the end, I keep the focus on Sutton—also known as taking the pussy way out.

Kodie: Good luck tomorrow. Hopefully, you'll secure a win too.

I shake my head as I let my cell drop to the bed.

I very rarely get nervous before games. I usually go through my routine exactly the same every time and I walk into the arena with my head held high and focused on what's to come. Okay, so recently the latter has been a bit of an issue, but despite being distracted by a certain blonde, I'm still not nervous.

But the morning of Sutton's games? Fuck. They're entirely different.

I'm a wreck.

I figured out a while ago that it's because I'm not in control.

In contrast, Sutton is as cool as a cucumber.

She also has her little routine. Same breakfast every morning before a game. Then she hits the gym with me to warm up. Then she has to get dressed in certain clothes, pack her bag in a specific order, and then we have to listen to the same playlist I helped her set up last summer.

She really is just like one of the guys—only, funnier and cuter.

"You're going to kill it today, Peanut," I tell her as we step inside the arena.

She doesn't respond, and I don't expect her to. Now that we're in the building, she's in the zone.

I'm smiling, both amused and incredibly proud of my headstrong and determined little girl. But as we move toward her coaches, my smile begins to fade, and those nerves return with full force.

Today isn't just another one of Sutton's games. It's a game with Casey as her coach. It's a game where I'm going to have to sit here and have my chest ripped in two as I watch them communicate—and hopefully, celebrate—together.

My two worlds have collided, and it's fucking me up.

It's creating ideas and images in my head of the kind of future that could possibly be there.

I'm trying not to let myself run away with it all, because it's a fickle dream that won't come true.

But what if it could?

What if there is a woman out there who could slot into our lives? Be a partner for me and an incredible role model for Sutton?

No.

I shake my head, dragging my hand down my face.

Don't go there, Rivers. It's too fucking dangerous.

"Good morning, Rivers," Casey calls once we're close enough to hear.

My heart skips a beat, and it only gets worse when I discover that she's not talking to me. All her focus is on Sutton. Right now, she's Rivers, number fifty-five. It's time for me to take a back seat, both in the game and with Casey.

62

CASEY

Man, I love hockey. It doesn't matter if it's men's or women's; professional, juniors, or youth.

I love it all.

And watching my own team of talented girls play...I think that might just be my favorite.

I've only been coaching them a couple of weeks, but I can see them improving with each training session and each game we have. The fact that I might just have something to do with that blows me away.

But as much as I love it, and as focused as I am on the game, at no point do I forget that Kodie is sitting in the stands.

He's not here for me. He has no interest in talking to me—he's made that clear enough the last two times I've messaged him. And it's fine; I get it.

I thrust myself into his life without his permission, and I kept something from him that I should have confessed the moment I found out.

As I lay in bed last night, reflecting on my embarrassing freak-out in the bathroom, I came to realize that it's probably for the best.

Kodie is everything I could possibly want in a man. He's the whole package. Sweet and caring, sexy, smart, incredibly dedicated and hardworking.

Therein lies the problem.

He's too good to be true.

I've been telling myself these past two weeks that this might be it, that after all these years watching him, pining after him, he could actually be the one.

But it's just a pipe dream.

He's exactly what he's always been.

A fantasy.

I should be grateful. I mean, I am grateful that I got to spend that time with him. And given a chance, I'd do it all over again in a heartbeat.

But I'm not going to be the kind of woman who continues clinging on to a man who doesn't want her.

It hurts.

It really fucking hurts.

But what else can I do?

I'm Casey fucking Watson, and I will not lose myself because the man I've fallen for doesn't want me.

It's not like he's a man I can have anyway.

When I find my gaze drifting in his direction as the second period comes to an end, I immediately rip it back.

I just have to get through this game, and then who knows when I'll see him again.

He's got another home game tomorrow night, followed by alternating home and road games that will thankfully see him miss both Sutton's Wednesday evening training and her game next Sunday.

I wanted to keep looking at their game schedule and try to predict when he'll be here, but I stopped myself, knowing that I'd get obsessed with the dates and waiting for him.

That is not the way to put him behind me.

Focus on a week at a time. Each one that follows will get easier.

Right?

I mean, it has to. I can't continue with the heart-wrenching pain in my chest right now.

Forcing my attention to stay on the game and not the man

taunting me across the rink, I get the pleasure of watching our girls dominate the game and finish with a very impressive six-two win.

Their small crowd erupts with cheers as the final buzzer sounds. The rest of the team joins those on the ice to celebrate before they shake hands with the visitors.

Megan and I watch with pride as they celebrate together before finally turning our way.

They race across the ice, jump through the gate, and surround us.

Sutton is the first to wrap her arms around my waist, and the second I glance down and her glittering eyes lock with mine, I swallow thickly as behind my nose itches.

"Incredible game, girls," Megan thankfully praises while I battle with the huge lump in my throat that refuses to budge. "We're so proud of you."

Parents begin to move closer as Megan says a few more inspirational words.

As I stand there listening, tingles race through my body, the side of my face begins to burn.

Shit.

Despite being aware that he's getting closer, I don't react. The last thing I need right now is for him to know just how in tune I am with him.

Stupid, stupid body.

The second Megan dismisses the team, I race around them to begin collecting equipment, and at the first possible opportunity, I disappear.

I can't bear to stand there and watch Kodie be sweet and attentive to Sutton. I just can't.

"Hey, are you okay?" Megan asks when she joins me in the equipment closet a few minutes later.

I don't want to say that I'm hiding in here, but I'm pretty sure she's figured me out.

"Of course," I say, forcing a smile.

She studies me for a beat before nodding.

"Great game tonight," she finally says, deciding that she doesn't want to dive into my issues.

"They were great."

"Are you ready for your first road game?" she asks as we put everything away.

"I'm excited to see them play on a different rink."

"I've got a good feeling about this season."

"Me too," I muse as I move back toward the ice.

I don't want to, but as we round the corner, I scan the space for Kodie.

My chest compresses as disappointment rushes through me.

I might have tried to push the thoughts away, but I'd be lying if I said that underneath it all, there was just a little bit of hope that he might have hung around to talk to me.

I suck in a shaky breath.

It really is over.

I didn't go to the home game on Monday night.

It's the first game I've missed in a long time.

But after a long day at work, I just couldn't face it.

Seeing Kodie would have been too much.

If I'm ever going to come to terms with everything, then I need some space—which is a really fucking hard thing to find, considering everywhere I turn at work, I see his face.

Literally.

I spent the day working on graphics that included all the team's new headshots, so for a good part of my morning, Kodie was staring at me through the screen.

All I wanted to do was sob. But I'm stronger than that.

So, instead of breaking, I focused and got his images completed first. Things got a little easier as I moved onto Linc and his cocky smirk. In the safety of my own home, I pulled on Kodie's jersey and watched the game from my TV.

They won, and I celebrated quietly by myself before crawling into bed and crying myself to sleep as I pictured him out with the guys.

It'll get easier, I continue lying to myself.

But as the week goes on, the lie only seems to get bigger and bigger.

I've only ever lost one person before, and that was Mom. I was ten when she passed, and while I was old enough to understand, it was impossible to come to terms with.

Of course, losing Kodie is very different from losing a parent, but some of the feelings are the same: the dark cloud hanging over me and the struggle to get up in the morning and go about my life like any other day. It reminds me of some of the days back then.

I hate it. But I also don't know what to do about it.

I'm not a kid now, and I need to keep putting one foot in front of the other.

It's ridiculous. He's just a man. A man who never promised me anything.

Hell, let's be honest—he did the exact opposite.

He told me outright that he couldn't offer me anything.

I accepted that because I was more than happy to get any little bit of him that I could.

I knew it would end up ripping me apart. I just very much underestimated how hard it would be to walk away from him when he's still such a huge part of my life.

The only one who understands is Parker, and thankfully, she's also been crazy busy with clients this week. We've spoken, but I haven't seen her. She knows I'm struggling, but she doesn't know the extent of it. I fear that the second she looks into my eyes, she'll know. I met up with Freya for dinner last night after work, and despite knowing she'd understand, I couldn't tell her anything. Instead, I focused on everything but the pain in my chest. To be fair, talking about men and relationships was the last thing she wanted anyway.

I stand in the front of the mirror with makeup littering my countertop and dread sitting heavy in my stomach.

I may have missed Monday's game, but I didn't stand a chance of missing tonight's.

Parker is picking me up in fifteen minutes, and I'm yet to decide what I'm wearing.

There's a part of me that wants to pull on a Seattle Bandits jersey with *Donnelly* on the back.

A laugh tumbles from my lips as I imagine Dad's expression if he caught me wearing anything but green and white.

Once I've done the best job I can at covering the circles under my eyes, I stand in my closet, assessing my options.

My heart wants me to wear *Rivers* on my back.

It's a Friday, so I can only assume that Sutton will be going as well, and something tells me that she'd get a kick out of me wearing her name and number.

"Fuck it," I mutter before pulling the jersey from its hanger.

That little girl has no idea, but she already has me wrapped around her little finger.

She was on fire at Wednesday night's practice, and I have no doubt that nothing will change before Sunday's game.

Inspired by what I've been doing at work this week, I dug out my camera and requested that Megan allow me to take headshots of all our girls.

They're already a great team with a fantastic reputation in the league. But I've got the power to push them even further. It didn't take a lot of convincing for Megan to give me the log-in for their social media platforms. All week, I've been working on a plan to overhaul everything and really get their name out there.

With thoughts of my girls spinning around my head, I finish getting ready before my cell rings.

My stomach twists as I swipe the screen.

"Do not tell me that you're not ready," Parker barks down the line.

"I'm just coming."

"Good. I haven't eaten all day. I need those tacos more than I need air right now."

With a laugh, I push my feet into my sneakers, throw my purse over my shoulder, and pull my door open.

"No margs for you until you've lined your stomach," I tease.

"Hey now, I never said that."

"See you in two," I say before hanging up on her and stepping into the elevator, staring at myself in the mirror.

To everyone else, I probably look fine. But Parker will see the truth.

Just get through this game, and then you won't see him again until next week.

After giving myself a little pep talk, I walk toward Parker's car and pull the passenger door open.

"Jeez, you took your—Oh shit," she curses when her eyes land on me.

"Can we not?"

"You're wearing his number," she points out with a frown.

"Nope, I'm wearing Sutton's number."

"Not sure Kodie will see it like that."

"Well, fuck him," I hiss.

"Yeah," she muses. "That's where this all started."

Shaking my head, I strap myself in. "Just drive before I change my mind about all this."

"You won't," she says confidently.

63

KODIE

"**S**he's wearing your number," Linc shouts over to me where I'm warming up before our game against Seattle.

I know.

I know Casey has turned up to my game wearing my fucking number again.

There might be close to eighteen thousand people in this arena, but the second I stepped out onto the ice, I could only see one.

Well, two. It helped that they were together once again.

I swear, they're colluding behind my back to torture me as much as possible.

I don't remember them ever sitting close before. But then I guess, I never really noticed Casey before the masquerade.

Fuck knows how. She's so beautiful she lights up the entire room.

I guess I was just following the rules before.

"I'm confused," Linc states, making me roll my eyes. "She's up there with your name on her back as if everything is okay, and yet you're still a miserable motherfucker, so..."

"There's nothing to sort out," I mutter. "I fucked up. We..." I shake my head. "She's not mine, and she can't be mine. There's nothing else to say."

He laughs, but there isn't much humor in it.

"Want to say that like you mean it?"

"Storm," I warn.

"What?" he asks, skating up next to me where I'm stretching out my hips. "I hate to fucking say this, but—" I scoff. Linc doesn't hate to say anything. He just says it how it is with zero fucks given. He narrows his eyes at me, his signature smirk playing on his lips. "You were a better person while you were fucking her."

A spray of ice hits my face, and I groan when I look up to see Killer smiling down at me.

"Holy shit. You're fucking someone?"

"Brilliant," I mutter before turning my back on them.

I realize my mistake instantly, because that puts me directly in Casey's line of sight.

Sutton waves at me with a beaming smile splitting her face.

I focus on her, using her excitement to fuel me.

Do not look at Casey.

Do not look at—

All the air comes rushing out of my lungs as my eyes shift to her.

She's got her hair pulled back into a ponytail, her face looks flawless, and she's wrapped in green and white. The beer in her hand is already half empty as she enjoys the beginning of her evening.

Just like at Sutton's game on Sunday, she looks...normal.

A sharp pain cuts through my chest as I stare at the evidence that Casey isn't suffering in the same way I am.

She might have been the one with the little fantasy and the slight obsession, but it seems only one of us lost a little more than they were willing to give during our short time together.

When she wasn't here Monday night, I stupidly thought that it might have something to do with me. But seeing her now, I realize I was wrong.

She was probably just busy.

Maybe she was on a date.

My lungs deflate with disappointment.

What if she was on a date?

There's nothing I can do about it.

Hell, she deserves to be.

She's...fuck, she's incredible. Any guy would be lucky to have her.

"You're a fucking idiot, man," Linc says, continuing our conversation.

I glare at him, hoping he'll fucking drop it, but all he does is grin at me.

"Look, I might not want to settle for one woman for the rest of my life, but if I did, I can understand why she'd be a good one to choose."

"Storm," I warn.

"What are you really scared of?" he asks, holding my eyes.

My lips part to respond, but the music changes around us, and we've got no choice but to get off the ice, pausing our conversation.

As I follow him toward the dressing room, his question rattles around in my mind.

What am I scared of?

"FUCK, YES," Linc bellows as the final buzzer sounds, announcing us as the hard-fought winners against the Seattle Bandits.

Linc and Rett might be childhood friends, but you'd never know it when they're on the ice together. They play like they hate each other.

We collide as we celebrate the end of a wild fucking game before the others dive on us. The arena is on its feet, shouting and screaming.

Breaking away from the crowd, I swallow my unease and skate toward the boards in front of Sutton and Casey.

Adrenaline buzzes through my veins, making it easy to forget reality.

Fuck, what I wouldn't give for a celebratory photograph tonight.

Or a video call.

Hell, an in-person visit.

We're both here.

I know how to get into her apartment. I could get there if I wanted to.

Fucking hell, I want to.

My eyes lock on Sutton as she shouts and screams like a madman.

I can't hear her over the rest of the crowd, but her little voice is loud and clear in my mind.

I pause at the boards and press my gloved hands to the plexiglass.

She continues to scream at me, Mom standing at her side with a proud smile on her face.

'Love you, Peanut,' I mouth.

Pressing my weight against the screen, I push myself back, ready to get changed and take her home to bed, but before I can turn around, my eyes jump.

My breath catches. Casey's face is flushed, and her eyes are wide as she chants along with the rest of the fans.

She's drunk.

But the worst thing about it is that she's acting like she hasn't even seen me standing here.

Wow. I guess we really are done.

With my heart in my throat, I continue skating backward before I spin around to shake hands with the Bandits before they disappear off the ice, leaving us to soak up the rest of our celebration.

"Fletch, Linc, you're both on press," Coach says as we make our way to the dressing room a while later.

"You got it," Linc agrees with a smile.

All the guys are in high spirits after the win, and despite flying out first thing in the morning for another game tomorrow night, they're planning to head to The Fractured Compass once they're showered.

"Rivers, you're in tonight, right?" Handsy asks.

"We've got a seven-a.m. call time," I mutter.

"Just one. You can be tucked up in bed by midnight, old man."

"Watch it."

"Come on, bro. First round is on Rett," Linc announces, causing a round of cheers to go around the room.

"I promised Sutton," I explain.

"What about Ca—"

"I'm taking my girl home," I state, cutting off Linc's words. He might have been saying them quietly, but I don't want her name so much as whispered in this room. Especially from someone else's lips.

Hearing the warning in my tone, Linc holds his hands up and backs away.

When I went up to collect Sutton and Mom last Saturday, Casey wasn't there.

I knew she watched the whole game. She was standing right next to my daughter the entire fucking time. But it seemed she bailed the second we left the ice.

At the time, I assumed it was because of me. Hell, I wanted to think it was; my ego and battered heart wanted her to be suffering, too.

But after what I saw tonight, I know I was wrong. And that is fully confirmed when I walk into the suite and find her sitting at the bar, looking right at the door as if she's waiting for me.

But despite her eyes landing on me, she doesn't so much as react.

Ouch.

Instead, she looks away, says something to Parker, and then lifts her drink to her lips and takes a sip.

"Daddy," Sutton screams, dragging my attention to where it should be before she crashes into me.

Wrapping her up in a hug, I kiss the top of her head and breathe her in.

For years, I told myself that she was the only girl I needed.

But I'm pretty sure I was lying.

As I lower her, my eyes shoot back over to Casey.

She's still ignoring me.

"Ready to go, Peanut?" I ask, dragging my attention away again.

"You know I'm not," she sulks. She always wants to stay longer and mingle with the guys. I can only imagine what she's going to be like as a teenager.

I can also fully understand why Coach warns every single player away from Casey.

"Come on, it's getting late," I say, earning myself a groan in response.

But despite wanting to stay, she takes my hand and walks beside me as we head for the door.

We're a few feet away when it bursts open as Linc and Rett make their arrival known.

"Rett!" a familiar voice shrieks behind me, and I glance back in time to see both Parker and Casey slipping from their stools and racing over.

"Hey, sis," Rett says, wrapping Parker in a hug.

I'm about to keep moving when he releases his sister and spins to Casey.

"Hey, Case. You're looking good tonight," he states, wrapping her in his arms.

I have to cough to cover the deep growl of possessiveness that rumbles in my throat.

My eyes follow his hands as he slides them low on her back. My fingers twitch with the need to reach out and rip him away from her.

"Would you prefer if I take Sutton home?" Mom asks softly behind me.

"No," I grunt. "We're leaving."

Forcing myself to put one foot in front of the other, I walk away before I do something really fucking stupid.

In a few short minutes, we're in the parking garage; Sutton is safely strapped in, and I drop into the driver's seat.

Mom glances at me, but thankfully, she doesn't say anything, instead allowing Sutton to do her game analysis from the back seat.

By the time we pull up at home, I feel like I've experienced the game for a second time tonight.

"Straight up to put your pajamas on," I say as Sutton hops out of the car.

"Aw, Daddy," she complains, but without another word, she races up the stairs to do exactly as she's told.

I don't follow. Instead, I make the mistake of marching to the kitchen for a drink, giving Mom a moment to say the words that have been on the tip of her tongue the whole ride home.

"Will you please talk to me, Kodie? I can see that you're hurting, and it's killing me."

I swallow the mouthful of water and lower the bottle to the counter, squeezing my eyes closed.

I take a couple of seconds to collect my thoughts before I look up and into her eyes.

"I wouldn't even know where to start."

"How about at the beginning?"

The alcohol flows just a little too easily. The buzz it gives is also just a little too addicting.

We started the night in The Fractured Compass. The Vipers refuse point-blank to go anywhere else. But seeing as they're all headed out of town tomorrow, all but two of them disappeared early, leaving us to party with the Bandits.

Fueled by vodka and the need to put everything about that game behind me, I allowed Parker to take my hand and drag me around after the team.

We're now in the VIP section of Club 52. The beat of the music thumps through the floor beneath me, vibrating through my bones as we dance.

My skin tingles with the attention of those around us, but I don't open my eyes to look.

I'm not interested in anyone here tonight.

The only man I want is currently at home, probably tucked up in his bed, fast asleep.

The strength it took to look unfazed by him this evening was almost too much.

But after last weekend's game, where I ended up freaking out in the bathrooms, I knew I needed to pull my mask on.

I can't keep falling apart whenever I see him. At least, I can't do it on the outside.

Whether we like it or not, our lives are entwined and will be for some time.

I don't have any intention of changing my job. Either of them. And something tells me Kodie and Sutton won't be going anywhere anytime soon either.

That means I'm going to have to find a way to be able to look at him and not feel like someone is shredding pieces of my heart, strip by strip.

"I needed this," Parker shouts over the music.

Cracking an eye open, I watch Parker as she moves to the beat. Her face is flushed, a few locks of dark hair sticking to her cheeks. She's taken her jersey off and now has it tied around her waist, leaving her in what is basically a bralette. And one glance around lets me know that I'm not the only one who's noticed.

She has the eyes of almost every man in the room on her.

I search the faces, looking for a familiar one who isn't going to be impressed with almost every single member of his team checking out his sister. But when I find Everett at the bar, he's more than a little distracted by two women.

I'm not sure why I'm surprised. Everett takes advantage of his position as a professional hockey player, leaving broken hearts in every city. LA is no different.

A breath gets caught in my throat when someone brushes behind me. I take a step forward to get out of their way, but I barely move before a large pair of hands grips my hips, dragging me back.

My back presses against a hot, hard chest before the man standing behind me begins moving his hips in time with the music.

"Relax," he murmurs in my ear. "We're all here for a good time."

As he says the words, another guy steps up behind Parker.

I recognize him.

Anderson Westly, starting forward for the Bandits.

Once again, my eyes flick to Everett. It might have been a while since Parker was regularly around his teammates, but he's too busy laughing at whatever the woman pressed against his left side is saying.

"What's wrong? You Viper girls too good to dance with the likes of us?" my new dance partner says.

The Bandits have a bit of a reputation for being rough and violent on the ice. While they might get some bad press for the way they play, as far as the bunnies are concerned, the Bandits are up there with the best players to snag. Fight hard, fuck harder is one of the many terms I've heard used to describe them.

Unfortunately for the guy behind me, I'm not interested in finding out if the rumors are true.

"If you think I'm here because I'm a bunny, you really need to reconsider," I shoot over my shoulder. Twisting a little farther, I try to figure out who I'm talking to.

Andrey Petrov.

I might not want him, but still, a little thrill shoots through me.

This man is a legend.

His stats are incredible. Top goal scorer the last two seasons running, and only a few games into this season and it's likely he's heading in the same direction again.

And he's here, dancing with me.

What the actual hell?

But as shocked and awed as I might be, there isn't an inch of my body that burns for him. Not a single flicker of interest.

His chuckle is dark and full of promise. I'm sure it works wonders on other women. But I'm not other women.

I'm Casey Watson, and there has only ever been one hockey player who's wormed his way in. And not just to my body. Kodie is deeply rooted in my head, my heart, and quite possibly my soul.

I let out a sigh as we continue moving.

I'm sure if I were to twist out of his hold, he'd let me go. But I don't.

I might not be interested in anything he has to offer, but I also can't deny how good his hands feel holding me, and how comforting his presence behind me is.

This week has been awful. Hell, everything since the moment Kodie found me with Sutton and the Polar Bears has been torture.

The pain in my chest, the longing...all of it is just too much.

How can someone make such a huge impact on your life in such a short space of time?

I groan before leaning back into him. For a few minutes, I let my eyes close and embrace the moment.

I try to ignore the constant ache in my chest and the disappointment that drips through my veins that the man behind me isn't the one I want.

The beat of the song changes, making Andrey move a little faster behind me, and I gasp when I feel him hard against my ass.

Surely not.

I blink, confused.

This man could literally have any woman on the planet, and right now, he's hard for me.

Talk about a headfuck.

But even still, I don't feel a freaking thing.

That's just how broken I am.

"Don't worry, I know exactly who you are, Watson," he groans in my ear, reminding me that I said something.

"Then why—"

He releases my hip with one hand before he grips my ponytail, directing my line of sight.

"See that redhead?" he murmurs.

I scan the sea of women, all trying to steal any of the players' attention.

"Yeah," I confirm when I find her.

"I needed to get away from her."

"Why? She looks more than willing," I point out as she gropes one of his teammates, not giving a single fuck about who might be watching.

"Stage five," he says simply.

"Ah."

"I'm all for playing with bunnies, but I draw the line at the craziest ones. No one needs a stalker."

I shake my head. I know this kind of shit happens. It's a real threat for all professional athletes. But hearing some of the lengths that women go through to try and bed a player blows my mind.

"Ah, so you're using me," I tease, wondering just how far my father's warning reaches within the league.

For so long, I kept away from this scene as much as possible, so I wasn't aware that anyone even knew I existed outside of the Vipers' arena.

"I wouldn't put it like that."

Knowing I'm safe with him, I keep moving, my eyes returning to the two people in front of me.

For a girl who says she doesn't want a hockey player, she's doing a very good job of making it look otherwise.

"Everett is going to lose his shit when he sees them," I muse. If they know who I am, there's little doubt they also know who Parker is.

Andrey laughs again.

"Asshole deserves it."

Spinning around, I put Parker behind me and focus on Andrey. His eyes are dark, his cheekbones strong and perfect, just like his jawline. There really is no denying the appeal.

"I would say good game tonight, but—"

He chuckles. "It was a close game. Your guys did good."

My chest puffs out with pride. "Yeah, they did."

The music continues, but we mostly block it out as we talk hockey right in the middle of the dance floor.

Everything is going well until a shadow falls over me a beat before a familiar angry voice growls, "What the fuck do you think you're doing?"

A hand wraps around my upper arm, and I'm dragged away from Andrey at the same time as Parker is pulled away from her dance partner.

I stare up at Linc, my head spinning from the number of drinks I've had tonight. I don't bother saying anything, because if I know my best friend at all, she's about to rip him a new one.

And to prove me right, Parker steps into Linc's space and shouts, "What the hell are you doing?"

"Stopping Rett from knocking Westie the fuck out," Linc seethes, looming over her with his eyes boring into hers.

"Rett's reaction to me dancing with a guy is not my issue."

Linc's jaw tics, his lips twitching like he wants to say something but is biting it back.

"Maybe it's not your issue directly, but do you want that on your conscience when he's out because of a broken fist?"

Parker rolls her eyes, a bitter laugh spilling from her lips.

"If Rett has an issue with my behavior, he can deal with it for himself instead of sending his minion."

Linc nostrils flare with irritation. "I'm taking you home," he states.

Parker's nostrils flare, her hands landing on her hips as she stares him down.

"I don't fucking think so. Case, let's go."

Before I know what's happening, she's got my hand in hers and she's dragging me away.

"We'll go downstairs. It stinks of over-inflated egos up here anyway," she shoots over her shoulder.

Twisting back, I glance over at the three men we left behind.

I allow her to pull me along, and the second we hit the ground floor, she leads me toward the bar, where she orders us shots. Twisting around, I look back up at the VIP area to see Andrey standing at the railing. His lips twitch into a smile before he lifts his hand to wave.

I shake my head. Such a player.

Surprisingly Linc doesn't follow, but something tells me it's not going to be the last we see of him tonight.

No sooner have we swallowed them is Parker on the move again, with me right behind her.

She battles through the crowd on the dance floor before coming to a stop and turning me to face her.

"Hockey players are assholes," she states.

I glance up at the VIP area and find one person leaning over the balcony, watching us closely.

But Linc isn't watching me. His attention is purely focused on Parker.

65

——————

KODIE

Rolling over, I reach for my cell and wince as the screen lights up.

I turn the alarm off, and my thumb hovers over the Instagram app.

I shouldn't look, I know that. But I also knew that the other million times I've opened it and tapped on Casey's name since I ended it with her.

I told myself that it would help me move on if I were to see her doing the same.

She may have only posted a couple of times, but seeing her smiling face had the opposite reaction.

It didn't make anything easier. Instead, it made the pain worse.

But apparently, I'm a masochist, and despite knowing it'll hurt, I do the same as all the other times I've opened this app.

This time, though, the pain in my chest when I see her isn't my only reaction.

Anger and jealousy surge through me at the sight of her with another man.

This is what you wanted, a little voice pipes up, my grip tightening on my cell and my heart rate becoming more and more erratic as I swipe through the images.

She's dancing with a Bandit.

471

And not just any fucking Bandit.

Andrey Petrov.

Fuck me. I might be straight, but even I can admit that the guy is good-looking. It's understandable why bunnies literally trip over themselves to get close to him.

But last night, he didn't have his sights set on a bunny.

He had his sights on what's mine.

I sit up straight, possessiveness taking over me as my hand trembles with my need to do something.

Each image is worse.

Acid swirls in my stomach as I look at someone else touching Casey.

My Casey.

"Fuck," I hiss before launching from the bed and racing to the bathroom before I vomit in the toilet.

You let her go.

She can be with anyone she wants now.

Casey doesn't hook up with players.

But images don't lie. And those pictures drip with evidence of what happened last night.

I retch again, but nothing comes up as the band that's been wrapped around my chest tightens once again.

I can barely fucking breathe without her.

But it's the right thing to do.

Using the sink for support, I drag myself to my feet. Running the faucet, I splash cold water on my face, hoping for a miracle.

I've got to be at the airport in an hour for our game tonight. I don't have time to lose my shit right now.

I need to focus on my job, not lose myself over the fact Casey has done exactly what I pushed her to do.

She's moved on.

"Fuck," Linc mutters as he drops into the seat beside me on the team's private plane almost two hours later.

Grabbing my cell that's sitting in my lap, I turn my music up.

I'm not one to talk during our flights. I prefer to put my AirPods in and get in the zone, ready for what lies ahead.

All the guys have their rituals, from where we sit, to what playlists we listen to, or what games we play. We thrive on it, and if anyone fucks up our routines...well, we all know we're risking our game.

"What the fuck?" I bark after Linc pulls one of my earphones free.

He smirks at me as he curls his fingers around the device, letting me know that I'm not getting it back anytime soon.

"Fuck you," I mutter, turning to look out the window as the last of the guys and staff board.

"It's not how it looked," he says quietly.

My teeth grind as I breathe deeply through my nose.

"I was there. Marilyn was too. Nothing happened with Petty, man."

I tense as his words and reassurance flow through me. But I still don't say a word.

"I know you're listening, and I know you know what I'm talking about. It's all over her fucking Instagram. She's gonna be pissed when she sees it."

I close my eyes, hating that his words are working.

Block it out, Rivers.

Focus on the game.

"Even if she was interested, I never would have let her out of my sight. I've got you, man," he says cockily.

"I didn't ask you to do that," I whisper, the words out before I can stop them.

He chuckles, happy that he's got me.

Dropping my head forward, I rest my brow against the wall as the plane begins to taxi.

Around us, the attendants begin their preflight safety announcement.

I can guarantee not a single person is listening.

We fly multiple times a week. It's just white noise to us at this point.

"You didn't need to. I've got your back. Hers too."

"You should have gone home and got a good night's sleep. We need you on form tonight."

"I'll be fine. Probably more than I can say about Casey. She was wasted by the end of the night."

Turning around, I glare at him.

All he does is fucking laugh.

"I'm sorry, I'm not seeing the fucking funny side of all this, Storm."

He shakes his head, a look that is a little too close to pity for my liking passing across his face. "That's because you're in so deep you can't fucking see straight. Jesus, Rivers. Pull your head out of your ass and open your fucking eyes."

"W-what?"

"You're in love with her," he states as if it's the most obvious thing in the world.

"I'm not—"

Linc throws his head back and laughs as we take off.

"Fuck me, you're so fucking delusional."

Giving me an out, he finally opens his palms, revealing my stolen AirPod.

"Fuck you, Storm. Fuck you," I state, snatching my earbud back and stuffing it into my ear.

He doesn't say anything else for the rest of the fight, but that doesn't mean his words don't continue to circle around my head.

What he said...

I shake my head.

Mom said the same.

She looked me in the eye, her face all soft and hopeful, and expressed her happiness that I'd finally found someone who made me smile.

She didn't care about all the reasons we couldn't be together. She said it was white noise.

Love and happiness are more important than the rules, she said.

But it's not that fucking simple.

The game is...awful.

Worst of the season so far.

We don't just lose. We get fucking annihilated.

And worse than that. It's my fault.

Two goals were scored against us while I was in the penalty box.

I'm fucking embarrassed by my performance tonight. And it only gets worse when I think about both Casey and Sutton watching it.

Casey is out there living her life, and here I am fucking drowning in front of the fucking world.

After an ass-ripping from Coach, I crash into our hotel room, ready to set the world alight.

Linc follows me in, his concerned stare burning into my back as I stalk toward the windows and stare out at yet another city.

After all my years of traveling, they've started to blur into one.

"Rivers, you need—"

"Stop," I beg. "Whatever you're going to say, just fucking stop."

"Call her," he says, ignoring my plea.

"I can't," I seethe. "It's over."

"Says who?"

I bite back my response, my teeth grinding and my fists curling.

"You? You're a fucking idiot. She fucking loves you, man."

Spinning around, I glare at him, my words spilling free. "Oh yeah? She wasn't fucking showing that last night, was she?"

"She's miserable."

"And she found comfort in the arms of another man."

"Fucking hell," he mutters, shaking his head. "Did you hear anything I said earlier?" he shouts as if I'm deaf.

"A picture paints a thousand words. I saw them all, Storm. I saw his hands all over her."

"Yeah? And do you know what you didn't see?" he says, prowling closer, his face set as if he's waiting for the puck to drop on our last chance to win a game.

My lips thin and my eyes narrow. I don't need to say anything; I know he's about to tell me whether I want to hear it or not.

"You didn't see me escorting her out of that club. Her and Parker. There were no Bandits in sight. She didn't want Petty. She wasn't interested in Westie, or any of them. All she wants is you, you fucking moron. I took her home and—"

I see fucking red.

I surge forward, my hands press against Linc's chest, forcing him back until he collides with the wall.

We stand nose to nose.

"What do you think I did, Rivers?" Linc taunts, staring right into my eyes.

My chest heaves as I fight to drag in the air I need.

"She was wasted. The bandit assholes wanted a piece—" A growl rips up my throat at his words. "But I wasn't letting that happen. No motherfuckers touch what's ours, Rivers."

His words touch something inside of me, and I relax.

"Ours?" My brows pinch.

"Yours," he corrects.

Silence falls between us, only the sound of our increased breathing filling the room.

"Call her," he finally says. "Tell her how you feel. Tell her you made a mistake. Tell her you fucking miss her."

I release a breath and I take a step back.

"I'm gonna go grab a drink with the guys. I'll message you when I'm leaving. If you need more time, I can crash with Handsy and Killer."

I stand at the end of my bed as if I don't belong while he strips out of his suit and pulls on a pair of jeans and a t-shirt.

"Good luck," he states before dropping his cell into his pocket and marching out of our hotel room.

The slam of the door echoes around me, but I still don't move.

I have so many reasons not to do as he suggests.

But...do any of them really matter?

Slowly and methodically, I strip out of my shirt and slacks before falling onto my bed wearing just my boxers.

I unlock my cell, and it opens on my pregame good luck message from Sutton. Disappointment in myself floods through me. She will have watched a good portion of the game tonight. She'll have seen some less-than-professional moves. Tonight, I wasn't a good role model, and I hate myself for it.

I let my anger and frustration get the better of me. I should be better than that.

Tapping out of our conversation, I scroll down and find my abandoned one with Casey.

My chest compresses as I read through our last words to each other.

Pain shoots through me.

I miss you.

Harboring every ounce of strength I have, I begin typing out a message.

66

CASEY

Watching the Vipers battle and then still lose like they did last night hurts.

I might have watched through a screen, but I could feel their anguish and desperation as if I were on the ice with them.

But as bad as last night was, standing here now, watching my team of fierce girls fight the same ruthless battle, is even worse.

The sad part is, they're not even the weaker team. They've just made a couple of mistakes that allowed their opponents to take advantage, and the ref doesn't seem to be on our side.

Frustration oozes from the team as they fight to get the puck toward the goal, but none of them are trying harder to turn this game around than Sutton.

She's a force to be reckoned with, but as of yet, she hasn't managed to make a difference.

I want it for her. Just like I wanted it for Kodie last night.

But I couldn't help then, and I can't now. All I can do is scream and shout my support and hope it's enough.

It won't be.

I woke up yesterday with the hangover from hell. I'm pretty sure it was the worst one I've ever suffered. It was long after lunchtime before I was able to drag my ass out of bed and function like a normal person. And Parker wasn't any better.

We ordered in coffee and food before collapsing on my couch with our heads pounding and stomachs swirling.

She was the one who found the images of me tagged on my Instagram account.

She also happily pointed out how hot I looked in the arms of Andrey Petrov and how Kocie would lose his mind if he saw them.

The thought made my heart flutter momentarily before it contracted painfully and I murmured that he'd moved on.

Parker didn't want to accept my words, but thankfully, our food arrived and cut the conversation short.

I stand there helplessly as the minutes count down to the end of the game. The score is three-zero.

My heart is in my throat as our girls push harder and harder.

I glance at the time.

One more play.

One more chance to score.

I watch as Megan tells the girls which play, and after brief words among those on the ice, they line up for the puck drop.

The puck is dropped, and for what feels like the first time tonight, we win possession.

Our center shoots it to Mila, who quickly takes off, but her mark is right on her, stopping her from even attempting to shoot.

She looks up, searching for options as Sutton breaks free.

Oh my god.

My heart is in my throat as hope blooms inside me. Of course, we're not going to win. But getting a goal in before the buzzer is still something.

Mila pulls her stick back, ready to pass, and I swear I watch in slow motion as the puck slides across the ice, right toward where Sutton is going to be able to pick it up and hopefully put it straight into the back of the net.

I swear, everyone holds their breath.

I gasp as the puck hits Sutton's stick and she shoots.

But I don't get to see if she scores—and neither does Sutton, because a defenseman from the other team suddenly slams into her, sending her flying backward.

"SUTTON," I scream as I watch her small body leave the ice.

Oh my god.

She hits the ice hard, her head taking most of it, and my blood runs cold.

I'm moving before I even realize, jumping the boards and racing toward her lifeless body with my heart lodged in my throat.

There's a flurry of movement behind me, but I don't register any of it as I drop to my knees beside her.

"Sutton, Sutton? Are you okay?"

Despite desperately wanting to touch her, to pull her to me and hold her, I don't. I know I can't. It fucking kills me.

But not as much as her lack of reaction to my words.

Her eyes are closed, her face pale.

Oh my god.

"Call 911. Please, someone, call—"

"It's okay," someone says from behind me, and when I look back, two EMTs are racing across the ice. "We'll take over from here."

Unable to do anything else, I take a step back.

My body trembles as I watch them check her vitals.

Despite her pads, she looks so tiny, so vulnerable.

That's Kodie's baby girl.

He's never going to forgive you.

A sob rips from my throat, my hand coming up to cover my mouth in a pathetic attempt to smother it.

The EMTs speak to each other before one lifts a walkie-talkie from his shirt and then speaks into it. I don't hear a word. I just watch in horror, praying that she'll open her eyes.

But she never does.

I glance over my shoulder, finding that Megan and the parents who traveled to this game are comforting the others, trying to keep them distracted, but their wretched expressions are clear from here.

"We're going to take her in," the EMT says, dragging my

attention back to where he's sitting alone beside Sutton. "Are you—"

"Her coach. I'm her coach. I'm coming with you," I say before he has a chance to continue. "I'll call her father; he'll meet us there," I say, but as I do, reality settles. He's on a plane right now, flying home from last night's game.

"What's going on?" Aurora's mom says, having left her daughter with the rest of the team to join us.

Her face is pale; her eyes wide.

She brought Sutton to this game, along with Aurora and Mila.

I close my eyes briefly, thinking of the times I'd carpool with teammates for road games. The drive home with friends after a win was such a high. Being together also made the losses sweeter.

None of these girls are going to experience that today, though. Not having witnessed this.

"They're taking her in," I say, my voice weak. "She's still unconscious." My eyes drop where she's still lying on the ice.

I want to help. I want to make it better. I want...I want everything I can't fucking do.

"She'll be okay," Aurora's mom says, her eyes also focused on Sutton's motionless body.

God, I hope she's right.

Calling Kodie to say there was an accident will be one thing, but calling him with worse news...

Acid churns in my stomach, burning up my throat.

No, that's not going to happen.

She's going to be okay.

Aurora's mom and I step back, allowing the EMTs to roll Sutton onto a stretcher.

"Look after the girls. I'm going with her," I say before hurrying after the stretcher.

"Casey," Megan cries. When I glance back, I find that she's untangled herself from the team and is racing after me.

"Look after the girls," I tell her. "I'll message you where we are."

"Are you sure? I can—"

I glance up at the horrified faces watching us.

"I won't leave her side. I'll call Kodie and Kathleen."

"No, I can—"

"I've got this. I'll message you," I call as I chase after the EMTs who rush down a hallway now that they're off the ice.

The second they have her loaded into an ambulance, I jump in beside her, taking her hand as we immediately take off.

"I've got you, Sutton. Everything is going to be okay. I'm going to call your dad and—"

"Don't," a little voice whispers.

My heart jumps into my throat, and I surge to my feet, ignoring the glare from the EMT.

I stare into her eyes, my muscles relaxing sightly.

"I'm okay," she says softly.

"Sweetie, you've been unconscious. You—"

"Please, please don't tell him. He'll worry."

My nose itches with emotion, my eyes burning as tears flood them.

"That's his job to worry about you," I assure her.

"He should be focusing on the game. Last night..."

I hang my head as her words trail off.

She saw Kodie losing his shit and getting thrown in the box.

"He's not...he needs..." I squeeze my eyes closed, hating that she's got to witness all of this. But then she says one final word that has my eyes popping open again. "You."

All the air rushes from my lungs as the ambulance takes a corner, making me stumble.

"Miss, please sit down," the EMT instructs.

I'm too stunned to do anything but what I'm told, and my ass hits the seat once again.

The next two hours are a blur of activity as Sutton is admitted to the ER and checked over.

I try calling Kodie, but as we both know, he's currently on a flight home.

He's going to lose his shit when he lands. I left a voicemail for him to call me. But the second he sees my name, he's going to know that something is wrong.

I speak to Kathleen and assure her that Sutton has been fully checked over and is okay. She took quite a hit and has a mild concussion. She was lucky, but there's no doubt that she'll feel it for a few days.

I press my hand to my chest, rubbing as I remember the pain of a hard hit.

Kathleen promises to be waiting for Kodie when he lands so they can drive here immediately.

As if turning his cell on to find a voicemail from me isn't going to be bad enough. Finding his mom waiting is going to finish him off.

After I've assured her once again that Sutton is okay, I promise to message her our new location and hang up.

My entire body is trembling with adrenaline and nerves.

"Is everything okay?" Sutton asks when I step back into her bay.

I smile at her, trying to smother how I really feel.

"Of course. Your gran is going to pick your dad up the second he lands, and they'll come here."

"They don't need—"

"Sutton," I say softly. "There is nowhere else in the world your father will want to be than by your side."

"But I'm okay," she argues.

Reaching out, I tuck a lock of her hair behind her ear. "Even when you're okay, it's his job to worry about you. You heard the doctor. They want to keep you here overnight just to be safe. He'll want to be right here with you."

She smiles, knowing that I'm right.

Suddenly, sadness washes across her face, and her bottom lip begins to tremble. I shift closer, my hand holding her tightly as her first sob breaks free. "I miss him," she cries.

Me too, Sutton.

Me too.

67

———

KODIE

I throw my bag over my shoulder and step out of the airplane, my eyes watering with the brightness of the sun. It's a vast cry from the miserable, gray day we left behind. But no amount of sun and warmth can soften the blow of what I find waiting for me at the bottom of the stairs.

The second my eyes land on her, ice floods through my veins.

Shoving Marilyn aside, I race down with my heart lodged in my throat.

"Sutton?" I bellow as I race toward Mom.

Her face is pale and her eyes are wide as she watches me approach.

"She's okay," Mom says, sounding more confident than she looks.

My heart continues to race, my hands trembling with fear.

"Then why—"

"She took a hard hit on the ice during her game."

Oh god.

I squeeze my eyes tight for a beat as all the fears I had about her playing ice hockey come rushing back.

I know how dangerous a sport it is. I've been fairly lucky with only a few breaks and pulls, but I've witnessed more than my fair share of players who've suffered worse.

It's a position I would never, ever want my baby girl in.

"She got knocked out, and they took her to the hospital."

My chest tightens to the point I can barely suck in a breath.

"Why aren't you there? She shouldn't be alone right now."

"She's not alone," Mom explains. "She's with Casey."

"Fuck," I breathe, sinking my hands into my hair and staring up at the clear sky.

"My car is in the garage. She went to the game with Aurora and Mila," Mom explains despite me already knowing this. "I got a taxi here so we can go together."

"Rivers, everything okay?" Coach asks, coming to join us.

"It's Sutton. She's in the hospital." Those are the only words I manage to get out before he's practically shoving me in the direction of the parking lot.

I take off running, forgetting that Mom doesn't stand a chance of keeping up. My only thought is getting to my little girl.

The second I'm at my car, I throw my bag in the trunk and climb inside.

I have the engine started and I'm ready to back out when Mom finally climbs inside, her breathing erratic.

"I've got...GPS..." She waves her cell at me. "Go. Just...go."

I don't need telling twice. I throw the car into reverse and spin out without looking to see if anyone is there.

Calm down, Rivers.

You need to get there in one piece.

Mom syncs her cell to my Bluetooth, and in seconds the map is up on the screen, telling me where to go.

Long, agonizing minutes pass before Mom speaks.

"She's okay," she assures me. "I've spoken to her. Casey has kept me informed from the moment it happened. She called you, but obviously—"

"My cell was off," I answer for her as the weight of the world presses down on my shoulders.

My baby girl needed me, and I wasn't there. I wasn't contactable and—

"FUCK," I roar out, slamming my palms down on the wheel,

but it does little to shatter the tension wrapped around me in a tight hold.

"I'll call her. You can hear her voice then, know she's okay."

I don't respond. I can't. The thought of hearing either of their voices right now is enough to push me over the edge.

But not a second later, a familiar voice hits my ears, and I realize that no preparation would have been enough.

"Hi Kathleen," Casey says lightly.

My entire body erupts with goosebumps as a chill races down my spine.

I need you.

"We've just left the airport. GPS is saying just over an hour."

"Did you hear that?" Casey asks. "Your daddy's on his way."

"Hi Daddy," a little voice says through the speakers, and I swear, my heart rips in two at the weakness in it.

"Hey Peanut," I breathe, speaking for the first time. "How are you feeling?"

"Pfft, it was barely even a hit. I'm fine."

"Said like a true hockey player," Casey teases.

"I'm sorry, Daddy," Sutton said.

"Peanut, you have nothing to apologize for. I'm sorry I wasn't at your game."

"Wait," Sutton says sounding a little more awake all of a sudden. "Did I score?"

"What?" Casey asks while a knowing smile curls at my lips.

"I took a shot; did it go in?"

A laugh bursts out of me. It feels so fucking good.

Mom looks over, her eyes burning into the side of my face.

"Yeah, it went in," Casey tells her.

"Yesss," she hisses.

I can't wipe the smile off my face as I shake my head.

"I stopped them from having a shutout. That's all that matters."

It's absolutely not what matters at all, but as a hockey player, I get it. I'm pretty sure Casey does too.

"Yeah, Rivers. That's all that matters."

There's some movement down the line before Casey explains that the doctor has just arrived to do some checks.

"I can call back after," she offers.

"No, let Sutton get some rest. We'll be there soon."

"Okay, sure. I'll grab coffees and—"

"Casey," I say, stopping her mid-sentence. "Thank you."

"Kodie, I—"

"Not now," I hiss, shooting a glance at Mom who's sitting in my passenger seat with a smile. "We'll see you soon. Make sure Sutton does as she's told."

"I'll do my best," she promises before hanging up.

"Kodie—"

"Mom," I warn.

She chuckles. "Okay, fine. You don't have to listen to anything I have to say. It's not like I'm older or wiser or anything. But please, talk to her. Be honest with her. Tell her how you really feel."

Oh yeah, because that's so fucking easy.

***

By the time we pull into the hospital parking lot, my patience to see my girl has all but run out. I park the car in the first space I find before racing out.

"Just go," Mom calls from behind me.

"Shit, I—"

"Go, Kodie."

Mom's not old and frail by any stretch of the imagination. In fact, she's in very good shape. She does yoga three times a week and walks with a group of friends. But even still, she's no match for a professional athlete.

I look back, torn between waiting for her and getting to Sutton. But when she tells me to go again, I take off running.

Thanks to Casey's message earlier, we both know what floor and ward Sutton is on.

Without looking back, I burst into the building and head for the stairs. There is no way I can be contained in an elevator. I don't need one; it's only eight flights of stairs.

By the time I hit the top, my chest is heaving and sweat glistens on my skin.

Okay, maybe the elevator wouldn't have been such a bad idea.

I step into the hallway, fighting to catch my breath and focus so I can read the ward names.

Finding the one I want, I take off running again, and in seconds, I'm rushing toward the nurses' station.

"Sutton Rivers," I force out through my heaving breaths. "She's here, she—"

"Kodie."

Casey's voice wraps around me like a warm blanket, and just for a moment, everything stops.

"Kodie, Sutton is right over here," she says again when I don't visibly react.

I pause, terrified to turn around. But time for hiding is over.

"Ko—" Her voice falters as my eyes lock on hers, the air between us crackling like a livewire. "S-she's in here," Casey whispers, pointing over her shoulder.

My legs move without instruction from my brain, my eyes holding Casey's until I'm forced to look at the door behind her.

"Daddy," Sutton cries from the bed.

She looks tiny in a huge hospital bed surrounded by stark white sheets.

"Peanut," I breathe, taking both her hands in mine. "Shit. Are you really okay?"

I can tell from the raised eyebrow at my swear word that she is. But I need to hear it with my own ears.

"And no hockey bravado. I'm not your coach. I'm your father."

She smiles softly at me. "I know, Daddy. My head hurts, but I'm okay. The hit wasn't that hard, but I lost my balance, and—" Tears fill her eyes, her bottom lip trembling. "I should have been able to catch myself."

Lowering my ass to the edge of the bed, I pull her into my arms, holding her as tight as I dare while she cries.

"It's nothing to be ashamed of. It happens to the best of us. You scored your team's only goal, and you're okay. That's all that matters, right?"

She shakes her head, sniffling. "I made you worried and you had to travel all the way out here after landing and—"

"Sutton," I warn. "I would go to the end of the earth for you. This is nothing."

Her little arms tighten around my waist as her sobs subside.

She keeps her face pressed against my chest, and thank fuck she does, because it means she can't see the tears that are flooding my eyes.

It's only now that I'm here with her in my arms that I fully appreciate just how fucking terrifying it was to see Mom standing there, waiting for me.

Yes, Sutton has a mild concussion, that is not something to celebrate. But it could have been so much worse.

Movement behind me has me looking over my shoulder, and my breath catches at the sight of Casey and Mom standing together, watching us. They both look emotional and exhausted, but it's Casey who's barely holding on.

The second her eyes find mine, a sob breaks free.

It fucking wrecks me, because I want to be over there with her as well as right here with Sutton.

Thankfully, Mom pulls her in for a hug.

"You did amazing, Casey. Thank you for looking after our girl."

I nod, agreeing with Mom as Casey watches me over Mom's shoulder.

After a few minutes, Sutton releases me, lying back down. She's pale and exhausted, her adrenaline running out faster than she can control now that I'm here.

I stay sitting on the edge of the bed as Casey hands me the coffee she promised.

Our fingers touch as I take it from her, sparks shooting up my arm from the small contact.

My lips part to say something, but a knock at the door has me swallowing the words.

Megan, Sutton's head coach, walks inside, her face hard with stress and worry.

"Mr. Rivers, I'm—"

"It's Kodie," I remind her, just like I do every time she addresses me so formally.

"Of course. I just spoke to the doctor again and everything is as it should be. They'd like to keep her in overnight for observation. I'll organize accommodation for both you and your mother."

"I can do it," Casey pipes up. "Go and look after the girls. We're all okay here."

"A-are you sure? I—"

"We're fine," I assure her. "Thank you for everything."

"When can I come back to practice?" Sutton asks, making us all smile.

"Let's see what the doctor says before you leave tomorrow and then make a decision from there."

"But we have another game next Sunday."

I let out a sigh, understanding all too well her desperation to push through this and continue as normal. Hopefully, she'll be doing that by her next game. But if there are any signs of this being more than a mild concussion, she'll have to get through me first.

"If you're well enough, you'll get some ice time," I promise her. "But only if you have medical clearance."

She stares at me but wisely doesn't argue.

"You'll be back on the ice before you know it," Megan promises. "Good job today, Sutton. And despite the obvious, that was a fantastic goal."

Sutton beams at the praise before Megan says her goodbyes and disappears.

"Right, well, I'm going to find a hotel," Mom says, pushing to stand with her coffee in her hand.

"Oh, no, I can—"

"Nonsense. You stay here. Catch up," Mom says looking

between us. If she's going for innocent, she's falling about an eternity from the mark. "I'm glad you're okay, sweetie," she says before kissing Sutton's cheek. "I won't be long. And who knows, maybe I'll find some candy on my travels."

Before we know it, Mom is closing the door behind her, leaving the three of us alone for the first time.

68

KODIE

I swear, as Mom closes the door behind her, she sucks all the air in the room out with her.

The weight of everything I've felt since stepping off that airplane and seeing Mom standing there with worry etched onto her face finally starts to ebb away.

Sutton is okay. Of course, even a mild concussion is something to be concerned about, but as an ice hockey player, they're inevitable.

I hate that she's involved in a sport that will result in injuries, but I'd never stop her from doing something she loves so much.

I just wish I could protect her at all times.

Movement at the end of Sutton's bed brings me back to the here and now, and my eyes shift between my daughter and the woman who's been at her side since the incident earlier.

The second my gaze lands on Casey, my heart contracts.

She looks exhausted, and something tells me it's not just the stress of the morning that's causing it.

I hate myself for it. But I can't deny that I want her to be struggling the way I am right now.

Doing the right thing fucking sucks.

My head knows I've done what I needed to do. It followed all the rules.

But my heart...

My heart is an entirely different story.

That is battered and broken, begging to be listened to. It doesn't care about the rules; it just wants to beat the way it did when Casey was mine.

I rub my chest, right above my broken heart.

Silence surrounds us, but despite the thousands of things I've dreamed of saying to her, all my words seem to dry up.

Instead, I stand there staring between the two girls who have changed my life in so many different ways.

We've never been alone in a room like this before.

Hell, I can count on one hand the number of people I've allowed this close to Sutton.

Having Casey here with us, knowing she's been taking care of my girl in my place...it makes my heart beat faster, and not in a bad way. In a really, really good way.

Casey shuffles forward again as I continue to battle to remember what words are.

"I...um...I should go," Casey whispers as she moves toward the door.

"Dad," Sutton begs weakly.

It's her voice that brings me back, and as Casey passes me, my hand shoots out, my fingers wrapping around her wrist, stopping her.

"Stay," I breathe.

The reality is that this is a hospital, and she's been here for hours already. It's probably the last place she wants to be.

The game finished hours ago. She'd probably almost be home by now if it weren't for Sutton.

I should let her go.

But I'm fed up with doing what I should do.

It's making me fucking miserable.

And now, she's right here, and it's where I want her to stay.

She freezes at my side, her breath catching in her throat at my demand.

It takes her a moment—a moment which feels like a fucking lifetime—before she turns to look up at me.

Her eyes are red rimmed from crying, the shadows beneath them dark with exhaustion.

Let her go, a little voice screams in my head.

But I can't.

"I'm sorry, I—"

"I can stay," she says softly, her eyes searching mine. I have no idea what she's looking for, or if she finds it, but after a moment, her shoulders relax.

A huge sigh of relief passes my lips, but I don't let go of her. I can't.

The warmth from her skin and the electric sparks that shoot up my arm are too addictive.

"Would you like another coffee?" she asks when no other words are said.

"Uh..."

"I'll go and get us some. Sutton," she says, ripping her eyes from me and focusing on my sleepy-looking daughter. "Would you like anything?"

Sutton shakes her head. "Gran's bringing me candy," she says with a smile.

"I'll be right back," she says before slipping from my grasp and moving toward the door.

The second she pulls it open and steps outside, I panic.

Spinning on the balls of my feet, I race after her.

"Casey," I call.

She turns around instantly, her eyes wide with panic, but when her eyes land on me, her expression softens.

"I'm just going for coffee," she says softly.

"Please come back."

I know I don't have any right to ask that of her. I've been an asshole. She deserves much better, but...I don't want her to leave.

A smile pulls at the corners of her lips.

"I'm coming back. Go in there and be with Sutton. I won't be long."

I hesitate, feeling like I'm being torn in two.

God, life was so much easier when my heart only belonged to one girl.

Letting her go, I step back into Sutton's room and rest back against the door. Closing my eyes, I take a few deep breaths.

I'm in love with Casey Watson.

The realization hits me out of nowhere, my heart pounding erratically inside my chest.

"Daddy?" a soft voice asks, dragging me from my thoughts. "Are you okay?"

Fucking hell. Today is wrecking me.

Ripping my eyes open, I focus on my daughter.

"Yeah, Peanut. I'm really good."

For the first time in a very long time, a little bit of hope trickles through my veins.

She mirrors my smile as I close the gap between us and lower myself back into the chair beside her bed.

"I really like Casey," she confesses, making my heart slam against my ribs once again.

"Yeah, you may have mentioned her being your new favorite coach."

"I don't just mean as a coach, Daddy."

Our eyes hold as understanding passes between us.

Sutton's maturity and awareness blow me away sometimes. But I know I only have myself to blame. She's spent her formative years surrounded by adults and grown-up conversation. It's no surprise she's in tune with what's happening around her, even if she doesn't fully understand it yet.

"I like Casey too," I agree, making Sutton beam.

"You know, it's okay if you want a girlfriend."

This girl...

"I love you, Sutton," I say, my voice rough with emotion.

"I love you too, Daddy."

We both fall silent, lost in our own thoughts, and only a few seconds later, her eyes fall closed and her breathing evens out.

"Fucking hell," I mutter, dragging my hand down my face and slouching back in the chair.

I watch her sleep, wondering how on Earth I was lucky enough to have a daughter as incredible as her.

I try my best not to think about the woman who gave her to

me, but every now and then, I can't help but think about how much she's missing out on.

Don't get me wrong, I don't want her in either of our lives, but she has no idea just how perfect her little girl is.

Long, silent minutes pass before the door behind me opens and soft footsteps move closer.

I don't need to turn around to know who it is. Her scent wafts over me as my body reacts to her proximity.

"Here," she says, passing me a takeout cup before walking around the bed with her own in hand.

"Thank you," I muse, my eyes tracking her every movement as she lowers herself into the other chair.

I want to demand she move it over so she can be closer to me, but I refrain.

I might have made a few decisions about where I want things to go with us, but I'm not under any illusion that she'll be on the same page after the way I've treated her.

She's here for Sutton right now, not me.

I want her to be here for me, though.

"She finally sleeping?" Casey asks, keeping her eyes on Sutton.

"Yeah."

"I tried to get her to sleep while we were waiting for you, but she refused until you got here."

My heart seizes.

"Well, I'm here now," I say like an idiot.

"Yeah," she mutters.

I keep my attention on Sutton for a few seconds, thanking any deity who'll listen to an asshole like me that she's okay. But my eyes inevitably drift to Casey again.

It's been the same since I ran into her that night at the ball. Our bodies are like two magnets that can't help but gravitate toward each other. The pull is ridiculous, and I don't think it's going to lessen any time soon. If anything, it's getting stronger.

"Casey," I whisper, forcing her eyes to lift to mine. "I'm sorry."

Her brows pinch, her throat rippling with a thick swallow.

"It's okay. I—"

"No. It's not okay. How I acted...nothing about that was okay."

Casey's eyes flick to Sutton briefly before she focuses back on me again.

"I should have told you. It was my fault. I blindsided you and—"

"Why didn't you?" I ask.

"Because it was just another reason why we shouldn't have been..." Her eyes jump to Sutton again, watching to see if she's still sleeping. "Doing what we were doing," she continues a little quieter.

"I was scared," I blurt, unable to keep the words in any longer.

She blinks, reaching up to tuck a loose lock of hair behind her ear as she contemplates my confession.

"Was scared?" she asks hesitantly.

I shake my head. "I am scared," I clarify.

Nodding, she twists her fingers in her lap, leaving me hanging on that confession.

As the seconds tick on, I regret saying it more and more.

But then, her lips part, and she whispers. "So am I."

Our eyes hold as the air in the room thickens. My chest heaves as I fight to drag in each breath. My body burns for her. I want to march over there, pull her into my arms, and never let her go.

Sutton whimpers in her sleep, and I'm dragged back to reality.

"Casey, I—" My words are cut off as the door behind me opens again and Mom rejoins us.

She looks between us with a frown on her brow.

"Everything okay?" she asks.

"Yeah," I say. "Sutton is sleeping."

Mom glances at Sutton before looking back at me with a raised brow as if to say, no shit.

She walks around me and places a huge bag of candy on the unit beside Sutton before moving toward the window and perching on the low sill.

"I should arrange a ride home," Casey says, rising from her chair with her coffee still in hand.

The thought of her leaving sends a bolt of panic through me.

"We can take you back tomorrow," I say.

Casey's eyes hold mine. I swear I see a little spark of something within them. "I have work tomorrow," she mutters, although there isn't much conviction in the words.

"I'm sure they won't mind if you go in a little late," Mom says hopefully.

"Mom," I warn, aware of what she's doing.

"What?" she asks innocently. "You have a game tomorrow night. You need to be back early. Assuming Sutton is okay, I'm guessing we'll be leaving early so you're back in time."

Casey looks between the two of us, indecision warring in her eyes.

"I can work remotely. I have my laptop and—"

"You've had a long day. Stay, rest, and then start over tomorrow," Mom says, her tone a little more commanding than I've heard for a while. I study her, trying to figure out what her game plan is here.

"What?" she mouths.

"A night in a hotel sounds like heaven right now," Casey finally admits.

"Exactly." Mom digs into her purse and pulls out a hotel keycard. "Go and have a bath. Relax."

"Oh, I can't accept that," Casey argues.

"You looked after our girl today. We owe you everything for that."

When Casey looks back at me, all I do is smile encouragingly.

"Okay," she concedes. "I know she's okay, but will you let me know if that changes?"

"Of course," Mom agrees while I sit there, mute.

Casey hesitates, but after a couple of seconds, she moves toward the door.

"I'll walk you out," Mom says in a rush, and not a moment later, they've both disappeared, leaving me with my sleeping daughter and my head spinning.

69

CASEY

I let out a sigh as I sink into the bathtub full of bubbles and a little too hot water. Soft music fills the air along with the floral scent of bubble bath I found waiting for me on the counter.

My body ached for this when Kathleen described it, but if anything, this is better.

She didn't hold back on the hotel room—it's massive and luxurious. I should feel guilty over accepting it, but as the warmth seeps into my muscles, I'm having a hard job feeling anything but relief.

I haven't had a bath since that day with Kodie, I've stuck with showers in the hope of banishing the memories. Instead, I've glared at my tub with disdain and self-loathing.

My pulse picks up when I think back to our brief exchanges earlier. The way he begged me to stay. How he told me that he was sorry before explaining how scared he was.

Just being in a room with him and Sutton like we were some kind of family was a big enough headfuck. But hearing him say all those things?

Fuck, it messed with my head.

I want him. Nothing has changed for me there. But despite it being my fault, he hurt me when he walked away from me.

He isn't the only one that's scared.

I've learned since that night at the ball that when it comes to Kodie Rivers, it's impossible not to fall for him.

Hell, I'm pretty sure I've been falling for him from afar since I was a teenager. Convincing myself that I could have a one-night thing with him and then move on was the biggest lie I've ever told myself.

He's too...well, Kodie Rivers for that.

He commands attention, adoration, and awe.

I never stood a chance.

I just get comfortable, losing myself in thoughts of what could be, when the music cuts and my cell starts ringing.

Anxiety twists me up inside because I already know who it is.

I didn't reach out to him after our game. In my defense, I was a little busy with Sutton.

I don't doubt that he knows all about it, seeing as Kodie was whisked away by Kathleen the second they touched down.

Nerves wrack through me as I prepare to answer his questions before I swipe the screen with a bubbly finger and put it on speaker.

"Hey, Dad."

"Hey, Care Bear. Is everything okay?"

I let out a sigh that I'm sure says a thousand words.

"Yeah. It's been a tough day, though."

His own sigh lets me know he understands.

"Seeing one of your players hurt is one of the hardest things to go through as a coach. How is she?"

"She's good. Mild concussion. I think her ego is bruised more than anything," I explain.

He chuckles. "Typical hockey player."

I can't help but smile.

He's right—and not only is she a hockey player, but she's her father's daughter.

"You were no different, you know that?"

"Dad," I warn.

"I'm serious. The first time you were injured...my heart stopped dead for a few seconds, I swear. It was awful."

"Dad," I whisper, emotion crawling up my throat.

"I ran onto that ice faster than I've ever moved in my life. I beat the EMTs. I was so fucking scared. But a couple of seconds later, you opened your eyes, looked up at me, and asked if anyone had managed to score."

An emotional laugh falls from my lips.

"That's the day I knew for sure that you had hockey in your blood. I also knew that your mom was going to kill me."

My eyes burn with tears at the mention of her. She supported me wholeheartedly, but that didn't mean she liked watching me play a sport that was so violent. She never said the words, but I'm sure she'd have been much happier if I'd wanted to be a ballet dancer.

"I tried calling Rivers, but it's going to voicemail," Dad suddenly says.

"He's with her," I explain. "She was sleeping when I left."

"Casey?"

"Mmm."

"Where are you?"

My silence says everything I don't.

"You're still there, aren't you?"

"Sutton asked me to stay, and I was worried about her, so—"

"Do you want me to come and get you?" he offers.

"No," I say in a rush. "I'm sure you've got more important things to be doing than chasing around after me."

"I'm never too busy for you, Care Bear. You know that."

A contented sigh slips past my lips. I do know that. He's the best father in the world. But right now, I really don't need him turning up here to take me home.

"It's fine. I'm having a night in a hotel. I'll head home in the morning." I say the words as lightly as possible in the hope he doesn't read into them.

They have a game tomorrow, I know he's about to offer again, but he doesn't have time to come and rescue me.

If I can't get a ride with Kodie—obviously my first choice—then I'll just call an Uber.

"Casey—"

"Honestly, Dad. It's fine. I've got an amazing room with a massive tub. I'm going to call room service and spend the evening working."

My heart flutters with other possibilities for my evening, but I attempt to shut it down.

That is not how my night is going to go.

"Call Parker, she'll come and get you. I don't like the idea of you being in an Uber with a stranger for that long."

I shake my head, a smile playing on my lips.

It doesn't matter how old I get; he'll still try to protect me like the little girl I was.

"I'll be fine. And I'll be back well in time for your game."

"That's not what's important.'

"Of course it is."

"Are you sure you don't want me to come? I can leave right now," he asks, trying again.

"I'm sure."

"Okay," he concedes. "Message me when you're back tomorrow."

"I will," I promise.

"I love you, Care Bear."

"I love you too, Dad. Have a good evening."

"You too."

Dad cuts the call, plunging the room into silence for a beat before my music returns.

Reaching over, I ignore my cell but grab the glass of wine I have waiting beside it.

I may have told Dad that I was planning on ordering room service tonight, but the truth is, I already have.

I hum in delight as the cool, fruity liquid hits my tongue.

Resting the glass on the edge of the tub, I sink a little lower in the water.

This might not have been planned, but it's very much needed.

Do I wish I had some company in the form of a sexy-as-hell hockey player? Hell, yes. But a little me time is almost as good.

I stay in the tub until the water is cold and my wine glass is empty.

My skin is soft and my muscles are loose as I lift myself out, letting the bubbles race down my body.

Reaching for the thick robe hanging on the back of the door, I snuggle into it before stepping up to the basin to remove what's left of my makeup.

Relaxed and ready for a quiet night, I pad through to the bedroom, grabbing my laptop from my bag as I go before settling in the middle of the huge bed.

Time drifts by as I continue working on my overhaul of the Polar Bears' Instagram.

I've taken inspiration from the Vipers' account, and I've been working on creating eye-catching graphics that I know resonate with hockey fans. My team might be small—in both size and stature—but that doesn't mean they don't deserve for the world to know who they are.

Our girls are talented, and if just one thing I post allows others to see that and helps to carve out their future, I'll be thrilled.

I have a whole grid designed with both headshots and action shots of the girls. I have quotes from them about how much they love their sport, their team, and their coaches. I have video content that I'm going to turn into reels, but that's going to be a project for another day. It's all coming together beautifully, and I'm proud of what I've managed to achieve so far. I just have to hope others are, too.

I add a few things to the to-do list before opening up the room service menu to select something for dinner.

I'm about to place my carb-heavy order when a noise outside the door catches my attention.

My eyes shoot up a beat before my heart jumps into my throat as someone lets themselves in.

What the fuck?

Heavy footsteps move my way as I stare in horror. I should be saying something, but shock and fear have me frozen.

But then, everything changes in a heartbeat when Kodie stalks around the corner.

The second his eyes land on me, his brows pinch, and his chin drops.

"Casey?" he questions as if he's seeing things.

"Hey," I say awkwardly, aware that I'm sitting here with the front of my robe gaping open while he's fully dressed and clearly not expecting to have company. "Is everything—"

"Little witch," he hisses, although there's a smile playing on his lips.

"What?"

"We've been set up," he says with a laugh before holding up a hotel keycard. "She told me this was for the room she'd booked for me and her."

A smile spreads across my mouth, hope and warmth flooding through my body.

"Ah." I knew I liked Kathleen. "How is Sutton?" I ask.

Reaching up to rub the back of his neck, he scans the room.

"Yeah, she's good. Mom refused to let me spend the night in the chair by her bed because of the game tomorrow and sent me here. She's going to stay with her."

"Good. That's good," I say, closing the lid on my laptop and pushing it across the only bed in the room.

"I can go and get another room," Kodie offers, although it's weak at best.

"Is that what you want?" I ask, shuffling to the edge and swinging my legs over.

"Uh." He combs his fingers through his wild curls, his eyes holding mine firm. "We should talk."

"Yeah," I agree, pushing to my feet and stepping closer to him.

He's not wrong; we really do need to talk.

But right now, he's standing before me looking lost and confused, and I'd rather show him what I want—what I need—instead.

Pressing my hands against his chest, I slide them up.

His breath catches as his eyes shutter at my touch.

"I missed you," I confess. "I'm sorry for not telling you about coaching Sutton. I—"

"I missed you too."

70

KODIE

My hand wraps around the back of her neck, and my lips crash down on hers.

My patience is gone.

Mom has spent the last few hours trying to convince me to take the keycard and get a good night's sleep.

I've got a game tomorrow, and the last thing I need is a night attempting to sleep in a chair.

I'd do it, though. For Sutton, I'd do anything.

But Mom insisted that she'd be the one to stay and all but shoved me out of the room once I'd run out of excuses.

I know Mom can be sneaky when she wants to be, but this is something else.

Casey whimpers as my tongue pushes inside her lips.

Desire fills every inch of me, my cock already hard and aching for her as her sweet scent floods my nose.

My grip on her waist tightens as her tongue eagerly glides against mine.

Her fingers twist in my hair before her nails drag across my scalp, making me shudder.

"Kodie," she whispers like a prayer into our kiss, and it's the final spark that lights my fuse.

Spinning her around, I press her back against the wall before hitching her leg up around my waist so I can grind into her.

She's right. We should talk, but I'm not sure I'm capable of forming words right now, let alone thinking.

"Oh god," she cries, breaking the kiss, her head hitting the wall as my lips graze across her jaw and down her neck. "Kodie."

I breathe her in as I kiss down the soft skin of her throat, wondering how I managed to go without her for so long.

"I'm sorry," I repeat. "I'm so fucking sorry."

"Me too," she gasps as I suck on the patch of skin beneath her ear. Her fingers twist in my hair, tugging tight enough to send a shot of pain down my neck. It hits me right in the balls. "I need you. I need you so badly."

"I didn't think I was going to get this again," I confess, the words falling from my lips. "You're all I've been able to think about."

"Then why were you ignoring me?"

"Because...because I thought it was the right thing to do."

I pull back and look into her eyes.

"It was the right thing to do," I tell her honestly. "But it's been fucking killing me."

"Me too."

"I've been fucking up on the ice," I say, although if she's watched any games, she's probably well aware. "You're all up in my head, Casey. Under my skin."

Her eyes glisten with moisture as she rolls her lips between her teeth.

After a beat, she nods, reaching for my hand that's resting on her waist and pressing it against her chest, right over her heart.

"In here," she whispers, her voice cracked with emotion.

My breath catches in my throat.

I've heard women say all kinds of things over the years in the hope of having me for more than a night. But I have never heard them said so sincerely. And they've certainly never affected me the way Casey's do.

My heart stutters in my chest, my stomach knots with a mixture of nerves and excitement, and my hands noticeably tremble.

I'm fucking scared.

Reaching for her other hand, I mimic her movements, pressing her palm to my chest.

"You feel that?" I ask, my voice deep and raspy.

It takes her a couple of seconds, but she nods.

"You terrify me, Casey," I confess.

She swallows thickly.

"This terrifies me," I add. "I've never felt like this. I've never wanted anything like this. My life...it's hard. My schedule, my daughter—"

"I don't care about hard, Kodie. Nothing can be as hard as not having you in my life. It was okay before when I was just watching you from afar. I knew you were incredible, but I didn't *know*. But now that I do, I don't know how to continue with my life without you in it."

"Fuck," I breathe, leaning forward and letting my head rest against hers. Her honesty floors me. She fucking floors me.

"I don't know what'll happen if we do this. Your dad...he could trade me. He—"

"Then I'll follow you," she says without missing a beat.

"But your job. Your life—"

"I can get a job anywhere. I can't find you anywhere."

"Why me?" I ask, hating how vulnerable I sound but powerless to do anything about it.

"Because you're you," she says, her big green eyes staring up at me. Honesty and desire flickers within them.

"Casey."

"Please tell me that this is it," she begs.

I swear, she may as well claw my chest open and rip my heart out at this point.

It's hers.

Everything is fucking hers.

"It's not going to be easy."

"It would be boring if it was," she counters.

"I'll fuck up."

"So will I."

"I can't put you first."

"You shouldn't. Sutton always comes first."

"Goddamn."

My lips find hers again, and I kiss her until we're both breathless and she's clawing at my shoulders, desperate for more.

"Kodie, I need you. Please," she begs.

I can't help but smirk against her lips. Will I ever get enough of her begging me? Fuck, I hope not.

She shrieks as I wrap both of my hands beneath her thighs and lift her from the floor.

Instantly, her legs wrap around my waist.

Pulling her from the wall, I walk her over toward the bed with her arms locked around my neck, as if she's scared I'll disappear if she lets me go.

Breaking our kiss, I let her back hit the mattress before reaching for her arms and tugging them free.

"I promise, I'm not going anywhere."

Standing to full height, I pull my cell from my pocket and put it on sleep mode. That way, the only person who'll be able to get through is Mom, and if she calls, it'll be an emergency.

Placing it on the nightstand, I reach over my head and pull my hoodie off, leaving my torso bare for her to feast on.

Her eyes trace every single line and muscle until she hits my waistband, and then a little lower.

I don't need to look to know that I'm tenting my sweats.

"Please," she whimpers before her hands go to the tie knotted around her middle.

"No," I command, pressing one knee to the mattress.

"No?" she echoes with a deep frown forming between her brows.

Pulling her arms away, I throw them back on the bed.

"I undress you," I state, letting my eyes track down her towel-covered body.

Fire burns through my veins just knowing what hides beneath it.

When I get back up to her face, she's biting down on her bottom lip, her eyes almost black with desire.

"Tell me what you want."

"You. Everything."

I quirk a brow, needing more detail than that.

"Your mouth. I want it on mine, on my neck, on my tits, my pussy. I want to come all over your face, and then I want you to kiss me after."

"Christ," I grunt as precum soaks into my boxers.

"Then I want you to fuck me. I want you to stretch me open and remind me just how well we fit together."

As she talks, I tug at the tie around her waist, finally freeing it.

Slowly, I peel the fabric back, revealing inches of her beautiful skin.

All the air in my lungs comes out in a rush as I stare down at her swollen breasts, her peaked nipples.

"Kodie," she whimpers, her hips grinding in her need for friction.

Reaching for her ankles, I place her feet flat on the bed before spreading them so I can see all over her.

Her pussy glistens and my mouth waters to follow her orders.

Patience.

"I haven't even touched you and you're dripping."

"I told you; I need you."

"Fuck," I mutter, scrubbing my rough jaw while my other hand squeezes my length. Her eyes drop, watching me. "The feeling is mutual."

"So, what are you waiting for?"

"I have no fucking idea."

Falling over her, I catch myself with a hand on either side of her head before ducking lower and claiming her lips.

She tastes like wine and my ultimate addiction.

Her hands burn as she runs them down my back, and I shudder when she drags her nails all the way back up.

"More," she begs.

"Needy little thing, aren't you?" I mutter into the sweet skin of her neck.

"For you, always."

Peppering kisses over her collarbone, I continue lower until

I'm sucking one nipple and then the other into my mouth. She arches off the bed, crying out as I nip her gently.

"Tell me you're mine," I demand, my eyes locked on hers.

"Kodie," she breathes. Just hearing her say my name does things to me. "I'm yours. I always have been."

"Fuck," I groan, descending to where I really want to be.

Pressing my hands against her inner thighs, I pin them to the mattress, giving my shoulders enough space.

"Did you want me to eat you, Trouble?"

"God, yes," she cries as I blow a teasing stream of air over her heated skin.

"Such a pretty pussy. I should feel bad about ruining it. But I don't. This is mine," I say, dragging a single finger from her clit to her entrance.

"Yours," she breathes, her muscles trying to suck me deeper when I tease her entrance.

"It's been too long," I muse before surging forward and licking the length of her pussy.

Her taste floods my mouth, and I groan in a mixture of delight and torture.

My dick hurts, it's so fucking hard.

I need her. But I'm the one who needs to prove himself. I'm the one with the huge apology to make, and I'm going to make sure she more than gets hers before I even consider getting mine.

"Kodie," she screams, her fingers sinking into my hair, attempting to drag me closer as I suck on her clit.

She writhes on the bed as I eat her like a man starved.

In only a few short minutes, she's trembling and on the cusp of her first orgasm.

"Have you been dreaming about this, baby?" I ask, my lips still on her.

"Yes, yes. Every night," she cries. "Please, don't stop."

With a smirk, I get back to work, and I don't come up for air until she's screamed out my name and fallen limp on the bed.

"Missed you," she muses as I sit back and stand at the end of the bed.

She watches me with hooded, exhausted eyes as I tuck my

fingers under the waistband of my sweats and boxers, and shove them down.

"Oh yeah?" I muse as I wrap my hand around myself and stroke slowly.

"You're beautiful," she tells me as I crawl onto the bed and between her legs.

"Not as beautiful as you."

Hitching her leg around my hip, I grind my dick against the burning heat of her pussy.

My eyes hold hers, the air crackling between us.

"You're everything, Casey. My everything."

"Kodie, I—"

I cut off whatever she's about to say, terrified it's going to be something I'm not ready to hear.

With our lips locked together, I reach down and find her entrance, coating myself in her juices before I push inside her.

One word hits me as I slide deep inside her body.

Home.

71

CASEY

I love you.

The words drift off as if they never had any intention of being spoken aloud as his tongue delves inside my mouth, kissing me as if he'd die without it.

"Oh god," I moan, breaking our kiss as he continues pushing inside me.

He's a tight fit, and he stretches me almost to the point of pain.

His eyes collide with mine as his body falls still.

"I've got you, baby," he whispers, "I'll wait all night for you to be ready."

Fucking hell.

This man.

"Mine." The word falls free without instruction from my brain as my hand lifts to cup his cheek.

He leans into my touch, and the sight makes my chest tighten.

This strong, powerful, unrelenting man is mine.

I shake my head as the craziness of that reality attempts to settle.

How can it be true?

It's too good to be true. It's—

"Yours," he rasps. "For as long as you'll have me."

My core tightens, the pressure sitting low in my belly making it almost impossible to lie still with him filling me up.

"Please, Kodie," I beg. "Fuck me."

His eyes hold mine captive, but that doesn't mean I miss the smirk that covers his mouth.

"Later," he rasps. "I'll fuck you like the dirty little whore you are later. Right now, I have other plans."

My breath catches as he drops down, his lips brushing over mine as he rolls his hips.

A loud groan rips from my lips, but he steals all of it with his kiss.

His moves are so tender and soft, yet utterly filthy at the same time.

I am so fucking here for it.

He kisses me until I'm breathless before pulling back and finding my eyes once more.

It's so intimate it makes my heart ache in the best kind of way.

I've never felt more connected to another person—and I don't just mean physically—than I do in this moment.

Everything he just said, I believe him.

I want this. I want him. And the part of me that thinks I can have it is growing faster than I can control.

Fuck the rest of the world.

Fuck the rules.

This, what we have together, is far more powerful than all of that.

He rests on his forearm beside my head before hitching my leg up around his waist.

I gasp as he hits me deeper, grazing that sweet spot inside me that's going to make me see stars.

"Yes," I hiss as his free hand begins to roam.

He pinches and twists my nipples, sending more and more heat to my core as his dick does its magic.

His hand brushes over my stomach before he finds my clit.

"Kodie," I whimper, my eyes urging him for more.

"You're so beautiful," he whispers, continuing his torturous pace. "So mine."

His words light a fire inside me.

"Yours," I agree.

"And I want the world to know about it."

It's the final push I need.

"Eyes, Casey," he demands the second they slam closed as my orgasm sucks me under.

Ripping them open, I let him see everything. Right down to my fucking soul.

This man has owned me unknowingly for years.

But now, he does know.

"Fuck yes," he groans. "Such a good fucking girl, coming all over my dick."

I nod, my lips parted as I ride out every wave of my release, my body convulsing and trembling beneath his.

I've almost come down from my high when Kodie stills, his loud groan bouncing off the walls around us before his dick jerks inside me, filling me up and making me his in the most primal way possible.

Aftershocks from my release shoot from my core as he continues. He collapses on top of me, his breathing erratic and his body limp.

"Fuck, Casey," he groans, his face tucked into my neck.

"Yeah," I muse, completely crushed by him but loving every second of it.

I've missed him so much. I've done my best to smother just how much his distance hurt, how large the gaping hole in my chest was, but now he's here, it's all too clear.

I sniffle as emotion burns the back of my nose and stings my eyes.

I fight it, I really do.

The last thing I ever want to be is one of those girls. But I can't help it; all of this is just too much.

I suck in a shaky breath that alerts Kodie to my fragile state, and he pulls his face from the crook of my neck, his brow furrowing as he watches a tear roll down my cheek.

"Casey?" he whispers, his eyes bouncing between mine.

"I'm okay," I say brokenly.

"You're crying," he states, looking completely out of his comfort zone.

"I know, but they're not bad tears."

That only makes his frown deeper.

As another falls, he leans forward and presses his lips against my cheek, catching it.

"I never want to make you cry."

"You haven't."

"Then why—"

"I'm just a little overwhelmed. All of this, you...I've wanted it so badly, and the last few weeks have been hard and—"

"I'm sorry."

Reaching up, I cup his jaw. "You don't need to keep apologizing. You haven't done anything wrong. In fact, you're doing everything right."

At my words, the most incredible smile spreads across his lips.

"I've never been in a serious relationship," he tells me.

I might already know that from the media over the years, but hearing him say it means so much more. He's opening himself up, allowing himself to be vulnerable.

It's everything.

He's everything.

"Nor have I," I confess.

"How? How is that even possible? Casey, you're amazing."

Heat blooms on my cheeks, the warmth spreading down my neck to my chest.

I shrug. "Just haven't found my person, I guess."

He releases a long breath, and it dances over my face. "I want to be him."

"Kodie," I whisper, my voice cracked and rough with emotion. "I think you are."

"Fucking hell," he groans before his lips find mine.

His kiss is soft, gentle and so full of everything I could only dream of before that masquerade ball.

I wished, but I never really believed he could be as incredible as I always made him out to be in my head.

The reality is, he's better.

I lose myself in his kiss, in the way his tongue glides against mine as he devours me. His free hand moves, skimming over my curves as if he's relearning them. All the while, mine do exactly the same thing. Not that I ever forgot. There isn't anything about Kodie that I could ever forget.

"Can't get enough of you," he mutters into our kiss. "Missed you so much."

"Me too."

Rolling onto his back, Kodie drags me with him allowing me to settle against his body. With my head on his chest, listening to the steady beat of his heart, I through my leg over his waist and hold him tight.

"What happens now?" I whisper, hating to ask but needing to at the same time.

He doesn't respond for a few seconds, but when it does, it's everything I want to hear. "Honestly, I don't know. But whatever it is, we're doing it together."

"Kodie."

"Thank you for today. Sutton, she—"

"I'd do anything for that little girl. It's not just her daddy who's wormed his way under my skin."

He chuckles. "I'm pretty sure Mom likes you too."

A heavy sigh passes my lips as thoughts of Kathleen morph into wondering what my mom would make of all this.

"You okay?" Kodie asks when I fall silent.

"Yeah." It's not a lie. I am okay, more than okay. But even all these years later, there are moments where grief hits me out of nowhere.

"Talk to me, Casey. What's been going on with you?"

"Other than missing you?" I ask, shooting a look up so I can see the smirk that is inevitably on his lips.

"Other than that."

We chat away about life for the longest time before my stomach lets out the loudest growl.

Kodie chuckles. "Think I'd better feed you before we go for round two."

As he says the words, he rolls his hips against me, letting his hard dick grind against my thigh.

"I can wait," I say, clawing at his back in the hope he'll forget about food and give me what I really need. As nice as it is lying here talking, we've got some lost time to make up for. "I'd rather have something else in my mouth."

"Dirty girl," he muses as he rolls over me.

For a moment, I think I've convinced him. But I should really know better, because what he does is grab the menu that's sitting on the nightstand.

"I'm ordering room service. Any requests?" he asks as he falls back to his side, his body still half on top of mine.

"Nope. As long as it's quick."

Ripping his eyes from the menu, he glances at me.

"Got plans, Trouble?"

Letting my gaze drop to his waist, I take in his impressive erection. My core clenches. What we did a few moments ago was perfect in so many ways. But I still want more.

Loving and passionate Kodie was incredible. He twisted me up in the best kind of way. But I want all sides of him tonight. Mostly, I want his kinky side.

"So many plans," I confess, pushing myself up on my elbow so I can kiss his jaw as he reads.

"Mmm," he groans, tilting his head to the side to give me better access to his neck.

"Go and start the shower," he suddenly commands.

"I'm okay here," I say honestly.

"Casey," he warns. The deep rasp of his voice makes my nipples pebble. "Be a good girl and do what you're told."

Shivers. Fucking shivers.

Putting on what I hope is a sexy voice, I ask, "What would you like me to do after I've put the shower on?"

He doesn't look at me. His eyes don't even falter from the menu as he explains, "You're going to put the shower on, and then you're going to wait for me on your knees with it raining down on your back."

My thighs clench.

"Yes, Sir," I breathe before planting a final kiss on his jaw and slipping from beneath him.

The second I stand, cum rushes down my thighs, reminding me of what we did not so long ago.

"Problem?" he asks, again, not looking up from the menu when I don't move fast enough.

"Nope," I say before rushing into the bathroom with fire licking at my insides.

I do as I'm told and rest my hands on top of my thighs as I wait for him.

My heart pounds against my ribs as desire sits heavy between my legs. I'm pretty sure my clit has its own heartbeat at this point.

My fingers curl with my need to spread my legs and deal with the situation myself. But I refrain.

There are times for being a brat, and right now isn't it.

I swear, the seconds feel like hours as I wait.

Time drags on and on, and I start to think he's not going to come.

My desire begins to turn into panic.

I'd know if he left. Surely I'd have heard him?

But with the water pounding down around me, maybe I wouldn't.

I'm debating what to do next when a shadow falls over the doorway.

My breath catches in my throat a beat before he appears.

All the air leaves my lungs as he stands there as naked as the day he was born, his attention on me.

He's so fucking beautiful, I can barely stand it.

His shoulders are wide, his arms strong and lined with veins and corded muscles. His chest and abs are the things of fairy tales, the muscles so defined and the dips and valleys so delicious, just asking to be traced with my tongue.

I follow those V lines to his impressive dick. It jerks under my attention as if he knows I'm looking and that my mouth is watering for a taste.

I keep going, my eyes running over his thick thighs and all the way to his feet. Even they're sexy. How the fuck is that possible?

But nothing is better than when he speaks. His deep, raspy, commanding voice fills the room, and I melt.

"Good girl."

My breathing is erratic as he strides toward me. The second he's in touching distance, he reaches out and sinks his fingers into my hair, holding my head exactly where he wants me.

I gaze up at him, waiting for my next instruction despite knowing what's coming.

In my peripheral, I see him reach out and wrap his fist around his cock.

"You look so perfect on your knees for me, Trouble. Are you going to be a good girl and choke on my dick?"

I nod—or at least, as much as he allows me to.

A needy whimper spills from my lips as he traces them with the tip of his cock, coating me with precum.

"Lick," he commands the second he pulls back. "Taste me."

I groan as his taste hits my tongue.

His cocky smirk is all the encouragement I need as I open my mouth and attempt to lean forward.

"Greedy girl," he chuckles. "So desperate for my cock."

I am—there's no lie in his words. But mostly, I want to do to him what he did to me on the bed. I want to bring him to his goddamn knees. I want to rock his world so fucking hard he's unable to ever get me out of his head or from beneath his skin.

"That's it, baby," he praises after allowing me to wrap my lips around his crown. "Suck me off like a good little whore."

Dead. I am fucking dead.

72

———

KODIE

I'm not sure how it's possible, but Casey is even better than I remember.

Being with her, everything else falls away. The stress of the season, the pressure of being the best father I can be. Everything is just so much easier.

I knew I was lying to myself when I walked away and ripped both our hearts out.

But I'm done lying.

I'm done pretending.

I'm going to embrace the fear and see where it takes me.

She's fucking it for me.

I've fallen for her so fucking hard, I barely even know which way is up.

Fuck what everyone else thinks. No one else matters.

Just us.

Us and our family.

I think of Sutton lying in her hospital bed and a bolt of guilt shoots through me.

The second I approach the nightstand, I swipe my cell up and check for notifications.

There are none. I already knew there wouldn't be, but still.

Opening my messages, I tap a quick one to Mom before locating my sweats.

522

I forgo my boxers, knowing that Casey will get a kick out of it.

What is it they say? Gray sweats are the way to a woman's heart.

Okay, maybe *heart* is the wrong part of their anatomy.

My cell dings and I grab it from the bed, staring down at the exact reply I expected.

> Mom: Sutton is perfect. You don't need to worry. Enjoy your night.

> Kodie: Nice trick with the keycard.

> Mom: You're welcome. Just remember you have a game tomorrow. You need to get some sleep 😉

My loud groan fills the bedroom.

Please tell me that my mom didn't just winky face emoji me knowing she gave me a hotel keycard that would give me access to the woman I can't get out of my head.

"Fucking hell," I mutter, dragging my hand down my face.

"Is Sutton okay?" Casey asks as she steps out of the bathroom with a towel tucked under her arms.

"Yeah, she's fine."

"So what's the moaning about?"

Turning my cell around, I show her the message stream.

She snorts a laugh.

"I like your mom," Casey says, her cheeks a little pinker than they were a few seconds ago. "I'm not going to be able to look her in the eye in the morning, though."

"Just wait until your dad knows what we've been up to."

"Oh god," she groans. "Can you not?"

"Cas—"

"Kodie, I want this. I want you and everything that comes with you. You said earlier that you want everyone to know. But..."

A frown tugs at my brows as I wait for her to continue.

"I do want everyone to know. I want to be able to come to your games and have everyone know that you belong to me. I want to walk down the street holding your hand and do all the things normal couples do. I just...I'm not sure I'm ready for it yet."

My lips part to respond, but she beats me to it.

"We'll never be just a normal couple. Your life, your public image, and your reputation mean that we're going to have a lot of attention on us at the beginning, and I want us to be solid before we have to deal with that.

"We have Sutton to think of. We have your career. My father. We need to figure all of it out before the rest of the world gets an opinion."

All I can do as she blurts all of this out is smile. "Okay."

She stares at me as if I've just grown a second head. "Okay?"

"Yeah. Did you expect me to argue?"

"I...uh...I don't know."

"Casey," I say, dropping my cell to the bed and walking around until I'm standing in front of her.

Taking both of her hands in mine, I stare down into her eyes.

"I want this. I want you. And we'll go at whatever pace you're happy with. You want me to call up a few reporters I know and tip them off so I can stand out the front of this hotel and shout at the top of my voice that I've fallen for Casey Watson, then I'll do it. You want to keep me as your dirty little secret a while longer, then I'll happily do that, too."

She squeezes my hands, a small smile playing on her lips.

"Promise me something."

"Anything."

Her smile grows. "Never, ever do anything even close to the first one."

A laugh rumbles in my chest before it explodes.

Wrapping her up in my arms, I hold her tight and press my lips to the top of her head.

"I can't promise things like that," I tease, my smirk growing.

"Kodie," she warns.

"Casey," I counter, lifting her hand and kissing her knuckles. "When the time comes, I want everyone to know you're mine."

"How are you so perfect?"

A self-deprecating laugh falls from my lips.

"Baby, I'm so far from that it's not even funny."

She shakes her head. "Not to me."

My chest tightens as she gazes up at me. I'm not sure anyone has ever looked at me and seen me the way Casey does.

It's as exhilarating as it is unnerving.

"If we do this, you might learn a few things to prove otherwise."

"If we do this?" she asks, concern pulling at her features. "I thought—"

"We're doing this," I confirm. "I just want to warn you that you might find something you don't like."

"That's a risk I'm willing to take."

A knock sounds at the door as my head lowers to kiss her, halting my immediate plans.

"Dinner's here," she whispers.

If she weren't so hungry, I'd say fuck it and eat her again instead. But my girl needs sustenance if we're going to have anywhere near the kind of night I'm planning.

"Get comfortable, baby," I say before releasing her and stalking toward the door. "I've ordered you a feast."

I wasn't lying. Even for a hockey player, I'd ordered an obscene amount of food.

We gave it our best shot though before we both slumped back on the bed, full and content.

We didn't have sex again; instead, we shuffled under the sheets and kissed and cuddled like a couple of teenagers. Under the cover of darkness, locked away together, talked about what we wanted, where we wanted to take things, and how we wanted it to go.

It turns out, we didn't have any answers other than the fact we want to do it all together.

When we eventually drifted off to sleep in each other's arms, I slept better than I have in a long time.

I had my girl back, and everything was going to be okay.

Knowing she was mine, that we were going to walk out of that hotel room together, made everything so much more.

My eyes lift to the rearview mirror, and as if she knows I'm thinking about her, I find Casey staring right back at me.

The air crackles between us, and I forget that we're not alone as I reach down to tug at my pants.

Casey's cheeks flame before Sutton's soft voice fills the car, dragging me back to reality.

We're almost back, and I'm not sure how I feel about it.

What I really want to do is drive home, taking everyone in the car with me. But I know I can't; Mom might be fully aware of what is happening between us, but that doesn't mean I can bring her into our lives, our family, without discussing it with both her and Sutton first.

A pained sigh passes my lips, earning a glance from Mom.

"Everything is going to work out. Have faith," she says quietly.

I don't respond. I can't. Instead, I grip the wheel harder and try not to think about what's about to happen.

Unfortunately, before long, Casey's apartment building comes into view and I'm pulling into one of the free spots in the parking lot.

The whole way home, her soft voice has filled the air along with happy giggles from Sutton.

Watching them laugh together in the rearview mirror had me fighting to suck in the air I needed.

It was too much but not enough, all at the same time.

"Can't Casey come home with us?" Sutton asks as I kill the engine. Disappointment is evident in her voice. I feel it all the way to my soul.

"Sorry, sweetie. I should be at work right now." Seeing her panic, Casey reaches over and squeezes Sutton's hand. "Making sure you're okay was more important than anything else. Make sure your daddy spoils you rotten today, okay?"

A smile spreads across Sutton's face. "I will," she promises before shooting a look in my direction. "He's going to win tonight, too," she states confidently. "And," she adds, looking pointedly at me, "he won't spend any time in the box. Will you, Daddy?"

"I'll try my best," I promise as I turn around to look at them.

Casey's eyes find mine, and my breath catches.

She doesn't want to go, either.

Fucking hell.

"I'll walk you in." The words are forced, and I hate them. But as much as I might want to take Casey home with us and play house, it's not that simple. As she said last night, we've got a whole lot of stuff to work through first.

"It's okay, I can—"

"I'm walking you in," I state, leaving no room for argument, before pushing my door open and climbing out.

By the time I get to her, she's already waiting beside the car.

Her hair is unstyled, and she doesn't have any makeup on—not that she needs it. But what really makes my heart race is that she's standing there wearing my shirt from yesterday. While Mom might have packed me a bag with spare clothes, Casey only had the clothes on her back, which is why she stole my shirt when we got dressed this morning.

Waking up with her naked body tucked against mine was the thing dreams are made of.

I could have stayed there all day with her. But reality was calling—or more so Mom, so that Sutton could talk to me.

In a few months' time when the season is over, we'll have the chance to laze around in bed all day. But for now, we've got to keep moving.

With her bag in one hand, I snatch her fingers up with my other and walk her toward the entrance.

She watches as I tap in the code for her building before pulling the door open and tugging her inside, aware that the tinted glass will give us some privacy.

"Thank you," I say, cupping her cheeks in both of my hands.

"You have nothing to thank me for."

I shake my head. "You're wrong. I have everything to thank you for."

She sighs, a smile playing on her lips.

"Sutton loves you."

"She's a great kid."

"Yeah. I lucked out."

"Nothing lucky about it. You're an incredible dad."

I wiggle my brows, happy to take the compliment. "Oh yeah? What else am I good at?"

She laughs, and the sound lights me up inside.

"You're coming to my game, right?" I've already asked her, but I need to hear it again.

"Yes, Kodie. I'm coming to your game," she confirms.

"And you're wearing my jersey?"

Her smile spreads wider, crinkling the corners of her eyes. "Yes."

"And I can come here after and celebrate?"

She tilts her head to one side teasingly. "If you win."

My breath catches.

"And if we lose?"

She shrugs one shoulder and taps my chest. "Then it's just you and your right hand, big guy."

"Hell fucking no," I say, dropping my hands to her hips, pushing her up against the wall, and kissing her in a way that will ensure she spends the rest of the day praying that we win so I can finish what I started.

When I finally leave the lobby of her building, I'm sporting a very inappropriate tent in my sweats, and my smile refuses to falter.

I haven't felt this good in a long time.

I just pray it continues, and I don't fuck it up again.

73

CASEY

They win.

No. They don't just win. They fucking dominate.

They're two goals up before the end of the first period, and I'm pretty sure a couple members of the other team spend more time in the box than they do on the ice.

As the game goes on, the hits get more and more brutal. So do the injuries.

Our guys took it like the champs they are. Only Linc ended up being coaxed into a fight. Not surprising, really. It isn't a Vipers game if Linc doesn't punch at least one person.

The whole time, Sutton stands beside me, shouting and screaming, cheering her dad and his team on as if the day before hadn't happened.

Kodie was reluctant to let her come, preferring she stay at home in the quiet, resting. But she wasn't having any of it, and in the end, he had to concede. Despite the brutality of the match, I'm glad he let her. It's safe to say that the arena is her happy place. I'm pretty sure the smile on her face hasn't slipped since the moment she walked toward me, as if us sitting together now is just how it's going to be.

I can't lie. The thought of spending the rest of the season celebrating wins and commiserating losses with this little pocket rocket makes it even more exciting.

It's late by the time the game ends, and despite Sutton's argument, Kathleen stands her ground and takes her home. Sutton wants to see her dad. I get it. Hell, I remember it well. But she should have been in bed long ago.

"Wait," Sutton cries when they're a few steps away from where Parker and I are still watching as the guys lap up the attention.

Her little feet pound down the row before she crashes into me and throws her arms around my waist.

"Night night, Coach C," she says.

Reaching out, I smooth my hand over soft hair.

"Night night, number fifty-five."

She beams up at me as warmth fills my chest.

"See you at practice," she cries after she releases me and rushes back to her gran. Kathleen gives me a little wave, a soft smile playing on her lips.

"Well, would you look at that," Parker muses from my side.

"What?"

"You're stealing all the Rivers' hearts." I can't help but laugh. "Come on, I want a drink with my bestie before she leaves me for a man."

"I'd never leave you for just any man," I tease.

She shakes her head. "No, a hockey god," she muses.

"Still think you're jealous," I tease. "You could have one of your own if you wanted, you know."

"Not interested."

"Monroe could be fun. He's got the same amount of energy as a Labrador puppy."

"Ew, no, thank you. If I'm hooking up with anyone, they at least have to have enough experience to get me off twice at a minimum before they blow."

"What's to say he can't have lexperience *and* energy?"

"Is he even old enough to graduate from college?" she deadpans.

"Just about." Monroe has the pretty boy next door look, but he is older—and who knows, maybe more experienced—than he looks.

"Yeah, thanks but no thanks."

"Handsy, then? Killer? Oh, you could be a bad, bad girl and take advantage of your brother's best friend."

"No, no, and hell no," she practically shrieks. "Just because you're happy bouncing on Rivers' hockey stick, doesn't mean that I have to follow suit. I'm more than happy with my current situation."

"First, keep your voice down," I hiss. We're surrounded by people who could either tell Dad or, worse, the media. "Secondly, I call bullshit that you're happy with your current situation with your vibrating boyfriend."

Parker glares at me. "The fuck did you just say about keeping your voice down?"

I bark out a laugh as we get closer to the family suite.

"Does he offer to clean you up after and wash your hair in the shower?"

"You're not funny," she sulks before throwing the door open and marching toward the bar.

We chat and laugh with everyone while waiting for the players to finish. The team might call themselves a family, but that can also be said for the people up here waiting for them. I love being surrounded by my Vipers family. I always have. Despite it just being me and Dad after Mom passed, I was never lonely. Especially when I was here. The WAGs of Dad's teammates always ensured that both of us were properly taken care of. They'd deliver food on almost a daily basis, and whenever Dad was travelling, there was always someone I could turn to if I needed something.

They all rallied together, just like I've seen them do numerous times since, and ensured that our family is well looked after. It's really quite something.

I guess it's only right that a member of our hockey family has stolen my heart.

As the minutes tick by, my nerves begin to increase.

He's going to message me when he's done, and I'm going to slip away, hopefully unnoticed, to the parking garage where I can hop into his car and get our celebration started.

It's risky, but he was adamant that he wasn't leaving the arena without me. And who was I to argue?

Pulling my cell from my purse, I check it again.

"He's not going to forget," Parker teases.

"I know, I just…" I let out a sigh.

"I love this look on you."

"What look?"

"The happy, sappy, in-love look. It suits you."

My first instinct is to argue. But I quickly discover that I can't force the words past my lips.

She's right.

I am hopelessly and shamelessly in love with Kodie Rivers.

My cell finally buzzes, and I practically fall off my stool.

"Go, just go," Parker encourages as I attempt to right myself.

"Oh, I am. Don't worry."

"Remember you have work tomorrow. Your legs need to work."

I roll my eyes. "I'd say the same to you, but we both know your boyfriend will need recharging before that happens."

"Harsh. I'll have you know, he has a very good recovery time."

I'm still chuckling as I walk out of the room and head in the direction of the parking garage.

I pass a couple of third and fourth line players. All of them say hello, but thankfully, no one stops me to talk. Well, not until Linc and Fletch waltz around the corner. Their deep laughter bounces off the green and white walls on either side of us, but it falters the second their eyes land on me.

"Lost, Watson?" Linc asks with a smirk.

"Nope. You seem to be, though. The bunnies are that way," I say, pointing in the general direction of the arena exit where I've no doubt they'll be lingering in the hope of snagging a player.

"Nah, it's too soon. The rookies can have first pick. All the best ones are willing to wait until the real men appear."

Fletch shakes his head, muttering, "I can't believe I used to be like you."

"Admit it—you miss it."

"I fucking well don't. Reese is the only girl I need. Speaking of, I'm going to find her."

"Good game tonight," I say as he continues forward.

"Thanks, Casey," he shoots back before disappearing down the hallway.

"So..." Linc starts with a knowing glint in his eye. "You're sneaking around the arena minutes after a certain player has just walked out of the locker room. A certain player who's suddenly stopped being a grumpy motherfucker..."

The strength it takes to keep the smile off my face as I stare deadpan into his eyes deserves a fucking medal.

"I don't know what you're talking about. Excuse me."

I attempt to slip past him as if he isn't a massive defenseman whose shoulders almost take up the entire hallway.

He chuckles before his fingers wrap around my upper arm, halting my escape.

"Linc," I complain, attempting and failing to escape his grip.

"I'm so fucking glad you both sorted your shit out. Now, please, from one hockey addict to another, do not break his heart again. The team can't take it."

"Linc," I repeat.

"I fucking mean it, Casey. I've never seen him happier than when he was with you, and I've never seen him more miserable when he was without you. We stand a real chance this season, but we need him fully focused and determined. That means you need to be in the stands as often as possible. He plays even better when he knows you're watching."

My cheeks heat as I wonder if it's the promise of what comes after his win that really spurs him on.

"Be good to him, Casey. He's a great guy who deserves all the love in the world."

As I stare at Linc, a guy I've known almost all my life, I realize that I don't really know him at all.

Is he...is he jealous?

Not because he wanted me, but of us. Of what we've found together.

I shake the thought away before it really lands, because it's ridiculous. Linc is and always has been a player. He loves it and the attention that comes with it.

"I couldn't agree more. Now, do you mind moving so I can get to him?"

"Fucking knew it," he laughs, finally shifting.

"Have a good night," I call.

"I'm sure it won't be as enjoyable as yours."

Spinning around, I smirk at him. "What? Haven't you heard? You're Lincoln Storm, a defenseman who loves nothing more than breaking hearts in every state. I'm sure you won't have any issues securing a wild night."

His face lights up at my words, but there's still something I'm not used to lingering in his eyes.

But as I round the corner, I spot the elevator that'll lead me to the garage, and I forget about anything but the man waiting for me.

The second the doors open at garage level, I'm slipping between them. My sneakers squeak on the concrete floor as my eyes scan the cars for his.

The rumble of an engine hits my ears, and the moment I spin around, I see him sitting behind the wheel of his car, moving toward me.

With my heart in my throat, I run toward him. No sooner has my ass hit the seat do I lean over the console, wrap my hand around the back of his neck, and slam my lips to his.

I kiss him right there and then in the middle of the arena parking garage where anyone could see us. And for the first time, I really don't give a shit.

Screw the consequences. This right here is more important than anything else in the world right now.

He groans into my mouth, and it sends a fire racing toward my core.

"Need you," he breathes.

"Then you'd better drive fast," I say, forcing myself to sit back in my seat.

I look at him with my heart racing and my temperature soaring.

He's fresh from the shower, his hair still damp, and he smells like sin.

"Kodie," I whimper when all he does is stare back as if I'm not really sitting here.

"I'm sorry. I just...this is everything. I know it's selfish, but I want you waiting for me after every home game. Maybe even a few on the road."

"I'm there," I agree.

"And no other name or number is ever going to be on your jersey again."

"Well...we'll have to see about that," I tease.

"Casey," he warns, his voice so deep its vibrations hit me straight between the legs.

"What? You love it when I'm a bad girl."

"I love it more when I know you're mine."

My smile spreads so wide, it hurts my cheeks.

"Great game tonight, Rivers," I praise as he finally hits the gas.

"I was playing for my girls."

74

KODIE

"**K**odie," Casey cries as I slam her against her closed front door, my lips finding hers and cutting off any other words she might want to say.

My hands grip her ass, and I lift her from her feet.

Instantly, her legs wrap around my waist, and I grind my aching dick against her.

Her entire body trembles. Needy and desperate. Just the way I like her.

Fire burns through my veins as my adrenaline from our epic win tonight continues to rage.

I need her. I need to be inside her as much as I need my next breath.

"Can't wait," I mutter as I kiss across her jaw, one of my hands slipping inside her jersey to find her tits.

"Please," she whimpers as I palm her, loving the feel of her nipple hardening at my touch.

"Why the fuck are you wearing jeans?" I complain as I pointlessly tug at her waistband.

"I...I didn't think—"

"I'm banning them from games," I say as I drag her from the door and move toward the couch with her in my arms. "Skirts or nothing."

"What if I want to make you work for it?" she taunts as I

lower her to her feet, my fingers immediately finding the button of the offending article.

My eyes shoot up and narrow in warning.

She smirks as her eyes glitter with mischief.

"Any other night, fine. Game night? Not a fucking chance."

Ripping her skinny jeans down her legs, I drop to my knees to pull off her sneakers and then free the fabric from her ankles.

"You want me to dress like a puck bunny?"

I freeze at her words.

"No," I bark. "And I never want to hear you ever refer to yourself as one. You're not—"

"I know, Kodie," she says, reaching out and combing her fingers through my curls. Her touch soothes me, but it does nothing to dampen the roaring fire within me. "Sometimes, though, I want you to fuck me like one."

My teeth clench, but this time there is no anger.

Only desire.

"Challenge accepted."

I tear at her panties, freeing them from her body and throwing them to the floor before my hands wrap around her hips, twisting her around. The second she's in position, I press my palm against her back, giving her little choice but to bend over the back of the couch.

My hands slide to her ass, and I squeeze, my fingers pressing into her skin.

"Please," she whimpers, wiggling her hips as if she'll find some friction.

"Spread your legs," I demand, my eyes locked on her pussy.

I haven't touched her and yet she's swollen and glistening, as desperate for me as I am for her.

I only took her this morning before we left the hotel room, but it feels like a month ago now.

My cock aches, precum soaking my boxers.

Fuck. I hope this need for her never ends.

It's still possible to feel like this about your girl when you're old and gray, right?

"So fucking perfect," I muse before spreading her with two fingers and licking her from clit to ass.

I circle her puckered hole with the tip of my tongue, loving the way she shudders.

"Oh god."

"Nah, baby. Number Fifty-Five."

"Cocky fu—shit," she gasps as I push just slightly inside her.

"This is mine, Casey," I say, replacing my tongue with my thumb, continuing to tease her. "I'm going to take you here. Not tonight. But one day soon, I'm going to watch my dick stretching your ass open. I'm going to feel you come harder than you ever have in your life all over it." She shudders, whimpering nonsense. "Is that okay?"

"Y-yes."

"Yes, what?"

"Yes...Sir." Pulling my hand back, I reward her with a slap to her ass.

She screams as my handprint blooms on her skin. Her ass is perfect, pale skin with just a few dimples here and there. I'm fucking obsessed with it.

I'm fucking obsessed with all of her, let's be honest.

"Perfect," I muse before diving back in, eating her like I'm starving.

I am. Fucking starving for my girl.

Despite her being ready to come about thirty seconds after I started sucking on her swollen clit, I don't let her fall. Instead, I bring her to the edge over and over until she's almost sobbing for relief.

Her legs tremble, and her juices drip from my chin.

It's fucking everything.

"Please, Kodie. Please."

I pull back, eliciting a loud moan of disapproval before stating, "You're not coming on my mouth tonight. You're not coming until I'm balls deep inside you."

"Then hurry the fuck up and get in my pussy."

I chuckle as I wipe my mouth with the back of my hand and climb to my feet.

My dick physically hurts confined behind the zipper of my suit pants.

Usually, I don't mind having to wear suits to and from games, but right now, I could really do with being in a pair of sweats.

Ripping my fly open with one hand, I slide the other up Casey's spine, over each ridge until I can sink my fingers into her silky blonde hair.

"Kodie, please."

"Fucking love it when you beg," I praise. "You're such good fucking girl."

She whimpers as I pull my dick out. I squeeze, giving it a few strokes, rubbing the precum into the head, but it does little to quell the ache.

"Yes," she hisses when I step closer and drag my dick through her folds, letting her wetness coat me.

The second I press against her entrance, her muscles ripple, trying to drag me deeper.

"Greedy girl. Tell me what you want."

"Your dick, Kodie. Please."

I shake my head. How the hell I managed to stay away from her and lie to myself for as long as I did, I don't know.

Will a relationship between us be easy? Hell no. But I already know it'll be worth it.

Being able to come home from games to this woman, whether at home or on the road, is going to be the best part of my job. And knowing that my daughter loves her too? Fuck. It's too much.

Thrusting my hips forward, I fill her in one swift move as my fingers tighten in her hair. Pulling her head back, I force her to arch her back, allowing me to take her as deep as physically possible.

"So full," she cries. "Kodie, yes. So deep."

I didn't know it was possible, but I swear I get harder, hearing her words.

"So fucking deep," I grunt as I pull out and push back in slowly, allowing her a few moments to adjust before I give her what we both really need.

"Yes," she cries, shifting her hips as if it'll pull me even deeper. "Fuck me, Kodie. Please, fuck me."

I don't need to be told twice. The next time I pull out, I wait a beat before I surge back in so hard and fast that her feet leave the floor.

Something settles inside me as the beast that was taking over subsides slightly.

"Fuck, Casey. Your pussy is fucking heaven."

I keep up my punishing pace, my grip on her hair getting tighter and tighter as her muscles contract around me.

"Come for me, Casey. Let me feel how addicted you are to my dick."

She cries out an unintelligible response as her release hits her.

Her pussy clamps down on me so hard, her muscles rippling in the most delicious way, that it takes every ounce of my restraint not to fall with her.

I need to feel this over and over before I finally give in. I want to prove to her that she made the right decision, forgiving me. That she's making the right choice by making me a part of her life, by making me hers, and allowing me to make her mine in return.

I fuck her slower through her release, allowing her to fall forward as she gasps for air and her body comes back to her. But the second she's done, my tempo increases again.

"Oh god," she whimpers.

I chuckle. "Have you forgotten already? Fifty-Five, remember?"

"So fucking cocky."

"Would you expect anything else? I'm a hockey player, remember."

She laughs, and it makes her muscles tighten again.

"Fuck, baby. Keep that up and I'm not going to deliver on my promise," I warn.

"Your promise?"

I smirk because I never actually told her.

"I scored three tonight, Trouble."

"Riiight," she muses, predicting where this is going.

"I score three, you get three orgasms before I get off," I explain.

"What about if you score six?"

"Then you get six."

"You're meant to be celebrating, not torturing yourself."

"Fucking you is far from torture, baby. Watching you come is one of my favorite things to do. I'd watch it all night if I could."

"I think you might kill me," she teases.

"You can take it. I'm not losing you again."

"Thank fuck for that. I didn't cope very well without you."

"Me either, baby. But tonight, we're celebrating, not looking back."

"CASEY," I roar as my release rips through me a while later.

After I confessed my plan, I'm pretty sure Casey did everything in her power to hold her next two releases as long as possible.

In reality, not much time has passed, but my balls are convinced it's been at least three hours.

I fall forward, squashing her exhausted, tiny body on the couch. I try to keep most of my weight off her, but it's easier said than done.

"I hope you win every game," Casey giggles, still on a high from her multiple releases.

"You and me both, baby."

Forcing myself off her, I reluctantly slip from her body and spin her around to face me.

Her face looks tiny as I cup her cheeks with my giant hands. Leaning forward, I press my lips to her in a sweet kiss.

"I'll never fuck you like a bunny, Casey. You mean too much to me."

A contented, happy sigh passes her lips, her warm, beer-scented breath rushing over my face.

"I promise to always fuck you in whatever way you need, though."

Tears fill her eyes, and I panic. I fucking hate seeing her cry.

"I used to imagine that you were the most incredible man. How is it possible that you're even better?"

A smirk kicks up one side of my mouth while one of my shoulder's pops.

"It really is a skill."

"And so modest, too."

Her eyes drop from mine, and they widen as if she's only just noticing that she's completely naked, and other than my dick, I'm still fully dressed.

"Get naked, Fifty-Five, I'm not done with you yet."

Releasing her, I hold my arms out from my sides and take a step back.

"I'm all yours. Do your worst."

Her teeth sink into her bottom lip, her cheeks brightening.

"I spent a lot of years fantasizing about you," she confesses.

"Oh yeah?"

Despite coming harder than I ever have in my life, my dick jerks back to life.

"Yeah. I don't think there's any situation I haven't thought about...gotten myself off to."

"Tell me more."

She moves closer, her delicate fingers reaching for the first closed button on my shirt.

"There is only one man I've thought of when I've gotten myself off since I was about fifteen."

"Considering our age gap, that's a little unnerving."

She shrugs, uncaring. "I knew what I wanted from the very first time I saw you play. I was addicted. It sounds crazy. No one has ever understood it. But I felt different watching you. I couldn't get enough. Every single thing you've done, every move you've made, I've read it all."

"Creepy little stalker, aren't you?"

"Guilty. You should probably run now while you have the

chance. For all you know, I have plans to lock you up in the basement and make you my sex slave for life."

Lifting my arms, I press my wrists together as if she's about to cuff me. "Lead the way. I'm yours now, however you want me."

Her fingers curl around my waistband and my entire body flinches as her knuckles graze my skin, my cock hardening.

But she doesn't do anything else. Instead, she just stares up at me, her eyes full of awe and disbelief.

"I want you exactly as you are, Kodie Rivers. You're perfect to me. You always have been."

75

CASEY

Despite falling asleep in the safety of Kodie's arms, I already knew I wouldn't wake in them.

As much as he wanted to stay, he had to be home for Sutton.

I don't know what time he slipped out. All I know is that when my alarm goes off the next morning and I reach for him, the other side of the bed is cold.

I more than understand his reason for leaving. Hell, I encouraged him to. But it still stings, waking up alone after everything we've done and promised each other.

I want him. I want a life with him and Sutton. There is not a single ounce of doubt in my mind.

At Wednesday's practice, despite advice that she should continue resting, Sutton was at the rink and ready to go.

I want to say I was surprised by her presence and a very exasperated Kathleen, but I wasn't.

Thankfully, though, Sutton was happy not to train; she just wanted to be with her team, even if she couldn't join them.

I already knew Sutton was going to make a fantastic professional player one day, but that just solidified it.

She spent the session doing light duties and helping me and Megan. She loved it. Of course she was frustrated not being on the ice, but she didn't let it hold her back or stop her from getting involved.

The way her little face dropped when our time was up and she had to leave...it melted my heart. It didn't help that Kodie was away on back-to-back road games. I was feeling his absence just as much as she was. I entirely understood her lack of desire to go back to a home where he wouldn't be. I missed his presence every time I walked into my apartment and he wasn't there.

He's only been a handful of times, but that doesn't mean his absence isn't palpable.

They lost their first road game before managing to pull off a tight-fought win last night.

Afterwards, I received a beautiful photo of him standing in front of a full-length mirror in only a very tight pair of boxers. And in return, I sent him a sexy shot of my ass bent over in my usual pair of lucky green panties. The phone sex that followed was almost as good as having him here in person. And now that Linc knows, there was no rush to end the call and we ended up chatting for hours afterward.

Unable to stop myself, I glance at the clock in the corner of my monitor for the millionth time today.

Kodie and the team boarded a flight from New York this morning. He's due back just before school pick-up and hoping to get there in time to make Sutton's day.

Butterflies flutter in my stomach as I think about how excited she'll be to see him standing there, waiting for her. I don't want to consider the fact he won't make it in time.

The minutes drag on slower than I've ever known.

I might not be seeing him until after he's put Sutton to bed tonight, but that doesn't stop me from wishing the day would whizz by.

There was a time when work would keep me distracted for hours, but it seems those days are long gone, because I find my attention drifting every few minutes, my mind full of memories of Kodie and hopes for the future.

We've got a few hurdles in our way until we might be able to embark on the kind of life I crave with him, but I know it's within reach. My heart flutters. I'm not the only one who wants it either. By some fucking miracle, Kodie seems just as obsessed with me as I am with him. I don't know how, or what I did to deserve it, but I'll take it.

I'm gazing at the wispy white clouds that dance across the bright blue sky on the other side of the window when my cell buzzes on my desk.

Absently, I reach for it, not expecting anything exciting.

> 55: Make an excuse and meet me in the dressing room.

> 55: Right.

> 55: Fucking.

> 55: Now.

"Oh my god," I whimper, my hand trembling as I hold my phone.

I look around my office, but despite the explosion of excitement inside me, no one even looks my way.

It's like they don't know the world just shifted from beneath my swivel chair.

I shouldn't go. I have a job to do, and I'm almost at the end of a series of designs that need to be complete and with Bianca by the end of the day.

But...Kodie...

"Fuck it," I mutter to myself before tucking my cell into my jacket pocket and rushing from the office.

If anyone asks, I had some dodgy fish tacos for lunch. I ate alone in a little place down the street, so no one will know.

I don't think anyone so much as glances up as I flee the room as if the hounds of hell are snapping at my ankles.

My heart thunders at a million beats per second as I slip into the elevator and jab my finger against the button that will allow me to descend to where Kodie is waiting for me.

My legs tremble as I move down the hallway to the dressing room. Thankfully, after disappearing inside the elevator car, I haven't seen a single person. I guess that's what happens when the entire team and every member of staff they need have just traveled back from two road games. They've all gone home to their homes and families.

But Kodie came for you...

Despite being in this building every day, it's been years since I've been this close to the players. When I was a kid, I'd often walk into the dressing room with Dad. Hell, I remember celebrating a couple of wins with the team when my sitter had to leave. I also remember Dad ripping them all a new one about their behavior while I was in the room. Not that they needed reminding; they were a great group of guys, many of whom were fathers themselves, and they were always respectful to me. Just like I know our team would be now if Sutton were there.

But this time, when I press my palms against the door to slip inside, there is no noise, no boisterous players, no loud music. It's silent. It still smells like sweaty boys, but after a lifetime of being surrounded by that scent, it doesn't really bother me. I step inside, my eyes scanning the stalls for my man.

My breath catches when I find him sitting in his stall, resting forward with his elbows on his knees and his dark eyes locked on me.

"Y-you're early," I stutter, my voice barely audible as my temperature rises.

Fuck, I missed him. It might have only been a few days, but it's been like losing a limb. There's a part of me that hopes it'll get easier, but at the same time, there's another part that wishes it won't. I always want to feel this incredible high when he returns. It's addictive, just like the man before me.

"Surprise," he rasps, a smile pulling at the corners of his lips.

"But..." I blink, watching as he stands to his full height and begins stalking closer.

"I can go, if you want," he offers, his eyes darting toward the door for the briefest moment.

"Hell no," I state. The second he's in touching distance, I reach out, twist my fingers in his shirt, and drag him closer. Or at least, I try. I don't stand a chance at moving his giant frame.

Thankfully, he takes pity on me and takes the final step,

closing the space between us. His hand wraps around the back of my neck and he tugs. I stumble forward until I'm pressed up against the hard length of his body.

"Missed you so fucking much, Trouble."

And then his mouth is on mine, our hands are everywhere, and getting closer to him is the only thing I can think about.

He lifts me off my feet, carrying me somewhere. I'm too focused on getting more to care about where we're going. To care about anything.

My back presses against a wall, and the next thing I know, my panties are being dragged to the side and his fingers are pushing inside me.

"Fuck," he groans, finding me wet and ready. "Thank fuck you didn't wear pants today."

"Please," I whimper, my head falling back against the wall as I stare at him with hooded eyes.

"Fuck," he repeats as he holds me up with one hand while tearing at his pants with the other.

He hasn't even gotten changed; he came straight here from the airplane.

He needed me that badly.

"Oh god, yes," I gasp as he drags his cock across my pussy, notching at my entrance.

"This is going to be fast. Later, I'll take my time and do it properly."

And with that, he thrusts forward, simultaneously dropping me so he fills me to the max, hitting me so deep it makes my eyes cross.

"Yesss," I hiss as he sets a punishing pace.

His lips meet mine, our kiss wild and frantic as we take what we need from each other.

In only seconds, the first tingles of my release awaken.

His grip on my ass tightens until I have no doubt I'll have his fingertips bruised onto my skin tomorrow. Bring it on. I'll happily walk around every day for the rest of my life with a Kodie brand on my skin.

I whimper as he squeezes my breast through my blouse before his hand slips upward until he's collaring my throat.

Heat races to my pussy at his possessive touch, and it only gets worse when his grip tightens a little.

"Give it to me, Casey. Come all over my dick. Show me how much you missed me."

One more roll of his hips and I'm done for.

My release slams into me. My lips part and a scream rips up my throat, but a beat before it passes my lips, Kodie slaps his hand over my mouth, smothering the noise.

As I clamp down on his dick, riding out my release, he stills before a guttural groan rumbles deep in his throat and he spills inside me.

Letting his hand slip away, he leans forward, tucking his face into the crook of my neck as we both fight to catch our breath.

"Needed that," he pants. "Needed you."

"Same," I confess.

For a few seconds, I remain there suspended between the wall and Kodie, blissfully unaware of my surroundings and where I am. But as my eyes flutter open, reality slams back into me.

"Uh...we just fucked in your dressing room."

When he pulls back, he's got the cockiest smirk I think I've ever seen.

"Kodie," I chastise with a light slap to his shoulder.

"I've been thinking about doing that for weeks."

My cheeks burn, but I can't deny that his words don't light me up inside.

"Anyone could walk in," I point out.

He shakes his head. "They've all gone home. We're safe."

"You don't know that for sure," I say, wiggling against him until he doesn't have a choice but to slip free from my body and lower me to the floor.

"Maybe not. But no one did, did they? And fuck, that was hot."

I tug my damp panties back into place as his cum slips from my body.

Staring up at him, I get lost in his excited eyes.

"Yeah," I muse. "It was hot." And I've no doubt a fantasy I'll revisit time and time again over the years.

Lifting his arm, he checks his stupidly expensive watch.

"Shit. I need to go," he says before tucking himself away and zipping up. "I want to surprise Sutton, too."

Grabbing my cell, I check the time.

"Fuck. How long have I been down here?" I balk. That was nowhere near as fast as I thought. "I need to go."

I spin around and take a step toward the door, but that's as far as I get, because his hot hand wraps around my wrist, halting my escape.

He turns me back around and steps up, cupping my cheeks.

"Don't eat. I'll bring dinner with me later."

"Okay," I breathe. "I'll be waiting."

His eyes flash with desire.

With one final kiss and a swat to my ass, he sends me on my way.

I swear, I don't suck in a real breath until I'm in the hallway and rushing toward the elevator.

But everything comes crashing down around me when a door opens up ahead and none other than my father steps out. He looks in the opposite direction first, but I don't have time to react — not that there's anywhere to hide even if I did. Inevitably, he turns my way.

His eyes widen the second he sees me, and I cringe, wondering what the hell I look like.

Probably similar to if I'd just been ravaged by a wild animal.

You were.

"Casey?"

Despite knowing he's there, the sound of his voice filling the hallway makes my heart sink into my shoes.

"What are you doing down here?"

His eyes bounce between mine before he gazes over my shoulder.

Please, please don't choose this moment to walk out of the dressing room. Please.

I need to tell Dad, and I will. Soon.

What I really don't need is for him to find out like this.

"I…uh…I came down to get a couple of photos for something I'm working on," I lie, hating myself for doing so. That isn't how Dad and I work. We're honest with each other. Always.

Or at least, we were until recently. My lies are stacking up faster than I can control.

His gaze drops lower, his brows pinching. "You don't have a camera," he points out.

"Oh. No. I…did it on my phone."

"Right, okay. Well, I'm not staying. I just wanted to grab something from my office before heading home. Breakfast in the morning?"

I nod. "Yes. Yep. Can't wait." That isn't a lie. But as the words continue to tumble suspiciously from my lips, I start to wonder if it's a good idea. If he suspects something, he won't shy away from asking. That isn't who my father is.

The thought of disappointing him, of going against everything he's ever told me, cuts deep. But I can't stop.

Kodie…he's…he's a part of me, and there is nothing I can do to stop that. He's in too deep.

"Great. I'll pick you up at ten?"

"Sounds great. Enjoy your night," I say before quickly darting around him toward the elevator that will take me to safety.

"Casey?" he says, forcing me to stop.

"Come here. I've missed you."

He pulls me in for a hug, and I squeeze my eyes closed, praying he can't smell sex and Kodie on me.

Something tells me that might be wishful thinking.

76

KODIE

"**F**ucking hell," I groan the second Casey opens her front door.

I had a feeling she'd do something to knock me on my ass when I got here, and I thought I was prepared. But apparently, nothing could have prepared me for the sight that greets me.

And being the little minx that she is, she gives me a little spin, aware that I can't reach out and drag her to me because my arms are full of bags.

"Approve, huh?" she asks as if it's not obvious from my expression.

"How could I not? You're wearing my fucking number."

I should have predicted it, because I know just how much this woman loves to torture me.

Kicking the door closed behind me, I follow her toward the kitchen like an excited puppy. There's a chance I have my tongue hanging out the side of my mouth and everything. I know for a fact I'm fucking panting.

Get a grip, Kodie.

It's just Casey.

It isn't just Casey, though, is it? It'll never be *Just Casey*. She's so much more than that. She's everything. And right now, she looks like a walking wet dream.

She's wearing my jersey with the side twisted up into a knot so it stops at the slimmest part of her waist. She's got on those green fucking panties that drive me wild, and she's wearing green and white athletic socks that are pulled up to her knees. Her hair is twisted up somehow on the top of her head with a few tendrils hanging around her face, and she isn't wearing a stitch of makeup. I fucking love that she doesn't feel the need to doll herself up for me.

It pissed me the fuck off when she compared herself to a bunny the other night.

She's not a fucking bunny. Not even close. And the fact she's not plastered in makeup right now is just more confirmation of that fact.

"What have we got there?" she asks, spinning around, her eyes locked on the bags in my hand. "I'm starving."

I know I've made her wait, but as desperate as I was to see her, I needed to spend the night with my girl first.

This afternoon was fucking epic. Not only did I get to surprise Casey with a little visit, but the look on Sutton's face when she came out of school and saw me standing there waiting instead of Mom? Fuck. It gets me every fucking time.

Okay, so Coach's surprise appearance at the arena wasn't a part of my master plan, but he hasn't turned up to kick my ass yet, so I'm assuming we got away with it.

Ice ran through my veins as I pulled the dressing room door open and heard his voice. I didn't so much as poke my head out to confirm that he was talking to Casey. I immediately closed it as silently as I possibly could and slipped out of the emergency exit unnoticed.

As fun as it might be, sneaking around like naughty school kids, we need a plan. A way to break our relationship to him that won't lead to me being in the hospital or run out of town.

"Chinese. I didn't know what dishes you like, so I got a bit of everything."

Casey laughs as I place the huge bags on the counter.

"We've been messaging all evening. You could have asked."

I shrug one shoulder as I begin pulling the containers out. "Didn't want to."

"Well, lucky for you, I love all Chinese."

After grabbing two bottles of water from her fridge, she hops up on the stool beside me as I pull the lids off and instantly dives for a spring roll.

"Ohmygodsogood," she mumbles.

I let my eyes trail over her. "I was thinking the same."

Reaching out, I fist her jersey and drag her closer so I can kiss her.

It might have only been a few hours, but I need my Casey fix.

"Can't wait to win tomorrow and claim my prize in person," I say, releasing her.

"And I can't wait for you to lose so I can claim mine."

I gasp in horror. "You don't mean that."

"Don't I?" she teases. "It's your first game this season against your old team. You beat them last time you played. They'll be coming with a point to prove. It's gonna be a tough game. Have you seen how well they're doing this season?"

"Of course. Should I be concerned that you have?"

She smirks. "You're cute."

"I am not cute."

"You kinda are."

I huff a laugh before stabbing a piece of shredded beef and pushing it past my lips.

"Have you heard anything from your dad?"

"Nope. He wouldn't message it anyway. He'll wait until the morning and do it face to face."

"What are your plans for Thanksgiving?" I ask, changing the subject, although the second shadows pass through her eyes, I kick myself for doing it. I already know she's dreading the next few weeks.

"We'll just be home. I'll cook," she says sadly. "It's not the same without Mom," she confesses.

"How old were you when you lost her?" I ask.

As we eat, Casey tells me all about her mom. She doesn't just tell me about the illness that stole her too soon, but she tells me what an incredible person and parent she was with a smile on her face and tears glistening in her eyes.

"Dad has never gotten over it. I wish he could move on. Find someone to share his life with."

"He will when the time is right and his person comes along," I say. I may not have lost Sutton's mom in the way Coach did Casey's mom, but letting someone else in was never a part of my plan. But then there was Casey. I hope Coach gets to experience the same thing at some point.

"What if Mom was it for him?"

"I love the idea that there is only one person out there for us, but then people like your dad and my mom wouldn't have another chance. They deserve that."

"They really do."

"So, what are your plans for Thanksgiving?"

"Mom will cook and Sutton and I will eat until we can't move."

Casey chuckles as she twists her fork in her noodles.

"Spend Thanksgiving evening with me," I blurt, needing to do something to put a smile back on her face.

She stills before looking over. "W-what?"

"After you're done at your dad's, and once Sutton is in bed, will you come to me and spend the night with me?" I don't know where the question comes from. I hadn't thought about it before now, but spending Thanksgiving without her doesn't sit right with me. Aside from Sutton and Mom, she's the person I'm most thankful to have in my life right now.

The widest, brightest smile spreads across her face and I love that just for a moment, I allow her relief from the sadness of spending another holiday without her mom.

"Yes," she blurts. "I'd love to."

My chest compresses with relief.

"Really?"

"Yes, Kodie. Really."

"Okay. Good."

"I'll make sure Mom makes herself scarce."

"Oh god," Casey laughs. "She'll be in the pool house, right?"

"Yeah. Worried you'll be too loud?" I tease.

"When it comes to you, anything is possible."

Pride washes through me. I fucking love making my girl lose control.

"So, we'll spend next Thursday night together," she states. "What about between now and then?"

"Well," I say, reaching out to drag her stool closer so she's sitting between my parted thighs. "I was thinking that I could make you come as many times as possible."

"Well, I was hoping that was a given."

"Home game tomorrow and Monday, and I have every intention of you being there, leaving with you, and then making you scream while wearing my jersey. Then we leave Tuesday afternoon for a road game on Wednesday night, which we'll win, and I'll get a sexy little photo again."

"You're really rating your skills, huh?"

"Don't even pretend that you don't know my stats better than I do."

Casey's cheeks brighten at that comment.

"What?" I ask, sensing there's something she's not telling me.

"I have notebooks with your stats in them," she confesses.

My eyes widen.

"Seriously?"

"Yep. And maybe a scrapbook or two with trimmings and photos." Her entire face glows now, and she quickly tries hiding it in her hands.

"Casey," I whisper, pulling her hands from her face. She looks up at me through her lashes, utterly mortified that she's told me.

"I'm sorry. That's really creepy. You can leave now if you want. I promise I'll stop stalking you."

My chest shakes with a laugh. As if it's possible to walk away from her now.

"Can I see them?" I ask, intrigued.

She looks away. "I...um...I don't know where they are."

"You're lying," I state, confident that I'm right by the way she's refusing to look at me.

I tuck two fingers under her jaw and force her to look at me.

She does so shyly through her lashes. I swear, it makes my heart skip a beat.

I am so in love with this woman.

"They're under my bed," she whispers.

"Can I see them?" I repeat.

She sighs. "Do you really have to?"

"Only if you're willing to show me. I won't make you do anything you don't want to do."

Slipping from her stool, she steps right into me, her arms wrapping around my neck.

"I'll show you if you promise not to mock me endlessly." I smirk. "You need to remember I was a teenage girl with the world's biggest crush."

I shake my head. "Why didn't I find you sooner?" I muse.

"Because then you wouldn't be the man you are now, and you wouldn't have Sutton."

My hands freeze on her back, halting their descent to her ass. The thought of a life without my daughter is horrifying. "So you're an everything-happens-for-a-reason kind of girl then?"

"Sometimes," she admits. "Other times, I think life is just shit beyond belief for no reason at all."

"Yeah," I muse. "Can't really argue with that."

Ducking down, I brush my lips against hers as my fingers twist in the hair at the nape of her neck.

I kiss her until I fear I'm going to make her forget about these scrapbooks.

She's panting and her lips are swollen when I pull back.

"Seriously?" she giggles, seeing what I want in my eyes.

"Yep."

Taking my hand, she steps away from my legs before pulling me toward her bedroom.

She drops to her knees and opens a hidden drawer beneath her bed, pulling out a box.

She places it on the bed and knocks the top off.

Inside are two bulging scrapbooks, and soon, I discover that Casey has recorded more about my hockey career than even my mother has.

It's impressive.

"This is—"

"Crazy and embarrassing?" she asks quietly as I flip through the pages.

"No, Casey. It's amazing. Sutton is going to love all of this. Thank you," I say before looking up at her through glassy eyes. "Thank you so much."

77

CASEY

For almost as long as I can remember, the days leading up to the holiday season get exponentially harder.

Every year, I tell myself that it'll get easier. Every year, I'm wrong.

I'm hopeful that this year might just be the one that the grief and loss won't be quite so bad. It'll be there. It'll always be there. But less, maybe.

Kodie has been the best distraction, as has his daughter.

As promised, he and the Vipers slaughtered his old team, winning yet another shutout game. They also won their next home and road games. They're killing it this season. They've got their eyes on the playoffs and the cup, and honestly, I think they've got a good chance.

But of course, better than all of that, Sutton and the Polar Bears won their home game, and there were no injuries or trips to the ER. I call that a double win. There was no way I could deal with a repeat of that experience quite so soon.

Kodie has mostly kept my mind off the impending holidays, but with him on the road and needing to be at home with Sutton, he's not here as much as I'd really like.

I miss him something awful.

I know it's early—we're not even public with our relationship yet— but I need more.

Does that make me a crazy-obsessed puck bunny who always needs more than players are willing to give? I really fucking hope not.

Showing him my scrapbooks the other night was the most mortifying thing I've ever experienced. Fuck knows why I told him.

His reaction, though...I never could have predicted that.

I shake my head, my heart so full of love for a man I've adored from afar for so many years.

I pull into Dad's driveway with a lump in my throat and emotion burning my eyes.

Holidays without Mom are awful.

It doesn't matter how many years pass; the hole she left is still as huge and raw as ever.

Pulling my cell out, I send Kodie one final message.

As much as I might want our exchange to continue, we both need to focus on our families today. I hope that maybe one day, we could be celebrating together as one big family. But today, we have to be strong for our parents and make the best of a day where we're to be thankful, even if those we love aren't with us.

> Casey: I can't wait until later. I'm so thankful for you and everything you've brought to my life.

The dots start bouncing immediately as if he is sitting waiting for a message.

> 55: That's a really lovely way to say you're thankful for my dick, Trouble.

I roll my head as a laugh huffs out of me.

> Casey: I'm thankful for a whole lot more than just your dick. I'll show you later.

> 55: Is it bedtime yet?

> Casey: Give Sutton a hug from me x

Dropping my cell into my purse, I push the door open and climb from my car.

To my disbelief, Dad didn't say a word about bumping into me at the arena the next morning. He didn't even look at me suspiciously.

Maybe I didn't lie as badly as I thought I had. Or maybe it was his exhaustion from road games and traveling. Whatever it was, I'm grateful, because it's given me a little more time to try and figure out how I'm going to tell him about Kodie.

There's a part of me that believes it'll be fine. Dad only wants the best for me, and being with Kodie makes me happier than I've ever been in my life. But also.. all he's ever told me is to stay away from his players.

And now, I've fallen in love with one.

With my heart in my throat, I make my way to my childhood home. I've got so many amazing memories under this roof. But I also have a lot of painful ones.

I understand why Dad never wanted to move out. Mom is everywhere we look. But at times, I've wondered if it's held us back.

As soon as I move toward the front door, it opens, and I find my dad standing there in a shirt and slacks, just like he still does for every holiday, because Mom loved it when we all dressed up.

"Care Bear," he announces, allowing me to hear the crack in his voice.

He might be putting on a good show, like he's done every year since she's passed, but he still feels the loss just as potently as I do.

"Daddy, Happy Thanksgiving," I say stepping into his arms and hugging him as tightly as he does me.

I want to say that the house smells amazing and my stomach rumbles on cue, but that's not the case.

"Did you put the turkey in at the time I told you?"

I look up just in time to watch guilt pass over his face.

"I forgot to set my alarm," he confesses.

"Dad," I laugh as I slip past him and into the house. "You promised you had it under control."

In the past, I've stayed over the night before to take care of the cooking. I'm not a good cook, and neither is Dad, but we've managed over the years. But last night, I couldn't be here. How was I going to sneak a six-foot-five hockey god into the house without anyone realizing?

Of course, I didn't tell Dad the real reason for staying away this year, and thankfully, he didn't question me. Instead, he just assured me that he had it all under control.

Apparently, he did not.

Walking straight over to the oven, I peer inside to find our turkey not quite as cooked or as golden as it should be by this time.

"So...dinner is going to be late then," I deadpan.

"Meh, it's not like we've got anyone else waiting for it."

His words are meant to be a joke, but they fall a little far from the mark.

"Right, well, roll your sleeves up, old man. We've got to prep the rest."

"Less of that," he mutters as he does as he's told and walks to the sink to wash his hands.

I chuckle, but it doesn't come as easy as it would on any other day.

We work seamlessly, getting the rest of our dinner prepped before we reward ourselves with a beer and head for the couch to watch the parade.

Dad sits in the spot he has for as long as I remember, and I curl my feet beneath me in the corner of the sectional where Mom used to sit. It weirdly makes me feel closer to her, knowing that if she were still here, this is exactly where she'd be. Well, unless she was fussing with everything in the kitchen to ensure we had the most perfect day. She always tried so hard, ensuring we had all the trimmings. But in reality, all we needed was each other. Dad and I didn't care about having the most succulent turkey or the perfect pumpkin pie. Thanksgiving was never about the food; it was about family, and it was never more obvious than the year we became a member short.

I let out a pained sigh as one of the alarms on my cell bleeps, uncurling my legs and standing.

"I know it's hard, Care Bear. But it's getting better, right?" The emotion in Dad's voice is like a knife through my chest.

He needs me to give him hope, but I'm not sure how much I have.

"She'd want us to keep living. She'd want us smiling, laughing, and making the best of life." I swear, I say something like this every holiday season, but it feels different this year. Something has shifted in me, and there's this nagging feeling inside me that I'm finally going to be able to enjoy the holidays again—all the while leaving Dad behind to continue grieving.

"It's okay to move on, Dad. To find happiness elsewhere. It doesn't mean you've forgotten or that you don't still love her."

He swallows thickly, his eyes glistening.

My stomach knots with regret. I hate pushing him. I know that when the time is right, when the woman is right, he'll do what he needs to do. It's just that sometimes...sometimes I feel like he needs to have my permission to do so.

He has it. And I'd hope he knows that—I've said it enough over the years. But hearing it and acting on it are two very different things.

A lthough it's a few hours later than planned, Dad and I sit down to a traditional Thanksgiving dinner. It's delicious and, like always, way too much food for two people.

While Dad watches football, I put the leftovers into containers and fill his fridge and freezer. At least it should stop him from ordering takeout every night when he's home for a while.

Guilt rushes through my veins every time I glance at my watch, my cell, or the clock on the kitchen wall. I shouldn't be wishing the day away, but my need to be with Kodie is getting unbearable. He's going to make everything that's awful about today better, and I can't wait.

When the time finally comes, I slip my feet into my heels and grab my purse from the hallway before walking into the living room.

There's a huge part of me that wants to change my mind when Dad looks up at me with sad eyes.

"That time already, huh?" he asks.

"I can stay." The words are out of my mouth before I have a chance to catch them.

A second passes, and then another as I wait.

"What? Don't be silly. You said it yourself earlier. She'd want us to be living our lives and laughing. Go, spend time with your friends. Family isn't just about blood, Casey. Family is also those we choose."

I nod, the lump of emotion in my throat too huge to force out any words.

"Go, Care Bear. Call me tomorrow?"

"Of course. Please try not to drink all the beer in the fridge."

He chuckles, which is basically confirmation that he will.

"And it's not too late for you to go out with friends as well, you know," I whisper as I kiss his cheek.

He mutters some kind of agreement that I know is a whole heap of bullshit before I leave him with a fresh bottle of beer, waiting for the next quarter to start.

"Love you, Dad."

"Love you too, Care Bear. Don't do anything I wouldn't do," he calls before I pull the front door open and slip out into the mild fall evening.

Yeah...we'll see about that.

The second I'm in my car, I set my GPS to the address Kodie gave me earlier and blow out a large breath.

Like Dad, he lives on the outskirts of the city. It's not too far away, and thanks to its suburban location, I shouldn't need to worry about the press catching me. Something I wouldn't be able to say if he lived in a fancy penthouse in the city center like Linc and most of the other guys.

In an attempt to distract myself from my nerves, I turn up the volume on my favorite playlist and press my foot to the gas.

In only a few minutes, I'm going to be inside Kodie Rivers' house, and hopefully soon after, his bed.

A laugh bubbles up, filling the car.

This could be up there as one of the best Thanksgivings I've ever had.

As I pull into his large driveway, his front door opens, revealing the man himself standing there in nothing but a pair of gray sweatpants, I upgrade that thought. And fuck, am I thankful.

78

KODIE

I was waiting at the window from the moment she messaged to say she was leaving.

Sad, I know. But now that Sutton is in bed and Mom has made herself scarce, I'm desperate.

Nerves rush through me like a tsunami as her car comes into view, her blinker telling everyone on my street that she's turning into my driveway.

My neighbors are great. They've always been respectful of my privacy and treat us like we're any other normal family. I couldn't be more grateful for them all allowing us to live our lives. But that doesn't mean they won't be curious if they spot a woman pulling up at my house. I'm not sure it's ever happened before.

I'm at my front door in a heartbeat, pulling it open and watching her behind the wheel of her car.

With a riot of butterflies in my stomach, I lift my trembling hands, wrapping my fingers around the doorframe as she slows to a stop with her eyes locked on me.

Was I playing fair by changing into sweats and nothing else before she arrived? Hell, no. Do I care? Also no.

Her eyes feast on me for a moment too long, and my need for her carries me forward and into the cool evening air. Not that I notice.

In a heartbeat, I have her driver's door open and I'm reaching out for her.

"Kodie," she squeals as I place her on her feet and crash my lips to hers.

She hesitates, and my heart sinks.

"Someone could be watching," she whispers. "Take me inside."

All the air comes rushing out of my lungs.

She's right.

Pulling back, I ask, "Do you have a bag?"

"In the trunk."

I nod, ripping myself away from her to collect it. "Go inside," I instruct before following her a few seconds later.

Kicking the door closed, I drop her bag at my feet and pause.

She's only standing in the entryway to my home, but she looks like she belongs.

"Your home is beautiful," she muses, her eyes finding me after scanning the space.

A chuckle rumbles deep in my throat as I step closer, the magnetic force between us drawing me in.

"I think it's a little early to make statements like that," I tease. "Maybe you should see a little more first."

Defying what I really want to do, I take her hand and tug her through to the main living area.

"Oh wow," she gasps, taking in the entire wall of glass that showcases my lit-up backyard.

I love the home we've created here.

When my trade was confirmed, Vipers management hooked me up with a local realtor. She was amazing, understood exactly what I wanted, and even though this place was at the very top end of my budget, I knew it was the one. From the first day we moved in when we were surrounded by boxes, I knew it was the best decision I'd ever made. Okay, best decision aside from signing Sutton's sole custody agreement. That will forever be at the very top of my list.

Stepping behind Casey, I wrap my arms around her waist and rest my chin on her shoulder.

"Have you had a good day?" I ask softly.

We may not have spent a whole lot of time together this week, but we have talked a lot, and she's been very open about how she's been feeling in the lead up to the holidays. Hell, we've both done a lot of talking about how we're feeling. It's something I've never really done before, but it feels good. I feel lighter because of it, and I can only hope she does too.

Losing a parent is heartbreaking. But at least I was an adult when we lost Dad. I can't even imagine how hard it must have been for Casey to lose her mom when she did.

"Yeah," she muses before a little laugh spills free. "Dad forgot to put the turkey in."

"Didn't you make him set alarms so he would do it?"

"Yeah. He didn't though, did he? Slept right through."

"Oh dear."

"It was fine. We just ate later than planned. What about you?"

"Same. Although dinner was on time because Mom is like a sergeant major when it comes to holiday meals."

She chuckles, the sound lighting me up inside.

"I'm not sure I can see it."

"Oh, trust me, the woman you've met is only one side of my mother. She's a force to be reckoned with."

She twists in my arms, reaching up to wrap her arms around my neck as her eyes lock on mine.

"I guess she has to be, with a son like you."

My brows hike. "What are you saying?"

Her lips curl, her eyes twinkling with mischief.

"Don't act all innocent with me, Rivers. You might be mostly living life in the slow lane now, but I saw you all those years ago."

My eyes bounce between hers, wondering why I couldn't have been lucky enough to meet her before now.

"Jealous, baby?" I tease. "You wanted a taste of me back then, huh?"

She shakes her head slightly. "I get a taste of you now. That's all that matters."

"Mmm," I hum before ducking down to steal the kiss I wanted outside.

As my tongue pushes into her mouth, she melts against me, and I can't help wondering if it's the first time she's fully relaxed all day.

I lose myself in her, in her sweet taste and her soft body. My hands roam, tracing her curves, learning everything about her.

"Did you have any plans for tonight?" I ask as I kiss across her jaw.

"No," she breathes. "I just...I just want to be with you."

"Are you hungry?" I ask before sucking on the sensitive skin beneath her ear.

"No. Well, not for food, anyway."

Music to my ears.

Gripping her ass, I lift her from the floor and carry her to my kitchen island.

"Kodie," she whimpers, keeping me pressed against her core with her legs twisted behind my back.

With my lips back on hers, I blindly attempt to undo her coat.

It takes longer than I'd like, but eventually, I push the fabric from her shoulders.

Pulling back, I look down and my mouth runs dry.

"Casey, you look—"

Resting back on her palms, she allows me a moment to look at her.

I swallow—or at least attempt to.

"Y-you've been wearing this all day at your dad's?" I rasp, my eyes glued to her cleavage.

She nods, a smirk on her lips.

"You cooked...in this."

"Uh-huh."

Taking all her weight on one arm, she trails a finger down the deep V of her knitted gray dress. Well, to be fair, dress might be pushing it. She might be in a compromising position right now, but it's riding so high on her that I can see her panties beneath. I have no doubt that this dress—sweater—barely covers her ass.

"Do you like it?"

"Christ, how are you so hot?" I knock her hand out of the way, and my lips descend on her breasts, kissing and sucking her sweet skin.

"Oh god," she cries, her head falling back as I tug both her dress and bra down, exposing her to me. "Kodie," she gasps as I flick her peaked nipple with my tongue.

My erection strains against the fabric of my pants, desperate to be released. It would be so easy to tug her panties aside and take her right here.

"B-bedroom," she forces out through her increased breathing. Shaking her arms from her coat, she sits up straight and loops them around my neck.

"Please, Kodie. As much as I want you to fuck me in your kitchen, it's probably not the best idea right now."

She's right. I know she is. But it fucking pains me to stop even just long enough to carry her to my bedroom. But I know I don't have a choice.

It's not often Sutton gets up during the night, but if we continue here, you can guarantee tonight will be the night it happens.

Tugging the fabric back in place, I lift her into my arms, striding across the kitchen toward the stairs.

"I can walk," she offers.

"Not a chance."

She holds on, her lips attacking my neck as we climb to the second floor. My body is on fire; all I can think about is stripping her naked and laying her out on my bed to feast on.

Despite imagining this all day—hell, all fucking week—getting inside her the second she stepped through the door wasn't actually my plan.

I was going to offer to at least feed her first. Sit and chat and watch some TV. You know, be an almost normal couple celebrating Thanksgiving.

But fuck...one look at her, especially in this dress, and I was fucked.

The food and TV can wait until later.

We're quiet as we hit the top of the stairs, and as quickly as I can, I carry her to the other end of the house and slip into my room, closing and locking the door. I've never used the lock before. The idea of keeping Sutton on the other side of it horrifies me, but tonight, should she wake up, it'll be for her own good.

"Where's your mom?" Casey asks, breaking the silence.

I don't respond, forcing her to pull her head from the crook of my neck and look at me.

"She lives in the pool house," I remind her.

"Yeah, I know. But she's out there, right? She's not going to—"

"She knows we want privacy."

"Oh god," she whispers before hiding once again.

"She gave me a hotel keycard to get to you," I remind her. "She knows what's happening."

"That doesn't make it any better," she complains.

"Any chance you could forget about her and focus on me instead?"

Her lips curl against my throat before she shamelessly wiggles herself against me.

"Make me," she breathes, her lips brushing the shell of my ear.

A groan rips up my throat as my need for her explodes.

Dropping her feet to the floor, my hands go to the hem of her dress, and I peel it up her body, revealing her—

"Fucking hell, Casey," I groan, taking in what is arguably the sexiest lingerie I've ever seen.

"You like?" she asks coyly.

"No, I don't like," I muse, stepping closer to her. "I fucking love." And I don't just mean the lingerie.

Wrapping my hand around the back of her neck, I kiss her breathlessly before I begin working my way down her body, unwrapping her like a gift as I go.

As good as the lingerie looks on her. Casey naked is unbeatable.

The second she's standing before me in just her heels, I gaze up at her from my kneeling position.

"You're beautiful," I tell her, needing her to know just how fucking incredible I think she is. Leaning forward, I press a kiss to one hip, and then the other.

She whimpers, her fingers sliding into my hair. But I don't allow her to take control. Instead, I look back up at her again.

"Get on my bed, Casey. On your back, legs spread. Let me see you."

As she does what she's told, I rise to full height and watch in awe.

"I've never had another woman in this house, let alone in my bed." The words tumble free without instruction, needing her to know just how big a moment this really is for me. "And there won't ever be another," I add as I push my sweats from my hips, letting them drop to my ankles, my cock springing free. "You're it for me, Casey."

She gasps as my confession hangs in the air between us.

"I know it's only been a short amount of time, but...this... you...it's everything to me. Tell me you feel it too?"

I know she does. Or at least, I think she does. I feel it from her every time she touches me—hell, every time she looks at me.

She nods, her teeth sinking into her bottom lip before she confesses.

"I feel it, Kodie."

79

CASEY

Sudden movement behind me startles me awake and has my heart jumping into my throat as my eyes fly open.

"We fell asleep," comes a panicked, raspy voice from behind me.

"Oh shit."

Blinking, I force my eyes to adjust, the digits on the alarm clock beside me coming into focus.

"Oh shit," I repeat as I throw the covers off and sit up.

The bed shifts as Kodie rolls off and stands to his feet.

For the very briefest of moments, I'm able to appreciate his insanely beautiful naked form. But then reality comes crashing back.

"Sutton," I whisper. "Fuck. I'm so sorry, Kodie. I didn't mean to—"

"Not your fault," he insists.

Our plan was to set an alarm so I could leave before Sutton woke up.

I said it was okay for me just to go home originally, but after snuggling in his bed, talking into the early hours, we agreed I'd get up early and slip out.

"Fuck," he barks, sinking his fingers into his hair and tugging until it has to hurt.

"It'll be okay," I whisper as I get to my feet and rush to him.

As I move, I swear every muscle in my body aches, but nowhere is as persistent as between my thighs.

Holy shit. Last night was epic.

"I know," he says, although the panic in his eyes defies his words. "I'm just...I'm not...how do I even begin to explain this to a seven-year-old?"

I smile up at him as I cup his rough cheeks.

Honestly, I have no idea. The only experience I really have with kids is from when I was one. But Sutton is smart and crazily observant. She already knows. That doesn't mean we should ambush her with it though. Kodie still needs to talk to her.

"Sutton is a smart kid," I assure him. "Trust her to understand in her own way."

His hands grip my hips as he leans forward, pressing a kiss to my forehead. His lips linger for a few seconds as warmth spreads through my naked body.

He takes a deep breath, trying to calm himself down.

"Being a parent is really fucking hard," he confesses. "I didn't think I'd have to deal with explaining adult sleepovers to my daughter for a few years yet."

I chuckle. "She doesn't need all the details. Right now, all she cares about is that you're happy."

"I am," he says quickly, cutting off whatever else I was about to say. "I'm so fucking happy, Casey."

I don't need to hear the words; I can see it in his eyes, in the curve of the small smile on his lips. Feel it in his touch. But still, the affirmation makes me feel lighter.

Right now, I am making this incredible man happy. It blows my mind.

"Me too," I agree. "And Sutton will be too. She loves me."

He groans, his smile growing.

"She sure does."

I swear, my heart swells in my chest.

"I could just sneak out?" I offer, still feeling like I need to talk him down from a ledge.

"Your car is in the driveway," he points out.

"She might not have seen it," I reason.

"Have you met my daughter? She'd know if a house plant had been moved."

I can't help but smirk. "You have house plants?"

He shakes his head. "Last night didn't really go to plan," he confesses. "I was going to give you a tour, try to make you feel welcome."

My smile grows. "We could have been anywhere, Kodie. You were there, and I'd have felt at home."

"Fucking hell," he groans, his grip on my hips tightening. "Okay, so how do you want to play this?" he asks, searching my eyes for suggestions.

Thirty minutes later and Kodie has his fingers wrapped around the door handle, but he hesitates opening.

"I can still try to slip out if you—"

"No. Let's go. Just...let me go in first and...yeah, just let me go in first."

I slip my hand into his. Our fingers entwine, and I give a little squeeze of support.

Silently, we make our way toward the stairs. By the time we begin descending, Sutton's soft voice floats up to us. Any hope that she might have slept in is squashed. Not that Kodie thought there was any chance of that.

Each of our footsteps sounds like gunshots, and my body trembles with nerves. It's like I'm a teenager again, trying to slip out of the house for a party I'm not allowed to go to. Only this time, the adult is trying to give the kid the slip.

The front door is right there; I could easily disappear unnoticed. But I trust Kodie, and of course, I don't want our relationship to be a secret forever.

Keeping it under the radar makes it seem like we're doing something wrong. Okay, so we might be breaking a few rules, but ultimately, we're just two people who are falling for each other. We're both consenting adults, and being with Kodie makes me happier than I ever remember.

Kodie's breath rushes over my face as we hit the ground floor, and he presses a kiss to my cheek.

"Wish me luck," he whispers before striding away before he can change his mind.

As he slips around the corner, I lower my ass to the bottom step and wait.

"Daddy, did you have a sleepover?" Sutton demands the second he walks into the kitchen, proving Kodie right. She saw my car.

"Uh...yeah, Peanut. I had a friend come over after you went to bed. It got late so she stayed here."

"Yesss," she hisses. In my mind, I see her pumping her little fists in victory like she does on the ice. "I knew it was Coach C."

I suck in a sharp breath, trying to predict Kodie's reaction.

"I've seen her car at the rink," Sutton explains despite no one asking her to.

"Is it okay that Casey stayed over?" Kodie asks hesitantly.

"Uh...yeah. She's awesome. Why wouldn't it be okay?"

My heart pounds against my ribs and I lift my hand to cover it, afraid it might burst right out of my chest.

"It's usually just us three here. I don't want to do anything that you don't like. This is our home."

"Yeah, but it's Coach C. Where is she, anyway? Don't tell me she left already."

"No, she's just coming. Aren't you, Casey," he calls, making my heart rate pick up.

Am I ready for this?

Fuck. Yes. I was born ready.

Pushing from the step, I race toward the door with a wide smile on my face.

All eyes turn on me as I step into the kitchen.

"Coach," Sutton shouts before jumping from her stool and racing over to hug me.

"Hey, Rivers. How's it going? Did you have a good Thanksgiving?"

"So good. Gran made the best pumpkin pie. I wanted it for breakfast, but she wouldn't let me.'

"Well, it's not really a breakfast food, is it?"

"It should be, the morning after Thanksgiving."

Unable to argue with that, I release her and move closer to the island where Kodie and Kathleen are watching us with soft smiles on their lips.

"Good morning, Casey," Kathleen says, her eyes twinkling. "I'm sorry to rush off, but I've got something that needs my attention now that you're up."

"Is everything okay, Mom?" Kodie asks, a frown tugging at his brows.

"Of course. If you need anything, I'll be right out there." She thumbs over her shoulder as she backs away. "Everything you need for breakfast is in the fridge. The coffee is ready."

Before Kodie can get another word in, she's gone.

"What the—"

"She's giving us space," I say, hyper-aware that Sutton is watching closely.

"Right. Okay. So...who wants breakfast?"

"Can I have pumpkin pie?"

We both look at Sutton before glancing at each other.

"Screw it, pumpkin pie for breakfast," Kodie announces.

"With ice cream?" Sutton adds, pushing her luck.

"Yeah, why not."

The smile on Kodie's face as he turns around is something I'll never forget.

"So, what did you two do last night? Watch a movie?" Sutton asks, pulling us from our thoughts.

"Um...yeah. We watched a movie and played some games," Kodie responds as he slides three pieces of pie onto plates.

"Without me," Sutton whines.

"We'll have a movie night another day," I promise, but the second the words are out of my mouth, I panic. What if Kodie doesn't want me here hanging out with them as if we're a fam—

"And a games night?" Sutton asks with hope in her eyes.

"Yeah, Peanut," Kodie agrees. "We can do both. We'll look at my game schedule and see when we can fit it in."

I look between father and daughter with my heart in my throat and tears burning the backs of my eyes.

They're the perfect little team, and the fact that they're willing to let me join them blows my mind.

"Are you okay?" Kodie whispers as he places my breakfast in front of me.

"Yeah," I agree, blinking back tears.

He studies me, not believing a word of it. Reaching for his hand, I give it a squeeze, trying to silently let him know how much being here right now means to me.

With a smile and a nod as if he understands, he turns back for his and Sutton's plates.

"Yesss," Sutton celebrates.

"Make the most of it. It won't happen again for another year."

"Worth it," she mutters before diving in.

"I think you might have just created a new family tradition," I tell Kodie as he takes his seat, his fork poised to cut off a piece of his pie.

He stills, his eyes lifting to meet mine. "No, Casey. *We* just created a new family tradition."

"We're going to do some practice in the yard, after this," Sutton explains. "Do you want to be on my team, Casey? Girls against boys." Her competitive smirk as she looks at her dad is everything.

"I'd love to. Your dad doesn't stand a chance."

We spend hours in Kodie's yard playing grass hockey. It might not be quite the same as being on the ice, but it's a lot of fun. And by the time we finished, I was exhausted. Hockey was not what my sore muscles needed.

Kodie made us omelets and a fruit salad for lunch, and after gently declining an offer from Sutton to play in her room, I let Kodie grab my things and meet me at the front door.

"Please stay a little longer," Sutton begs.

I'd love to. Hell, I'd happily stay here forever if I could. But

Kodie doesn't get to spend all that much time with his little girl during the season, and I've already taken up enough of it.

"Another day, I promise I will. I've got plans with my friend this afternoon." I didn't have any plans earlier in the day, but one message to Parker earlier and she insisted she needed to know every detail about my sleepover with Kodie. If I don't get moving, she's going to beat me to my apartment.

"Parker Donnelly?" Sutton asks.

"Yeah."

"She's cool. So is her brother."

"Oh yeah?" Kodie asks. "I thought you were a Viper through and through."

"I am. But Donnelly is good. Really good. I think your D line could definitely use him. I've mentioned it to Coach a few times now. Just waiting for him to realize it."

"I'll have a word too," I offer.

Sutton lights up. "Really? You think I'm right?"

"Yeah. I think he'd be a good addition to our team. And I know Parker would love having him around."

Sutton beams with pride.

"Sutton, we need to pop to the store; can you go and get your shoes on please?"

"Ow, really?" she complains.

"Really."

Reluctantly, Sutton disappears up the stairs, leaving us alone for the first time in hours.

Kodie steps forward, pinning me to his front door with his hips, his forearms on either side of my head.

"She likes you," he teases.

"I hope she's not the only one."

"Nope. I'm pretty sure Mom likes you too."

"And what about you?" I tease, tilting my head to the side.

"Oh, Trouble. I more than like you." The air between us turns charged and my heart rate increases. "I—I like you a whole lot, Casey Watson."

"I like you a whole lot too, Kodie Rivers."

Our eye contact holds, our breaths mingling as desire crackles between us.

"We've got an early game tomorrow. Can I take you out after?"

"Like...on a date?"

"Yeah, Trouble. Like on a date."

"B-but—"

"I won't take you anywhere someone can see us. You can trust—"

"I do. I trust you."

"So, is that a yes?"

"Yes, it's a yes."

He leans forward, and his lips just brush mine when footsteps race back down the stairs.

"Cockblocked," Kodie whispers, making me laugh. "I'll make it up to you tomorrow night," he promises before taking a huge step back.

"I don't doubt that. Enjoy the rest of your day."

"I'll see you at the game tomorrow, Casey?"

"Yep. It's a date."

Two dates with two Rivers in one day. What could be better than that?

80

CASEY

I look down the street, watching as the cars pass, waiting for the one I want.

The game finished a little over an hour ago, and after one drink with Parker, I excused myself for an "early night."

After getting caught by Linc on my escape to the parking garage last time, we decided it might be safer if I left. It's only for a little longer. We're going to tell Dad soon, and then there will be no more secrets or sneaking around.

My foot taps against the ground as my impatience gets the better of me.

This seemed like a good idea at first, but I forgot about the logistics of hanging around, waiting for him.

He's left. He messaged me ten minutes ago.

So why isn't he here?

A horn startles me, and I narrow my eyes at the huge black truck it came from.

I swear to God, if some asshole tries to pick me up, I'll—

"Kodie?"

He pulls obnoxiously onto the sidewalk and waves me over.

Oh my god.

I take off running before pulling the passenger door open and climbing up.

"What the hell is this?" I ask, my eyes raking over him as he sits with a backward cap hiding his curly hair, which I suspect is still damp from his post-game shower. Aviators cover his eyes, he's sporting a few days' worth of stubble, and he's still in his game-day suit. The image as a whole is delicious.

"Our date night transport. What does it look like?" he says, his voice deep and gravelly as he finally uncurls his fingers from the wheel, instead wrapping them around the back of my neck and dragging me over the massive center console.

"Missed you," he confesses before kissing me the way I've been dreaming of since walking away from him yesterday afternoon.

"Kodie," I moan, gripping his tie as I lose myself in his kiss.

A horn from a car behind us finally forces us apart.

"Get moving before someone looks too hard," I say breathlessly, sitting back in my seat.

"Fucking hell," Kodie groans, tugging at his tight slacks.

"Problem?" I ask innocently as he pulls away, his grip so tight on the wheel that his knuckles are white.

"Tease me and you'll end up bent over with it in your mouth, Trouble."

"Do you hear me complaining?"

He gives me a double take.

"Fuck. You're serious, aren't you?"

I smile at him.

"Christ."

"Good game tonight," I say, changing the subject before I do end up ass up, sucking him off as he drives.

As wet as my panties are from just thinking about it, we can't risk it.

Would be a hell of a way to announce our relationship, though...

"Yeah, everything lined up for us tonight," he says, playing off their solid win like it's nothing.

"Sutton was hyper when I saw her after."

I can't help but laugh. "She was hyper the whole time. She reminds me so much of me. I remember leaving Dad's games with a sore throat and no voice."

"You were his number one fan, huh?"

"Just like Sutton is yours."

He smirks as he briefly glances over.

"I thought you were fighting it out for the position?"

"She's your number one. I'm your longest and most obsessed."

"You're both number one to me. Sutton because she doesn't have a choice, and you because I want you to be."

I smile, my heart fluttering in my chest. I love it so much when he says these things. He makes me feel so treasured and important.

I've always been loved. Mom and Dad always did a fantastic job on ensuring I was. Dad especially, as he was forced to take on the role of both parents. But that kind of affirmation hits different when it's from someone who has chosen you.

And out of all the women on the planet, for some reason, Kodie Rivers has chosen me.

"I'll be whatever you want me to be," I tease as he takes a left at an intersection that'll take us out of town.

"Are you going to tell me where we're going yet?"

"Nope. But you might want to get comfortable. We've got a while to go yet."

"Hmm...interesting."

I glance at the screen, but despite it showing a map, there's no navigation on. Wherever we're going, Kodie knows the directions without instructions.

"Sutton wanted to know if you were staying the night again," he says after we drive for a few minutes in a comfortable silence.

"Glad she wasn't too traumatized by finding me in her house yesterday morning."

"Traumatized? She was elated. You were all she talked about for the rest of the day."

"She's awesome."

"So?" Kodie asks.

"So what?"

"Are you staying tonight?"

When he asked me on this date, he didn't mention anything about that, so I'd assumed this was an evening-only thing.

"I-I don't know. I didn't realize it was an option."

"Having you in my bed is always an option."

"You're always welcome in mine too."

"I like your place. But seeing you in my bed Thursday night... fuck, Casey." He wrings the wheel as if he's trying to contain himself. And when I look down, I find that he's hard all over again. "If I had my way, you'd be in it every night."

"Taking it slow, remember?"

"I know. Fuck, I know. It's just..."

"Hard?" I offer.

"Yeah. Really fucking hard."

"If you're happy for me to stay tonight, I'd love to. I'm just aware that I'm intruding on a family, on a little girl's life. We've got a game tomorrow, though, so I'll need to leave early."

"Maybe we actually set an alarm this time," he suggests.

Pulling my cell from my pocket, I open my clock app and set one right here and now.

"Done."

"I love your eagerness."

And I love you...

"K odie?" I question when he pulls up into some woods and puts the truck in park. "Where are we?"

"Somewhere no one will find us." My brows lift as I stare at him. "Okay, that sounded creepier than it was meant to."

"So, you're not going to kill me and leave me here for no one to find?" I confirm.

"Hell no. I need someone to have phone sex with when I'm on the road next week."

"Glad I come in useful for something," I tease. "So, what are we doing here?"

"It's a surprise," he says, pushing the door open and climbing out.

"Well, okay then."

I pull the handle to follow him, but it doesn't do anything.

Twisting around, I try to look out of the window behind me, but it's too dark, only flickers of moonlight peeking through the trees.

"Kodie?" I cry.

Not two seconds later, my cell vibrates in my pocket.

55: Trust me, baby.

Casey: You'd better not be getting your axe out...

55: Not sure if that was a euphemism or not.

I chuckle. I'm not sure if it was either.

The sound of the tailgate cover rolling back catches my attention before the vehicle dips. He moves about doing... something...before the entire thing bounces, I assume when he jumps off.

"What are you doing, Kodie Rivers?" I ask myself.

A couple more minutes pass before a shadow moves outside my window.

The locks disengage and the door opens, letting in a rush of cool evening air.

A shiver runs down my spine and my nipples pebble, but it's not from the cold. It's from the man standing before me.

He's lost the suit, now dressed in sweats and a hoodie, his hat sadly missing.

What is it about a backward cap?

"Hey, are you ready for your date?" he asks as he holds his hand out to help me down.

"So ready. And curious."

A stream of moonlight hits the side of his face, allowing me to see his smirk.

"Come on then."

I barely take a step when I see the lights.

"Kodie, what have you done?" I whisper as he leads me around the back of his truck to reveal his handiwork.

He's turned his tailgate into the perfect date.

There are lights strung up everywhere, giving the space a warm glow. There are blankets and pillows and a picnic basket.

Tears sting my eyes as I take it all in.

"You did all this?"

Glancing over, I find him rubbing the back of his neck nervously.

How the hell could he possibly be nervous? This is the thing romance books are made of.

"Well, my number one fan helped out a little. She chose the blankets and pillows."

I sniffle and he steps in front of me, ducking down so he can look into my eyes.

"Casey," he says softly.

"I'm sorry. I'm just...a little emotional."

"You like it, though?" he asks, a slight frown marring his brow.

"I love it. It's perfect. Thank you."

Wrapping my hand around the back of his neck, I pull him down for a kiss.

"I'm kinda pissed about this, though," I confess, tugging at his hoodie as I pull back.

"You prefer me in the suit?"

"I'll take you in either. I was more talking about you changing without letting me watch."

"If you're lucky, I'll give you a repeat later." Stepping around me, his huge hands wrap around my waist before he says, "Up you go," and effortlessly lifts me.

I crawl toward the stack of pillows and lie back, waiting for him to do the same.

"This is the best date I've ever been on," I confess, rolling onto my side so I can see him. "Thank you."

"It's the only date I've ever been on," he counters.

"W-what? How is that possible?"

Copying my position, he reaches out, wraps his arm around my waist and tugs me closer.

"You already know I don't date, baby."

"I don't believe everything I've read online about you."

"Does that mean I can try to convince you that I wasn't a fuckboy before Sutton came along?"

A laugh bursts out of me.

"You can try if you want, but no one needed words to learn that. A picture paints a thousand words, after all."

His eyes darken before he looks down for a beat.

"I'm not that person anymore. I haven't been for a long time."

"Kodie?" I cup his cheek and force him to look at me. "I don't care about the past, or all the things you did in your rookie year that you'd rather forget." One side of his mouth twitches as I'm sure more than a few memories fill his head. "What I care about is the man before me now."

"We all have a past that's full of bad decisions and regrets. But they're nothing to be ashamed of, because they're what makes us the person we are today. And, I for one, think you're an incredible person.

"In fact, I might go as far as to say that you're my favorite."

"You're my favorite too," he whispers, leaning forward and brushing his nose against mine.

"Don't let Sutton hear you say that."

"It's okay, I think you might have overtaken me as her favorite person."

"Never. You're her hero."

"Can I be yours too?" he asks, kissing the corner of my mouth.

"Always have been."

He rolls me onto my back, deepening the kiss as the sound of the wind rustling through the trees surrounds us.

I shiver as his hand slides from my hip and under my jersey— with his name and number on, of course.

"Can't get enough of you, Casey," he groans as his lips trail across my jaw and down my throat.

"Same."

He shifts so he's between my legs and I hook one around his back, allowing him to grind against me where I need him most.

"You drive me crazy," he continues, building me higher with

his words as well as the movements of his body. "You've changed my life in a way I never thought I'd experience."

"Kodie," I gasp as he pulls back and gazes down at me.

His eyes are dark and full of desire. His lips are glistening and swollen from our kisses.

"Casey," he rasps, his eyes searching mine. "I'm...I'm falling in love with you."

81

KODIE

I will never forget the glassy, wide green eyes staring up at me as those words spill from my lips.

They've been teetering on the edge for days, desperate to be released.

But this time, I couldn't hold them back.

She looks so beautiful under the soft light of the fairy lights I've covered my truck in.

I shake my head, unable to believe where I am and what I've done.

All for her.

Everything is for her.

"Kodie," she whispers, bringing me back to the here and now. I flinch when her warm palm covers my cheek, her thumb grazing my skin tenderly.

"I've been falling for you from a distance for years. But nothing could have prepared me for how hard I'd fall when you were right in front of me."

I exhale as if her words are like a physical blow to the chest.

"Casey."

"It's crazy," she whispers.

"Yeah," I agree. "This, you...none of it was a part of my plan, but now that you're here, I can't imagine anything else. I want you by my side, Casey. I want you in my bed. I want you sitting front row at my games, wearing my jersey, and I want to have you waiting for me when I'm done. I don't care whether we win or lose; knowing I get to go home with you every night means I'll be celebrating.

"You're perfect, everything I didn't know I wanted or needed in my life. And you're mine. All." Kiss. "Fucking." Kiss. "Mine."

Her hands slide down my sides until she grips my hips, tugging me closer. Or at least, she tries to.

"Please, Kodie," she begs, arching her back to get us closer.

A smirk kicks up the corner of my lips.

"Here?"

"Yes. Right here."

I drop my weight onto her, and she instantly wraps her leg around my back, pinning us together.

"I need you, please."

"Anyone could see you out here, Trouble." I mean, it is possible. We are in public woods, but I'm confident that the chances are slim to none.

"You won't let them," she gasps as I roll my hips, letting my erection graze her clit. "Oh god."

"Too fucking right, I won't let them. You're mine, Casey. Mine."

"Yes, yes," she cries as I push up the fabric of her jersey, my hands splaying across her stomach before sliding up to cup her breasts. "More."

"So fucking sexy when you beg, baby."

She whimpers as I lean forward, sucking her pebbled nipple through the lace of her bra.

"Kodie, stop teasing me." I smirk. I might be just as desperate for her, but I fucking love this. Hearing her pleas for more, feeling her body tremble with need...

"Love how hot for me you are."

"Years of pent-up lust right here," she laughs.

"Fuck, I hope it never runs out," I groan as my fingers find the waistband of her jeans. "What did I say about skirts?"

"Just take them off," she demands impatiently, lifting her ass to allow me to pull the fabric down.

I chuckle, my cock weeping with need as I do as I'm told.

"Good boy."

My eyes shoot to hers as shock rocks through me.

"Now, rip my panties off and put your dick inside me. I'm so fucking wet for you already, Rivers."

My chin drops, but I can't deny that her dominating tone does things to me.

I've always wanted to be the one in charge. It allows me the control I need. But with Casey, everything is different.

Of course, I love telling her what to do. But this...I can get on board with this as well.

"What are you waiting for?" she asks when I don't move.

"Fuck, you're so perfect."

"Prove it."

"Damn, controlling Casey is something else."

Doing as she said, I twist my fingers in the sides of her panties and tug. The sound of ripping lace mingles with the rustling of the trees, and she gasps the second cool air rushes over her heated skin.

"So pretty," I muse as I push my sweats over my ass, pulling my cock out.

"Oh god, please. Please," she cries as I drag myself through her folds, coating myself in her juices. "Kodie, now. Please."

Shuffling forward a little, I press against her entrance.

Her hands grip my forearms as I hold her hips, her nails digging in hard enough that I know I'll be left with little crescent indents later. Bring it on. I'll proudly wear any mark that Casey wants to give me.

She whimpers as I push inside her. The sweet sound combined with the feel of her wet heat sucking me in is too much.

My hips punch forward, desperate to be as connected to her as possible.

She cries out as I still, fully seated inside her.

"Fuuuck," I groan as her walls ripple around me. "Baby, you feel so fucking good."

"Move, please. Fuck me, Kodie. I need you."

With my hands planted on either side of her head, and my eyes locked on hers, I give her exactly what she's demanding.

I set a punishing pace, which I'm sure has my entire truck rocking with the force.

Casey whimpers, mewls, and cries out my name.

It is fucking everything.

Gritting my teeth, I force myself to hold back. I'm there. I'm right on the fucking edge. But I can't come. Not before she does.

"Touch yourself. Show me how you tease that pretty little clit when I'm on the road."

Without hesitation, her hand snakes down her stomach before two fingers begin to rub hurried circles on her swollen bundle of nerves.

"I need you to come, baby. I'm there. I'm right fucking there."

"Yes, yes. I am. Fuck, Kodie. Fuck."

Her pussy clamps down on me so fucking tight as she falls into her orgasm that I don't stand a chance of holding back any longer.

I throw myself off the cliff with her, freefalling, but confident that we'll land together.

"Fucking hell," I groan, dropping over her body and tucking my face into the crook of her neck, breathing in the sweet scent I'm so obsessed with.

"Yeah," she muses.

It takes me a few seconds before I find the strength to roll off her, not wanting to crush her small body into the bed of my truck.

Tugging my sweats up, I reach for one of the blankets to cover us. It's not cold out here, but there's a chill in the air, and the last thing I want is for her to be cold.

"This is nice," she says, snuggling into me.

"Yeah?"

"Yeah. You did good for your first date. I hate to say it, but you've set the bar pretty high."

I groan lightly. "I didn't think about it like that. I guess I shouldn't tell you about the champagne, strawberries, and melted chocolate I've got in the basket then."

"Umm...no. You can always tell me about those."

Kissing the tip of her nose, I reach for the picnic basket Sutton helped me prepare.

"Whoa, there's a lot more in here than you just suggested," she teases.

"I wasn't sure how hungry you'd be or what you'd fancy, so..."

"You brought everything?"

"Something like that. I wanted to make you happy, make our first date special."

"Kodie, you've already done that. The food is just a bonus."

"I love you," I blurt, the words coming easier now that I've said them once.

Her eyes soften and this sappy smile that I can't get enough of appears on her lips as she starts shaking her head.

"What?"

"I just can't believe it. I always hoped that dreams could come true, but I never really believed it. But you're proof they do."

"Casey," I whisper. "I'm no dre—"

"You are so much more than you know, Kodie Rivers, and I love you too. So much."

Unable to stop myself, I abandon unloading the basket and drag her in for another all-consuming kiss.

"The only thing we need to figure out now is how we tell the rest of the world."

"You mean your dad?" I correct.

"Yeah, that," she muses.

We won tonight, another epic shutout game for Handsy. He's fucking killing it this season and is well on his way to a shot at the Vezina Trophy this year. I'd fucking love to see him win it. It would mean everything —not only to him but also to our entire team. Our family.

It may have only been a few days since Casey and I finally exchanged those three big words we were both holding back, and it might sound like a cliché, but I swear, everything has changed.

I'm happier.

Even happier than I was when we started hooking up.

Multiple people have commented on it, but mostly my teammates.

I'm playing better, too, which is a bonus.

Everything is just better.

Every laugh feels lighter and more genuine. Every conversation flows better. It's fucking bizarre, but I'm here for it.

But while I'm flying higher than I ever have, Casey is struggling.

Tomorrow is her mom's birthday, and she's dreading it.

I get it. Dad's birthday earlier in the year ripped me to pieces.

I just wish there was something I could do to make it easier for her.

I'm glad we're getting a red-eye back home tonight so at least I can be there when she wakes up in the morning.

We've got almost two weeks' worth of home games ahead of us once we land back in LA, and Casey and I have agreed that once she and Coach have got over these painful few days, we're going to tell him about us.

I'd be lying if I said I wasn't nervous. I'm fucking terrified. But we can't keep our relationship hidden anymore.

I want Casey to be a part of my life. To be a part of our family. Not my dirty little secret. She deserves so much more than that.

Sunday...Sunday is going to be the day. Coach and I both have a day off. Casey is going to invite him to breakfast with her, and if it all goes well, I will then join them for dinner later in the day. Or if it all goes wrong, I may be packing up my house and getting ready for my trade to the East Coast, as far away from Casey as Coach can get me. Only time will tell...

The second my cell buzzes on the table, I leap up, swiping the screen as I go, running out of the noisy hotel bar so I can hear her properly.

"Hey, baby. How are you doing?"

Her pained sigh on the other end tells me everything I need to know.

Finding a couch in the corner of the quiet lobby, I block everything out and focus solely on her.

"I wish I was there," I say honestly, hating the miles separating us.

"Me too. What are you doing?"

"Been having a drink with the guys. You know, for a bunch of assholes, they can be fun."

She laughs. "Don't let Linc hear you say that."

"Casey?"

"Yeah."

"I just want you to know that you make me a better person."

"Kodie," she whispers, her voice cracked with emotion.

"It's true. Everything in my life has gotten better since the night of the ball."

"I agree. Stealing Dad's ticket was the best decision I ever made."

Exhausted from our overnight flight, I silently slip into Casey's apartment. I planned to go home to see Sutton and take her to school. But Casey needed me more.

I messaged Mom to make sure she was okay doing the school run should I not return in time. She didn't ask why, but I can assume she knows.

I don't want to wake her, but she's going to need support today, and I'm more than happy to slip into her bed and hold her until she feels strong enough to get up.

There's a niggling awareness that something is wrong as I pad toward her bedroom. I figure it's just her sadness making the apartment feel cooler than usual. But the second I step into her room, I discover the reason.

"Casey?" I call as my hand slides across the wall to find the light switch.

I blink back against the brightness, but I find what I already knew as my vision adjusts.

Her bed is empty, and Casey is nowhere to be found.

But there is only one place she could be.

82

CASEY

My cheeks burn and my chest heaves as I bring myself to a stop in the middle of the rink.

I couldn't sleep.

Memories of Mom were spinning around my head, morphing with how badly I was missing Kodie.

I really need him today. Hell, I needed him last night. Having his voice in my ear was nice. But it wasn't enough.

In the end, I gave up trying to get any rest. And I knew I wouldn't cope being confined to my apartment, so I pulled on a pair of leggings, a sports bra, and a hoodie, and after making myself a very strong coffee, I grabbed my skates and my stick and headed here.

My haven.

I felt a little better from the moment I stepped into the building. The cold air filled my nose as I sucked in a deep, calming breath.

The entire place was deserted. Hell, it still is.

Tilting my head to the Jumbotron above me, I close my eyes and just breathe.

The grief, although painful, is more manageable than it once was.

Most days, I don't recognize it. But this time of year...today.

Fuck, it hurts.

I give myself a few minutes before I grip my stick tighter and take off again after the puck I sent shooting across the ice not so long ago.

When I was a kid, I used to do this for hours. Mom would sit front row and watch me as I took shot after shot into an open goal.

On really good days, Dad would join me and make it a little more challenging.

She never complained. Not once.

She just watched.

A smile pulls at my lips as I think about Sutton. I bet Kodie would do that for her. He must hate that he's not around enough during the season to do it more.

I'm going to, though. If he allows me.

I'm going to bring her here and just watch her.

Hell, I'll do one better than that. I'll get out here with her. For as long as she wants.

Mom hated skating. She hated the feeling of losing control.

I understood, but it was never something that bothered me. I always felt more at home on ice than I did on firm ground.

I keep tight control of the puck as I move toward the open goal, my eyes locked on my target.

I'm vaguely aware of a bang somewhere around the rink, but seeing as no one is booked on here yet, I don't bother looking over.

When I'm confident I can make the shot, I line up, pull my stick back, and watch it hit the back of the net.

Despite it not meaning anything, adrenaline still races through me. I'm pretty sure it always will when it comes to hockey.

Skating forward, I collect the puck and circle the goal before heading for the other end of the ice.

A shiver runs down my spine as if I'm being watched, but I don't let it distract me. Instead, I focus on shooting again.

"Yesss," I whisper-hiss to myself, feeling like a child again as I spin around, only this time, I look up.

I gasp as my eyes collide with a pair I wasn't expecting to see for hours.

"Oh my god," I breathe, my stick hitting the ice with a clatter as I stare at the beautiful man standing at the entrance to the ice. "Kodie, what—"

He moves, and it's not until he glides toward me that I realize he's also wearing his skates.

How long has he been watching me?

He doesn't say a word as he skates closer, and his eyes don't waver from mine.

The air turns thick between us; my nose begins to itch and my eyes burn.

I don't want to cry.

I want to feel anything but sadness and grief.

His lips part, and I hold my breath, more than ready for the deep rasp of his voice to flow over me. But his words never come. Instead, he wraps his hand around the back of my neck, dragging me forward until our skates and mouths simultaneously collide.

His scent surrounds me as his lips part and his tongue sweeps into my mouth.

Reaching for him, I twist my fingers in his dress shirt.

He came straight from the airport.

He knew I needed him, and he came.

A sob bubbles up, but he catches it. His free arm bands around my back, pinning me against him as our kiss continues.

We're right in the middle of the rink. Anyone could see us.

Dad could walk in at any moment.

But I don't care.

The only person I care about in this moment is Kodie.

My Kodie.

My everything.

"You scared the shit out of me," he confesses when he finally breaks our kiss, resting his brow against mine as we fight to catch our breaths.

I blink, trying to force my brain into action.

"I came to your apartment. But you weren't there."

"I-I'm sorry."

"Baby," he whispers, cupping my cheek tenderly.

I smile up at him, my eyes glassy with the tears I don't want to shed.

"What do you need?" he asks, studying me closely. "Want to get out of here or—"

"Want to play with you," I blurt, cutting him off.

"Well," he teases. "I'm never one to say no, but I think we might need to find somewhere more private first."

I laugh, and fuck, does it feel good. Gently slapping his chest, I say, "That's not what I meant and you know it."

"Do I?" he asks, wiggling his brows. "I know how much you like playing with me."

"Have you got something to change into?"

He looks down at himself as if he's only just remembering he's wearing suit slacks and a shirt.

"You okay to keep practicing for ten minutes?"

"Yeah, although I must warn you, that'll give me an unfair advantage."

"Hmm...I think I can handle it."

Bending down, he picks up my forgotten stick and hands it over.

"I'll be back. Tighten up your shot, though. Really focus on where you want it to land. You were a little sloppy," he says as he skates backward toward the gate.

"What? There's nothing sloppy about my shots," I cry incredulously.

The most incredible smile appears on his face before he steps off the ice.

"You're perfect, Casey. And that ass in those leggings..." I laugh as he lifts his fist to his mouth and bites down before jogging away.

The second he's out of sight, I find the puck and do exactly what he just said.

I've played against numerous members of the team over the years, but suddenly, I feel the pressure.

I want to impress Kodie. Prove to him that I'm a worthy coach to his daughter. It's been years since I played properly, and I have no doubt that I'm a little rusty.

Doing as he said, I set up shot after shot, trying to hit my mark every time.

It works. By the time he emerges in his Vipers training gear, I'm feeling all kinds of confident to take him on.

Plus, I like to think I have the upper hand compared to his usual teammates.

I know how to play really dirty.

"I hope you're ready for this, Watson," he warns, his game face in place.

"I was born ready, Rivers," I taunt back as we meet at center ice.

I stare up at him with my heart pounding and excitement fluttering in my stomach.

This is exactly what I need today.

Of course, the sadness is still there, but it isn't all-consuming in the way it was earlier.

Kodie makes everything better.

Holding the puck out between us, I continue to hold his eyes.

The air crackles with chemistry and competition, and just when I think he's too distracted by me, I drop the puck.

"Loser," I shout over my shoulder as I take off, my stick handling almost perfect. Or at least, it is until the second I'm aware of him chasing after me.

Fuck, this is actually quite scary.

As quick as the wind, he shoots around in front of me, stealing the puck almost before I've even noticed.

"Asshole," I cry.

"Never play a player, Watson. I thought you already knew that."

I give chase, putting my all into catching up with him. But it's hopeless; he's too strong and fast for me.

Even during my best years, I wouldn't stand a chance.

Thankfully, he tones it down a little after his first goal, and we play a much more even match.

He even allows me to score a few points, which is nice of him, considering it really should be a whitewash.

"Oh my god," I pant as I collide with the wall. My chest is heaving, and I'm soaked with sweat. This is more of a workout than I've had in years.

But while I might be battling to catch my breath, I can't keep the smile off my face. It's so wide, it makes my cheeks hurt.

"Kodie, oh my god," I cry as he comes barrelling toward me.

I curl in on myself as if that'll help make me smaller and lessen the pain of our inevitable collision.

But right at the last second, he stops himself.

His palms land on the plexiglass on either side of my head, his hips pressing my ass into the boards.

"Good game, baby," he breathes.

I give myself a little mental high five, because despite him being better than me in every possible way, he is actually a little out of breath. I'll take that.

"Were you able to keep up?" I ask.

"Only just. You're a beast on the ice."

"Well, I don't like to brag, but my father is a professional, don't you know?" His eyes twinkle with mischief.

"Is that right? I guess that explains it."

Ducking down, he steals a quick kiss.

I chase his lips when he pulls back again, needing more. But he doesn't allow it.

"We should go," he says. "We might not have training today, but that doesn't mean some of the guys won't turn up."

Realization rocks through me, and my eyes jump to the clock on the Jumbotron.

"Shit, is it really that late?"

"Come on, you're all sweaty. I need to clean you up."

"Oh yeah, you definitely need to do that," I eagerly agree before allowing him to tow me off the ice.

This is going to really hurt tomorrow.

"Sit down," he demands, nodding to the bench the second we step onto firm ground.

I do as I'm told and watch in delight as Kodie drops to his knees and begins unlacing my skates.

"You're fucking sexy, Casey. But seeing you out there, bossing it? Fuck, baby. Made me so goddamn hard."

I watch his fingers as he unties my laces. His hands are massive, but he works with skill and precision. I guess he does do this multiple times a day.

"Now you know how I feel during every single one of your games."

"Every single one?"

"Every. Single. One."

A groan rumbles deep in his throat before he surges to his feet and sits beside me, working on his own skates.

"Let's go," he says after I've put mine away. "I've got plans for you."

Side by side, hand in hand, we leave the deserted arena behind.

It was still dark when I arrived in the early hours of the morning. But now the sun is rising, casting a beautiful pink hue across the city I love.

"It's beautiful out here," I muse as I follow him to his car.

"Not as beautiful as you." My heart flutters as he opens his passenger door for me, allowing me to climb in.

He leans in, pinches my chin between his thumb and forefinger, and plants a lingering kiss on my lips.

"I hope you've still got some energy, Trouble," he teases before jogging around to join me.

I was right. Kodie always makes everything better.

83

KODIE

We stumble through my front door hand in hand, laughing like school kids.

Casey's quiet laughter bounces off the walls around us, making me wish my home was always filled with the sound.

Maybe one day.

That thought hits me out of nowhere, but it isn't even close to as terrifying as it should be.

Having Casey here in the home that Sutton and I have made for ourselves in LA feels so natural. So right.

I feel as light as a feather—which is saying a lot, considering how much I do actually weigh—as I run up the stairs with Casey right behind me.

My daughter's internal clock is faultless, and we've got exactly twenty-eight minutes until she gets out of bed and goes looking for breakfast.

Sure, she's capable of getting herself a bowl of cereal, and considering I haven't been home yet or in touch with Mom, she's probably assuming I'm not back. The last thing I want is for her to walk into my house to look after my daughter as Casey's cries of pleasure ring out.

"Shhh," Casey shushes me as we get to the top of the stairs.

Biting on the inside of my lip, I move as quickly as I can to my bedroom.

The second I discerned Casey wasn't in her apartment, I knew exactly where she'd be. She's told me before about her visits to the rink. I wasn't surprised to find my little troublemaker cutting up the ice with her very impressive skills. I know I gave her shit, but honestly, she was really fucking good. I'm pretty sure if she'd carried on playing, she would have gone pro.

It makes me wonder if Sutton will stick with it to achieve her childhood dream. It's hard. Really fucking hard. But also, it's so fucking worth it.

"Get naked," I demand the second I close and lock my bedroom door.

"Kodie," Casey shrieks as I spank her ass, urging her forward.

"Now, Casey. We have twenty-seven minutes."

"Any they say romance is dead."

"I hate to break it to you, but it is when there's a child about to wake up down the hallway. Nothing glamorous about parenting."

"Twenty-seven minutes it is," she agrees as she pulls her hoodie off, revealing her fitted black sports bra that does magical things to her tits. "Hey, hands off. No time for that," she chastises, tugging her leggings from her feet. "Twenty-six minutes now. You really should move."

Her bra hits the floor a few seconds before her panties join them, and then naked and shameless, she waltzes into my bathroom.

"Shit," I hiss, quickly shedding my clothes and following her.

"Twenty-four," she warns. But despite the ticking clock, my steps falter and I freeze, staring at her standing in my huge shower with water sluicing down her body.

What a fucking vision.

I stand there naked with my cock hard as steel and just take her in.

She's mine.

All fucking mine.

"Kodie, are you joining me, or am I going to have to take care of myself?" She quirks a brow, and my feet instantly begin moving.

"One day I'll take you up on that offer and watch you get yourself off. But today isn't the day. I need to be inside you too badly."

I march right up to her, gather her up in my arms, and lift her from her feet.

"Watching you out there on my rink...fuck, it did things to me, baby."

"Yeah, I can feel that," she quips as she wiggles her hips against me, teasing us both as my cock grazes her pussy. "Take me, Rivers. Show me what else this powerful body can do."

She shrieks as I press her back against the cold tiles.

"Hold tight. We've only got twenty minutes now," I mock before holding her up with one arm so I can guide myself to her entrance.

"Plenty of time. I have faith in y-you," she stutters as I thrust forward, filling her in one move. "Oh god."

"That's it, baby. Take it. It's just you and me. Feel how deep I am?"

She nods frantically as her nails claw at my back.

"Fuck. Scratch me up, baby. I want to wear your brand with pride."

"Yes, Kodie," she cries as she begins to climb toward her first release.

"Find your clit, baby. I scored twelve earlier. You've got a lot of orgasms to have in eighteen minutes now.

She laughs as she does as she's told, and the second her fingers collide with her sensitive skin, she clamps around me, making my head spin.

"You're good, Rivers. But you're not that good."

"We can start now, and I'll finish up later."

"Oh god," she moans.

"That's it. Such a good girl for me. I want to feel you coming now."

I circle my hips, hitting that spot inside her that makes her fall almost instantly.

"Yes, yes. Right there. Right fucking—" I slam my hand over her mouth, afraid that she might cry out just a little bit too loud, even with the sound of the running water smothering us.

Her pussy tightens around me, making my eyes cross as she rides out her first release.

"One," I count. "Give me another, then I'm spinning you around and fucking you raw," I rasp in her ear before replacing my hand over her mouth with my lips.

Only a few minutes later, she gives me her second before I follow through on my promise, drop her feet to the floor, spin her around, and fuck her from behind.

By the time I've finished, her legs are trembling and she's barely able to hold herself up.

As I massage shampoo into her hair, she's wearing a satisfied smile and staring up at me with glassy, sated eyes.

"How are you feeling?" I ask, aware that she's hurting.

"Right now, perfect. Thank you for coming to find me."

"Anything, Casey. I'd do anything for you."

Sutton squeals in excitement when she bounces into the kitchen and finds Casey and me at the island, nursing coffees.

Turns out, we didn't need all twenty minutes.

I lift my mug, hiding my smirk.

"Good morning," Mom sings from behind us. "Casey, what a surprise." The knowing lilt in Mom's voice tells me that she isn't surprised in the slightest. "It's so lovely to see you." Mom's eyes are full of genuine happiness. The sight has emotion burning the back of my throat.

Now it's time for her to find someone as well. As weird as it'll be to see her with someone who isn't Dad. It's time.

She has so much love to offer. It deserves to be spread wider than just the people under this roof, Casey now included.

"You too, Kathleen. I love your dress."

"It's so pretty, Gran, is it new?" Sutton joins in.

I sit there watching their exchange with the widest smile on my face, but also...

"Uh...I'm here too, you know."

Their conversation stops, all three sets of eyes turning to me. Casey and Mom wear knowing smirks, but guilt washes over Sutton's face.

"Daddy," she cries rushing to me. "I only watched the first period last night." She shoots Mom a glare that makes us all laugh. "Tell me you won," she begs. "Their D line was a mess."

I chuckle. "Yeah, baby. We won."

"Yesss," she hisses before giving me a hug. "Missed you," she whispers so only I can hear.

"Missed you too, Peanut. Is it okay if Casey has breakfast with us? Maybe comes with to take you to school?"

She looks at me emotionlessly for half a second before her eyes roll. "Of course it is. Did you even need to ask?"

Laughter ripples around the room.

"Right then, seeing as you don't need me, I'm gonna head out," Mom says.

"You can stay," Casey offers.

"You three enjoy your morning together. I'll see you later."

A couple of moments later, the door closes behind her.

"She didn't need to leave on my account," Casey says, looking concerned.

"She didn't. She does far too much for us. She's escaping while she can."

"Fair enough."

"She'll head to her favorite diner and have someone else cook for her."

Casey sighs. "She's awesome. You're so lucky to have her."

"I know," I admit. "Right," I say, changing the subject before Casey thinks too much about the hard things today. "Who wants eggs and bacon?"

"What? No pie?" Casey asks teasingly.

"Or pancakes and ice cream," Sutton pipes up.

"So, eggs and bacon all around?" I ask, shaking my head at them.

We can't start a new unhealthy tradition every time Casey stays for breakfast. Sometime soon, all we'll be eating every morning is sugar.

"I can help," Casey offers as Sutton hops up onto the stool next to her.

"Nope. You just hang out with my girl there. I've got this."

As I move around my kitchen, Casey's eyes follow me despite being locked in conversation with my daughter.

I look over my shoulder and my eyes collide with hers, her cheeks brightening at being caught.

I blow her a kiss before focusing back on breakfast.

So this is what it feels like to be truly happy...

It's fucking addictive.

After convincing Casey to braid her hair, they both disappear upstairs so Sutton can get ready for school, leaving me with the clean up.

Maybe Mom had the right idea.

I feel guilty for saying it, because I know Casey is hurting, but I had the best fucking day.

We took Sutton to school together, and I won't lie, I got a little choked up when Sutton wrapped her arms around Casey, giving her a big squeeze just like she had me before racing across the playground toward her classroom.

Seeing my daughter falling just as hard and fast for Casey is incredible.

After stopping at her place so she could change and grab a few things, we got takeout coffee and then went home.

Walking in together felt so natural. Seeing her in my space felt so normal and yet electrifying at the same time. It made me realize that this house hasn't really been a home at all. It was missing something.

We curled up on the couch, watching highlights of last night's games, and before I knew it, Casey's breathing evened out and she drifted off to sleep on my chest.

I held her tighter and pressed my lips to the top of her head, breathing her in.

I hate that she's hurting, but I also love that she's relaxed enough with me to get the rest she needs.

Losing her mom will always hurt, just like losing Dad will for me. But together, I hope we can make those harder moments a little more bearable.

Together, we slept for hours, and only woke when my cell alarm started blaring, reminding us that we needed to collect Sutton from school.

Later that evening, the three of us sit at the dining table like a real family, eating enchiladas while listening to Sutton's drama of the day.

Of course, it's focused on Adrian.

Sutton tells Casey all about what a little shit he is, and they bond over the fact Sutton is dealing with some of the same issues Casey did when she was younger.

Everything is great. Perfect, even. Until I send Sutton upstairs to get showered.

My cell buzzes in my pocket and I pull it out, wanting to put off cleaning up a little longer.

> Storm: Did you manage to get in there first?

I frown.

> Kodie: With what?

But even as I type the letters, dread begins to seep through my veins.

"Is everything okay?" Casey asks, her eyes on me.

> Storm: Telling Coach that you're tapping his daughter.

All the air rushes out of my lungs, and it only gets worse when Linc's next message contains a link.

A link to an article that is full of images of us outing our secret relationship for the world to see.

84

CASEY

I stare at Kodie, my heart slamming against my chest.

Something is wrong.

No. Something is really wrong. All the blood has drained from him face.

"Kodie? What is it? What's—" He reaches out and turns his screen around, showing me a news article. I frown. It takes me a second to process, but the moment I do, the world crashes down around me.

"No," I gasp, my hand flying up to cover my mouth as I stand from the chair so fast, it topples over and crashes to the floor behind me.

"I'm sorry, baby. I'm so fucking sorry. I had no idea they were there. If I did—"

"N-not your fault," I whisper, my vision blurring as I study the images.

The first ones are of us walking out of the arena hand in hand this morning. Then there's another at Sutton's school, saying goodbye to her. Getting our takeout coffee. And it continues. Our entire day has been documented by some asshole.

Acid fills my stomach before burning up my throat. But as angry as I am at someone doing this to us, mostly, I'm angry at myself.

I've lived this life long enough to know better.

I've seen photographers hiding outside our house when I was a kid, trying to get a glimpse of Dad when he was at his peak. I've seen the way they clamor for any shot they can get as the players both arrive and leave the stadium.

I just...

Fuck.

I didn't even think.

"Casey," Kodie says softly, but I barely hear it. The only thing I can focus on is how fucking stupid I've been. How careless. How selfish.

I was so lost this morning. And then Kodie turned up and everything changed.

The pain and grief became bearable as other emotions took over.

Happiness. So much happiness.

His warm hand cups my cheeks, and I suck in a shaky breath.

"Casey, look at me," he commands, his voice deep and steady. "Everything is going to be okay."

"M-my dad," I whimper.

If he sees this and learns that I've been lying to him...

Oh god.

He's going to hate me.

A sob erupts.

We don't lie to each other.

We never lie to each other.

"He'll understand, baby. He's a good person."

"B-but..." My words trail off as I spiral again. "I need to go to him. I need—"

"Sutton wants you to read her a bedtime story," he reminds me.

The memory of her asking me to do tonight's story flickers through my mind, and my heart swells as love rushes through my veins.

I feel so wanted here. So loved.

I never want to leave.

"While you do that, I'll speak to Mom and see if she's okay to come over, and then I'll drive you to your dad's."

"I-I can go," I offer weakly. "I'm not sure you being there—"

"You're not going alone, Casey. You're mine, and we fight our battles side by side. If he wants to get rid of me, he'll have to say it to my face."

Another whimper spills free. "Please don't say that."

His brow wrinkles. "I'm sorry. It won't happen. Everything will be fine."

He's lying.

He's as worried as I am. He just doesn't want me to see it.

If Dad trades him, sends him across the country...

I blow out a long, slow breath.

I'd follow him. I'd follow him to the ends of the earth if necessary.

"If the worst happens, I'll come. No matter where it is. You and me, Kodie. We're it."

"Casey," he whispers, leaning forward to press his forehead against mine and closing his eyes, savoring our closeness.

When he opens them again, they're glassy and full of emotion, which makes my heart race faster and my stomach knot harder.

"I love you, Casey. I love you so fucking much."

"But?" I prompt, feeling like there's more that he doesn't want to say.

"But..." The word punches all the air out of my lungs. My grip on his upper arms tightens as I wait for what he needs to say. "I could never ask you to uproot your entire life. LA is your home. Your jobs are here. Parker is here. Your Dad."

"I don't care. My dad and Parker will always be here, and at the end of a phone. I can get new jobs. But I can't get a new you. I love you, and I have no intention of living my life again without you. And plus, you're not asking me to do anything."

"Fucking hell," he groans. "What did I do to deserve you?"

I don't respond. I'm pretty sure it's a rhetorical question.

"Everything is going to be okay," he repeats as if him saying it over and over will make it true.

Leaning forward, he presses his lips to mine. It's the sweetest, most heartfelt kiss I think we've ever shared, and it ensures more tears spill from my eyes.

He doesn't deepen it, and neither do I.

The connection between us in this moment is everything we need.

It's almost an hour later by the time I step out of Sutton's bedroom, letting her drift off to sleep.

After her shower, I braided her wet hair so it'll be pretty in the morning. Then, she pulled out her favorite hockey book for me to read.

Although I love that she wanted me to do this, and I've enjoyed every moment of it, half of my head was focused on what the rest of my night is going to hold.

The rational side of me believes that Dad will be okay. We'll turn up and he'll see how in love we are, and he'll just let it go.

But then there's the other side. The rule-follower side. The side that is terrified of letting him down. That side is fucking petrified that he's going to be beyond disappointed in me and make me choose.

My body is trembling as I make my way down the stairs. Hushed voices float from the kitchen, where Kodie and Kathleen are discussing something—probably me—but I'm too in my own head to even attempt to eavesdrop.

Their heads snap up as I step into the room, their concerned expressions softening.

The sight does nothing for the unease raging inside me.

"Everything okay?" Kodie asks.

"Of course. She was incredible, as always."

He smiles as he slips from the stool he was perched on and walks toward me.

"I'm going to kiss her goodnight, then we'll go."

I swallow thickly. The thought of standing before my father and confessing my sins makes me feel like a seven-year-old myself.

The only difference is that when I was seven, I always had Mom in my corner. She was always the more lenient parent. Dad has always been the stricter one, something I've always respected...until this moment.

I watch Kodie go before my chest compresses on an exhale, and I lower my head.

"Your dad will understand, Casey," Kathleen says, startling me.

Looking up, I meet her soft, empathic expression.

"He'll be able to see how much you care about each other. He'll be happy for you."

God, I hope she's right.

"But what if he's not?" I whisper, terrified to even ask the question out loud.

"Then make him," she says fiercely. "Love and relationships aren't always easy. But if you've found the right person, they're always worth fighting for."

I nod as I blow out another long breath. At some point, one will work and help settle me.

The sound of Kodie's footsteps pounding down the stairs ends my time hiding here from reality.

"Ready?" he asks, looking as confident and as self-assured as ever.

"Is that a serious question?" I ask.

"Trust him, Casey," Kathleen says from her spot at the island. "Trust him to know you well enough to know when something is really important."

I nod. It's all I'm capable of as Kodie takes my hand and leads me to the hallway. I slip my feet into my sneakers, and together, probably being photographed, we leave his house and make the journey to my childhood home.

The butterflies in my stomach get wilder and wilder the closer we get to Dad's.

Kodie's grip on my hand gets tighter, and the sick feeling gets worse. There is a solid chance that I might vomit on him before I manage to get a word out.

We've barely said a word to each other during the drive, and I know it's because Kodie is freaking out as much as I am. He doesn't want to show it, but he is. If Dad takes this badly, his entire life will be thrown into chaos.

The second we turn into the driveway, every muscle in my body tenses at the sight of his car sitting there.

He's home.

At least if he were out, there'd be a chance he wouldn't have seen the pictures circling the internet.

I haven't looked, but I know for a fact that the hot new gossip about Kodie Rivers isn't restricted to one site. It'll be going viral right as we speak.

"Okay, let's do this," Kodie says, killing the engine and reaching for his door handle without taking another second to think about it.

"No," I cry, making him twist back to look at me. "No, can I just...I need to go in there alone first."

"Casey," he warns.

"Please, Kodie. I need—"

I don't know what he sees in my eyes or in my expression, but he cuts me off in agreement.

"Thank you. I'll message you."

His jaw tics as his eyes search my face, silently begging me not to do this.

But I need to. It's been Dad and me against the world for so long. It's important I find the courage to do this alone.

"Okay," I say, sucking in a deep breath through my nose and then out through my mouth. "I can do this."

I push the door open, one of the only times I've ever done that in Kodie's car, and step out.

"I love you, Casey. Don't forget that."

"Impossible. I love you, too."

Before I talk myself out of it, I slam his door closed and march toward the house.

My entire body trembles as adrenaline shoots through my veins, but nowhere is it more noticeable than in my hand as I reach out to knock in warning and then open the door.

"Hey, Dad," I call out, my voice breaking. Even if he hasn't already seen, he's going to take one look at me and know something is wrong. "It's just me."

I head for the kitchen first when I don't get a response, and my steps falter when I find him sitting at the island with his phone before him on the counter, his eyes immediately on mine.

"H-hey, how are you?"

He quirks a brow.

He knows.

Holy shit. He knows.

I attempt to discreetly shake my arms at my sides as if it'll help dispel some of my nerves.

"So...um...I'vegotsomethingtotellyou," I say in a rush.

"Go on," he says, his voice firm and cold.

Oh god. He hates me.

I've lied to him, and he hates me.

I fight to keep breathing and lick my dry lips as I figure out what to say next.

"I'm seeing someone, and it's serious. I'm in love with him and—"

"Where is he?" Dad asks, cutting me off.

I glance back over my shoulder as if just seeing where he is will give me the strength I need to get through this.

"Umm...out in the car. I thought it would be best if—"

"Do you love him?"

"Yes. I love him so much. He's...he's everything to me."

Something flickers in Dad's eyes, but it's gone so fast I can't identify it.

"Go and get him."

My mouth opens and closes like a fish before I spin around and summon the man I hope isn't about to be traded as far away from me as possible.

85

CASEY

I shriek when I open the front door, because Kodie isn't in the car waiting for a signal to join me. He's standing right there as if he was just about to barge in the house.

"I'm sorry," he mutters. "I couldn't just sit out here. I—"

"He asked me to come and get you."

"Did he know already?"

"I think so."

Taking his hand, I march him through Dad's house until we're standing side by side and hand in hand in the entrance to the kitchen.

Dad's face doesn't show a single emotion as his eyes flick back and forth between us, alternating between our faces and our entwined hands.

The silence in the room is deafening, ensuring my heart continues to pound faster than I'm sure it should.

A million words dance on the tip of my tongue, but none of them fall free.

In the end, it's Kodie who breaks it.

"Sir, I know this isn't what you want to hear, and I'm sorry for not coming to you sooner, but I need you to know that I'm in love with your daughter. She is the most incredible, intelligent, funny, talented, beautiful woman I've ever met, and over the past couple of months, she has made me happier than I've ever been in my life."

Dad's lips press into a thin line the moment Kodie mentions a timeline, and I panic.

"Dad, I—"

Dad holds his hand up to cut me off. "Let him finish."

"I-I...um..." Kodie stutters, having lost his flow.

Dad frowns slightly, and Kodie thankfully finds some words.

"I know that I'm not the kind of man you hoped for, for your only daughter. I know I'm a disappointment, but I promise you, sir, I will protect her with everything I am. Every single day, I will strive to make her as happy as she makes me. I want to give her the life she's always dreamed of. I know that'll include me being away for games, and that fucking kills me, but sir... I can't live another day of my life without her in it. I love her," he says before ripping his eyes away from Dad and turning to me.

His hand still holding mine squeezes while the other lifts so he can tilt my chin back with two fingers.

"I love you, Casey. I've loved you from that very first night. I might not have known who you were, but I knew you were going to change my life in ways I never could have imagined."

My breathing is erratic, and the moment I press my hands to his chest, I feel the heavy beat of his heart against my palms.

Tears fill my eyes as I replay everything he just confessed. It's everything I've always wanted to hear from him, but something I always thought would be a dream.

"I love you, too, Kodie. I always have."

"Goddamn it," Dad suddenly barks, and we turn just fast enough to catch him wiping his eyes.

"Dad?" I whisper, desperate for him to say something. Anything.

But he doesn't. Instead, he slips from the stool he was sitting on and marches over.

Kodie and I tense as he closes the space between us.

I stop breathing.

Dad's going to hit him. I'm going to be forced to watch Dad pound into my man, and knowing Kodie, he'll take it.

It won't be the first time I've seen Dad fight. It used to happen almost every game back in the day. But he hasn't hit anyone in years. As far as I know.

But as he comes to a stop in front of Kodie, no fists fly. Instead, Dad holds his hand out for the man at my side to shake.

Kodie hesitantly slides his palm against Dad's.

"Welcome to the family, Son. It's been a long time coming."

All the air rushes out of my lungs.

"What?" I ask, as Dad releases Kodie and turns to me.

"I'm so proud of you, Care Bear," he says, his voice cracked with emotion as his arms wrap around me.

"Thank you, Daddy," I whisper, clutching him tightly as my tears soak into the soft fabric of his ratty Vipers tee.

Long seconds pass before he pulls back and wipes his face, turning his back on us in favor of sticking his head in the refrigerator.

"You okay?" Kodie asks, wrapping his arm around my waist as I also dry my tears.

"Yeah, I think I am. He's...he's happy about this, right?"

Kodie chuckles. "Yeah, baby. I think he is."

Turning to look up at him, I find the same amazement and bemusement I feel reflected in his eyes.

"Okay, good. That's how I took it."

"You both want a beer?" Dad asks, finally emerging with three bottles in hand.

"Uh, yeah, sir. That would be great."

"Kodie, for fuck's sake. Stop calling me sir. It's James while you're under this roof."

Kodie nods, looking thoroughly chastised.

"Living room," Dad states before walking off with the beers, leaving us both to trail behind.

"So..." Dad starts once he's positioned in his favorite spot while Kodie and I take the couch opposite. "You two have some explaining to do. Earlier, during your very heartfelt speech—good work there, by the way. Got me right here," he says, slamming his fist against his chest. "You mentioned that this had been going on for months. Talk me through that."

I groan, aware that I've got a few more confessions to make.

"I may have made use of your masquerade ball ticket this year."

Dad's brows lift slightly in surprise, but that's as much of a reaction as I get. "I see."

"I dyed my hair, chose a mask that covered enough of my face that I hopefully wouldn't be recognized, and...well..."

"We hit it off but I had no idea who she was," Kodie finishes.

"And when did you learn who she was?"

"About a week later. She came down to the rink to see you and...one look at her and I knew. I didn't think I'd ever find her again. And there she was, right under my nose."

"I tried to do the right thing. I tried to follow the rules, but...I couldn't. Not this time."

Dad frowns. "Rules? What rules?"

"What?" I ask on a laugh. "The rule that I should never get involved with one of your players."

I expect Dad to remember and agree, but what I don't expect him to do is throw his head back and laugh.

"What?" I ask, confused and a little offended by his reaction.

"Casey, you are a fully grown woman. I'm not controlling who you can and can't spend time with."

"B-but—"

"Yes, there were a few years when I warned you to stay away from my team. You were young and impressionable, and I'm sure Kodie will be the first to agree that hockey players aren't always the best role models. Sure, there are many of my players I'd rather you steer clear of because the chances are that you'd end up hurt. But I can assure you, Kodie isn't one of those."

I blink, utterly speechless.

"And anyway, I knew the minute he moved to LA there was a chance you'd go after him," he admits.

"W-what?" I blurt.

"Oh, come off it, Casey. You've been in love with Kodie since you were about twelve years old." My expression must tell him what I'm thinking. "You didn't think I knew you had his posters stuck everywhere, or that you suddenly paid more attention to college hockey than you did any of my games?"

"I...um..."

"Casey, I know you. Clearly, better than you think I do." He laughs again, amused by my utter cluelessness. "Why do you think Kodie was traded here in the first place?"

"Because he's an amazing winger. Any team would be lucky to have him."

"Well, yes. I wouldn't bring a shit player to my team. But...I brought him here...for you."

All the air rushes out of my lungs.

"Of course, I didn't know this would happen," he says gesturing between us, his eyes locking on our joined hands again. "But I knew you'd get a kick out of getting to spend time with your hero."

"You're my hero," I counter.

"When you were a child, maybe. But as I said, you're an adult now, Casey. You get to make your own choices and decide your path.

"I just wish you would have told me sooner instead of allowing me to find out online."

A regretful sigh passes my lips. "I'm sorry. We wanted to tell you, but it was all so new and...I was scared."

Dad's eyes darken with regret. "Casey," he soothes. "I'm so sorry. I only ever warned you off the guys to try and protect you. You know what they can be like, how quickly they go through bunnies. I didn't want that for you. I never meant to scare you into thinking you couldn't tell me if one of those guys was the one for you."

"So you're not disappointed in me?" I ask quietly.

"Care Bear, I could never be disappointed in you. I'm so proud of you for everything you've overcome and achieved." I smile as I fight back my tears. "And Kodie," he says, turning his eyes to my man. "I *know* I warned you off my girl. But if you wanted her, I needed you to fight for her. Only someone very special comes before hockey." Kodie nods in understanding as tears continue to burn my eyes. "I'm proud of you, too. Being a single parent is hard, but being a single father in our world is almost impossible. You're doing an incredible job; Sutton is a credit to you. She reminds me so much of this one at that age," Dad says with a fond smile.

"Bossy and know-it-all," Kodie says lightly.

"Yep, that's it," Dad laughs. "She has good ideas, though."

"Don't tell her that or she'll never stop. She wants you to get Donnelly from Seattle. Have you heard that one yet?"

Dad's thoughtful for a moment. "Indeed I have," Dad confirms.

"Yeah. Don't worry, it'll be someone else next week. I'm happy as long as she isn't trying to get Nash in a Vipers jersey."

Dad laughs again.

"We don't have a game next Saturday; will you all come over for dinner? Sutton and your mother, as well."

I look at Kodie, unable to wipe the smile off my face.

"We'd love to," Kodie confirms before lifting his beer to his lips.

"So...what else do I need to know?" Dad asks, his eyes bouncing between us.

We glance at each other. I don't know about Kodie, but I'm certainly thinking of what happened all those weeks ago right above our heads. "Oh, um...I'm not sure there is much to tell really. We're taking things one day at a time and figuring it all out. I've never had a serious relationship before so it's all new to me," Kodie explains while Dad eyes him suspiciously.

"You might want to get your story figured out, by the way. Everyone is going to want to hear from you about this. You can't tell me that your cell isn't already blowing up."

Kodie's face pales, giving us all the answer we need.

"I may have had a few missed calls from Hailee and my agent."

"Hailee will sort you out. She's a good one. Anyone want another?" Dad asks, lifting his empty bottle in the air.

"No, thank you," we both say, watching as he leaves us alone.

"Well, that could have been worse."

"I can't believe it," I say with a laugh and a shake of my head. "All this time, he brought you here for me."

"See, you've been underestimating him."

"Yeah," I muse. "I think I have."

CASEY

"Oh my god, Case. This is crazy," Parker screams as we attempt to make our way into the arena.

This is the Vipers' first home game since the news broke about our relationship, and it's wild.

There are reporters and fans everywhere.

Everything has been a whirlwind since those first images were released and we were forced to confess to Dad.

The next day, Hailee turned up at Kodie's house along with a photographer and her social media manager, ready to spin up the best love story the world had ever seen.

Kodie was grumpy as hell having others in his home. He reminded me so much of the man I used to admire from afar. Now, though, I know differently. He is so much more than the grump he portrays. I can't deny that version of him is just as sexy as the others, though.

After they selected the perfect spot, they had us pose before we worked together to write up an approved CliffsNotes version of our relationship.

The internet was already buzzing with the news, but the moment Kodie posted our official announcement, things hit a whole new level.

I get it. If I were still just a Kodie Rivers' fan and I was watching all of this unravel, I would be losing my mind. I'd also be incredibly jealous. Thankfully, though, and by some kind of freaking miracle, I wasn't sitting at home reading the article. I was the woman in the photograph.

People scream and shout. I hear my name above it all. Demands for me to look their way. Questions about our relationship, about the season, and how Kodie was feeling before this game.

A wave of nerves rushes through me.

We're playing Vancouver again tonight, which means Kodie and Nash are going to be facing off.

Their rivalry is no secret. Everyone who follows ice hockey knows that there is no love lost between the two of them.

I don't know Nash. I've never met him. But something tells me he's going to be gunning for Kodie tonight. Especially after all the press he's got this week.

Up until this week, Kodie's only weakness has been his daughter, and while hockey players can be brutal, generally they're decent people and will leave young kids out of their chirping. A new girlfriend, though...I can only imagine the kinds of things Nash is going to say tonight to try to rile Kodie up.

My stomach knots, dread sitting heavy on my chest.

Kodie has been killing it this week. They've already secured one road win because of a hatty from him. He was on fire, and I was gutted that I was forced to watch it through a screen. There was one bonus, though—I had the best and most excitable buddy to watch it with. It was also my first night staying at Kodie's without him. It was weird. Although, I can't deny that it felt so good to crawl into our bed for our celebratory phone sex after he gave a press conference that was almost as hot to watch as his game. The second his raspy voice hit my ears, even through the screen, I was burning for him.

I don't respond to any of the questions. Instead, I smile for a few photographs before Parker and I walk into the arena arm in arm.

"It's like you're a freaking celebrity," Parker shrieks once we're safely inside.

"I'm not, but I'm dating one," I counter.

"I can't believe it's official. This is so exciting. Your first home game wearing a real Kodie Rivers jersey as his girl."

My stomach flutters wildly.

For years, I've worn Kodie's jerseys, but they've always been the ones from the team store. But not tonight.

Tonight, I am literally wearing one of Kodie's jerseys.

It's massive and completely swamps me, but I wouldn't have it any other way.

He's played in this jersey. He's won in this jersey. And now, it's mine.

I brush my fingers over the stitched number fifty-five on my front. It's stupid, it's only some fabric, but wearing this makes me feel so much closer to him.

"Are you ever going to stop smiling like that?" Parker teases as we make our way toward the rink.

I always have good seats thanks to Dad, but now I'm even more hooked up than I was before.

Tonight, we have front-row tickets.

Okay, so it has more to do with Hailee than it does Kodie. She wants to drive the fans wild with footage of us being cute, and that wasn't going to happen if I was a few rows back.

Instead, I'm on the bench..

I'm going to be able to touch him when he walks past.

This time, it's not only the butterflies in my stomach that are fluttering.

"Smiling like what?" I ask innocently.

"Like a lovesick fool," Parker laughs.

"I really hope not. Just think, if we can find you a man then we can have matching grins."

"Not happening," she sings as the sound of blades on the floor hits my ears.

I twist around, watching as the Vipers emerge from their dressing room to come and warm up.

Fletch is first, followed by Linc, and Kodie.

His face is stoic, focused, until his eyes land on mine. Everything about him lights up in that moment, and I swear, it almost makes my heart explode in my chest.

I push to my feet, needing to be closer to him.

"Casey," Fletch says with a respectful nod as he passes me. Linc, on the other hand, he decides to play up to the cameras that are no doubt pointed in our direction. Opening his arms, he pulls me in for a hug.

"Donnelly," he grunts over my shoulder when he spots my best friend probably glaring at him in distaste.

One second Linc is there, and the next he's not—he's being dragged away by a very sexy, very pissed-off Kodie.

"Get your motherfucking hands off my girl, Storm."

"Oh shush," Linc teases. "It's not my fault I have more to offer. Someone needs to make sure Casey is aware that she's settled with second best."

"Fucking asshole," Kodie grunts, shoving his teammate toward the ice and stepping closer.

The entire arena and all the noise surrounding us fades to nothing as he steps into me. His scent floods my nose, and heat floods between my legs.

"Nice jersey," he rasps, his eyes holding mine captive.

"Thanks," I say, biting down on my bottom lip coyly. "It's my boyfriend's."

Desire darkens his eyes as he wraps a hand around the back of my neck, pulling me in for a kiss.

He's usually well over a foot taller than me, but with his skates on too, I practically need a ladder.

"Get a move on, Rivers," a familiar voice bellows from the tunnel.

"Gotta go, baby. I love you."

"I love you, too. Go beat Nash's ass."

"I don't need telling twice," he says, continuing toward the gate.

The rest of the team must have slipped past while he'd stolen my attention, because they're all out on the ice already, leaving only the coaching and medical staff to follow.

"Are you distracting my players?" Dad asks, coming to stop in front of me.

"As if I would," I tease, batting my lashes innocently.

"If we lose tonight, I'm placing the blame solely on Hailee for thinking that putting you in his eyeline was a good idea."

"Nah, if we lose tonight, it's because your team isn't up to it, old man," I say, patronizingly tapping his chest.

"Watch it. I can still trade his ass."

I smile up at my dad, not believing a word of his threats. I might have been nervous—okay, terrified—about his reaction to Kodie and me dating, but he's proven to me in just a few days that he's more than happy with welcoming Kodie into our lives in more ways than just being a part of his team.

"Then you'd definitely lose," I point out.

He smiles down at me, and I eagerly return it.

Any concern I had about his feelings toward my boyfriend has long vanished. I'm excited about our family dinner on Saturday night. I have a feeling it's going to be the beginning of something beautiful.

"Yes, come on," I scream, my palms slamming against the plexiglass as Linc shoots across the ice in front of us. The game is tied at three apiece, and there are only two minutes left on the clock.

Vancouver has played dirty, taking their lead from Nash. But our boys have hit back just as hard.

I don't think I've ever heard a whistle blown or seen as many penalties in a single game before. It's as exciting as it is nerve-wracking.

Every time we take the lead, they come back at us, leveling the score.

"No, you fucking asshole," I bellow as a Vancouver defenseman crosschecks Linc and sends him flying. He hits the ice hard, causing the entire crowd to gasp, but apparently, it looked worse than it was, because he's back on his feet almost before the ref has had a chance to blow his whistle.

The clock continues to count down as the D man earns himself a minor and stalks toward the penalty box like a petulant toddler. I swear, the girls take their punishment better than that asshole.

There's just over thirty seconds left as Fletch gets into position for the last face-off of the game.

"Come on, we've got this," I scream, my eyes on Kodie.

He's focused, his eyes locked on where the puck is going to hit the ice, ready with whatever play Fletch called.

My heart slams against my ribs, and I swear it stops altogether when the game restarts.

Fletch wins the puck, fakes right and shoots left, sending it directly to Kodie.

Time slows to almost a stop as I track the puck across the ice.

It hits Kodie's stick, and he taps it a couple of times, lining up the perfect shot.

Nash is right on his ass, but Kodie is stronger, faster, and he pulls back and shoots a second before Nash takes him down.

Kodie hits the ice at the same time the cherry lights up and the arena erupts.

"Kodie," I scream despite the fact he won't be able to hear me.

He shifts his legs and then rolls over so he's facing me.

The moment I see his wide smile and the excitement in his eyes, I know he's okay.

Lifting the arm he's not lying on, he points at me. "For you, baby," he mouths before his teammates pile on him.

He humors them, celebrating that incredible last-minute win, but the second he can break away, he's shooting across the ice, his sights set on me.

"Goddamn, I want a man who looks at me like that," Parker mutters.

I laugh. She might claim she's not interested, but I call bullshit. She's just done with sifting through the fuckboys to find the one.

Despite knowing it's about to happen, I startle when Kodie collides with the plexiglass, his helmet abandoned somewhere on the journey over.

His curly hair is dripping with sweat, his eyes are electric, and his cheeks are glowing.

"We did it," he shouts.

"Hell yeah, you did."

I mirror his movements as he edges toward me. The second he's there, I jump into his arms, his lips finding mine.

Another round of cheers erupts, and when he finally lets me up for air and I glance at the Jumbotron, I find the whole thing was broadcast for everyone to see.

Previously, that would have terrified me. But nothing seems so scary now that I've got Kodie by my side.

KODIE

I follow Coach and Fletch into the press room after the game to an explosion of flashes and excited chatter.

Fuck, it feels good.

Obviously, winning is always a high, but beating Nash, and having my girl in the front row to see it, was fucking euphoric.

The only person that was missing was Sutton. But despite her protests, we decided that it was better for her to watch from home until things calm down a bit.

I'm aware that I'm never going to be able to keep her out of the media. It would be easier if she wasn't so hockey obsessed and always begging to be at the arena. But it is what it is. I'll do everything in my power to protect her, but I won't squash her dream.

"Congratulations on your win tonight," the first reporter says once we're settled.

My eyes scan the room as question after question is fired toward us. Thankfully, Coach and Fletch are keyed in, and they answer each as I search for my girl.

She said she'd be here.

She no longer needs to hide in the shadows and pretend she doesn't have a vested interest in one player. Now, she can support me as openly and as loudly as she likes. Just like I can her.

"And how did it feel to take the final shot and secure the win for your team tonight?" one reporter asks, focusing on me.

"It feels fantastic. The whole team really did a fantastic job tonight."

"We all know the rivalry between you and Cooper Nash. I can only imagine how sweet that victory must taste."

I smirk, but keep any words locked down. Everyone might know that there's tension between us, but I've never voiced anything about our relationship to the media, and I never will.

Nash might be okay with letting everyone know how much he dislikes me, but I'm not so petty.

"You've been killing it on the ice these past few weeks. Can we assume that might have something to do with the new lady in your life?"

Now my smile grows, and as it does, the crowd parts in just the right way, allowing me to see Casey standing toward the back of the crowded room. She looks phenomenal in my jersey.

Her eyes meet mine, and a smile spreads across her lips.

"Proud of you," she mouths, making me feel all warm and fuzzy.

"Yes," I state confidently. "How I'm playing, how I'm feeling, has everything to do with the new woman in my life. She not only makes me a better player, but a better person, and I couldn't be more grateful that she gave me a chance."

Heads spin around, noticing where my attention is focused, and Casey's cheeks blaze as they find her.

"We're happy for you, Kodie. And long may it continue. Keep up a winning streak like this, and we could have a first-class ticket to the playoffs."

The questions continue, and I listen as Coach explains how proud of his team he is, and Fletch focuses on what we need to tighten up going into the next games. All the while, my eyes are on Casey.

I can't fucking wait to get her home tonight and have her lying on my bed in nothing but that jersey.

I'm so lost in my own thoughts that I don't even realize when our time is up. Coach teasingly slaps me on the shoulder, and when I look over, he and Fletch are already standing to leave.

"Shit," I hiss, making Coach chuckle.

His hand clamps around my shoulder, stopping me from retreating to the dressing room once we're free of the press room.

"I'm proud of you, Kodie. As a player, as a part of my team, and as my future son-in-law. You're not the only one who's happier. Casey is, too." My chest expands as I take in a deep breath. "I didn't say it the other night, and I'm sure it doesn't even need saying, but Casey is my little girl, she means everything to me. If you don't take care of her properly—"

"I will," I promise, cutting off whatever threat was about to spill from his lips. "I swear, I fucking will."

His scowl slowly turns into a smile. "I know. I just felt the warning needed to be said. I'm not sure I could say I'm a father without it."

"God, I'm already dreading the day I'll have to give that very same speech to some asshole."

Coach laughs. "It comes around all too quickly, Rivers," he states, clapping me on the back as we begin walking again. "Enjoy celebrating tonight. Make sure you're all at my house at six tomorrow evening."

"We'll be there, si—James. Thank you."

Just before I duck into the dressing room to grab my things, I catch the genuine smile on Coach's face.

I know Casey was worried. But there really was no need to be.

He'll support her to the end of the earth as long as she's happy. It's exactly what I hope to do for Sutton.

<hr>

The second Fletch and I walk into The Fractured Compass, a cheer erupts. Everyone who's waiting for us raises their glasses. I scan the familiar faces and see that every member of the team has come out tonight.

But I don't want to see any of them.

I want Casey.

My heart races as I search the sea of hockey players before me.

She's here—I know she is. She messaged to say that she and Parker were getting a lift with Linc.

There's movement along the left-hand side of the bar, and I spot a flash of blonde hair hiding behind Marilyn.

My fists clench at the thought of anyone but me getting close to my girl.

I surge forward, shoulder-checking a couple of the guys in my way.

The second my eyes land on her fully, everything inside me relaxes.

She's sitting on a stool but leaning back against the wall behind her with a cocktail in her hand and a soft smile on her lips.

Marilyn is talking, but she's paying him zero attention. Instead, her eyes are locked on me.

Heat floods my veins, my body buzzing with desire, my need for my girl growing with every step I take.

At some point, Marilyn must realize he's lost her, because he turns, looking over his shoulder.

He rolls his eyes the second he finds me, but I quickly look away again, focusing on who I really want.

"Hey, Trouble," I say as I step right up to her, nudging her knees apart with my thigh so I can step between them. "Do you have any idea how many times I've been here and wished I could do this?"

She tilts her head to the side in thought. From the flush of her cheeks, I'd say she's already had a few drinks. "It can't be many, because you never used to come out with the team."

My lips twitch into a smirk.

"From what I've heard, nor did you," I counter.

Yeah, okay, so I may have done a little detective work of my own about Casey Watson.

"Of course not, because unlike you, I was a rule follower."

"That sounds pretty boring, don't you think?" I muse, sliding my hand up her arm until I'm cupping the side of her neck.

"Yeah, it was awful. I much prefer breaking all the rules."

"Me too," I agree, ducking down and stealing the kiss I've been desperate for since the moment I walked away from her earlier.

Having her so close while I was playing was incredible but the biggest tease I've ever experienced. Every time we made a shift change, all I wanted to do was pull her into my arms and kiss the life out of her.

Each stroke of her tongue sates a little bit of the need that's been burning through me for the last few hours.

Her fingers twist in my shirt at my sides, clinging to me as if she's afraid I'll walk away.

Never.

I am never walking away from this woman.

You couldn't pay me enough.

Eventually, I pull back, my lungs screaming for air.

"This is so unfair," Marilyn grunts behind me as I rest my brow against Casey's and stare into her eyes. They're dark and full of hunger. The sight does little to stop the semi I'm rocking from going full mast.

"What was that, Rookie?" I tease, ripping myself away from Casey to glance over my shoulder at him.

"She was meant to be off-limits. And anyone who touches her will be traded."

"Yeah, too fucking right. Casey is mine, and any motherfucker who tries anything will be traded."

Marilyn shakes his head, his hair flops around his ears, making him look like the little puppy dog he is.

"I need a girl."

"Dude, we're surrounded by bunnies. Go find one."

"I don't want one of them. I want a real woman."

Casey giggles beside me before shouting, "Parker, get over here."

"Oh, shit. Is Donnelly fair game now?" he asks with wide, almost terrified-looking eyes.

"You two are disgustingly cute," Parker says, trying and failing to look appalled as we cling to each other. "What's up?"

"You know, Marilyn, right?" Casey asks.

"The rookie, yeah. Why?"

She looks at him with a blank, uninterested expression while Marilyn's eyes do a full-body sweep.

"Uh...oh no. I don't think so, buddy," she says, backing up.

"Aw, Parker, he just wants to know what it's like being with a real woman," I tease, earning myself a glare from Marilyn.

Dragging some confidence from somewhere, Marilyn suddenly stands.

"Dance with me, Donnelly?"

Parker's mouth opens and closes a few times, her eyes looking between the puppy before her and the dance floor on the other side of the bar.

"Fine, but only because I want to dance. If your dick so much as grazes me, we are done. That is not on the table."

Gripping his hand, she drags him away.

Casey and I both laugh when he looks over his shoulder, showing us his wide smile.

"He's going to be disappointed. She never hooks up with hockey players."

"Why?" I ask, more than aware of Parker's aversion, even though most of the team would be more than willing to keep her company.

"One broke her heart," Casey explains while watching her friend dance with our rookie.

"Come on. I want to dance with my girl," I say, taking her hand and dragging her toward them. I find us a bit of space before pulling her into my body and dropping my lips to her ear. "And lucky for you, you can graze my dick all you like."

With a smile, she reaches up on her toes, wraps her arms around my neck, and presses her lips to mine.

I groan as I wrap my arms around her back and pin the length of her body against mine.

This is how we celebrate a win.

"I love you, Casey. Thank you for being my longest and most obsessed fan."

She giggles happily, her eyes alight with excitement.

"Always, Kodie. I love you, too."

Our lips melt together again as our bodies sway to the music.

Eventually, she pulls back and looks up at me with dark eyes and swollen lips.

"Can I take you home yet?"

She smirks. "Nope. We're having fun with our friends. Reminding you just how good it can be to spend time surrounded by others."

"I know," I grunt. Although the truth is, I've only been remembering it since she came into my life. I've been doing a whole load of things I never used to think I wanted.

"Good. Now dance with me, boyfriend."

Her smirk turns wicked before she spins in my arms and thrusts her ass into my crotch.

"Fucking hell," I groan, watching as she dances.

My skin prickles with awareness, and when I glance around, I find almost everyone watching her—us—but none of my teammates are looking at her like they want her. Their expressions are mostly of awe and jealousy. I'll fucking take that.

Forgetting about our audience, I focus on my girl.

Sweat runs down my spine, and my heart pounds steadily in my chest as song after song passes.

Casey laughs, her smile so infectious that mine hasn't faltered once.

"This is fun," she says, resting her head back against my shoulder as the tempo of the songs slows.

"Anything with you is fun, Trouble."

She hums in agreement as Linc storms across the dance floor.

"What's he—" My words are cut off when he steps up to Marilyn and drags him away from Parker without saying a word. "Well, okay then."

I watch for a few seconds longer as Parker barks at Linc in irritation, but the brush of Casey's soft lips on the underside of my jaw distracts me.

"Take me home, boyfriend," she breathes. "I'm ready for our real post-win celebration."

Taking her hand I turn my back on Linc and Parker before pulling her through the crowd and toward the door, ready to spend the rest of my life worshiping the woman who's proudly wearing my number.

Who knew breaking the rules could be so much fun?

EPILOGUE

Casey

Christmas Day

I'm already awake when I hear the first soft footsteps coming our way.

I haven't been this excited about Christmas since I was a little kid myself.

It was never the same once I grew up, and then it was even worse after Mom died, when Dad and I were too busy trying to survive than celebrate.

Mom loved the holidays. She decorated a week before Thanksgiving, and every week, there was an addition to her beloved collection. A collection that has been gathering dust in the garage ever since.

Well, not this year.

This year, all of her decorations are out on display to be enjoyed as they should have been. Only, they're in a different house.

In the days that followed the first Vipers game with us as officially a couple, Kodie asked me to spend the holidays with him and Sutton. Of course, I agreed, but only if Dad could come as well.

What I didn't know was that Kodie had already spoken to my dad about it, and that they'd been scheming up how to make this Christmas the best one yet.

The last thing I expected when I walked through Kodie's front door after work one day was to find boxes and boxes of familiar decorations filling his living room.

My heart stuttered when I saw them, because I knew exactly what they were.

Kodie stepped up behind me and told me that he understood if I wasn't ready, or didn't want to, but that my dad had given him the boxes because he felt like it was time to celebrate Christmas properly, as a family.

I broke down right there and then in front of all my mom's decorations.

But they weren't sad tears. Okay, not all of them were sad tears. Mostly, I was just so overwhelmed and grateful, and so fucking in love with the man doing this for me, I couldn't contain it.

Together, along with Sutton, we spent the next two days decorating the entire downstairs of Kodie's house.

They both listened dutifully as I explained the story behind almost every piece—where Mom had bought it, why, and where it had lived in our home over the holiday season.

Tears streamed down my cheeks as we carefully unpacked each box, but as much as my heart hurt, I could also feel it being put back together at the same time.

What I used to know as family hasn't existed for a long time, and there will be a part of me that will forever mourn that. But times are changing, and family to me now includes the incredible people who live under this roof.

Kodie's bedroom door creaks a little as it's pushed open. The little footsteps are getting closer.

I crack my eye open to check the time, and I fight a smile when I see that it's one minute past five.

Of course it is.

Kodie gave a strict no-earlier-than-five-AM wake-up time. I'll bet anything that Sutton has been sitting in there, staring at the clock and begging for it to move faster.

Kodie's arm tightens around my waist, silently letting me know that he wasn't sleeping either.

I bet he's just as excited as I am.

Gift shopping with him for Sutton was so much fun. He put so much thought into each of her presents, and I know he's going to enjoy watching her reactions to them just as much.

Excitement flutters in my stomach as a very soft, "Daddy," fills the room.

Kodie groans as if she's waking him up.

"Daddy, he's been. Santa's been."

Be still, my beating heart.

"W-what was that, Peanut?" he asks, rolling over to face her.

"Santa, Daddy. He came. Wake up, please," she begs before her shocked shriek rips through the air as he suddenly lifts her from the floor and drops her between us on top of the sheets.

Reaching over, I flick the bedside light on.

"Santa came?" Kodie asks with a frown. "What do you mean?"

"It's Christmas Day, Daddy. Come on, wake up." She rolls her eyes as I laugh at her.

"Of course he came, sweetie. You've been so good this year."

She beams. "I tried really, really hard."

Oh my god, I love this kid.

"We know you have, Peanut. Shall we go and see exactly what he's left?"

"Yesss," she squeals, scrambling off the bed and racing toward the door in her elf pajamas.

Kodie rolls back over, pulling me into his body and rocking his erection against my ass.

"Hmmm, wish there was time for me to give you a special gift to start the day."

"I know we're good at quickies, but I don't think even we have time right now."

He groans, pressing his forehead to my shoulder.

"Later," I promise before slipping from under his arms and standing at the side of the bed in my own elf pajamas. It was weird sleeping with Kodie while fully dressed, but we knew we were going to get an early morning visitor, and we agreed it would be best not to terrify Sutton.

"Elf pajamas shouldn't be that sexy," Kodie groans, his eyes running down my body as if I'm naked.

Flipping the sheets off him, I take in his shirtless chest and then his green-and-white striped pants that are barely containing his morning wood.

"Yeah, I see what you mean."

A wicked glint flashes in his eyes, and the second he swings his legs off the bed, I take off running to the bathroom.

He catches up to me in front of the sink where I'm about to brush my teeth, but he doesn't allow it. Instead, he cups my jaw and slams his lips to mine, morning breath be damned.

"Daddy. Casey," Sutton shouts. "Are you coming?"

"Sadly not," Kodie mutters after ending our kiss.

We quickly brush our teeth before joining Sutton, who's waiting for us at the top of the stairs with the stocking she left at the end of her bed last night. Only now, it's full of gifts from the big man.

I swear to God, I have never in my life been as scared as I was attempting to sneak around last night doing that.

Sutton usually sleeps through anything. But knowing we could be caught at any moment was terrifying. I don't want to be the reason she loses the magic too soon.

But seeing the wide smile on her face, and the excitement in her eyes, I know I passed the test.

Kodie takes the stocking, and together we make our way toward the Christmas tree in the living room.

"Oh my god," Sutton squeals, finding more gifts that have appeared overnight. "Is this one a bike?" she asks, pointing at a huge, flat box propped up against the wall.

"I don't know, Peanut. Let's all grab a drink and then we can get started."

Sutton huffs impatiently, but she doesn't argue as I fire up the coffee machine and Kodie makes her a hot chocolate loaded with cream and marshmallows.

Only a few minutes later, we're all sitting on the floor in the living room, and Sutton is practically vibrating with excitement.

"I'm doing the big one first," she squeals before tearing at the paper with two hands.

As she predicted, there's a new "big girl" bike inside.

"Yesss," she squeals before hitting her stocking.

She takes her time gently unwrapping each one and spends a minute or two focusing on each gift. She explains every single one of them to us as if we weren't the ones who chose them and tells us all the reasons she wanted them and loves them.

She's about halfway done with her gifts when she suddenly pauses.

"Daddy, we should give Casey hers now," she states with her hands on her hips like she owns the place.

"Yeah?" Kodie asks.

Sutton dives under the Christmas tree, stretching right to the back where they must have hidden it.

She passes it over before stepping back. Kodie reaches for her and sits her on his lap, both of them watching me impatiently.

"Go on then," Sutton encourages when I don't make a move to open it.

Curious, I carefully unwrap the paper, finding a small white box inside.

I glance up, my eyes narrowing at the anxious expressions on their faces.

What have they done?

Forcing my eyes away from them, I gently pull the lid off and then peel back the tissue. Inside, sitting on a velvet cushion, I find a key inside attached to a little metal house keyring. Written on that house are three names.

Kodie.

Casey.

Sutton.

"Baby," Kodie says softly, shuffling them both closer. "Make it official. Move in with us?"

My eyes bounce between his before dropping to Sutton's.

The lump in my throat is so huge, I can barely breathe.

I nod, my smile spreading across my face.

"Yes?" Kodie asks, needing verbal confirmation.

"Yes. Yes," I cry, reaching for both of them.

We hold each other for the longest time as we prepare to embark on the next chapter of our lives as a family. When we eventually part, I look between them and confess, "My gifts are going to be such a disappointment after this."

Laughter rings through the house, and it stays the same way for the rest of the day.

Dad and Kathleen join us, and Kathleen and I take charge of the kitchen, melding our family traditions together into a whole new one.

Everything about the day is perfect. There is so much love and happiness. It's exactly what Dad and I have been missing.

Sutton eventually concedes and lets us put her to bed an hour after her usual time. The four of us play games, drink, and laugh until the early hours before Kathleen retires to her pool house and Dad heads to one of Kodie's guest rooms.

Alone at last, I climb onto Kodie's lap on the couch and wrap my arms around him before tucking my face into the crook of his neck and breathing him in.

"I've had such a good day—thank you."

"We didn't ambush you too much earlier?" he asks, forcing me to pull my head up and look at him.

"It was perfect. You are perfect. Sutton is perfect. We are perfect. Thank you for opening your life and your family to me."

"We weren't a family before, baby. Something was always missing. We were just people battling our way through life. You being here is what makes us a real family."

"I love you."

"I love you, too, Trouble."

Pushing to stand with me in his arms, he walks toward the stairs, promising to end the day as we always should. Together. And maybe, just every once in a while, breaking a few rules while we're at it.

One Year Later...

Nostalgia hits me the second I hear Sutton's first steps out of her room.

As she moves closer through the darkness, my smile grows.

This past year has been incredible.

Kodie and Sutton have given me a life I never thought I could have.

The love, the laughter, the endless hockey talk and happiness.

It's been everything I was only ever able to dream about.

No. Actually, it's better.

Sure, not everything has been easy.

Loving and living with a not only professional hockey player but also a father and his daughter has been challenging.

At times, it feels like we're all being pulled in different directions, when all we really want is to be together.

But once all our obligations are over, and we do finally find ourselves under the same roof once again, everything settles back into place.

For a few months after I officially moved in last Christmas, Kathleen stayed in the pool house, but as we settled into a routine and I found my footing with school runs and all the other things Sutton needed while Kodie was on the road, she started looking for a place of her own.

She hasn't gone far. She's only down the road, and for one reason or another, she's still here almost every day. But it's given her the space and the life that she deserves. Although this morning, she's right down the hall. My dad is too.

Warmth spreads through me as I think about spending the whole day as a family.

The door creaks as it always does when Sutton steps into the room.

I remember last year fondly as she tiptoed around the bed to get to Kodie, beyond excited to tell him about Santa's visit.

But this year, her steps slow sooner, and when I crack an eye open, she's standing right in front of me.

Her eyes find mine in the darkness, and her already beaming smile grows wider.

"He's been," she whispers excitedly. "He's been."

My heart swells in my chest. Watching this little girl grow and learn is such a privilege. She amazes me every day with her kindness, her compassion, and her love.

"Oh yeah? Has he left you lots?" I ask.

She nods. "Daddy? You need to wake up."

Kodie chuckles behind me.

"Daddy, are you pretending to be asleep?" Sutton chastises.

Suddenly, he releases the death grip he had on my waist and sits up, dragging the sheets away from me.

"Are you kidding? It's Christmas morning. I've been waiting for you to wake up."

Bullshit. He was snoring only a few minutes ago.

I keep that little nugget to myself, though.

"Have you?" she asks suspiciously with her hands on her hips.

"Go and wake Gran and James, then get your stocking. We'll meet you downstairs."

Kodie hasn't finished talking before Sutton spins on her heels and races toward the door.

"Don't start without us," I call as she disappears.

The second she's gone, the door swinging closed behind her, Kodie rolls over, pressing the weight of his body against mine.

I groan, loving the way we line up as he trails kisses across my jaw and down my neck. A shudder rips through me as I drag my legs from beneath him and wrap them around his waist.

"Oh god," I moan when he grinds his morning wood against me.

"You keep forgetting, baby. It's Kodie. Kodie Rivers."

I chuckle. I swear, there isn't a week that goes by where he doesn't remind me of this. Whether he's here or on the road, it's a constant, mostly because I love to tease him mercilessly.

"Mmm, yeah. I sleep in Kodie motherfucking Rivers' bed every night."

"Every motherfucking night," he groans as the sound of Sutton making her way downstairs floats around us.

His kisses continue, ensuring my temperature continues to rise.

But as much as I need him, we don't have time.

"Kodie," I whimper, my hand skating down his side, loving the goosebumps that erupt from my touch.

"Better," he teases as his lips close in on mine.

"We need to get up."

"One taste, baby. Just one—"

His tongue sweeps into my mouth, teasing my own into action. My hold on him tightens as I quickly forget about what we should be doing and focus entirely on him.

My man.

My everything.

"Daddy. Casey. You'd better not be asleep again," Sutton warns as the house begins to wake up around us.

"We're coming," I call back, trying and failing to shove the ginormous man off me.

"I can assure you, we are not."

A giggle erupts and I finally manage to slip away.

"Come on, your girl is waiting," I say, righting my Santa pajamas.

Behind me, the sheets rustle before Kodie stands to full height. Unable to stop myself, I spin around, getting my fill of him and his tented red Santa pants.

"Our girl."

"W-what?" I stutter, my brain barely functioning.

It's not fair; it's too early, and he looks like that.

"Sutton. She's our girl."

My lips open and close, but I don't find any words.

Kodie steps closer, wrapping his arms around my waist and holding my eyes as he gazes down at me.

"You're incredible with her, and she loves you so much."

My eyes burn and my nose itches. "I love her too."

I didn't know it was possible to love two people this much. But I do. Every day, I wake with my heart so full thanks to my new family.

We may not be related by blood, but we are in every other way that matters.

"You were the best gift either of us could have asked for," he says, his voice deep and raspy.

"Kodie," I breathe.

"I'm serious. You are the best thing that's ever happened to us. I can't imagine our life, our family without you."

"I love you so much," I say, resting my cheek against his chest and holding him tight.

"I love you too—but we'd better move before she comes back and starts threatening us."

With a laugh, we drag ourselves apart, clean up, and then head downstairs.

Just like last year, there are gifts everywhere, almost all of them with Sutton's name. But it isn't the sight of them all that really takes my breath away. It's the house. No, the home.

And it's only made better by the two people who come wandering in with mugs of coffee in their hands.

"Thank you," I say, taking one from Dad and immediately lift it to my lips for a sip.

With a free hand, Dad wraps his arm around my shoulder. "Merry Christmas, Care Bear."

"Merry Christmas, Dad."

Mom's decorations are everywhere, and every time I look at them, I feel a little closer to her.

She may no longer be here with us, but I also know she never left, and she never will. She's just as much a part of this new phase of my life, and I know she's just as proud of me as Dad is.

"Oh wow, Peanut. You weren't lying; you really have been good this year," Kodie laughs as we join her.

"Can I start?" she asks eagerly.

"Of course you can."

Kodie and I sit side by side in our matching pajamas with our fingers entwined while Dad and Kathleen get themselves comfortable on the couch as she unwraps gift after gift.

She pauses after opening a new set of hair brushes and looks at me.

"Are you okay?" I ask, sensing something shifting.

"Daddy, can I?"

"Of course," he says, his hand squeezing mine.

Okay, what is happening?

Looking over, I search Dad and Kathleen's faces for clues, but if they know, they're not giving anything away.

Sutton rummages around under the tree until she finds the gift she wants before shuffling to me on her knees and handing it over.

Memories slam into me of this time last year, when I was handed a key to the house and they asked me to move in.

It blew my mind in the best possible way, and I can only imagine what they've planned this time.

"This is for you," Sutton says, holding the gift out toward me.

I take it give it a little shake, seeing if I can guess before I rip into the paper. Everyone watches me closely, and I glance between them all nervously.

Whatever is in here is important. I can tell by the hitch in both Kodie and Sutton's breathing.

Inside, I find a box. And then inside the box, whatever it is is wrapped in bubbles.

But the second I slide the contents out, my breath catches.

"Sutton," I breathe, staring down at a photo of the two of us at a Vipers game in a frame that is engraved with *Mommy and Me*.

Tears flood my eyes.

Kodie reaches over and squeezes my hand in support.

"Peanut, you have something you want to ask Casey, don't you?"

Ripping my eyes from the frame, I stare at her, noting the tears in her eyes, too.

"Casey, will you...will you be my mommy?"

"Oh my god," I cry as I place the frame to the side and gather her up in my arms, holding her as tight as I dare.

Her entire body trembles against mine, and I can't say I'm in a much better state as I fight to suck in air through my sobs.

"Oh, Sutton, I'd love nothing more," I tell her when I'm finally able to pull back and look into her eyes. Reaching up, I wipe away the tears on her cheeks with my thumbs. "I love you so much, sweetie."

She mimics my move and wipes my tears too. "I love you too... Mommy."

My heart is in pieces as she tests out the word, she has never called anyone before.

Kodie's hand shifts on my back, reminding me that he's here in this moment with us.

"You knew about this?" I ask weakly.

"Of course. Sutton asked me a few weeks ago how I thought you'd feel about it."

"You two wreck me in the best kind of way," I say, wiping my cheeks again because the tears won't stop.

"I've got another matching gift here too," Sutton explains as she pulls another wrapped box from beneath the tree and walks toward Dad.

Ripping his tear-filled eyes from me, he focuses on the little girl approaching him. "I think it's time I got a grampa too."

"Sutton," he rasps, barely holding it together as she passes him an identical sized box to mine.

"What do you say, Coach. Want to be my grampa?"

Without opening the gift, Dad pulls Sutton onto him lap and holds her tight, all five of us crying the happiest of tears.

Family.

Totally worth breaking all the rules for.

EXTENDED EPILOGUE

Parker

New Years Eve

"You owe me," I slur, throwing my arms around my best friend.

I've barely had a chance to speak to her tonight; if she hasn't been attached to Kodie's hip then she's been chasing around after Sutton.

I love seeing my girl so happy. It lights me up inside, seeing her smiling like she does now. But it also showcases just how fucking lonely I am.

"Why do I owe you?" Casey asks.

"We made a bet, remember."

Her brows pinch.

"Uh...did we?"

"Yep. At the beginning of the season, I said something like, I bet that by the end of the season, you'd have fucked Kodie again. Well, Missy. It's New Year's, the season is far from over and you have just moved in with him. A la...you owe me."

Casey's quirks a brow, her smile growing as she thinks about her man.

Ugh, there's that happiness again.

It's a good thing I love her so much.

"That doesn't constitute as a bet, and it certainly doesn't mean I owe you anything."

I narrow my eyes at her.

"Why aren't you as drunk as me? If you were, you'd agree."

She shakes her head. "What is it you want for winning?"

I blow out a long breath through my nose as I think.

"I don't know."

"Okay, so the point of bringing it up was..."

"Proving a point that I was right, I guess."

"Well, congratulations, Miss Donnelly. You were right. Now, have you figured out who you're going to be kissing in..." Casey checks the time. "Six minutes."

I groan.

"This room is full of hockey players."

"So? It's New Years. It's all about new starts remember."

Excitement stirs in my stomach as I think about what the New Year holds for me already.

Casey wasn't the only one to have her dream come true this year.

By some miracle, I've managed to achieve mine too.

In three days, I am officially starting my new position as the LA Vipers' newest—and obviously hottest—athletic trainer.

"My new job is even more reason why I shouldn't be kissing any of these guys," I point out.

Drunk or not, I will not be forgetting the promise I made to myself all those years ago.

No hockey players. Not again.

Ever.

"Baby, it's almost time," Kodie says, stepping up behind my best friend so he can steal her away for their midnight kiss.

"Please, Parker," Casey begs, her eyes all soft and pathetic. "Next year is your year, I can feel it. Please don't start it alone."

"Go, just go," I say, waving them off before turning to the bar and gesturing to one of the servers for a new drink.

My spine stiffens as someone steps up beside me.

I don't need to turn around to know the looming presence belongs to a hockey player; I can tell by the expensive scent of their cologne.

My only question is...which one.

"Thank you," I say as my double Jack and Coke is placed in front of me.

"Something wrong with all the champagne that's being passed around?"

Closing my eyes, I silently will the man next to me away.

But I already know I'm not that lucky.

Lifting my drink to my lips, I swallow a gulp, hoping it'll help me deal with the man beside me.

My skin heats under his attention, but I refuse to give him the satisfaction of knowing he affects me in any way other than annoying me.

"I guess this is the problem with parties the team owner throws, he doesn't invite bunnies," I taunt, finally twisting around to look at the player who dared to come over and ruin the last few minutes of this year.

The smirk that pulls at Lincoln Storm's lips makes my teeth grind.

He thinks he so special. So hot and...okay, fine. He is hot. But the fact he knows it counteracts the whole situation. That along with a whole list of other things.

"It's not really an issue when you're in the room, sweetheart."

"If you think that kind of line is going to get you anywhere with me then you really need to think again."

"It's almost midnight, Donnelly."

"And that means what, exactly? You going to turn back into a pumpkin?"

One side of his mouth kicks up in amusement.

"I didn't have you down as a fairytale fan."

I sneer at him.

"You're even hotter when you're drunk."

"I'm done here," I say, lifting my glass from the bar and walking away.

I make it four steps before everyone around me begins counting down.

Ten.

Nine.

Eight.

I look around the room, finding couples and groups of friends excited to welcome in a new year.

I understand why the Vipers are happy. They're having their best season in years. There is a very good chance that the year we're about to go into is going to be the first in almost a decade that they make it to the playoffs.

Seven.

Six.

Five.

Fletcher has his arms around Reese's waist. Kodie is gazing into Casey's eyes.

The other couples on the team are ready.

Four.

Three.

Two.

And I'm standing here with only my drink to celebrate with.

Fuck. I hope Casey is right. I hope next year is my year.

One.

Cheers erupt as kids pull party poppers shooting confetti everywhere. I'm about to lift my drink to my lips in a private celebration with myself when a hand wraps around the back of my neck.

Before I know what's happening, a warm pair of lips press against mine.

It takes me a second for my brain to catch up, and the second it does, I raise my glass higher and dump the contents all over Lincoln Storm's head.

"The fuck, Donnelly?" he barks as my Jack and Coke soaks his hair and runs down the sides of his face.

"Happy New Year, Storm. Let's start as we mean to go on, yeah?"

What will happen next for Linc and Parker? You can find out in their story, Playing the Game.

Want more Kodie & Casey? Sign up to my newsletter for a bonus Scene! Get your copy here.

Psst... want to see Sutton and Adrian come head to head on the ice? You can read this scene, and more, over in my Happily Ever After Book Club on Patreon.
Become a member now.

BROKEN SAINT
SNEAK PEEK

Colton

From our very first play, we fucking owned it. We played like a well-oiled machine of savages. The Bulls didn't stand a chance, and every time Sawyer's eyes locked on mine, he stoked the determination burning bright within me.

We had their defense running circles around themselves as we scored over and over. It was fucking majestic, and exactly what I needed to remind myself of what I was doing with my life.

As the fans roar in the excitement in the stands around us, I close my eyes for a beat, feeling the steady thrum of my heart in every inch of my body.

Last play of the game and the chance to put the final nail in the Bulls' coffin.

We line up, the adrenaline of the win already coursing through our veins.

Luca calls the play as I glare Sawyer dead in the eyes, promising him a world of pain for the dirty tackle I can see him planning.

I shake my head, warning him against it before the whistle blows and we spring into action.

Luca fakes a throw in Kane's direction. The Bulls' defense

follows it—well, all but Sawyer. His attention is still locked on me as Luca passes off the ball and I take off running.

My catch is flawless, and I tuck it under my arm as Sawyer attempts to take me down. But I've already got him, and we both know it.

The roar of the crowd rises to astronomical levels as I make the touchdown—but in only seconds, it becomes a blur as my teammates dive on me in celebration.

"Fucking yes," Luca screams in my face, bumping our helmets together as he holds the sides of my neck.

The last few seconds count down on the Jumbotron before the Saints' fans lose their shit once again over our epic win.

With Kane and Luca on either side of me, I'm turned toward the crowd, or more specifically the seats where Letty and Peyton sit for every single game we play.

They're both dressed in their boys' jerseys, jumping up and down, screaming in celebration. Even Kyan is beaming, his little chubby cheeks red with excitement as if he knows his dad is a fucking legend, in more ways than one.

But it's not my teammates' wives or cute little Kyan who catches my attention.

It's the woman standing right in the middle of them.

Wearing. My. Fucking. Number.

As if she can feel my attention, her gaze finds mine.

It's been years since I laid eyes on her. But the second our gazes meet, my dark to her honey, it's like no time has passed.

That tether I'd thought I'd finally managed to sever pulls between us. It's just like I remember. No. It's worse than that. It's stronger. More powerful.

And as I stand there locked in her stare while everyone around me celebrates our win, there's only one thought in my head.

I'm fucked.

Totally fucking fucked.

I'm jostled to the side before Kane leans in closer.

"Surprise, Rogers. Looks like your night just got even better."

Broken Saint is now live and available with kindle unlimited.
Download your copy now

ABOUT THE AUTHOR

Tracy Lorraine is a *USA Today* and *Wall Street Journal* bestselling new adult and contemporary romance author. Tracy has recently turned thirty and lives in a cute Cotswold village in England with her husband, baby girl and lovable but slightly crazy dog. Having always been a bookaholic with her head stuck in her Kindle, Tracy decided to try her hand at a story idea she dreamt up and hasn't looked back since.

Be the first to find out about new releases and offers. Sign up to my newsletter here.

If you want to know what I'm up to and see teasers and snippets of what I'm working on, then you need to be in my Facebook group. Join Tracy's Angels here.

Keep up to date with Tracy's books at
www.tracylorraine.com